S.M. STIRLING

THE STONE DOGS

But I praise and love every one who does nothing base from free will. Against necessity, even gods do not fight.

Simonides of Keos
c. 468 BC

THE STONE DOGS

Copyright © 1990 by S.M. Stirling

A Baen Books Original

Baen Publishing Enterprises
260 Fifth Avenue
New York, N.Y. 10001

ISBN: 0-671-72009-0

Cover art by Paul Alexander

First Baen printing, August 1990

Distributed by
SIMON & SCHUSTER
1230 Avenue of the Americas
New York, N.Y. 10020

Printed in the United States of America

DATE: 07/06/67
FROM: Techspec IV Carnot Alden, Virunga Biocontrol
Institute
Project [*Classified*]
TO: Techspec VIII Carmen Fougard, Archona
University
Biocontrol Department
RE: Project [*Classified*]
Viral Coding Subsection, Ituri Retro-66b6-03

[*Technical data deleted by order of Security Directorate.*] . . . I tell you, Cammie, when I saw the specs on that virus I nearly fainted, and then I nearly heaved my breakfast. *Damnedest* retrovirus complex you ever saw—even managed to work its way into the lymphatic matter. Dormancy period—you won't believe this—up to ten years! The wild version would just rip the shit out of a human immune system; anyone who got it would be wide open for opportunistic infections. . . . Possibly even an insect vector. The thing that gives me nightmares is the thought that it might have broken out into the general population when we swept the blacks there out into the compounds. They were just starting to do blood-transfusions in the 1880's, so *we* might have got it, and back then they'd have had no earthly prayer of beating it, they couldn't even have identified it. Could have been the Black Death all over again. The gods own luck most of those went into destructive-labor camps. Of course, it's lucky some survived in the Ituri pygmies, too. Anyway, it's given us a ten-year jump on the SD project, this is the perfect source of our basic viral carrier—particularly since there are direct neurological effects. Once you finish tweaking this, it'll be like a ripe fig stuffed with botulism.

Acknowledgments to Jerry, Jim, and all the bixen for their assistance with the technical data; mistakes are purely my own.

Dedication:
To Jan with love

Timeline of the Domination of the Draka and the Terran Dispersal

1947– Fisson power reactors; breeder reactor under construction.

1948– Frederick and Marya Lefarge born, Hospital of the Sacred Heart, New York.

1954– Yolande Ingolfsson born, Claestum Plantation, Italy. Myfwany Venders born, Arethustra Plantation, Sicily.

1955– Ramjet suborbital missile exceeds Mach 8.

1959– First scramjet flight to orbit.

1961– Space stations.
First "perscomp" marketed in Alliance, by Pacific CyberSystems

1962– Manned moon landings; first permanent Lunar settlements.

1963– Successful activated transfer of mammalian genes, Virunga Biocontrol Institute.

Alliance tests nuclear-fission pulsedrive vessel. First-generation drive, using modified tactical weapon and graphite-sheathed steel thrust plates.

Domination tests pulsedrive.

1964— Alliance, Draka expeditions to Asteroid Belt, Mars. High-boost probes to Venus, Mercury, outer planets launched from Earth Orbit.

1965— Magnetic catapult launchers on Luna, supply of minerals to orbital fabricators in zero-G.

1966— First free-electron laser boost to orbit from Earth.

1968-9— Two-ship *Van Riebeck* expedition to Jupiter; one lost.

First Apollo-group (Earth-crossing) asteroid captured, brought into Earth orbit.

1970— Second-generation pulsedrives; subcritical plutonium pellets compressed by collision from railguns. Liquid reaction mass used to cover carbon-carbon/steel thrustplates.

Permanent Draka settlement on Mars; orbital stations, mining operations on Martian moons.

1972— Space-generated solar power beamed to Earth via microwaves.

1975— Secession of Indian Republic from Alliance for Democracy. Draka conquest of India.

1980— Third-generation pulsedrives; fission pellets compressed by lasers.

Fourth-generation pulsedrives; deuterium-tritium fusion pellets imploded by laser/electron beam system.

1989— First planet-based fusion reactor, Nova Virconium, Mars.

1996— Fifth-generation pulsedrive; deuterium-boron-ll fusion pellets.

PROLOGUE

VIRUNGA BIOCONTROL INSTITUTE
WEAPONS RESEARCH DIVISION
WEST RIFT PROVINCE
DOMINATION OF THE DRAKA
MARCH 1, 1969

"This is the first series," the project manager said; a stocky brown-haired woman in her thirties. The wall lit up with a three-dimensional rendering of a virus molecule. It was color-coded, black and scarlet. "Yo' see how we've replaced —"

"Doctor Melford," the Senator said, with soft courtesy. The other members of the audience turned slightly to catch his words. "We've all absorbed as much technical info'mation as possible from the prep-files, and while I'm sure the computer projections would be very interestin', perhaps . . . ?"

He was a tall man, eagle-faced, with silver-streaked blond hair and mustache, conservatively dressed in indigo velvet and white lace. There was no impatience in his posture, leaning back at his ease in one of the two dozen swivel chairs that lined the little auditorium. Still, the woman in the white lab coat flushed slightly, coughed to cover it; her fingers moved on the controls.

"Well," she said. Her vowels had a rather crisp tone, an East African accent; she had been born in these highlands. "Well, here are the recordings of the chimp results."

The screen blanked for a moment and split. "The left is our control sample, an' the right is the Series 24D group."

Two enclosures, sealed under glass but green with flowers and trees, like giant terrarias. The left showed a group of chimpanzees foraging, grooming, playing; one male reared up on his hind legs and then ran screaming down a slope, flailing the ground with a bamboo, a threat display. On the right, nearly the same.

1

"This is an hour after the introduction of the activating factor; yo' understand, there has to be stress fo' the altered enzyme chain to . . . Ah, here."

One of the chimps in the right-hand group had snatched a palm-heart from her neighbor. The victim rolled back and bared her teeth, then suddenly leaped. Both animals went over in a blur of limbs and grass and shrieking.

"This is highly atypical, yo' see. Chimps do fight to the death, but very seldom—yes." The victor had risen, the blunt almost-human face wet with blood; she was dancing on the dying animal's form, with leaps and arm-waving. The others were visibly agitated, hooting and moving back and forth in distress. Then two more began to fight; a mother picked up her infant and slammed it on the ground, over and over, until a big male leapt on her back and began tearing . . .

The Senator watched, stony-faced amid his silent aides. The plainly-clad woman at the heart of the other clump laughed aloud. A minute passed, and nothing living remained on the right-hand screen. To the left, a picture of the innocence before the birth of man.

"It seems," he said, "that yo've been makin' progress, Doctor."

She nodded eagerly. " 'Specially since yo' got us the new computer," she said, one hand caressing the row of pens in her breast pocket with a nervous gesture.

The Senator smiled for the first time. "Thank the Yankees; it was the best we could steal," he said dryly. "How confident are yo' that these-here results can be transferred to humans?"

"Very, yes," the geneticist nodded. "Chimps are the best possible test subjects, they're so close to us. Ninety-eight percent genetic congruence, only five million years since the last common ancestor, which . . . Yes. We've managed to move the focus of the infection from the immune to the limbic systems without'n much trouble; the original affected the neurological . . . Well, it wasn't much trouble. The problem is gettin' it activated with the sort of arbitrary external stimulus yo' wanted, sir. We've gotten promisin' results usin' particular frequencies of strobe-lightin', the *grand mal* trigger effect, yo' know? The endorphine response is modified into a feedback loop. That still needs work."

The woman to the Senator's left spoke, in a flat Angolan accent: "What's y're success rate?" She was younger than the

Senator, perhaps forty-five, head of a committee in the House of Representatives that attracted little public attention.

Melford nodded at the right-hand screen. "Ovah 99%; no point in 'finin' it down further until we moves to human subjects."

"In y' professional opinion, is this project go or no-go?"

"Go." A decisive nod. "Provided we get the necessary fundin' an' personnel. Mo' work on the vector—we're still relyin' on blood to blood—and the secondary keyin' sequence. Four years, eight maximum, an' we'll have it on-spec."

"Chiliarch," the Senator said. A man in the olive-green uniform of the Security Directorate spread his hands and laid his fingertips on the desk before him.

"It's tight. Jus' this one facility, an' the Institute's normal activity is good cover. The computer's not physically connected to any datalink. Nothin' certain in my line of work, but I'd bet mah tender pink ass this'un can be kept close. Until operational deployment, of course."

"Ah." The Senator dropped his chin onto the steepled fingers of both hands, and the lids drooped over his narrow gray eyes. "Doctor, what about keepin' it from the Yankees when we deploy it against the Alliance?"

"Well." A frown. "Well, they're not as, ummm, sophisticated at biotech as we are. Those Luddite fanatics of theirs who keep protestin' every time they try to use somethin', and then again they can't test humans to destruction the way we can. Sloppy. Still, they've got some good people."

She paused. "Very unlikely fo' the virus to be discovered —I'm assuming nothin' goes wrong with the clandestine operations side. We'd have trouble findin' that bug iff'n we didn't know what to look for. These retroviruses are cunnin' critters at concealin' themselves, and we've tweaked it until even the immune system is completely fooled. Yo'd have to puree the subject's nerve tissue an' do a congruent-DNA sample test series . . . unless it was activated, of course. That'd produce gross abnormalities and yo' could follow them back. It's less a disease than gene-surgery, really."

The Senator looked across to his colleague; she nodded and spoke: "What'll yo' need?"

"Ummm, more funding. More personnel, as Ah said. And experimental subjects, of course. Several hundred humans, assorted gender an' age in the postpubescent range, pref'rably the same ethnic mix as the target population. Very delicate, to get it contagious but with a failsafe turn-off. Don't want it becomin' a global pandemic, do we?"

"Wodan, no," the Senator said. "Well, Doctor Melford, certain othahs will have to be consulted, but unofficially I think yo' can take it that the project will be approved fo' further development." He rose. "Service to the State."

"Glory to the Race," the scientist answered absent-mindedly as the audience left; she was keying the machine again, reviewing the additional resources that would be needed.

"Well, how do y'like it?"

"Nice view," the Senator said, nodding down from the terrace toward the lake and drawing on his cigarette.

The Virunga Biocontrol Institute was built in the hills overlooking Lake Kivu, at the southern edge of the Virunga range. A century old now, almost as old as Draka settlement in these volcanic highlands. Low whitewashed buildings of stone-block, roofs of plum-colored tile, almost lost among the vegetation; the gardens were flamboyantly lovely even by the Domination's standards, fertile lava soils and abundant rain and a climate of eternal spring. National park stretched north and west, to the Ituri lowlands: haunt of gorilla and chimp, elephant and hippo and leopard; of the Bambuti pygmies also, left to their Old Stone Age existence.

Plantations stretched widely elsewhere across the steep slopes, green coffee and tea and sheets of flowers grown for air-freighting elsewhere; the air was scented with them, cool and sweet. The city of Arjunanda lay two thousand feet below by the waters, turned to a model by distance: buildings white and blue and violet with marble and tile, avenues bordered with jacaranda and colonnades roofed in climbing rose and frangipani. Even the factories and labor-compounds that ringed it were comely, bordered by hedge and garden. Sails speckled the waves, and they could see the pleasure boats beating back toward the docks, and dirigibles lying silvery in the waterfront haven.

"It's a famous beauty-spot," the woman said with elaborate sarcasm, indicating the sun setting behind the mountains to their right, amid clouds turned to the colors of brass and blood. "No mo' games, man."

He flicked the butt of the cigarette over the railing. *Like her, to be cold even when she's angry. You can see why our enemies nicknamed us "snakes," looking at her.* The burning speck fell like a tiny meteor, to lie winking for a second before one of the Institute outdoor serfs arrived to sweep it up.

"It might work," he said quietly.

"It *will* work. This time yo' suspicions of biotech don't wash. And this project was mah price fo' supportin' yo' pet schemes."

"Granted."

They gave each other a glance of cool mutual hatred and turned again to the view beneath. Shadow was falling across the city and the lake as the first stars appeared above. The streetlights of Arjunanda flicked on in a curving tracery, and the lamps of the plantation manors scattered down the hills. An airship had cast off from the haven, and the thousand-meter teardrop rose from darkness into light as it circled, bound northward with cut flowers and electrowafers, strawberries and heavengrape wine.

"Have yo' ever wondered," the Senator said meditatively, "why we Draka love flowers so?"

The woman blinked, her fox-sharp face shadowed in the dim glow. "No, can't say as I have," she said neutrally. "Why?"

"They're safer to love than human bein's," he said thoughtfully. "An' unlike humans, they deserve it." He turned. "I'll be in contact aftah I speak to the Archon."

CHAPTER ONE

Representatives of the Alexandria Technological Institute today announced that the fetal-transplant process has been cleared for Citizen use after extensive testing. "Ova may now be stored indefinitely in frozen form, either before or after fertilization, then warmed and implanted in either the donor or a host-mother." Eugenics Directorate officials are enthusiastic about the technique, which they say removes the last biological constraints on the reproduction and improvement of the Citizen population. Clinics offering transplant services will be established throughout the Domination; healthy serf wenches to act as host-mothers will be provided for those who have none suitable in their own households. In addition, Citizens with outstanding mental and physical characteristics will be asked to make contributions to sperm and ova banks. Once brought to term in host-mothers, the infants will be offered for adoption into selected Citizen families or raised in the Education Directorate's existing orphanages. It is expected that over the next twenty years, these measures will at least double the present Citizen birthrate of 24 per thousand, enabling Citizen women to do their reproductive duty to the Race without interfering with their military and other commitments. Even greater improvements are to be anticipated shortly, when gene-engineering becomes practical.

Alexandria Herald
May 8, 1962

CLAESTUM PLANTATION
DISTRICT OF TUSCANY
PROVINCE OF ITALY
DOMINATION OF THE DRAKA
SEPTEMBER 1, 1964

Eric von Shrakenberg paused at the edge of the steps, looking up at the constellations of the northern hemisphere. This was the north front of his sister Johanna's Tuscan plantation manor; the stone pathway wound up to the crest of the hill under ancient trees, oak and cypress and chestnut. They had been here long before the Eurasian War, but the new masters of Europe had changed the patch of forest to suit their tastes. He could hear the tinkle of water ahead, smell the damp scents of new-cut grass and flowers; roses, he thought, opening their blooms to the hot Italian night. Sweat tickled his flanks under the linen of his *djellaba* robe, under the leather of the shoulder-holster harness beneath it.

For a moment, he considered going back to the birthday party, rather than seeking out his sister and her husband. *No,* he decided. The people were salt of the earth, no doubt about that. Local planters, of course, overseers, Combine and League execs from the nearby towns . . . not many of them personally known to him. *And face it, provincial,* he thought. *And politics keeps me in Archona too much, and Johanna and Tom seem to have grown on to this place like a pair of barnacles.*

He would not have thought it of her, or of Thomas Ingolfsson either, when the man had been a neighbor and a friend and a rakehell fighter pilot in his sister's squadron, back during the War . . . *Well, time and marriage and children do change us,* he thought, and walked up the steps. The stone was smooth and warm and slightly gritty under his bare feet.

"Shhhh, Lele!" Yolande Ingolfsson hissed.

The night was quiet on this side of the hill; the house was visible only as a glow through the treetops ahead of them, the noise of the guests less than that of the crickets and nightjars and the slow rubbing of branch and thicket. Away to her right in the valley were the lights of the Quarters, but the party there would have ended sooner, the plantation-hands had to be back at their work tomorrow, getting ready for the vintage.

The serf girl beside her looked subdued. Yolande sighed to herself as she squirmed on her stomach past the topiary bush. This whole birthday party for Ma had been *boring*. The gifts were stupid stuff, mostly: statues and paintings and jewelry, or Combine shares and like that. She gritted her teeth. And her cousin Alexandra von Shrakenberg had been put in charge of the children's part of the celebrations, and that was . . . was . . . *impossible*, she decided; that was the word. Being ten was impossible, too.

Alexandra's only thirteen, that's only three years older than me, she thought resentfully. *Stuck-up*. Because she was in Senior School; all she could talk about was the *serious* things they had to study and the *boring* love affairs at school and how her parents' estate in France was prettier than Claestum . . .

Yolande heard voices and string-music from uphill. There was a waist-high circle of clipped hedge ten meters before them. Her eyes *estimated the ground* the way the instructor at school told the children. The slope here was down from the wooded crest, and to the north; there was an artificial stream coming down, falling through a stepped marble trough in a chuckling tumble. Cypresses on either side, opening out into circles around the pools, each with its benches and flowerbeds, and the hedges around those. So.

She looked back at Lele. The serf girl was nearly her age. Deng the foreman's daughter, one of *Yolande's* birthday presents, given to her like a puppy five years ago. *I'm getting too old to play with serfs*, Yolande decided. Tantie Rahksan's son Ali had been fun, always ready to climb and stuff, but he had gotten all sullen and close-mouthed lately. Lele was better, but she was so weak and slow . . . All serfs were, of course. Yolande sighed imperiously, then led the way at a stop-motion leopard crawl toward the hedge; they were on clipped grass, which made it easier to move quietly. Reconnaissance was fun; there was a thrill to spying on the grownups, and you could hear things they wouldn't say in front of a child.

Dew chilled her chest and stomach as she crawled; mouth open and breathing light and regular, the way the trainers said. Test your path, touch it lightly. Don't look at anything bright, it cripples your night-vision. She reached the hedge, rolled under the bench and curled her body to lie under it, a hand's-breadth back from the prickly leaves; it was white-thorn, not the shaggy multiflora used for field-boundaries out in the working part of the plantation. Lele followed more clumsily; they lay head to head, feet pointing in opposite directions along the circle. Yolande applied her eye to a natural gap.

Ooops, she thought. It was her mother and father, sitting at their ease in the pool; a housegirl was on one of the inner benches in the background, strumming on a mandolin. The pool itself was a circle of white-and-green marble two meters across, with water entering and leaving by the top and bottom ends. Tantie Rahksan was there, too, laying out a tray with wine and fruit and a waterpipe. That was unusual: Tantie had been with Ma *forever*, and she never did menial's work. Supervised the house staff, and she had run the nursery before the Ingolfsson children were of school age. She was quite old, too, nearly as old as Ma, nearly forty. From Afghanistan; you had to look in the history books for that, it wasn't there any more.

Oh. Tantie Rahksan had drawn her tunic over her head, and gotten into the pool, too; all she had on was a string of beads around her waist. It was funny, she didn't look all that old. Field wenches were just solid and brown and lumpy when they were forty, and the ones in the Great House got fat, mostly, but Rahksan was all curvy still. Her breasts floated up when she sat between Yolande's mother and father, handing them each a glass of wine. They drank some, and gave Rahksan sips out of their glasses, and passed the mouthpiece of the waterpipe back and forth. Yolande made a face; kif, she could smell it. Children weren't supposed to use it; she had snuck a quick puff once, and it had just made her feel heavy and sleepy.

I'd better leave, she thought. Pa was kissing Rahksan, and Ma was touching her breasts. Tantie Rahksan was sort of squirming and making sounds, and her hands were stroking the Draka on either side of her. Yolande felt her ears burn, as if they were turning bright red at the tips, and a weightless feeling in her stomach. There were books and tapes about sex in biology class at school, of course, but children weren't supposed to watch, and it was *really* impolite, and Ma might strap her if she found out.

Yolande looked up, and met Lele's wide eyes. She laid a finger across her lips and prepared to squirm backward, when she heard a voice from beyond the other side of the pool.

Trapped! she thought. A tall man at the north side could see the stretch of lawn they must cross to get to the next downslope terrace. *Oh, boy, I'm really going to get into trouble now!* Longingly, she thought of her bed in the tower room and the new *Young Draka's Illustrated Odyssey* Uncle Eric had brought her. *Oh,* shit, *that's Uncle Eric!*

"Oh. Sorry," Eric said, seeing that his sister and brother-in-law were busy, and half-turning to go.

"No matter," Thomas Ingolfsson said. "Just amusin' ourselves. Settle in, if yo' were lookin' fo' us."

"Was at that," Eric said. Rahksan emerged dripping from the pool to take his robe; he looked her over with reminiscent pleasure. *Still a fine figure of a wench,* he thought, remembering times on the ancestral von Shrakenberg estate in southern Africa. She gave him a pouting smile and folded the cloth by the pool's curb, the Tolgren 10mm neatly on top.

"Ahh, that feels good," he said as he sank in across from the pair. The cool water seemed to wash more than his skin, relaxing tensions he had not known were there. He ducked his head under and threw the wet hair back from his forehead. "Good to slow down fo' a while, too," he continued, lying back against the glass-smooth marble and sliding down on the underwater shelf that acted as a seat.

"No more news about Sofie?" Johanna said, taking up her wineglass.

"Thank yo'," Eric murmured as Rahksan waded across with another for him. "No, not since this mornin'. Those lung transplant operations are still tricky . . ."

"Wouldn't have minded if yo'd stuck it in Archona," Johanna said. Eric nodded gratefully; his sister had always liked Sofie, even though his wife came from what passed as a lower class among the Citizen caste.

"Yo' know Sofie, wouldn't hear of it," he said. A scowl: "Wouldn't stop smokin', either."

Tom shrugged. "Iff'n I knows our Sofie"—his voice made an attempt at a hoarse soprano—"*People who expect to live a long time don't join the paratroops, and if I hadn't done that I wouldn't have met Eric.* And think that clinches the argument."

"Well, *now* she's goin' to quit," Eric said, and for a moment his voice went entirely flat. Then he shook off the mood. "Relief to get away from all the politics, too."

"Well, Archona *is* the capital," Johanna said. "Some grapes, Rahksi . . . which is why I stay away from it as much as I can." She cocked an affectionate eye at him. "Yo' know, brothah dear, I always figured Pa pulled in his polit'cal debts to get yo' the Senatorial seat just so yo' could write those damn subversive novels without gettin' a pill from the headhunters."

A Senator had a certain immunity from the Directorate of Security, even for offenses that would merit a pistol-bullet in the back of the head for an ordinary Citizen.

Eric turned his hands up from the edge of the pool and raised the palms. "Think that's how *he* thought about it." Eric's own war record had not hurt, but that was something he preferred not to remember. "I . . . it's a matter of responsibility." He grinned. "Service to the State," he added.

"Glory to the Race," they muttered back, in the obligatory formality.

"Well, just between thee an' me, the headhunters are still tryin' to trip me up. Tried to block me from the Science and Technology section of the Strategic Plannin' Board, but failed."

"Oh, *ho*, we are movin' up in the world," Tom said. "Why, though?"

"Well, partly . . . yo' heard of Louise Gayner? SD Merarch, 'fore she retired. Representative from North Angola, now. Has it in fo' me, personal. Damn it, the headhunters spend half their time tryin' to steal research from the Yankees; how do they expect us to *apply* it, iffn we don't make mo' use of the serfs? We've got to keep this creakin' anachronism of a social system workin' *somehow*. Field hands don't need to know how to read, factory-serfs can do without it. Even ordinary Janissary infantry soldiers could, though it's inefficient and we're givin' them all basic now. Bookkeepers an' secretaries and technicians, we could get away with rote-learnin', but times are *changin'*. Computers and space between them, they're the frontier of power . . . less than a hundred million Citizens in the Domination, a billion and a half serfs, we need millions with *real* education—"

He stopped, relaxed once more. "Sorry, didn't mean to launch into a campaign speech." *Though it wouldn't hurt to have friends in the local sections of the Landholders' League and the Party*, he thought. That brought sadness; would there never be a time again when he could wholly discard his work? *Probably not*, he decided.

"Tell me 'bout it," Johanna said. "Just got one of those tin brains ourselves; wonderful, if we didn't have to have the League send round a technician every month. Speakin' of

space," she continued, "how we doin'?" She looked up; was
there an edge of wistfulness there? Eric suspected flying the
family plane did not leave his younger sister *completely* satisfied . . .

"Not bad, not bad at all. The scramjets are workin', and the
Technical Section people say the next lot will even be as safe
as Russian roulette. That giant magnetic catapult dingus on
Mt. Kenia is on schedule. And we're copyin' that Yankee
pulse-drive thing. Sounds insane, throwin' atomic bombs out
behind yo' ship fo' propulsion, but evidently it works."

He yawned, slightly tired, slightly disoriented still from
the long flight up. Always a little bewildering, to go from
winter to summer. It made you conscious that you really did
live on the surface of a globe. Eric glanced up; none of the
new moving stars in Earth's firmament was visible just now,
but they were there. The Alliance and his people had two
orbital platforms each now, and the tiny new stations on the
moon. *It changes your perspective*, he thought. *How I envy
those youngsters up there.*

Johanna sighed. "Better be gettin' back to bed," she said.
She and her husband rose, and Rahksan moved to towel them
down and hand them their clothes.

"Mistis?" Eric looked up; the Afghan was crouched by her
owner's feet, fastening the sandals. "Mmmm . . . maybe Mastah
Eric want an attendant here?"

Eric smiled. "Don't let me deprive y'all," he said politely.
There was a rustling sound; the Draka froze and reached out
for their gunbelts. A moment passed.

Tom laughed, and snapped fingers for the serf with the
mandolin. "Fox, or a rabbit. Haven't had bushman trouble
here fo', oh, seven, eight years . . . Yo' stay here then,
Rahksi; we can always teach Elizabetta heah a new tune," he
said. Johanna chuckled and threw an arm around his waist.

"See yo' in the mornin', brothah," she called over her
shoulder as they left.

Rahksan moved the refreshments closer and slid into the
water again. "Masta Eric, yo' hasn't changed one li'l bit," she
said, half chidingly. He smiled at the familiar accent. It was
the serf dialect of the Old Territories, below the Zambezi,
the speech of his childhood, the sound of home.

"Neither have yo'," he said. Not *quite* true: the full breasts
no longer stood out without benefit of buoyancy, and there
was a little gray in the strong coarse black hair. And genuine

friendliness in the curve-nosed, roundly pretty face. More warming than any number of younger and more comely bodies, when you could not know the thoughts behind the eyes.

"I means up here," she said, touching him on the forehead. "Yaz still thinks too much, Mastah. Hurts yaz inside." She grinned, slow and insolent, and the hand stroked teasingly down to grip him below the water and knead. He put his hands around her waist, and she swung to face him, knees astride his waist. "And I knows how to make yaz stop thinkin', f'whiles," she whispered.

They nearly heard us, Yolande thought, forcing herself not to shake. She had been glued to the hedge while they spoke; this was great stuff, about *spaceships*—and then Lele had nearly spoiled things by trying to crawl away too soon. *I'm going to switch her*, Yolande decided, glaring at the abashed half-Chinese serf. She had never actually beaten Lele, but . . . *Oh. I'd have to tell Ma or Tantie Rahksan why I wanted to switch her*. Children had no disciplinary authority over servants, even their own, until well into their teenage years. *I'll just yell at her.*

She put her eye back to the hole in the hedge. Tantie Rahksan and Uncle Eric were face to face, moving. Just then the serf gave a cry, and her feet came out of the water, locking around the man's lower back. He stood, water cascading off the linked bodies, and Tantie Rahksan had her hands dug into his shoulders and her head right back . . . *I had really better go*, Yolande decided. This wasn't at all like the pictures. *It's confusing and scary and their faces look so . . . fierce*, she thought, squirming back.

Below the lower terrace, they rested for a moment. Yolande looked up, through the moving leaves. *Stars*, she thought. *That would be* something.

FROM: CLAESTUM PLANTATION
      DISTRICT OF TUSCANY
TO: BAIAE SCHOOL
      DISTRICT OF CAMPANIA

PROVINCE OF ITALY
DOMINATION OF THE DRAKA
SEPTEMBER 1, 1968

It's too crowded in here, Yolande Ingolfsson thought irritably.

The crowding was not physical. The van was an Angers-Kellerman autosteamer from the Trevithick Combine's works in Milan, a big six-wheeler plantation sedan like a slope-fronted box with slab sides. There were five serfs and one young lady of landholding Citizen family in the roomy cabin; the muted sound of the engine was lost in the rush of wind and whine of the tires. None of them had been this way before.

Young Marco the driver was chattering with excitement, with stolid Deng sitting beside him giving an occasional snarl when the Italian's hands swooped off the wheel. The Oriental was a stocky grizzle-haired man of fifty, his face round and ruddy. He had been the House foreman since forever; Father had brought him from China when he and Mother came to set up the plantation, after the War. Saved him from an impaling stake, the rebel's fate, or so the rumor went, but neither of them would talk about it. Bianca and Lele were bouncing about on the benches running along either side of the vehicle, giggling and pointing out the sights to each other.

Not to me, Yolande thought with a slight sadness. Well, she was fourteen, that was getting far too grown-up to talk that way with servants.

The van had the highway mostly to itself on the drive down from Tuscany, past Rome and through the plantations of Campania; Italy was something of a backwater these days, and what industry there was clustered in the north. There was the odd passenger steamer, a few electric runabouts, drags hauling linked flats of produce or goods. Nevertheless the road was just as every other Class II way in the Domination of the Draka, an asphalt surface eight meters broad with a graveled verge and rows of trees on either side; cypress or eucalyptus here, but that varied with the climate.

Fields passed, seen through a flicker of trunks and latticed shadow slanting back from the westering sun, big square plots edged with shaggy hedges of multiflora. Fields of trellised vines, purple grapes peering out from the tattered autumnal lushness of their leaves; orchards of silvery gray olives, fruit trees, hard glossy citrus, and sere yellow-brown grain stubble. Fields of alfalfa under whirling sprinklers, circles of spray that filled the air with miniature rainbows and a heavy green smell that cut the hot dust scent. Melons lying like ruins of streaked green-and-white marble tumbled among vines, and strawberries starred red through the velvet plush of their beds.

Arch-and-pillar gateways marked the turnoffs to the estate manors, hints of colored roofs amid the treetops of their gardens. Yolande felt what she always did when she saw a gate: an impulse to open it. Like an itch in the head, to follow and see what was there, who the people were, and what their lives were like. Make up stories about them, or poems.

Silly, she thought. People were people; plantations were plantations, not much different from the one she grew up on.

Words and surfaces, hard shiny shells, that was all you could know of people. Yet the itch would not go away. You thought that you knew what they were like, especially when you were little; then a thing would happen that showed you were wrong. She shivered. Like that time years ago at the party; she had been peeking down through the banisters when Mother and the stranger began quarreling. Their voices had gone hard, then very quiet. The man began a motion to hit Mother, and the slap of her hand on his forearm was very loud.

A second before the main hall had been noisy with talk and music, then quiet had gone over it, rippling the way wind did through ripe wheat. Yolande had watched her mother's face go strange, very still and smiling. Not moving at all, even when the others talked and then some houseserfs came with her gunbelt and the man's. The two of them had walked out the French doors into the garden, Pa and a friend with Mother, two guests with the one who had tried to hit her. Two shots, so quick, before she had time even to be afraid, to think that Mother might be *dead*. Then she and Pa had come walking back through from the garden; Mother was laughing, and she had her arm around his waist. Some of the house servants had come in carrying the stranger on a folding garden chair; there was blood glistening and seeping from a pressure-bandage on his stomach, and his face looked yellow and waxy.

Yolande shook the memory aside. *It was just because it was so sudden*, she reminded herself. Duels were not that common—years could go by without one—and the insult had been gross. *I was too young to understand.*

The senior maidservant Angelica was sulking, but she was quite old, twenty at least, probably missing somebody back

home. It would have been good to have someone to talk to,
reading in a car had always made her nauseated. Lele gave a
giggle that was almost a squeal at something the other maidservant, Bianca, said, and Deng turned back to scowl at *her*.
Lele stuck out her tongue at him, but lowered her voice.
Lele was Deng's get; usually it was anybody's guess who
fathered a housegirl's children, but the foreman was the only
Oriental on the estate. You could see it in the saffron-brown
tint of her skin, the delicate bones and the folds at the
corners of her hazel-tinted eyes.

The Draka girl leaned back with a sigh, feeling heavy and a
little tired from the going-away party last night. She had the
rear of the autosteamer to herself, a semicircle couch like the
fantail of a small yacht. *Nearly* to herself: her Persian cat
Machiavelli was curled up beside her. He always tried to
sleep through an auto drive; at least he didn't hide under a
seat and puke anymore. . . . The windows slanted over her
head, up to the roof of the auto, open a little to let in a rush
of warm dry afternoon air. She let her head fall back, looking
through the glass up into the cloudless bowl of the sky, just
beginning to darken at the zenith. Her face looked back at
her, transparent against the sky, centered in a fan of pale
silky hair that rippled in the breeze.

Like a ghost, she thought. Her mind could fill in the
tinting, summer's olive tan, hair and brows faded to white-
gold, Mother's coloring. Eyes the shade of granulated silver,
rimmed with dark blue, a mixture from both her parents.
Face her own, oval, high cheekbones and a short straight
nose, wide full-lipped mouth, squared chin with a cleft; Pa
was always saying there must be elf somewhere in the bloodlines. She turned her head and sucked in her cheeks; the
puppyfat was definitely going, at long last. She was still
obstinately short and slight-built, however much she tried to
force growth with willpower.

At least I don't have spots, she mused with relief. Her first
year at the new school, and her first in the Senior Section, as
well.

"Bianca, get me a drink, please," Yolande said, shifting
restlessly and stretching. The drive had been a long one, and
she felt grubby and dusty and sticky; the silk of her blouse
was clinging to her back, and she could feel how it had
wrinkled.

The air had a spicy-dry scent, like the idea of a sneeze.

Yolande sipped moodily at the orange juice and watched as the auto turned south and east to skirt the fringe of Naples: just a small town now, badly damaged in the War, and afterward most of the non-historic sections had been torn down. The low bulk of Vesuvius was ahead of them, twin peaks notching the broad cone of the volcano, and the road swung west toward the impossible azure blue of the Tyrrhenian Sea. Her mouth was dry despite the cold drink. She handed the glass back to the servant girl and wiped her palms down the sides of her jodhpurs, hitched at her gunbelt, ran fingers through the tangled mass of her hair, adjusted her cravat.

"Bianca, Lele, my hair's a mess," she said. "Fix it." There was a sour taste at the back of her mouth, and a feeling like hard fluttering in her stomach.

The two servants quieted immediately and knelt on the cushions to either side of her. The feeling of their fingers and brushes was familiar and comforting, even if it hurt when they tugged at the snarls. Yolande used the forced immobility to practice the breathing exercises, driving calm up from the body into the mind. There was something oddly soothing about having your hair combed, a childlike feeling of trust.

Don't fidget, she told herself as the tense muscles of her shoulders and neck eased. *It's serfish*. It was emotional to be frightened of going to a new school; they weren't going to hurt her, after all. Children and serfs were expected to be emotional; a Citizen ruled herself with the mind. Bianca was humming as she used the pick on the end of her comb to untangle a knot. Yolande's hair had always been feather-soft and flyaway.

The school was on the Bay itself, surrounded by a thousand hectares of grounds. A chest-high wall of whitewashed stone marked the boundary, overshadowed by tall dark cypresses; the van slowed as they passed through the open wrought-iron gates and past the gatekeeper, bowing with hands over his eyes as the law commanded. Then the wheels were crunching and popping on the gravel of the internal road. Lawns like green-velvet plush spread around them, flowerbanks, clusters of stone-pine, oak, clipped hedges of box and yew. A herd of ibex raised their scimitar-horned heads from a pool, muzzles trailing drops that sparkled as they fell among the purple-and-white bowls of the water lilies.

"Turn right," Yolande said, unnecessarily; there was a servant in the checkered livery of the school directing traffic.

The sun had sunk until it nearly touched the horizon, and the light-wand in the serf's hand glowed translucent white. More servants waited at the brick-paved parking lot, a broad expanse of tessellated red and black divided by stone planters with miniature trees. The van eased into place, guided by a wench with a light-wand who walked backwards before them, and stopped; Yolande felt the dryness suddenly return to her mouth as she rose.

"Well," she said into air that felt somehow motionless after the unvarying rush of wind on the road. "Let's go."

Deng pushed the driver back into his seat. "Not you, Marco," he said.

The younger man gave him a resentful glare but sank down again. Deng was not like some bossboys, he did not use the strap or rubber hose all the time, but he was obeyed just the same. He flicked a match-head alight between thumb and forefinger as he climbed down from the cab, lighting a cigarette and puffing with grateful speed, then unclamped the stairs beneath the side door.

Yolande ignored the acrid smoke and the stairs as well, stepping out and taking the chest-high drop with a flex of her knees. The servants followed more cautiously, passing the parcels and baggage out to Deng and taking his offered hand as they clambered down the metal treads. The Draka girl stood looking about as the pile of luggage grew. There was activity enough, but nobody seemed particularly concerned with her. An eight-wheeler articulated steamer was unloading a stream of girls; that must be a shuttle from Naples, the ones coming in from the train and dirigible havens.

They were all dressed in the school uniform, a knee length belted tunic of Egyptian linen dyed indigo blue, and sandals that strapped up the calf. She felt suddenly self-conscious in her young-planter outfit, even with the Togren 10mm and fighting-knife she had been so proud of. They were mostly older than her; all the Junior Section would have arrived yesterday. Their friends were there to greet them, hugs and wristshakes and flower-wreaths for their hair . . .

Yolande swallowed and forced herself to ignore them, the laughter and the shouts. A few private autos were unloading as well, sleek low-slung sports steamers, and two light aircraft in an empty field to the east. Tilt-rotor craft, civilianized assault-transports; as she watched one seemed to tense in place, the motors at the ends of the wings swinging up to the vertical. The hum of turbines rose to a whining shriek and brown circles appeared in the grass beneath the exhausts as the long propellers blurred. Burnt kerosene overwhelmed the scents of steamcar distillate, flowers, warm brick. Then the airplane bounced five hundred meters into the air, circled as the engines tilted forward to horizontal mode, shrank to a dot fading northward. Navigation lights blinked against the pale stars of early evening.

She blinked; in half an hour it would be past Sienna. Past Badesse, past home. Over the tiny hilltop lights of Claestum; her parents might look up from the dining terrace at the sound of engines. Tantie Rahksan with her eternal piece of embroidery . . . Moths would be battering against the globes, and there would be a damp smell from the pools and fountains. Warm window-glow coming on in the Quarters down in the valley, and the sleepy evening sounds of the rambling Great House. Her own bedroom in the west tower would be dark, only moonlight making shadows on the comforter, her desk, airplane models and old dolls and posters . . .

This is ridiculous, she scolded herself, working at the knot of misery beneath her breastbone. The quarrel at the old school had *not* been her fault; even if somebody had to leave, it should have been Irene, not her. Would have been, if they had not valued peace over justice.

"Hello."

She looked down with a start; a girl her own age was standing nearby, hands on hips and a smile on her face.

"You're Yolande Ingolfsson, the one from up Tuscany way?"

She nodded, and grasped the offered wrist. Then blinked a little with surprise, feeling a shock as of recognition.

I must know someone who looks like her, she thought.

"Myfwany Venders," she was saying. "Leontini, Sicily. I'm in yo' year, and from out-of-district, too, so I thought I'd help yo' get settled."

The other girl was a centimeter taller, with brick-red hair and dark freckles on skin so white it had a bluish tinge, high cheekbones, and a snub nose; big hands and feet and long limbs that hinted at future growth. She grinned: "I know how it is. They pitched me in here last year and I went around bleating like a lost lamb. It's not bad, really, once y' get to know some people."

"Thank yo'," Yolande replied, a little more fervently than

she would have liked. Myfwany shrugged, turned and put thumb and forefinger in her mouth to whistle sharply.

"It's nothing, *veramente*. Let's get the matron."

"Missy."

Yolande stretched and turned over, burrowing into the coverlet.

"Missy. Time to get up."

That was Lele with the morning tray. She was wrapped in a robe, her own half-Asian face still cloudy with sleep.

"Thank you." The Draka yawned and stretched, rolled out of bed, and drank down the glasses of juice and milk.

It was still quite early, with only a faint glimmer of light through the glass and drapes along one side of the bedroom. She walked over and drew back the curtains, yawning again, and walked out onto the terrace. This section of the school faced the sea, with a series of garden-terraces running down to the beach. The sun was behind her, still hidden by the bulk of the inland mountains; a mild breeze was setting in from the ocean, smelling of salt, oleander, rosemary. Gray-blue water stretched to meet dark-blue sky; Jupiter and Venus were fading overhead, and lights winked from the water. A hydrofoil ferry going out to Capri, fishing boats, a tall-masted freighter raising sail; above, along the horizon, were the long whale-shape of a dirigible and the distant pulsing of engines.

Yolande stretched again, turned back into the bedroom. The white-and-green marble tiles were cool under her feet. She worked her toes into the Isfahan carpets and looked around. It was not large, twenty feet by fifteen, part of the usual five-room Senior School suite. Schools had the same facilities, but they were not built to a set pattern. Pale-blue stone walls, plenty of room for anything she wanted to put up; some of her hangings and pictures were still boxed in corners. She walked through the olive-wood door and down the corridor. Different marble on the floor, patterned in geometric shapes. Doors: a study, a lounge, cupboards, a washroom. A room for her servants; she had checked that last night.

Mother's voice in her mind's ear: *You make their choices. It's your responsibility*.

A vestibule, before the outside door. Deng and Marco were waiting, ready for the trip back to the plantation. The Oriental bowed slightly, and the younger man looked down and flushed. Yolande blinked in puzzlement, then realized she was naked. *Oh*, she thought. Serfs were strange about that sort of thing. Especially here in the New Territories; Marco had not been up from the Quarters long, and that mostly in the garages.

"We leaving now, Mistress Yolande," Deng said, crumpling his cap in one hand and bowing again. His eyes flickered past her, to Lele . . .

"A quick journey back and a happy return," Yolande said. "Tell the Mastah and Mistis I'm well settled in, not to worry, I'll call soon. Give Tantie Rahksan a kiss fo' me." She felt the familiar wince of guilt; she was a terrible correspondent, missed her parents bitterly, could never seem to remember to call . . . Home was a prison that you longed to escape, and your safe warm place as well; seeing Deng go was like losing another bit of it. "Don't yo' worry either, Deng, I'll take good care of her." She patted his shoulder; it was like tapping the edge of a boulder.

"Thank you, Missy," he said, with a rare smile.

She could remember him smiling that way when he played tossup games with her, when she was a toddler; now her eyes were level with his. The two men left, and the door closed with a sough.

The other score or so of girls in her Year and section were already gathering in the courtyard, dressed like her in rough cotton exercise tunics and openwork runner's sandals, talking and yawning and helping each other stretch. Baiae School was laid out in rectangular blocks running inland from the water's edge; it was slightly chilly in the shade of the colonnade that ran around three sides of the open space, and the sun was just rising over the higher two-story block at the east end. The low-peaked roof was black against the rose-pale sky, and the sound of birds was louder than the human chatter. In the center of the court was a long pool; water spouted from a marble dolphin, and she could feel a faint trailing of mist as she walked out into the garden beside it among the flowerbeds and benches.

A few heads turned her way as she rummaged among the equipment on a table. Weights for the ankles, and to strap around her wrists; she bound back her hair with a sweatband, and sniffed longingly at the smells of coffee and cooking that

drifted over the odor of dew-wet grass and roses. No food for
an hour or two yet.

"Ingolfsson!" It was Myfwany Venders, the redheaded one
who had greeted her at the parking lot. "Come on over here,
meet the crew." The girl from Sicily continued to her knot of
friends: "This is Yolande Ingolfsson, down from the wilds of
Tuscany." She turned to the newcomer. "This is—"

Yolande struggled to match names with faces as the intro-
ductions were made; it was important, she was the outsider
here. Most of the others were from south-central Italy, daughters of planters and overseers, civil servants and Combine
execs. A few from farther away—that was government policy—
from the French and Spanish and Balkan provinces, even
from the older territories on the south shore of the Mediterranean. Most humiliatingly taller than her, *why* was she
still short . . .

"Look out," Myfwany muttered. "It's Bruiser and the Beak."

Two adults were walking toward them from the administration block at the head of the courtyard. A woman in white
cotton pants and singlet with a towel around her neck; stocky-
muscular, broad in hips and shoulders, big-busted for a Draka,
with a hard flat face and golden-brown hair. The man beside
her was much taller and almost thin, with a close-cropped
mat of black hair shot with silver and a face that would have
been handsome except for the eagle swoop of his nose. He
was stripped to the waist and his body looked wiry and very
strong, long ropy muscles moving easily under tanned skin.

"Teachers," Myfwany continued, *sotto voce*. "Married.
She's Unarmed Combat and Hand Weapons, he's Firearms
and Tactics."

The students fell silent. "Keep stretching," the woman
said, walking and appraising. "Some of you need it." The man
dropped forward, caught himself on three fingers and a thumb
and began doing one-handed pushups. His wife stopped in
front of an apprehensive-looking girl and poked her below the
ribs with one finger. "Too much pasta this summer, Muriel.
Yo'll regret it."

Well, she is a bit plump, Yolande thought. Not fat, but
with a smoothed-at-the-edges look, serfish. Stupid to let yourself go like that over the holidays; it just made school harder
. . . and you lost respect, too.

Myfwany held out linked hands. "Hamstring?" she said.

"Thanks." She swung the heel of her right leg into the

other's fingers. "Higher," she said, rolling back the toes and laying the ball of her foot in line with the shin, kicking position. Myfwany bent her knees and raised it slowly until Yolande's foot was pointing at the sky. That brought their faces close together, and she whispered:

"What're they like?"

"Beak's not bad," the redhead whispered back. "Used to be a tank commander in the Third. His classes are pretty interesting. Bruiser's fair even with her own daughters, but sort of strict. Doesn't much care for excuses; she was in a recon cohort."

The former scout-commando came to stand behind the new girl. "Good extension there," she said. "Try the other leg." Yolande switched feet. "Well, yo' limber enough. Here." Her accent was flat and a little nasal, north-Angolan or Katanga.

Yolande shook out her legs and took the offered hand; it was like gripping a piece of carved wood. She squeezed as strongly as she could, admiring the thick wrist and smooth flat ripple of the teacher's forearm.

"Not bad," the instructor said, releasing her. "Stronger than yo' looks; little ones fool yo', sometimes."

The girl's ears burned. *Why does everyone have to comment on my height?* she thought.

"Right, fo' all the new ones here, I'm Vanessa Margrave, and this is my husband Dave." The man dropped onto the fingers of both hands and flicked himself upright, using the strength of his arms only.

"That's *Miz* Margrave to yo' little horrors. We're goin' to get on fine, as long as certain things are remembered. Back home on Pappy's plantation, yo're all princesses an' the apple of every eye. Here, we learn discipline." She grinned, and a few of the girls swallowed nervously. "Yo've all had seven years of the basics; now Mr. Margrave an' I are responsible fo' turnin' y'all into killin' fighters. Yo' *will* do it, and all become credits to the Race. And in the process, yo' *will* suffer. Understand?"

"Yes, Miz Margrave!" they chorused.

"Now, it's six kilometers befo' breakfast, and I'm hungry. Let's *go*."

Yolande hesitated at the entrance to the refectory, one of several scattered throughout the complex. There were seven hundred students at Baiae School, half of them in the Senior years, and Draka did not believe in crowding their children. In theory you could pick the dining area you wanted, from among half a dozen. In practice it was not a good idea to try pushing in where you were not wanted, and she had tagged along with Myfwany's group from the baths where they had all showered and swum after the run.

I feel like a lost puppy following somebody home, she thought resentfully. Back at the old school she had had her recognized set, her own territory. Here . . . *Oh, gods, don't let me end up a goat,* she thought. Yolande knew her own faults; enough adults had told her she was dreamy, impractical, hot tempered. School was a matter of cliques, and an outcast's life was just barely worth living.

The dining room was in the shape of a T, a long glass-fronted room overlooking the bay with an unroofed terrace carried out over the water on arches. Yolande hesitated at the colonnade at the base of the terrace, then closed the distance at a wave from one of Myfwany's friends. There were four of them, five with her, and they settled into one of the half-moon stone tables out at the end of the pier. It was after seven and the sun was well up, turning the rippled surface of the bay to a silver-blue glitter that flung eye-hurting hints of brightness back at her like a moving mirror, or mica rocks in sunlight.

There was shade over the table, an umbrella shape of wrought-iron openwork with a vine of Arabian jasmine trained through it. The long flowers hung above their heads translucent white, stirring gently in the breeze that moved the leaves and flickered dapples of dark and bright across the white marble and tableware. Yolande stood for a moment, looking back at the shore. You could see most of the main building from here, stretching back north. It was a long two-story rectangle like a comb with the back facing Vesuvius; the teeth were enclosed courtyards running down toward the sea. The walls were pale stone half-overgrown with climbing vines, ivy or bougainvillea in sheets of hot pink, burgundy, and purple.

Formal gardens framed the courts and the white-sand beach. At the north end of the main block another pier ran out into the water from a low stone boathouse; little single-masted pleasure ketches were moored to it, and a small fishing boat that supplied the kitchens with fresh seafood. Beyond that she could see a pair of riders galloping along the sea's edge, their hooves throwing sheets of spray higher than the manes.

"Pretty," she said as she seated herself.

"Hmmm? Oh, yes, I suppose it is," Myfwany said, pressing a button in the center of the table. "Everyone know what they want?"

"Coffee, gods, coffee," one of the others said as the serving wench brought up a wheeled cart.

Yolande sniffed deeply, sighing with pleasure. The scent of the brewing pot mingled with the delicate sweetness of the flowers over their heads and the hot breads under their covers, iodine and seaweed from the ocean beneath their feet, and suddenly she was hungry. For food, for the day, for things that she could not know or name, except that they made her happy. She looked around at the faces of the others, and everything seemed clear and beautiful, everyone her friend. Even the serf, a swarthy thick-set woman with a long coil of strong black hair; the identity number tattoo below her ear showed orange as she bent to fill the cup, and the coffee made an arc of dark-brown from the silver spout to the pure cream color of the porcelain.

"Thank yo'," she said to the servant, with a bright smile. "I'll have some of those—" she pointed to a mound of biscuits, brown-topped and baked with walnuts "—and the fruit, and some of those egg pies."

"Grapefruit," Muriel said sourly, watching with envy as the others gave their orders and Yolande broke a roll. It steamed gently, and the soft yellow butter melted and sank in as soon as it was off the knife. The plump girl had lagged badly when they sprinted the last half-kilometer of the run, and bruised herself doing a front-flip over one of the obstacles. The wench put two neatly sectioned halves before her. "I loathe grapefruit."

"Then don't be such a slug, Muri," Myfwany said ruthlessly, looking up from a clipboard. "You were doing quite well last year, and then spent all summer lolling about stuffin' yo'self with ricotta and noodle pie."

Somebody else giggled, and Muriel's face went scarlet; her expression went from sullen to angry, and then her eyes starred with unshed tears.

"Honest, Muri, everyone's just tryin' to help—" one girl began.

There was a rattle of crockery as Muriel pushed her half-eaten plate away, rose, and left at a quick walk that was almost a run. Myfwany scowled at the girl who had tittered.

"Veronica Adams, that was *mean*."

"Well, I didn't call her a *slug*, anyway."

"An' I didn't laugh at her. Are we her friends, or not? I thought yo' two were close."

Veronica frowned and pushed strips of chicken breast and orange around her plate. "Oh, all right," she muttered. A moment later: "I'll tell her I'm sorry." A sigh. "It's just . . . all the trouble we went to, an' she slides back down the hill when we stop pushin'."

"Things aren't easy fo' her," Myfwany continued, expertly filleting her grilled trout. Aside, to Yolande: "Her parents are religious."

Yolande kept silent for a moment, biting into the biscuit and catching a crumble beneath her chin with the other. Myfwany was obviously the leader of the group, and it would not do to offend . . . not while she was on probation.

There was a slight taste of honey and cinnamon to the pastry, blending with the richness of the butter and the hot morsels of nut. The egg pies looked good, too, baked in fluffy pastry shells with bits of bacon and scallion; she ate one in three swallows, feeling virtuous satisfaction. Her body felt good and strong and loose, warmed from the run and the swim, relaxed by the masseur's fingers.

It would not do to look tongue-tied, either. She swallowed, looked up and raised a brow. Religious . . . That *was* unusual, these days. "Aesirtru?" she asked. You still found a scattering of neopagans about, though even in her grandfather's time it had been mostly a fad.

"No, worse. Christians."

Yolande made a small shocked sound, one hand going unconsciously to her mouth. *Very* unusual, and not altogether safe. Not forbidden, precisely. After all, only a few generations ago most Draka had been at least nominal Christians. But now . . . it was enough to attract the attention of the Security Directorate. Believers were tolerated, no more, provided they kept quiet and out of the way and gave no whisper of socially dangerous opinions; the secret police took the implications of the New Testament seriously, more so than most of its followers ever had. And it could kill any chances of a commission when you did your military service, even if the *krypteia* could do no more to you than that.

She felt the eyes of the others on her. "Well, she's a Citizen," she said with renewed calm, undoing her hair and shaking it out over her shoulders. The sea breeze caught it and threw it back, trailing ends across her eyes. "She's got a right to it, if she wants to."

Myfwany smiled with approval. "Oh, it didn't take," she said, waving her fork. "That's part of the problem, we talked her out of it last year—partly us, some of the teachers helped— and then when she went home it was one quarrel with her parents after another, and she was gloomin' all the time. She'll snap out of it." Another hard look at Veronica. "*If* we help her."

"I *said* I'd say I was sorry," the girl snapped back, then bridled herself with a visible effort. Softly: "I *am* sorry." She was broad-shouldered, with a mane of curly dark-brown hair and the sharp flat accent of Alexandria and the Egyptian provinces. "What's today?"

"Intro Secondary Math 8:00 to 10:30," Myfwany said, glancing back at the clipboard. "Classical Lit from 10:45 to 12:15. Historical Geography till lunch, rest period, and then we're back to Bruiser and The Beak. Shouldn't be too bad, Beak's givin' us a familiarization lecture on rocket-launchers today."

"Moo," the third girl said. "Secondary Math." Yolande fought to remember the name. *Mandy Slauter.* Tall and lanky and with hair sun-faded to white, pointed chin propped in one hand. "Tensor calculus, an' Ah had trouble enough with basic. Euurg, yuk, *moo.*"

"Y'can't make flying school without good math," Myfwany said, reaching for a bunch of grapes from the bowl in the center of the table. She stripped one free, flicked it up between finger and thumb and caught it out of the air with a flash of white teeth. To Yolande: "Yo've fallen in among a nest of would-be spacers."

They all gave an unconscious glance upward. It had only been a few years since the first flights to orbit, but that was a strong dream. Only a few thousand Draka had made the journey beyond Earth's atmosphere as yet, and rather more Americans, but it was obvious that the two power blocs who dominated the planet were moving their rivalry into space. There would be thousands needed when the time came for their call-up in half a decade.

Yolande flushed. "Me, too," she said. "Both my parents were pilots in the War." With shy pride: "Pa was an ace.

Twelve kills." Some of the others looked impressed. *Thank you, Pa*, she thought. Well, it was impressive.

Mandy shrugged. "But tensor calculus . . . Sometimes Ah'd rather just settle fo' the infantry. Not so much like school, anyway." She reached for a passionfruit, cracked the mottled egg-shaped shell, and dumped the speckled greyish contents into her mouth.

"How can yo' eat those things with your eyes open?" Veronica said. "They look like a double tablespoon of tad-poles glued together with snot." In an aside to Yolande: "Mandy's boy-crazy already, that's why she's considerin' the infantry." The pilot corps was two-thirds female, while the ground combat arms had a slight majority of men.

Mandy laughed and raised the fruit rind threateningly. "Ah am *not* boy-crazy—"

"Aren't we all a little old fo' food-fights?" Myfwany said, looking at her watch. "Class time."

CHAPTER TWO

. . . sorry it took so long to write but it's been a bit of a whirl. The school is very pretty here on the bay, and my rooms are fine. I checked on the servants' quarters and food and everything, like you said. Bianca complains about the cooking but that's just because it's Neapolitan, and they all have trouble understanding the Italian around here (so do I) which isn't like Tuscan at all. The school servants can mostly speak English anyway, since they come from all over. A lot of them can read, too. The classes are about like the old school on Elba, but we've got a really tough Unarmed instructor and I'm learning a lot. You have to or she thumps you, which I suppose is fair.

The other girls are mostly nice and I've made some friends already, especially Myfwany and Muriel and Veronica and Mandy. People are calling us the Fearsome Five, and we're all going to try for pilot training and the space program. Can I invite them up to home for the Novembers?

Anyway, I miss you all the time, Mother, and Pa, too, and Edwina and Dionysia and even John but don't tell him or he'll be even worse than he usually is. And Tantie Rahksan and Deng, too, and the house and everything.

Love,
Yolande

P.S. The stables are pretty good here, so could you send down Foamfoot? The school hacks have all got mouths like saddle leather.

Letter from Yolande Ingolfsson to her parents
Dated: October 21st, 1968
From: Contemporary Poets Series
Trackways of the Heart
Archona Press, Archona, 1991

BAIAE SCHOOL
DISTRICT OF CAMPANIA
PROVINCE OF ITALY
DOMINATION OF THE DRAKA
SEPTEMBER 18, 1968

The classroom was comfortably cool, even though the day was growing sultry in the hours after noon. Half the frosted-glass panels of the inner wall were folded away, leaving gaps between the slender pillars of white-streaked rose marble; beyond was the shade of the inner colonnade, and hot white light on the courtyard's gardens and fountains. Yolande still fought to stifle a yawn; there was a feeling of drowsiness to the hot air. It smelled of cool stone, seawater, and the summer-scent of pine resin baking out under the unmerciful sun. Her eyelids fluttered down, and she brought herself back up with a jerk. It had been like that since her periods started a year before. Wild energy, and then sleepiness in the middle of the day; despair and happiness switching on and off like a light-switch.

And I don't even have breasts yet, she thought resentfully, looking down at a chest still almost as flat as a boy's. She looked over at Mandy, in the next desk. *She already looks like a woman and she's tall, too. It isn't fair!*

Myfwany hissed at her and she rose as the teacher walked briskly through the colonnade, followed by a serf with a double armful of books and papers.

"Make yo'selfs comfortable, girls," the instructor said. There was a rustle as they sat again. "Just leave it all, Helga," she added to the servant.

How elegant she looks, Yolande thought, watching the teacher as she arranged the materials. *Sort of distinguished.* Sixtyish, with graying brown curls cropped close to her head; slender, with a scholar's well-kept hands and an athlete's tan, dressed in a long gray robe with a belt of worked silver vine-leaves. And a miniature gold circlet pinned over her heart; the *corona aurea*, the Archon's highest award. Awed, Yolande wondered what it was for. Usually for bravery-above-and-beyond, or some really important accomplishment for the Race.

"Service to the State," the teacher said formally.

"Glory to the Race," the students murmured in perfunctory unison.

The class was a little over average size, twelve pupils seated at desks of African flame-cedar in irregular clumps across a floor tiled in geometric patterns of blue and green, facing the rear wall and the teacher's station.

"I'm Catherine Harris," she said, sitting with one hip on the edge of the green malachite slab that was her desk.

There was a big display-screen on the wall behind her, one of the new crystal-sandwich types; she touched a control on the desk and it lit with a world map in outline. The smaller screens on the students' desks came alive as well, slaved to the master control. Countries were shown in block colors: black for the Domination, with the Draka firelizard sprawled across it, and shades of green for the nations of the Alliance.

"We'll start with a regression. This is the situation today, with more than half the world under the Yoke." All Africa, all Europe, all of mainland Asia except the southern peninsulas running India-Malaysia-Indochina. "Now before the Eurasian War, in 1940." The area of black shrank; now the Domination was mostly Africa, with the Middle East and Central Asia and only a toehold in the eastern Balkans. The names of vanished lands reappeared on the screen: Germany, France, Russia, China.

"Now 1914, before the Great War. Which, difficult as it may be to imagine, infants, I can remember." Muffled laughter, and the screens showed Africa alone in black, with outliers in Crete and Cyprus and Ceylon. "Ten-year intervals back to the beginning." The dark tide receded, from the western bulge of the continent and from the interior. 1800, and Egypt went pale. Two decades more, and there was nothing but a tiny black spot around Cape Town in the extreme south.

Yolande stirred uneasily at the sight. The sequence was familiar, but showing it in reverse was not. Usually the maps *started* with the tiny speck, and then it flowed irresistably forward. Doing it this way seemed vaguely . . . improper, somehow. She glanced at the servant, who was sitting on her heels by the side of the desk, hands folded neatly in her lap and eyes cast down. A wench in her twenties, blond and with

a Germanic-looking pallor, very pretty—what Pa would call a
hundred-auric item—with the serf-number standing out orange beneath her ear.

I wonder what she *thinks of the course*, the Draka girl
thought suddenly. *The wench must have heard it dozens of
times.* Some people said serfs didn't think at all, except about
things like food and sex and their work, but that wasn't true.
Serf children played quite freely with the offspring of the
Great House when they were young, and Yolande had learned
all their gossip; the stories, whose mother yelled and hit, and
whose father drank too much smuggled *grappa*. Deng thought
a lot, he was really smart even if he wasn't very talkative.
Rakhsan, Mother's Afghan maidservant, she could tell you
things about times way back before the War. It was the older
fieldhands who kept so quiet, never speaking unless you
asked them something, the ones old enough to remember the
War and the times right after it, the purges and the camps.

". . . Sure yo're quite familiar with it," the teacher was
saying. "What I'm goin' to teach is the realities beneath it.
Question: how did we get from *that*"—she moved her head
toward the screen—"to *this*." A hand indicated the school.

Myfwany raised her palm. "We won, Miz Harris," she
said, and there was another muffled giggle.

Harris smiled herself, and reached into the folds of her
gown for a gunmetal cigarette case. "Pardon the bad example," she said sardonically at their round-eyed stares. Draka
of their generation did not often smoke, at least not tobacco.

"I was raised befo' we knew it was bad for yo'. Yes, Myfwany,
we won. But war isn't the explanation, it's the result. We're a
warrior people, and our weakness is that we tend to think too
much of battles and not enough of the things which lead up to
victory. There are problems that don't yield to the butchershop
logic of the sword. Yo' can say a man dies because his heart
stops, but it doesn't *explain*. We need to know the *why*."

She turned slightly, leaning back against the desk and
cupping her right elbow in the left hand. "School is trainin',
and not just to fight."

"Yo', girl." She pointed at Mandy. "How many Draka are
there?"

The tall girl started. "Hum, ah, sixty million? Roughly."
Under her breath: "I hope. Moo."

"Fifty-eight million, nine hundred and twenty thousand-
odd. How many serfs?"

"Lots, ah, a billion and a half?"

"Correct. So we're about three percent of the total; that's not countin' the billion or so wild ones in the Alliance countries. It's not enough to be strong an' fierce, good fighters. Necessary, but not enough; to use the old cliché, we aren't a numerous people and nobody loves us. We have serfs enough in the Janissary legions for brute force, to carry rifles and die. Yo' are Citizens, and need to be able to *think*."

A meditative puff. "History is process; like dancin', or an avalanche. Sometimes it's . . . too ponderous to move, just grinds on regardless. Sometimes it balances delicately, and a minor push can turn it. Other times, yo' can turn even a pretty heavy movement with a small force by findin' the right lever to magnify yo' strength.

"That's how we dominate. Leverage . . . and this class is goin' to teach yo' how the process works. Look to either side of the screen, now."

Murals flanked the two-meter square of the display panel, a landscape of hills rocky and steep and covered with the olive-green scrub bush of southern Africa. A labor-gang was building a road through it, black men in leg-hobbles swinging picks and sledgehammers; others pushed wheelbarrows full of crushed rock, chipped granite blocks for the curbs, pulled stone rollers beside yoked oxen. Draka worked with surveyor's transepts and spirit levels to mark the course, swung their whips over the bent backs of the serfs, sat mounted and armed to guard.

"Question," the teacher said. "Date this mural and place it."

Yolande blinked at it, dredging at her memory. No powered machinery, just ox-wagons and horses. *Probably* before the 1820s. Her eyes switched to the right, a close-up of a horseman. Canvas-sided boots, baggy leather pants, a coarse cotton shirt, and a jerkin of zebra-hide; long yellow hair in a twisted braid down his back to the waist. A saber at the belt, and a saw-hilted flintlock pistol in his right hand, double-barreled and clumsy-looking. Two more in holsters at his saddle-bow, and a fourth tucked into the high top of a boot. The long-barreled musket slung across his back was the same as the heirloom antique Mother had brought north from her family's plantation in the far south, a Ferguson breech-loader.

Her hand went up. "1790s?" she said, when the teacher glanced her way. "Uhhh, somewhere north of the White-ridge? Limpopo valley, I think." Myfwany glanced her way, and Yolande caught the thumb-and-forefinger gesture of approval with a flush of pleasure.

"Excellent," Harris said. She looked down and tapped again at the controls set in the stone, and a map of Africa appeared on the screens. It jumped as the focus shifted, narrowing down to the southeastern corner of the continent, and a red dot appeared. "1798, in the Northmark." That was the province north of the Limpopo. "Not far from where I was born, just south of the Cherangani mountains. A wild place and time."

Yolande looked at the man in the picture again. There was a trick she knew, of getting inside someone's head. You had to think *really hard*, and imagine you were wearing their skin, feeling what they felt. Sometimes it worked; sometimes you could even put it down in words, and that was the most magical feeling there was. She fixed her eyes on the face in the picture, made herself forget that it was pigments on a flat surface.

There was pale stubble on his cheeks, and she could see the sheen of sweat on it; the hand that held the pistol was tight-clenched, with half-moons of black under cracked nails. He would stink, of sweat and leather and gun-oil and sulfury black powder, and his hands would have the sweet-sour pungent smell of brass from the hilt of his sword. It was a good picture . . . *no, not a picture, that's how he looked.*

Eyes slitted, they would be flickering ceaselessly back and forth. At the laborers, there were hundreds of them, big muscular men with heavy hammers and picks in their hands. Captured warriors, not meek born-serfs. At the dense bush all around; rough stumps and edges where it had been cut back from both sides of the road, but it rose dense enough to block sight within javelin-cast. She felt the unseen hating black eyes on her back, and pink-palmed hands gripping the hafts of iron-bladed spears. Trapped in close thornbush country, eight shots and then hand-to-hand with cold steel . . .

"Ah, I see yo' understand," Harris said softly as she blinked the present back into her eyes and met the teacher's.

Yolande's mouth was dry, and she drank from the glass of lemonade beside her screen. "No radios or tanks, no helicopter gunboats or automatic weapons. Tell me, how did you place it?"

Yolande willed the sour taste of fear to leave her mouth. The feelings lingered just below the surface of her mind, an adrenaline-hopping intensity of focus, of anger and ferocity. "Ahh . . . it couldn't be earlier. The way they're wearing their hair, and the zebra-skin. But that's an early-model Ferguson, my Mother's got one just like it, see how the trigger-guard has only a little knob to turn it and open the breech? Later on they made them with a bigger handle sticking down from the buttstock."

"To increase the rate of fire," Harris said. "We were the first to adopt the breech-loader, because it shot further an' faster. Gatling came to the Domination, because we'd use his invention . . . because we were always outnumbered, and had to be able to kill them faster than they could charge. Right, now someone else. Which is the richest continent? Yo', Veronica."

"Uh, Africa?"

Harris grinned. "Sorry, trick question. Wealth is a subjective quantity. Fo' example, the Congo river generates as much hydropower as the whole of North America . . . if yo' can get at it, through jungles crawling with diseases."

Her hand reached to the screen controls again. "This is a disease map of Africa, before we cleaned it up. Sleeping sickness. Ngana. Malaria. Yellow fever. Dengue fever, river blindness, bilharzia. Now we'll overlay it on the political sequence-map I showed befo'. Muriel, what do you see? Patterns, remember. Process."

A frown and a long pause from the student whose parents followed the proscribed faith. "The south's healthiest, the areas south of Capricorn. Then the high country all the way north and east to the Ethiopian provinces, then the far north."

"Right. Now the sequence again."

"They . . . they overlap. Not always, but the conquest starts in the south, then leaps 'way north to Egypt, then it goes across North Africa and in both directions down the rift highlands. For a long time, anyway."

"Good, Muriel. Most of this part"—Harris' finger indicated the western coast of Africa—"is a deathtrap for Caucasians without modern medicine. It ate them alive. Now, when was the first European settlement at the Cape?"

Yolande raised her hand again. "1654, Miz Harris. The Dutch."

"Right, the Dutch East India Company. Feeble little colony, and after a hundred and fifty years there were only ten thousand of them. Why?"

"They weren't interested in it?"

"Right again, they never sent mo' than a few hundred colonists; it was so healthy that they multiplied fast. Some of us are descended from them, though they got swamped pretty quick. Next significant date."

"1779," Myfwany said. "The British annexed the Cape."

"Conquered. The formal annexation was in 1783 after the Peace of Paris. But our ancestors were already arrivin'."

The screen flashed a montage: American Loyalists being driven from their homes by revolutionary mobs, Loyalist regiments and their families boarding sailing ships as the British evacuated Charleston and Savannah and New York, Hessian mercenaries sitting idle in camp as the war for which they had been hired wound down.

"Question: with about twenty thousand fightin' men—it was all men in those days—our forebearers conquered a half-million square miles of southern Africa in about a decade. We've seen it was possible partly because the environment didn't kill them; but two generations later, it took a hundred thousand men *two* decades to conquer North Africa for us . . . with better weapons an' organization, too. There were two million strong an' warlike blacks in the southern provinces. Why were they relatively easy to break to the Yoke? Yes, Berenice."

"Mmmm, blacks are stupid an' backward?"

Harris laughed. "A comfortin' lie that was obsolete when I was yo' age, girl." She called up the world map again. "What's the most relevant fact about that area, all things considered? Think about it, Berenice."

"It's . . . far away from everywhere?"

"*Correct*. As far as yo' can get, failin' Australia. Societies grow an' develop by competition, same as species, only the process is Lamarckian not Darwinian. The inhabitants of this area were barely neolithic, 'cept for havin' iron spears an' hoes. No political unit larger than a few villages, no written language, no horses, no wagons, an' a magical-ritual worldview. Four thousand kilometers of mountain, jungle, an' fever-bush protection; then three millennia of progress arrived overnight by ship, with the result that they became our cattle."

She glanced at her wrist. "Class over. Fo' the next, I want a short essay, outlinin' why plantations became the standard rural unit." A hard look. "I do *not* want a rehash of chapter 7," she added, tapping the brown-jacketed text before her,

The Domination: A Historical Survey. "Yo' *own* thoughts. Give yo' a hint: look at where the most of the Loyalists came from. Then look at the figures in the appendix on soil fertility an' erosion in the far-southern provinces, and the demographics chapter. See yo' Thursday, girls. Service to the State."

"Glory to the Race," they answered. The desks hummed and began to spit printouts of the maps the teacher had summoned into the receiver trays.

Wheeee! Yolande thought, slowing to a handstand on the parallel bars. Her body was straight as a plumbline, toes pointed to the ceiling and arms a rigid Y on the hardwood poles. Then she let her weight fall back, a long swoop that accelerated like a sling's circuit into speed that pulled the blood out of her head, flung her *up* and her hands came off the bars and she twisted in midair, body whirling like a top. *Slap* and her hands were back on the bar, almost in the same position but facing the opposite direction.

Five, she thought. That was enough; her arms were starting to tire. There was no sense in risking an injury. Instead she spread her legs in the air and lowered her feet, placing them neatly just behind her hands. The damp skin touched oak; she took a deep breath and sprang, backflipping in the air and landing on the balls of her feet, knees bending slightly to take the shock as she touched down on the hard rubbery synthetic of the *palaestra*'s floor.

There was applause. Startled, Yolande looked up as she reached for a towel. Several of the other girls had stopped and were clapping, halting for a moment the stick-fighting or free weights or exercise machines that their individual programs prescribed. She blushed and bent her head to dry herself off; she was slick-wet with sweat from face to feet, a familiar enough sensation and rather agreeable. The embarrassment was not, and she was glad that the exertion-glow would hide it. She finished and drew on the rough cotton trousers and singlet, pulling the drawstring of the pants tight with fingers that trembled slightly. Half irritation, half a pleasure that was almost painful . . .

I am good at the bars, she thought. *I just wish . . . it's nice to be good, but I wish it didn't make you* stand out. *Why can't I ever just fit in . . .*

"Not bad," Margrave said. The instructor was dressed in *pankration* practice-armor, shiny black leather and synthetic,

and a padded helmet with protective bars across the face.
"Ever thought of trying for the Games?"

"Yes, Miz Margrave," Yolande said. The Domination had
little in the way of professional sports, but amateur athletics
had high prestige. She had daydreamed it, standing on the
rebuilt plinth at Olympia with the golden olive-wreath resting on her hair . . . but that would mean giving up all her
spare time, and . . . "There are too many other things to do."

Margrave nodded, and jerked a thumb over her shoulder
at the rack of pankration equipment on the far wall. "Such as
that. Suit up, I'd bettah check yo' style."

Yolande swallowed dryly and trotted to obey; that was one
of the rules, you ran everywhere. This palaestra was a severly
plain box two stories high and open on one end to face a turf
running-track and a long vista of fields and woods; the interior was finished in white tile, with mirrors and stretching-
rails around most of the perimeter, climbing-ropes and rings
dangling from the ceiling. "Thanks," she muttered to Myfwany,
as the other girl helped her on with the armor.

"Level?" she asked the instructor as they faced off.

"Full contact far as yo' concerned," Margrave said. "Startin'
. . . *now.*"

Yolande dropped into fighting position, feet at right angles
and knees bent. Breath in through the nose, out through the
mouth. Muscles relaxed; you could make yourself faint with
exhaustion in minutes if you tensed. The weight of armor,
boots, and gloves was familiar; you never practiced without
them, for protection's sake and because real-world fighting
wasn't done in gym clothes. The teacher quartered, and
Yolande responded with a pivot on her front foot. *Don't let
the opponent push you back*, she reminded herself.

A kick. Straight hop-kick forward, toward her stomach. She
moved into it, parrying with her left hand and swiping upward with her left elbow towards the chin . . . No, that was a
mistake, Margrave was too tall . . .

The teacher's kicking leg had come down aside, leaving her
in a wide horse-straddle stance. Her hands clamped down on
Yolande's arm, elbow and shoulder; she hip-twisted to leave
her right leg as a trip-bar and threw the student forward and
down. That was simple enough, so simple that she could
think while reflex ingrained since her fifth year tucked her
head down and made her throw herself *with* the motion.
Time slowed as she fell. *Impact* on the shoulders. Rolling to

break the hold, rolling forward curled into a ball to preserve momentum.

"Can't get up fast enough," she muttered, vocal cords following thought without conscious intervention. She was watching between her own feet as she rolled, watching the teacher's machine-fluid rush after her. *Slap*, and her forearms went down on the mat in a neat V; her body curled on top of them, its own weight coiling it back like a spring. A *hunnh* of effort, and she drove both legs back, toes curled towards her shins and heels together.

They struck, heelbones driving into the teacher's solar plexus. *That hurt*, she thought; it was like kicking a concrete-block wall, and it jarred every bone in her body down to the small of her back. *Move, move.* Margrave was folding backwards bending at the middle, moving like a stone dropped into thick honey. Yolande let the impact stop her own body in mid air, curled her knees towards her chest and roll-bounced upright. The teacher was just straightening; the girl swung forward in a flying scissor, pumping the left knee up for momentum and then down as the right foot whipped around in a torquing circle, aimed for—

Blackness.

"*She's all right*," a voice was saying. Yolande blinked and started to shake her head. That was a mistake, and she was barely able to contain the surge of nausea that followed. Flecks of glitter drifted past her retinas, and her vision quivered as hands undid the helmet and slid her head free.

A finger peeled back one eyelid, while a hand clamped her head steady. "Good—even dilation. No concussion."

A cool cloth touched brow and cheeks: Myfwany. "Yo' were just out fo' a sec," she said, her voice anxious. Margrave removed her own practice helmet and threw it to one side, leaning forward again to probe at Yolande's neck and shoulders with expert fingers.

"Nice work. Iff'n I hadn't had the breastplate yo' might have put me out with that back-kick."

"Sorry," Yolande mumbled, squinting against the multiple images. Margrave grinned.

"Nevah say sorry fo' doin' it right." She looked up to the circle of students. "That was the *right* move. 'Specially against superior weight an' strength. The follow-up was the problem; those-there high-jumpin' kicks don't do it, 'less'n the other

side's immobilized anyways. Don't get fancy." Margrave came
up on one knee, leaned over with elbow on thigh.

"Good work, Ingolfsson," she continued. "Yo' really pushed
me a little. Rest easy fo' a while." To the others: "Right, pick
partners an' face off. No contact."

It was full dark now on the beach, and the driftwood fire
crackled, sending sparks flying up with sharp popping sounds.
The flames were blue and red and orange, a white-crimson
over the bed of coals below; the smell was dry and hot.
Inland the trees and shrubs rustled, shadows dark and moving against the lesser dark of the sky. The waves were breaking in a foam of cream, glittering in starlight and moonlight,
surge and retreat. The sound of them was like heartbeat in
her ears, like lying beside some huge and friendly beast. Out
beyond her friends were still diving and playing, flashes of
white bodies otter-sleek among the water. Their voices dropped
into the warm dark, no louder than the cicadas and nightbirds.

Yolande laid her head on her knees and wiggled her toes
over the edge of the blanket. The powdery white clung to
them like frosting; she tapped her feet together and felt the
grains trickle down her insteps, tickling or clinging where the
skin was still damp from her swim. Looking up, the moonpath
lay on the water like silver, almost painfully bright. The stars
were sparse around the moon, abundant elsewhere; the lights
of men were far too few to dim them. A faint glow west across
the bay was Naples, and she could make out the long curve of
the coast by the wide-scattered jewels that marked the towns
and manors of her people. Elsewhere the shore was quiet and
lightless, fields and groves and orchards.

She lay back on the striped wool and smiled, stretching her
arms above her head. Stars . . . there was a trick to that. A
mental effort, and the velvet backdrop with its glowing colored lights vanished; instead there was *depth*, an endless
dark where great fires hung burning forever amid the slow-
fading hydrogen roar of creation. Her lips parted, and she felt
a sensation that might have been delight, or a loneliness too
great to bear; she forced herself to hold the wordless moment, mind suspended in pure experience. Moisture gathered slowly around her eyes, trickling in warm salt streaks
down the wind-cooled skin of her temples.

"Woof!" Mandy's voice. "I'm turnin' into a *prune*. Come on!"
Yolande started as the others dashed out of the ocean,

wiping away the not-quite-tears with the back of her wrist.
They ran past her to the freshwater fountain at the edge of
the beach, laughing and splashing each other around the
stone basin as they sluiced off the salt. The darkness closed
around as they threw themselves down on the blankets about
the fire; now it was a hearth, the tribe's fortress against the
night. Myfwany sat cross-legged beside her, leaning back on
braced palms. She was still breathing deeply from the swim;
from Yolande's position her face was shadowed against the
backlit dark-red curtain of her hair. The drops of water that
ran down her flanks glistened with the rise and fall of her
chest, changing from blood-crimson to lemon-yellow.

"You're quiet, 'Landa," she said. "Head still troublin'?"

"Mmmmm . . . no. Hammerin' great headache yesterday,
couldn't hardly move this mornin'. Now it's just a bit stiff all
ovah. No, I's just lookin' at the stars and thinkin'."

Myfwany probed at her neck, tracing the cords down to
her shoulders; she shivered slightly at the touch, still cold
and wet. " 'S right, stiff," Myfwany said definitely. "Maybe
swimmin' wasn't such a good idea. Muriel, give me a hand?
Roll ovah, 'Landa."

Yolande turned onto her stomach and laid her cheek on her
crossed hands, feeling a painful warmth in her stomach.
"Thanks," she muttered. Massage was usually serf's work,
although everybody learned it; it was something you did for
close friends, a sign that status was put aside. Two pairs of
hands began to work on her, one starting on the soles of her
feet, the other where the neck-muscles anchored on the base
of her skull. She felt uncomfortable for an instant, as the
pressure made her aware of soreness she had been ignoring,
then surrendered to the sensation.

"Y'all bein' mighty nice," she said sincerely. Myfwany
snorted, and Muriel laughed and slapped her lightly on the
calf.

"Yo' the one bruised the Bruiser," Mandy said. She was
kneeling by a basket across the fire, rummaging within. "Never
seen her move so fast; mean of her to thump yo' head,
though."

"No, that's the point," Myfwany said. "Bruiser *had* to
move fast, an' react automatic-like."

"Jus' so —*Veronica, watch where yo' puttin' that dirt!* I's
got *scallops* in heah!"

The stocky girl had been raising the fine sand in double

handfuls, letting it trickle down over her body. She laughed and bent backward from her kneeling position until her head touched the blanket behind her, a perfect bow, stretching.

" 'Salright," she said as she rose. A sigh. "Ah jus' *love* this time of year. Perfect, just cool enough fo' a fire, but not cold. Look! There it is!"

She raised a hand. They followed the gesture, and saw a moving star crawling slowly across the southern horizon.

"That our'n or their'n?" Mandy asked. The Domination and the Alliance had both put up another dozen orbital platforms in the last few years; the rivalry was pushing development hard.

"Ours," Myfwany said, sinking back on her elbows. "Oh, ours." Her voice became dreamy. "I wonder . . . How do the stars look from *there*?" To Yolande: "What were yo' thinkin' of, starwatcher?"

"Lots of things," Yolande said abstractedly. "How we can't see the stars, jus' the light they sent long ago. Like readin' a book, hey? An' . . . how far away, an' how perfect."

"Perfect?"

"There's no right or wrong with them," Yolande continued, almost singsong, whispering. "No lovin' or hatin'; they just . . . *are*."

They were silent for long minutes, each staring upward past the fire-glow and the dancing sparks.

"Well," Mandy said, her hands moving again in the basket. "Who's fo' lemonade, and who's fo' wine?"

"Mmmm, I'll take the wine," Yolande said.

"Lemonade first, I'm too thirsty fo' drinkin'," Myfwany said. "That enough, 'Landa?"

"Feels nice," she replied.

Veronica and Mandy were making skewers from a pile of willow-switches, sharpening the ends and threading on pieces of scallop and shrimp wrapped in bacon; they handed the limber sticks around, with wicker platters of soft flat Arab bread, and glasses. The five girls drew closer to the fire. Yolande sat up, watching the flames. The breeze had picked up slightly, and gusts of it blew the tongues of colored flame toward her. She sipped at the wine as the bacon sizzled and dropped fat to pop and flare on the white coals; it was cool from the earthenware jug, rather light, slightly acidic. A southern vintage, she thought, probably from Latium.

"Strange," Muriel said, hugging her knees and leaning back, letting her head fall against Veronica's shoulder.

"What?" Mandy asked.

"I was thinkin' . . . Here we are. In twenty-odd years our own daughters will be here, or someplace like here. Maybeso raaht here; maybeso doin' and thinkin' just what we are. Strange."

"What brought that on?" Myfwany said. She brought the skewer close, examined the seafood critically, and used a piece of the flatbread to pull it off. "Mmm, these are *good*."

"I was . . . I was thinkin' about history class. An' about the things Ma and Pa used to tell me, yo' know, those religion things." Muriel stuck the butt-end of her skewer into the sand and rolled the wine-cup between her hands. "I mean . . . if yo' believes all that, the God stuff, then"—she frowned —"then it would all look different. It would be *comin'* from somewheres, and *goin'* to somewheres. Like-so a story, hey? An' if yo' don't believe it, then it's . . . all sort of, well, it just *happens*."

"Iff'n yo' believes it, we're all goin' straight to hell," Veronica laughed, giving a light tug on Muriel's brown curls.

"Pass the wine, will yo', hey?" Yolande said. There was a clink of stoneware. "Thanks, Mandy. Well, the way Harris says it, it's the story of the Race; where we came from an' where we're goin'.'"

Muriel rested her chin on the edge of the cup. "That sort of depends, don't it? I mean, the *Race* didn't have to happen; Harris says so herself. History's a story leadin' up to *us*, but only on account we happened. If the Yankees killed us all off, then it'd be a story about *them*, an' we'd just be part of their history."

"But we did happen, an' the Yankees aren't goin' to win; we are," Myfwany said definitely.

Yolande chuckled. "So the story has an endin' and a meanin', because we're tellin' it." A pause. "Us here, too. It's . . . true because we make it true, eh? So we tell history like ouah own story, like we was writin' it. Like God."

The others looked at her. "Say, that's really pretty clever," Myfwany said.

Yolande flushed and looked down into her wine cup, continuing hastily. "Speakin' of which, what *are* we goin' to do once we've conquered the Yankees?"

Myfwany laughed. "My brothah, Billy? He likes the Yankee movies; says the girls look nice. Says he's goin' buy a dozen when we put the Yoke on them."

"Euuu, yuk, *boys*," Mandy said. "Ooops, this is over-done . . ."

"Ah thought yo' *liked* boys," Veronica said. She bent her head to whisper something in Muriel's ear, and the other girl giggled and worked her eyebrows.

Yolande looked at Veronica and flushed again; the Alexandrian girl was no older, but she had definite breasts, and the dark-brown hair between her legs was thick and abundant. It made her conscious of her own undeveloped form again. And . . . *strange about sex and things*, she mused. *When yo' young, yo' know about it an it isn't all that interestin', and all of a sudden it's scary and important.* She shook her head; at least there was a while before she had to worry about that sort of thing. *Freya's Curse, I hate being shy!*

"I do like boys," Mandy said. "At least, I sort of like the *idea* of 'em. But they still sort of yucky, too. Yo' know, my brothah Manfred, he only a year older than me, an' he's got ouah *cook* pregnant? Ma found him ridin' her in the pantry, an' cook's *thirty*, with a bottom a meter across an' a mustache. I mean, we're not planters, we've only got a dozen houseserfs, but Pa bought him a regular concubine when he turned thirteen, and still he goes an' does things like that." She brooded for a moment. "Yucky."

"My Ma," Yolande began, "says it's on account of they don't have enough blood." She grinned at their blank looks and held out a hand, palm-up, then slowly curled up her index finger. "Yo' know, all the blood rushes to they crotch, their brains shut down fo' lack of oxygen, an' they stop thinkin'?"

There was a moment of silence, and Yolande felt a flash of fear that her joke had fallen flat. Then the laughter began and ran for a full half-minute, before trailing off into teary giggles.

"Aii, that's a good one," Muriel said. She glanced up at the stars again. "When we've beaten the Yankees, we'll put up mo' of those power-satellites my Pa's workin' on."

"Build cities on the moon!"

"Turn Venus into anothah Earth!"

"Give Mars an atmosphere!"

"Hollow out asteroids an' fly 'em to Alpha Centauri!" The comments flew faster and faster, more and more outrageous, until everyone collapsed into giggles again. Myfwany rose, and pulled out a velvet case from their bundles.

"This is your'n, isn't it, 'Landa?"

"Yes—careful!" Yolanda took the long shape in her hands;

they moved toward it with unconscious gentleness. "It's a mandolin."

Muriel whistled between her teeth. "An' Archona's a city. Old one, hey?"

"My great grandma's," Yolande said. She put the pick between her teeth while she arranged the case across her lap, then settled the instrument and slipped it onto her hand. "On my Ma's side; she Confederate-born. Had it fancied up some . . ." She tuned it quickly; the strings sounded, plangent under the fire-crackle and *shhhhh* of the waves. The wood was smooth as satin under her fingers, the running leopards inlaid in ivory around the soundbox as familiar as her own hands.

"Well, give 's a song, then," Myfwany said.

"I don't sing all that well—"

"C'mon," Mandy said. "We'll all join in."

"Oh, all right." Yolande bent her head, then tossed it as the long pale ripple of her hair fell across the strings. She swept through the opening bars, a rapid flourish, and began to sing: an alto, pure but not especially strong.

> 'Twas in the merry month of May
> When green buds all were swellin',
> Sweet William on his deathbed lay
> Fo' love of Bar'bra Allen—

The ancient words echoed out along the lonely beach; everyone knew *that* one, at least. They all had well-trained voices as well, of course; that was part of schooling. Myfwany's sounded as if it would be a soprano, rich and rather husky. Muriel's was a bit reedy, and Veronica's had an alarming tendency to quaver; Mandy's was like her own, but with more volume. They finished, gaining confidence, and swung into "Lord Randal" and "The WesterWitch."

"What next?" Veronica said. "How about something modern?"

"Alison Ghoze?" Muriel said.

Mandy made a face.

"Oh, moo. Call that modern? It's a hundred years old; modern iff'n yo' count anythin' after the land-takin'."

"I—" Yolande strummed, forced the stammer out of her voice. "I've got somethin' new, care to hear it?"

The others nodded, leaning back. *Calm. Breathe deep. Out slow.* She began the opening bars, and felt the silence deepen; a few seconds later and she was conscious of nothing at all but the music and the strings.

It ended, and there was a long sigh.

"Now, *that* was good," Myfwany said. She half-sang the last verse to herself again:

> "An' we are scatterin's of Dragon seed
> On a journey to the stars!
> Far below we leave—fo'ever
> All dreams of what we were.

"Who *wrote* that, anyways?"

"I—" Yolande coughed. "I did."

They clapped, and she grinned back at them. Mandy laughed and jumped to her feet.

"C'mon, let's dance—Muriel, get yo' flute out!"

The silver-bound bamboo sounded, a wild trilling, cold and plangent and sweet. Yolande cased her mandolin and joined the others in a clap-and-hum accompaniment. The tall girl danced around the outer circle of the firelight, whirling, the colored driftwood flames painting streaks of green and blue across the even matte tan of her skin and the long wheatblond hair. She spun, cartwheeled, backflipped, leaped high in an impossible pirouette, feet seeming to barely touch the sand.

"C'mon, yo' slugs, *dance!*" she cried.

> " . . . as we dance beneath the moon
> As we dance beneath the moon!"

Myfwany came to her feet and siezed Yolande's hand in her right, Muriel's in her left. "Ring dance!" she said. "Let's dance the moon to sleep!"

"Oh, wake up, Pietro," Veronica said, kicking the serf lightly in the side. He started up from the grass beside the little electric runabout and loaded the parcels as they pulled on their tunics and found seats.

"Do y'know," Mandy said, tying off her belt, "that the Yankees wear *clothes* to go swimmin'?"

Veronica made a rude noise. "And fo' takin' baths, too."

"No, it's true, darlin'," Muriel said. "My Pa visited there, an' they do." She outlined the shape of a bikini. "Like underwear."

"Strange," Myfwany said. They settled in for the kilometer ride back to the main buildings; nothing else moved on the narrow asphalt ribbon of the road, save once an antelope caught in the headlights for an instant with mirror-shining eyes. It was much darker now after moonset, and they rode with an air of satisfied quiet.

"Go into Naples tomorrow?" Veronica said. Tomorrow was a Sunday, their only completely free day.

"Fine with me," Mandy said; Muriel nodded agreement, and Myfwany nudged Yolande with an elbow.

"How 'bout it?" she said casually.

"Why—" Yolande smiled shyly; this was acceptance, no longer tentative. "Why, sho'ly."

The runabout ghosted to a silent halt by the eastside entrance. They made their farewells and scattered; Yolande blinked as she walked into the brighter lights of the halls and colonnades. It was after twelve and there were not many about; twice she had to skirt areas where the houseserfs were at their nightly scrubbing and polishing. Her own door, looking more familiar now somehow.

"Missy?" That was Bianca, yawning and blinking up from a mat by the entrance, tousled in her nightgown. Machiavelli yowled and circled until she picked him up; the cat settled in to purr as she rubbed behind his ears, sniffing with interest at the shrimp scent on her fingers.

"Jus' turn down the bed, put this stuff away, then go to sleep," Yolande said, padding through to her bedroom. *How do I feel?* she asked herself, with relaxed curiosity. Tingly from the swim, tired from that and the dancing. Relaxed . . . *Happy,* she decided. *Maybe that's part of growin'.* When you were a child happiness was part of the day, like sadness over a skinned knee or sunlight on your face. Then one day you *knew* you were happy, and that it would pass.

"Tomorrow's also a day," she muttered to herself, setting the cat down on the coverlet. She yawned hugely, enjoying the ready-to-sleep sensation; that was odd, how it felt good when you knew you could rest, and hurt if you had to stay up. The bed was soft and warm; she nuzzled into the pillow, and felt the cat arranging itself against the back of her knees. "Tomorrow . . ."

CHAPTER THREE

The War? We didn't think about the War while it was on. We thought about the next mission, then staying alive for the next five minutes. Get back and we thought about sleep or food or a cigarette, or getting laid. Maybe about "after the War," but that was a daydream . . . but when it was really afterward, yes.

Then we thought about it. Something as big as the Eurasian War can't be understood from the inside, not while you're in the belly of the beast. What did we think? We were . . . shocked, I suppose. We were a more matter-of-fact generation than yours, you know. You youngsters have grown up with things getting really *strange* —yes, you're tired of hearing that. The War was something new under the sun, though; there'd never been a world war in an industrialized world before. A tenth of humanity died in those seven years, that's just numbers, but we up at the sharp end, we *saw* it. Worse than that, because it was concentrated. No fighting on our soil, thank Wotan, not much on the Yankee's, either. Elsewhere, though, by '46 it was a charnel house. I'm not using a metaphor, you could travel hundreds of miles and not get out of sight of human bones. You'd see a city, and someone would say it was Shanghai or Minsk or Bruges or Heidelberg, but it was all rubble, just mounds of dirty brick and stone with bits of reinforcing-rod standing out. Sometimes melted by firestorms, and the *stink*, Freya bless . . . tens of thousands, hundreds of thousands of bodies down under the buildings, smothered by the fire or nerve-gassed.

We were tired, by the end, very very tired. Tired and sick of it. Gods know, we're not a squeamish people, but . . . It changes you, that much killing. First you stop even thinking about alternatives. Life in the abstract loses its meaning, then your *own* life does. Life and death, good and bad, it all starts to blur.

It takes a lot of rest to recover from. If you ever do.

From: *Notes to My Children*
Journal of Thomas Ingolfsson:
April, 1950

CLAESTUM PLANTATION
DISTRICT OF TUSCANY
PROVINCE OF ITALY
APRIL, 1969

The aircar was a Trevithick Meerkat, a little crowded with six. Shiny new and smelling of fresh paint and synthetics; civilian production had just gotten under way, and they were still expensive enough that only the more affluent Citizens could afford them. Yolande, Myfwany, and Mandy were squeezed into the backseat, with Muriel in the front and Veronica on her lap, careful not to jostle the driver. He was a serious-looking young serf, thin and very black, flying cautiously. Trained at the Trevithick Combine's works in Diskarapur in the far south; a pilot and two mechanics had come with the aircraft.

"Oh, hurry up, boy," Yolande said irritably, as he banked the car into a circle at a thousand meters and began a slow descent, the ducted-fan engines turning down for lift. They had been slow getting away; the eight-month academic year was ending, and the Baiae landing fields had been crowded. Of course, an aircar like this could be driven by road and take off from any convenient open space, but serfs operated machinery by the book. Her hands itched to take the controls; this was all fly-by-wire, you *couldn't* redline it, the computers wouldn't let you . . .

"Just yo' parents to home?" Veronica asked, turning her head and resting it on Muriel's shoulder.

"Mmm-hm," Yolande replied. "Edwina and Dionysia both turned eighteen last year; they in Third Airborne, stationed near Shanghai. John would've been out, but they picked him fo' officer's trainin'." That meant an extra year's active service beyond the usual three, or possibly more. "He might be back on leave soon, though . . . Ma said her cousin Alicia's up from the south; she's in textiles, Shahnapur. Just got divorced, up here restin'-like. May move up."

The sound of the fans altered as they came to a halt a hundred meters up and lowered with a smooth elevator sensation.

"Oooo, woof, nice," Mandy said from her right, as their descent gave a slow panorama of Claestum manor. "I like it when they use the old things."

There were admiring murmurs as the aircar extended its wheels with a cling-*chung*, and Yolande felt a warm glow of pride like sun on bare skin. They had landed at the southern entrance of the main building, where the road widened into a small plaza after its winding journey up from the Quarters and through the gardens. Ahead was the house complex, and the tall oaks and chestnuts that crowned the hill and tumbled down the northern slope.

It is pretty, she thought, trying to look at it as a stranger might. Her parents had laid out the Great House in the shape of a U along the south-facing slope, with its apex open to the woods at the crest. Both flanks were old Tuscan work from the pre-War town, each ending in a tower; weathered red tiles and sienna-colored stone overgrown with flowering vines. The newer buildings knitted them together, and the southern end of the U was closed by a curved block in classic Draka style; two stories of ferroconcrete sheathed in jade-green African marble. Fluted pillars of white Carrara ran from the veranda past the second-story gallery to end in golden acanthus leaves at the roof, and the windows behind were etched glass and silver.

"Oh, it's all right," Yolande said casually, as the gullwing doors of the aircar soughed open. She put a hand on the rim of the passenger compartment and vaulted out.

Home, she thought, swallowing. *It smells like home.* Green, after the filtered pressurized atmosphere of the aircraft; the mildly warm fresh-green scent of a Tuscan spring. Odors of stone, dust, flowers, water from the two fountains that flanked the wrought-iron gates into the central courtyard. The piazza of checkered brick beneath her feet was where she had learned to ride a bicycle, the trees flanking it were ones she had watched grow. Her parents had been waiting beneath the gate, out of reach of the miniature duststorm an aircar made in landing. They came forward as their daughter's friends clambered out of the Meercat. Yolande swallowed again and drew herself up calmly, cleared her throat.

"Hello, mother, father," she said. One of the housegirls behind the Landholders was coming forward with a curtsy, bearing a courtesy tray with a carafe and glasses. Yolande smiled with a flush of pleasure. There would be a formal greeting; her parents were treating her friends as adults, not casually as children.

"Service to the State," her father said. He was a stocky man and rather short for a Draka, no more than 175 centimeters, dressed in planter's working clothes: boots and loose chamois trousers, cotton shirt and gunbelt, and a broad-brimmed hat in one hand. Hazel eyes, and gray streaks through seal-brown hair and mustache. "Thomas Ingolfsson, Landholder, pilot, retired," he continued.

"Johanna Ingolfsson," her mother took up, handing out the glasses and raising her own. "Landholder, pilot, retired. Glory to the Race." She was a finger's breadth taller than her husband: a wiry-slender blond woman in her forties with a handsome hatchet face and scarring around her left eye, dressed in a long black robe with bands of silver mesh at neck and throat. They all poured out the ceremonial drops and sipped, murmuring the formula. The wine was a light, slightly sweet white; not the *clasico* vintage that was Claestum's pride, but that was a red dinner wine and unsuitable as an aperitif. "Well, do the honors, daughter."

"Myfwany Venders, Arethustra Plantation, Sicily," she said. Myfwany clasped forearms with both the elder Ingolfssons. "Mandy Slauter, from Naples; Veronica Adams, Two Oaks Plantation, Lusitanica; Muriel Quintellan, Haraldsdal Plantation, Campania."

Her parents went through the ritual gravely. Then her mother turned to her and smiled, spreading her arms. "But *yo'* are still my baby 'Landa, hey?"

Yolande flung herself forward, and felt the familiar slender strength of her mother's arms around her, pressed her face into the hard curve of neck and shoulder. It smelled of soap and a faint rose perfume and the clean summery odor of

Johanna's body, the scent of comfort and belonging. "Hello, mama," she whispered. "Thanks awfully." Her mother held her out at arm's length.

"Yo' *are* fillin' out," she said. Yolande grinned with pride, then gave a whoop of surprise as hands gripped her under the arms and swung her in a circle.

"Y'are indeed, but still bird-light," her father said, laughing up into her indignant face.

"Daddy! Put me *down!*" He laughed again, giving her a toss; she felt the strength in his hands as he lowered her, gently controlled and as irresistible as a machine.

"Greetin's, child," he said. To the others: "Y'all will fo'give me, ladies; I've got an overseer gone and broke her leg, and fo' hundred hectares of vines to finish prunin', while my wife lazes about." He nodded and strode down the plaza, where a groom led a horse forward.

"If he thinks wrestlin' with that accountin' computer and those League bureaucrats—" Johanna shook her head. "Well. Friends of my daughter, y'all are to consider Claestum yo' own, and make yo'selves to home. Veronica an' Muriel, I'm puttin' yo' together?" The friends were standing hand-in-hand; they exchanged a glance and nodded, smiling. "East tower, then; yo' servants an' baggage arrived safe last sundown. Or pick another if it doesn't suit; one thing this stone barn's not anyhow short of, it's space. 'Landa, I'm puttin' y'other two friends directly either side of yo' old rooms over t' the west tower. Rahksan heah will settle yo' in, and see y'all at lunch."

"Oh, it *is* good to be home," Yolande said, throwing her gunbelt on a table and sinking into a wicker chair. "Shut up, cat; iff'n I'd taken yo' by air, yo'd have puked."

Machiavelli looked up from the cushions of the chair opposite, giving her a cool green-eyed stare of resentment before ostentatiously grooming. He had been sent ahead by train with her luggage and maids, and would be a while forgiving her. The Draka girl shed her boots with a push of instep against heel, and let them drop; she peeled off her socks with her toes and rubbed the sole of each foot down the drill fabric of the opposite pants-leg.

Rahksan laughed, scooping up the holstered pistol and racking it neatly on the stand beside the door before picking up the boots. "Good to have yaz back, Mistis 'Landa," she replied, examining the scuffed heels. " 'T cat Ah could do without."

Yolande sighed, linked her fingers behind her head and stretched, wiggling bare toes against the edge of the reading table as she watched the serf drop the footwear outside the entranceway to the corridor and begin unpacking the hand case she had brought with her in the aircar. She could feel her mind settling into the familiar spaces, at rest with every cranny of the rooms that had been hers since she moved down from the nursery. There was the old tower above, with its spiral staircase; the rooftop aerie, a private study below, then her bedroom. This lounging room on the ground floor, lined with bookcases and the tapestries Uncle Eric had looted from Florence during the War and given for her naming-feast. Her desk, over there in the corner; a video screen, her own retrieval terminal to the House computer, the new digital sound system she had gotten for her thirteenth birthday. Chinese rugs on the gray-marble tiles of the floor, glowing in the bright morning light that streamed through the glass doors of the terrace.

Rakhsan came back from taking her toiletries through into the bathing rooms. Yolande looked at her more closely. The Afghan had been a fixture of her life as long as she could remember. Ma had been given her as a present by an uncle when they were both five, to raise as she might a puppy or a kitten, a ragged girl-child pulled out of the rubble of a gassed village during the conquest of her wild and mountainous homeland. She was a short woman, round-faced and curve-nosed and slightly plump, big-breasted and -hipped, with curling dark hair still glossy despite the silver streaks.

"Yo' lookin' good," the young Draka said affectionately. Rahksan had done much of the day-to-day rearing of the Ingolfsson children, and supervised the serf nursemaids. "Younger, or at least thinner."

"Tanks kindly, Mistis," Rahksan said, running a complacent hand down from silk blouse to pleated cream-colored skirt. With a slight grimace: "Had to live on rabbit-food, an' swim ever' day 'til I thought mebbeso I'd grow fins, but I shed five kilos." A sly wink. "Certain person said it'd be *all* lonely nights iff'n I didn't."

Yolande smiled and closed her eyes, surprised at her own brief embarrassment. She had always known that her mother slept with Rahksan occasionally, at least since she was old enough to be conscious of such things at all. It was nothing unusual. For that matter her father had probably sired Rakhsan's own son; he had the look. *But it's sort of uncomfortable to imagine Ma and her actually* . . . *doing it*, she thought. And it still sounded a bit strange to hear "Mistis" instead of the child's title of "Missy."

"How's Ali?" she asked, changing the subject. "Drink, please. Yo'self, too."

Rakhsan slapped her forehead. "Ali! That boy!"

There was a sideboard near the stairs with a recessed chilling unit, the usual. The serf poured two glasses of lemonade, handed one to Yolande, and sank gracefully to her knees, sitting back on her heels; it would not have been fitting for her to use the chair, of course.

"Ah *swear* he do things jus' t'grieve his ma —" She shrugged. "Do mah best fo' him, and whut do Ah git? Trouble an' gray hairs. He workin' in the House stables now." A sniff, and grudging admission. "Doin' right well, Mastah say he natural with horses, mebbeso Head Groom somedays. Still, he doin' field-hand work when he coulda lived clean an' been clerk o' somethin', here in t' House."

She drank, and rolled the cup between her palms. "I tell him yo' 'quires, Mistis, tank y'kindly."

Yolande cleared her throat. "Did Myf . . . did my friends like they rooms?" she asked.

"Why, sho'ly," Rahksan said blandly, finishing her juice and rising to replace the etched-glass tumbler on the counter; her back was to Yolande for a moment. "They all settled in good." A pause. "That Mistis Myfwany, she a fine young lady," she continued. "Mos' particulah interested in yo', Mistis, ask questions an' all." Another pause. "Powerful pretty, too."

"We're good friends!" Yolande snapped. "All of us," she added.

"Did Ah says different? A body'd thinks mebbeso yo' was sweet on somebody . . ." She turned, a wide grin flashing white against her olive face.

"Oooo—!" Yolande half rose, flushed with anger, then sank back, joining helplessly in Rahksan's laughter. "Yo' *impossible*, Rahksan!" she said, throwing a pillow.

"No, jus' impudent an' triflin'; comes a' havin' wiped yo' butt an' changed yo' diapers . . ." The smile softened. "Didn' mean hurt yo' feelings, sweetlin'," she said warmly, laying a hand on her shoulder.

"Yo' didn't," the girl said, throwing her arms around the short woman's waist and laying her head on the comforting softness of her bosom. "Oh, Tantie Rahksan, maybe I am sweet on her, a little . . . I don't know, it's all mixed up, don't know *what* I want." A sniffle that broke into a sob. "Why can't everything be simple, like it used to?"

"There, chile, there," Rahksan replied, stroking her hair. "My little 'Landa growin' up, is all." She hummed softly in her throat, rocking the Draka girl for quiet minutes. "Some day yo' looks back on *this* as y' happy an' simple time. Be happy in it; growin' is painful sometime, but believe me, bettah than agin'." A rueful chuckle. "T'ings works that way, sweetlin'. Wait fo', five years an' yo' starts gettin' interested in boys, now *that* complicated. They a lot mo' different."

Yolande giggled tearily and made a mock-retching sound. The serf bent and kissed the top of her head. "Y'change y'mind somedays, girl. They necessary, an' mighty nice in they own way. Anyways, take things as they come. Here."

The serf produced a handkerchief, and proceeded to wipe Yolande's face. The girl surrendered to the childlike sensation, but reclaimed the linen to blow her own nose. She *was* grown-up, or almost, after all.

"Thanks, Rahksan," she muttered. "Sorry I was so silly." Looking up, she saw the blotch her tears had made on the front of the other's blouse, and winced with embarrassment. "Didn't mean to be such a waterin' pot." That prompted remembrance: she felt in her pocket. "Got somethin' fo' yo' in Palermo last month."

Rahksan unwrapped the tissue and opened the small blue jeweler's box. "Why, Mistis 'Landa!" she exclaimed, lifting out the locket. It was a slim oval of pale gold rimmed in pearls, on a slender platinum chain. She opened it, holding the cameo up to the light; a Classical piece in the modern setting, translucent white against indigo blue glass, a woman's head wreathed in a spray of tiny gold olive-leaves. "That beautiful, sweetlin'; nice to remember y' ol' Tantie Rahksan."

"I'll nevah fo'get yo', Rahksan," she said quietly.

"Well." The serf put the chain around her neck, then bent to kiss Yolande on the forehead. "Whenevah y'needs somebodies t' talk to . . . o' cry on, Mistis . . . Ah'm theah." A glance at her watch. "Bettah get goin'. Mastah John's rooms need a check; them useless bedwenches of his neglects things somethin' aweful. That Colette, particular."

Yolande watched her leave and finished the lemonade, vaguely ashamed of the display of emotion. *I'm too old for tears, really* . . . The sadness was gone, though. Now she felt truly relaxed; this was her home ground, after all. She undid her cravat and pulled it loose to finish wiping her face, then tossed it aside, undid the top button of her shirt, and held the Egyptian linen away from her skin. *I am filling out*, she thought with satisfaction. Not much, but then Ma wasn't much bigger, and she was the most beautiful person in the world. What had she said? "Anything more than a handful is a waste." Curious, she touched the smooth shallow curve with the pads of her fingers. In biology class the teacher said breasts were mostly an ornament, like a peacock's tail. The touch had a sort of shivery feel to it, almost like an itch.

Her fingertips brushed across the pointed pink cone of the nipple, and she jerked the hand away; it was the sort of sensation that could feel good or bad, depending. Too strong, anyway.

She rose to her feet and paced, letting her hand trail across the bookshelves. Good friends here; *Gulliver's Travels*, her *Alice Underland* and *Looking-Glass World*, family heirlooms in smooth leather and stamped-gilt titles. Some she could remember her mother reading to her at bedtimes; others she had discovered herself. The old books had a rich scent all their own, leather and the glue of their bindings and a slight hint of dust that reminded her of summer afternoons. She opened one and smiled to herself; there was a vine-leaf still pressed where she remembered, brown and gossamer-fragile. They had seemed so big, then, filling her lap, the smooth paper with the dyed edges transparent gateways to wonder. Verne, Stevenson, Lalique, Halgelstein, Dobson. Illustrated histories, and the *Thousand and One Nights*; most of all horse books: riding, breeding, showing.

There were models on the shelves as well, from the time when flying had won co-equal place in her heart with the stables. Early machines: Pa had gotten the model of the *Ahriman* for her; it was nearly a hundred years old and had been made when the first war-dirigible was launched. An odd looking machine, cigar-shaped with the spiral wooden framework dimpling the fabric covering, and big room-fan type propellors jutting out from the gondola. Miniatures of her parents' Eagle fighters, from the Eurasian War. Pencil-slim twin-engined planes, perfect down to the blackened exhaust-trails behind the big prop engines and the kill-marks on the wings; they had been going-away gifts from their ground crews. A plastic suborb missile she had put together herself from a kit: a slender sinister black dart. And a scramjet fighter, long slim delta shape banking in frozen motion on its stand. She touched that, symbol of freedom from earth's bounds and gravity's pull.

There were data-plaques piled beside her terminal. Yolande grimaced at the size of the stack of the palm-sized wafers, in school colors; enough to keep her busy several hours a day. She put her palm against the screen for the identity check and pushed a wafer into the slot beside it. The machine chimed: *Introduction to Evolutionary Ecology.* Text and pictures flickered by, moving diagrams showing energy-flows, reconstructions. Feathered dinosaurs and ground-apes from Olduvai—and space for the data she would be entering, answers, and essays. That would be interesting, at least, but mind and body rebelled at the thought of more study now.

She turned through the open glass doors to the ground-level terrace instead, and reached overhead to grip the steel bar just outside. Moodily she began a series of chin-lifts, stopping at fifty to hang with her knees curled close to her chest and controlling her breathing to a deep steady rhythm. Bruiser said it was the best way to clear your mind for thinking: let the muscles soak up and burn the hormonal juices the body tried to cloud your mind with. *It's a good remedy for confusion,* she thought wryly. *If I could be sure what I'm confused* about.

"Hio, 'Landa." The terrace outside her rooms ran all along the west front of the building, but her section was separated by a carved-stone screen that ran out to the low balustrade. Myfwany's face leaned around it, smiling. "Want company, or yo' set on devolvin' into a gibbon?"

"C'mon ovah," Yolande said. She raised herself to chest-height against the bar, counting twenty slow breaths, then dropped to the ground, acutely conscious of her rumpled state. "Everythin' all right?"

"Better than that," Myfwany said, swinging around the balustrade. "Been lookin' forward to seein' yo' homeplace quite some time, now. Can't know a person till you've seen where they come from, hey?"

The other girl had shot up these last six months, and flat-footed on the tile pavement Yolande's eyes were level with her nose. She had changed already, into a round-necked

cream-silk sleeveless shirt and fawn trousers; there were bracelets in the form of curled snakes pushed up on her upper
arms, and a fillet of the same silvery metal holding back the
red curls that fell to her neck. They walked to the balustrade
together, leaning on the stone and looking down. Yolande
cast a covert eye to her side, admiring the way the platinum
snakes seemed to ripple as the muscle moved beneath the
freckled skin of Myfwany's arms.

"Utilities an' such?" the redhead asked, nodding downslope.

The hill fell away gently to the northwest. There was a
strip of lawn three meters below them, then terraces behind
low brick retaining walls, flowerbanks and cypresses, fountains and stairways. At the base of the slope the buildings
began, two rows of them built back into the slope so that the
pale yellow tile of their roofs made steps leading down to the
pool at the bottom. They were half-hidden from here by the
trees planted about them, chestnuts and oaks.

"House stables, toolsheds, garages, some sleepin' quarters," Yolande answered. Most of the housegirls bunked in
the attics, but not the garden staff. The plantation's transformer was down there, too; electricity came in by underground cable, brought down from the hydro plants in the
mountains. She laid a hand on Myfwany's. "Thanks . . . thanks
fo' comin' along, Myf. Missin' goin' to yo' home, and all.
Would've been lonely, without."

Myfwany turned her hand palm-up and squeezed for a
moment before releasing the other girl's fingers. "No great
sacrifice," she said quietly, not looking around; she smoothed
the wind-tossed hair back from her face. "Got to get it cut
. . . My stepmother an' me don't get on so well, anyhows."

Yolande tried to imagine what it would be like, for her
mother to die and a stranger take her place, and shivered.
"Come on, there's time for a swim befo' lunch."

There was a shout from the pool. Johanna Ingolfsson looked
up from her papers, and saw her daughter balanced on her
red-haired friend's shoulders. The other girl reached up; they
clasped wrists and Yolande did a slow handstand, grinning
downward through dangling strands of wet blond hair.

"Now!" she said.

Myfwany pushed up and Yolande twisted, doing a complete 360 turn before arrowing into the water headfirst. Johanna nodded approvingly as the sleek body eeled along the

bottom of the pool for a dozen meters before breaking surface and crawl-stroking for the far end. Myfwany followed. They paused for a moment, treading water and hyperventilating, then dove for a game of subsurface tag. Johanna quirked a lip. *Not the only type of touching friend Myfwany has in mind, if I can still read the signs*, she thought.

"Looks like my youngest might make a pilot; got the reflexes, at least," she said musingly. "About time, the first three bein' in the ever-lovin' *infantry* of all things."

Rakhsan chuckled; she was sitting on a cushion at the bottom of the lounger, embroidering a circle of silk held in a wicker frame. "Mebbeso she pick the Navy, eh, Mistis?"

Johanna snorted and reached for the glass of cooler. The outdoor pool was set along the eastern flank of the Great House, along the outer rim of the terrace built up and out from the hillside. It had been convenient; the space beneath provided room for things best tucked away, the heat-pump system, the fuel-cell for the war-shelter deep in the rock beneath the manor, the armory, a laundry . . . a pleasant place for an outdoor lunch, as well. One hundred meters by twenty-five, with a basic pavement of black onyx marble they had gotten cheap after the War, stripped from ruined *palazzi* in Sienna. The rough stone of the wall behind them was overgrown with bougainvillea, bright now with pink-purple garlands; low limestone troughs held banks of clematis, pearl rhododendrons, azaleas; there were stone bowls with topiaries and small trees, or lilac bushes for the scent.

The older Draka returned her attention to the documents. There had been *another* change in the League accounting procedures for olive-oil delivery, specifically the extra-virgin first pressing Tuscan that Claestum produced for the restaurant trade. The Landholders' League bureaucrats never seemed to tire of searching for the perfect paperwork solution.

"Lady Freya bless," she muttered. "Some day the civil service will grow right over the Domination like-so coral on a reef, an' we'll all freeze in place." She made a notation, signed and snapped her fingers. "Guido, take these an' give them to the bookkeeper; we have to have *written acknowledgment* from the Florence office, tell her that." Next thing would be to do a check on the irrigation piping in the orchards, hands-on work, but that could wait until after lunch.

Stretching, she looked back at the pool. Yolande was sitting on the edge of the little island at its center; there was a two-meter high alabaster vase in the center of that, with water cascading down from a spout in its center. She was smiling and swinging her legs, talking to Myfwany as she floated nearby; Johanna could hear their laughter over the sound of the fountain. Her mother turned her head to the other lounger where . . . Mandy Slauter, that was her name. Lying up on one elbow under the dappled shade of the pergola, fanning herself with her hat; a nice enough girl, a bit citified, but it was good that Yolande was making friends outside Landholder circles. Some people liked to pretend it was still 1860, but the Domination had changed; unless you were prepared to rusticate all your life, connections in the urban classes were essential.

Johanna nodded in the direction of the pool. "They two seem to get on very well," she said. Mandy nodded. "Are they sleepin' together yet?" she continued casually.

Mandy blinked and coughed, would have squirmed if etiquette permitted. "Ah, Miz Ingolfsson, they, ah, that is—"

Johanna's cousin spoke without raising her eyes from the book in her lap. "Gods, Jo, y'always were as subtle as a steamtruck. Spare the girl's feelin's, hey?"

Johanna chuckled; adolescent affairs were a long-standing tradition for Citizen-class women, but there was an ancient convention of not mentioning them before adults. Probably a survival from times when such things were strongly frowned upon, but it had been silly even in her youth. "Younger generation's less discreet than we was, Alicia," she said. To Mandy: "Hard though it is to imagine, girl, I went to school, too. Jus' inquirin'."

"Ah, no. I don't think so," Mandy said. Under her breath: "Moo."

"Well, as they please," Johanna said contentedly.

Yolande had never been very popular at school in her younger years: too much the loner and dreamer. It was reassuring to see her fitting in so well and making friends. A lover was only to be expected given her age, although Johanna had never thought much of the hothouse-romance atmosphere of Senior School herself. In theory it was supposed to be emotional training for adulthood, but she had never seen the point in falling in love with someone you couldn't marry. Not that school sweethearts necessarily drifted out of touch; ex-lovers who were godmothers and unofficial

aunts to each other's children were a staple of Draka life . . .
But it was all no preparation for how *different* men were.

Well, I was always eccentric, she mused comfortably. Deciding who you were going to marry at sixteen was decidedly
unusual, even if he was a neighbor's son. She smiled down at
Rakhsan; that was an entirely different matter, of course. As
the Roman poet had said, it was pleasant to have it friendly,
easy, and close at hand . . . friendly especially, otherwise it
just wasn't worth the trouble, usually.

Rahksan smiled back, laying aside her embroidery. "Yo' got
anythin' fo' me to do, next hour or two, Mistis?" she asked.

"No, not particular, Rahksi. Why?"

"That boy of mine," she said. "Wants particulah to have a
talk with me, says it impo'tant. Allah, most of the time he don'
give me the time of day, an' now he jus' *has* to have a chat."

Johanna pursed her lips; Rahksan's son was a classic pain in
the fundament. Spoiled from house-rearing, restless as a cat
on hot tiles, and sullen; a lot of young serfs went through a
stage like that, particularly the males, but he was considerably worse than average. It was no help that Ali had been
sired by Tom. Contraception had been more difficult then,
and Rahksan careless about it; the three of them had been play-
pleasuring, and the Afghan had decided to keep it on impulse.
Not that half-Draka bastards were uncommon, but mostly they
grew up in Quarters and it made no particular difference. Ali
had run tame in the manor; looking at it from his point of
view, she supposed it was natural enough for him to be more
discontented than most. To make it worse, he was completely
besotted with Colette, her son John's new French concubine.

*Who is a gorgeous mantrap and a teasing bitch of the first
water*, Johanna thought sourly. The wench had been a present from her cousins Tanya and Edward, who had a plantation west of Tours in the Loire valley; John certainly hadn't
complained—he indulged the wench—but his mother was
beginning to think her kin had unloaded a troublemaker.
Tanya's bloody sense of humor, she mused.

"Rahksi, that boy needs some serious talkin'-to," she said.
"Half a dozen times I've talked Tom out of kickin' his butt
good an' proper. Fightin', drinkin'; he's first-rate with the
horses, but he's back-talked the head groom enough to get
anyone else triced up to the frame fo' ten-strokes-an-' one.
Freya, honeybunch, I cain't let him ruin discipline." Bending
the rules too far for a favorite was an invitation to trouble.

"Ah knows, Mistis." A deep sigh, and the serf's brows drew together. "Blames myself, really do. Too easy on that chile; I get set to rake him down, an' then remembers him so little an' sweet. He too kind treated, never reminded strong of his place; it better iff'n y'learns that young."

Rahksan looked suddenly older; Johanna sat up and gave her a gentle squeeze on the shoulder. "Isn't easy bein' a mother, Rahksi. Don't worry, we'll straighten him out."

The Afghan shrugged and smiled ruefully. "I'll tells him yo' threatenin' to sell him to the mines," she said.

Johanna snorted. "Bettah use somethin' he'll believe," she replied. The Ingolfssons and her own von Shrakenberg clan had definite ideas about managing their serfs; they did *not* sell them to strangers, except as punishment for some gross crime like child-abuse. Such extreme measures had not been necessary on Claestum since the brutal days of the settlement, right after the War. Besides which it would break Rahksan's heart, which was not to be contemplated.

"Say we might send him down to the boats fo' a year," she continued. Claestum had a part-share in a tuna-fishing business on the coast, run in cooperation with a half-dozen neighboring estates. The Landholders oversaw their hired managers carefully, but it was rough work.

Rahksan winced slightly and made a palms-up gesture. "Tell yo' true, Mistis, I've thought on that. Might do him good t'see how soft he's had it, an' get him away from his momma's skirts. But—"

"I know, he's yo' own and yo'd miss him." Johanna rested one of her own hands on the serf's. "Look, Rahksi, this just an idea. Tom was sayin' Ali makes a terrible houseboy but might do well as a soldier; we could get him a Janissary postin', if he volunteered."

And it would be just what he needs to make something of himself, she thought. *The boy's strong an' smart enough, it's the attitude's the problem.* An induction camp's hard-bitten Master Sergeants had no interest in the anguished sensitivities of the adolescent soul, or anything else beside results.

"Eehh." Rahksan bit her lip. "That generous, but they mighty rough an' he ain't nohow used to it." A talented serf could rise far in the military. Not just to non-commissioned rank in the subject-race legions; Janissaries had opportunities for education, training of every sort. There were ex-Janissaries throughout the serf-manned bureaucracies that ran the Domination, below the level of the Citizen aristocracy. "Though . . . I wouldn't see him much, that way," she finished softly.

"Rahksi," Johanna said seriously. "He's not yo' little boy no' mo'. Ali's a grown buck, an' he has to learn to look his fate in the eye. He cain't hide behind yo' fo'ever. Else he'll do somethin' we can't overlook, an' . . . ." She shrugged. "Ahhh, well, run along an' try reasonin' with him. But think about it. We'll talk it ovah mo' tonight."

Johanna put the matter out of her mind as Rahksan left; time enough later. She could hear Olietta directing the wenches setting the table behind her, and glanced at her watch. 1258 hours; Tom would be in from the fields any time now. It was a house rule that the family ate together; otherwise you might as well be living in a hotel.

"C'mon, yo' two!" she called to the girls in the pool.

"That was fun," Yolande said, as they slid out of the water. The verge was covered in the same blue-and-green New Carthage tiles as the pool; they felt warm and slick under her feet, and the dry air cooling on her wet skin. It had turned out to be a not-quite-hot day, just right for outdoors.

" 'Twas," Myfwany agreed. "I'm *nevah* goin' be able do that circle-flip like yo' can, 'Landa."

Yolande grinned with pride as the servants came forward with towels; Bianca and Lele, her own. The deep pile of the cotton was a pleasure in itself, smelling crisply fresh and slightly of the cherry-blossoms they had been laid on in the warming-cupboard. She had always rather enjoyed being dried; there was less distraction than when you had to do it yourself, and after a swim it made you feel tingly and extra clean. Like wearing new-laundered underwear, only it was your own skin. She reached down and absently patted Lele's head as the Eurasian serf worked over her feet.

"How's Deng?" she said.

"Still poorly, Mistis. Gives many tanks fo' the crystallized ginger yo' sent up last month." Lele looked up and grimaced. "Says he hasn't seen any since China. I tried it. I kin see why." Yolande laughed and held up her arms for the serf to slide the Moorish-style striped *djellaba* over her head. The fine-textured wool settled against her skin like a caress, and she ran her fingers through the damp mass of her hair to spread it over her shoulders.

The serfs gathered up their towels and left; Myfwany looked

up from adjusting her belt-tie. "Yo've got wonderful servants," she said sincerely, shaking back the wide sleeves. Disciplined obedience could be bought from any good labor agent, but enthusiasm was not as common. "Spirited but not spoiled."

"My parents' doin'," Yolande said in disclaimer. "They had the hard part, back right after the War. Had to kill a few, even; but now we go six months at a time without so much as a floggin'; Pa doesn't hold with whippin' much, says it's the last resort of stupidity an' failure."

"Good teacher still needs good pupil," the other girl replied with a slow smile. "Yo've got the nature, like Marsala wine: strong but sweet."

Yolande smiled back, and then the expression faded. There was a feeling like cold under her breastbone, yet it was hot as well, cramping her lungs. She could feel her lips paling, and her arms and legs wanted to tremble; her vision grayed at the edges until Myfwany's face loomed in a tunnel of darkening night. There was a moment when the whole surface of her skin seemed to prickle, drum-tight, then the world snapped back to normal. Or almost normal; the hot-chill sensation in her stomach settled lower and faded to warmth, and she put a hand to the side of her head, gasping for breath.

"Yo' all right? *'Landa?*" Myfwany's voice was sharp with concern, and she gripped her friend by the shoulders.

"I—yes, just felt funny fo' a second." She shook her head. "Little scary . . . must've held my breath too long underwatah. Anyways, let's go eat; I'm starvin'." She had, suddenly, a bottomless hollow feeling almost like nausea. It was worrying, even if they had only had rolls and fruit with their coffee that morning. No run, after all, and only a couple of hours in the water . . .

A serf struck with quiet precision at a tiny bronze gong by the table. Another seated herself at a harp nearby and began to play softly as the Draka assembled. The table was near the house wall, the usual rectangular slab of polished stone on curved wrought-iron supports, shaded by oleanders. Yolande dropped into her wicker chair and grabbed at a roll from a basket, breaking the soft fresh bread and eating it without benefit of butter. The taste was intoxicating, and she finished it off and took another, more slowly. Muriel and Veronica had arrived, looking sleekly content; they nodded around the table as they drew their chairs closer.

"Where *is* yo' father?" Johanna asked, as the serfs handed around the first course; it was iced beet-and-cucumber soup, for a warm day. "And are they starvin' yo' down at that school, child?"

"Mmmph," Yolande said, then swallowed to clear her mouth. "No, I just had a . . . really strange sensation. It's funny, I was lookin' at Myfwany an' thinkin' on how nice she is, then all of a sudden my head was swimmin', and my knees felt watery and my skin went cold an' I broke out in a sweat; and then my stomach felt strange. Figured I must've not noticed how hungry I was . . . What are y'all laughing at?" she concluded with bewildered resentment.

Her mother had put fingertips to brow and her shoulders shook. Aunt Alicia was coughing into a napkin; Myfwany looked back and forth between them, blinked in understanding, and then focused on carefully pouring herself a glass of white Procanico wine. Mandy looked at her owl-eyed.

"Y'are joshin', 'Landa?" she asked, and turned to Veronica and Muriel. "She is joshin', isn't she? Please, tell me, nobody could be that ignor—"

"Johanna!"

It was her father's voice, from the french doors that gave onto the terrace from the main house.

"Look-see who *I've* brought to lunch!"

". . . so it turned out they were just Keren tribesfolk who wandered across the border," her brother was saying. "It's pretty wild there in south Yunnan, mountain jungle. Of course, they could have been Alliance operatives *pretendin'* to be tribesfolk, so we turned them over to the headhunters." He grinned and buffed his fingernails. "And my tetrarchy got extra leave fo' stumblin' across them. Scramjet shuttle to Vienna, overnight dirigible to Milan, caught the train to Florence an' so forth."

The soup was removed and the next course arrived: seared sea-scallops with asparagus, stuffed Roman artichokes and truffled walnut oil, then *insalata* in cumin vinaigrette and a paella salad on the side. Plain country food; her parents disapproved of the modern Orientalizing fashion of bits and pieces of this and that, saying it was bad for the digestion and distracted the attention from the real pleasures of dining and conversation. Hunger satisfied, she touched a finger to her wineglass for a refill and watched the others. John was getting

respectful attention in his description of an impromptu tiger-
hunt in the rhododendron thickets of the Yunnan mountains,
up on the Nepalese border. Mandy was drinking it in, with
her chin resting on her hands.

Well, he is pretty dashin', Yolande thought critically, glancing at her brother. Tall and long-limbed, which showed to
advantage in garrison blacks. Russet colored hair and close-
cropped beard, straight high-cheeked features and gray eyes
against brown-tanned skin, set off by tasteful ruby ear-studs
and the silver-niello First Airborne Legion thumb-ring.

" . . . so I ought to be able to squeeze in a week here to
home," he finished.

Johanna signed for the serf to remove her plate and lit a
cigarette. "We'll be havin' some people over next Tuesday, if
yo' haven't lost the taste fo' countryside jollifications . . . I'm
goin' over the orchards this afternoon. They're in bloom; why
don't yo' come along and help show Yolande's friends about?"

"Hmmm." The serfs were bringing coffee and deserts,
blueberry lemonade sorbets and almond flan with fruits and
cheeses. "Actually, mother, I had somethin' else planned fo'
this afternoon. Glad to, tomorrow. Sorry." He grinned
unrepentantly.

Yolande looked up at the harpist. Colette, her name was. A
gift to John on his twenty-first birthday from the von
Shrakenbergs of Chateau Retour, over in what had been
France; they were kin, first cousins on her mother's side and
more remotely on her father's, as well. The wench's mother
was a serf-artist of note, a singer trained pre-War at the Paris
conservatoire. Colette had inherited some of the talent, and
her looks as well. Tall, slender, dancer-graceful; softly curled
hair the color of dark honey to her waist, and huge eyes of an
almost purple violet. Priceless, and faultlessly trained, but
Yolande had never liked her; conceited, given to dumb insolence, and unpopular with the other servants, which was
always a bad sign. Except for a few of the bucks hopelessly
infatuated with her, of course.

The serf met the Draka girl's eyes for a moment, smiled with
an almost imperceptible curve of the lips, then dropped her
gaze to the instrument. Sunlight worked in flecks through the
flowers overhead and patterned the white samnite of her gown.

Yolande's father laughed. "Give the boy a few hours to . . .
settle in, darlin'," he said. Johanna smiled and slapped her
son on the shoulder.

"Don' wear yo'self out befo' dinner, then," she said as he rose.

"If there's anythin' left of yo' tomorrow, yo' might help with a problem, son." Thomas Ingolfsson said. "We've been losin' sheep, over to Castelvecchi."

"Ah." His son turned back, alert. "Wolves? Wildcats?"

"Leopard, from the sign." Yolande saw her father's eyes narrow in amusement at the sudden prickle of interest around the table. "Yes, they must finally be breedin' enough that they're spreading out of the Apennines."

The upper hill-country had been stripped bare of population after the War; that was standard practice, for security reasons and because such areas were seldom worth the trouble of cultivation by Draka standards. The Conservancy Directorate had reforested most of the abandoned lands, and introduced appropriate wildlife. The Italian reserves were still not as rich as North Africa's, where a hundred and fifty years of care had left the mountains green and teeming with game, but there was enough to allow limited culling. Draka loved hunting with a savage passion, and were preservationists accordingly, but letting the big cats into densely populated farming country was excessive even by their standards.

"In fact, the Conservancy people said go ahead an' take them, not worth the trouble of trappin'."

John sat down again; behind him, Yolande noticed Colette playing with an irritated vehemence.

"I could ride over tomorrow morning with the dogs; take Menchino and Alfredo . . . Join me, Pa?" he said eagerly. "Ma?"

His parents shook their heads reluctantly. "Winnifred went and broke her arm, can't spare myself," Thomas Ingolfsson said.

At John's frown, Johanna added: "Can't come myself either; we're sortin' the yearling colts fo' the Sienna show. Tell yo' what, though, Johnny, why don't yo' take Yolande and her friend Myfwany?"

"Thanks—" Myfwany and Yolande began in chorus, then broke off with a giggle. John opened his mouth to say what he thought of taking his baby sister and an unknown teenager along on a leopard hunt, caught his mother's eye, and nodded.

"Glad to, sprout. An' yo' too, Miz Venders," he added.

"Thanks awfully," Myfwany said. "No leopards on Sicily yet, an' my elder sister got one down in Kenia last year an' she's always on about it."

Johanna turned smoothly to the other girls. "Best not to cluttah up a huntin' party too much; I'd be honored if y'all would come with me and assist at selectin' the yearlings, we're rather proud of our ridin' stock here at Claestum . . . An' to be sure, pickin' out one each fo' yo'selfs, as well."

Mandy smiled with delight. *John-boy, you still can't compete with horses*, Yolande thought satirically. Muriel and Veronica were enthusiastic as well: *of course, they like anything they can do together*. She suppressed envy and hunted a last blueberry around her plate.

"I'm sure there'll be one left yo'll find suitable, Miz Venders," Johanna continued. " 'Landa's been half-livin' in the stables since she was knee-high, she can help yo' pick."

"That was beautiful," Myfwany said.

They were riding their horses through the Quarters, but blossom from the orchards still clung to their shoulders and hair. Yolande could see them starring the other's dark-red mane, pink cherry and white of apple and peach; the blossom season had overlapped this year, which was a little unusual.

"Y-" Yolande cleared the stammer from her throat with an effort. "Yo' are beautiful."

"No," Myfwany said fondly, looking around. Side by side with their boots touching, they were just close enough for private talk. "I'm good-lookin', just. You are beautiful." A smile quirked her mouth as the other girl shook her head in a spray of flowers.

A companionable silence fell, and Yolande enjoyed the feeling of communicating without speech. The roofs of the Great House were just visible on the distant hilltop, over the cypresses and the outer wall of the gardens; some plantations tucked the serf village away out of sight, but the Ingolfssons were Old Domination and not shy about the foundations of their wealth. The cottages were native stone, tile-roofed and closely spaced along brick-paved streets; shade trees flanked the lanes, and each four-room house stood in a small patch of garden, vegetables and often enough a few flowers. It was getting on towards evening, and the Quarters were noisy enough to drown the clop-clatter of hooves and the occasional metallic kiss of stirrup-irons.

Heads bowed towards the riders from passing serfs, dutiful routine deference to the Landholder and her daughter, curiosity towards the guests. Folk were back from the fields and the compulsory evening shower, work-gnarled older men in shapeless overalls, short thickset women brown as berries and seemingly built of solid muscle. Younger ones with enough energy left to throw jokes and snatches of song at each other as they scattered to their homes. Children played run-and-shout games along the sidewalks, or helped their mothers carry home baskets of round loaves that gave off the tantalizing scent of fresh baking. Cooking-smells came from the cottages, tomato and garlic and hot olive oil. They reined in to the little plaza where the lane joined the main road to the manor, and Yolande called to her mother:

"Ma!" Johanna Ingolfsson reined up. "Ma, Myfwany and I'll go right around to the stables an' walk up."

The Landholder raised one brow; the grooms could take their mounts from the Great House steps just as well. A touch at her stirrup made her look down; Rahksan was there, and gripping her ankle. She frowned slightly at the lapse in decorum and bent low to listen to an agitated whisper.

"Please yo'selfs, girls," Yolande's mother said after a moment. She extended a hand; the serf gripped her wrist, put a foot on the toe of Johanna's boot and swung up pillion behind her owner. The Landholder looked around, abstracted. "Two hours to dinner," she finished, and touched heels to her horse. There was an iron clatter of hooves as Johanna and their friends spurred up the road.

Myfwany and Yolande walked their horses across the square. There was a small fountain in the center, Renaissance work salvaged from some forgotten hill-town. The public buildings of the Quarters lined the pavement, the larger houses of the Headman and senior gang-drivers, the school, the infirmary, the bakery, and baths. There was a church as well, a pleasant little example of Tuscan baroque reassembled here at some little expense, and another building that served as a public-house with tables set outside; a few workers sat there over a glass of wine or game of chess. Serfs never touched money, of course, but Claestum had an incentive-scheme that paid in minor luxuries or tokens accepted at the inn. *Farming is skilled work*, Yolande remembered her father saying. *Difficult, and easily spoiled. Needs the carrot as well as the stick.* She nodded to the priest in his long black gown and odd little hat as they passed, and he signed the air.

"Funny," Yolande said, as they turned their mounts left to

the laneway that skirted the base of the hill. "Nothin' much has happened today, but it feels special, somehow."

"Know what yo' mean, 'Landa." Myfwany ran her hands through her hair and rubbed them together, shedding bits of petal. "Smell."

Yolande leaned her head to the other's extended hand; it carried hints of soap and leather, overlain by the spring-silvery scent. Like a ghost memory of the orchard, tunnels of white froth against black branches, sun-starred with water diamonds and rainbows from the sprays. Her heart clenched beneath her ribs and she felt suspended, floating in a moment of decision like the arch above the high-dive board. She bent to kiss the soft spot inside the wrist, and felt cool fingers brush across her lips. Glanced up, and their eyes met.

The moment passed and they laughed uneasily, looking around. The garden wall was still on their right, whitewashed stone along the gravel of the road. The lawns were a vivid green beyond it, trees and flowerbanks, groves and summer-houses, ponds and statues. Hedges and onyx-jade cypresses gave glimpses of the workaday area to their left, barns and pens, round granaries and the sunken complex of the winery, smithies and machine-shops. The sun was sinking behind the Great House and they lay in the shadow of its hill, an amber light that turned the dust-puffs around their horses' hooves to glinting honey-mist. They passed under an arched gate and Yolande waved her riding-crop to the one-armed man who bowed from the veranda of the cottage next to it.

"Evenin', Guido," she said, as they passed. A boy had run ahead, and they turned downslope into an area of low stucco-coated stables and paddocks fenced in white board. The horses side-danced a little at the smell of home and feed, eager for their evening grooming and mash. Yolande smoothed a hand down the neck of her mount as stablehands came up to take the reins.

"Nena, Tonio," Yolande said as they swung down.

"Mistis Yolande," they replied. "*Buono* ride, Mistis?" Tonio continued, with a flash of white teeth against olive-tanned skin.

"Tolerable good," Yolande said, grinning back. Both Draka gave their mounts a quick once-over before turning over the reins, and Yolande slipped a piece of hard sugar to hers. Slipping into local dialect: "Did that barn-cat have its kittens?"

The young man shrugged and spread his hands apologetically, but his sister dipped her head. "Stable four, Mistis," she said. "Up in the loft, I heard it."

Myfwany looked at her with raised brows; the patois on her family's Sicilian estate was different enough to be a distinct language.

"Cats?" she said.

"Kittens," Yolande replied. "Have a look?"

"Meeeroeuuw!" the cat said warningly. It had been reasonably polite, but it was *not* going to tolerate strange fingers touching the squirming, squeaking mass of offspring along its flank.

The two young Draka backed away on hands and knees across the loft's carpeting of deep-packed clover hay. It had a sweet smell, still green after a winter's storage. They flopped back on the resilient prickly softness; the long loft of the stable was almost night-dark, the last westering rays slanting in through the louvered openings above them. Yolande stretched, feeling the breathless heat as a prickle along her upper lip. There were soft sounds of shifting hooves through the slatted boards beneath, and the clean smells of well-cared-for horses. There were a dozen of the long two-story stables here below the hill: personal mounts for the Landholders and their retainers, used for the routine work of supervision, or the hunt or pleasure-riding.

Yolande turned on her side, watching her friend's face and probing at her own feelings. *Happy*, she decided. Myfwany's face was a pale glimmer in the darkness, her eyes bright amber-green. *Scared.*

"Yes," she said, to a question not spoken in words.

They moved together, embraced. Yolande gave a small sigh as their lips met; a shock went over her skin, like the touch of the ocean when you dove into an incoming wave. Their arms pulled tighter, and her mouth opened. She tasted sweat-salt and mint.

"Gods," she murmured, after an eternity. "Why did we wait so long? I'd've said yes months ago. Didn't yo' want to?"

Myfwany chuckled softly. "Almost from the first," she said, and laid her hands lightly on the other's flanks. "Beautiful, muscle knitted to yo' ribs like livin' steel . . . Waited because the time wasn't right." Yolande shivered as the hands traced lightly up to her breasts.

Voices from below, jarring. Yolande fought down a surge of anger; what did they have to do for some privacy, go check into a hotel? A dim light shone up through the floorboards; the voices of serfs, angry and quarreling.

"Send them away," Myfwany breathed into her ear.

Yolande controlled her breathing and crawled toward the big square hatchway that overlooked the tack-room; a little light was coming up from below, a hand-lantern's worth. Not that it was any serf's business what she did or with whom or where, but she was suddenly tooth-gratingly conscious that the estate rumor mill would be passing news of every straw in her hair and undone button before morning. Whoever it was—sundown was after plantation curfew, and there had better be a *good* excuse for this, or somebody was going to be sorry and sore. She recognized the voice as her head peered over the timber frame of the trapdoor, and the anger left her like a gasping breath: Rakhsan, and her son Ali. She was five meters above their heads; it was unlikely in the extreme that they would look up. Myfwany caught her tension and froze beside her.

Ali's voice, speaking Tuscan. A tall young buck, in groom's breeches and shirt and boots, tousled brown hair. He had run tame with the House children when she was younger, a little rambunctious but fun. Sullen past his early teens, with that buried-anger feel you got from some serfs, always quarreling with the other houseboys. Semi-serious trouble once or twice, pilfering or breaking curfew. A friend of his beside him in driver's livery; she hunted for the name: Marco. Understudy pilot for the aircar.

Rahksan put the lantern down and stood with her arms crossed. Underlighting should have flattered the well-kept prettiness of the serf's face, but somehow brought out the High Asian cast of the strong bones. The voice was as familiar as her own mother's to Yolande, but the tone was one she had never heard the Afghan use. Flat, level, uninflected; she replied in the Old Territory serf-dialect.

"Ali," she said. "This isn't trouble yo' in. We not talkin' whippin' here, we not talkin' sniffin' around Masta John's bedwench an' havin' her laugh at yaz." She leaned forward, and her clenched fists quivered by her sides with throttled intensity. "Goin' bushman means *death*, boy. The greencoats ties yo' to a wheel an' breaks yo' bones slow with an iron rod, an' then they rams the stake up yo' ass an yaz *dies*, it kin take *days*, the crows pick out yo' eyes an'—" Her voice broke and she grasped for control, panting. "Oh, Ali, my baby, my chile, *please* listen to me."

Ali jerked; Yolande could sense threads of argument reaching into the past, like walking into a play halfway through. "I—It's worth the risk, to be free."

"Free." Then there was emotion in the woman's voice, an anger and hopeless compassion. She pressed her fists to her forehead for a moment, then looked up. "Ali," she said, her voice calmly serious. "We beyond gamin' an' twistin' words to make points. This the time fo' truth."

Marco made an impatient sound; Ali cast him an appealing glance and gestured before returning his gaze to his mother and nodding gravely.

"Did I have a magic stick, I'd wave it an' send yo' to England. Break my heart to lose yo', son, but I'd do it. Yo' happiness that impo'tant to me. Does yo' believe me?"

"Yes, Momma," he said, with warmth in his voice.

"*But I don' have no magic stick!*" She buried her hands in her hair. "Allah be merciful, whats can I say to a boy of nineteen? Yo' doan' believe yaz can die . . ." Rahksan stepped to her son and reached up to take his face between her palms. "Ali, my sweet, my joy, I knows yo' full of pride an' shame. What yo' think, I says *cast them out* 'count it makes trouble fo' me?"

She kissed his brow. "Son, that sort o' hard pride, that fo' Draka; an' I wouldn't be Draka iff'n I could, I seen what it make them into. It ain' no shame to be serf! We not serf 'count of bein' bad, or worthless, it just . . . kismet, our fate." She paused, licked her lips, continued. "Mebbeso the Mastahs take the world, like they dreams. Mebbeso they loses, an' then they dies, on 'count they don' accept they can ever lose. Win or die, every one; think on it, boy, does yaz see strength or weakness in that? Whatevah happen, *we* still be here. That the honor an' pride of serfs; to *live*. We is *life*, boy. Yo' wants pride . . . *Look* at this place. Who built it? We did, our folk. Who builds everythin', grows everythin'? Our folk. We *is* the world. *That* cause fo' pride."

"Momma . . ." Ali gestured helplessly. "Momma, maybe . . . you could be right, but I *can't*, I just can't. Please, come with us. I want you with me there, Momma; I want to see you free, too. I know it's risky, but maybe they *won't* catch us."

"Oh, son," she said, in a voice thick with unshed tears. "They caught me long ago. I'm bound with chains softer an' stronger than iron. I'd send yo' if I could, but my life is here."

"Don't listen to her, Ali!" Marco burst in. "She's a Draka-lover. Be a man!"

Rahksan straightened and glared at Marco, glanced him up and down. "Man?" she said with slow contempt, and the Italian flushed. "Big man, makes his momma an' poppa stand an' watch while the headhunters break his bones, an' they gots to watch and cain' do nothing."

Her voice went whip-sharp. "Yaz poppa, Marco, *he* a man. Live through the War, an' help yo' momma live. Right after-wards, they was hard times, plenty folks dyin'; yo' poppa keep othahs from gettin' theyselves killed, riskin' a night-time knife in t'back to do it. Then I hears him myself, talkin' to the mastahs, respectful an' firm, askin' fo' let-up so's the rest don' do nothin' foolish. There're Draka who'd've skinned him fo' that. Ours wouldn't, but how he know then? He settle down with yaz ma, t'make the best of what fate give him; yo' doan' think that take a man? Works hard, helps her raise their chillen. *That* a man. Yo'? Yaz not even much of a *boy*."

Marco clenched a fist, would have swung it at the begin-ning of any movement. "Julia and I can never have children of our own," he rasped, and his flush of anger faded to white around his mouth. "Is a *man* supposed to lie down for that?"

Rahksan touched her stomach. "Yo' don't have chillen, boy. We do. Julia, she can go down t' the clinic ever' six months, same as any wench on the plantation, an' get a shot. I does, regular. She fo'get o' don' care, have her two while she a housegirl, so they ties her tubes. Mebbeso yo' wants to get six mo' with her to prove yaz a *man*, then see them sold off to the serf-traders when they turn fourteen? The Ingolfssons don' breed us fo' market. An' I notice *Julia* ain't here, hmmm?"

Rahksan extended a finger toward him, and he flinched. "Marco, like I said, I'm no Draka; so I won' take no pleasure in seein' yo' die. But I savin' my sorrow fo' yo' folks. My boy Ali here, he bein' bull-stupid, but it honest stupid. Yo' doin' this outa bent spite, lyin' to yo'self an' draggin' my son in to make yo'self feel bettah about it. Mebbeso yaz got cock, balls, an' voice likeso a jackass, but that don' make yo' much of a *man* t' my way a' thinkin'."

She turned back to Ali. "Tell me honest, son. Bring it out. Yo' agreein' with his opinion of yo' momma what bore you?"

"I—" The boy's eyes hunted back between them. "You—" He stopped, then the words burst free. "You love *her* chil-dren, you always have, better than you love me; it was smiles and stories for them, and lectures for me! Isn't that being a Draka-lover?"

"Ali." Rahksan forced her son's head back toward her. "Yo' my son. Nine months beneath my heart, inside my body. Blood an' pain when I bore yo', an' the midwife laid yaz on my belly. My milk fed yo'. *Yo' the dearest thing in all the world to me!* Iff'n I been hard on yo' sometimes, that love, too, tryin' to teach yaz how to live. Loves yo' mo' than life."

She took a deep breath. "No, I'm not a Draka-lover. Yes, I love the Mistis' children. They *children*, Ali." She put her hands beneath her breasts for a moment. "One I gives suck to. All I cleans, an' picks up when they cries. Holds they hands when they learnin' walkin'. Plays with. Hears they babblin' an' first words. Comforts when they skins they knees o' they pet rabbit dies; same's I did with yo'. Woman who don' love a chile aftah all that, *she don' have no lovin' in her heart!*" A wry smile. "There some othah Draka I likes, o' anyway respects; that not 'lovin' the Draka.' As fo' the Mistis— a shrug "—we best friends, always have been."

Ali spoke with ragged calm. "How can you say that, say that you're the *friend* of someone who owns you, uses you, who—" He paused, continued almost in a mumble. "I can't . . . can't stand to see them touch you. It makes me feel ashamed."

"Oh, chile," she sighed. "How can she and I be friends? It ain't easy, is how. I a serf, Ali; I cain' change that, neither can she. She own me; law say she can sell me, whup me, kill me. Forty years in t' same house, same room mostly, how often yo' thinks we gets riled with each othah? How often she work to hold her hand? How often I make myself not use that to hurt her? She still a Draka, chile, an' that mean arrogant as a cat an' near as cruel, sometime, 'thout even' knowin' it."

She paused, made a sound halfway between laughter and pain. "As to touchin' . . . Ali, I knows it shockin' to every boy t' learn this, but mothers don' stop wantin' and needin' when they has their sons. Fo' the rest—look at me, Ali. No, *look* at me."

He obeyed. "I is forty an' four, Ali. Still right comely, but there dozens, mebbeso hundreds, younger an' better-lookin', would dearly like to get on right-side with the mastahs by lyin' down with them. Why yo' think Mistis still want me? An' I her, Ali. 'Cause we has *likin'* fo' each other; knows each other to the bone. The pleasurin' nice, but it comfort, too, and bein' with someones yo' shares memories with."

Rahksan crossed her arms on her chest and continued calmly. "Love yo', son. Give my life fo' yaz, but I won't lie about what I is, o' pretend to bein' ashamed of it. Nevah did find a man I wanted full-time; wish I had, might have been bettah fo' yo' to have a Pa. But I didn't, an' there nothin' wrong with takin' what's available along the way.

"Now, Ali," she continued. "It's time, son. Fo' my sake . . . an' fo' yo'rn . . . give this up. *Please*. It madness. I wants to see yo' happy, see yo' give me grandchildren. Iff'n yo' cain' be happy here, there other places; we can work somethin' out, *but I can't let yo' kill yo'self, Ali.*"

Marco stiffened in suspicion. "She's betrayed us, turned informer!" he snapped. "Quick, get the ropes! We can get her to the car, it's two hours until that black bastard Nyami is back, I've got the keys, *hurry!*"

Rahksan hurled herself forward, gripped her son in a fierce embrace. "Allah, be merciful—Ali, Ali, I'd die fo' yo'; I'd give yo' up an' never see yo' again iff'n yo' had a chance to do this crazy thing. *Ah, god, yo' crackin' my heart in two!*" The last was a wail, and tears were running down the face she raised to her son. "Even kill yo' love fo' me, my chile. Even that I'll do fo' yo'."

Marco grabbed for her. Ali's arms were around his mother, uncertain whether to comfort or confine. Rahksan struggled against both of them, or shuddered in her weeping. Above them the two Draka girls tensed as one, ready for movement, but Yolande's hand pressed her friend back. There was someone at the door of the stable.

"Well." The serfs froze, the footsteps halted by the stable doors, and a hand flicked on the lights. The horses stirred, whickering and stamping in their stalls. Yolande slitted her eyes to make out the figure in the entranceway: her mother, still in the black riding leathers. The silver rondelles on her gunbelt shone like stars against night, and her face seemed to float detached as she skimmed the broad-brimmed hat aside. The boots went *tk-tk* across the brown tile as she walked to within arm's reach of the serfs. There was a cigarette in her left hand; the other stayed near her gunbelt, the fingers working slightly.

The Draka spoke again, in a tone of flat deadliness. "*Take—those—hands—off—her.*"

The two young men released Rahksan and stepped back reflexively; Ali's eyes followed his mother as she moved to the side, tears running down a face that might have been carved in olivewood. Then back to the Landholder, standing stock-still with explosive movement packed ready beneath her skin.

Johanna spoke to Rahksan, with infinite gentleness. "Yo' don't have to watch this, Rahksi."

"Yes, I do, Jo. It my fault. This my punishment."

Johanna nodded. Even then, Yolande felt shocked at Rahksan's use of the first name without honorific; a privilege that could only be exercised in strict privacy. Her eyes turned back toward the two serf males. Evidently they were no longer considered witnesses.

The Landholder blew meditative smoke from her nostrils as she stared at Marco. When she spoke, the tone was almost conversational.

"Buck, yo' are just too stupid to live. Plannin' to take that lumberin' cow of an aircar to England? Yes?" Marco gave a frozen nod. "Across the heaviest air defenses in the world? Boy, they can see a *bird* movin'. England? Yo'd be lucky to make it halfway to Florence. Lucky to be blown out of the air, mo' likely forced down. Free out of Ingolfsson hands then, into Security's."

The serfs flinched at the mention of the secret police, and Johanna nodded. "Try convincin' them yo' don't know anythin' political. Talk to the scalpels, an' the wires, an' the drugs. Three weeks, maybe they'd believe yo' and send yo' to the Turk." They flinched again at the obscene nickname for the impaling stake. Marco was shaking now, white showing around the rims of his eyes.

The Draka sighed. "Haven't had to have a killin' on Claestum since befo' yo' birth, boy. I really regret this." Her voice became more formal. "One choice that can never be taken away, an' that's to die rathah than live beneath the Yoke. Marco, as yo' owner an' an arm of the State, I hereby judge yo' a threat to the welfare of the Race and so, unfit to live," she said. The serf made the beginnings of a motion, perhaps an attack, perhaps only an attempt to flee.

Even to the Draka watching from the loft what followed was a blur, a dull smack of impact and Marco was sinking to the floor clutching his groin, face working soundlessly.

She pulled it, some reflexive corner of Yolande's mind thought. Otherwise there was no room for thought, for movement, scarcely even for breath. Heartbeat hammered in her ears.

"Yo' should listen to yo' momma, boy," she said quietly to Ali with voice full of calm, considered anger. " 'Stead of to Marco, who can't even commit suicide on his ownsome without takin' his friends with him. Gods preserve me from friendship like that-there. Understand me, boy? Louder, I cain't hear yo'."

"Yes, Mistis." A breathy whisper.

"Are yo' *listenin'* to me, boy?"

"Yes, Mistis."

"Nineteen years old, Freya . . . Forty years yo' mothah and I've been together, Lord, forty years. Youth an' age, night an' day, war an' peace . . ." She touched the scars around her left eye where the ridges stood out under the overhead floodlights. "She helped put me togethah again aftah this. Helped midwife my children, an' I was there when yo' were born. Incidental, I was there when yo' were conceived, too." A shake of her head. "Yo' momma worth ten of yo', buck. Mo' guts, mo' brains, mo' *heart*." Very softly: "Times was, when she was the only thing kept me from freezin' solid."

She leaned forward, and her index finger tapped him on the nose; from above, Yolande could see him jerk at the touch, and the sheen of sweat on his skin. Her mother's voice became calmer still:

"So she's what's kept Old Snake off yo' back, many a time. She's why I'm bendin' strict law, accordin' to which the Order Police should be here now. Bendin' it enough that I'd be in some considerable shit myself if it came out. But we comin' to the hard place, boy, between wish and will and duty, the place where I got no choices left. Rahksan dear to my heart, but I live here; my children do, my husband, my kin. I can't keep a mad dog in my household, or sell it into someone else's. Are yo' an Ingolfsson serf, or a wild bushman? No, don't look at her, or him. This is the narrow passage; here there's no brothah, no friend. *Decide*."

A long pause.

"Yes, Mistis."

"Louder, boy."

His voice cracked. "I am yours, Mistis. Mercy, please!"

Johanna nodded, and her mouth twisted as at the taste of some old bitterness. "Gods damn yo', Ali, why couldn't you have thought on that befo' things come to this? We nevah asked fo' yo' likin', just obedience. Now I have to kill part of yo' to save the rest." Almost kindly: "I know yo' sorry now, Ali. I know yo' frightened. It's not enough, now; yo' a brave boy, an' stubborn. Fear isn't enough, because it don't last. Yo' has to show me, and show yo'self, right down where yo' soul lives, who an' what you are." Her face nodded toward the wall. "Pick up that shovel, an' come back here."

Ali's face had gone gray-pale with understanding; he stumbled to the wall, took the long-handled shovel from the rack. Marco had risen to his feet, still clutching at himself. His breath whooped between clenched teeth. Johanna moved again, kicking twice with delicate precision. The point of her boot drove into Marco's solar plexus and straightened his body up in paralytic shock. The edge flicked up into his throat, and he dropped to the floor bulge-eyed, jerking and twitching.

"Kill him, Ali." The Draka drew her pistol; the chunky shape of crackle-finished steel glittered blue-black. "If not, I'll make it quick."

Rahksan turned her back, hands over her face. The shovel went up, hesitated. Ali was shaking almost as much as his friend, who strained to draw air through a half-crushed windpipe and made noises that were part pleading, part choking. Strengthless hands rose from the floor to ward off the iron.

"No!" Ali screamed. The shovel swung down and struck, clanged. Marco's body jerked across the floor like a broken-backed snake. Rahksan twitched where she stood, as if the impact had been in her. "No! No! No!" Another blow, and another; it took six until the other man stopped moving and Ali was able to drop to his knees in the blood and vomit himself empty.

"Serf." Johanna's voice cut through the spasms, and Ali looked up, wiping at tears and blood and vomit on his chin. Horses moved and whinnied in the stalls, frightened by the scent of death. There were voices in the distance, and other lights coming on. The Draka's face might have been carved from some pale wood; she gripped the side of his head, hair and ear, and jerked him close.

"Yo' bright enough to understand that yo've found the way to compel me, to hurt me; by makin' me hurt yo' mothah through you. *Look*." She jerked his head around, forcing him to face Rahksan. "Is it worth it? That's yo' doin'." Another twist, toward Marco. "So is that." Back eye-to-eye.

"Now. This is what happened. Marco went crazy, and

attacked yo' momma. Yo' had to hit him, an' it was all ovah by
the time I got here. Nobody will say otherwise; go get Deng,
an' the priest. They'll fetch the Mastah and do what's needful. Get out of here, boy. *Remember, and don't yo' ever make
me do this again.*"

He stumbled out into the awakening night. Johanna's calm
evaporated; she threw the cigarette down with a gesture of
savage frustration and ground it out beneath her heel as she
slammed the pistol back into its holster.

"Shit, shit, *shit!*" she swore venomously. Then, gently:
"Rahksan."

The other woman turned from the wall and let her hands
fall. Her face had crumpled, and there were fresh lines
beside her mouth. "Did we have to?" she asked, in a thin
small voice. "Oh, Allah, Jo, did we have to?"

"Rahksi—" Johanna held up her hands, a helpless motion.
"There wasn't time . . . another hour, an' too many would
have known. I'm sorry, I'm truly, truly sorry. There was
nothin'—He had to learn, Rahksi, it was that or kill him."

Rahksan nodded as the tears spilled quietly down her
cheeks. "I know, Jo. I should've taught—" Then she was
moving, stumbling forward intb the outstretched arms.

"Oh, Jo!" They clung fiercely, and Rahksan's gray-shot
head was pressed against Johanna's throat. She was sobbing,
a harsh raw sound of grief that shook her like a marionette in
the puppeteer's fist.

"It'll be all right, Rahksi, my pretty, shhh, shhh," Johanna
said, stroking her hair. A moment. "Cry fo' him, Rahksi. Cry
fo' all of us. I wish I could."

"My baby, Jo, my baby!"

"I won't let anyone hurt him, I promise. Shhh, shhh."

Yolande felt an overwhelming guilt and grief, sensed
Myfwany stirring likewise beside her. Her skin crawled; this
was something they were never meant to see, something that
was *wrong* to see, something that could never be forgotten.
They shared a single appalled glance and began cat-crawling
backward, using the growing clamor to fade into the welcoming night. Behind and below them the two figures remained
locked together, the Landholder's cheek resting atop the
serf's head as she crooned wordless comfort.

CHAPTER FOUR

Contrary to hoary myth, the Domination is not antitechnological; after all, it began its industrialization at about the same time as the United States. The lower "social visibility" of its cities and factories was partly due to the sheer size of its inhabited area, and more to the fact that they developed under the sponsorship and control of the landed gentry, rather than as alien incursions in a rural world. Nor is the more recent myth of an anti-scientific bias in Draka culture wholly accurate. The autosteamer, the dirigible airship, the turbocompound engine and—characteristically—the machine-gun are all Draka inventions, after all. It is true that until the Eurasian War the Domination imported many of its research and development personnel; also true that in certain areas of pure research, particularly physics and electronics, they still depend on pirated American research to a substantial degree. However, we should remember that in some fields—biotechnology above all—the Domination remains a world leader. Its process and heavy industry, capital goods production and basic transportation are all highly efficient. Draka engineers and technologists are second to none, if not their pure researchers.

Why then the widespread belief in a ruralist, anti-urban Domination? The most obvious reason is the lower per-capita output and productivity of the Domination's economy. But "productivity" is anything but a neutral, objective term; instead, it is culturally determined. The Draka maintain a huge unmechanized farming sector because it is, in their terms, highly rational. Shifting to mechanized agriculture would simply transfer serfs from field labor to making and servicing farm machinery, or into supplying and servicing the resulting industrial workers. The net result, from the viewpoint of the Landholders, would be to transfer income from landed to industrial capital, increase the drain on the planet's non-renewable resources, and decrease the gentry's quality of life. That it would also greatly increase the overall standard of living is, *from a Draka point of view*, utterly irrelevant; to a Draka, the reason for having industry is to meet the military and security needs of the State, and *that* the Domination's economy does very well. Here we meet another cause of misunderstanding: the aesthetic and conservationist. Many Alliance citizens assume the importance the Domination attaches to environmental controls implies an antitech attitude similar to our "deep ecologists."

The social roots of Draka environmentalism are wildly different from ours. First, this is an aristocrat's conservationism; a collective projection of the Landholder's desire to preserve and improve the family estate. Second, the Draka are long-term thinkers by tradition and inclination. Third and most important, they can afford it. An economy where industrial productivity is high but even skilled labor very cheap has a greater disposable surplus for sewage-plants and underground transmission lines. It is significant that the one area where the Domination is grossly inferior to the Alliance is in the production of modest consumer durables—our dominant sector, and the driving motor of our economy. There is very little environmental impact to a lavish standard of living when it is confined to a flyspeck of aristocracy; it would never have occurred to a Draka to invent the dishwasher. Here the fundamental truth of the myth we have been demolishing becomes apparent. The Draka are perfectly capable of research and innovation, but a few specialists aside, they do not *like* it. The Draka elite would have been perfectly satis-

fied if all technological progress had come to a
halt in, say, 1910; they have continued to fund
research heavily for power-political reasons, not
any dynamic internal to their own society. The
Draka innovate in response to a perceived need;
when the need is satisfied, they stop. Our restless worship of change for its own sake is alien
to them, alien and repugnant. In a Domination-
ruled world, progress would probably gradually
taper off and cease within a few generations.

Only the Alliance can take humankind to the
stars.

*The Mind of the Draka: a Military-Cultural
Analysis*
Monograph delivered by Commodore Aguilar
Ernaldo
U.S. Naval War College, Manila
11th Alliance Strategic Studies Conference
Subic Bay, 1972

CLAESTUM PLANTATION
DISTRICT OF TUSCANY
PROVINCE OF ITALY
DOMINATION OF THE DRAKA
APRIL, 1969

"Mistis."

Yolande stirred and blinked her eyes; Lele was at the foot
of her bed, touching the mattress to wake her. Machiavelli
was there, too. The cat rolled, flexed its feet in the air and
tucked itself into a circle on the other side, tail over nose.

I wish I could do that, Yolande thought, swinging her feet
out and taking the juice, yawning and stretching.

"Mornin', Lele," she said, rising and walking over to the
eastern window and leaning through the thickness of the
stone wall. There was just a touch of light over the trees, and
the last stars were fading above. The air was cool enough to
raise bumps on her skin, but there were no clouds. It would
be a warm day, and sunny.

"Terrible about Marco, Mistis," Lele said. News spread
fast on a plantation. "Whatevah could he want to hurt Rahksan

fo'?" She began laying out Yolande's hunting clothes. There was indignation in her voice; violent crime was very rare in the countryside. And Rahksan was very much a mother-figure to the younger housegirls, which said a good deal. Favorites were not always so popular.

"Who knows?" Yolande said, forcing the memory out of her mind and starting her stretching exercises; she felt sluggish this morning, and sleep had come hard in the dark loneliness. She lay down on the padded massage table, and felt the blood begin to flow under the serf's impersonally skillful hands.

"Ali quite the hero, Mistis," Lele continued in a dreamy tone, pausing to rub a little scented oil into her palms. Rahksan's son was popular with the younger wenches, too, for entirely different reasons.

"Lele, *be quiet*," Yolande snapped. The serf subsided, quelled as much by the sudden tension in the young Draka's muscles as by the tone. "Is Mistis Venders up yet?"

"Yes, Mistis," the serf replied. "She—" There were footsteps, and Yolande turned her head to watch as her friend climbed the stairs. She was already dressed in hunting clothes, boots and chamois pants, pocketed jacket of cotton duck with leather pads at the elbows, wrist-guards and a curl-brimmed hat.

"How y'feelin', sweet?" Myfwany said softly.

"Pretty good," Yolande replied, and realized it was true, suddenly. The achey feeling was gone, and her body was rested and loose. She arched her back against the masseuse's fingers, sighing with contentment as her friend perched one hip on the table by her shoulder and began braiding her hair with swift deft motions.

"Ever taken the big cats befo'?" Myfwany said.

"Nnnno," Yolande replied. "Little harder there on the small of the back, Lele . . . No, just wildcat. Foxes, of course, an' wolves now and then. Plenty of deer. John has, though, lion an' tiger an' leopard, gun an' steel-huntin' both." Her people usually took game smaller than Cape buffalo on horseback, with javelins or lances, terrain permitting.

Lele finished the massage, carefully rotating knees and ankles to ensure suppleness, and brought the clothes. Yolande turned to look over one shoulder; Myfwany was watching her dress with frank pleasure, still half-sitting on the table with one leg swinging. Draka had little body-modesty—the nudity taboo had been dying in her grandmother's day—but the feeling of being watched with desire was strange. *I like it*, Yolande decided. It was like being stroked all over with a heated mink glove, tingly and comforting and exciting at the same time.

"Ready fo' some huntin'?" she asked, buckling the broad studded belt and holstering her pistol. Automatically, her hands checked it; ejected the magazine, pressed a thumb on the last round to make sure it was feeding smoothly, worked the action, reloaded, snicked on the safety, and dropped it back into the holster, clipping the restraining strap across behind the hammer.

"Ready fo' that, too," Myfwany said. "Where's that brothah of yours?"

"C'mon, let's go roust him out; much longer and the sun will dry out the scent."

They clattered down the stairs, jumping four or five at a time with exuberant grace. Out through her rooms and down the corridors, past the sleepy early-morning greetings of the House staff, up and about their sweeping and polishing. They passed through the library complex, a series of chambers grouped around an indoor pool, two stories under a glass-dome roof; galleries ran back from it, lined shoulder-high with books, statuary, paintings. This had always been one of her favorite indoor parts of the manor, for reading or music or screening a movie; last year they had gotten a Yankee wall-size crystal-sandwich unit, the first in the region.

Off to one side a group of serfs was sitting about a table littered with papers, printout, coffee-cups, and trays: the senior Authorized Literates, managerial staff at their morning conference.

"Hio, Marcello," Yolande said, waving them down as they made to rise. That still felt a little strange. "No, go on with yo' breakfasts, everybody."

Marcello was Chief Librarian, a lean white-haired man in his sixties who had been a university professor before the War. Normally that meant Category 3m71, deportation to a destructive-labor camp, but her mother had thoughtfully snapped him up from a holding-pen while scouting out the estate on recovery-leave in '42. Yolande returned his smile; he had been an unofficial tutor of sorts when she was younger. Not that she was under house-staff direction anymore—no Draka child was once he turned thirteen and carried weapons—

but there were fond memories. She nodded to the others she recognized: the paramedic from the infirmary, the school-teacher—these days, even a plantation taught one child in five or so their letters—and the librarian's son and daughter, understudying as replacements in the usual way.

"We're off huntin'," she said to the elderly Italian serf. "Tell the Lodge we'll be there in 'bout half an hour, an' have somethin' sent to the armory, coffee an' a snack, will you?"

"Gladly, Mistis," he said. "I'll see to it." His accent was odd, much crisper than the usual serf slur, and as much British as Draka in intonation; she remembered some of the neighbors saying he talked too much like a freeman for their taste. He hesitated, then continued:

"Will, ah, any of the Family be at the funeral, Mistis?"

Yolande scowled, then forced her features straight and her mood back to where she wished it. "No. I wouldn't think so, all things considered."

Usually the Landholders of Claestum put in a brief appear-ance at such affairs, as a token of respect. The other serfs at the table exchanged glances, then returned their eyes to their plates and documents. Some estates would have hung an attempted murderer's body up in the Quarters for the birds to eat, as an example.

"John's through here," she continued, as they came out an arched doorway and into a long arcade. Cool air and dew from the gardens to their right; they cut through, and into her brother's rooms. "Hio, Johnny?" she called.

The lounging room was empty, with only the sound of moving water and music playing. A Gerraldson piece, quiet and crystal-eerie, the *Conquest Cantata*. Yolande had never liked it, it always made her think of the way serf-women cried at gravesides, which was odd since the sound wasn't anything like that. But somehow there was laughter in it, too . . . The outer room of John's suite was larger than hers, since he used it for entertaining, and surfaced on three sides with screens of Coromandel sandalwood inset in jade, mother of pearl, ivory, and lapis; they could be folded back to reveal the cabinets, chiller, and displays. The furniture scattered around the lavender-marble floor was mostly Oriental as well; there were a few head-high jade pieces, Turkestan rugs, and a familar bronze Buddha in the ornamental fishpond that ran through the glass wall into the garden beyond.

"Slug-a-bed!" Yolande said indignantly. "An' there he was,

goin' on about how we should make an early start. Come on, Myfwany, we'll tip him out an' throw him in with those ugly carp."

There was a colonnade through the garden, which was mostly pools and and lilies. "Ah, 'Landa, maybe we should call ahead—" Myfwany said as they pushed through carved teak doors and down a hallway.

"Johnnnny!" Yolande chorused, clapping her hands as they turned past the den into the bedroom. "C'mon, yo' big baby, sun's shinin' and we got an appointment with a kitty-cat! Oh."

John Ingolfsson was sitting half-dressed in one of the big black-leather lounging chairs. Colette was kneeling across his lap, and wearing nothing but anklets sewn with silver bells. They chimed softly as her feet moved. Her owner's mouth was on her breasts, and her hands kneaded his shoulders; the tousled blond hair fell backward to her heels as she bent, shuddering.

She gave a sharp cry of protest and opened her eyes as John raised his head and looked at his sister with an ironical lift of eyebrows.

"Yo' *might* knock, sprout," he said dryly, lifting the wench aside and setting her on her feet as he rose. "Or even, iff'n it isn't askin' too much, use the House interphone."

Yolande tossed her head, snorted and set her hands on her hips. "All afternoon, all night an' yo' *still* can't think of anythin' else?"

She eyed the huge circular bed. John's other two regular wenches, Su-ling and Bea, were there in the tangled sheets. Bea was sitting, yawning and rubbing her face, smiling and making the slight courtesy-bow to the two Draka girls. She was a big black woman, Junoesque, older than John, a present from relatives in the southlands given when he turned twelve. Yolande nodded back. She had always rather liked Bea; the wench was unassuming and cheerful and unsulky about turning her hand to ordinary work. Su-ling made a muffled sound and burrowed back into the sheets. Well, who could blame her . . .

"Should see what we'uns had to make do with in those border camps," John said. He stretched, naked to the waist, showing the classic V-shape of his torso. Smooth curves of rounded muscle hard as tile moved under tanned skin, like a statue in oiled beechwood. Not heavy or gross, the way an over-muscled serf who could lift boulders might be; graceful as a racehorse in motion. She felt a glow of pride. Even by Citizen standards, he was beautiful.

"Men," Yolande continued. "Hmmmph. It's a wonder we let yo' vote."

Colette was standing panting and ignored, sweat sheening her long taut dancer's body. Yolande caught a glare of resentment from the huge violet eyes, frowned absently at her. The serf glanced deliberately from Myfwany to Yolande and back, smiled ironically and made the full obeisance from the waist, palms to eyes and fingers to brow. The Draka girl gritted her teeth. The wench needed a good switching; John spoiled her.

"Colette did sort of distract me," he was saying mildly. "Meet you in the armory in, oh, no mo' than five minutes."

"Sho'ly, John," Myfwany said, touching Yolande on the arm. She giggled as they left the bedroom, flapping one hand up and down in a burnt-finger gesture. "Oh, hoo, hoo, quite a sight!" she said.

Yolande blinked surprise at her. "Who, Colette?" she asked. "Needs a belt taken to her rump."

"That might be interestin', but I was thinkin' of yo' brother, sweet, in an aesthetic sort of way," Myfwany said, twitching at the other's braid. "Yo' a good-lookin' family."

"I'll tell him yo' thinks so," she said, grinning slyly. "I mean, seein' as Mandy's makin' moon-eyes at him already . . ."

Myfwany laughed and slapped her shoulder. "Don't yo' dare; swelled heads runs in yo' family, too."

The armory was a single long room on the lower level, a twenty-by-ten rectangle smelling of metal and gun-oil, and of coffee and hot breads and fruit from the trays on the central table. The kitchen-wench had put it down and scuttled out; ordinary serfs were not allowed past the blank steel door with its old combination-lock and new palm-recognition screen. There were no windows, only a row of glowsticks along the ceiling. Military-model assault rifles along the left wall, a light machine-gun, machine-pistols, helmets, body-armor, ammunition, communications gear and nightsight goggles. Benches at the rear held the tools of a repair shop. Ismet sat there: a big balding ex-Janissary, the plantation's gunsmith and one of the four licensed armed serfs on Claestum, although he was technically State property, rented rather than owned.

The hunting gear was on the other wall. Broad-headed boar spears, javelins, crossbows, shotguns. And rifles of the type Draka thought suitable for game when cold steel was impractical, double-barreled models.

"Here," Yolande said. "This is my other Beaufort style . . . unless yo'd like somethin' heavier?"

"No, 8.5mm's fine fo' cat, I think," Myfwany said, popping a roll of melon and prosciutto into her mouth and dusting her hands together. She accepted the weapon and looked it over with an approving nod, thumbing the catch that released the breech; it folded open to reveal the empty chambers. The barrels were damascened, the side-plates inlaid with hunting scenes in gold and silver wire, the rosewood stock set with figures in ivory and electrum.

"Nice piece of work, really nice. Sherrinford of Archona?"

"Mmmm, yes," Yolande said, taking down her other rifle. They were part of a matched set, and Sherrinford worked only by appointment; you had to be born a client. Over-and-under style, like a vertical figure-8; her parents thought that made for better aim than the more usual side-by-side. She watched as her friend snapped the weapon closed and swung it up to dry-fire a few times. *How graceful she is.*

Her brother finished taking down three bandoliers. "I'm usin' the 9mm, but 8.5's fine as long as yo've got the right cartridge. A big male leopard can go full manweight, an' we're talkin' close bush country here. These're 180-grain hollowpoint express, ought to do it. There's a range with backstop at the lodge, Myfwany, so yo' can shoot-in on that gun."

"Lovely," Myfwany said.

The balloon tires of the open-topped Shangaan hummed on the pavement as they wound east from the manor. The road was like the broad-base terraces on the hills, and the stock-dams that starred the countryside with ponds: a legacy of the Land Settlement Directorate and the period when the estate had been gazetted, right after the War. The labor-camps were long gone, and the work of the engineers had had time to mellow into the Tuscan countryside. Babylonica willows trailed their fierce green osiers into the water, and huge white-coated cattle dreamed beneath them with the mist curling around their bellies. Roadside poplars cast dappled shade, and the low stone walls of the terraces were overgrown with virginia creeper.

"I like this time of year," Yolande said. "It's . . . like waking up on a holiday mornin'."

She inhaled deeply; the air was still a little cool as the sun rose over the Monti del Chianti to the east. The olives shone silver-gray, and the vineyards curved in snaking contour rows of black root and green shoots along the sides of the hills; the shaggy bush-rose hedges were in bloom, kilometer upon kilometer of tiny white flowers against the lacy thornstalks. Their scent tinted the air, joining smells of dust, dew, the blue genista and red poppies that starred the long silky grass by the roadside verge, the scarlet cornflowers spangled through the undulating fields of wheat and clover. The air was loud with wings and birdsong, plovers and wood doves, hoopoes and rollers. The white storks were making their annual migration southward, and the sky was never empty of them in this season.

"It's beautiful any time of year," John said; he was at the rear of the fantail-shaped passenger section of the steamer. Yolande looked up; his voice was completely serious, different from the bantering tone he usually used with his youngest sister. "Yo' love this place, don't yo', John?" she said.

He smiled, shrugged, looked away. "Yes," he replied musingly. "Yes, I do. All of it."

They were passing through the lower portion of the estate, as close to flat as any part of Claestum, planted in fruit orchard, dairy pasture, and truck gardens. A score of three-mule plow teams were at work, sixteen-hand giants with silvery coats and Roman noses, leaning into the traces with an immemorial patience. The earth behind the disk-tillers was a deep chocolate color, reddish-brown, smelling as good as new bread. The work gangs were there already, unloading flats of seedlings from steam drags, pitchforking down the huge piles of pale-gold wheat straw used for mulch, spreading manure and sewage-sludge from the methane plant, or wrestling with lengths of extruded-aluminum irrigation pipe. Some of them looked up and waved their conical straw hats as the car passed; the mounted foremen bowed in the saddle.

"Y'know," he continued, and shifted the rifle in the crook of his arm, "we say 'Claestum,' and think we've summed it up. It all depends who's doin' the lookin'. A League accountant looks at the entry in her ledgers and sees forty-five hundred hectares, yieldin' so-and-so many tonnes of wheat and fodder, x hundred hectoliters of wine and y of olive oil per year. Security's District Officer down t' Siena calls up the specs on a thousand-odd serfs an' checks fo' reported disorders. An ecologist from the Conservancy people thinks in terms of"—a flight of bustards soared up from a sloping grainfield and glided down to a hedgerow—"that sort of thing."

"Ma and Pa?" Yolande said. *Damn, can't get to know your own brother until you grow up*, she thought.

"They see it as something they made," he replied. "Almost as somethin' they fought and broke. I can understand it; every time they look out they can say, 'we planted these trees,' or 'it took five years of green-manurin' to get those upper fields in decent tilth.' Pa told me once it was like breakin' a horse; yo' had to love the beast or you'd kill it in sheer exasperation."

"And yo', Johnny?" she continued softly, careful not to break the mood.

"It's . . . home," he said. "Some people need that feelin' of creation. I don't. I love . . . it all; sights and smells and sounds, the people an' the animals and the plants and . . . oh, the way the sun comes over the east tower every mornin', the church-bell soundin'— Shit, I'm no poet, sprout; yo're the only one in the family with ambitions in that direction."

He smiled ruefully. "I suspect I love this place mo' than any individual, which may say somethin' about yours truly. At least, a community an' place is longer-lived than a person. I won't change anythin' much, when it's mine. A bit of tidyin'-up here and there, maybe bring in a herd of eland, it'd do well . . ."

"Mr. Ingolfsson?" Myfwany asked.

"John," he said.

"Thanks, John . . . I was wonderin', don't mean to pry, but if yo' like it here so much, why did yo' volunteer fo' officer trainin'?" Everyone started equal in the Citizen Force, three years minimum and a month a year until forty, but not everyone wanted to prolong their spell in uniform.

"Payback," John said, opening a thermos of *caffé latte* and passing it around. Myfwany made an inquiring sound as she accepted a cup of the coffee.

"I pay my debts," he amplified. The road was winding upwards again, through fig orchards and rocky sheep-pasture dotted with sweet chestnut trees.

"Down at that school, they're probably fillin' y'all up with yo' debt to the Race and the State." He shrugged. "True enough. I likes to think of it on a mo' personal level. A plantation can feel like a world to its own self, but it isn't. It only exists as part of the Domination. The Race makes possible the only way of life I know, the only world I feel at home in, the only contentment I can ever have."

He laughed. "Not least, by controllin' change. It must be powerful lonely to be a Yankee; by the time one of *them* is middle-aged, everythin' they grew up with is gone. Like havin' the earth always dissolvin' away beneath yo' feet. Cut off from yo' ancestors an' yo' descendants both. Here, barrin' catastrophe, I can be reasonable sure that in a thousand years, what I value will still exist."

"It's here because Ma and Pa an' others like them fought fo' it, bled fo' it. A decade of my life is cheap payment. I wouldn't *deserve* this unless I was ready to die fo' it, to kill fo' it." He blinked back to the present, and the gray eyes turned warm as he smiled at his sister. "It'll always be here fo' yo', too, sprout, when yo' come back from that space-travellin'."

The lodge was pre-War Italian work, only slightly modified; the plantations fronting the hill nature-reserve maintained it jointly, part of their contract with the Conservancy Directorate to manage the forest. Vine-grown, it nestled back into the shadow of the hill, flanked by outbuildings and stables and a few paddocks surrounded by stone walls. The huntsmen were waiting in the forecourt, with the horses and dogs, beside a spring-fed pool. A dozen liondogs, the type the Draka had bred to hunt the big cats in the old African provinces: black-coated, with thick ruffs around their necks and down their spines. Massive beasts, over a meter at the shoulder and heavier than a man, thick-boned, with broad blunt muzzles and canines that showed over the lower lip. They rose and milled as the car stopped, straw-yellow eyes bright with anticipation, until a word from the handlers set them sinking back on their haunches in disciplined silence.

"Menchino, Alfredo," John said, nodding. The huntsmen were brothers in their early thirties, one fair and one dark, with the slab-sided, high-cheeked faces of the Tuscan peasantry.

"Master John," Menchino said, making the half-bow as the Draka stepped down from the car and the driver pulled away in a *chuff* of steam and sough of pneumatics. There was a smile on his face; hunting was the brothers' religion, and

John Ingolfsson had been a devout fellow-worshipper since he was old enough to carry a rifle.

"Missy—" Alfredo began. "Mistis," he corrected, as she frowned and tapped her gunbelt in reminder of her adult status. Adult as far as serfs were concerned, at least. A slight glance out of the corner of his eye to the other serf, the hint of a shrug; she suspected it was the thought of two young females going after a dangerous beast. Italian serfs were funny about things like that, and Ma said it would take another generation or two to really break them of it.

They had learned not to let it *show* some time ago, of course.

"We'll probably be back fo' lunch," Yolande said to the middle-aged housegirl on the veranda. "Myfwany, yo' pick y' mount?"

The serfs lead the horses over, and the Draka checked their tack. Light pad-saddles, with molded-leather scabbards for their rifles; the huntsmen had much the same, though without the tooling and studs. The two Ingolfssons and their guests slid their weapons into the sheaths and fastened the restraining straps. Their pack was sitting quiet, but the dogs knew what that meant; tails began to beat at the gravel of the drive, and deep chests rumbled eagerness.

"I'll have the dapple," Myfwany said, reaching for the bridle of a spotted gray mare. It blew inquisitively at her, and politely accepted a lump of brown sugar. She turned eyes bright with excitement to her friend. "Less'n yo'd rather?"

" 'S fine," Yolande said, gathering her own reins and vaulting easily into the saddle one-handed. The brown gelding sidestepped, then quieted as she gathered it in and pressed her knees. She ran a critical hand down its neck, checking the muscle tone, and turned an eye on the others. They were fresh but not rambunctious, which meant the lodge staff had been exercising them properly.

"Keep the dogs well in hand," John said to the huntsmen. "They not used to anythin' bigger an' meaner than they are."

"That's it!" John said, reining in on the bank of the little stream. The sound of the pack had changed, the deep *gerrr-whuff!* barking giving way to a higher belling sound. "They've sighted."

"Less'n they've taken out after a deer." Myfwany grinned, reaching down beyond her right knee. The rifle came out of the scabbard with an easy flip, and she rested the butt on one thigh. The other Draka followed suit.

One of the Italian serfs snorted, and the other coughed to cover it. John laughed. "Not this pack," he said. "Not when we gave them a clear scent."

They heeled their horses down the slope in a shower of gravel and dust. Two hour chase had brought them deep into the high hills; the Monte del Chianti were mountains only by courtesy, more like steep ridges, few more than a thousand meters high. It was just enough to keep the air comfortably crisp as the morning turned clear and brilliant. The forest was shaggy and uneven, part old growth, much new since the conquest; you could see the traces of old terracing, or the tumbled stones of peasant houses. Oak and chestnut covered the lower slopes, with darker beech and pine and silver fir above; feral grapevines wound around many, and there were slashes of color from the blossom of abandoned orchards.

This spot was cool under tall black pines, full of their chill scent. There were poplars along the stream; the mounts stepped through cautiously, raising their feet high as horseshoes clattered on the smooth brown rocks. Spring rains and sun had brought a brief intense flowering where sun reached through the trees; the far slope was too thin-soiled to carry timber, and it blazed with wild field lilies, grape hyacinths, and sheets of purple-and-yellow crocus. Yolande rose slightly in the stirrups as the gelding's muscles bunched to push it up the hillside in a series of bounds. The bruised herbs raised a sharp aromatic smell, of sage and rosemary and sweet minty hyssop that shed anthrophora bees and golden butterflies in clouds before the horses' hooves.

"Hiya*aaaaaa*," Yolande shouted, as they broke onto an open ridgeline and swung into a loping canter. One of the serfs sounded a horn, *taaa*-brrrt, and the sound of the dogs rose to a deep baying roar; the prey was treed or at bay. She could feel the blood pounding in her ears, and the wind cool after them; it tugged her hat down and blew streamers of pale hair free of her braid, flickering at the corners of her vision. The horse moved between her knees like a beating heart, a long weightless rocking and then the rhythmic thumping of hooves, snort of breath, a creak of leather, and rattle of iron.

"Whoa-*hey*," John said. The dogs were raving, just out of sight ahead, and then the voice of one rose to a shrill scream of pain, cut off sharp as a knife. Another sound, a wild saw-edged snarling shriek that never came from a canine mouth, and the cries were echoed and re-echoed as if from stony walls, fading to a harsh far-distant clamor. Yolande's horse laid back its ears and shook its head slightly, and she tightened her legs to reassure it.

The horses slowed to a fast walk as they went under the shade of a stand of tall fir, then again as they emerged into a semicircle of open space surrounded on three sides by trees. The ridgeline was broken here, with a steep slope that turned into a cliff ten meters high. The spot had been improved slightly, the sort of thing the Conservancy Directorate did to encourage the game: a spring had been dug out halfway up the cliff and funneled through a stone lion's mouth, leaping out to feed a pool and the trickle that drained down toward the creek. A big maple grew out of the cliff near the spring, thick twisted roots gripping at the rocks like frozen snakes, the trunk sweeping out almost horizontally and then flaring upward. Six of the liondogs were leaping and calling beneath the trunk; five more were clustered around the base of the tree.

"Merda!" Alfredo swore. One of the pack was lying at the base of the slope, still twitching but with its intestines hanging gray and pink out of its rent belly. It was plain enough what had happened. The five dogs at the tree were barking frantically toward the dense foliage farther out, making short dashes out the broad sloping surface of the trunk and then retreating, as if daring each other. Through the leaves the hunting party could see a flash of brown and orange, and the yowling screech of the leopard. Only one dog could approach at a time. A liondog might outweigh a leopard, but its jaws alone were no match for the big cat's claws and speed.

"Call them in, Alfredo," John said, without taking his eyes off the tree.

The Draka all dropped their reins, and the horses froze into well-trained immobility. Nervous, though, and sweating with it, their eyes rolling at the scent of carnivore so close. Alfredo blew a series of notes on his horn, and his brother rode among the dogs snapping his whip. They milled, bellowing, then drew back with a rush, standing in a clot with their muzzles raised toward the tree. Discipline kept them motionless and quiet, but there was a straining eagerness in their posture, and they shifted weight from foot to foot as unconscious whines of frustration slipped between their fangs.

Yolande worked her mouth, suddenly conscious of its dryness. The glade grew quiet; there was the soft background surf-sound of air through the trees, and the incongruously soothing rush of water into the pool, the small noises of the horses and dogs, and for a moment the fading echoes of Alfredo's horn. *Gods, this is exciting*, she thought. The branches shook as the leopard moved restlessly, then settled, and she could see its amber eyes peering through the leaves. *Exciting*. Quiet outside, inside a torrent of feelings: pity for the dead lionhound, awe and pity for the great deadly beast twenty meters away. The peculiar combination of sorrow and deep happiness she always felt hunting, but raised to a new level, an aliveness that seemed to reach out to encompass every speck of dust in the slanting beams of light, every movement of leaf and shadow. As if she could track the bees by their humming, or know every rock and crevice of the cliff . . .

"Fist fo' it," John said easily. He drew his binoculars left-handed and focused. "Hooo, lordy, that's a big one. He-cat, old an' mean. He *not* happy at all." Her brother laughed softly with pure pleasure as he returned the glasses to their case at his saddlebow. "Sprout, yo' first."

They both beat their left fists through the air, then opened them simultaneously.

"Scissors beats paper, towhair," John said. "Miz Venders?"

"Myfwany," she corrected, raising her hand. "One, two, three—"

The girl's hand came out closed: rock. The young man's was scissors again; he swore good-naturedly.

"Yo' win, Myfwany. Remember, he'll come down *fast*; that's, oh, thirty meters. Ten in the leap from the tree, then a couple bounds to us. Got it?"

"Mmmmm-hm," the redhead said. There were two spots of crimson high on her freckled cheeks as she kicked one leg over the neck of her horse and slid down, then went to one knee. The muzzle of the rifle stayed pointed half-down, and rock steady. The breeding pairs for the Italian leopards had been imported in the late '40s from the Atlas and Kayble mountains, and not much hunted since; they would have little fear of men. Still, it was possible this one knew what a gun meant; if nothing else, the scientists used dart-guns for tagging specimens. She was equally careful not to stare directly at their prey.

"Yo' next, sprout."

Yolande brought her right leg over the low horn of her saddle, rested her left hand behind her and eased herself down to the ground. The springy turf gave beneath her boots; it was a long way down, a fifteen-hand horse and a short person. She dropped the reins, which meant "stand still" to a gun-trained mount, and brought her Sherrinford to high port. Her brother waited a few seconds and then dismounted, careful to make no abrupt movements.

"Menchino," he said, in the same soft, conversational voice. "Take yo' rifle, circle around and come up behind that tree. Don't shoot less'n yo' has to. Iff'n yo' has to, don't hesitate."

"*Grazie*, Mastah," the serf said; some Draka might have sent him up there unarmed. He drew his own plain single-shot hunting weapon and dropped back to follow the edge of the trees around the clearing and approach the maple from behind.

"Spread out," John continued. The two Draka fanned out from Myfwany, leaving her directly facing the tree. Alfredo snapped leashes to the collars of the lead dog and bitch, drawing them to one side to anchor the pack. They could all hear the leopard moving restlessly in the branches, a coughing grunt and an occasional snarl, glimpses of patterned hide.

"Mastah, there's a cave back here," Menchino called from the dense scrub at the base of the slope. The soil was thin there, but the rock was damp with seepage and carried dense thorny *maquis*, rock-rose and broom. "Sign and scat."

"Lair," John called. "Ignore it." He waited until the huntsman was well-positioned at the base of the tree. "Can yo' see him?"

"Yes." There was a tight quality to the serf's voice. "Jesu and Maria, Mastah, he's a big one. Two and a half meters long, easy."

"Good. Now send him down."

Menchino shouted and began kicking the underbrush around the base of the tree; he roared insults, waved his arms, skated rocks out toward the thicker branches. Yolande wiped her hand on her jacket and took a firmer grip on the rifle. To a cat, noise and motion were threat; it would probably break forward. And predators were more sensible than humans, they were dangerous when cornered or where their young were concerned, but they rarely attacked something except in self-defense or to eat. Leopards were an exception sometimes, though . . . The serf fired his rifle into the air; then she could hear the hasty sounds of his reloading. Again.

That brought the cat out into the open, out along a thigh-thick branch that had only a tuft of leaves at the end. Flowing out, liquid metal in motion, then halting blinking in the sun. The light seemed to catch fire on its coat, hot spotted gold rippling like living metal, and the tawny pools of its eyes with the pupils slitted against the sun. *Wotan, it* is *a big one*, she thought delightedly. The North African breed were larger than the sub-Saharan variety, but this was exceptional even so. An old male, one ear chewed to a stump. Not a happy one, either; the head was forward and the ears laid back, the tail lashing. Menchino fired again, into the upper branches of the tree, and cut twigs pattered down.

That's decided him, Yolande thought, with a pins-and-needles sensation that ran down to the small of her back. The long body froze, tail extended and rigid, and then the haunches moved, settling and gripping. She could see the muscles bunch, the claws extend and dig into the rough pale bark. The leopard screamed.

And leapt. An impossible distance out from the branch, soaring as if in flight. Myfwany's rifle came up, seeming to drift with the deceptive calm of a motion that is fast but very smooth. The muzzle halted, steady, and the flat *crack* of the heavy game round broke the air with a startling suddenness. The yellow grace recoiled in midair and fell, hitting the tall grass with an audible thump; it thrashed, sending stalks and wildflowers and divots of turf flying amid a wild squalling that set the horses shuddering and the liondogs growling like thunder. Then it was up again, flowing like swift water across the open ground, stretching and bunching. Yolande brought her own weapon up, and saw the fangs barred in the V of the backsight. Myfwany fired again, and the predator seemed to stumble with a grunt, fall, sliding into the ground shoulder-first, tumbling end-for-end, then lying still. Time began again.

"Wait fo' it!" John called. They waited, in a moment that seemed forever. Yolande met her friend's eyes, bright in a flushed face, and felt a shock that seemed to run down to the pit of her stomach.

Myfwany glanced away. "He's not breathin'," she said, slightly hoarse. Yolande looked at the leopard; it was smaller, somehow. The eyes and mouth were open, the tongue lolling like a pink flag; blood pooled out, and there were flies on it already. She walked over to Myfwany, putting a hand on her shoulder, and together they looked down at the dead leopard. It was a little past its prime, marked with the scars of its prey and of mating fights, but still sleek and strong. Triumph and a huge sorrow mixed to make a feeling that was wholly pleasure; she took a deep breath and let it out in a sigh, letting the moment pass with it.

John came up and clapped Myfwany on the back. "Nice shootin'," he said heartily. " 'Cross the loins with the first round, an' right through the lungs with the second," he continued, pointing out the wounds with his toe. "Want to skin him out?"

"Nnnno," the redhead said, breaking open her rifle and letting the spent brass tinkle down to ping on rock and bounce off the warm skin of the cat. Loosening the sling, she hung it muzzle-down across her back. "I'll water the horses, iff'n yo' don't mind."

The young man nodded, slung his own weapon and drew the long clip-pointed Jamieson from its sheath along his leg. The honed edge glinted in the morning sunlight, a line of silver along the blackened steel of the narrow blade.

"Alfredo, give me a hand," he said, kneeling and holding the hilt in his mouth while he rolled back the sleeves of his hunting jacket.

Yolande let the barrel of her rifle fall back onto her right shoulder, reaching left-handed for the reins of her mount. Myfwany collected the other four, soothing them with words and a firm stroking hand on nose and neck, leading them carefully around the bloody bodies of dog and leopard. They shied slightly at the smell as they passed, then quieted a little; the wind was from the hillside, and she thought it must still carry the dead cat's scent, if it had been denning here. She gathered the reins and pulled her horse's head around, following her friend.

"*Masta! Look out!*" Menchino shouted.

She looked up, and for a second perception warred with knowledge; the leopard was dead, but a leopard was charging toward her from the shrub beyond the pool. Running in long low bounds, the tail swinging to balance it, fluid and sure. Menchino fired from above, and his bullet kicked dust and spanged off stone by the animal's side. It swerved slightly, the platter-sized feet spreading and gripping in automatic adjustment; swerved toward Myfwany. The horses were rearing and neighing. Myfwany's hand was tangled in their reins; she was fighting to free it, clawing with her other for the pistol by her side. Alfredo's rifle was still in its scabbard on his saddle; John's was across his back, and his hands busy with the skinning.

Yolande felt the reins burn through her left palm. The Sherrinford's muzzle came forward as she yanked at the stock with her right hand, but slowly, so slowly, caught in air thick as honey. Only the leopard was moving at normal speed, the bounds lengthening. Myfwany's face was chalk-pale, the green eyes enormous. *Slap* and the forestock of her rifle hit her palm, *hold* the breath *squeeze* the trigger. *Bam!* and recoil hammered at her shoulder, another spurt of dust by the cat's forefeet, and now it was rising in the final leap, head high, Yolande let the muzzle drop again *straight-on shot* ran through her head and *bam!*

Then she was running toward the tangled figures on the ground, rifle held high by the barrel, shouting wordlessly. She swore as she ran, every muscle tensing for the single blow, then froze. The leopard was not moving, but neither was Myfwany . . . Yolande dropped the rifle heedlessly, buried her hands in the cat's ruff and strained backward, heaving at a limp unresisting weight that was like a roll of damp canvas; the animal's bones and sinew moved in their natural courses, but flopping loose without a directing mind, hampering. She heaved it half off the other girl and dropped to her knees, hands smoothing blood-matted hair back from blood-slicked skin.

"*Myfwany!*" she said frantically. "Oh, gods, Myfwany, are yo' all right, *please* be all right, I tried, oh please, I yo', *please!*"

"Phffth," Myfwany said, spitting blood to one side. The matted lashes fluttered open. "It's—*pfhth*—not my blood, an' get this thing *off* me!" She kicked and shoved, freeing herself, then sat up and caught at Yolande's shoulders. "And I love yo', too." Suddenly they were laughing, embracing, with kisses that tasted of rank blood and fear and joy.

"Touchin'," John said, dryly and a trifle breathlessly. The girls broke apart and rose, leaning on each other. Yolande's brother heaved the animal over on its back. "Female, nursin'." The teats along its belly were enlarged. "In through the lung, an' a perfect heart-shot," he continued. "Dead in the air."

Myfwany gripped Yolande harder, and gave way to a single

deep shudder. "Felt like someone fired it at me like a cannonball, an' it was sprayin' blood."

Yolande felt her stomach knot with fear-nausea, and pushed it down; there had been no time before, and now it would be foolish. She slipped her arm down to rest around Myfwany's waist, unwilling to break contact, unwilling to let go the concrete feeling of life.

"Bet there's kits in that-there cave," she said.

The leopard cub mewled, and Machiavelli danced back from the box that held his fascinated regard, hissed, then turned tail and bolted up the tower stairs. Yolande heard Myfwany laugh, and gripped harder at the stone of the balustrade, biting at her lip and choking back a sob.

"Sweet, what is it?" Myfwany asked.

Yolande turned, to see her framed by the opened French doors of the lounging room; behind her the servants were scurrying out. The afternoon wind blew up from the gardens, cuffing with warm soft hands at red hair still damp and dark from the baths, plastering the thin cloth of the robe to her body.

"I—" she breathed deeply, winning back control. Her head felt light, only vaguely connected to the rest of her. "I just realized again, yo' might have *died*, Myfwany. Yo' might be *gone*, right now."

"So." The other smiled, warm and fond; then her expression grew serious, and she stretched out her hands toward the other, palms up. "Come to me. I'm here."

The cub was looking doubtfully at the bottle. Yolande looked up from fastening her eardrops as it hissed.

"Come on, *eat*, yo' little moron!" Myfwany said, pushing the bottle toward the spotted form. It tumbled backward in the blankets, crowding toward the back of the improvised cage the plantation carpenter had knocked together for them. The huge amber eyes were opened wide, and it made a pathetic gesture of menace with the too-large paws.

"Oh, the poor thing!" That was Sofia, Myfwany's maid. She reached toward the leopard and yanked her hand back, sucking at the scratches and spitting curses in Sicilian.

"Here," Yolande said, laughing. She picked up the comforter from the rumpled sheets of her bed and threw it over the cub, then clamped the wriggling form through the thick fabric while the others tucked it into a bundle.

"Now, let's get the head free . . . right. Give me the bottle, darlin' . . ." The cub was glaring and hissing again; she waited until it quieted a little, then dribbled milk on its muzzle. It squalled, but licked its fur as well, and she could almost see it pause mentally at the warm almost-familiar taste. "There, little tiger, that's bettah, isn't it?" Yolande moved the rubber teat closer, then gently brushed it against the cub's lips. It hesitated, then began to suck strongly; she let it feed for a moment, then brought the fingers of her other hand close enough for it to smell, rubbing along its jaw.

"Lele, Sofia, *that's* how y'all does it," she said. "Ready to go down to dinner, darlin'?"

"Sho'ly, love," Myfwany replied. The word was still new enough to send a stab of pleasure. "How do I look?" She stood and turned, holding out her arms.

They were both dressed in evening wear, the neogrecian gowns that had been standard formal dress for Citizen women since the Classic Revival a century and more ago. The draped and folded chiton still felt a little strange; children did not wear such. The right shoulder was bare, and the end-fold hung over the left elbow. Myfwany's was a warm bronze color, edged in a turquoise that matched her eyes. Yolande had decided to stick with ivory-cream; ash-blonds tended to look washed-out in anything lighter.

"Yo' look wonderful," Yolande said, running her fingers gently down the other's neck. "Ready to face the music?"

"I didn't know yo' meant it literally," Myfwany said.

Dinner was indoors today, it being still a little cold for dining on the terrace after sunset. The two girls had halted in the corridor outside the lounge where the family gathered before the evening meal, and they could hear the sound of harp and flute through the tall carved-ebony doors.

"Oh, yo'," Yolande said. Then: "Oh, *yo'*." She made a few last-minute adjustments to the hairpin in the psyche-knot above her left ear. "I'm nervous. I mean, I feel, yo' know, *different.*"

"Love, yo' didn't have a big 'V' fo' 'virgin' stamped on y'forehead, anyhows." Myfwany smiled heavy-lidded, and leaned forward to plant a gentle kiss on the skin between

Yolande's breasts, above the drape of her gown. "Besides, it's only fifty percent deflowerin'."

"No fair, I cain't grab when we're all dressed up!" Yolande whispered, then chuckled.

"What's so funny?"

"Well . . . It wasn't like I expected. I mean, I knew it was a *pleasure*, everyone's always goin' on about it, but I didn't expect it to be so much, oh, *fun*. Like a tickle-fight, hey? An' I feel so much *bettah*."

Myfwany joined in her laughter. "I think that depends on who, sweet," she said, and held out a hand. "Shall we go in?"

Yolande took the hand in both of hers. "Myfwany, I want yo' to know something. As long as our names are spoken together, I'll never do anythin' to make yo' ashamed of me."

"Nor will I," Myfwany said, equally grave. They linked arms and turned.

The door swung open easily with a hand-push against one of the silver lion's heads that studded the night-black Calamander wood, into a space more dimly lit than the corridor. The room within was a long L-shape; the inner wall held bookshelves and a huge fireplace, the outer Flemish tapestries between tall windows. Cedar logs burned with an aromatic crackle, their light ruddy on the couches, settees, and low tables. The serf musicians were gathered unobtrusively in a corner, the Draka grouped around the hearth: her father and mother and brother, of course, and Aunt Alicia; her friends from school; the three overseers. This was a semi-formal occasion, to celebrate the successful hunt.

"Greetin's," her father said with a slight bow, raising his brandy-snifter. "Honor to our leopard-killers." He was smiling, but there was real pride in the gesture.

Yolande nodded back to the stocky figure in the dark velvet jacket and lace cravat, feeling a rush of love. The others raised a polite murmur and joined the toast before resuming their conversations. A housegirl brought round a tray of aperitifs, and the girls accepted glasses of chilled white wine with their free hands as they joined the loose grouping around the fire. She sipped, marveling at the tart refreshing taste, the sensual pleasure of fire-warmth on her skin; everything seemed new, everyone sharing her joy.

"Congratulations again," John said, taking a wafer dabbed with beluga from a passing servant. He looked at their linked hands. "On all counts."

Her mother looked up from a lounger; she had been talking to Rahksan, who sat beside her on a stool working listlessly at her inevitable embroidery.

"Well, here's a cat that's found its way into the dairy," she said dryly. "Took long enough."

"*Mother!*" Yolande said, with a sound halfway between affection and exasperation.

Veronica had been leaning against the mantelpiece. "An' about time," she added, grinning.

Myfwany leaned closer to give Yolande a kiss on the cheek. "My sentiments exactly," she said aloud. In a whisper: "They just teasin', sweet."

"Don't I know it," Yolande replied, and realized that this time at least she did not mind; her heart knew as well as her head did that the words were without intent to hurt. Today nothing could diminish happiness, except the knowledge that today must end.

She looked down at Rahksan; the serf's face was drawn tight around the eyes and mouth, a look of suffering. *Poor Tantie.* She gave her friend's arm a squeeze.

"Just a second, love," she murmured, then crossed to sit on the lounger. "Y'all right, Tantie?" she asked softly, putting a hand on her shoulder. The official story was that Rahksan had been attacked, which would account for her being shaken. The Draka girl grimaced mentally at the memory of the scene in the stable, then put it aside with adolescent ruthlessness; nothing seemed strong enough to cast a shadow on the changing of her life. "Anythin' I can do fo yo'?"

"No, thank y' kindly, Mistis 'Landa," Rahksan said. Some life returned to her face, and she reached up to pat the girl's hand. "I jes' need a little time, is all."

"Which reminds me, time fo' an announcement," Johanna said casually. "In recognition of his quick and decisive action, Rahksan's son Ali is bein' recommended as a candidate fo' State service, an' will be leaving in two months fo' preliminary testin' at the Janissary base in Nova Cartago."

There were raised eyebrows among some of the Draka. The number of recruits needed was limited in these days of peace, and there was fierce competition for the available slots among the one and a half billion of the serf population. Recommendation was a privilege usually only given to exceptionally deserving cases, and Ali had been notorious as a troublemaker, aside from this latest incident. Of course, the

Janissaries were not house serfs or field-hands, and qualities which made a man unsatisfactory on a plantation could be valuable in the armed services . . .

Rahksan nodded deferentially to the congratulations, murmuring thanks. "I jes' hope he do well, Mistis," she said to Johanna. "He never goin' be happy here, that sure. Maybeso this the makin' of him." She blinked, her lashes wet. "But I don' see much of him now, that sure too."

"Hey, don' be sad, Tantie," Yolande said, concerned. "He get leave now an' then, yo' sees him as often as Ma sees me or Edwina or Dionysia or John."

A sigh. "That true." The Afghan smiled, wearily but with genuine warmth. "Congratulations fo' yaz an' y'friend, Mistis 'Landa. Good to see m'other chile's growin' strong an' happy."

"Thank yo', Tantie," Yolande said, touched.

Her mother reached out a finger and touched Rahksan's cheek, taking up a teardrop. "Speakin' of children, why don't yo' go an' talk to y' boy some, Rahksi?" Johanna looked up to meet her husband's eye; he nodded slightly, smiling. "See yo' later this evenin'."

The Landholders and their guests walked through into the dining room—one of the smaller ones; there would be no point in eight people losing themselves in the halls meant for entertainment. This was spacious enough but cozy, a round rosewood table and sideboards; the white linen and burnished silverware shone beneath the chandelier, and the housegirls were laying out the appetizers: smoked salmon and foie gras and oysters nestling in beds of crushed ice. Yolande found herself and Myfwany seated to the right of her parents, the senior positions. The smells suddenly made her mouth water; it had been a long day, and she had skipped lunch.

"My, that looks good," she said, as the serf laid salmon and capers on her plate. Another poured the first wine, a Valpolicella the color of straw. She sniffed, sipped.

"Fifteen an' hollow legs," Johanna said. "Children . . . Oh, speakin' of which, Tom an' I have *anothah* announcement." She reached across and took her husband's hand. "We're havin' some mo'."

Yolande choked on her wine. Myfwany thumped her back, but she could still hear John's glass hit the table with a heavy *chunk* as she coughed.

"Yo' *what*, ma?" she gasped. She was the youngest of the

four, and had had fifteen years of hearing Johanna's fervid
relief that that particular duty to the Race was complete.

"Loki yo' say!" her brother added, with a snort. "*That's* a
surprise."

Her father laughed, deep and rich. "Soul of the White
Christ, everyone's Methuselah to their offspring," he said,
leaning back and grinning at their discomfiture. "Frig and
Freya, boy, yo' goin' so slow on the grandchildren, we thought
we'd show yo' how."

"An' we're not exactly too old *yet*," Johanna said, raising a
brow. Then, relenting: "Yo' youngsters do tease easy. Oh, we
not doin' it *personal*; that would be too risky at my age,
certain-sure. Not to mention barbaric an' uncomfortable. We
had a couple dozen frozen ova stored by the Eugenics people, just goin' have them warmed up and borne by host-
mothers, brooders. *Finally* they figured a way of havin' the
unpleasant part done by the serfs." A bland look at Yolande.
"Provided yo' approves, of course."

"Certai— Oh, *moth*er," Yolande said, casting an appealing
eye at her friends. It was bad enough being teased by your
contemporaries, but parents were much worse. She saw suppressed laughter, as her schoolmates examined their plates or
the ceiling.

"It'll be nice to have babies around again," she said. That
was true enough; babies were even more fun than kittens.
"An' they're no bother, after all."

"Sho'ly will be nice," Johanna agreed, nodding. "The
Eugenics people talkin' about improvements, as well. Now,
about the party next week—"

CHAPTER FIVE

DATE: 07/06/67

FROM: Techspec IV Carnot Alden
         Virunga Biocontrol Institute
         Project [*Classified*]
         West Rift Province

TO: Techspec VIII Carmen Fougard
         Archona University
         Biocontrol Department
         Archona Province

RE: Project [*Classified*]
         Viral Coding Subsection
         Ituri Retro—66b6—03

[*Technical data deleted by order of Security Directorate.*]

. . . and I tell you, Cammie, when I saw the specs on that virus I nearly fainted, and then I nearly heaved my breakfast. *Damnedest* retrovirus complex you ever saw—even managed to work its way into the lymphatic matter. Dormancy period—you won't believe this—up to ten years! The wild version would just rip the shit out of a human immune system; anyone who got it would be wide open for opportunistic infections. From the anthro evidence and the analysis of cognate primate carriers (green monkeys, mainly) I'd say it crossed over into the Ituri population just about eighty to a hundred years ago. I'll be fucked if I know how, you'd need some sort of blood exchange, or body fluids at least. Human-human transmission would be easier, not pneumatic or contact, but sex would do it. Possibly even an insect vector. The thing that gives me nightmares is the thought that it might have broken out into the general population when we swept the blacks there out into the compounds. They were just starting to do blood transfusions in the 1880s, so we might have got it, and back then they'd have had no earthly prayer of beating it, they couldn't even have identified it. Could have been the Black Death all over again. The gods' own luck most of those went into destructive-labor camps.

Of course, it's lucky some survived in the Ituri pygmies, too. Anyway, it's given us a ten-year jump on the SD project. This is the perfect source of our basic viral carrier—particularly since there are direct neurological effects. Once you finish tweaking this, it'll be like a ripe fig stuffed with botulism.

> *Biopsych Warfare: An Interdisciplinary Approach*
> by Professor Colin Demoreaux von Sternheim
> Archona University Press, Archona
> 2004

PROVINCE OF SARMATIA
DOMINATION OF THE DRAKA
CRIMEAN MILITARY RESERVE
AIR TRAINING SECTION
15,000 METERS
MARCH 10, 1973

"Beep. Beep. Beep." The missile lock-on warning repeated itself with idiot persistence, a drone in the silenced cave-world of the pilot's helmet, sharper than the subliminal moan of the engines.

"*Shit,*" Yolande muttered to herself, throwing the aircraft into a series of wild jinks and swerves, just enough to keep the *beeps* from merging into the continuous drone of launch.

She was half-reclining in the narrow cockpit of the Falcon VI turboram fighter, immobile in a hydraulic suit that cushioned her against acceleration and a clamshell couch that left nothing mobile but fingers and head. The sky above her was blue-black through the near-invisible canopy, here on the fringes of space; ahead was the smooth semicircle of crystal-sandwich screen, the virtual control panel with its multiple information displays. Mach 3.5 and climbing, and *nothing* on the fucking screens, nothing at all.

It was a testing exercise, another name for sadistic mental torture. They *might* have programmed an error into her machine. Or simply cut the input from its electrodetectors; it was resentfully acknowledged that the Alliance was ahead in ECM and sensor-technology, and this could be a test of how she would deal with that in combat. Her lips curled away from her teeth behind the facemask. The Domination was *not* behind in engines and materiels, so use that . . .

Her hands moved on the pressure-sensitive pads inside the restrainers. The Falcon pitched forward and power-dove, straight down. Something soft and heavy and strong gripped her and *pushed*, pushed until she could feel the soft tissues trying to spread away from her bones and gray crept in at the corners of her eyes. The suit squeezed, fighting the G's and pressing the blood back toward her brain, but nothing could make it easier to breathe or stop the feeling that her ribs were about to break back into her chest. Mach 4, and the altimeter unreeled; 15,000 meters was *not* far at these speeds. The indicator hesitated in its maddening *beep*, then resumed.

"*Now!*" she yelled to herself, and yanked at the pads, pulling the Falcon up in a wrenching curve that stressed it to ten tenths of capacity. The pressure grew worse, crushing, vision fading, hands immobile but the AI would continue the curve, *hold Wotandammit hold don't grayout not* now *you stupid cow*— The red telltales blinked back to amber; Mach 3.8, 6,000 meters, half the altitude gone in seconds. The orthodox maneuver, and not good enough, the lock-on was still sounding and altitude was so much easier to lose than regain. Airbrakes. Dump velocity, emergency mode, cycle the vent. The high-pitched roar of the ramjet faltered, stopped.

The airplane shuddered, thrumming, rattling her teeth, ramming her body forward against the clamshell as it slowed; not as good a fit as a body-tailored squadron unit would be. Might be, if she passed. Her mind drew a picture of how it would look from outside: the long oval of the fighter's fuse-lage, the stubby forward-swept wings, edges flexing and thuttering as the spoilers popped open along the trailing edge.

Far below serfs in the plantations of the Kuban valley paused for an instant at the flash of silver overhead, the rolling *crack-crack* as the fighters passed, then bent again to the immemorial rhythm of their hoes; it was a familiar thing, and the bossboys were watching.

Mach 1 and dropping. *Lost him—shitshitshit!* The scanning warning started up again, the *beeps* coming closer and closer together. The rubber taste of the mouthpiece was bitter against her tongue; he must be *close* now, very close. *Still* nothing on the detectors.

"Override stops," she said. The computer acknowledged with a patterned light, releasing its control of maneuvers that threatened the integrity of the aircraft. *Threatened to leave me as a long greasy smear on the landscape*, she thought, and pushed it away.

Fingers moved, like an artist's on the piano. Left-two-right-one-one. Fractional seconds, time floating by so calm, so leisurely. Touch, touch, crack the vent and bleed air into the turbines for low-altitude boost. Bring the vectored-thrust louvers online, still closed. *Now.*

The fighter flipped up, presenting its belly to the axis of flight. In the same moment the underside jets cut in, super-heated air pumping out like retrorocket thrust. Shock struck, like hitting a brick wall, and this time she *did* grayout, felt the jolt of the medicomp pushing stimulant into her veins. Something in the airframe *pinged* audibly, and a warning light began strobing crimson.

And something flashed by outside, above, a streak from one side of the sky to the other. "*Eeeeeeeeeeeehaaaaaaa!*" she shrieked exultantly, and pushed at the throttle. Speed crawled back up, then the ram cut in, building to maximum thrust, and the giant was back on her chest. Too low for optimum burn, too rich a mixture, the ramjet sound was wrong, thready. But the enemy was on her screens now, the thermal signature of a ramscoop engine centered in the weapons section. He had still been decelerating when she did the kick-up; Yolande's Falcon must have disappeared from his board as if teleported out.

The release of tension was like neat brandy on an empty stomach, like orgasm after a long teasing tumble.

"Die, yo' shit, fuckin' *die!*" she screamed happily. Closing,

closing; the rearward sensors were less powerful than the ones in the nose, and her own ECM would help. Visual range, nothing fooled the ol' Eyeball Mark I, they were both accelerating fast but she had the edge. A touch and the gunsight sprang out on the weapons screen, with the green blips at the lower corners; a Falcon had two 30mm gatlings at the wing-roots, a concession to the dogfighting days. *Not going to give him a lock-on warning*, she thought. Closer still, and she remembered her mother's advice: *an ace is someone who climbs right up the enemy's asshole before they shoot*.

He dodged, too late and too point-blank now. Her fingers danced on the pads, and the slim form of the fighter was one with her, dancing in sky. The triple line of the vents filled the sight, and she fired. *Ping-ping-ping*, and the computer stitched a line of hitmarks across the instructor's fuselage; his own machine went rock-steady and began a careful circle back to base, sign that the AI had acknowledged defeat and taken control for landing. Yolande pulled her own plane back and drove for the upper levels.

She was halfway through the second victory roll when the weakened tail-vanes blew.

"That was without any shadow of doubt, the most stupid, arrogant, purely *moronic* thing yo've done, in a course of study marked by mo' than its share of fuckups, Ingolfsson."

Yolande swallowed. The ejection had produced instant unconsciousness; the next thing she remembered was the murmur of Russian as the fieldhands lifted her out of the pod, their broad weathered faces whirling against a nauseatingly mobile sky. A day in the infirmary had taken the worst of the sting and ache away, but her neck still felt as if it had been wrenched all the way around twice and every vertebra in her back seemed to have been squashed into its neighbor. The medicomp weighing down her right forearm clicked and dribbled something into her veins, and the pain behind her eyes eased—the physical pain. Her stomach twisted, and she could taste acid at the back of her throat. Clammy sweat ran down her flanks from the armpits, and the light fabric of her garrison blacks was a clinging burden.

"Yes, ma'am," she said, bracing to attention and staring over the head of the seated Chief Instructor; she fixed her eyes on the crossed flags behind the desk. The national flag, the

Drakon, a crimson bat-winged dragon on a black background, clutching the slave-fetter of mastery and the sword of death in its claws, a green-silver-gold sunburst on the shield across its chest. The Air Corps banner, the skull of an eagle in a circle of gold on black, with flames in its eye-sockets.

The Chief Instructor's office was a plain white room in what had once been the Livadiya Palace, here in Yalta, looking out over the garden and with a view down to the Black Sea. The Livadiya was more than a century old, once a resort for Russian nobles. The time of the Czars had passed, and it had been a playground for the more exalted of the Soviet *nomenklatura*. The Eurasian War came, and now for thirty years the Crimean peninsula had been a training reserve of the Directorate of War.

"Well, have yo' anythin' mo' to say fo' y'self?" Merarch Corinne Monragon was a small woman, no taller than Yolande; in her fifties, with an ugly beak nose and a receding chin and gray hair streaked with an indeterminate mousy color. There was an impressive array of ribbons over the left breast of her garrison blacks: the Flying Cross, for more than six confirmed kills in air-to-air combat, and the Anti-Partisan medal.

Freya, not a washout. Disgrace, at this stage. Everyone carefully avoiding talking about it, not-friends commiserating. Two years driving some lumbering gun-truck groundstrike monstrosity with damn-all chance of space training. No chance of being posted to the same base as Myfwany Black edged in around her sight.

"Ah . . ." Yolande pulled on her training, clamping inwardly on the tremors that threatened to make her voice shake. Her face was expressionless, save for the beads of moisture along her hairline, and that could have been the crash-trauma. The windows behind the big desk were slightly open on a pale winter noon gray with cloud, and chill damp air cuffed at the heavy silk of the banners, slid across her face.

"Ah, I *won*, ma'am."

The officer sighed and touched a screen on the desk before her. "Records, Ingolfsson, Yolande, pilot-trainee." She examined it in silence for a moment, then looked up.

"There *is* that, Ingolfsson. There is also *this*." Her hand tapped the screen. "Which contains good news an' bad, apart from the good-to-passable academics." She folded her fingers and leaned forward, the nose with its pearl stud like the beak of a bird of prey. "The good is that when yo' good, yo' very, very good indeed; a shit-eatin', bird-stompin' wonder of a pilot." The merarch's voice rose slightly. "And when yo' bad, *yo' is fuckin' awful!*"

Another sigh. "So this time, yo' suckered the best pilot-instructor we got. Wonderful. Then yo' turned a 1,750,000-auric trainer into a large, smokin' hole in a cherry orchard outside o' Krasnodar by doin' acrobatics—just didn't *notice* the airframe alarm, eh? We have an *enemy* to shoot down our aircraft, Ingolfsson, but yo've decided they don't deserve the privilege, eh? Well."

Wotan, Yolande thought, impressed despite herself. That was half the price of a fully-stocked plantation. Some imp of the perverse spoke in her ear: *They aren't going to dock it out of my pay, are they, ma'am?*

The instructor took a deep breath. "Well, yo' application fo' scramjet or deep-space trainin' is, of course, denied." Those postings were reserved for people with squadron experience.

"I suspect if it weren't fo' yo' friend Venders's steadyin' influence, yo'd have washed out into ground-support work, or even the infantry, a while ago." A pause which grew long. The five friends who had entered pilot-selection training were down to three now; Muriel and Veronica had transferred out. "As it is, yo've made it. Just. Barely. See the adjutant fo' yo' orders; the usual two months' leave, then report fo' squadron service."

"Yes, *ma'am!*" Yolande threw a cracking salute, right fist to chest. *Calm. Why do I feel so calm?*

"An' Ingolfsson?"

"Ma'am?"

"Flyin' fighters isn't a game, Ingolfsson. I know there's a killer instinct somewheres inside of yo'; find it. Or it may turn out to be a *very* good thing fo' the Race that we have a deposit of yo' frozen ova, understand?" She rose and came around the table. "Congratulations," she said, and they exchanged the wrist-grip Draka handshake. In her other hand was a box with Pilot's rank-tabs.

"Thank yo', ma'am." The ruby bars clipped onto the epaulets, and she tucked the old silver cadet's pins into a pocket of the tunic. Yolande forced her face to graveness as she pulled the peak-billed cap from her shoulder strap, unfolded it, and settled it home on the regulation recruit's inch-long haircut.

Now I can grow it long enough to comb, she thought gleefully, as she did a smart about-face and marched into the outer office, past the desks and the gray-uniformed serf Auxiliaries. Out into the corridor, past the two motionless Janissaries, like giant insects in segmented impact-armor and visored sensor helmets. She looked down; her hands were shaking. *I didn't even notice*, she thought. She concentrated a moment; the floating feeling at the back of her skull diminished. Down the arched colonnade, thin rain falling on tiles and potted trees on her left, bas-reliefs of the Eurasian War on her right. Through more offices, into a waiting room.

Her pace picked up as she saw Mandy and Myfwany, turned to a jog as they saw her grin and wave. Then she was running, dodging tables and people in uniform, and flinging herself into the air, heedless of the jar to her bruises.

"*Wuff!*" Myfwany caught her in midleap; Yolande wound her legs tight around her friend's waist and propped her elbows on the hard muscle of her shoulders. "Why, Cadet Ingolfsson, someone might think yo'd had good news."

Yolande clasped hands behind the redhead, as close-shaven as her own, and kissed her. It turned long and passionate, until she felt herself as breathless as in a high-G turn, lost in touch and scent and taste. Taste of salt, as two tears slid down her cheeks to the meeting of their lips. She turned her head aside and buried it in the collar of the other's uniform.

"Yo' hurtin', love?" Myfwany whispered into her ear.

"No. Happy. We'll be together." Her hug turned fierce.

"Oh, *moo*," Mandy said. "Y'all are always at it. Good news, yo' make out. Bad news, yo' make out. Nothin' else to do, yo' make out. C'mon fellas, we've all gotten through Selection, let's go *celebrate*."

Yolande unlocked her legs and slid down to stand. "Well," she said huskily, smiling up into Myfwany's turquoise-green eyes. "Myfwany an' I could celebrate by goin' back to our room an' fuckin' our brains out—*oof*." She broke off as the blond jabbed her under the ribs with her fingertips.

Myfwany laughed. "Do we complain at the boys y' always draggin' in?" she said.

"No, y'all steal 'em," Mandy said.

"That's not fair, we just *borrowed* a few; they are reusable, yo' knows," Myfwany replied. "Anyways, yo' know what they say: 'Men fo' amusement, women fo' pleasure, cucumbers fo' ecstasy.' "

Yolande sighed, closed her eyes, and leaned into her friend's side; they were just the right height for that, about a handspan's difference. As far as she was concerned, Mandy could keep the men—it was as often uncomfortable as enjoyable—but she supposed Myfwany was right, you had to broaden your experience. *I guess I'm just a prude*, she thought regretfully. For that matter, she didn't much like sleeping with serfs, either; it was always difficult to tell whether they really wanted to, and if they didn't why bother?

"There's always the Flamingo Feather," Mandy said.

The Crimea had been taken by amphibious assault in the fall of '42, early in the War, and had become a major base area for the drive west, since the harbors had fallen relatively intact. Between the Germans and the Draka and the general chaos, there had been little of the native population left; when the European section of the Eurasian War wound down in '45, it had seemed sensible to make it a military reservation, and the remaining locals were moved out to provide labor on the wheat plantations of the Ukraine. There were mountains, plains, seashore, forest, and steppe, a reasonable facsimile of a Mediterranean climate along the southern shore for barracks, and every other type of weather and terrain within easy reach. Recruit-training became the major occupation as the settlement of the lands west of the Volga proceeded, and the Citizen population built up.

So the Crimea was not really part of the Province of Sarmatia; not really of any specific location. It was Army, an island in the archipelago, a way-station in the Domination's largest institution, and a cog in the slaughterous efficiency that had conquered two-thirds of the human race. That meant more than barracks and armories.

"Hoppin' tonight," Mandy said, as they pushed through the bead curtain. The Flamingo Feather was an aviator's hangout, a dozen linked public rooms with the usual facilities, palaestra and baths and bedrooms.

"Everybody glad to be off restriction," Myfwany replied. Few Draka used enough of anything to endanger their health; it was stupid, and illegal besides. Pilot-trainees were on an altogether stricter regimen, enforced by the medical monitors they wore at all times; there were even restrictions on sex, leading to a good deal of resentful graffiti about the Orgasm Police.

Yolande looked down on the sunken room. There was a haze of blue smoke under the rooftop lights, a little tobacco, considerably more Kenia Crown *ganja*. Tables scattered around the edges, a dais for the musicians and singer; dancers going through their paces in the center. Big murals on the walls, holograph-copies. She recognized one: it had been done by her mother's uncle's daughter Tanya, who had been a cohortarch in the Archonal Guard until '45. Gray shattered buildings under gray sky, with a column of tanks going through, mud squelching up from under their treads. Hond III, mid-Eurasian War models. The hatches were open, and the Draka crews showed head-and-shoulders out of the turrets. Wrapped and muffled against the cold, looking with a weary and disgusted boredom at the skeletal corpses lying rat-gnawed along the avenue.

"Euugh," she said, as they handed their rain-cloaks to the serf and walked down the stairs. She had seen her share of bodies—Draka children were taken to public executions fairly early to cure them of squeamishness—but this was just purely ugly. "I like that one bettah." The other side was a picture-holo. A tropical beach, palm-fringed, backed by jade-green sugarcane and dark-green mountains beyond; the sun was setting over a stretch of purple sea speckled with white foam-crests, in a riotous banner of clouds in cream, gold, and rose. "Nosy-Be, isn't it?"

They found an unoccupied table in a nook, settled back in against the cushioned settees. The attendants had seen their new-minted Pilot's bars; this was Graduation Week, after all. A bucket of ice with a bottle of champagne appeared, and finger-food, grilled spiced prawns and crawfish.

"I think so," Myfwany said. "Which raises the interestin' point, where do we go after the Great Escape?" The next two months would be the longest leave they would have before they mustered-out on their twenty-second birthdays.

Yolande halted with the glass halfway to her lips and set it down again on the smooth stone of the table. "It's real," she said dazedly. "It just hit me, *we're adults.*" Her eyes were wide, and she felt a slight tug of alarm. The speeches and parades would come later that week, but it was official enough now. "We can . . . oh, we can vote. Get elected Archon."

She took a gulp of the wine, then slowed down as the chill piquant sweetness hit her mouth.

"Watch the sacrilege there, that's Old Klik," Myfwany said, and took up the game as she sipped at her own. "Or we can get called out in a duel. At least while we're not Active Service."

"Apply fo' a land-grant. Or get married," Mandy said, propping her chin on a hand with a distant look.

The other two exchanged glances; their friend *had* been getting an awful lot of letters from Yolande's brother John. It was a bit May-September, but the difference in ages mattered less as they grew older.

"Well, not much point in that," Yolande said. "Yo've got to live in barracks fo' the next twenty-six months at least. Not really practical to have children, either."

"Oh, I don't know," Myfwany said. "Use a brooder fo' the children. These days, no need to incubate yo' own eggs. But it's true there's no point in marryin' until yo' can set up house together; I wouldn't consider it fo' another three, five years, myself."

Yolande felt a chill that ran down her spine and settled under her ribcage. With too-familiar effort of will she shoved it aside and sprang up. "C'mon, love, let's dance," she said. "Shadowdance."

Myfwany grinned back at her, the strong-boned young face the most beautiful thing in the world. "Sure, sweet," she said.

They rose and threaded their way hand-in-hand to the dance floor, their soft boots rutching on the tessellated mosaic of the surface. The band were just setting up for a new number: Hungarian Gypsies by their look, and in native costume, playing violin and flute and czembalom, something like a hammer-dulcimer. Except as horse-handlers, Gypsies made poor workers, but they were fine entertainers and the leisure industries had bought up a good many of them. The lights dimmed. The music began low and sweet, with a swinging lilt; then it grew wilder, sorrowful, and with a hint of dark empty places and wind through faded grass. The singer stepped up to the edge of the dais and began a soft throaty lament; the hoop earrings bobbed against the toffee-colored skin of her neck, and the multicolored silk flounces of her dress glittered.

The two Draka stood face to face and extended their arms

until their hands touched, very lightly, at the fingertips. Shadowdancing was a development of the martial arts, originally a method of training in anticipating another's movements. Yolande half-closed her eyes and let the music take her, the gentle pressure on her fingertips, the whole-body *sense* of the other. They turned, circling, swooping, bending, the lead passing from Myfwany to Yolande and back with each dozen heartbeats. She felt the boundaries of her self blur; motion was uncaused, unthought, total control merging into total abandonment of will. The tempo picked up, and they were whirling, leaping, then suddenly slowing to half-time and a languorous drifting. It was a pleasure halfway between flying and making love, and like both it translated you outside yourself. They slowed almost to a halt, palm against palm on either side of their faces, feet skimming the tile with cat-soft precision.

The music stopped, and Yolande returned to herself with an inner jerk, like walking down a step that wasn't there. Sensation returned, and she knew she was breathing deeply, felt the prickle of sweat on her skin. The other dancers had emptied a circle around them, and a few were applauding. Myfwany was close enough for her to watch the pupils contract from their concentration-flare, close enough to smell the clean warm scent of her body, like summer grass and fresh sheets.

"I watched you, not the teacher, all that long summer's noon
    Though he taught Leonardo, with loving respect
 I was blinded by knowledge of where we'd be soon
    And my eyes wandered dazed on the curve of your neck
 Oh, statues and portraits, now to me you're a part
    Of my golden Myfwany; kisses and art."

AIRCAR
100 KM SOUTH OF NANTES
LOIRE DISTRICT, TOURAINE PROVINCE
DOMINATION OF THE DRAKA
APRIL 5, 1973

Nantes in ten minutes, Yolande thought, banking the aircar north toward the Loire estuary and beginning the descent. *Chateau Retour in another fifteen after that.*
The little aircraft dipped smoothly; the whole top was set

transparent down to waist-height, crystal-sandwich luxury. Poitou wheeled beneath them, broad squares of plowland and vineyard and straight dusty roads, patterned with the shadows of a few fleecy white clouds on this bright spring morning. She had a temptation to swoop down and barnstorm—the aircar was as responsive as a fighter at low altitude—but resisted it with a caressing motion on the sidestick that waggled the wings.

She is a honey, the Draka thought happily. A six-seater Bambara, Archona-made by Dos Santos Aerospatial. The very latest, twin ceramic axial flow turbines, vectored-thrust VTOL, variable-geometry wings that could fold right into the oval fuselage. Supersonic, just barely, though she ate fuel like a stone bitch if you tried to cruise above .9 Mach; obscenely comfortable by comparison to any sort of military issue. The four rear seats were recliners, swivel-mounted around a table-console and bar. Myfwany's parents and hers had clubbed together to buy it for them, as a graduation present.

Myfwany and she had spent the first month of their furlough traveling in the Bambara. Money was no problem; they had the basic Citizen stipend now, their pilot's pay, and their families had put them on an adult's allowance from the joint enterprises, about as much again. Yolande looked over her shoulder at her lover, curled asleep on one of the rear seats with her hand under one cheek. It had been like school holidays again, only better, with nobody to tell them what to do. They had rented a little island for a week. Sleeping during the hot days, watching impossibly lurid sunsets, spearfishing, grilling their catch on the long empty white beach while the surf hissed phosphorescent under the huge soft stars, making love by moonlight and lying entangled under the palms until dawn. Visiting distant relatives had been fun, too: the parties and sports, the cities and museums and galleries and plays. Giving each other presents—Myfwany had found her a signed first edition of *Ravens in a Morning Sky* in Damascus, and Yolande had dug up a Muramachi blade someone had left in a dusty shop in Shanghai.

The serf sitting behind her craned to see the semicircle of the control panel, smiling a little uncertainly as the Draka caught her eye. *Jolene, dammit, remember the name*, Yolande told herself. Jolene had been their latest impulse-buy. They had picked *her* up at an auction in Apollonaris, on the coast of western Africa, two days ago. Yolande frowned a little; it had been Myfwany's idea, and in her opinion it was a bit reckless just to buy a serf like that. Ingolfssons did not sell their human chattel except for gross and deliberate fault, which meant you had to be careful.

Mind you, traveling from base to base, they *would* need at least one literate bodyservant, someone in Category IV or V, trained to handle communications equipment and secretarial business. Jolene was well educated and beautifully trained, creche reared and certified by Domarre & Ledermann, who specialized in high-skilled and fancy items. Very pretty besides, in a broad-nosed, high-cheeked Mandingo fashion—and pilots had a certain status to maintain in their personal gear. Skin the shade of ripe eggplant, almost purple-black, with natural yellow-blond hair and eyes like hot brass, the result of some sport of wandering genes. Yolande rather liked her; she was eager to please without being fawning, glad to be in good hands, and charmingly agog at seeing the world beyond the strait confines of the creche.

"Nantes control, this is A7SD24, approachin', requestin' clearance fo' in-district release," the Draka said, touching the smooth surface of the control panel. "Headin' upstream to Chateau Retour plantation."

"Is that—" the voice hesitated, as the ground-sensor computers queried the machine's. "Greetings, Citizen." A French accent, some serf technician. "Feeding clearance data for approach routes; central control under two thousand meters."

"Ovah to AI," Yolande said, lifting her hand from the stick. The aircraft turned east and then north to enter the in-city approach path, sliding down an invisible line in the sky and weaving its way among the busy low-level traffic over the Loire estuary. A Bambara did not extend to that sort of computer, but Nantes ground control would be handling it from here. She nodded toward the other forward seat. "C'mon up front, iff'n yo' like," she added.

"Thanks kindly, Mistis," Jolene said, sliding forward and buttoning her blouse; she and Myfwany had been necking in a desultory sort of way until a little while ago. Alertly, the serf studied the controls. She was a Category V Literate, authorized to operate powered vehicles, but this board was all-virtual, touch-sensitive simulations of dials and screens, and that was just now coming in for the top-line civilian market. "May I?"

At Yolande's nod, a slender black finger touched the upper

quadrant of the central screen. She ran through the menu quickly until a map of Nantes appeared; then another of the Loire valley as far east as Tours. A light flicked on the bank of the river.

"This where we stayin', Mistis?"

"Fo' a few days. Meetin' my second cousin Alexandra an' my brothah John, a friend name of Mandy, family gatherin'," Yolande said. "Then up east a ways, boar-hunt."

The aircar was slowing down to 500 kph and banking in for the approach path; you could always tell when a computer was flying . . . Jolene touched the screen again and hesitated until the Draka signed permission with a flick of her wrist. The sale contract from Domarre & Ledermann scrolled up.

"800 aurics?" Jolene said, disappointment in her voice. Ten times what a prime unskilled laborer cost, but less than might be expected for a special item like her.

"Notice," Yolande said, indicating two clauses. "We suckered them. See, a buy-back option fo' yo', and a first-purchase option on any of yo' children." At the serf's questioning look, she continued: "We're . . . my family doesn't sell, 'cept in-house."

"Oh." The serf looked relieved.

Probably afraid we'd just picked her up for the holiday, Yolande thought.

Then, after a pause: "Yo' don't intends to breed me, either, Mistis?"

"Not fo' sale, anyhows, or if yo' don't want. Like children?"

"Oh, yes," Jolene said, with a shy smile. "I helped out in the nursery a lot at the creche. I"—another hesitation —"I was sort of hopin' to be a nurse, had some of the trainin', but . . ." She made a gesture towards herself. The startling hair hung halfway down her back in a mass of loose curls; she had the long-limbed African build, slender neck, high firm breasts, buttocks that were rounded but showed the clench of muscle in the tight trousers. Carefully exercised, with a pleasant glow of youthful health.

Yolande nodded; not much chance the Agency would sell her at three hundred aurics as a medical technician when they could get two or three times that for a fancy.

"Well," she said, "we might find yo' work in a plantation infirmary, later. Plannin' on keeping yo' with, while we're in the Service."

"Thanks, Mistis, I was . . . hmm, I was afraid I hadn't been pleasin'."

"Oh, that," Yolande shrugged. "Don't worry, that's my fault. I'm sort of inhibited that way. Need to get to know yo' better befo' it works proper fo' me. Myfwany certainly enjoyed yo'. Not the main reason we bought yo', anyhows."

Reassured, the serf smiled. "Glad to hear it, Mistis. I's lucky." At Yolande's questioning look: "Nightclubs and suchlike were biddin' on me, too." She made a slight face. "Rather belong to folks I can get to know personal. . . . Glad to get the auction an' such ovah with 's well, I mean, the waitin' once yo' passes eighteen an' all. : . . We meetin' yo' old servants down theres, Mistis?"

The Draka nodded; the other staff were nearly as important to a fresh purchase's life as the owners, and just as much a matter of potluck. She thought for a moment; as Pa used to say, a little consideration went a long way in getting first-rate service. Besides that, as *Ma* always said, serfs were inferiors, but inferior people, not machinery; there was no point in making their lives more difficult than necessary.

"Lele, my maid, she won't give yo' any trouble," Yolande said judiciously. "Sensible wench. Sofia, she's Myfwany's, she gets, ah, a little jealous sometimes." In fact, Yolande thought that deep down there were times when Sofia got jealous of *her*, which was ridiculous beyond words. Pitiful, in fact. "Don't stand any nonsense, and I'm sure yo'll make friends soon enough." That prompted another thought. "Oh, remind me when we get in, I'll have yo' cleared with Central Communication to call back to yo' creche, talk to yo' friends there when yo've a mind to."

"Oh, *thank* yo', Mistis," Jolene said, her face lighting.

There was a stirring behind them. "Thanks fo' what?" Myfwany asked. The serf rose and slid back into the body of the aircar; Yolande heard a brief yelp-giggle before her friend sank down in the bucket seat, yawning and rubbing her hands over her face and hair, the red locks now just long enough to curl. They exchanged a brief kiss before the other Draka turned to run a quick eye over the displays.

"Damn, down to twenty-five percent, need to refuel again," she said.

"Could be worse; they could have made this thing run on hydride 'stead of kerosene," Yolande said, and laughed. Turboram and scramjets ran on hydrogen compounds.

"Not until they build 'em orbit-capable . . . What's so funny?"

"Oh, nothin'. Just happy, is all. Wishin' this holiday could last fo'ever." She stretched with her hands over her head, watching the other's green eyes narrow in a silent grin. Myfwany's face had more freckles now, and a faint golden bloom that was as much of a tan as her complexion and SolaScreen would allow, much lighter than Yolande's toast-gold. The flight-school pallor and gauntness were gone; she looked relaxed, fit, sleeker.

"Know how yo' feel, love," Myfwany said gently, brushing the back of her hand on the other's cheek. "Though we'd get bored with it, soon enough."

A beep from the machine, and they looked back to the board. The middle of the main screen had switched automatically to an underbelly shot, showing a city center of garden-green interspersed with roofs of umber tile and black slate. It shifted as the aircar banked, and then a message flashed: *Manual control below one thousand.*

"Jolene, number between one and ten," Myfwany said, and looked at Yolande. "I'm six."

"Fo'," Yolande said.

"Mistis Yolande wins," Jolene said; her voice was slightly muffled, as she pressed her face against the side of the canopy.

"Shit," Myfawny replied good-naturedly, and sat back. Yolande let her hand fall on the sidestick. "Initiatin' sequence," she said, and touched the consol. "Manual."

"Cleared, Citizen," the Nantes control answered; a trifle grumpily, she thought. *Probably prefer me to let the computer do it. Fuck that.*

She throttled back to 400 kph, and the wings slid forward to right-angles with the fuselage. The river wound below them, blue shimmer marked with the gold teardrop-shapes of sandbars and the metallic silver of shallow water. Levees flanked the wandering braided stream, although the level was down from the wintertime floods; Yolande brought the aircar down to three hundred meters, close enough to see details. Much greener than Tuscany, where you could sense the earth's dry hard bones even in the rains. They passed over Samur on its white cliffs, the pale stone of the castle blinding in the morning light; then the banks sank lower, only subtle changes in crop and growth showing where the sandy flood-plain gave way to upland *gatine*.

"This it?" Myfwany asked.

"Mmm-hmm," Yolande replied.

Unmistakable, an old chateau built in checkerboard of white stone and red brick, with black Angers-slate roofs; four towers, and a big pool-reservoir behind the Great House with landscaped banks. The Quarters were to the east, the cottage roofs almost lost among the trees. Around the manor grounds were blocks of orchard, pink and white froth of apple and apricot and peach; dairy pasture down by the river, green-blue wheat and dark-green corn farther north, and long low slopes of vineyard black-shaggy with new growth. A hoe-gang looked up as they passed, faces white under the conical straw hats, then bent again to their work.

"There's the House landin' field," she continued. A square of asphalt among trees, on the border between the manor gardens and the croplands. She touched the transmitter control.

"Chateau Retour, Yolande here," she said.

"Mistress Ingolfsson." A serf's voice, the plantation radio watch. "Please—"

"Hiyo." A Citizen . . . yes, Aunt Tanya. A courtesy aunt, Yolande's mother's first cousin technically. "Y'all cleared. Yo' stuff arrived yesterday."

"Thanks, Tanya. See yo' in a bit."

The near-inaudible whine of the turbines altered, as the slotted louvers beneath the aircar's body cycled open. Motion slowed, turned sluggish as the Bambara dropped below aero-dynamic stallspeed and shifted to direct vertical lift. The inship systems balanced it effortlessly, and Yolande began to relax her grip on the pistol-trigger throttle built into the control column. It didn't require much in the way of piloting, really, just a steady hand . . .

And memory, she thought, reaching out to touch the by-pass fan initiator. There was a *chung* sound from behind the compartment, and a lower-pitched toning as the engines transferred some of their energy to pumping cool air through the lift-nozzles. Ceramic turbines were adiabatic, they ran *hot*. Hot enough to melt metal; that was what made them efficient. Also hot enough for the exhaust to damage an asphalt landing-stage, and Edward and Tanya von Shrakenberg would *not* appreciate that. *Sometimes I think I need a computer just to keep the relations straight*, she thought idly.

The altimeter unreeled. She touched another part of the smooth glassy surface before her, and the wings folded back and in, disappearing in their slots as the wheels lowered. Engine noise mounted, and wisps of dust flew off the smooth pebbled surface of the stage. An indicator blinked as the wheels touched down. Yolande touched the groundmode button, and the console rearranged itself; Bambaras were theoretically road and surface-water capable, although she felt that was a needless flourish.

The canopy above them split into three segments and half retracted to the rear. Air poured in, spring-chill and fresh, smelling intensely of blossom, greenery, very faintly of burnt fuel. Quiet struck, the ears ringing with the engine's silence after so many hours. Nothing was louder than the *ping* of cooling metal; there was the murmur of wind in trees, birdsounds, no backround city-sound of engines. She had missed that country quiet, these last few days.

The landing field had a low hangar at one end, overshadowed with trees and vine-grown; Yolande could see a twin-engine winged tilt-rotor craft within, a couple of ducted-fan aircars. Plantation servants were already loading a dolly with the suitcases from the Bambara's luggage compartment. She and Myfwany rose, buckling their gunbelts and donning the Shantung silk jackets they had picked up in China. That prompted a thought; Yolande looked back and saw Jolene standing and staring about with an expression of half delight and half bewildered terror, the small carrying-case that held all her kit in one hand.

And getting goosebumps. Yolande snapped her fingers for the serf's attention, then took her hand and laid the palm against the screen. "Scan, identify," she said. That would access the personal file from the Labor Directorate net. "We'll have to have the plantation seamstress run yo' up a few outfits, Jolene."

The two Draka vaulted out of the aircar; the compartment was only chest-high above the pavement, not worth the effort of opening the door, and Jolene clambered down more slowly to where Myfwany could grip her at the waist and swing her to the ground. Yolande could feel the residual heat of the jets on her legs through the linen of her trousers as she flipped up an access plate and touched the panel within. The canopy slid back above the passenger compartment and flashed from clear to mirror to a dull nonreflective black.

"Thumb here, Jolene," Yolande said, and keyed. "All right, yo've got vehicular access." Not to the controls, of course. Raising her voice, she called one of the porters: "Yo', boy." The stocky middle-aged French buck looked up from laying a cylindrical leather case of hunting-javelins on top of the pile of baggage and bowed. "See this wench to our rooms along with the rest of our things."

"Yolande Ingolfsson, kitten-adopter, small birds rescued to order," Myfwany said fondly, as they strolled arm-in-arm to the pathway that lead to the manor.

"I'll spoil my half an' yo' can flog the othah," Yolande replied dryly.

"Nothin' wrong with a kindly heart, love," Myfwany said, and yawned again, stretching. "Now let's lunch."

CHAPTER SIX

The Protracted Struggle is as clear-cut an example of a struggle between good and evil, freedom and slavery, as human history affords. Or to put it another way, never have two so clearly antithetical worldviews stood in such immediate opposition. At stake is not merely political power, but the power to define and, in a sense, create the human race. That this is so is indisputable. That it has hazards for us of the Alliance is not so generally realized. Because the cause we represent and fight for is so indisputably good, there is a widespread tendency to assume that our *actions* are necessarily correct. This is perilously close to the Draka ethical maxim that to desire an end is to desire the means necessary to achieve it. Consider how some of the institutions we have come to take for granted might appear to generations before the Eurasian War: compulsory National Service for both sexes, for example; a peacetime military of over 20 million; a single police-intelligence-counterintelligence agency, the OSS, with an unaccountable budget of over five percent of our collective GNP. This is not to say that these measures were not necessary; simply that we should not assume therefore that they are good in themselves.

We must also beware of the tendency to define ourselves solely in opposition to the enemy. Much of the neopuritanism of the postwar years, only now fading, was the result of Draka counterexample. More seriously, popular revulsion at the Domination's eugenic and biocontrol experiments has seriously hindered our own re-

search in these areas. Knowledge is power, a
fact which the Draka keep in mind only too well;
it is in the *use* to which power is put that the
ethical element resides.

from: *Notes to a History of the Human Race*
Horton Newsby-Wythe, Ph.D
Oxford University Press
1994

BOMBS AWAY TAVERN
ALLIANCE SPACE FORCE ACADEMY
SANTA FE, NEW MEXICO
UNITED STATES OF AMERICA
ALLIANCE FOR DEMOCRACY
AUGUST 25, 1969
0100 HOURS

"Hey, Freddie! I say, Freddie old man!"
The voice bellowed inches from Frederick Lefarge's ear,
and was barely audible. The Bombs Away was the trainees'
watering-hole of choice, and the graduation party was still
going strong; the quieter spirits had mostly left with their
families in the afternoon. Every table was full, and the bar
was packed six deep; smoke drifted under the piñon-pine
rafters, about half tobacco, and the air was solid with the
Yipsatucky Sound music roaring from the speakers, the noise
of several hundred strong young male voices. Speaking every
language of the Alliance, though English and Spanish pre-
dominated . . .
"What?" Lefarge screamed back, halting in his forward-
tackle drive toward the beertaps. The air was solid with smell,
too, sweat and sawdust and liquor.
It was "Randy Andy" McLean, a transfer student from the
British national military, and a few years older than the run of
students; it was common for candidates to take lateral transfers into the direct Alliance service. Short, slight, unbeliev-
ably freckled, and newly-assigned Junior Power Systems
Engineer on the *Emancipator*. That was the first and to date
only example of the second generation of pulsedrive spaceships, a plum posting for a new-minted Academy graduate;
McLean had been celebrating his success ever since the
assignments were announced, or drowning his sorrows at the

prospect of joining an all-male branch of the Service. The pulsedrive ships were opening the area beyond Luna to Alliance exploration and development, and the cruises tended to be long.

"*I say, who are those two stunners waving at you, you dog?*" he continued. The Scot's nickname was not undeserved, and represented a real achievement in Santa Fe, with its heavy surplus of young men.

Stunners? Lefarge thought. He had a few friends among the female tenth of the Academy's student body, but he wouldn't consider any of them worthy of *that* particular appraisal; besides, they were supervised like Carmelites, and none of them would be *here* tonight. Santa Fe was a government-research-military town, families and young single men mostly . . .

"Excuse me!" he bellowed at his two nearest neighbors, putting his hands on their shoulders and levering his feet to knee-height off the ground. There *were* two young women waving at the cantina's courtyard door.

"*Well?*" McLean said. Lefarge began to laugh, and pulled his friend closer by the high collar of his uniform jacket. "It's my sister," he shouted into the other man's ear.

"You lie!" A pause for thought. "Well, who's her friend, then?"

"My godfather's daughter, we grew up together!"

The redhead's face fell, and the native burr showed under his carefully cultivated Queen's English. "Yer a fookin' traitor to the Class of '69 and men in general, ye know," he said with mock-bitterness. They worked their way steadily toward the door, and the trace of cooler air that found its way in.

"Well, I can still introduce you," he said in a more normal tone. "Just watch your step, Randy, or I'll break the offending hand."

"That bloody Unarmed Combat prize went to your head," McLean said, pausing to adjust his jacket and pull the white gloves from his belt. "Lead on, old chum, and fear not: once a McLean, always a gentleman."

"Meaning you never pay your tailor. *Marya! Cindy!*"

His sister gave him a quick strong embrace and a kiss on the cheek. They were twins, and looked it, the same high-cheeked oval face, straight nose, dark-gray eyes, black hair, long-limbed build. She was three inches shorter than his six feet, with a graceful tautness that suggested dance classes and gymnastics; her hair was in a plain ponytail, and she wore a sneakers-jeans-windbreaker outfit that made her look far younger than her twenty-one years.

He turned to Cindy Guzman and put his hands on her shoulders. "How's Mexico City?" he said softly. She was nineteen and . . . *McLean's right*, he thought breathlessly. *Stunner*. Anglo-Mayan looks, olive skin and greenish hazel eyes, hair the color of darkest mahogany. Figure curved like—*down, boy!* he told himself sternly. *Remember Don Guzman and his machete*. Cindy's father had been a submariner in the Eurasian War and after had retired a Commodore . . . and had never abandoned certain of the attitudes he learned as a farmboy in Yucatan.

Not that my intentions aren't of the most honorable, he thought dismally. *Lieutenants just can't marry*. Not if they had any concern for their careers, and while he would be willing to risk it, Cindy would not. Captains could marry, of course. That had been a considerable element in his academic success. A good report never hurt.

She hugged him and exchanged a long but frustratingly chaste kiss. "Mexico City's still as crowded and nasty as ever," she said. It was the fourth-largest city in the United States, after all, and the postwar growth had been badly handled. "Luckily, I don't have to leave campus very often. Who's your friend?"

"The Honorable Andrew McLean of McLean, fifth of that ilk," Lefarge said. McLean bowed with his best suave smile, somehow suggesting a kilt, with gillies and pipers in the background. Cindy and Marya extended their hands, found them bowed over and kissed rather than shaken.

"Och aye, an' my friend Frederick, he wasna joking when he said that here would be two flowers fairer than any the Highlands bear," he said.

Lefarge smiled, remembering his friend's description of the family's seldom-visited ancestral hall, late one night after a few beers:

Built by cattle thieves for protection against other cattle thieves. Och, it's this ghastly great drafty stone barn, uglier than Balmoral if that's possible, and if y' ken Balmoral . . . the land? Bluidy pure. Heather, beautiful and useless. Great-great-great gran'ther drove out all the crofters and tacksmen in the Clearances and then found it wouldn't even feed sheep to any purpose. We've lived off renting the deer-shooting and the odd bit of loot ever since.

"Shall we find a table?" Lefarge said. The Bombs Away had several outdoor patios.

"Ah, Fred, Cindy wanted to go back to the hotel. She's staying with *Maman*, and doesn't want to be out late." Marya made a slight shooing sign with her fingers as she spoke. There was something puzzling in her face as she looked at McLean, as well; it was *too* smoothly friendly. His sister was not a naturally outgoing girl . . . Well, it had been nearly a year, and people changed.

"Andy," he said, slapping the smaller man on the shoulder. "Be a brick, would you, and see Cindy back to her room. She's staying with my mother," *who you know is a dragon—* "and I'm sure she'd appreciate it." *And I know where you live, you cream-stealing pirate.*

"A pleasure and an honor," the other graduate said, extending his arm and sweeping a bow to Marya. "Until we meet again."

Brother and sister watched them go, then moved out onto the patio. This was an old building, Spanish-Mexican in its core; the original had been built in adobe brick around a courtyard, then extended to an H-shape later.

"Uncle Nate's here," Marya said quietly. "With his working hat."

"Oh." Lefarge felt a chill shock run into his belly, like the moment before you went out the door on a parachute drop. Nathaniel Stoddard had taken turns with Commodore Guzman in being the father they had never known; he was also *General* Nathaniel Stoddard, Office of Strategic Services . . . and now their commanding officer as well. "Let's go."

The older man was sitting at a table in the outer courtyard, hard up against the wrought-iron fence; it was dark there, with only candles in glass bubbles on the tables. Stoddard rose with old-world courtesy as they approached, a lanky figure in a conservative houndstooth-tweed suit and dark blue cravat; as Eastern as his Bay State accent. The face was pure New England as well, long and bony, with faded blue eyes and gray-streaked sandy hair; the face of an extremely mournful horse. There was an attaché case with a combination lock on the table before him, half-open; Lefarge caught sight of equipment he recognized, a detector-set that would beep an alarm if any of the active long-range snooper systems were trained on them. The younger man glanced up quickly at the parking lot visible through the grillwork: it was full of Academy student steamcars, battered Stanley Jackrabbits and cheap Monterrey Motors Burros; also a few very quiet, systematically inconspicuous men.

"Marya, Fred," Stoddard said, shaking hands with them both. They sat: a waitress in synthetic-fabric pseudo-Southwestern cowgirl costume brought coffee for the younger pair.

"Anytheek for you, sir?"

"Nh-huh," Stoddard said, touching his glass of water. "Fine, thank you."

"Mike's not here?" Lefarge asked. Stoddard's only son was Air Force, stationed in Asia, but he had been planning to take leave. Marya's face froze, and Lefarge looked up in sharp alarm.

"There was a brush over the South China Sea," Stoddard said. He was staring at his water, voice flat. "Trawler out of Hainan lost its engine, drifted into Draka-claimed waters; one of their hovercraft gunboats came out after it. We sent in fighters, so did they. Mike's wingman reported him hit." A pause. "Missing, presumed dead. Hopefully dead." The enemy recognized no laws regarding treatment of prisoners; their own military were expected to fight to the death.

"Oh, Jesus, Uncle Nate," Lefarge said, crossing himself.

His sister followed suit. "Jesus."

Stoddard raised the glass to his lips; the hand was steady. The homely face was emotionless as he sipped, but there was an infinite weariness in it.

"How's Janice?" His daughter-in-law.

"In Hawaii with the baby, waiting for news," Stoddard said, and sighed slightly. "So, Fred, you'll see I couldn't make the graduation ceremony."

Lefarge nodded slightly, groping within for a reaction; grief, anger, hatred. *Nothing*, he thought. *I must be dazed.* There were continual border skirmishes along the line that divided the Domination from the Alliance; even in space, recently. But that was like traffic accidents or cancer; you never thought of it as something with a relation to *you*, you and the people you knew.

He was a good joe, Lefarge thought. *Bit too solemn, but he always put up with me.* He remembered the older boy patiently explaining to the visiting New Yorker how to use a fly rod, and letting him hold a safely unloaded birdgun. Later

Mike and Uncle Nate and he had gone on long hunting trips up to the Maine woods, and—

"Jesus," he said again, shaking his head.

The sky above was clear and full of stars; this city was at seven thousand feet, and far too small for the lights to dim the sky the way they did at home, in New York. When he had lain in the hammock on the veranda at the Maine cottage, Mike and his father had taught him constellations. There was a far-off growl like thunder, only it did not end; another star was rising, from the mountains to the northeast. Rising on a pillar of light, laser light, into the sky: a cargo pod from the launcher at Los Alamos. He followed it with his eyes, up toward the moving stars. Space platforms, and these days weapons platforms armored in lunar regolith. Suddenly the stars were very cold; reptile eyes, staring down with ageless hunger.

"Ayuh," Stoddard said. "To work."

Only someone who had known him all their lives could have seen through the mask of calm; Lefarge did, and now anger flushed warmth into his skin. Stoddard would grieve in the manner of his kind, with a silent reserve that encysted the pain, preserving it like a fly in amber.

His hands were sliding a file out of the attaché case. "First, one thing, Fred. Do you still want the Service?"

Lefarge nodded, slightly surprised; that commitment had been made long ago. Not that the OSS recruited openly; to his classmates and most of his instructors, he was just one more astronaut-in-training, with a specialty in cryptography and information systems. One who went somewhere else for the holidays, most of the time. Plus a more-than-fair halfback . . . *Concentrate*, he reminded himself. An astronaut could not afford to let anything break his mind's grip on a problem, and neither could an Intelligence agent.

"Then look at this," Stoddard continued.

He pushed an eight by eleven glossy across to Lefarge. The younger man took it up and inclined it towards the candle, then accepted a pencil-flashlight. His lips shaped a soundless whistle. Ultra-chic, somewhere between twenty and thirty. In a strapless black evening gown, a diamond necklace emphasizing the long slender neck without distracting from the high breasts beneath. Smooth, classic-straight features, dark blue eyes, glossy brown hair piled high; one elegant leg exposed to the knee by the slit gown, with a daring jeweled anklet. Holding a champagne glass in one gloved hand, gesturing with the other, laughing. At some sort of function; black suits, very expensive dresses. An old-looking building, with a Georgian interior.

"European?" he said. She had that look. Millions had made it out of Western Europe during the last phases of the Eurasian War; his own mother had, in 1947, although that had been a special case. The Draka serf identity-tattoo on the neck could be surgically removed. "In London, recently?"

Stoddard nodded with bleak satisfaction.

Marya spoke: "Marie-Claire Arondin; that's actually her name. Elder brother is Jean-Claude Arondin; refugee from Lyon. Got out in '48, officially, stowaways in a cargo container aboard a dirigible. Established a machine-parts business in London, and made a fair go of it, despite occasional alcohol problems. The sister went to English schools, latterly a fairly expensive boarding establishment. Did her National Service as an assistant nurse in a West End hospital; the alcohol-rehabilitation ward, where she made some . . . interesting contacts." His sister's voice had a dry tone he recognized; someone reciting from a file.

"Set up a small dressmaking concern after studying design at the University of London; soon, not so small, due to discreet gifts from several prominent men with whom she became discreetly involved." Her right hand was resting in her lap; the fingers of the left tapped the table. "A very classy and high-priced courtesan, if you examine the record."

"Agent?"

Stoddard nodded. "Ayuh. Her brother was a sleeper—he died in '66—and she was trained in London. Financed very carefully from the Security Directorate's cover-assets in the Alliance." The British capital was the world center of espionage and fashion, if of little else these days. "The usual thing, pillow talk leading to compromise, then blackmail to keep it coming."

"How did—?" he stopped; if there was a need-to-know, he would be told the method of discovery.

"Her mother was still in the Domination; that was their lever. She died. We started suspecting one of Marie-Claire's . . . clients, when one of *our* sources on the other side turned up data only he could have leaked."

Stoddard slid another package across the table. Lefarge

broke the seals and pulled out the first envelope. It was a set of assignment orders, in his name.

"Assistant Compsystems Officer on the *Emancipator!*" His eyes narrowed. "This had to come from the Service, right?"

The general nodded wearily. "Because she told us the latest of her conquests, Fred," he said, with a tired disgust in his voice. "Open the next package."

Lefarge obeyed with fingers suddenly gone clumsy. There had to be a reason he, of all people . . .

Lieutenant Andrew McLean, RN, Alliance Space Force. "Oh, shit, God, Andy would never sell out!"

"He didn't," Marya said, an impersonal pity in her tone. "She met him at some social affair when he was on leave from Portsmouth, before he transferred here, and hit him like a tonne of cement. Far too expensive for him, and she guided him to some of the best clipjoints and casinos in Britain. Then found 'friends' to tide him over with loans, then . . . By the time she let the hook show, he was in over his head." She hesitated. "She told the debriefers she's convinced he's in love with her, as well. Gave him a long story about the threats the Security Directorate were holding over her family, that sort of thing."

"It doesn't matter," Stoddard said quietly. "For money, for a promise of Draka Citizenship, for love . . . it's treason, Fred."

"Why hasn't he been arrested?" Lefarge said, but felt the knowledge growing in his gut, a cancer of nausea.

Stoddard nodded. "We turned Arondin, and the Security Directorate doesn't know it. Won't for several years, during which we'll feed them a careful mixture of accurate data and disinformation . . . but the stuff she's been getting from McLean has a short halflife, Fred. Nothing too important yet, but the *Emancipator* is the best we have. He can't return from that cruise, and it has to look like an accident. You're the best-placed operative."

Lefarge opened the rest of the sealed packages. An Execution Order. "I . . . don't like it," he said hoarsely.

"I don't like it either," Stoddard said. "The personal approval of the Alliance Chairman and a quorum of the High Court . . . It's still a secret trial, and that wasn't what this country was founded for." More gently: "And I know he was your friend, Fred."

"He was." Lefarge slammed his fist into the wall beside

him, then looked in shock down at his own bleeding knuckles. "The bastard, the stupid, stupid brains-in-balls *bastard.*"

Marya looked away. Stoddard continued. "Can you do it?" Lefarge pressed his fingertips into his forehead. Could he kill a friend, a man who trusted him? Another thought twisted the knot below his stomach tighter. He would have to live at close quarters with him. Laugh at his jokes, pass the salt, never let show that anything was different . . .

"I can," he said. And that was a bitter thing to know about himself, as well.

Marya relaxed, and brought her right hand up from under the table. Lefarge's eyes widened; there was a gun in his sister's hand, an ugly stubby little silenced custom job. For the first time in his life, he felt his jaw drop with surprise; she flushed and looked down. Stoddard reached out and slipped the weapon into his own hand, pointed it out into the night and pulled the trigger.

Nothing. The young woman's head whipped around, and she gave the general an accusing stare. "You claimed there was evidence he might be involved!" she said.

"Circumstantial evidence," the general replied. He snapped the clip out of the weapon and thumbed the square rounds of caseless ammunition out. "He was a close friend of someone we *knew* had gone over. Actually, I never doubted him."

He smiled bitterly. "Fred, you just passed a test. Your test is willingness to eliminate McLean. This little charade was hers. Marya was lucky; the information we gave her about you wasn't real. We just needed to see how she would react if it *was* real." The expression lost all resemblance to good humor. "This is what I told you, long ago. This business of ours, it takes . . . a different sort of courage from a soldier's. A soldier"—his voice stumbled for a moment—"may have to sacrifice his life. More is asked of us; we get the danger without the glory, such as that is. For us, there's the dirty business that has to be done; we may have to sacrifice a friend, a brother . . . our own sense of honor." He slid the material back into the attaché case, stood. "I'll be in touch."

Stoddard left by the back gate, walking toward an inconspicuous steamer. Two of the silent men followed, one taking the wheel. There was an almost imperceptible *whump* of water hitting a flash-boiler, and the vehicle slid away.

"Shit, what a night," Lefarge said, a shakiness in his voice.

"Shit." A hand fell on his, and he looked up to meet his sister's eyes. "Would you have shot me?"

"If I thought you were a traitor?" she said, gaze level. "Yes." The eyes glimmered suddenly, in starlight and moonlight. "I'd have cried for you after . . . but yes."

The moment stretched. "Thank you," he replied. Their fingers met and intertwined. "*Merci, ma soeur*," he said again, in their mother's native tongue.

Presently he sighed. "Look . . . can you drop me back at Maman's hotel? I'd . . . like to see Cindy again."

"I understand. It's not far from mine."

"But not the same hotel as Maman?" he said, with a faint smile.

His sister's was more wry. "Maman's never going to accept that I don't have a vocation, Fred," she said.

"Christ, when the Sisters sent that bloody *delegation* around to explain you were a perfectly good Catholic, just not suited—!" It was an old anger, a relief to slip into it.

Marya shrugged. "Hell, I might as *well* be a nun, the chances I'm going to get in this line of work . . . Fred, Uncle Nate told me a little bit more about how he got Maman out of France, back in '47."

"Oh?" *Thank you for changing the subject*, he thought. *I need something to calm me down first.* "Her resistance work and so forth?"

"Fred . . . Maman was in the Resistance, all right. But she wasn't Uncle Nate's contact. She wasn't supposed to come out at all."

"*What?* Look, I know there was an agent in place, I'm *named* after the man, but—"

"Shh. That nun that Maman told us about, Sister Marya? *She* was the Resistance contact. Maman just got dumped in the same place, bought out of a Security Directorate pen in Lyons by a planter. She . . . found out about the operation they were on—you can guess it was weapons research—and . . . well, threatened to blow the cover unless she was pulled out of there. The whole extraction phase went sour; your namesake was killed, so was the nun . . . Had to kill themselves, rather. Maman's considered it her fault, ever since."

"Mary mother. No *wonder* she was so set on getting you into the Order!"

"Expiation, and more than that, Fred. There wasn't any husband killed by the Snakes."

"You mean she wasn't pregnant then?" He blinked bewilderment. *Maman? Maman had an* affair *after she got to New York?* He had never seen his mother miss Mass or confession in all his life; and he still remembered the thrashing she had given him when she caught him with that women's-underwear catalog under the bed.

"Yes, she was . . . We're half-Draka, brother."

For a moment Frederick Lefarge saw gray at the corner of his vision, and then his skin crawled as if his body were trying to shed it. Oh, it made no legal difference; by Domination law, only those born of Citizens on both sides were of the ruling caste. But— He made a wordless sound.

"I know," Marya replied. "I threw up when I heard; I've had a week or so to get used to the idea now. But you can see why, why she's never looked at another man, why she was so dead set against me going into intelligence work. Any sort of field where there was a chance I might be captured." She pressed the button for the waitress. "I think you need a stiff one; then I'll drive you over.

   "Cindy, Cindy!"
   "Honey, what is it?" Shock and concern, and fear of what could have harrowed him so.
   "Hold me, will you? Just hold me."

CHAPTER SEVEN

In theory, the Alliance for Democracy began as just that: an alliance of sovereign democracies—some, such as the Empire of Brazil, democratic by courtesy only. In fact, it was an arm of American policy, the creature of the United States. By 1941 all Europe and most of Russia were under German control; Japan had taken Hawaii, invaded Australasia, and was raiding the coastal U.S. as far south as Panama. The Domination of the Draka was mobilized, visibly awaiting an opportunity to jump. Britain, her Indian dependency and the Australasian Federation were glad to follow the American lead; the only choice was to be eaten alive by one or the other of the predators. South America had known it lived on American sufferance since the U.S. finally pushed its borders to the Isthmus of Panama in the 1860s. When the Eurasian War ended with the Domination in control of three-quarters of the planet, everyone realized that the Alliance had to be made permanent; the alternative was the Draka labor compounds and a serf identity-tattoo on the neck.

Paradoxically, it is the transformation of the Alliance into a quasi-state which has caused our present problems with the Indian Republic. Member nations retain considerable autonomy, but the Grand Council and Assembly of the Alliance now control interest rates and other macroeconomic levers as well as setting military policy. For most members, this has been opportunity rather than hardship; the low-tax, minimal-regulation approach which even the Democratic-

Progressive party here in the U.S. embraces has proven widely popular. Some feel too popular, as the rocketing growth-rates of the smaller members of the Alliance erode the relative dominance of the United States. India has proven the exception to the general rule, mired down by the fanatical unwillingness of its religious groups to coexist, and by the Fabian socialism its ruling class inherited from the British. Despite prosperous enclaves such as Bombay, most Indians remain subsistence peasants, the last large group of peasants in the world. Poverty breeds demagogic charges of exploitation and cries of "corruption" by American "materialism." The growth of neo-Gandhian pacifism, with its claim that the nuclear balance of terror is absolutely immoral, is especially worrying.

And the Domination, with its usual cold cynicism, is actively fishing in these muddied waters.

The Indian Republic: Achillies Heel of
the Alliance
by Ernesto Perez
U.S. Weekly Chronicle
Nation's Bilingual Newsmagazine Since 1912
Managua, Nicaragua
November 1, 1972

NEW YORK CITY
FEDERAL CAPITAL DISTRICT
DONOVAN HOUSE
NOVEMBER 20, 1972

"Not going to the Inauguration, general?"

Nathaniel Stoddard snorted without turning from the window and brushed at his mustache. It was nearly solid gray now, only streaked with sandy brown, like the rather untidy mop of hair he kept in an academic's shag-cut. *Getting older*, he thought. *Older and creakier and more weary . . . Is it time to retire?* He probed at himself, with the same ruthless analysis he might have used on an agent under strain. *No. Still flexible, not making too many mistakes.* You couldn't overvalue yourself either; if you were indispensable, you weren't doing your job properly.

"Work to do," he said, in a voice that carried the flat vowels and drawl of Boston. "The OSS never sleeps."

Frederick and Marya Lefarge were waiting patiently in their seats, still in tropical kit, looking a little rumpled from the two-hour flight from India, a little worn from tension and sleeplessness. Harder than they had, after the work he had put them through these past four years. Easy with each other, and that was important; this had been their first mission together. There were jobs a team like this had an advantage in.

"And its agents don't get any sleep either," Fred was saying. "Here we are, just off the Calcutta shuttle, and you don't even give us time to stop off at O'Toole's for a beer."

Donovan House was at the northern edge of the Federal District, the series of interlinked squares and parks that occupied the center of Manhattan island. More and more of the capital's swelling bureaucracy was being moved out to Long Island or the Jersey shore, but the Office of Strategic Services preferred staying close to the centers of executive power. This office was twelve stories up, overlooking Jefferson Avenue; from here you could see north and south to the Hudson and East rivers. The parade was still moving down the six-lane avenue, between sidewalks and buildings black with the crowds. Paper confetti spun through the air, and the noise was loud even through the sealed double-glazed panes. Another flight of fighters went by ten thousand feet up—contrails and a brief silvery flash—and their sonic booms rattled the furniture.

My, aren't we noisy today, Stoddard thought.

The marching youth groups were past, the cheerleaders and bands, the cowboys and *vaqueros* and Hibernians . . . Troops now. Squat tanks with their long cannon swiveling in hydraulic pods above the decks, APCs, huge eighteen-wheeler tractors drawing suborb missiles on mobile launchers.

It's a good thing the infantry aren't marching, he thought dryly. *Messy, after all those horses.*

He took a sip from the coffee cup in his hands, thankful for the warmth. Thankful that he was inside, and not out there in the raw weather; it was damp and cold, the sky stark blue with streamers of cloud. An aircar went slowly by outside the window, down the length of the procession: a light open-topped model with ABS markings, and six ducted-fan propellers in swivel mounts spaced around the flattish oval body.

The drone of its engines hummed through the air between them, and he could see the blue tinge to the faces of the televid crew in the little four-seater.

"Better you than me, friends," he said.

"Sir?" Marya's voice, cool and neutral. *In a juster world, maybe she would be my successor*, Stoddard thought. *She's . . . not harder than Fred. Cooler, less of a closet romantic. This line of work will do that for a woman. But then, in a juster world she wouldn't have had the extra toughening.*

Stoddard grinned at his protégés. "Just feeling each and every one of my sixty-eight years, Fred, Marya," he said. "And glad I'm not out there courting arthritis." The use of the first name had become a signal between them to drop formality.

They were all in the wolf-gray uniforms of the Alliance military today: high green collars and epaulets and the American eagle on their cuffs. Frederick Lefarge had a captain's bars, his sister Marya a lieutenant's. The older man a general's oak-leaf clusters, although his position here made his authority nearly equal to that of a member of the Alliance Combined Staff.

"Not missing the distinguished company?" Frederick had a little more accent than his sister's, Academy mid-American, with a slight trace of East Coast in the vowels; Stoddard noted absently that a linguist would immediately place him somewhere between New York and Baltimore. "The Pope's there."

"And all sixty-two State governors," Stoddard said, turning back to his desk.

It was severely plain, like the rest of the office. Plain dark wood, in-out baskets marked "hate" and "love" a telephone, a scriber, the screen and keyboard of a retriever terminal. There was a table and settees for guests, bookshelves that held a mixture of mementos, leather-bound volumes and color-coded ring-binders. Two paintings on the walls, New Hampshire landscapes by Parrish, the chilly perfection of his late period. And two photographs on the desk: one of a plain middle-aged woman and three children standing beside a weathered saltbox home, the other of a young man in a flight suit. That was bordered in black.

Stoddard gave it a glance as he sank into the swivel chair and filled his pipe. "And the College of Cardinals," he continued between puffs. "The Chief Rabbi, Her Honor the Mayor, half the Alliance Grand Council, the Combined Chiefs, His Majesty Georgie the Fifth, the Prime Minister of Australasia . . . bit of a dog's breakfast. Not to mention the speeches."

"Bilingual, yet," the other man said, sitting by the table and reaching for a manila folder. "It would make more sense to have them in French or Yiddish, in this town. Or deep Yorkshire."

Stoddard nodded, blowing a cloud of aromatic blue smoke. A fifth of the United States was Spanish-speaking, but that was mostly in the states carved out of old Mexico. New York had always been a polyglot city; the great magnet during the immigrant waves of the 1890s and 1920s, then the primary center for the millions of European refugees just after the War, the lucky ones who made it out before the Draka had the coasts of Western Europe under firm control. The English were the latest wave all along the Atlantic coast; the British Isles were the Alliance's easternmost outpost, and not a very comfortable place to live, these days. It was a little embarrassing, for an old-stock Yankee. He could remember when a British surname was an elite rarity here; now every second waiter, hairdresser, and ditchdigger was a new-landed Anglo-Saxon. Not to mention prostitutes, pimps, street-thugs, and the gangs who were pushing the Mexicans and Sicilians out of organized crime . . .

"Well, India's patched up for the moment," Frederick Lefarge said, riffling the folder. "That little scandal about Rashidi and the hamburger killed the *Hindi Raj* party deader than Gandhi." He laughed sourly. "Why didn't he smuggle something safe, like heroin? For a Hindi nationalist, running a clandestine beef trade . . ."

Marya frowned. "Well, I was mostly working with the *Indra Samla* people," she said. "They were ready enough to believe the bad about Rashidi. Too many Moslems in his background, besides him being their main rival. Still and all, a lot of them had trouble believing he could make a blunder that big."

"Double-blind," Stoddard said. "He didn't. We framed him."

The captain sat bolt upright. "Jesus! If *that* ever gets out—"

Stoddard took another draw on his pipe. "You were the test, Fred. You took a first-rate team there for the investigation; if you couldn't find our sticky fingermarks, who could?"

The younger man shook his head and pursed his lips slightly. "I don't . . . It's not what we're supposed to do."

"What's the alternative?"

"He would have won the election. And left the Alliance." A long pause. "How could he be so . . . stupid's an inadequate word. Are the Snakes bribing him?"

The general gestured with the stem of his pipe. "Fred, Marya, when you've been in harness as long as I have, you'll learn two things: first, human beings don't have to be stupid to act stupidly, they just need to feel strongly about something. Second, conscious evil is actually quite rare, even rarer than deliberate hypocrisy."

He cradled the bowl of his pipe between the heels of his hands. "Rashidi is no fool, he's just convinced that American influences are sapping and undermining Hindu culture." A shrug. "He's right, too."

"Did he think the Snakes would be better?"

Stoddard smiled sourly. "Actually, there are some similarities between their system and the old Indian caste setup, and the doctrine of *karma* is the most diabolically effective mechanism for keeping the lower classes in order ever invented . . . No, the Hindi Raj people certainly didn't want a Draka conquest—they weren't insane. They thought a neutral India could stand off the Domination by itself—with unacknowledged help from us—and successfully industrialize behind tariff barriers without having to accept the, hmmm, *culture of individualist rationalism,* isn't that the way Rashidi used to put it?"

"That's insane."

"No, just wishful thinking. Actually, there are only two possible alternatives for human beings on this planet now. Us and the Domination. One is going to utterly destroy the other and incorporate everything else. It's one of the truths everybody knows and nobody says. The nationalists in India simply refuse to believe it, because believing that would mean that they *cannot* have what they most want."

"Stupidity."

Marya had leaned back in her chair and closed her eyes; now she opened one and chuckled. "Brother, while you were out playing astronaut"—he winced slightly—"I've been doing more straight political work. Your training's made you overestimate the role of rationality." A wry grin. "Also, you've never had an observer's chance to see how stupid most men are with their pants down."

Stoddard nodded. "Not stupidity, humanity. Which means

this is a battle won, not a war. The discontents continue, and they will find another vehicle."

Lefarge shook his head. "Hindi Raj is a dozen quarreling fragments; the Progressives will win the next three elections without trouble." A wolf's grin. "And some of those fragments *were* being paid off by the Snakes. We can use that if they start building momentum again. So much for deliberate evil."

"A rather petty evil. I've got the reports, and none of them were selling anything vital." He leaned back and blew a smoke ring at the ceiling. "Grafters like that are the political equivalent of tax frauds. They cheat, relying on the fact that most people don't, so they keep their money and get the benefit of the services, too . . . The Draka lose there by their own racial prejudices. They may not care about the color of the people they enslave, but they do when it comes to granting Citizen status. Best bribe they have. That's the way they got Ekstein."

"The filthy little traitor," Frederick Lefarge said, flushing with anger. "Even so . . . I've never understood how he could do it. Why would anyone want to become a *Snake*?"

"Captain, now you're allowing prejudice to blind *you*." A gentle laugh. "If you don't mind me asking, when did you lose your virginity, Fred?"

He blinked in surprise, then smiled reminiscently. "Junior High. I was fifteen."

"Ekstein never did."

"I'm not surprised."

Stoddard nodded. "He was an obnoxious, ugly, sweaty little toad with all the inherent appeal of a skunk and an overcompensated inferiority complex as big as all outdoors. Smelled like a skunk at times, too. No friends, and no female in her right mind would have touched him without being paid, which he was too terrified to do. Also one of the most unhappy and lonely young men I've ever met. It's the reason he went into electronics design; that was something he could do without face-to-face contact and get a certain degree of respect for. It was our fault the Draka were able to contact him; they gave him a palace in France and a harem. Not your idea of paradise or mine, but Ekstein's happy."

Marya made a *tsk* sound. "We should have fixed him up. I would have, if I'd been his case officer . . . even have volunteered myself, which shows you my devotion to duty." She raised an eyebrow at her sibling's discomfort. "Tool of the trade, Captain Brother Sir . . . Who *did* we have working on him?"

"A Sector Chief, *ex*-Sector Chief now, domestic surveillance. Very sincere fellow. Baptist." They all winced. "It was slick, I must admit. Off to England for a design conference, and the next thing we know his bed hasn't been slept in."

"I suppose it's too much to hope he stopped producing over there in the Snake-farm," Fred muttered.

"Ayuh. Tapered off a mite at first, then better than ever. The Maxwell and Faraday Combines are rushing his latest microwafer designs into production on a maximum-priority basis, or so our sources tell us."

"Damn!" The younger man shook his head again. "It was our job to prevent it . . . and I always hate to see them get their hands on our technical secrets. Technology's our big advantage over them, after all."

"Particularly the sapphire-silicon and gallium arsenide stuff they're doing up on the orbital platforms," Marya put in. "And Ekstein was in that up to the zits on his earlobes."

Stoddard shrugged. "We're ahead in some respects. Those tanks out there"—he pointed with the stem of his pipe towards the window—"*we* copied from Draka designs. Same with our small-arms. They're ahead in mining, ferrous metals, some machining, basic transport equipment. About equal in aeronautic power systems. Way ahead in biotechnology. We've got a commanding lead in agricultural machinery, synthetics, electronics, particularly circuit-wafers." He smiled sourly. "And in household appliances."

Fred flushed, opened his mouth to speak and paused, after a glance at his sister's relaxed form. "Wait a minute, general. I know your methods; you're trying to get me to think through something by pretending to defend the Snakes."

"Draka. That's one part of the lesson, son: calling them 'Snakes' is a way of denying that they're human beings. Which leads to underestimating them, which is fatal."

"They don't *act* like human beings."

"They don't act like *us*." Stoddard dug at the bowl of his pipe with a wire. Meditatively, he continued: "Ayuh. It's a handicap for you in the younger generations, growing up in so . . . uniform a world." He shook his head. "Just the fact that you can go anywhere on the globe and get by in English makes it a different planet from the one I grew up on. It's made us, hmmm, not less tolerant, but less used to the concept of difference. One of the reasons I sent you to India was to meet people who were genuinely *alien* in the way they thought and believed, seeing as the rest of Free Asia's gotten so Westernized . . ."

Fred ran a hand over his crewcut. "It did that, general. Do you know, some of those Muslim types wanted to secede from the Alliance so they could declare a *jihad* against the Sna . . . against the Domination? Crazy."

"Just different; when you really believe that dying in battle gains you instant admission to Paradise, it gives you a different perspective. Also, they're quite right that nobody in the Western countries gave a . . . rat's ass—isn't that the younger generation's expression?—about them until the Draka attacked Europe. As long as it was niggers and wogs and chinks and ragheads going under the Yoke . . ."

The other man winced. "Ancient history, though try convincing those stupid bastards of that."

"Fred, Fred . . . historical amnesia is an American weakness. Most people have a longer collective memory. The Draka certainly do."

"Quite true," Marya put in, without opening her eyes. "I spent more time with *Maman* and the refugees, Fred, while you were out proving how assimilated you were. You wouldn't believe some of the things they raked up and threw at each other; stuff nobody but history professors knows here."

"Don't *Draka* have any weaknesses?"

Angry, but controlling it well, even tired as he is, Stoddard decided. *Good.*

"Certainly," he said. "They don't understand *us*, not even as well as we—some of us—understand them." He laid the pipe down and leaned forward, laying his hands on the blotter. "They could have lulled us to sleep so easily, so easily . . . Fred, the great American public doesn't *like* being confronted with evil, or with a protracted struggle. We're not a people who believe in tragedy; history's been too good to us. Evil is something we conquer in a crusade, and then everybody goes home a hero."

Lefarge snorted, and his mentor nodded. "Yes, I know, but we're professionals, Fred. And you have personal reasons to keep the truth fresh. All the Draka would have to do is ease up, tell some convincing lies, and we'd have our work cut out for us keeping even a minimal guard up."

A sour twist of the mouth. "You wouldn't remember it, but

there were substantial numbers who refused to believe the truth about Stalin, until Hitler and the Draka between them released the pictures and records of his death camps. The Draka could have railroaded our credulous types just as easily. Instead they've virtually flaunted what they are, and pushed at us every chance they got. Trying to scare us, but Americans don't scare easily. It's the flip side of our weakness; we're the Good Guys, and therefore have to win in the end. All the stories and the movies and the patriotic pablum the schools dish out instead of history prove it. God help us if we ever lose a big one; we'd probably start doubting we were the Good Guys after all."

"I thought you said the Draka were smart?"

"Ayuh. Very smart, and very, very tough. But they don't *understand* us; some of them do, intellectually, but not down here." He touched his stomach. "Our reactions don't make sense to them, emotionally, any more than theirs do to us, and they're . . . a little less flexible. They know it, they repeat it to themselves, but it's . . . hard . . . for them to really believe anyone could fudge a power contest, could *want* to fudge one. For them, life is lived by the knife. That's reality for them. They believe in enemies; they don't have our compulsive need to be liked. For a Draka, if you've got an enemy you destroy or subjugate them; it's their lifework. Subconsciously, they assume that everybody else is the same, only weaker and less cunning."

Fred grinned wolfishly. "The way we assume that deep-down everyone is just plain folks, and you can always make a deal and square the differences, and the guy in the black hat either repents or gets shot five minutes before the hero's wedding? That's the point of these Socratic dialogues you've been putting us through?"

"More like Socratic monologues, I'm afraid," Stoddard said. "Also the temptation is, when we realize somebody isn't like that, to hate them. Which interferes with the task at hand."

"Elucidate, as you Ivy League types would say."

"The task of wiping every last Draka off the face of the Earth," Stoddard said calmly, and touched a control on the surface of his desk. A printer began to hum, and pages spat out into a tray with a rapid *shft-shft* sound.

The younger man snorted. "Glad to hear you say it, Uncle Nate; the sweet reason was beginning to wear a little."

The general paused with his finger on the control. "Ayuh,

not so sweet, Fred." A pause. "I grew up in a world where the Draka were a blot, not a menace. I've had to watch the Domination grow like a cancer, metastasizing. Watch my children"—he paused again, face like something carved out of maple—"nieces and nephews and *their* children grow up in the shadow of it."

His eyes met the younger man's. Frederick Lefarge had seen danger. Leading an incursion-team ashore in Korea, to snatch a fallen reconaissance-drone from the coastal hills. Once on the surface of an asteroid, when a friend turned around and saw his hands reaching for the air-controls of the skinsuit. Never quite so strongly as now, in the gentle horsey face of the New Englander. There had been Stoddards who signed the Mayflower compact, stood at Bunker Hill, helped break the charge of the Confederate armor at Shiloh. *Certain things you shouldn't forget about Uncle Nat*, he reminded himself. The memories were real, visiting the New Hampshire farmhouse, snowball fights and treeforts and sitting in the kitchen with Uncle Nat and Aunt Debra . . . and this was real, too. Every man had his god; Stoddard's was Duty, and he would sacrifice both the Lefarges to it with an unhesitating sorrow, as he had his own son, as he would himself.

Stoddard blinked, and the moment passed. "It doesn't pay to get emotional about it, is all. You'll be happy to know the Ekstein problem is what I want you working on. He has to go."

"I thought you were sorry for him, general?"

"I am. What's that got to do with the barn chores? I've selected a partner for you, too; Captain Lefarge will be your backup on this one."

"*Captain* Lefarge?" Marya sat bolt upright at that.

"You deserved it," Stoddard said. He pulled a small box out of a drawer. "This job has a few compensations, anyway.

"And here's the Ekstein file," he continued. "All but the eyes-only portion. Marya, you covered this before you left for India."

"Yes, sir, partially." Marya said. "Need to know," she added to her brother. "He's really quite formidably good. And I attended a few lectures of his at the Institute."

Frederick looked a question at the general.

"MIT, their Reserve Training Program." Fred nodded, he had known *that* much. "We wanted her to qualify as an electronics specialist, microwafer design and compinstruction both." Fred blinked surprise; it was not at all common to be an expert in designing computers and in the instructional sets that ran them as well.

"We put the captain through MIT under an assumed name, and fudged the physical records on her military service; enough to keep the Security Directorate from tagging her with a routine border scan."

"You *have* been a close-mouthed little sister," Fred said.

"Need—"

"I know, I know. Why do you think I never asked where you were, when you dropped out of sight for three months at a time?" The general's last words sank home. "We're going *in?*" he asked sharply.

"Certainly." Stoddard rose and walked to the window again. "You'll both be in for intensive briefing, starting Monday. Take the next few days off, rest. This may get messy, but we certainly can't afford to let them keep Ekstein much longer." The general looked aside at the black-bordered portrait of his son, whose P-91 had taken a seeker-missile over the Pacific. Just a skirmish, border tension . . . and a valuable indication that the Alliance electronic counter-measures were not as good as they had hoped. "Not much longer at all."

VON SHRAKENBERG TOWNHOUSE
ARCHONA, ASSEGAI BOULEVARD
ARCHONA PROVINCE
DOMINATION OF THE DRAKA
NOVEMBER 21, 1972

"Gayner's next," the assistant said.

Senator Eric von Shrakenberg tipped his chair back from the desk. "Spare me," he muttered, rising and pacing with a smooth graceful stride.

It was a warm summer's afternoon, and the windows of the office room were open on the sloping gardens that overlooked the city below. The von Shrakenberg townhouse was old; the core of it had been built around 1807, in the time of his great-great-grandfather, when Archona had been new. He tried to imagine it as it had been then, a vast rocky bowl on the northern edge of the great plateau; olive-green scrub, dense thickets of silverleaf trees around the springs and the Honeyhive River. A chaos of muddy streets and buildings going up by fits and starts, mansions and hovels and forced labor compounds, bars and brothels and fitting-out shops for the miners and planters, the hunters and slavers and prospectors pushing north into the great dark bulk of Africa.

"Why exactly do yo' detest Gayner, suh?" the assistant asked. She was just back from the yearly reserve-maneuvers of her Legion in the Kalahari, bronzed-fit with rusty sunstreaks through her black hair. "Apart from her bein' a political enemy."

"Why?" Eric stroked a finger over his mustache in an unconcious gesture of thought. "Because she's totally ruthless, insanely ambitious—personally, as much as for the Race—and has no more scruples than a crocodile."

"Yes, but what does she *want*? And . . . we're idealists?"

"No, Shirley, we're utterly unscrupulous for the greater good," Eric said, smiling without turning. At fifty he was a generation older than his assistant, dressed in a gentleman's day-suit: jacket and trousers of loose cream-silk brocade trimmed in gold, ruffled shirt and indigo sash, boots and a conservative ruby stud in the right ear. The clothing brought out the lean shape of his body: broad shoulders tapering to slim hips. The long narrow skull bore faded blond hair worn in an officer's crop, short at the sides and back, slightly longer on top. His eyes were gray, set over high cheekbones in a face that was handsome in a bony beak-nosed fashion.

"What does Gayner want? I suspect she doesn't know herself; at a minimum, all this."

He nodded out the windows. The reception office was on the second story, and beyond lay Archona. It had long outgrown the original site; there were twelve million dwellers now, Earth's greatest city. Hereabouts were mansions and gardens, like this the townhouses of country gentry, used when business or politics brought them in from their plantations for a few weeks; for the whirl of social life in season as well. Tile roofs set amid green on the low slopes below him, red and plum-colored, the flash of sunlight on water or marble. Quiet residential streets, lined with jacaranda trees as municipal law required. A mist of purple-blue in this blossomtime, spreading down over the hills and into the valley below and up the far slope, kilometer after kilometer. There were few tall buildings, and those were for public use.

The blue haze of the flowers sank into the languorous sienna-umber tint of the high-summer air, giving a translucent undersea look, as if the Domination's capital were Plato's lost Atlantis still living beneath the waves. At the center the House of Assembly loomed, a two-hundred meter dome of stained glass on thin steel struts, glowing like an impossible jewel amid its grounds. From there the Way of the Armies ran east to Castle Tarleton, west to the Archon's Palace, each set on the bordering rim overlooking the old city. He could recognize other landmarks: the cool white colonnades of the University, the libraries and theaters, pedestrian arcades lined with shops and restaurants . . . gardens everywhere, small parks, streets lined with marble-and-tile low-rise office structures. More parks beneath the tall pillars of the monorail. A train slashed by with the smooth speed of magnetic induction.

There was little noise, a vague murmur under the nearer sound of children playing. Draka hated blaring sound still more than crowding, and even in the central streets voices and feet would be louder than traffic. The air smelled freshly of garden, hot stone, water; there was only the faintest underlying tint of the vast factory-complexes that sprawled north of the freemen's city, the world of the Combines and their labor compounds. Decently hidden away, so that nobody need visit it except when business took them there. His mind filled in the other hidden things: the vast engineering works that brought in water from the Maluti mountains and the headwaters of the Zambezi a thousand kilometers away, the nuclear power-units buried thousands of feet below in living granite . . . He had known this city all his life, and still the sight was enough to catch at the breath.

"What wonders we've built and dreamed," he said softly. The aide leaned closer to listen. "Wonders and horrors . . ." Above the horizon tall summer clouds were piling, cream-white and hot gold in the fierce sunlight. Aircraft made contrails high overhead, and the long teardrop shapes of dirigibles drifted below. "Gayner . . . it's a melodramatic word, but she *lusts* for control over the Race. And she'll never have it, because to rule them she would have to . . . love this world we've built. And to do that she'd have to understand it, understand how beautiful and how utterly evil it is . . ."

"Suh?"

"Forget it," Eric said. "Just keepin' up my reputation as a heretic." He turned, and his face went as cold as the flat gray eyes. "At seventh and last, I hate Gayner because she's a distillation of our bad qualities without our savin' graces; like a mirror held up to the secret madness of our hearts." A pause. "And if she and hers had their way, there'd be nothing human on this earth in a hundred years. Things that walked on two legs and talked, but nothin' we'd recognize."

Louise Gayner snapped the box-file shut and sank down in the rear seat of the runabout. It was a hired vehicle rented by the month. She preferred them: less bother than maintaining your own. Her house was temporary, too, a modest four-bedroom rental in the eastern suburbs. Archona was not her home; she was city-bred, but from the west coast, Luanda. And not interested in luxury for its own sake.

Unlike some I could name, she thought sardonically as the car turned under the tall wrought-iron gates of the mansion. The wheels rumbled on the tessellated brick of the drive, a louder sound than the quiet hiss on asphalt.

Five hectares; the von Shrakenbergs had arrived early, and kept wealth and power enough to preserve what they took. A slope, on the southern side of the basin that had sheltered the original city. Generations of labor had turned the stony ground into a fantasia of terraces and tiled pools, fountains, patios. Native silverleaf and yellowwood, imported oaks and paper birch towered to give shade, and the high wall that surrounded the estate was a shape beneath mounds of rose and wisteria. The car soughed to a halt before the main entrance.

"Why are we bothering?" her assistant said, as they emerged into the dazzle of sunlight, then gratefully forward into the shade of a huge oak.

Gayner flicked her wrists forward to settle the lace, adjusted her gunbelt. "It's like dancin', Charlie," she said flatly. "Yo' have t' git through the steps. Speakin' a' which—"

The half-moon of the drive was fronted by a last stretch of rock-garden, with topiaries in pots. The stairway ran up the middle of it, polished native granite casting sun-flecks back at them; dark foreshortened strips of shade lay slanting across it, from the Lombardy poplars along the edges. Servants came forward as they disembarked, one to show the driver the way to the garages; two more knelt smoothly to offer glasses on trays.

Gayner looked down at them, holding her gloves in her right hand and tapping them into her left. Wenches, a matched set; about nineteen, their movements as gracefully polished as the silver and crystal in their hands. One an ash-blond Baltic type, the other the gunmetal black of a Ceylonese Tamil, both in tunics of colorful *dashiki*, hand-embroidered cotton from the Zanzibar coasts.

The two Draka took the wine and poured out ceremonial drops before sipping. The aide's eyebrows rose. "Constantia," he said.

Sweet, with a lingering aroma as of flowers. Priceless; there was only one estate which produced it, down in the Western Cape province, and that was preserved as a historical landmark by the Land Settlement Directorate. Gayner smiled grimly as she replaced the glass; it was all faultless Old Domination manners, emphasizing that they were guests of the house. The finest of welcoming cups, presented with art . . . but no Citizen to greet them, subtly reminding her of status. Von Shrakenberg was a senator, she merely a committee-head of the House of Assembly. He a retired Strategos, a paratrooper four times decorated, while her military service had been with the Security Directorate. Her family moderately obscure Combine execs and bureaucrats, descended from rank-and-file Confederate refugees; his among the oldest in the Domination. The von Shrakenbergs had been mercenaries in British service during the American Revolution, and they had arrived in the then Crown Colony of Drakia with the first wave of Loyalist refugees. And every generation since had produced a leader, in war or politics or the arts.

"Up," she said to the serfs. They rose with boneless grace and led the way, up the steps and into the colonnaded veranda, into the cool shade past the ebony doors. A housesteward bowed them in; he was elderly, a dark-brown man with a staff of office that he had probably borne for thirty years. Estate-bred, she decided; he had the look common in the southern Police Zone.

"Mistis, Mastah," he said, with a deferential smile. "My Mastah bids yo'z free of his house. Does yo' wish to be shown to the reception room at once, oah is there anythin' yo' desire first? Rest, refreshments?"

"No," she said dryly. "It's excellent wine, but we didn't come here to drink." Tempting to keep the senator waiting, but childish. Nor did she wish more conversation with this relentlessly polite serf, who spoke far too much like a Citizen for her taste.

He bowed again. "A case has been sent to yo' cah, Mistis . . . This way, if it please."

Through rooms and courtyards, up a spiral staircase. Portrait-busts in niches, von Shrakenberg ancestors from the time of the Land-Taking on.

Dead men, she thought flatly. *All long dead; as useful as a plantation-hand's fetish.*

Or perhaps not. Dead as human beings able to help or harm; powerfully alive as myths. *The question being, is von Shrakenberg using the myths or being used?*

The upper corridor ran the length of the building, glassed at both ends, with a strip of skylight above. The steward swung the door wide, stepped in to announce them.

"My Mastah, the Honorable Louise Gayner, Representative for Boma-North," he said. "Centurion Charles McReady, of the Directorate of Security."

"Gayner," Eric said.

They had met often enough at official functions that no more was necessary. She was a slight woman, a decade younger than he. Reddish-brown hair, hazel eyes, a sharp-featured foxy face, freckled and with a pallor that spoke of a life spent indoors. Nothing soft in her stance, though; she had the sort of wiry build that always seemed to quiver on the brink of motion. Dressed with almost ostentatious plainness in pale-green linen, no more than a single stickpin in her cravat. A statement, in a way; so was the gun. Not an ornamental dress weapon. A Virkin custom job, worn higher-slung than usual and canted forward in a cutaway holster, the molded grip polished with use. A duelist's weapon, and the four tiny gold stars set into the crackle-finished black metal of the slide were a reminder of the ultimate argument in Draka politics.

Well, I'm not the only one who can deliver a hint, he thought with self-mockery, rising to grip forearms.

"Von Shrakenberg," she replied. "Kind of yo' t'make time fo' me, Senator."

Did I always dislike that Angolan accent? It was ugly, a nasal rasp under the usual soft-mouth drawl of the Domination's dialect of English . . . but that might be subconscious transference from the decade they had spent in political sparring.

"No trouble at all," he said.

Which was true enough; VTOL aircars cut the commuting time to his family's plantation to less than an hour. Not like the old days . . . ox-wagons then, a once-a-year trip. Moving the capital here from Capetown had been the first of the notorious Draka *faits accomplis*; the British Governor-General had protested all the long wagon-journey through the mountains of the Cape and across the high-veldt plateau. Unavailing protests, since the local Legislative Assembly held the power of the purse, a purse England needed desperately while locked in its death-struggle with Napoleon.

The two leaders' aides were laying out papers, treating each other with rather less courtesy than their elders. Eric watched in amusement as they bristled; his assistant was visibly looking down her well-bred nose, and the Security officer responded . . . *exactly as you'd expect*, the senator thought. He looked to be the sort of thug-intellectual the headhunters usually recruited, anyway.

"About the legislative docket—" Eric began, and halted as the doors swung open again.

"Oh, sorry, pa." A group of Draka adolescents in tennis whites or the loose bright-colored fashions the younger generation favored. Eric's smile turned warm as he greeted his eldest.

"A last-minute appointment, Karl," he said. Turning to Gayner: "My son, Karl. His aunt Natalia"—the politician blinked at the teenaged girl until she remembered that Eric's father had remarried late in life—"my sister's daughter Yolande, and her friend Myfwany, down from Italy." Eric's eyes swung back to Gayner, narrowed slightly.

"Karl," he continued, "Miz Gayner and I were just about to discuss somethin' private. Why don't you and yo' friends show Centurion McReady an' Shirley around fo' about an hour or two? We should be through by then, and we can be down to Oakenwald by dinnertime."

Gayner stared back at him for an instant, then gave an imperceptible nod to her subordinate, waiting until the door shut before speaking.

"What's y' game, von Shrakenberg?"

"An end to games," Eric replied. He walked to the desk, pressed a switch beside the retriever screen. "Private; my word on it."

Gayner inclined her head: "I believe yo'," she said neutrally. *Fool* was left unspoken.

"Gayner, between us we command the largest single voting-blocs in the Party . . . That's our power, and that's our danger."

"Party unity's an overworked phrase," she said.

"Because the Front has been in power too long; the other parties are shadows. Which means that everyone who wants office or powah crowds in, which undermines unity. But contemplate the consequences of an open split, an' an electoral contest."

She nodded warily. At the very least several years of uncertainty, while the factions settled who had most backing among the Citizen population. And it might not be her own group who came out ahead . . .

"What do y' propose?" Gayner said.

Eric seated himself across from her and leaned forward, tapping one finger on the papers. "On the budget an' the next six-year plan, we can compromise easily enough. It's all technical, after all. I still think yo' radicals are too ready to approve megaprojects. The Gibraltar dam worked out, but we're *still* patchin' and fittin' on the Ob-Yenisey diversion to the Aral Sea . . . Still, we'll let it pass. We agree on shiftin' mo' of the military appropriations to the Aerospace Command; we can compromise on the *amount*. Let's get on to the real matters, an' start the horse-tradin'."

She tapped paired thumbs and looked aside for a moment. "Y' right, dammit." A long pause. "Of the truly difficult . . . the new Section fo' serf education an' selection."

"Yo' don't think it'll work?"

"Too well. We're concerned with the long-term implications."

Eric sighed and rubbed a hand across his face. "Look, Gayner, the pilot program has been yieldin' excellent results; *that's* why we got the votes to put it through. We *need* mo' specialists, we *can't* raise them all from childhood in creches, an' psychological testing is a crude tool at best. Competition an' selection are necessary if we're to get results; we can only substitute quantity fo' quality so far and no further." A hard smile. "Or do yo' really think we can point to this one or that an' say: 'Drop the hoe, lay down that jackhammer, now go an' write compinstructions fo' our missile computers?'" He shrugged. "We've always picked out the mo' promisin' serfs for further trainin'. This just systematizes it a little mo' than the Classed Literate system."

"What about those who get some trainin' and then *aren't* selected? What about 'rousin' expectations we can't satisfy?"

"That's what the Security Directorate is fo'; let the head-hunters cut off a few mo' heads, then. Thunor's *balls,* woman, *we need those serfs trained!* If fo' nothin' else, to increase automation. We've always tried to keep the urban workin' class small as possible, here's our chance."

"Reducin' total numbers at the cost of buildin' up the most dangerous section. The fields we're talkin' shouldn't be serf work at all, nohow. We Citizens're producin' too many architects, too many so-called artists who sit an' draw their stipends and 'create.' "

Eric raised his hands, palm-up. "This is an aristocratic republic, not a despotism," he said dryly. "Citizens are free to pick they own careers, providin' they do their military service. We get enough career soldiers, enough administrators. Even enough scientists, usin' the term strictly. It's *routine* skullwork that's unpopular, and which we're short of. A matter of choice . . . unless yo' were plannin' on makin' some changes?"

"That'd be electoral suicide." *Fo' now,* she continued to herself with a tight smile of hatred.

Eric nodded. "Which is why that program has solid backin' among the independents," he said. "Not much of a concession fo' yo' faction to drop their opposition. Brings us to the court reforms."

"An' *that's* a matter of principle," she said. "That proposal *isn't* popular. Citizens have rights, serfs do not. At most, privileges revokable at will. If administrative changes are necessary, let the owners an' Combines make them."

"Well," Eric said softly. "Nobody's proposin' to let the serfs have access to our courts, or to limit the power of owners. Or to limit the rights of Citizens in general." The Code of 1797 had given the free Draka as a body power of life and death over every individual of the subject races; the privilege was jealously guarded. "All that we're askin' fo' is a set of tribunals to regulate ordinary administrative punishments by serf supervisors. *Not* fo' convicts or labor-camp inmates; just fo' the labor force in general."

"Why?"

"*Because as it stands every little strawboss can do as they fuckin' please!"* He gathered control of himself. "An' if yo' thinks *that* don't impact on productivity and worker morale, talk to somebody in any of the industrial branches." Eric's finger brushed at his moustache in a quick left-right gesture. "Harsh regulations can be lived with, harsh enforcement, but there has to be some *regularity* to it."

"It still sounds like rights to me," Gayner said with soft stubbornness, watching him closely. "An' it sets up mo' classes within the serf caste; we've got too many as it is. I can see why Janissaries an' Orpos need special treatment, but extendin' it beyond that is bad policy, whatevah the payoff." She waited, still as a coiled mamba, before proceeding silken-voiced. "That's what I believe . . . an' on *this* issue, *I've* got the independents behind me, I'm thinkin'."

Her paired thumbs tapped together. "It's *quid pro quo* time, von Shrakenberg. What're yo' givin' me, to take back to my people when they ask why we're not fightin' yo' in caucus?" Silence stretched. "I want the Stone Dogs, an' I want the trial run on the psychoconditionin'."

"No." His voice was quiet, a calm that matched his face and the relaxed stillness of his body. "I'm willin' to have yo' new toy used as an alternative to the traditional drugs-an'-lobotomy fo' incorrigibles, but no mass application an' no accelerated research."

Her palm cracked down on the teakwood. "Gods *damn*, von Shrakenberg, yo' the one always goin' on about catchin' up technologically; biochemicals an' genetics are ouah *strengths*, an' yo' fight every time we try to apply them!"

"Incorrect. I pushed as hard as yo' fo' eugenic improvement of the Race, and fo' the reproductive techniques. I'd've thought that would count fo' somethin', especially fo' those not inclined to the traditional methods."

Eric watched with satisfaction as Gayner flushed. She had never married, or borne children herself—which was odd, since according to his reports she was heterosexual to the point of eccentricity for a Draka woman . . . As little as a decade ago voluntary childlessness would have ruled out a serious political career, but now one's duty to the Race could be done by proxy, via a deposit of frozen ova with the Eugenics Board.

"An' as far as the long-term genetics projects fo' the serfs are concerned, I'm all fo' them *as long as they're selectin' from within the normal range*. Wotan knows we've been scatterin' Draka genes among the wenches fo' generations; breedin' the serfs for bidability might make . . . harsher measures . . . less necessary. But I say *no* to lowerin' general intelligence, an' *no* to direct intervention to remove the will."

"Why?" she asked; he thought he heard genuine curiosity in her voice, beside the hard suspicion.

"Well." He inclined his head toward the obligatory bust of Elvira Naldorssen, the Domination's philosophical synthesist, and the copy of her *Meditations* that rested beside it. "What did she say? That it was the mark of humanity to domesticate subsapient animals, and of the Race to domesticate humanity? We rule our human cattle—though they outnumber us forty to one, though even most of our soldiers an' police are serf Janissaries—by dominatin' their wills with ours. Where's the pride of the Race, if they're not human beings, with potential wills of their own?"

Gayner rose and walked to the opposite wall, looking at the pictures hanging there. Portraits of Eric's parents, of his wife and children. One of a serf wench, a Circassian in a long white dress.

"Yo' know," she said slowly, without turning, "that argument goes ovah well with the dinosaurs in yo' group; even with some of my people . . . Tickles their vanity. Yo' and I both know it's bullshit. Which leaves me with the question, why do you use it? I think yo' soft, von Shrakenberg. Weak-stomached. The serfs are organic machinery, no mo', and runnin' them all through a conditionin' process would eliminate major problems an' costs. I know, I know"—she waved an unstated objection aside—"there's still unacceptable side effects on ability. But those are just technical problems. Genetic manipulation to remove the personality is even mo' promisin'. Y' real objection is squeamishness. Soft, I say."

Eric rose, too. "Yo' not the first to think that, Gayner," he said flatly. "Those that did, mostly found I could be as hard as was necessary."

"P'haps so," Gayner said. Her gaze had gone to a battle scene beyond the portraits. It showed the ruined mountain-pass village Eric's Century of paratroops had held against two days of German counterattacks, back in the opening stages of the Eurasian War. "This-heah certainly covered up yo' earlier peccadillos." She jerked a thumb at the picture of the Circassian. Eric winced inwardly; she had been his boyhood concubine, and he had sent the child she died bearing out of the Domination. To America, to freedom . . . to the hereditary foe of the Race.

It hasn't helped that little Anna grew up to be a prominent novelist, he thought between irritation and pride. He had had works of his own win prizes; it seemed to run in the blood.

"I hope yo' not threatenin' to bringin' *that* up again," he said dryly. The Archon of the time had publicly said his action in the pass had saved the Domination ten thousand Citizen lives; and the Draka were a practical people.

"Oh, no, I'm makin' no threats," she said. She turned, and her eyes slid over him from head to toe. "There's an old rumor, that the Security Directorate tried to have yo' arrested 'by administrative procedure,' right after that there battle. Befo' yo' became the untouchable hero with the *corna aurea,* of course. Even sent an officer to do it."

"His mission was classified," Eric said with the ease of long practice. There were very few left who knew the truth of what had happened . . . *By the White Christ, was it really twenty-six years ago?* "In any case, moot; he shouldn't have wandered about an unsecured combat zone."

"Two Walther 9mm slugs," Gayner agreed. Another pause. "I used to wonder about how my brother died," she continued, approaching with steps that were soundless, leaning on the table until her face was inches from his. "But yo' know, fo' the last fifteen years I haven't *wondered* who fired that pistol, at all."

Eric kept his face motionless. Inwardly he felt a chill wariness that reminded him of going into close bush-country after leopard.

"I presume," she continued, moistening her lips, "that this means yo'll agree to the Stone Dogs project, von Shrakenberg?"

With an effort of will Eric forced himself to clear his throat and speak.

"Quite right, Gayner. It's still insanely risky, but it does oppose our strength to Alliance weakness, an' if war *does* come, it'd be invaluable. I was hesitatin' because I thought it might provoke the conflict itself, if they discovered it."

She nodded, still without taking her eyes from his face; the intentness of it was akin to love, a total focusing of attention on another human being. Her pupils expanded, filling the light hazel of her eyes with pools of black, and the small hairs along his spine struggled to stand.

"That's agreement in outline, then. I'll get my people to drop their opposition to the trainin' and tribunal motions; yo' agree to puttin' the Stone Dogs through the Strategic Plannin' committee; we shelve the chemoconditionin' trials. Agreed?" He nodded. "Let's have our subordinates draw up the draft proposals, then. I'll be goin'."

"Wait." She turned; he was standing at unconscious parade rest, with his hands clasped behind his back. "Yo' think I'm soft. What's more, yo' think the Domination's gone soft, don't yo', Gayner? Not like the hard, pure days back in the '50s?"

"In danger of it," she said, with her hand on the handle of the door.

"Yo' should read some history, Gayner; about what things were like just befo' the Great War, when we'd had two generations of peace . . . but think on this, Gayner. Let's do a best-possible-case heah; let's say the Stone Dogs work, an' we destroy the Yankees. Cast yo' mind forward of that, say we've pacified them; say the Domination is coterminous with the human race, as we've always dreamed. *Whose policies do yo' think the Race will find most agreeable then?*"

She blinked at him in surprise for a moment, then relaxed. "Well, then, we'd have only our *personal* matters to attend to, wouldn't we? In any case, by then other . . . hands may be at the tiller. A very fond, an' very *anticipatory* farewell, von Shrakenberg."

She swept out the door, and Eric went to his desk, sat, thumbed the record switch and dictated a digest of the legislation to be drafted. He flicked it off, thought for a moment, then thumbed it again:

"Note to Shirley. We've won, two out of three," he said. "Why is it that I don't feel too happy about this?"

CHAPTER EIGHT

In considering the Domination, the biological metaphors of mutation and evolution come irresistibly to mind. Not simply in terms of the popular image of an anachronism surviving past its time, as if in a Vernian romance where dinosaurs were found in an Amazon swamp. It is more useful to think in terms of alternative possibilities. Probabilities, rather; evolution is a probabilistic phenomenon, it depends on *chance*. The path taken is not the only possible one, nor even necessarily the most likely. We are now fairly certain that a flurry of cometary impacts was responsible for the extinction of the widespread and successful dinosaurs. Of course, if we were confronted *now* with the dinosaurs as they were *then*, we would have no trouble in handling them. But then, they faced no real competition from our remote ancestors; and if they had been spared the hammer from the skies, what bipedal tool-user might have evolved to gaze curiously starward with reptile eyes? Likewise, the particular form of society that developed in early-modern Europe spread and seized the habitats of other cultural "species," aborting the possibilities of their evolution . . . except in the singular case of the Domination, where an eccentric fragment of that expansion was, by a political and military accident as arbitrary as the fall of comets, given time and space to grow.

We are not confronted with an archaic society that somehow has survived unchanged; if that were so, we could be as confident as humans with rocket-launchers faced with tyrannosaurs. Instead, we are faced with the *evolved descendant* of another type of society—a far more serious matter. To use another analogy, consider the human brain. We are a recently arrived, cobbled-together species. Our humanity resides in the outer, forward layer of our brains; below that is the mammalian brain, below that the reptile, the amphibian. So too the Domination. The rulers of a slave society might not have chosen a path of change and development of their own accord; the satisfied rarely do. But confronted with the necessity of either changing or becoming first a helpless irrelevance and then prey, they *did* change. Unwillingly, haltingly, incompletely, but with each challenge a new layer was added to the pristine simplicity of the original social organism.

Without time for assimilation, or full integration. On the primary conquest society of estates worked by slaves was applied the monstrous machine-tyranny of the First Industrial Revolution; on that, the iron bureaucracies and armies of the age of steel and petroleum. The process continues to this day.

> *The Mind of the Draka: A Military-Cultural*
> *Analysis*
> Monograph delivered by Commodore Aguilar
> Ernaldo
> U.S. Naval War College, Manila
> 11th Alliance Strategic Studies Conference
> Subic Bay, 1972

NEW YORK CITY
FEDERAL CAPITAL DISTRICT
UNITED STATES OF AMERICA
NOVEMBER 20, 1972

"Good to be back in the old home town," Marya said.

They were strolling along Seventh, away from the Inauguration crowds. The blustery day had begun to clear, with patches of bright sky between the tall buildings. Around here they were mostly from the '20s and '30s, Mechanist style, stepped back like wedding cakes and capped with anodized-aluminum spires. Nobody noticed two more officers out for a post-parade stroll, not in this town; take away the military and the bureaucrats, and it would be a minor port-city—although he would have expected a woman with Marya's looks to attract more notice. He glanced aside at her, and his eyes narrowed; she had shortened and chopped her stride, hunched shoulders, made subtle changes in the set of her head and the way she carried her arms. Years older, and five notches down on the turn-your-head scale.

Excellent, he thought. *Maybe this will work, after all.* It was going to be a finesse operation, not a smash-and-grab. The almost open warfare of the 50s and 60s had given way to more subtle methods.

"You still think of Nu Yawk as home?" he said lightly. *Do I?* he thought. *Not really.* America was home; the whole Alliance, perhaps. He glanced up at the half moon, just visible against the cool blue of the sky; it was only a few years since the last of the old coal plants had closed down, but the air was already cleaner. *Thank God for the breeder reactors.*

"Yes," she said. They stopped by a stand and bought hot salt-pastry with mustard; the vendor took their change, thanked them in broad Lancashire and touched his cap. "Oh, yes, it's home." She gave him a wry smile. "I'm glad we're together on this one, too, Fred. Scared shitless, of course, but glad. Not that I blamed you for getting out of the house as much as you could, and after I left home, well . . ."

He shrugged. "I was glad to get off to the Academy, soon after that."

"*Naturellement*," she said. "That's . . . one reason this is still home. I'm afraid some of that stuff Maman tried to hammer into us took, with me." A bitter laugh. "Homesick for a country that no longer exists . . . and New York is as close to France as you can get, these days."

European refugees and their children were common enough; nearly ten million had made it out before the end in '44, or in the confusion just after the Draka reached the Atlantic. Most had moved on to the United States, and many had stuck here in New York City, grouped in their enclaves, organizing around their newspapers and cultural societies . . . bitter, aging people, facing the long slow drain as their children and grandchildren broke free into the greater world beyond. The Pacific basin cities, and now space: that was where the action was.

Marya squinted down at the pastry and took a meditative bite. "Remember her insisting that we speak French at table?"

Fred rubbed fingers across his forehead. They sat down on a bench in a postage-stamp corner park, bare but beautiful with the spare lines of winter roses and a single stone urn, a legacy of Mayor Olmstead's obsession with gardening, back in the last century.

"And I'd yell at her that I was an American—except I got so mad I yelled it in French?"

"I was angry, too. Oh, I know I didn't show it . . . Well, the convent school was all right, until she started pushing me about becoming a postulant. It was a good school, anyway; they didn't skimp on the math; no boys to hog the equipment the way it happens in the public system. Christ, though, I got mad when she wouldn't let me go to slumber parties with the other girls, or out to the sock hops and the soda fountain. Forever penned up in that apartment with those frowsty-smelling old ladies and men in berets, talking about *avant-la-guerre*."

She wiped her hands. "Yet, you know, Fred, she was right. You'll talk English with Cindy when you have kids. And in a generation or two, the only people left on earth who speak French will be serfs. Nobody will read it but linguists and historians. Maman and the others, they had this continous feeling that nobody really *understood*. Even here. Nobody except each other.

"They know so little of it," she continued, nodding to the passers-by.

Fred jerked his head in agreement as he looked out at the street and its traffic. The Stanleys and Hashimotos slid by, low hum of electrics and quiet machine-whir of closed-cycle steam. The crowds thronged the sidewalks and the glassed overhead walkways that laced the upper stories, burst floodlike from the subways. Conservative fashions, canary-yellow suits and white cravats, snap-brim fedoras, pleated skirts and padded shoulders and four-color shoes. Quieter than he was used to; New York had always been a staid well-mannered town, the civil-servant mentality, and there was nothing like the driving energy you felt in the Pacific Rim cities, far from the closed and guarded Atlantic. But even here most people thought little about the Domination. Yes, it was terrible; they *tsk-tsked* over atrocity photos, ate up secret-agent dramas where straw-men Draka were invariably defeated by Yankee ingenuity . . .

"That's about the level of their interest," he said sourly. There was an Odeon across the street, old and shabby but with a brand-new crystal sandwich display. *SEX SLAVES OF ARCHONA*, it screamed, showing a platinum-haired starlet in implausible lingerie cowering on a bed with the shadow of a whip falling across her. "Funny, if they're showing someone getting hurt, it's always a blond. When they show a black serf, it's a Janissary or a policeman."

"We brunettes are obviously an inferior race," Marya said, as she rose to throw the napkin in the wastebin; the usual obsessive New Yorker neatness. *I guess this really is still home to her.* To his surprise, she laughed outright at the marquee.

"Maman still gets really upset at that sort of thing; spits in the street and crosses to the opposite side. Not surprising, all things considered." More seriously: "Particularly after she opened up to Anna about what happened to her; a lot of it was in *The Kisses of the Enemy*, remember the sensation that one made?"

Fred nodded. Anna von Shrakenberg was uniquely well-placed to write a novel set in the Domination, having been born there herself, a serf concubine's bastard.

"Maman admired the book," he said. For certain someone would have told him if Marya and their mother were talking enough to discuss that sort of thing. "Even if she couldn't read it more than a page at a time. But when ABS-Pathway started sniffing 'round for a movie contract Anna had to spend a solid day convincing her she wasn't going to sell out. You know," he considered meditatively, "I've always wondered . . . You're a lot closer to Maman than I ever was, really. You fought with her less. Why was it you were the one who ended up barely talking? Not that Maman and I can really *talk*, but she tries."

She gave a sigh. "*Because* she and I were more alike. She didn't try to live through you, and I had to fight harder to break away. Good old Latin double standard, too . . ." A pause. "How do we kill Ekstein, by the way?"

Fred suddenly felt the chill of the November afternoon, and turned up the collar of his uniform greatcoat. "Well, we'll have to be careful how we use local assets. Remember Paris."

She winced. That had been in 1951, just after her fourth birthday, but nobody in the OSS was going to forget. A team had gotten into the household of the Draka military governor of northern France and poisoned her and her staff at a banquet. Felice Vashon had been an animal even by Draka standards; the idea had been as much humanitarian as anything, a threat to restrain the worst mass-murderers.

"Bad tradecraft," she said. "Even worse psychology." The Domination's aristocrats did not respond well to threats, and the Security Directorate had caught some of the locals who helped insert the OSS specialists. Ten thousand serfs from the pens and compounds of Paris had been impaled along the avenues, dying slowly on wooden stakes rammed up the anus. "Remember Barcelona, come to that."

Barcelona had risen against the Yoke in '52; hundreds of Citizens had died, and the last survivors had been pulled out by helicopter. An hour later, the city had gone up in a gout of radioactive flame.

"The Snake idea of riot control, a one-megatonne sunbomb," he said.

"Necessary, from their point of view," Marya said dispassionately. "They probably hated to do it, in their own backyard. Europe was shaky then, still primed to explode at the slightest sign of weakness. I doubt that they'd do that now, especially since the locals are all *owned* by somebody. Vested interests, you see."

He laughed. "You *have* been around Uncle Nate a lot recently, Captain Sister. I recognize that detachment."

"Detachment?" She turned and looked at him. "Actually, I've been researching more of the family history." She reached inside her greatcoat, carefully tore a strip of gum in half and began to chew. He noticed suddenly that her nails had the slightly lumpy appearance of a reformed biter. The Mexican habit of gum-chewing had been spreading north since smoking went out of fashion.

"She never told you? Maman wouldn't. She saved that for Anna, more than got into the book. Anna told me; we're still friends. There . . . was a gang-rape in Lyon, when Maman was arrested; her and her little sister. Didn't know we had an aunt, did you? Still over there, under the Yoke."

A long silence. "Detached? No, I'm not in the least detached. I'm going to warn you straight up, brother, what I am is a fanatic. A reasoning fanatic. *I've got a debt to collect.*"

"Remind me never to establish a credit account at your bank, ma soeur," he said. "Lunch?"

"Why not. As long as it isn't the canteen," she replied.

That's the problem with a French mother, it sort of spoils you for fast food, he thought.

CHATEAU OF MOULIN
PROVINCE OF TOURAINE
DOMINATION OF THE DRAKA
FEBRUARY 8, 1973

The chateau was south of the Loire, in the Sologne; a nobleman by the name of Philippe du Moulin had built it five centuries before. For most of the time since it had been a hunting seat, for the Sologne was an area of poor acid soils, of marsh and forest. When the Draka came they decided that the effort of reclamation was not worth the cost. Too many richer lands lay desolate, their tillers dead in the slaughter-house madness of the Eurasian War; the remaining French peasants were deported elsewhere, or set to planting oak trees. For two decades the mansion lay empty, until the Security Directorate needed a place of refuge for a defector with very specific tastes.

"Here he is," the Farraday Combine representative muttered with throttled impatience. "At last."

The Tetrarch from the Directorate of Security shrugged and raised her hands in a gesture of helplessness, then let them fall back to the surface of the table. There were three terminals and keyboards built into it, the only outward sign of modernity in the room with its tapestries and suits of plate armour.

"Hi!" David Ekstein said, as he bounded in. The Security officer winced and looked away. *Not quite so disgusting as he was*, she thought resignedly.

"Dave, it's really *impo'tant* not to keep people waiting," the officer said.

"Oh, gee, sorry, Cathy," Ekstein replied. He was in his mid-twenties but already the wiry black hair was thinning on top: a short man with a sticklike figure that turned pudgy at face and waist and buttocks. Acne-scars, and his skin was still wet from the pool, mottled brown from the sunlamps. Bitterly, she told herself that the defector probably thought he was fitting in with Draka custom by coming to the business meeting in a black pool-robe . . .

Tetrarch Catherine Duchamp Bennington gritted her teeth

and smiled back at him. Officially she was Security liaison here. *Actually, I'm bear-leader to this little shit*, she thought. Much of her effort was spent keeping him away from Draka. He was officially an honorary Citizen, but half an hour in normal society would have left him with a round dozen challenges to pistols at dawn.

Not that he was nasty, just . . . *like a damned smelly fat puppy*, she thought. Providential that a castle in France had been his private daydream, so they could immure him in the middle of this hunting-preserve. Even better if they could have stuck him in an SD property in Africa or Russia, but the orders were for soft-hand treatment. You could see why. Creativity was so delicate a quality, and this slug was a hothouse flower of the first order.

"Mei-ling was playing handball with me, and I really wanted to win," he continued.

At least that was going well. The Directorate had bought him two dozen concubines, every one of them from the top creches and with special training to boot. The Domination wanted full value from David Ekstein, and the wenches were leading him with patient subtlety into healthier habits. He had already lost a good deal of weight. It was unlikely that Ekstein would ever be anything remotely resembling what a Citizen should be, but with luck, in a few years and fully dressed he could avoid arousing actual disgust. His social skills had been marginal at home and were nonexistent here, but with careful management that could be handled. The Eugenics people had a sperm deposit in their banks, anyway.

"So, what's your problem?" he continued, rubbing his hands and turning to the exec. "I thought those designs were pretty good, really." Servants bustled in with trays of coffee, fruit, and breakfast pastries.

"Ahhh—" the exec began. The electrowafers were excellent, and had opened up a whole new range of near-space applications, not to mention the eventual civilian uses. "Well, we're havin' real quality problems. Seventy percent rejection rate, even on our best fabricators, an' we *needs* those wafers." He caught himself just in time, not mentioning the use to which the sensor-effector systems would be put. The American—the *ex*-American, he reminded himself—was a defector, after all, and quite startlingly naive politically, but it was better not to remind him of certain things without need.

Ekstein frowned, took the data cartridge from the man and

slipped it into the table unit. His hands skittered over the keyboard and the ball-shaped directional control; Bennington noted how their clumsiness vanished, turning to fluid skill. "Hey, no problem," he said after a minute. "It's the amorphous layer that's causing it. You're getting uneven deposition. How do you—"

Tetrarch Bennington tuned out the technical discussion and stared moodily out the mullioned windows of the salon. It was a cold bright morning outside; the courtyard's brick pavement was new-swept, white snow in the mortar-grooves between herringbone red brick. Gardens laced with white-ice hoarfrost, fairy-silver grass, and black treetrunks beneath hammered-metal branches, flowerbeds pruned back and dormant beneath their coats of mulch-straw. The edge of the forest was a black wall, and the surface of the moat clear gray ice. It would be warming soon, though. She was a bananalander from Natalia, born in Virconium, and the clear freshness of the Northern spring never failed to enthrall.

"Oh," the exec was saying. She glanced up with a start. Her coffee had gone cold, and she signed for the serf to bring another.

"Oh, well . . . Why didn't we think of that?" He looked down at the screen, rubbing his brow in puzzlement.

The American grinned. "Hey, man, it always looks that way. That should get you down to, hmmm, fifteen percent rejections, easy. Null-G applications of amorphous silicon deposition are tricky; it's not my specialty, you know, but I think that's the way to go. Especially with EV channels and particle-stream etching, you know."

"Many thanks, suh," the exec continued, as the terminal downloaded the details into his attaché case and clicked completion. He shook hands with the ex-American. "Service to the State."

"Have a nice d—h, Glory to the Race," Ekstein replied.

The room fell silent as the exec left. There was a crackle from the big fireplace, a glimmer of flamelight, and pale winter sun on polished stone and wood. Ekstein sighed, shifting restlessly and then moodily taking another croissant. The serf moved in deftly to sweep up the crumbs around his plates. She was a pert little thing, in a uniform of short skirt and white cap and bib-apron that had been another of Ekstein's eccentricities. He ran a hand up her thigh, but half-heartedly, even when she leaned into the clumsy caress and smiled.

That's a bad sign, Bennington thought. *He's not screwing anything that moves, anymore.*

"What's the matter, Dave?" she said quietly as the serfs left.

He slumped in the chair, hands resting loosely between his knees.

"Oh, I don't know," he said, frowning. "I . . . I feel lonely, I guess."

"Hmmm, I thought yo' were lonely befo'," she replied. Every word and gesture was going down on record for the SD psychs to mull over, but you had to get a personal gestalt to really know an individual. Besides, he *was* like a puppy; you wanted to see him wag his tail. "Yo' girls not givin' satisfaction?"

"No, no, they're great!" he said. "Mei-ling and Bernadette especially." His face puckered a little. "Yeah, I was real lonely. Only . . . Well, sometimes Bernie and Izzy and Pedro would come over, and we'd have beer and peanut-butter-and-jelly sandwiches, and play Knights and Sorcerors on my old Pacifica. I sort of miss it, I guess. I can play against myself here, but it's not the same."

He looked up, and his eyes were misty. "Say, Cathy, maybe you could get me an online terminal, and I could patch into PanNet? Then I could play them remote."

Bennington sighed inwardly; you had to swat a puppy if it piddled on the rug, but it wasn't pleasant. She forced a warm smile. "Mmmm, Dave, I don't think we could do that. I mean, the other end wouldn't allow it." Probably true, and no *way* the SD would let an OSS op get a line on this prize.

He blinked. "Look," she continued, "yo've been workin' too hard, Dave. What say, in a month o' two, we fly down to Nova Cartago or Alexandria. We'll go out to some of the nightspots, meet a few"—*carefully selected*—"people, relax, hey?"

He nodded, halfway between interest and listlessness. She crossed around the desk, put an arm about his shoulders. "An' in the meantime, we'll have cook make us up some peanut-butter-and-jelly sandwiches"—*Mother Freya, the things I do for the Race*—"an' yo' can teach me how to play Knights and Sorcerors, Mei-ling and Bernadette will sit in."

OSS SAFEHOUSE
STATE OF VIRGINIA
UNITED STATES OF AMERICA
JANUARY, 1973

"Goddammit, my brains are going to run out my nose!" Marya said, and grunted as she bench-pressed the weights again. "Ninety-nine, *one hundred.*" The link-rod fell back into its rest with a clang. She took a deep breath; the room smelled of sweat, hers and others, of oil and machinery and the straw matting on the floor. The lights were sunlamps, to give them the appropriate tan, and the walls were lined with mirrors.

"That's, '*Gods curse it,* mah *brains* is goin' *run out* mah *nose,*'" the instructor said. "Repeat it, Lefarge."

She lay back on the padded exercise bench and repeated the sentence in Draka dialect, turning her head to watch the instructor. He was a defector from the Domination, about twice her age: an unremarkable man, medium-brown hair and eyes and an outdoorsman's weathered face. He was doing one-handed chinups while he listened with a slight frown of concentration on his face.

"Bettah," he said. "But remembah, don't drawl *too* much. Brains is *buh'rains,* not *braaains.* The dialect has roots hereabouts, but it's changed in different directions since the 1780s. Over to the cycle."

She groaned and swung herself up, walking over to the fixed exercise cycle. Her sweatsuit was soaked and chafing; she wiped her face on the corner of the towel around her neck. Her brother was using the Unitorso machine beside it, with his forearms against the vertical spring-loaded bars, pressing them in to his chest, holding, then slowly out again. The muscles of his chest and stomach stood out, moving fluidly beneath the fair skin. Marya felt a sudden sharp stab of affection, oddly mixed with the sort of aesthetic admiration you might feel for a statue or a sunset.

Damnation, she thought dismally. The number of eligible males around was small, and seemed either gentlemanly or disinterested. A man could marry outside the field, as long as the wife didn't mind not being told a lot of things. For a female agent, another agent was about the only game in town. *It's like being tall,* she thought. *You have to go for the tall boys, but the short girls poach on them, too.*

Of course, she could start asking them herself . . . Her mouth twisted wryly. Sex was a tool of the trade, and she was sure enough she could do anything required in that line, but somehow it was different in a social setting. *Benefits of a Catholic upbringing. Shit.*

The instructor had finished his second sequence of fifty and dropped lightly to the ground, landing silently on the balls of his feet. He was dressed as they were, in loose felted cotton exercise clothing and soft shoes, but he seemed to flow as he walked.

"Get to it," the Draka said. "Yo' wind needs it." He stopped by Fred, looked him up and down appraisingly. Then he seemed to blur, and his fist struck the man low in the belly. Marya winced at the hard *smack*, and her brother doubled over with a grunt. His hand had come down to block and stayed suspended three-quarters of the way to completion.

"Better," the Draka said, then chuckled. "Back home, they'd envy me mah chances, gettin' to beat up on Yankees fo' a livin'."

Marya pedaled grimly. "If yo' loves us so much, why're yo' heah?" she enunciated carefully.

The Draka looked at her. "Good. Treatin' yo'r's' right, now."

It isn't a lack of expression, she thought, puzzled. Like most Draka she had seen, the instructor somehow gave an *impression* of stillness even when he was moving. *Ah. No unintentional gestures*, she decided. The hands moved only when he wanted them to, and the body stayed rock-still unless ordered to move. No twitches, jerks, shifts.

"It was a mattah of circumstances, luck an' opportunity," he continued. "I's an only chile, and mah mothah died early. Pa away most all the time, no relatives near. Raised by serfs mo' than most, didn't fit in well at school. Eventually realized that all the people I really cared about had numbahs on they necks, and that I was spendin' my life grindin' them down." He grinned, a gaunt expression. "Had an opportunity to get out, took it. Doesn't mean I've got any particular affection fo' Yankees or Yankeeland. The air stinks, everythin's ugly, there's no decent huntin', and the people are soft an' contemptible."

He checked the medical readouts built into the cycle: heartbeat, respiration, neurological profile. "Good enough. Two of you are gettin' as near passable as yo' ever will in the time available; toward the top of the bottom one-fifth of

Citizens. Pity, yo've both got good potential. Bettah than average."

Fred was using the Unitorso again, the mark of knuckles a fading red mark on his stomach below the solar plexus. "If . . . that's . . . so . . . why're we . . . so . . . godsdamned . . . rotten?" he asked, careful to keep his tone neutral.

The Draka looked up at him. "Time," he said. "Y'all didn't start early enough; that affects y'whole system. Bone-density, fo' example, basic body-fat ratios, metabolic rate an' so forth. Mah genes is no more than middlin', athletics-wise, but y'all will never catch up. If yo'd been in the *agoge* from age five, yo'd be notable excellent."

ABOARD AIRSHIP DOULOS
APPROACHING NANTES AIRHAVEN
LOIRE DISTRICT, TOURAINE PROVINCE
DOMINATION OF THE DRAKA
APRIL 3, 1973

Frederick Lefarge had not flown by airship since he was a child; in the Alliance countries lighter-than-air was used mainly for freight, these days. The Domination had its own turbojets and scramjets, but simply attached less importance to haste, and neither of the Powers allowed overflights by aircraft of the other. London-Nantes was the sole passenger link between the Alliance and Europe, maintained by the Transportation Directorate; the Alliance had accepted the arrangement, but insisted that only slow and easy-to-monitor dirigibles be used.

"Welcome home, Mastah, Mistis," the serf customs clerk said, handing him and Marya the forms.

The ferry dirigible was still at five thousand feet, time enough to complete the paperwork and to spare, but the American agents had come early to the lounge. That was in character for their *personas*, Draka eager to be home.

It is a comfortable way to travel, he mused. *But it gives you too much time to think.* He had been learning something of the nature of fear, this trip. Swift flashes, like the moment they passed the barricades in London and stepped onto territory that was Draka by treaty. The first green Security Directorate uniform, with the skull patches on the collar. Watching the Channel dwindling away below. A slow gnawing; every moment increased the danger, and there were a *lot* of moments to come.

Still, dirigibles are comfortable. Particularly compared with
being strapped into a windowless hypersonic tin can, boring
through the stratosphere at Mach 12 with the leading edges
cherry-red. The *Doulos* was a teardrop of fiber-matrix composite five hundred meters long; near the bow a semicircular
strip of the lower hull had been made transparent, as windows for the main lounge. The clear synthetic curved sharply
outward for nearly two stories above his head, and from his
seat at the edge of the deck he had a view that would have
made an agroaphobe cringe, straight down. Countryside for
the last few hours, and now the broad greenbelt that always
surrounded a major Draka city. There were a quarter million
people in Nantes.

None of the jumbled mixed-use fringe you saw in the
Alliance; plantation fields, then parks and public gardens and
manicured forest. Transport-corridors, more rail and less highway than he was used to. The industrial sector was to the
east, along a section of the river that had been dredged for
shipping. Anonymous factories with their labor-compounds of
three-story flats grouped around paved courts. Shipyards bristling with overhead cranes, warehouses, all along an orderly
gridwork of paved streets and rail sidings. Some of the streets
were tree-lined; that grew more numerous towards the west,
in residential districts reserved for the serf elite of technicians
and bureaucrats. Then the Citizen quarter, a cluster of public
buildings and a scatter of homes wide-spaced amid gardens.

He turned his attention to the paper:

Name. Antony Verman.

Place and Date of Birth. Archona, 1947: a Citizen population of over two million, which cut down the chance of
meeting someone who should know a personality that existed
solely as pits and spots in a read-only optical memory bank.
Quite a good cover; they had worked hard to slip it into the
files.

"Flagged," the instructor had said. *"If the Security Directorate checks it, they'll get a warning you're War Directorate
Military Intelligence; the War Directorate will be told you're
a krypteia hotshot."*

The Domination's two armed services liked each other only
marginally more than either loved the Alliance, and talked no
more than they had to. Of course, the cover would still not
stand up to detailed investigation; there were two many
records, in too many separate files.

Military Service. Infantry, XXI Airmobile; as close to anonymous as you could get.

Occupation. Ceramic design consultant; luxury manufactures like that were generally handled by small businesses, not the omnipresent Combines. A designer was doubly independent, was more free to be a rolling stone with no connections. Better still to have no occupation, but without a good excuse a person who just lived on their Citizen stipend was a figure of some suspicion and contempt, and would attract attention when traveling.

Purpose of visit abroad. Reviewing samples of American ceramics, of course. There was an interesting collection in the memory of the impeccably Draka *Helot-IV* analogue/ digital personal comp in his attaché case, and anyone making inquiries would find a string of design studios and shops with perfectly genuine memories of the two young Draka. That had been the beginning of their assignment, seeing if they could fool Americans first. And pass the critical gaze of the Draka defectors who had been their final instructors, in everything from etiquette and gossip to fighting-style and sexual technique.

He glanced aside at his sister. *Tradecraft's good enough to fool me*, he thought. They had both had minor cosmetic implants to make their faces unrecognizable to anyone who knew their genuine identities, hormone treatments to change their body-fat ratios, but it was more than that. Most of all the look, the hard-edged glossy *feel* of one of the Domination's elite. Not even just Draka; looking at her with his *persona*'s eyes he could place her, city-born, probably from the southern provinces.

He finished the form and snapped his fingers for the serf. The lounge was growing a little crowded. Two hundred or more; thirty or so Draka, settling in around them, and the rest from the Alliance, mostly Americans and English. Some on business, others well-heeled tourists prepared to pay highly for sights and experiences only the Domination could offer; Fred looked at them with a distaste most of the Citizens around him seemed to share. The Domination allowed a trickle of closely-supervised visitors, as much for the Intelligence opportunities as for the Alliance dollars they brought.

There was a subliminal change in the vibration of the hull; he looked back and saw the big turbocompound engine-pods swiveling. Distant pumps went chunk-*whir*, compressing hy-

drogen to liquid and draining it into the insulated tanks along
the keel. Fred's mouth was dry as he felt the slight falling-
elevator sensation of descent; he sipped at his glass of spar-
kling mineral water. They were over the airhaven now, passing
rows of dirigibles in their cradles, acres of concrete and rail.
The tall cylinder of the docking tower was ahead of them, and
the *Doulos* slid toward it with the calm precision of computer
piloting.

Contact, and a dying of machine-noise that had been imperceptible before. More movement but with a different feel,
heavier than the cushiony grace of lighter-than-air, as the
airship established negative buoyancy and sank into its cradle; more chunking noises, as the fuel and gas lines connected. The scene outside sank to four stories above ground
level, then pivoted slowly as the cradle turned the airship and drew it toward the waiting terminal. There were
three others with their noses locked into the huge cone-
shaped depressions in the giant building's wall. The *Doulos*
glided into the fourth docking bay and halted; there was a
whine as a ten meter broad section of the forward window
slid up.

"Let's go," he said.

Home—in a way, Marya thought, as they walked through
the gate into the terminal. *France. The country where we
were conceived.*

Although this terminal was post-War, pure Domination.
Probably built in the early '50s to a standard pattern. A huge
barrel-vaulted passenger terminal, the coffered ceiling in pale
blue and silvergilt tiles; the walls were murals, landscapes,
the floor streaked gray marble. Pillars around the walls, trained
over with climbing plants. The Citizens' section of the great
building was relatively small; most of the traffic was over the
other side of the low stone balustrade. *There* it was busy,
swarming even. Most of the serfs there were in overalls of
varying cut, livery, color-coded Combine suits with identify-
ing logos on the backs. Or uniform, green for SD internal-
security, dove-gray for the serf component of the Directorate
of War. Management level, authorized to travel alone.

And a coffle, forty or fifty people crouched within a rope
barrier. Young adults with children, and a few ranging up to
middle age, in cheap cotton overalls or blouses and skirts.
They were mostly dark, with high cheeks and slant eyes:

Asians, brought in from the main resevoir of surplus labor in the Far East. Nantes was a shipbuilding center, and Intelligence said that the submarine yards were being adapted to produce components for the second generation of Draka pulsedrive spaceships. The nuclear-powered deepspace vessels were more *like* ships than aircraft, no need to shave ounces when total payloads were well over five thousand tonnes.

Enough. Not your mission. She forced herself not to notice how a woman grabbed her child and winced as a guard walked by with a shockrod. They walked across to an information kiosk. The clerk covered his eyes and bowed, then smiled.

"Yo' will, masters?" He pronounced it *mastaire*; a Frenchman. A little overweight, unremarkable. The number stood out below his ear, glaring. His fingers hovered over a keyboard below the stone-slab counter; there was a screen on their side as well.

"Hotel Mirabelle," Fred said. "And a car, please. Fourseater, suitable fo' country drivin'. And a weapons store."

"*Phew,*" Fred muttered. His sister could read his thought: *Made it.* Another milestone: nothing flagged on the Security net attached to their identities.

Marya stopped with him at the bottom of the stairs, and took two glasses of mineral water from a refreshment stand. They drank, hardly noticing the taste except that it wet dry throats. Looked about: they were in a broad corridor, open to the roadway in front and lined by shops at their back. The serfs who moved about them mostly looked to be personal servants on errands, or airship haven staff. Steamcars were pulling up and leaving, parcel-delivery trucks, boxy little electric town runabouts. The Draka they saw were largely travelers, intent on their destinations.

Safe, she thought; or as safe as they could be on enemy soil. That had been something it took the OSS a long time to learn: that an agent was safer and more effective posing as a Citizen than as a serf. It went against common sense. There were so *many* more serfs, but most of them were plantation hands, or compounded workers; they just didn't *move* very much. Most of the ones who did travel were tightly integrated into some organization, known faces, and for a serf the Domination was a bureaucratized labyrinth, with monsters waiting at every corner to eat you if you made a wrong step . . .

Whereas a Citizen had fewer day-to-day constraints than the average American, if you didn't count things like the right to open a newspaper. Once that had mattered little, when the Domination and its ruling caste were smaller. But the Citizen population was no longer the tiny tight-knit band it had once been. Seventy-odd million was more than enough to be anonymous if you kept moving and avoided your supposed hometown.

They returned the glasses and walked into *Sanderton's Arms and Hunt Supplies*.

It was big, cool, and dimly lit; the aisles were separated by low glass-topped display cases, the ceiling covered in stained-glass hunting scenes while the floor bore plain sisal mats that rutched under their boots. Spotlights flooded the examination tables, granite columns with polished teak tops; there was a slight scent of well-kept machinery. Marya glanced over the merchandise in the displays and wall-racks with professional appraisal; to her, weapons were tools but not particularly interesting otherwise. A wide selection of sidearms. They would have to pick up some; their lack of gunbelts had attracted a few glances. The hunting weapons themselves were single shot rifles or double-barreled models, bolt-action repeaters in light calibers for small game, bird-shotguns. Spears, lances, various types of knife and bow.

Their needs were otherwise. "The proprietor, please," Marya said to one of the attendants. Most of those looked to be decorative, young women in short tunics. One of them whispered to an older man, black, shaven-headed, and massive; he bowed and used a desk phone.

Frederick Lefarge made a minuscule sign with his fingers: *I'll deal with this one.*

His eyes were appraising the . . . shopowner, he supposed. A Draka, of course, in this line of business. Well past fifty, in loose trousers and a sleeveless shirt. Tall and deeply tanned, face square and with an outdoorsman's weathered look. A formidable collection of scars; the American's eye picked out shrapnel on the arm and shoulder, a well-done reconstruction job on cheek and jawbones, a missing finger from the left hand, and what looked to be knife-scars on the torso. Impressively springy, despite the age that had turned the body gaunt and stripped any smoothing of subcutaceous fat from the long muscles. No gun at his waist, but a long knife strapped hilt-down along his right flank.

"Donal Green," the man said, gripping their wrists. "Trooper, Special Tasks, Long-Range Reconaissance, retired. Late of Mobaye-North."

That was a province north of the Congo river, thinly settled. Probably a hunter; it would go with the military specialty. There was an interval for the usual pleasantries. The black came up behind the Draka, and waited with something of the same relaxed patience.

"What can I do fo' y'all, Citizens? Sidearms?"

Fred had an uncomfortable feeling that the remote brown eyes were recording them both inch by inch. It prickled between his shoulderblades; machinery was tireless, but it only asked the obvious questions, and it had no intuition. Every contact with a potential informant risked bringing those uniquely human facilities into play.

"Yes, please. Just back from a trip outside the State." To Draka, there was only one. "We're doin' some huntin', as well," he said.

"Ah." Genuine interest in the Draka's eyes. "Local? We've got some fine boar, deer, wolf, and leopard territory hereabouts. Or if y'all're interested, my family runs a wild-country outfit down in Mobaye-North."

"Sorry. We're booked, fo' the Archangel Reserve."

More than a little interest now. "Tiger?"

"No, bushmen." The ideal cover story, for someone buying what they needed.

There were still bands of partisans, Finnish and a few Russians, in the great taiga forests that stretched from the northeastern Baltic up into the Arctic Circle: *bushmen*, in Draka dialect. The OSS even had contacts with them, few and sporadic, when a submarine could elude the ever-improving surveillance. Few Draka had ever wished to settle in those remote and desolately cold regions, and even the timber Combines worked only the most accessible parts. The military had hunted down the most dangerous bands in the early '50s, and as for the rest . . . a Citizen who wanted game more exciting than any on four legs could book a tour. It even made sense, for a people who hunted lion with cold steel. One of the many ways used to keep the edge from rusting in an era of peace.

Not peace, he told himself. *Just an interval between battles.*

To the Draka, there would be no peace until they ruled the human universe. *Or until we kill the last one.*

"Lucky yo'!" Donal Green said. "Y'all be wantin' somethin' special, then . . . Price range?"

"Show us what yo've got," Fred replied.

A wide grin. "As it just so happens . . . Bokassa, fetch the new models." He led them to one of the examination tables. "Now, we've gotten a shipment of the latest stuff. They're retirin' the Improved Model Holbars now, yo've probably heard; replacin' it with a caseless round? Well, the prototype production run got sold, and bought up an' customized down in Herakulopolis." That was the bridge-dam-city across the straits of Gibraltar.

The black man arrived with a case, folded it back. His master lifted the weapon within free.

"Lot of it's space-made," he said. In appearance it was a virtually featureless rectangular box; there was a barrel at one end, with a thinner rod above, and a cushioned buttplate at the other; a pistol-grip below, and a stubby telescopic sight above.

"Loads from a cassette, two hundred rounds," Donal continued, and slid a long box through an opening just above the buttplate. "Three-point-five-millimeter, but hypervelocity, prefragmented tungsten slug, designers say it'll only come apart in a soft target. Barrel's a refractory superalloy, an' it has a linin' of single-crystal diamond."

A smile. "They tryin' to use that fo' spaceships, thrust-plates, but even in vacuum and microgravity it's stone tricky. Thissere's an intermediate use. Charge the first round by turnin' this knob in a complete circle. The slide here sets cyclic rate, up to two thousand rpm; at that, yo' gets a three-round groupin' less than twenty-five-millimeter apart at eight hundred meters. Max effective range 'bout one thousand. Here," he continued, unloading the weapon, "sight on somethin'."

Fred took the weapon in his hands; it was superbly balanced, although it felt a little odd to have the action right by his ear and the grip halfway down the rifle. No heavier than the Springfield-12's he had trained on, lighter than the IM Holbars-7's the Domination was using now. The sight lit as his eye came into line, with the peculiar glassy brightness of electro-optical imaging . . . and a red dot in the center of the field. The Draka heard his surprised grunt.

"Laser sightin'," he said. "Where it falls, there yo' hit. Frequency filter in the sight, yo' can see it an' the target can't. Adjusts fo' range, as yo' up the magnification."

"Excellent, we'll take two," the American said calmly, fighting down his glee. *This* was an advantage a Draka agent wouldn't have anywhere in the Alliance.

"Ah . . . I'm afraid they're six thousand Aurics each."

He pretended a wince; quite a sum, by Draka standards. A little more than the basic Citizen stipend. And a standard low-skilled serf could be bought for a hundred and seventy-five.

"Hmmm . . . well, yo' want the best, goin' after bushmen. They do have rifles, aftah all. Yes, two. An' the usual; nightsight goggles, some light body armor."

"Well, the measurin'-rooms are this way—"

"Jesus, I just can't believe it was that *easy*," Marya said.

Her brother laughed, guiding the Bushmaster down the access ramp and onto the road marked *City Center*. That tone meant she had completed the sweep; the instruments in their perscomps were swift and thorough. For the moment he felt good, relaxed and strong and confident. The air rushing in through the opened window was cool, smelling of brackish river and warm asphalt pavement; the greenery and bright-colored buildings of the freemen's city showed ahead.

"No . . . Did you know, there was a time when you could get guns like that back home?"

The road was four-lane and raised on a five-meter embankment, narrower than a limited-access route in the US; more steamdrags, more buses, fewer private cars. And the Domination used rail transport more than his people. A checkerboard of streets was passing on either side, residential from the look of them. Brick-built walkups, patterns of red and white, an occasional square of decorative tile. Elite housing, individual family apartments for the literate class of industrial serf. Sidewalks, trees lining the streets. He could see the odd building that looked like a church, others that might be schools or stores . . . No, ration centers, the goods would be distributed rather than sold. It might almost have been an older suburb of an American city . . .

Marya touched his arm. There was an iron cage hanging at one of the intersections below, with a man in it, almost level with them. The sign wired to the bars read *saboteur*; there was a crowd of children gathered below, watching or throw-

ing rocks. At first he thought the man inside was dead—
nothing so skeletal could be alive—but then one of the stones
bounced through the bars and a stick-arm waved.

"*Shit,*" he said softly. Pictures were not like the real thing.
Something prickled at his eyes, and he turned them back into
the windstream as the car went past. *His head just rolled on
his shoulders. He couldn't have been watching us.*

"You were saying?" Marya continued. He glanced aside at
her: flawlessly composed. Of course he couldn't see past the
dark sunglasses . . .

"You're a cool one," he said.

She turned her head to look at him, smiled. He felt a slight
chill wash away the nausea. "I'm saving it up," she said.

"Yes . . . oh, the guns. Back before the War, you could
buy military-style rifles, handguns, the lot. The Constitution,
you know: 'A well-regulated militia . . .,' the right-to-bear-
arms clause."

She frowned in puzzlement. "Oh, you mean the Army
Reserve? Well, even these days, a lot of them keep the
personal weapons at home."

"No, nothing to do with the military. Those are under seal
and inspected pretty often, anyway. Not just people in hunting clubs, either. *Anybody.* Cheap pistols, sawed-off shotguns, the lot."

She shook her head. "Live and learn . . . I know why the
Draka always carry iron, they want to be able to kill at any
time. What possible use could—" A shrug. "Never mind.
Let's check in, and then we'll start working magic on the
hotel infosystem." She pulled off the sunglasses and chewed
meditatively on one earpiece. "Because I suspect magic is
what we'll need."

CHAPTER NINE

A tenth of the human race died in the years 1939–1946; after the Eurasian War, the total population was barely 2,500,000, no more than it had been in 1920. Growth in the postwar period was quite slow, and unevenly distributed. In the Domination, there were continuing decreases in the serf population of the newly conquered territories until the late 1950s, due partly to continuing partisan and guerrilla warfare, and partly to sheer despair. As living standards improved and the memory of past freedoms faded, growth recommenced at a modest level; this was accompanied by a continuing *geographical* shift, with China and to a lesser extent Western Europe, Russia, and Central Asia/ Western Siberia expansion was greatest in Iberia-Morocco, due to the Herakulopolis project, and in east-central Europe, Russia and Central Asia/ Western Siberia. There was also a substantial relocation of agricultural labor eastwards, especially to the vast irrigation developments of Central Asia. The Citizen population of the Domination increased fairly rapidly in the postwar period, from c. 40,000,000 in 1946 to approximately 60,000,000 by 1970; thereafter, growth was more rapid and the total approached 110,000,000 by the mid 1990s. Much of the increase was in the new territories taken in the Eurasian War.

In the Alliance the picture was much more complex. The United States, after a brief postwar "blip," showed steady but slow growth, tending to level off after the 1970s; totals reached 220,000,000 by 1995. There was also a steady

185

shift from rural to urban areas, and from the eastern and north-central to the southern and western states. Mexico City, for example, went from 1,000,000 in 1946 to 4,500,000 by 1990, causing severe problems of housing and water supply; Los Angeles showed even more remarkable growth, from 350,000 to 2,000,000 in the same period. South America's growth was more rapid, but the fall-off after 1970 more pronounced. In 1995, the four nations of the southern American continent totaled 230,000,000, larger than the US for the first time, over half of those being in the Empire of Brazil. Japan's gruesome war losses were never fully replaced, and the island nation stabilized at approximately 70,000,000 in the 1980s. Britain's population declined, and the Australasian Federation increased, in close synchronization; equality (in the 40,000,000 range) was reached by 1990. The most startling demographic change was the steep decreases in birthrates in the Asian members of the Alliance; the Indonesian and Indochinese Federations reached steady-state by the 1980s. Tragic India continued to grow rapidly, reaching a peak of 300,000,000 in 1975; the casualties of the Incident and the mass sterilizations and deportations which followed reduced this to 200,000,000 and falling by 1995.

The last factor to become significant in this era was the creation of significant human populations off Earth, first in orbit and on Luna, and then in the remainder of the Solar System. Starting with a few hundred in 1965, growth was proportionately extremely rapid, and by 1996 total resident population beyond Earth's atmosphere reached perhaps 3,500,000—4,000,000, the majority in the Earth-orbit/Luna complex, with the asteroid belt following closely and Mars last. The remainder were outposts of great future potential but limited size; of the extraterrestrial settlements, the Domination accounted for approximately 60% and the Alliance the remainder.

World Population Geography
Alliance PostSecondary Standard Texts
Ch. 1: An Overview
Democracy Press, San Francisco
1997

HOTEL MIRABEAU, NANTES
LOIRE DISTRICT, TOURAINE PROVINCE
DOMINATION OF THE DRAKA
APRIL 4, 1973

God, that thing's ugly, Marya thought, looking at the ghouloon. The transgene animal was *big,* for one thing, about three times her brother's weight. Basically a giant dog-headed baboon, four-footed most of the time but able to walk or sprint on its hind legs. The thumbs on feet and hands were fully opposable, and the forehead was high and rounded. The biocontrollers of Virunga had started with Simien mountain baboons, then added something from leopard and gorilla and the *jag hond* . . . but there was more than an animal's intelligence behind those eyes. Human genes as well, a mind that knew itself to be aware and could think in words. It wore a belt, and a long knife and pouch.

They were in one of the dining courtyards of the hotel, out under the mild midmorning sun; little fleecy clouds went by overhead, like something out of a Fragonard painting. Her brother and her and the Draka they had met: Alexandra Clearmount, a woman in her thirties, nearly their own age: a geneticist. The ghouloon was of the first "production batch." It had attracted a good deal of attention, although Draka considered it ill-bred to stare; the serfs were frankly terrified of it.

". . . mass production," she was saying. "So costs ought to come down pretty steadily. The War and Security Directorates've got large orders in already."

"They can be used in combat?" Fred sounded politely skeptical. A waitress brought their platter of shrimp and *crudités.*

"Fo' some things. Not much technical aptitude, not intelligent enough, but they'll make killer infantry. Eh, Wofor?" She laughed and tossed a shrimp.

The ghouloon caught it out of the air with one hand,

holding it between finger and thumb and sniffing curiously. Then he ate it, exposing intimidating fangs, and a long pink tongue washed the black muzzle. "Wofor *good* fighter," he said. The voice was blurred but understandable. "Wofor brave. Wofor smart." He slapped at his chest with his hands, a drumlike sound.

For a moment Marya's eyes met the bronze-gold slit-pupiled gaze of the transgene; she could see the lids blink, and the wet black nose ruffle slightly to take her scent. *Abomination*, she thought. That was what the Church taught, and for once she agreed wholeheartedly. The Draka woman was talking to Fred again, leaning forward with interest.

Lucky, Marya thought. Lucky that they had stumbled on someone heading for the Sologne forest-preserve. The Conservancy Directorate usually rented out the hunting rights to the smaller preserves to groups of neighboring Landholders, in return for maintenance work. Very economical, but it made it difficult for an outsider to get a permit, and Draka law and custom were not easy on poachers. This Clearmount had connections with the local planters—*she might even be a relative*, Marya thought ironically—and could get them into a hunting party. *Even more lucky that she's interested in Fred and not his sister*. Not that she wasn't prepared to make the supreme sacrifice, but . . . *better him than me*.

Citizen sexual mores were a tricky subject. Their instructors had gone into detail, tracing it back to child-rearing patterns . . . One thing Draka had never been was puritans; sadomasochistic hedonists, that was the term the psychs used. The boys had concubines from puberty on, or casual sex with any serf woman they wanted; that was a tradition dating back to their Caribbean origins and beyond. Not many pious middle-class Protestants in the bloodlines of *this* nation. Citizen women had been legally barred from any contact with serf males until quite recently, though, and it was still socially unacceptable. Given the sex-segregated boarding schools, the Draka neoclassicism and the near-total lack of erotic inhibition otherwise, she supposed a tradition of homoeroticism was natural enough. For that matter, young women generally wanted more romance in the mixture; that didn't seem to hit men until true adulthood. So young Draka women faced a perpetual shortage of interested men. Marya's mouth quirked, remembering her own teenage years.

I always suspected courtship was something adolescent males put up with because it was the only way to get laid, she thought. *This more or less confirms it*.

Draka teenage boys got all they wanted, and tended to be profoundly indifferent to females of their own caste, who could say no. So girls were thrown back on each other; they were supposed to grow out of it in their early twenties, theoretically. Most did, to the extent of marrying and bearing children; granted, there was really strong social pressure to do that, as well. The agent grinned to herself. The Draka woman's come-on to Fred had been disconcertingly blunt. *That's logical, too*. In the Alliance countries sex was something that women had and men wanted, and men had to conform to the indirect approaches women preferred. Here, precisely the opposite.

I wonder what hunting boar with a spear is like? she thought meditatively.

SOLOGNE HUNTING PRESERVE
PROVINCE OF TOURAINE
DOMINATION OF THE DRAKA
APRIL 10, 1973
1030 HOURS

"*Shit!*" Myfwany said, reining in her horse. "What a complete cockup!"

Yolande nodded agreement, switching her reins to the spear-hand and wiping her hair back from her forehead with the other. The rain had given way to a steady drizzle, just enough to keep them soaked and replenish the low mist drifting through the trees. They had halted in a clearing, a hectare or so of knee-high purple heather amid old-growth oak; the chill cut to the bone beneath the leather and wool of their hunting clothes. Discomfort could be ignored; they were also lost, which was rather more frustrating. She reached for her hunting-horn and blew, a dull *rooo-rooo-rooo* sound through the endless patter of rain on leaf. The air was raw and full of the smell of marsh, vegetable decay and wet horse.

"Hear that?" she asked, standing in the stirrups and cupping a hand to an ear. Their mounts stamped and blew, shaking their heads in a jingle of bridle and bit. Beyond it, far and far, came the belling of hounds.

"Sa," Myfwany said, her head coming up. "Think they caught the scent again?"

"We can hope. C'mon, this way." The Sologne was a half-million hectares of wilderness, but the keepers tended to the paths at least.

SOLOGNE HUNTING PRESERVE
CHATEAU OF MOULIN
PROVINCE OF TOURAINE
DOMINATION OF THE DRAKA
APRIL 4, 1973
1000 HOURS

"*Out!*" the Security Tetrarch said. The serf flinched back from the deadly quiet of the tone. "Yo' brainless slut, yo' supposed to keep *track* of him!"

Mei-ling swallowed and straightened. "Mistis, Mastah Dave doan' like it, when we keeps him too close. We supposed to make him happy, aren't we? Anyways, Bernadette with him."

The greencoated secret police agent looked down at her control board and keyed a sequence. "Then why isn't she carryin' her transponder? Oh, hell." Another touch on the board. "Decurion, turn out the ghouloons, let's see them earn their keep. No alarms, our little electronics wizard don't like the bars of the cage showin'." She stood, shrugging into a waterproof jacket. "Come on, wench. *Show* me where they might have gone."

"Where the hell have yo' *been*?" Mandy asked, as Yolande and Myfwany reined in. John looked up from overseeing the serf huntsmen who were rigging the nets between the big beech trees, waved, went back to work.

"Where have *we* been?" Myfwany grinned and waved at the surrounding forest. "Y'all were supposed to keep everyone in sight or hearin' of the dogs. Fo' that matter, where the hell are we *now*?"

A faint shout came from the woods ahead. The trees were tall here, thirty meters or more, but widely enough spaced that patches of underbrush flourished, spiny thorn and witch hazel. They all swung down, dropping their reins. Yolande swallowed and took a firmer grip on her boar-spear; it was a head taller than she, with an oval head as broad as her hand

and a steel crossbar beneath to prevent a tusker from driving itself up the shaft to gore a hunter. The nets made a deep funnel, with them at the apex . . . it was a slightly disconsolate feeling, as the servants led the mounts away to safety.

Damn, but I'm still light for this, she thought. No more than a hundred fifty tall; strong for her weight, but wild pig had *heft*. "Shut up, yo' crybaby," she whispered to herself under her breath, inaudibly. Aloud:

"Where are those citybred, the ones Alexandra picked up?" There was a slightly patronizing note to her voice; the pair had seemed nice enough, but she thought her cousin could do better . . . and had been a little undiscriminating, since her divorce. *Oh, well, not everybody can find the right one*, she thought charitably, sparing a quick glance for Myfwany. They all faced the gap in the net, spreading out to twice arm's length, just close enough to give support. A horn blew ahead of them, and John came trotting back towards them.

"Don't know," Mandy said with a shrug. John stopped to give her a brief hug before taking center position; Yolande noted how they were almost of a height, now. *Mandy's really filled out*, she thought, with a slight envy. *I'm always going to be like a sylph beside her*. And it looked as if she might be a sister-in-law . . .

"Alexandra lost track of them herself, an' said she was goin' lookin'."

"Shit. Oh, well, could be worse. Could be rainin'."

The wind picked up, blowing into their faces, and the cold drops came more thickly.

Myfwany laughed. "Yo' had to say it, eh, sweetlin'?"

"Sign!" John said sharply.

They fell quiet, leveling their weapons in a two-handed grip. The boarhound pack was in full cry not two hundred meters ahead, and then there was an enraged squealing sound. The dogs stopped. *No fools they*, Yolande thought, as the squeal sounded again, closer. No way of telling which way the boar would go, either. Wild pigs were omnivores, like people; much more likely to go looking for trouble than a meat-eater like wolf or lion. She stamped the rough-soled boots deeper into the slippery leaf mold and emptied her mind, letting her vision flow. The tips of the bushes quivered, against the wind.

"He's breakin'," she called.

"Got him," John said, grin white against his tan.

He moved slightly forward from the line. The bushes tossed again, and the pig came out. He stood motionless, three-quarters on, watching them with tiny red eyes. The massive head was held close to the ground, and the curved tusks stood up like daggers of wet ivory. Bulky and bristling, the shoulders moved behind as weight shifted from one cloven hoof to another. The pink snout wrinkled as the animal tried to take their scent; an organic battering-ram twice the weight of a heavy man, knife-armed, faster than a horse and many times as intelligent. The dogs bayed again, nearer; the shouts of the huntsmen ran beneath that harsh music, and the sound of their horns racketed from the trees. John leveled his spear and moved forward, dancer-light.

"Come on, yo' ugly son-of-a-bitch," he crooned. "Get past me and yo' home free. Come *on*."

The boar seemed to sink lower against the wet grass and heather of the forest edge. Then it moved, springing forward as if shot from a catapult, stumpy legs churning the leaf mold, and nose down to present nothing but weapon and heavy bone. Yolande's breath caught as her brother took two swift strides forward, poised the spear, thrust. Another squeal, louder, full of pain and rage; blood bright under the wan sun, and John was pushed back two bodylengths before he could brace the iron butt of the boarspear against the ground. The animal stumbled, and she could see its mouth wide open in a spray of blood and saliva; then it went to its knees for a second, but the hind legs were still pumping it forward. Mandy closed in to the side. Her spear lifted, body and weapon a perfect X across raised arms, braced legs. Yolande saw the point dip, then vanish into the boar's ribs with a precise snapping thrust.

"Hola!" Yolande cried, and saw her friend's rapt smile as she and the man pushed the beast backward, still fighting. Words formed in her mind; half-consciously she began to work them into form. *Arms together/blood and love—*.

" 'Ware!" Myfwany shouted.

Another boar had followed in the footsteps of the first; it broke cover, grunted uncertainly at the scent of blood, then angled around the struggle. Myfwany sidled off, and Yolande moved away from her, closing the beast's escape-route. She could see its eyes roll from one of them to the other, and a hoof pawed at the ground. *Is it a little smaller than the other one?* she thought. *Maybe. Wotan, I hope so.* Myfwany was beside her; unthinkable to flinch. Yolande could feel the coiled vitality of it, like raw flame. Then it was coming at her, bouncing off tensed hindquarters, and there was no time for thought of anything.

Keep low. From above a boar was all bone and leather and gristle-armour over its vitals. She stooped, crouching, spear held underhand. The ashwood shaft was smooth on the shark-skin palms of her gloves, and the broad point seemed to follow a scribed curve to the juncture of neck and shoulder. *"Haaaaaaa!"* she hawk-screamed, and the point bit. Then the weight of it struck her through the leverage of the spear, and it was like running into a wall at speed, like trying to stop a steamcar. *"Ufff!"* she grunted, and found herself scrambling backward. Then she went over on her tailbone, white pain flowing warm-chill across the small of her back. The spear-head was half-buried in the tough muscle and blood welled around it, but the beast was pushing her backward with her backside dragging, squealing ear-hurting shrill and hooking savagely at her feet as they dangled within striking distance of the tusks.

"Hold him, hold him!" Myfwany shouted, racing alongside and trying to find a target for a lunge.

"Yo' fuckin' try it!" Yolande was half-conscious of screaming.

The spearshaft wrenched her from side to side as the boar lunged and twisted, it was as if she was on the end of a ruler somebody was pounding against trees and dirt with negligent flicks of the wrist. With a supreme effort she threw her weight down on it, using the impetus to draw her feet back and up; the tusk clipped her heel, sending her body sprawling sideways. At the same instant the butt of the spear dug into the turf, caught in the crook of a root. The boar staggered, squealed again as its own momentum drove the razor-edged steel deeper into its body. Instinct brought its head around, as it tried to gore this thing that bit it. She could smell it, heavy and rank.

Myfwany moved up beside her, throwing herself forward. The wet metal gleam of her spearhead met the taut curve of the animal's neck. The Draka went to her knees as jugular blood spurted down over the bar of the weapon and along the shaft, and the boar seemed to grow lighter. Yolande panted with a sudden joint-loosening rush of unacknowledged terror as the beast's death-tremor shuddered up the spear. It sprawled, toppled over on its side; the little savage eyes grew misted. She rose, feeling exhaustion and bruises for the first time, braced her foot on the animal's body and tugged the spear free. There was blood speckled on her lips, salt-tasting.

"Wuff." Yolande leaned on the spear and hugged Myfwany one-armed. "*Wuff!*" Her friend returned the embrace.

"Yo' had me frightened for a moment, there, Yolande-sweet," she said.

"I had *me* frightened," Yolande replied, laughing with relief. Suddenly she broke free with a whoop and tossed the spear up into the air, then rammed it point-first in the earth and kissed the other heartily. "Makes yo' feel alive, don't it?" she asked, when they broke free. She looked over to her brother. "Shouldn't we be about findin' the others? I could use a nice long soak an' dinner in front of the fire."

Frederick Lefarge swung a hand behind himself, palm-down. *Stop.* Marya halted, then eased forward to follow the pointing muzzle of his assault rifle.

Ah, she thought. Barely perceptible at waist-height, a line of light. Laser light, only showing because of the mist; modern systems were selective enough to take that and not trip until interrupted by something more substantial. And beyond that at ankle height a camouflaged sensor clipped to a tree, capacitordetector. She went to one knee and swung her backpack around before her; it had been her responsibility to come ahead and cache their equipment. Not difficult to "lose" themselves in the woods, not when everyone else was following the sound of the dogs.

This would be the difficult part. She stripped off her gloves and flexed her fingers to limber them before assembling the apparatus. A light-metal frame to hold the clamps, *so*. Close the circles of wire around the beams, *so*. Her finger hesitated on the switch, then pressed. A modest green light flashed once on the black-box governor. Marya exhaled shakily, letting her palms rest on the cold damp leaves. She looked up, and the cold drizzle was grateful on her cheeks.

Her brother slapped her once on the shoulder, and they nodded. Marya caught up her rifle and followed as he hurdled the gap in the sensor chain she had created.

The two OSS agents froze in unison at the hoarse cries from the path ahead. Then voices, a man and a woman's, laughing. These woods were more open than those outside the guarded perimeter; they had had to halt half a dozen times to identify and disarm sensors. Marya slowly drew a map from a pocket on the side of her leather hunting-trousers and glanced at it, nodded to the other American. They were right on target . . . if the information they had received from the underground was correct. If not, there might be nothing waiting for them but a Security Directorate capture team.

Frederick Lefarge stepped through the last screen of brush. The rain had stopped, but there were puddles on the flagstones of the pathway; beyond it he could see banks of flowers, and then a screen of hedge marking a pavilion. It was obvious enough what the pair had been at; the woman had mud on her knees and was still adjusting her underwear, the man fastening his belt. For a moment Lefarge felt a surge of panic; this did *not* look like David Ekstein. Too thin, too tanned, the complexion too clear . . . then the bone-structure showed through. The other man's face was liquid with surprise as he stared at the two figures in hunting leathers.

"Hey," he said, drawing himself up. "This is *my* place!" A neutral Californian accent. Then, as if remembering a lesson: "Uh, Service to the State, Citizens."

Lefarge felt himself smile, and saw the other man flinch.

"Glory to the Race," he said, and the smile grew into a grin.

The serf girl nodded to the two agents, then stepped back. He stepped up to Ekstein, pushed the muzzle of the rifle into the defector's stomach and fired twice. Recoil hammered the weapon into his hand, augmented by the gases cushioned in flesh. Ekstein catapulted backward, jackknifing, the leather of his jacket smouldering. Back and spine fountained out in a spray of bone, blood, and internal organs; the air stank of burned flesh and excrement. The body fell to the earth and twitched, was still.

So simple, he thought. Always a surprise. So different from the viewer, rarely any dramatic thrashing around, no last-gasp curses, not with a wound like this. The body fell down and died, and it was over. A whole universe within a human skull, and then nothing. *Jesus, I hate this job.* It was done. Now they must escape; the easy way, if they could get back to the hunting party, or the hard way, switching identities and oozing out through the underground net.

"*Merci.*" That was the serf woman. "*Et moi aussi.*"

"What?" he said sharply in French, looking up. She was young, barely in her late teens; cool brunette good looks, face unreadable as she looked down into Ekstein's final expression of bewilderment.

"Now me," she said, looking up at him. "Surely you were told, monsieur? If you do not I must contrive it, and they will suspect everyone if I suicide. Most are blameless—I am the underground contact here—but that will not spare them interrogation, and I know too much."

He felt his mouth open, and the muzzle of the rifle drooped. "*Merde!* Nobody said a word about that to us!"

She swallowed, and he saw a slight tremor in the hands that smoothed back her disordered hair. "Please, quickly." She turned her back, looked up into the wet sky with fists clenched by her side. "There is not much time before he is missed."

"I—" Lefarge felt himself lock. There was white noise in his mind, caught between *must* and *cannot*. Marya stepped past him, with a soft touch on his arm.

"As you wish," she said to the serf girl, an infinite tenderness in her voice. "As you wish."

"I wish we hadn't had to drop the rifles," Marya said. The rain was lifting, finally this time by the rifts in the clouds. Their horses had been waiting where they were left, damp and restless and turning large brown eyes full of reproach on the humans.

Frederick Lefarge shrugged, guiding the big animal with the pressure of his knees; Draka used a pad-saddle and an almost token bit. It would be like carrying a "guilty" sign to have the weapons when the police came around. Not that either of them could stand a close questioning, but if they could slip back into the hunting party . . . They walked the mounts out into the open; out of the continual patter of moisture from the wet canopy above, but the air was colder where the wind could play. Six cars, parked along the verge. Two big steamtrucks for the horses and dogs, two vans for the huntsmen, two tilt-rotor dual-purpose jobs for the people . . . *Draka*, he told himself. *Don't get too much in character.*

The tall fair teenager was leaning against the open door of one aircar: Mandy, the just-graduated pilot. And his Draka persona's lady-love, Alexandra, supervising the loading of two dead boar; her ghouloon attendant lifted one under each arm and slung them casually into the bed of the truck. The van jounced on its springs under the impact, and the American felt a slight crawling sensation across his shoulders and down the spine. *That thing's as strong as a gorilla*, he reminded himself. Rather stronger, in fact, and much faster. It snuffled at its hands, licking away the blood and turned to its owner; standing erect it was easily two meters tall.

"Eat?" it said, in that blurred gravelly tone. "Eat?"

Alexandra laughed and slapped it on one massive shoulder. The sound was like a palm hitting oak wood. "Later," she said, and the transgene bobbed its head in obedience, tongue lolling and eyes turning longingly toward the meat; drops of rain spilled from the coarse black fur of its lionlike mane.

He turned a grimace into a smile as she looked up at him and waved. It would not do to appear unenthusiastic. Actually, it had been interesting, at least the sex had. *That* was like coupling with a demented anaconda. The smile turned into a rueful chuckle; it was also the first time he had been called "charmingly shy" in bed.

"Hiyo!" he called, as he and Marya handed their boarspears down to the servants. "Sorry we got separated."

"Whole damn party did, Toni," Alexandra said. "John's out gatherin' them all up, with Yolande and her girlfriend. Ah'm gettin' hungry as Wofor."

"Wofor *eat*," the ghouloon said.

"I—" Mandy began, and was interrupted by a chiming note. She leaned in to take the microphone of the aircar's com unit. "Wonder what the headhunters're sayin'?" she said curiously.

The American felt a sensation like an ice-drill boring through the bottom of his stomach. That was the Security-override alarm. Casually, he whistled the first bar of "Dixie," the code-signal. Marya swung down from her horse and turned toward the aircar; he slid the pistol from his gunbelt and checked it. A late-model Tolgren, 5mm prefragmented bullets, caseless ammunition and a 30-round horizontal cassette magazine above the barrel. He slipped the selector to three-rounds and set the positions of the Draka in his mind. The youngster leaning into the lead aircar. Alexandra ten meters back, by the steamtruck. The serfs could be ignored, they would hit the ground at the first sign of violence and stay there.

"Not bushman trouble 'round here?" he said, with a skeptical tone.

"Gods, no," Alexandra replied. Her hand had gone to the butt of her sidearm automatically, but it dropped away again as she twisted around to look toward Mandy. "I's born not a hundred clicks from here"—*news to me*, the American thought—"and the last incident was the year I born."

Time went rubbery, stretching. His body felt light, almost like zero-G, every movement achingly precise, the outlines of things cut in crystal. Mandy was speaking again.

"Oh, *moo*. Some sort of escape or somethin' from a head-hunter facility. Everyone's to stay put an' report movement until further notice. Eurg, mo' waitin' in the rain."

"Damn," the American said. "And I's real anxious to get out of here."

Wofor gave a growl, and Alexandra began to turn back, a casual movement that turned blinding-fast as her peripheral vision caught the muzzle of his Tolgren. Even then, it cleared the holster before the flat *brak* of his weapon stitched a line of fist-sized craters from breastbone to throat. *Falling*, she was falling away in a mist of blood and *roar* the ghouloon leapt from the rear of the steamtruck, its great hands outstretched and jaws opened to nearly ninety degrees. *Flying* toward him, the huge white-and-red gape, and two pistols fired in the background and he was levering himself backward off the horse. Inertia fought him like water in the simulator tank, back at the Academy. Then he was toppling, kicking his foot free of the stirrup.

The horse shied violently at the ghouloon's roar and the crack of the firearms, enough to throw him a dozen paces further as he fell. Damp gravel pounded into his back, jarring, but he scarcely noticed. Not when the the transgene struck the horse at the end of its flight; the big gelding went over with a scream of fear, and for a moment the two animals were a thrashing pile on the surface of the road. Just long enough to flick the selector on his pistol to full-automatic and brace it with both hands. Wofor rose over the prostrate body of the horse, looming like a black mountain of muscle and fur, yellow eyes and bone-spike teeth.

Even with a muzzle brake, the Tolgren was difficult to control on full-automatic. The American solved the problem by starting low enough that the first round shattered a knee and letting the torque empty the magazine upward into the transgene's center of mass. Wofor's own weight slewed him around when the knee buckled, and the massive animal slammed into the ground at full-tilt, a diagonal line across his torso sawn open by the shrapnel effect of the prefragmented bullets. The earth shook with the impact. Lefarge yelled relief as the pistol emptied itself, screamed again as the ghouloon's one good hand clamped on his ankle. Dying, it still gripped like a pneumatic press, crushing the bone beneath the boot leather and dragging his leg toward the open jaws. The human twisted, raised his other leg and hacked down on the transgene's thumb with the metal-shod heel of the boot; once, twice and then there was a crackling sound. He rolled, pulled free, came to his feet with a stab of pain up the injured limb.

Boot will hold it, he thought with savage concentration, as his hands slapped another cassette into the weapon.

Marya was running down the line of cars; the blond Draka lay on the ground, her hands to her belly. Lefarge hobbled forward, felt a stab of concern at the spreading red stain on the side of his sister's jacket.

"Just a graze, first car in the row, go, go, *go*," she shouted. At each car she paused just long enough to pump three rounds into the communicator; even so, she was in time to help him into the first as he hop-stepped to safety.

"Let's *go*," he snarled, wrenching at the controls as she tumbled through the entrance on the other side. The turbines shrieked and the aircar rose on fan-thrust, just high enough to clear the treetops before he rammed the throttles forward. The SD would not shoot down a planter's car, not until they got confirmation, and Marya had delayed that a vital fifteen minutes. At worst, a clean death when a heatseeker blew their craft out of the sky; at best, they would make it.

"We did it," he breathed. Something slackened in the center of his body, and pain shot up the leg from the savaged ankle.

"We—did," Marya replied. She was fumbling in the first-aid box. "We . . . *did.*"

"I didn't know that," Yolande said, looking down at the body of her cousin.

The eyes stared empty upwards into the rain, and the steady silver fall washed the blood pale-pink out of the sodden cloth. The ambulance took off with a scream of fans; Mandy would be in that, and John riding beside her. Myfwany put an arm about her shoulders.

"Yo' couldn't, sweet," she said. "Iff'n Alexandra couldn't tell, how could yo'? Y'hardly met them."

"Oh?" Yolande shook her head, and indicated the ghouloon; Wofor was not quite dead, though far beyond help. He had crawled the ten yards from the broken-backed horse with one good arm and one leg, trailing the shattered limbs and most of his blood. Now he lay with his head at Alexandra's feet, and Yolande crouched to shelter his head from the rain.

"Not that," she said softly, as the last trickle of sound escaped the fanged mouth and the labored breathing stopped. Her hand indicated the ghouloon, touched its muzzle. A bubble of blood burst at the back of its throat. "I didn't know these could cry, is all."

CHAPTER TEN

Draka serfdom is legally a rather severe form of chattel slavery, much like that of Classical times, except that there is no manumission. In terms of institutional history it descends from the plantation system of the Caribbean and the southern portions of the 13 Colonies, as absolute a system of bondage as any. However, there is slavery and slavery; slave status is a different thing in a society where the institution is rare and marginal than in one where it is nearly universal. In the Domination, over 93% of the total population are serfs; serfs labor in immense numbers as fieldhands, miners, factory workers, and domestic servants. But they also work as soldiers and police, foremen and boss-boys, machinists and clerks and bureaucrats. Existence in a mine compound can be very grim; plantation life depends on the whim of the owner, but is tied to the seasons and their demands as in any unmechanized farming system; domestic service is absolute personal subordination. The bulk of the urban working class have seen a slow improvement in their conditions since the Eurasian War—families now have rooms of their own, rather than bunks in a barracks, for example—but their work is long and their lives monotonous and closely disciplined, more by serf administrators than by the Citizens themselves. Their world is one of impersonal bureaucratic regulation.

For the ambitious or lucky there is the possibility of advancement; in the military, the police, the technical and administrative services of

the Combines or the State. Bright young men
and women are picked out and educated, and
those already at the top of the heap make stren-
uous efforts to see that their children do likewise. The rewards are great, more interesting
work and shorter hours, leisure, power. The top
echelons enjoy a living standard comparable to
the wealthy of the Alliance countries if not to the
Citizens: large homes, privacy, even servants.
Of course, the unsleeping gaze of the Security
Directorate rests on them more closely than any
others, and a single slip can mean death.

The Mind of the Draka: A Military Cultural
Analysis
Monograph delivered by Commodore Aguilar
Ernaldo
U.S. Naval War College, Manila 11th Alliance
Strategic Studies Conference
Subic Bay, 1972

NEW YORK CITY
FEDERAL CAPITAL DISTRICT
UNITED STATES OF AMERICA
DECEMBER 31, 1975

"Should auld acquaintance be forgoooot—"
  "I hate that bloody song," Frederick Lefarge muttered,
taking another sip of his drink. The room was hazy with
smoke, and flickering light and music came through the door
from the dance-floor; the room smelled of tobacco and beer.
More and more of the patrons at the bar were linking arms
and swaying, attempting a Scottish accent as they sang.
  It reminds me of Andy. Forget that.
  O'Grady's was supposed to be picturesque, a real Old New
York hangout and Irish as all hell. The wainscotting was dark
oak, and the walls of the booths were padded in dark leather
as well; there were hunting prints on the walls, and landscapes. It was *crowded* as all hell tonight, and noisy, but
Cindy had swung a private booth just for them; some noncom
friend of her dad's ran the place. The food was better than
passable, and the sides of the booth made conversation possible. There was a viewscreen on the opposite wall, showing

the crowds outside in Jefferson Square, and the big display clock on the Hartmann Tower. Ten minutes to midnight, and the screen began flashing between views. Different cities all over the Alliance, São Paulo, London, Djakarta, Sydney. The Lunar colonies—they could almost be called cities themselves, now—and the cramped corridors of the asteroid settlements. A shot from low orbit, the great curve of Earth rolling blue and lovely.

"Don't be such a grouch, honey," Cindy said, and nibbled at his ear. Lefarge laughed and put an arm around her waist, always a pleasant experience. "You were happy enough after dinner."

"There were just the two of us then," he said.

"Grrr, tiger!" Another nibble on his ear. "And I've got some news for you, darling."

"What?" he asked, raising the glass to his lips.

Cindy Guzman had had only two glasses of white wine with seltzer, but there was a gleam in her eye he knew of old. She was sitting in a corner of the booth, looking cool and chic in the long black dress with the pearl-and-gold belt. Her legs were curled up under her; the glossy dark-red hair fell in waves over her shoulder, and the diamond-shaped cutout below the yoke neck showed the uppper curve of her breasts. The glass in his hand halted and he sat motionless, utterly contented just to look. She gave off an air of . . . *wholesomeness*, he thought. Which was strange, you expected that word to go along with some thick-ankled corn-fed maiden from the boonies, not the brightest and sexiest woman he had ever known. It was like a draught of cool water, like . . . coming home.

"Miss?" Lefarge started slightly. It was old Terrance Gilbert, the proprietor, a CPO on one of Cindy's dad's pigboats, back when. He gave the young woman a look of fond pride, and Lefarge one of grudging approval. "Will there be anything else, Miss?"

"Not right now, Chief," Cindy said. "Happy New Year."

"And to you, Miss. Sir." Lefarge was in uniform tonight, the Major's leaves on his shoulders; the owner nodded before he disappeared into the throng.

"Finish your drink, darling," Cindy said.

He sipped. "What was the news, honey?" he asked.

"I'm pregnant."

He coughed, sending a spray of brandy out his nose; Cindy

thumped him on the back with one hand and offered a handkerchief with the other.

"The devil you say!"

"Dr. Blaine's sure," she said tranquilly. "Aren't you happy? We *will* have to move up the wedding, of course."

She flowed into his arms, and they kissed. Noise and smoke vanished; so did time, until someone blew a tin horn into his ear. Cindy and he broke from their clinch and turned, he scowling and she laughing. It was Marya and her current boyfriend—*cursed if I can remember his name . . . yeah, Steve. Wish she'd pick a steady*—in party hats and a dusting of confetti.

"It isn't 2400 yet," Marya said, sliding into the other side of the booth. Her face was flushed, but only he could have told she had been drinking; there was no slur in her voice, and the movements were quick and graceful.

She's a damned attractive woman, Lefarge thought. In a strong-featured athletic way, but there were plenty of men who liked that. Plenty who liked her intelligence and sardonic humor, as well, but she seemed to sheer off from anything lasting. *Hell, this isn't the time to worry.*

They all turned to watch the screen again; it was coming around to time for the countdown to midnight. It blanked, and there was a roar of protest from the crowd, redoubled when an NPS newscaster appeared. Sheila Gilbert, he remembered; something of a star of serious news analysis, a hook-nosed woman with a patented smile. She looked . . . *frightened out of her wits*, he thought suddenly. And it took something fairly hairy to do that to a professional like Gilbert. There was a sudden feeling like a trickle of ice down his stomach to his crotch: fear. Lefarge and Marya glanced at each other and back at the screen.

" . . . President Gupta Rao of the Progressive Party has committed suicide."

"Shit!" Lefarge whispered.

"I repeat, the President of the Indian Republic has shot himself; the body was found in his office only two hours ago. The suicide note contains a confession, confirmed by other sources in the Indian capital . . . " More shouting from the customers, but less noisy; Lefarge strained to hear, and then the volume went up. " . . . *Hindi Raj* militants have documentary proof that OSS agents were responsible for planting the information which led to the Hamburger Scandal and the disgrace of late Presidential candidate Rashidi. Riots have been reported in Allahabad and —"

It was a full ten seconds before Lefarge felt Cindy's tugging on his arm. Gently, he laid a finger over her mouth and looked at his sister.

"We'd better —"

"*Attention!*" The civil-defense sigil came on the viewer, cutting into the newscast. "*Alliance Defense Forces announcement. All military personnel Category Seven and above please report to your duty stations. I repeat—*"

DRAKA FORCES BASE ANTINOOUS
PROVINCE OF BACTRIA
DOMINATION OF THE DRAKA
JANUARY 14, 1976
1500 HOURS

" 'Tent-*hut!*"

The briefing room was in the oldest section of the base; built fifty years before, when this had been part of newly-conquered northern Afghanistan. Built for biplanes, ground-support craft dropping fragmentation bombs and poisongas on the last *badmashi* rebels in the hills, when the Janissary riflemen had flushed them out. Yolande blinked at the thought: two generations . . . her own parents squalling infants, way down in the Old Territories. Her birthplace still outside the Domination . . . A few banners and trophies on the walls, otherwise plain whitewash and brown tile.

Fifty years from biplanes to the planets, Yolande thought as she saluted. *Not bad.*

"Service to the State!"

"*Glory to the Race!*" A crisp chorus from every throat.

"At ease." The hundred-odd pilots sank back into their chairs.

The hooting of the wind came faintly through the thick concrete walls, and the air was crackling dry. There was very little outside that you would want to see. Pancake-flat irrigated farmland hereabouts, near the Amu Darya, and the climate was nearly Siberian in winter; even more of a backwater than Italy, unless you were interested in archaeology. The hunting was not bad, some tiger in the marshes along the river, and snow leopard in the mountains. Quite beautiful up there, in an awesome sort of way; the Hindu Kush made the Alps look like pimples. Otherwise nothing to do but fly and study, almost like being back at the Academy. She and Myfwany had both passed their Astronautical Institute finals last month, and could expect transfer soon. Now *that* would be something . . .

"The balloon's going up day after tomorrow."

The squadron-commander grinned at them with genial savagery. Her nickname among the pilots was *Mother Kali*, and not without reason. There was a collective rustle of attention. Yolande felt a lurch be**low** the breastbone, and reached out to squeeze her lover's hand.

"Here's the basic situation." The wall behind her lit with a map of the Indian subcontinent; the Domination flanked it to the north and west, the Indian Ocean and the ancient Draka possession of Ceylon to the south.

"The Indians pulled out of the Alliance last week, aftah the headhunters revealed the little nasty the Alliance OSS pulled on they last election . . . but it's almighty confused. Burma—" an area in the lower right corner shaded from white to gray—"counterseceded back to the Alliance, and there was fightin' in Rangoon. Alliance seems to have won, worse luck. We've stayed conspicuously peaceful"—a snicker of laughter ran through the room—"which put the secessionists firmly in power in New Delhi. Just long enough fo' the ground an' air units the Indians were contributin' to the Alliance to transfer their allegiance to the new Indian Republic, but *not* long enough fo' them to settle their share of the orbital assets. We've recognized the new government, an' they've reciprocated. Nice of them."

Another wave of chuckles. "Which means as of the present, *everybody* has recognized the new government as sovereign. *But.*" The squadron commander tapped her pointer into a gloved hand. "But, the Alliance hasn't yet signed a defense treaty with the Republic, which has no credible nuclear strike force *or* defenses. We've got a window of opportunity; now we're goin' jump through, shootin'. Calculation is that the Alliance will run around screamin' and shoutin' and do fuck-all fo' the week or so we need to overrun India. We'll carefully avoid any provocation elsewhere, or in space. Now, befo' I proceed to the tactical situation, any questions?"

"Ma'am?" A man's voice, from the seat on the other side of Myfwany.

Yolande turned to look at him. Pilot Officer Timothy Wellington; a slim man of middle height, with a conservative side-crop and a seal-brown mustache, a jaunty white scarf tucked into his black flight-overall. She gritted her teeth and fought back a flush. Not that he was a *bad* sort. City boy, from Peking; knowledgeable about the visual arts, worth talking to on poetry. She had even quite enjoyed the several occasions when Myfwany had invited him over for the night. *I just wish he'd learn not to presume on acquaintance*, she thought. *Also that Myfwany would slap him down more often*. He had been hanging around entirely too much lately.

"What if the Alliance treat it as an attack on they own territory?" Wellington said.

The commander shrugged. "Everybody dies," she answered. "Any other questions?"

He sat down and leaned over to whisper in Myfwany's ear; she turned a laugh into a cough. Yolande keyed her notebook and poised to record, elbowing her friend surreptitiously in the ribs. *This is important*.

"Our role will be to interdict the medium-high altitudes. We're doin' this invasion from a standin' start, can't mobilize without scaring the prey back into the Yankee camp. We expect the Alliance to continue feedin' the Indians operational intelligence. No way we can complain of that as hostile activity. Our preliminary sweep will be—"

"Woof!" Myfwany said, as they cleared the doorway. "And to think, only yesterday I was complainin' on how *dull* everythin' is around here!"

Yolande nodded, standing closer for the comfort of bodywarmth. "Some of that schedulin' looks tricky; we're dependin' hard-like on the groundpounders takin' the forward bases."

She stretched. "Well, let's go catch dinner." Their squadron had always been theoretically tasked with neutralizing Alliance turboram assets in India . . . in the Final War nobody had been expecting. *This won't be the Final*, she told herself firmly. Images of thermonuclear fire blossoming across Claestum painted themselves on the inside of her eyelids, and she shivered slightly. *Nobody's that crazy, not even us. I hope*.

"Ah—" Myfwany hesitated, then leaned against the corridor wall. "Ah, actually, sweetlin', Tim sort of invited me ovah to his quarters fo' the evenin' and night. Yo' don't mind, do yo'?"

"Oh." Yolande swallowed. A pulse beat in her neck. "Mmm, was I included in the invite?"

"I'm sure Tim wouldn't mind 'tall, iff'n yo' wants to, sweet."

"I—" Yolande looked aside for a moment. "Let's go, then."

CENTRAL INDIAN FRONT
15,000 METERS
JANUARY 16, 1976
1400 HOURS

"Shitshitshit," Yolande muttered to herself. *Myself and the flight recorder*, thought some remote corner of her mind.

The canopy of the Falcon VI-a went black above her for an instant. Automatic shielding against optical-frequency lasers—the Alliance platforms in LEO had decided that that did not constitute intervention, and all the Draka orbital battlestations could do was to respond in kind. She banked, and acceleration slammed her against the edge of the clamshell, vision graying. The Indian P-70 was still dodging, banking; they were at Mach 3, and if he went over the border into Alliance airspace the battlestations would not let him back in. There was no way to dodge orbital free-electron lasers; they could slash you out of the sky in seconds . . . as the Alliance platforms would do to *her* if she followed the Indian too far.

"*Bing!*" Positive lock on her Skorpion AAM.

"Away!" she barked. The computer fired, and the Falcon shuddered, on the verge of tumbling as the brief change in airflow struck. The canopy cleared, and she had a glimpse of the missile streaking away. Then her fingers were moving on the pressure pads; *cut* thrust, bank-turn-dive, and the red line on the console map coming closer and closer. Closer, *too* close.

The squadron override sounded. "*Ingolfsson, watch it.*"

"I am, I am," she grunted, feeling the aircraft judder. Blood surged under the centrifugal pull, and she could feel a sudden sharp pain at the corner of one eye, a warm trickle; a bloodvessel had burst. *Fuckin' insane, these things aren't designed for this limited airspace.* Like playing tackleball on a field of frictionless ice, with instant cremation the penalty for touching the sides. A turboram could cross India from edge to edge in thirty seconds or less.

The calm voice of the machine. "Impact on target. Kill."

There was no time even for exultation. "Myfwany, yo' pickin' up anythin'?"

"Not in our envelope." Her voice was adrenaline-hoarse. "Yo' gettin' too low, 'Landa."

"Tell me."

The edges of the wing-body were starting to glow cherry-red, and the sensors told the same story. Ionization was fouling up her electrodetectors, too; she might be too fast for the low-altitude turbojet fighters, but anything optimized for the thicker layers that happened to be in the right position would eat her.

"Come on, yo' cow," she muttered to the aircraft. "*Up we go.*"

The ground was shockingly close, and she was still far too fast. *All right, double Immelman and up.* Her fingers cut thrust, and the aircraft flipped. G-force snapped her head back, and for an instant she was staring at the maplike view of the subcontinent below. A point of blue-white light blinked against the brown-green land, and the console confirmed it. *.5 kiloton.* A blast of charged particles. *Radiation bomb.* A nuke warhead designed to maximize personnel damage, wouldn't want to mess up the new property, *shitfire I'm glad I'm not down there . . .*

Pulling up, six G's, seven. Nose to the sky, open throttle and here we go, fangs out and hair on fire, *heeeeeeee-aaaaah.* Feed thrust, overmax; speed bottoming out at Mach 1.7 and climbing, 2.1, 2.2, 2.8. The screens showed Myfwany closing in to wing guard position. And—*damn.* The canopy went black. *Petty. Very petty.*

The squadron commander broke in again. "No bogies, I repeat, no bogies our quadrant. Good work. Check fungibles."

Her eyes went back to the console. "Fuel .17, no Skorpions. Full 30mm drums." Close combat was proving to be something of an anachronism.

"All MK units, all MK units, squadron is cleared fo' alternate E-17, mark an' acknowledge."

The exterior temperatures were not falling the way they should; they must be tweaking the laser up there. Yolande spared a moment's snarl for the invulnerable enemies above. *Your day will come, pigs.* E-17 came up on the landscape director, down by her left knee; northern Punjab, enemy base. Status showed heavily cratered runways, fires, no actual fighting and low radiation count, but massive damage to the facilities. *No runways, vertical landing*, she thought unhappily. Which meant no takeoff at all, until the unit support caught up with them; that would burn the last of the fuel. The follow-up waves would be using their base back in Bactria, logical but unpleasant.

"All MK, take yo' birds in," the commander's voice continued.

Yolande felt a vast stomach-loosening rush of relief, and pushed it back with a savage effort. "It isn't ovah 'till it's ovah," she told herself. Aloud: "Acknowledged."

"*CRACK.*"

Marya Lefarge threw herself flat and rolled, over the edge of the wall. The ditch was two meters down, but soft mud. She leopard-crawled, did a sprint and forward roll over a bank of shrubs, fell to her belly again, rolled down a short slope and raised her pencil-periscope to look back. Smoke, smoke rising against the far blue-white line of the Himalayas that towered over the Punjab plains. Sunset already beginning to tinge the snowpeaks with crimson. The line of the retaining wall, and . . . helmets. Enemy, ridged fore-and-aft and with two short antennae at the rear. Their IV and millimetric scanners would be looking for movement, for human-band temperature points.

Two Draka troopers had vaulted down from the terrace. The building above it had been the HQ offices of Chandragupta Base; now it was burning rubble, after the cluster-shell hits. The troopers were bulky and sexless, visored helmets and articulated cermet armor; they went to their stomachs and scanned back and forth across the flat runway before them. Nothing moved on it, nothing except the smoke and flames from smashed aircraft that had been caught on launch; one had gotten into the air before the homing missile hit, and its ruins sprawled across half a kilometer. The air was heavy with the oily smell of burning fuel and scorched earth.

There were smashed revetment-hangars across the way. Something *was* moving there. A trio of low beetling shapes moved out onto the pavement, their gun-pods swiveling; light tanks. The two Draka infantrymen rose and trotted towards them, and more followed over the retaining wall. They moved with impressive ease under their burdens of armor and equipment, spreading out into a dispersed formation. *Good*, Marya thought. *They'll be concentrating on the link up.* She waited a hundred heartbeats, then a hundred more. Waiting was the worst. Running and shooting you didn't have time to be frightened . . . *Mission first*, she reminded herself. A bollixed-up mission to save remnants from the worst disaster in decades; there was data in the base computers which must *not* be allowed into enemy hands.

Marya rose into a crouch. She was wearing a standard Alliance base-personnel grey coverall, with Indian markings. That fitted her cover identity; the bomblet launcher in her hands did not . . . Runway to her left and rear, hectares of it, swarming with enemy troops now. HQ complex ahead, and she would just have to take her chances. A deep breath, and *now*. She sprinted back along her path, leapt, caught the lip of the wall and rolled over it. Nothing on the way back, nothing but a steamcar in the middle of the gardens, bullet-riddled and . . . not empty. A body lying half-out the driver's door, a pistol in one hand. She moved quickly from one cover to the next, feeling lungs hot and taut despite the dry-season cool of the air.

In through the front doors, and there were more bodies, enough to make the air heavy with the burnt-pork-and-shit stink of close combat. Past the front offices, and the light-level sank to a dim gloom, shadows moving with uneven flamelight. She stopped in a doorway long enough to pull the filter over her nose and mouth, then froze. Steps coming down the hall, booted feet.

Sorry if you're a friendly, she thought, and plunged out into the corridor with her finger already tightening.

Schoop. The launcher kicked against her shoulder, and the 35mm projectile was on its way as the Draka assault rifle came up. Marya went boneless and dropped, as the round impacted on the center of the soldier's breastplate. That was a ceramic-fiber-metal-synthetic sandwich . . . but her bomb-let was shaped-charge. The finger of superheated plasma speared through the armor, through vaporizing flesh, splashed against the backplate. Body fluids turned to steam and blew outwards through the soft resistance. Marya threw herself upright and ran forward; she tried to leap the corpse and the spreading puddle around it, but her boots went *tack-tack* on the linoleum for a minute afterwards.

Nothing moved as she tracked through towards the command center. *Critical window*, she thought; the moments between the assault-landing and the arrival of the Intelligence teams. Soldiers had a natural preference for dealing with the things that might shoot back at them, and so might leave an area already swept lightly guarded. She turned another corridor, came to a makeshift barricade. The bodies beyond were Indian, a scratch squad of office workers and one perimeter guard in infantry kit; they bore no wounds, but lay as if they had died in convulsions. Marya's skin itched, as if insects were crawling under it. *Contact nerve agent*, she thought, and put an antidote tab between her back teeth. That might work . . .

The stairs that led down into the control center were ahead. It would be guarded, but . . . She turned aside, into an office. It was empty, with a cup of tea still on the desk and the screen of the terminal flickering, as if the occupant—*Ranjit Singh*, from the nameplate on the door—might return any second. A quick wrench with her knife opened the ventilation shaft. The American pulled a pair of lightmag goggles out of a pocket and slipped them over her head. Darkness vanished, replaced by a peculiar silvery flatness. Marya slung the bomblet-launcher down her back, took a deep breath, and chinned herself on the edge of the ventilator.

Just wide enough, she thought. *Just.*

The Draka working over the base computer had the gearwheel emblem of Technical Section on her shoulder; so did the two gray-uniformed serf Auxiliaries helping her. They were all in battle-armor, though, a technical commando unit tasked with front-line electronic reconnaissance. Marya could see them all, down the short section of vertical shaft; she was lying full-length in the horizontal passageway above, with only her head out. That ought to make her nearly invisible from below, with the wire grille in the ceiling between her and them. And . . . yes, movement just out of sight. Probably troopers, guarding the tech. The peripheral units of the Alliance computer were open, and boxes of crackle-finished Draka electronics set up about it, a spiderweb of plug-in lines and cross-connections.

The OSS agent strained to hear.

"Careful, careful!" the Draka was saying. "Up ten . . . Fo'
mo'. Right, now keep the feed modulated within ten percent
of those parameters, and she won't blow when Ah open the
casin'."

Another figure, a middle-aged Indian in uniform, with his
arms secured behind his back. A bayoneted rifle rested between his shoulderblades, jabbed lightly.

"Yes, indeed," he babbled in singsong English. "That is
the way of it."

Too bad. The black-uniformed TechSec specialist pulled
the visor of her helmet down and took up a miniature cutting
torch. *Cracking the core unit,* Marya thought grimly. The
embedded instruction sets of a central computer and the
crucial hard-memory were physically confined in its core,
even on civilian models. This was a maximum-security military Phoebos, and it would be set to slag down unless you
were *very* careful.

Careful is the word, Marya thought. This mission was
important enough to make her expendable . . . but there was
no point in being reckless. Her lips moved back from her
teeth behind the mask. What was it Uncle Nat used to say?
"A good soldier has to be ready to die. A suicidal one just
leaves you with another damned empty slot to train someone
for."

If I push the launcher over the edge at arm's length, she
thought, *and then drop the satchel charge right away, the
ceiling should shelter me from most of the blast.* That would
certainly take care of the mission, now that the Draka had
conveniently opened up the armored protection around the
core. *Then I can go back up the shaft, and try and make it
out.*

Soundlessly, she whispered: "And maybe the horse *will*
learn to sing."

Millimeter by millimeter, she inched backward until only
the end of the launcher tube was over the lip of the vertical
shaft. Her other hand brought the explosive charge up, plas-
tique and metal and soft padded overcase. It scraped gently
against the tube wall in the narrow space between hip and
panel, and the sound seemed roaringly loud. No louder than
the beat of blood in her ears. *Stupid, stupid,* a voice called at
the back of her mind. *You volunteered, you're too stupid to
live, you could be* home *now.*

"Fuck it," she said, and pulled the trigger.

*   *   *

"Mistis—" the Janissary decurion began, as the canopy of Yolande's fighter slid back and she rose from the opening clamshell restraints. The cool air of the Indian night poured in, lit by a swollen moon and the lingering fires. Then eye-drying warmth as the inflow crackled across the fuselage of her aircraft. The Draka picked up her ground-kit, machine-pistol, and helmet. There were a half-dozen figures in infantry armor, with a flat cart of some sort.

Then the serf soldier's voice altered. "Mistis Yolande!" He saluted and flipped up the faceplate of his helmet.

Yolande stared for a moment; it was an unremarkable face, heavy beak nose and olive complexion . . . then memory awoke.

"Ali?" she said. "Rahksan's Ali?"

His grin showed white as she stepped up onto the rim of the cockpit and jumped down, careful to avoid the savage residual heat of the leading edges.

"The same, Mistis. Swears it like home leave to see yo'."

"Freya bless, small world," she continued, and gave him a light punch on one shoulder. Her gloved fist rang on the lobster-tail plates of his armguard. The legion blazon on it showed a hyena's skull biting down on a human thighbone; that was the *Devil Dogs*, one of the better subject-race units. "An' yo' comin' up in it, Ali. I tells yo' ma, first thing."

His fist rang on the breastplate as saluted again, then noticed his squad glancing at each other. Myfwany's Falcon lifted its canopy.

"Ah, Mistis, we got field-shelters set up over to there." He pointed, and she saw prefabricated revetments on an uncratered stretch of runway. Two big winged tilt-rotor transports, as well; one began reving for takeoff as she looked. "We's gotta get y' plane towed ovah there. Yo' support team's comin' through, later tonight. We's got perimeter guard."

"Myfwany, yo' remembers Ali, from Claestum?" The red-head came up, with a bounce in her stride, despite the sweat that plastered the curls to her forehead. "Coincidence, hey?" The squad was hooking the cart's towing hitch to the nose of her aircraft. "Carry on, decurion; nice to know mah bird's in good hands."

"Eurrch," Yolande said. "C'mon, love, why don't we turn in?" Most of the squadron was there, but it would be a day or two before they had anything to do but stay out of the way. In the meantime, they had been assigned quarters. The original occupants certainly had no need of them . . .

The prisoners were being held in a messhall; sorted in groups by rank and age, in squares marked off by colored rope. The guards were Security Directorate, Intervention Squad specialists, but there were a fair number of Draka making inspection; Citizen officers of the Janissary legion, pilots from their outfit, others. She looked at the captives with mild distaste; they had been stripped of their uniforms as a precautionary measure, and secured with the old-style restraints, chain and rod links that bound elbows and wrists together behind the back. Indians, mostly. Base techs, the sort of work that was done by unarmed Auxiliaries in the Domination's armed forces. A few had the glazed look of shock, or docilizing drugs; most were openly terrified, even *crying*.

"Yo' can turn in iff'n you wants to, 'Landa," Myfwany said. She was smiling, and there was a glitter to her eyes; Yolande swallowed past a hollow feeling. *I love you dearly, but there are times when you make me angry enough to* spit, *sweetheart*, she thought resignedly.

"Oh, all right," Yolande said. "Let's take a look."

They walked down the edge of one of the green-rope enclosures. Green for lowest-priority, younger specimens. She supposed they would be sold off, after the fighting, or sent to work camps, something of that sort. Her nose wrinkled; they stank of fear, and from the pungency, some had pissed themselves. Across the room there was a high scream. Yolande looked up and saw the Security troopers dragging an older prisoner out of the red-corded pen for interrogation. A paunchy type in his fifties, already babbling. *Glad they're not doin' it in public*, she thought idly. *Headhunters, eurgh.* Necessary work, she supposed, but disgusting.

"This one looks interestin'," Myfwany was saying. "On yo' feet, wench."

Yolande looked back. The prisoner had risen easily despite the restraints. In her late twenties, she estimated; much lighter-skinned than most of the others. Good figure, very nice muscle tone for a serf; cropped black hair, expressionless dark eyes . . . The neck was number-bare, that looked unnatural. *Sixty aurics basic*, Yolande thought. *Depending on where she's sold, of course.*

"Who're yo'?" Myfwany asked the serf. Silence, and then the Draka struck. *Crack.* The open-handed blow rocked the prisoner's head back; Yolande was surprised she kept her feet. Sighing, she glanced aside. *Myfwany gets too rough with them, sometimes,* she thought unhappily. Of course, this one was feral and had to be taught submission, but still . . .

"Marya Lenson." *Crack.* A backhanded blow this time.

"That's Marya Lenson, *Mistis,* serf." The Security guard glanced up, came over idly twirling the rubber truncheon by the thong around his wrist.

"Mistis." The serf's voice stayed toneless-flat.

"Indian?" Myfwany put a finger under the serf's chin, turned her head sideways. "Europoid, I'd swear."

"My parents were from California, Mistis."

Myfwany turned to Yolande. "A Yank! What say we sign this'n out and play with it, 'Landa?" she said.

Yolande sighed. "Oh, come on, sweet," she said exasperatedly. *I hope we're not going to have a fight, like we did when you wanted Lele.* It had taken two days of not speaking to each other before Myfwany realized she was serious about letting the servant say no. "Where's the fun in that?"

"We can use aphrodizine," Myfwany said impatiently.

"Eurg." Not that the aphrodisiac didn't *work,* but . . . "Look, sweet, yo' just got after-fight jitters. Yo' don't really want to—"

Myfwany released the serf and spun to confront her friend. "Look yo'self," she hissed. "I'm not yo' keeper, Ingolfsson, and yo' not mine. Yo've got somethin' better to do, go do it." The green eyes turned heavy-lidded. "Tim or someone be glad to help me out."

Yolande felt shock close her throat. This was fear, not the hot sensation of life-danger up in the clouds, but dread coiling at the pit of her stomach. She forced a smile.

"Oh, don't get so heavy 'bout it, love!" A glance aside at the serf. *Myfwany'll probably get tired fairly soon.* "Iffn' yo's set on it, certainly." *Not as if there was anything actually wrong with it, after all. You have to compromise on differing tastes.* "Let's . . . let's take a walk an' check on the birds, first, hey? Get some fresh air."

"Sure, 'Landa-sweet," Myfwany said. She smiled and took the other Draka's hand. Yolande felt the knot in her stomach melt. *Or most of it,* she thought. *Oh, well.* "I've got a rotten temper. Don't know why yo' puts up with me, sometimes."

She called the guard over, palmed the identifier clipped to his belt. "Send this one ovah to our quarters, would yo'?"

Frederick Lefarge felt the sweat trickle down from the rim of his helmet, itching under the armor and camouflage smock. He glanced at his watch; 2000 hours. The pickup squad was in a stand of tall pale-barked trees not far from what had been the perimeter wire of Chandragupta Base. A dozen of them, with nothing but their fieldcraft and two boxes of very sophisticated electronics to keep them out of the tightening Draka net. Two were wounded, and he didn't think Smythe was going to make it, he'd been far too close to a radiation bomb yesterday, when the rest of them had been sheltered in the cellar. Vomiting blood was not a good sign, at least.

"Sor." Winters, the Englishman. Professional NCO in the Cumberland Borderers before transfer to the OSS special forces. Very reliable. "Sor, it's past time."

She isn't going to make it, he thought. *Either she's dead or she should be*. He fought down the hot flash of rage, let it mingle with fear until it became something cold and leaden in his gut. Something that would not interfere with the job at hand . . . He remembered a moment in Santa Fe, and the pistol in Marya's hand unwavering upon him. *We always knew the price*, he thought. *Go with God, ma soeur*.

And *her* mission accomplished—the explosion in the base HQ proved that—but nothing beyond. He raised the visor of his helmet and bent to the eyepiece of the spyglass. There were pickups all over the operational area, where his men had left their optical-thread connectors. The fires were mostly out now. Those had been from the initial blitz, suborb missiles with precision-guided conventional explosives. Dibblers for the runways, earth-piercers for the hardened weapons points, then a rolling surf of antipersonnel submunitions. The assault-troops had come on the heels of those—1st Airborne Legion, Citizen Force elite troops, but they had moved out once the area was secured, now there was a brigade of Janissaries doing clear-and-hold. And support personnel, Intelligence, transports, two squadrons of low-altitude VTOL gunboats, another of Falcons.

And now they think it's secured, he thought grimly. *Time to disabuse them*.

"Hit it, Jock," he said.

*   *   *

"And we—" Myfwany stopped. "What the fuck was *that*, Ali?"

They and the Janissaries were standing outside a dugout. The explosion was a kilometer away, across the base. A flash, and the muffled *whump* a second later, a ball of orange flame rising into the soft Indian night. The troopers went into an instinctive crouch, and Ali cursed, rolling back into the sand-bagged slit and reaching for the groundline com.

"Suh?" he said. "Post Six, second tetrarchy—shit, it out!"

Another explosion, and another; a rippling line in an arc along the perimeter opposite them. Yolande and Myfwany exchanged a glance and pulled on their ground-helmets, slipping down the visors and turning the night to a pale imitation of day. Each had a tiny dot of strobing red light at the lower left-hand corner; jamming. Then a *real* explosion; the two Draka threw themselves flat at the harsh white glare. Even reflected around the edges of their visors it was enough to dazzle, and the shockwave lifted them up and slammed them down again hard enough to stun and bruise on the unyielding pavement.

Yolande heard one of the Janissaries shouting. "Nuke? Dec, was that a nuke?" Her eyes darted down to the readout on the sleeve of her flight suit. No radiation above the nervous-making background already there, and a spear of blue-white flame was already rising from behind the broken hangars. Secondary explosions bellowed, like echoes of that world-numbing blast.

"No, it ain't," Ali was saying. "That the fuel store."

Liquid hydrogen and methane, Yolande realized. High-energy fuels for high-performance craft, difficult to transport. One of the reasons the attack plan had made this base a priority target in the first place. And—

"The birds!" she shouted to Myfwany. Fatigue and worry vanished in the rush of adrenaline, at the thought of the turboram fighters caught helpless on the ground. The Falcons were two thousand meters distant, behind the parked assault-transports.

Myfwany nodded. "Ali, yo' tasked with that?"

The burly Janissary was climbing back out of the revet-ment. He hesitated for a moment; he was, but having two Citizens along out of the regular chain of command was *not* a good idea . . . The two Draka women saw him shrug and nod, accepting what could not be changed.

"Let's go," he said. "Marcel, Ching, Mustafa, come with me. Brigitte, Nils, Vlachec, hold the position an' report when the com comes back up."

"Now!" Frederick Lefarge kept to one knee and watched the dozen OSS special-ops troopers scurry by. In *toward* the base that now swarmed like a kicked-open termite mound. Their only chance . . .

He rose to his feet and followed. There they were, ten *Buffel* tilt-rotor assault transports, standing ready with their turbines warm. Nobody around them but unarmed ground-crew. The Alliance soldiers could charge on board and take off in ten different directions; the Draka IFF would hesitate crucial seconds before overriding their own electronic identification . . . and the battle was still a chaos of Draka and Indian-held pockets from here to Burma. Just insane enough to have some chance of success. The Springfield-15 seemed light as a twig in his hands; his gaze hopped across the flat expanses of the airbase, watching for movement. *There*. Light armor, moving out of laager in the vehicle park, coasting toward them with air-cushion speed. His hand slapped a switch at his waist.

"Down!" Yolande shouted, when the lines of fire erupted upward out of the stand of trees to their right. She and Myfwany threw themselves apart and forward without breaking stride; she could hear the light impact of her lover's body on the concrete, and seconds later the pounding slam of the Janissary heavy infantry hitting the pavement.

The weapon that had fired was some sort of rocket automortar; she watched the trajectories arch and then plunge back down. Down toward the trio of Cheetah hovertanks that had been approaching them; a hundred meters up the self-forging warheads exploded in disks of fire, sending arrow-heads of incandescent metal streaking for the thin deck-armor of the Draka tanks. The impacts were flashes that would have been dazzling without the guard-functions of her visor. The air-cushion vehicles bounced down as if slapped by the hand of an invisible giant, then exploded in gouts of fuel-fire and ammunition glare. Hot warm air struck her like a pillow, and a pattering rain of cermet armor and body-parts began to fall around the soldiers of the Domination.

" 'Landa!" Myfwany called. "Look right, are those hostiles?" Yolande halted and went to ground, concious of the others following the pilot's extended arm.

Frederick Lefarge threw himself to the ground and rolled to one side as the group running on an intercept vector with his opened fire. Muzzle flashes strobed before the silvery light-enhanced shapes of enemy soldiers. Shrapnel flicked at his exposed legs and arms, nothing serious, but he could feel the blood trickle behind the sharp sting. *Can't stop for a slugfest*, went through him. His special-forces unit were only lightly armored, and there was no cover on this artificial concrete desert.

"Eat this!" the OSS trooper beside Lefarge cried, flipping up to his knees and firing a grenade from the launcher beneath the barrel of his S17. It burst with an orange flash behind the enemy firing line; one of the rifles stopped, and there was a scream of pain. Then a chuttering flash from directly ahead; machine-pistol, not the louder growl of a T-7. The trooper who had fired pitched backward, torn open. Lefarge snapped off a burst toward the source and began leopard-crawling forward. Another sound came from near where he had fired, a scream that raised the tiny hairs along the back of his neck.

"Keep them occupied!" he shouted to his men, heading for the cockpit ladder of the *Buffel*. It had a 25mm gatling in its chin turret; if he could reach that . . .

"Keep them occupied!" a voice shouted. Yolande ignored it, braced behind an overturned supply-cart.

"Myfwany?" she called, looking over to where the other Draka had snap-fired last. "Hey, Myfwany?"

There was no movement. A long shape lying motionless on the concrete; impossible to see detail at this distance. Machine-pistol resting on the ground, no movement.

"Myfwany?" Yolande said, this time a whisper. Then she was moving, a sprint that leaned her almost horizontal to the ground. She forward-rolled the last five meters, rolling in beside her friend. "Myfwany?"

The body moved into her hands, infinitely familiar, utterly strange. Moving loosely, slack. Blood flowing down her hands from the band of black wetness across Myfwany's chest. Bits of soft armor, bits of bone and flesh; something bubbling and wheezing. Yolande tore off her own helmet, to see by natural light. There was enough to show the lashes flutter across the amber eyes, focus on her. The lips below moved, beneath the rills of blood that covered them. Perhaps to say a name, but there was no breath left for it. She slumped, with a total relaxation as the wheezing stopped. Yolande felt a sound building in her throat, and she knew that everything would end when she uttered it.

The firefight hammered through the darkness; Lefarge flipped his visor up for better depth-perception and ran crouching. He was almost on the two Draka before he saw them. Lying on the pavement, one with the utter limpness of the newly dead, the other holding her. His rifle swung round, clicked empty; the magazine ejected itself and dropped to the runway with a hollow plastic clatter. For a moment only the eyes held him. Huge, completely dark in a stark-white elfin face daubed with blood, framed in hair turned silver by the moonlight. They saw him; somehow he knew they were recording every detail, but it was as if no active mind lived behind them. Then he was past, his feet pounding up the aluminum treads of the transport's gangway.

"Hunh!" Marya jerked awake, surprised that she had slept at all. Dawn was showing rosy through the window; the air smelled of cool earth, explosives and fire and dead humans. And the door had swung open.

A Draka stood there. One of the ones who had looked her over in the prisoner pen earlier. Short, slender, and blond. Different; her uniform was smoke-stained, grimy; there were speckles of dried blood across her face. The face . . . the eyes were huge, pupils distended with shock. The American felt a clammy sensation: not quite fear, although that was in it. As if she was in the presence of something that should not be seen . . . The dead-alive eyes focused on her, and Marya saw a spray-injector in the other's hand.

"It's yo' fault." The words came in a light, soft voice. Almost a whisper, and in utter monotone. "I was weak, squeamish. She wanted to play with yo', and I didn't, so I got her to go fo' a walk, thought she'd fo'get the idea. She's dead. I saw his face . . . he's not here. They got some of the planes, but she's ddddd—" A brief stutter, and the marble perfection of the face writhed for an instant, then settled back. "Dead."

The Draka touched the controls of the injector, held it to her own neck and pulled the trigger. Shuddered. A degree of life returned to the locked muscles of her face as she lowered it and changed the controls.

"This is fo' yo'," she said, her voice slightly thick now. "Relaxant, muscle weakener, maximum safe dosage of aphrodizine." The cold metal touched Marya on the arm, but she scarcely felt the sting of the injection. It was impossible even to look away from those eyes, like windows into a wound. Something flowed across her mind, warm and sticky, pushing conciousness back into a room at the rear of her head. Fingers as strong as wire flipped her onto her stomach and began to unfasten the restraints.

"We're goin' to have a sort of celebration in memory of her, just this once," the Draka said. "And then I can think up somethin' else for yo' to do."

CHAPTER ELEVEN

NEGOTIATORS REACH AGREEMENT [NPS]. Sources close to the Alliance Chairman's office reported today that a negotiated settlement to the clashes with the Domination in the asteroid belt is within reach. "We've reached a mutual standoff," our source said, in response to questions. "We can each inflict about the same amount of damage, but without strategic results. It probably wouldn't have started except for the upsurge of popular anger after the Indian Incident."

Details remain to be settled, but the basis of the agreement is said to be a mutual recognition of the status quo; no armed action is to take place as long as neither side attempts to enter "zones" of varying size around the present points of occupation in the belt. While complex, these arrangements will essentially give the Alliance control of about 75% of the material orbiting within the proclaimed limits of the "belt" (an area defined roughly as the space between the orbits of Mars and Jupiter), and an even higher proportion of the highly valuable larger objects. Free transit to the outer system will be guaranteed for both parties. Space Force experts insist that this agreement gives the Alliance a considerable victory. As economic and military activity beyond Earth increases geometrically, demand for the resources available in the asteroids will soar. The Draka hold on the Saturnian and Jovian moons does not offer comparable advantage, while Mars, Venus, and Mercury are too heavy-gravity to be of immediate use.

The New York Times
World In Review
Sunday, August 15, 1977

TRANSIT STATION SEVENTEEN
MASAHD, PROVINCE OF HYRCANIA
DOMINATION OF THE DRAKA
JANUARY 23, 1976

Marya Lefarge looked up. The train was slowing, and there
was a stirring in the cramped darkness. It had been three
days on the train. That was the first thing she had been aware
of since the drug-haze lifted: being pushed off the truck and
onto the train in Kabul. West and north since then; smooth
steady hum of wheels on welded rail. Cold, but not freezing,
and they all had thick rough overalls. Ration bars, water
enough for drinking, and a chemical toilet. The forty prisoners were a mixed bag from all over India, city-folk mostly,
with a fair sprinkling of military. None past middle age or
younger than their teens.

The smell was not too bad, now that the dociline had worn
off the last cases, enough that they could clean themselves
and use the toilet; natural leaders had taken charge, gotten
the car organized and arranged rosters to look after the inca-
pable. Sleep had been difficult; the metal floor was hard and
many screamed in their sleep. *And the nightmares were
bad—* Forget that. Watch and wait, opportunity would come.
She put her eye to a crack along the doorframe. The railcar
was well-made but old, much-repaired. Nobody challenged
her post by this drafty spot. Obviously the car had been made
for its present purpose; impossible to break out of without
cutting tools . . . There had been mountains outside, for a
while, then flat desert. Now it was afternoon, and they were
traveling along a river valley. Wide flat fields, wheat and
alfalfa stubble, or cornstalks, thinly drifted with snow; boundaries were poplar trees, and she could see occasional piles of
irrigation pipe by a crossroads.

A road ran by the right-of-way, plain black asphalt;
steamtrucks passed now and then, sometimes a private car.
The traffic was thickening, and now they were passing through
a belt of open parkland. Other rail tracks converged, until
they were in a broad field of them. Other trains, too; freight

cars, flatbeds with standard-sized cargo containers. A set of double-decker cattle cars, loud and odorous with their bawling freight. *Like us,* she thought, and smiled savagely, pulling the handcuffs taut between her wrists. Military traffic, logistics trucks and armored personnel carriers chained down to flats, moving east; reinforcements for India, probably. The open fields beyond the rail gave way to buildings, low-slung factory types, gray concrete with skylights; she might almost have been in a textile town somewhere in Ohio.

Darkness; they were in a covered station-building. Marya worked her way back into the crowd. A rattle outside, and they all blinked at the harsh fluorescent lights. There was a blast of slightly warmer air.

"Out, out, everybody out," an amplified voice shouted. Marya could see the plank barricades on either side of the door; the rest of the train was invisible noise.

Hands reached in and dragged the nearest through; the rest crowded to follow. Marya kept to the center of the mass, head slightly down so as not to attract attention, eyes flickering to collect data. *Study everything. Knowledge is survival.* They were being herded down wide bleak-lit corridors of concrete block, between lines of guards. Not armed, not police; serfs in boots and gray wool overalls, swinging hard rubber truncheons.

"Stop!" The end of the corridors, a gate.

Collisions, cursing, blows directed at random. Through a stamped-steel door into a room with multiple exits, and a green-uniformed Orpo guard running a reader over the bar-coded plastic labels stapled to the breasts of their overalls. More greencoats along the wall behind him, and these had machine-pistols and shockrods in their hands.

"Left," the man said, and gave her a shove; she staggered into another prisoner. A gateway there, with an observation camera and some cryptic letter-number code above, stenciled on the bare concrete. In front of her a young man turned, tried to run back; one of the Orpos stepped forward and slashed at him with the shockrod. He shrieked and convulsed, falling face-first to the floor.

"Pick him up, freshmeats," the guard snarled at the two prisoners nearest. "Or yaz get fuckin' same!" The Orpo was a short wide-shouldered man heavy with muscle, a flat snubnosed slavic face and shaven skull that gleamed in the bright lights. Marya darted forward and bent to help the fallen man;

someone else took the other arm, and they carried him, dazed, into the next room. Blood was running down his face from the broken nose, but after a dozen paces he was able to walk.

"That's it." Another bellow and the steel grille slammed shut behind them. "Line them up."

This time they were in a rectangular room a hundred meters by twenty. There was no immediate roof; instead the walls ran up three times a man's height and ended in steel walkways with guards pacing along them. Far overhead were girders and panels, like a warehouse, with arc-lights glaring down. Squinting, she could make out more cameras, and what might be automatic guns. Certainly gas dispensers. Hands shoved at her, and she returned her attention to the ground level. There were twenty turntable-mounted chairs along the opposite wall, like dentist's chairs without padding, each surrounded by instruments swung out on jointed booms from the chairs. A serf technician waited by each—neatly dressed serfs this time, without the bruiser-muscular look of the others she had seen since the train.

The guards were forming them up in lines of five in front of each chair, between painted white marks; there was a fair amount of shoving and shouting, but with two greencoats for each line it went quickly. For the first time she had time to notice the smell of the place, a combination of locker room and factory and slum police station, cheap soap and disinfectant and fear. And old concrete and metal; this place had been here for a long time, generations. She could see discolorations in the floor, places where partitions and wiring had been changed.

"Shuck to the waist," a guard shouted. The guards demonstrated on those first in line; overall unzipped and allowed to fall back. Marya complied, feeling her skin roughen in the dry chill. A few resisted, and there was the sharp frying-bacon sound of shockrods in action, choked moans from throats clamped tight. Echoes from above, off the roofing; this whole vast building must be divided into chambers like this.

"First rank, to the chairs." Marya swallowed dryly and looked away, realizing what this must be. There were unindentifiable machine sounds . . . Some of those waiting stared at the process before them, others at the ground or their feet or the walkways above. Few would meet her eyes.

"Next!"

She walked forward, feeling detached, feeling the pulse beating in her throat and ears. *Maman never had her number removed,* she remembered. *She could live with it. So can I.*

The chair was more cold plastic. Bands fastened around her, and a helmet-like arrangement came down over her eyes. The technician fiddled with a screen and keyboard fixed to the rear of the chair as it tilted back.

"Keep y' eyes open," he said. A singsong accent under the Draka slur, probably local. Something flickered at her eyes; retina scan. Marya felt a tug at the loose fabric bunched around her waist; that must be the serf feeding the bar-coded tag into his machine. "Blood sample next," he said; she could hear a yawn through it. Something sharp stabbed her in the forearm, then a cold medicinal-smelling spray. "Spread y' hands on th' grips." A hum; finger and palm prints.

A metallic sound, and a cold bar of metal touched her neck below the right ear. "This hurts," the bored serf's voice continued. More clamps immobilized her head.

"Ssss!" That forced out of her before she could clench her lips together.

More cries of pain along the line of seats, someone wailing. Cold stabbing along the bar pressed to her skin, then the bar of metal swung away, and another medicinal spray; this time it stung sharply, with a sensation that did not go away. The hood swung up, and she squinted at the lights. The technician was rummaging in a bin by his keyboard, full of dull-metal bracelets. They were jointed; he put two around her wrist before grunting satisfaction and snapping one closed. It was about half an inch thick and two broad, featureless except for a small jack-receptor hole on the upper edge. He plugged a lead into that, and she could hear him keying behind her; then the jack was removed, replaced with a threaded plug. The auto-tattooing machine hummed and extruded a piece of paper. The technician peeled off its backing and slapped it adhesive-down on her arm.

She looked down. **marya-I33M286**

The guard overseeing the room put the megaphone back to his mouth, as the bands released her. "Up!" he barked, and she stood beside the chair. "Dress." The twenty newly neck-numbered serfs zipped their overalls. "Yaz numbers is onna tag. Learn 'em quick." A cage door on the opposite side of the long room opened. "Out through there, move, move,

move." Marya forced her hands down, not to touch the patch of rawness on her neck.

About three hundred of us, Marya estimated. It had taken an hour for the big room to fill; this one was square, under the same warehouse roof. Absolutely blank, except for a waist-high dais and comp terminal at one end. Four of the big steel-mesh doors, one in each wall. No chairs, of course. No talking allowed; one prisoner had persisted, and the guards had picked her up and thrown her into the wall, just hard enough to stun, and the shockrods were always there. There was another white line around them on the floor; the prisoners had learned enough to treat it like a minefield. Marya had worked her way to the second line from front with slow, careful movements. *They're going to give us some sort of information,* she decided. *I'll get it all, and make my own use of it.*

This place had the depressing regularity of a factory; it was designed to make you feel like sausage-meat. *That is information, too.* The door behind the dais opened, and two more Orpos stepped up on it, one going to the terminal; she laid a hand on the screen, then made a few keystrokes. A tall woman, hard to tell age with the shaven head. The uniform was a little more elaborate, with a sidearm and complicated equipment on a webbing belt; she had the traditional metal gorget around her neck on a chain. *Chain-dog,* Marya remembered. *That's what the serfs call the Order Police. Appropriate.*

"All of them supposed to understand talk," Marya heard her say to her companion. *Talk must mean English.* She filed the datum away.

"Right." The voice boomed out over the huddled crowd, amplified now. "Listen up, cattle." The face scanned them; tight skin stretched over bone, a white smile. "Y'all are serfs. I'm a serf. There are serfs and serfs; y'all are cattle, I'm yo' god, understand?" An uneasy silence. "Yaz all from India. Yaz here because our noble mastahs"—Marya's ears pricked; was that a note of sarcasm? *Listen. Wait.*—"are souvenir hunters. That what yaz are. Trinkets. We shippin' yaz fo' that. Sometimes, trinkets get broke."

The Orpo jerked a thumb towards one of the crowd. Marya recognized the young man she had helped earlier, with dried blood caked on his lower face and the nose swollen. A Bengali, slight and dark and with a nervous handsomeness apart from the injury, about twenty. A junior officer in the Indian ground forces, from his mannerisms. The crowd parted to leave him in a bubble of space as the guards closed in, shoved him roughly to the edge of the dais. The Orpo noncom had lit a cigarette; now she flicked ash off the end and looked down at the Indian.

"Just in case yaz thinkin' y'all too valuable to hurt," she said, and nodded.

The guards moved in; Marya could see their elbows moving, hear the heavy thuds of fists striking flesh. A moment, and the young man was hunched over when they parted, dazed. The Orpo with the cigarette nodded again, and her companion on the dais stepped forward, pulled a wire loop from his belt and bent to throw it around the man's neck. Marya drove her teeth into her lower lip and made herself watch.

The greencoat grunted and lifted the slight Bengali youth without perceptible effort, holding the toggles of the strangling wire out with elbows slightly bent. The youth bucked, heels drumming against the dais, made sounds. His face purpled under the brown, tongue and eyes bulging, sounds coming from him. From behind her, too, she could hear vomiting. A stain spread down the front of the Bengali's overall, and she could smell the hard shit-stink as his sphincter released; see the thin smile on the executioner's face as he jerked the wire free of the man's neck and cleaned it lovingly with a handkerchief. Blood trickled down Marya's chin.

I will remember you, too, my friend, she thought grimly.

"Yaz nothin'," the amplified voice continued. Gray-suited attendants came in, threw the corpse on a wheeled dolly and took it away. The door slid shut behind them with an echoing clang. "Y'all barely worth the trouble of keepin' alive. Yaz cattle, meat, dogshit. Understand?"

The man who had used the wire noose bellowed: "That's *Yes, thank yo', ma'am,* apeturds!"

Marya opened her mouth and shouted with the others. *Words are nothing,* she told herself.

"One lesson, an' it all yaz need. *Do what y' told.* Anything y' told, anythin' at all. Right now yaz total worthless; with hard work an' tryin', mebbeso yaz work up to just worthless. Understand?"

"YES, THANK YOU, MA'AM!" the prisoners screamed. Someone behind Marya was crying again, slow racking sobs.

"Oh, one mo' thing." The Orpo noncom pulled a flat crackle-finished box from a pouch at her waist; it was roughly the size of a pocketnovel, and a miniature keyboard showed when she opened it. "Them pretty-pretty bracelets. They new. Space research, monitors. Traze yaz anywheres, identify yaz to the comps. Take readin's, heartbeat. And a little nerve hookup, inductor. Right to a center in yaz brains, if y' got any." Her fingers stabbed down on the controller.

PAIN. Marya fell limp and boneless to the floor and her head cracked on the concrete and the skin splitting was wonderful because for a single fractional second it blocked the PAIN but then there was nothing but the PAIN and there had never been anything but PAIN and her heart and lungs were frozen and death would be wonderful but there was no death only PAIN onandonandonandonandon—

It stopped. Marya drew breath, screamed, blood and tears and mucus covering her face, and then she curled around herself and hugged the hand with the controller bracelet and laughed because it *stopped* and the bleeding from her cheek was heaven and the stabbing behind her eyes was better than orgasm and the sensual delight that it had *stopped* and she knew she could never feel pain again because that had been *pain* not the pain of anything not surgery without anesthetic not grief not longing not fear, it had been everything and nothing and pure, purest simple *pain*.

"Up and quiet, or I give yaz anothah five seconds. Now, wasn't that wonderful!" A shriek. "*Understand?*"

"YES, THANK YOU, MA'AM!"

They were all up, quiveringly silent. All except for one woman who lay motionless while the serfs with the dolly came and removed the body, and some of the others looked at it with envy.

"Most places, it's bettah to live than to die. Here, we can make it bettah to die than to live. Remembah that, cattle."

The van doors opened. "Out," the serf guard said. Marya slid forward and looked around; they were in the Citizen section of Mashad. Startling after five days in the blank steel and concrete of the Transit station. The guard pushed her ahead, through a revolving door into a hotel lobby. *Warm.* The first real warmth since Kabul, and a fear worse than the gnawing anxiety of the cell came with it. Across the ornate marble-and-tile splendors of the lobby; the walls were sections from the mosques that had once made this city a wonder of Islamic architecture. An elevator, bronze rails and fretwork, that took them up five stories. Down a corridor, past through a teakwood door. Her mouth was paper-dry again; she called up strength from the reservoir within.

But what do I do when it's empty? she thought for a moment. Then: *Never.*

A serf came to meet them in the vestibule, a room of pale glossy stone walls and floors covered in rugs of incredible colors. She was odd enough to snap Marya's attention aside for a moment; a black woman with yellow eyes and a flamboyant mane of butter-blond hair, in a white robe. There was pity in the brass-colored eyes, and in her soft voice.

"I'm sorry," she said, after signing the invoice the driver presented. "I'm really sorry. I . . . tried."

More corridors, then out into a double-storied lounging room, massive inlaid furniture and a glass wall looking out over a cityscape coming alive with evening lights, reflected on the falling snow. A Draka waiting in a reclining chair, smoking a water-pipe, dressed in a striped *djellaba* with the hood thrown back. The face from Chandragupta Base. Thinner, with dark circles under the huge mad gray eyes; Marya lowered her own to hide the sudden stab of fury she felt. *Looks older.* Marya knew the lines that grief drew. *Good.*

"Stop," the Draka said. "Look at me, serf." Marya looked up. "I'm Yolande Ingolfsson. Remember me?"

"Yes, Mistis," Marya said with equal softness. A smile twitched at the Draka's lips. The American swallowed a sour bubble at the back of her throat.

The black serf spoke, hesitantly. "Mistis—"

"Jolene," Yolande said, "I heard yo' out. I said no. Now if yo' don't want to watch, get out. I'm not angry with yo'. Yet."

The African bowed silently and left; Marya could hear her steps quickening to a run.

"Take off the overall, and stand ovah there," Yolande continued. Marya moved to obey, found herself in the middle of a three-meter rectangle of clear plastic sheeting; the rug scrutched underneath it, feeling bristly-soft to her bare feet. "Oh, it's good to see yo' again. Took a while, gettin' leave, and I don't have long until I have to report to the Astronautical, but it's *good* to see yo', Yank. Yo' fault, it is.

"Now," the Draka continued. "There's somethin' I want from yo'. Guess?"

Marya looked up sharply. The other's eyes were fixed on her with a curiously impersonal avidness.

"Are you . . . going to abuse me again, Mistis?" she asked flatly. There was no sign of a drug injector.

Yolande chuckled; it had a grating sound. "Oh, not that way. That was a special occasion . . . No, there's something else I want yo' to do fo' me. It *was* yo' fault, aftah all."

Her free hand pulled something out of a pocket in her robe. Crackle-finished in black, the size of a small book. Opened it. Marya felt herself begin to tremble, heard a moan. Knew that in a moment she would beg, and felt a brief stab of shame that she felt no shame, because *nothing* was worse than that.

"What—" she choked, swallowed to clear her mouth of saliva. "What do you want me to *do*?" she asked, clamping her hands together to halt the shaking.

Yoland opened the controller and poised her finger. Her eyes met the American's, and Marya could feel them drinking.

"I want yo' to scream," she said, and pressed down.

NEW YORK CITY
DONOVAN HOUSE
FEDERAL CAPITAL DISTRICT
JANUARY 21, 1977

"I still say it stinks, General," Frederick Lefarge said. His body somehow gave the impression of tension, even when he sat relaxed in the stiff government-issue office chair.

Nathaniel Stoddard nodded, considering the man who sat across from him. *Thinner*, he thought. *And not just in body*. Pale as well, with the pallor that comes from long months inside a submarine, or a spaceship.

"I agree, but . . ." He pressed a spot on the desk screen, and a thinfilm rectangle slid up along one wall.

"India hurt us," he said quietly. "Not so much physically— it was the sinkhole of the Alliance—but in our souls. Our first major brush with the Domination, and we lost. Granted it was the Indians' own damn fault; that disinformation campaign wouldn't have produced secession if they hadn't been completely irrational about it. Granted, but we still *lost*, and another three hundred million went under the Yoke."

He rapped the desk with his knuckles. "First, we needed a victory, and the asteroid agreement *is* that. What we have to guard against is not treason, that's the *enemy's problem*. What we have to fear is *defeatism*; the turning-away from useful work into hedonism, because people don't think there *is* a future. That's the real danger, in the short term."

"I'd rather have kicked the Snakes out of the belt and everything outward."

Stoddard shook his head. "Not feasible, Colonel. It was turning into a struggle of attrition, and they outnumber us." He produced his pipe, took comfort from the ritual of lighting it. "Nor can we fight full-scale near Earth, not anymore. India took us to the brink of that, and it's only the sheer insanity of Draka ruthlessness that let it get that far." He puffed. "Now, list for me the *positive* aspects of these miserable few years."

Lafarge shrugged. "The Alliance will stand, now."

Stoddard nodded; the constituent nations had agreed to a full merger of sovereignty. A pity in a way—he had always regretted the increasing uniformity of life in the Alliance—but necessary.

"And not just among the electorate, either." His expression became wholly blank. "Now, I'm about to tell you something that requires complete commitment. If I'm not satisfied by your reactions from this point on, then the only way you will leave this building is as a corpse."

Lefarge sat upright, a slow uncoiling motion. His eyes met the other man's for a long moment.

"You're serious," he said flatly.

"Never more so. Want me to continue?"

The moment stretched. "Yes."

Stoddard cupped the bowl of the pipe. "We—that is, the permanant staff just below the political level—we've become convinced that if things go on as they are, we're headed for the Final War. If only because the limits of the Domination's ability to adapt to technical progress are on the horizon, and they'll bring everything down in wreck rather than see us reduce them to irrelevance."

Lefarge smiled. "Then the only alternatives are annihilation or surrender?"

"Surrender *is* annihilation, certainly for freedom, probably for humanity," he said, nodding agreement. "And the Final War is annihilation, too, It's the seeping realization of that that's been paralyzing our leadership echelons." He touched another spot on the screen, and a starfield lit the rectangle that hung from the ceiling.

"Tell me, Fred, what do you know about fusion power?"

Lefarge blinked narrow-eyed at the older man. "Controlled? Still a ways off. Plasma-confinement, we just reached break-even, possibly a workable reactor by the turn of the century. Inertial confinement shows some promise. Solid-state tunneling reactions are tricky and we still don't understand them; much longer."

"Look at this, then." A schematic appeared, a huge sphere with a tube protruding from each end, like a straw through an orange. "Build a big sphere; doesn't matter much of what, as long as it's thick enough. Throw fusion bombs in through this magnetic catapult. Set them off; we've got an electron-beam system that looks likely to work, but uranium's cheap off-planet these days. Bomb goes off, vacuum, no blast. Just radiant energy; shell absorbs the energy, you *extract* the energy, then beam it anywhere you want via microwave. Simple, robust, nearly as cheap as solar past Mars . . ."

"Useful," the younger man said without relaxing his lynx stare. "Particularly in the belt. With that, we could really set up a self-sustaining system, and *fast*. But that isn't what you had in mind."

"No. Incidentally, we think the Draka are using a much cruder form of this to mine ice from Sinope or Himalia, off Jupiter." Another tap on the screen. The artifact that appeared this time was a simple tube of coils and large-scale industrial magnets floating free in space, contained by the outline of an enormous box. "What's buried in New Mexico and eats power?"

"Linear accelerator . . ." His hands gripped the rests of his chair. "*Antimatter*, by God!"

"Right the first time, give the man a cigar." The stem of the pipe pointed. "And that's the *first* of the secrets you'll be expected to guard. You think, Fred. *Think*."

Slowly. "It can't be for bombs. We've *already* got bigger weapons than we can use." A pause. "Spaceship drives?"

A nod. "Paahtly. The ultimate reaction drive. We've tested models with the minute amounts we've made here Earthside. A great advantage, even over the improved pulsedrive mod-

els we're working on. Even over the fusion models that we'll
have in a decade."

"But not *enough*," Lefarge said. "It'll never be enough, a
better weapon, more weapons, even when we've got a lead
we're too gutless to use it."

The general frowned. "Fred, the price of open war is *too
high*. And getting higher! They can at least copy what we
do." He shook his head, waited for a second, then summoned
up another image. "All right, look at this."

This was a spaceship, with an outline he recognized beside
it for comparison; a *Hero*-class deepspace cruiser, the type he
had been operating out of in the Belt. Those had a 7,000-tonne
payload . . . and this one was dwarfed by the model beside it.
A huge cylinder, basically; a wheel and a ball at one end, at
the other a long stalk and a cup.

Awareness struck him. "Judas Priest!" he wheezed. "A
starship!" For a moment he was a boy again, watching Bat
Markam, Alliance Future Patrol, planting the blue-and-gold
on a planet of green-tentacled aliens . . . Then his teeth
skinned back. "Shit." A *bolthole*.

"How do you feel about the idea, Fred?"

"Jesus . . ." He ran a hand over his face. "General, could
we do it?"

A shrug. "Ayuh. Theory's all right, the engineering is big
but nothing radical. Have to test the drive, but the math
works. Alpha Centauri in forty years. And, Fred, they've been
looking that way with the Big Eye." That was the fifty-
kilometer reflector at the L-5 beyond Lunar farside. "There's
a planet there."

The excitement surged again, mixed sourly with bitterness
at the back of his throat. "Inhabitable?"

"Mebbe. Mebbe not. It's got an oxygen-nitrogen atmosphere, water vapor, continents and oceans . . . Yes, the
definition's that good. A little smaller than Earth and further
out; and the orbit's funny, what you'd expect." The Centauri
system had three stars; that *must* be complex. "A Mars-type
as well, subjovian gas giants, moons, asteroids we *think* from
the orbital data. A planet by itself isn't enough these days."
More slowly: "How do you *feel* about it, Fred?"

Unconscious of the general's stare, the younger man rose
and paced, running a hand through his close-cropped black
hair. "Christ. I love it; that's something I've dreamed since I
was a kid. When the news flash came through about the

Conestoga reaching orbit, I was on my first date, you know? Sheila Washansky. Her folks were away for the afternoon, we were on the couch upstairs, I had my hand up her *skirt* and the TV on downstairs—and I dumped her on the floor, I got up so fast. Never even noticed her walking out the door. Thirteen, my first chance to score, and I never noticed: *that* shows you how I feel."

He stopped and drove a fist into one palm. "And I hate it, the idea of running away. Even as a last resort"—he swung towards the general—"It *is* a last resort, isn't it?"

"Ayuh."

"Just to get a few hundred clear—"

"More like a hundred thousand, Fred."

At his surprise, Stoddard continued: "The other side aren't the only ones who do technological espionage. They've about perfected a reduced-metabolism system that works; down to less than one percent of normal. Our biology people say they can work out the remaining bugs without using their methods." They both grimaced slightly; one reason the Domination made faster progress in the life sciences was its willingness to expend humans.

"So the passengers age less than a year. Crew in rotation; no more than five years each. Seeds, animals, frozen animal ova, tools, knowledge, fabricators . . . all the art and history and philosophy the human race has produced. Enough to restart civilization; *our* civilization. America was started by refugees, son. What's your say?"

Lefarge nodded once, then again. "Yes. As a last resort, because too much is at stake. It's not as if the resources were crucial. The Protracted Struggle isn't going to be tipped by a percent here or there."

Stoddard sighed with relief, and his smile was warm.

Hell, that's Uncle Nate's smile, Lefarge noted with surprise.

"Fred, you just past the test," he said, coming around the desk to lay a hand on his shoulder. "And I can't tell you how glad I am."

"Test?"

"Yes. Look, Fred, we've got *lots* of anti-Draka fanatics; the Domination produces them like a junkyard dog does fleas. They're useful; that's one reason India cost the Draka the way it did. But fanatics are limited; they can't really think all that well, not where their obsession is concerned, and *they aren't reliable*. They've got their private agendas, which is fine if

they happen to coincide with the command's, and if not—"
He shrugged. "This is too big to risk."

Lefarge nodded slowly. "And I've just shown I'm not a
fanatic? General, don't bet on it."

"Mebbe there's a difference between that and a good hate."
He made a production of refilling the pipe. "Well, that was a
big enough secret?"

"Oh, sure." Lefarge grinned like a wolf. "Out with it."
Another secret, went through him. *And this one has to be a
weapon. Something that can well and truly upset the balance.*

"Nh-huh. You *are* going out there. With a promotion to
lieutenant colonel. Security chief, overall command with War
Emergency Regulation powers. The rank will go up as the
Project builds up."

Lefarge whistled silently. War Emergency Regulation. Power
of summary execution!

"You see, Fred, you're perfect. Good technical background;
good record with the OSS. Known to be space-trained. But
not prominent enough to make the Security Directorate flag
you, particularly. Not more than they watch fifty, a hundred
thousand other officers." There were twenty million in the
Alliance military.

"Just the right type to be put in charge of a middling-
important project. Like a fusion-power network for the asteroid belt; like an antimatter production facility. Like a fleet of
antimatter-powered warships. Layers like an onion; by the
time, which God forbid should ever happen, they come to
the *New America*"—Lefarge nodded at the name—"you'll be
senior enough to oversee security work on *that*."

"And?"

Stoddard leaned backward against the desk, cupped an
elbow in a hand. "And that's as much as anyone on Earth
knows, except me, thee, and a few technical people. Damned
few know *that* much. The technical people will be going out
with you; they'll brief you when you get there. All the Chairman and the President know is we're doing *something*, and
the appropriations are in the Black Fund."

"Yeah. Everyone's feeling rich these days." Even with the
military burden, taxes had been cut and cut again in recent
years, as wealth flowed in from new industries and from
space. Economists kept warning that the budget surplus would
wreck the economy if prices went on falling the way they
had. "They won't miss it."

"You'll get everything you need. We're encouraging development of the belt, you may have noticed, and doing it *hard*. That'll give more background to camouflage you, and more local resources to draw on in the later stages. This project is going to be a black hole, and you're the guardian at the event horizon. Nobody comes back. Nobody and *nothing*. Except you, occasionally, and you report verbally to me or my successor. I don't tell anyone anything. Not until it's ready."

For a moment, for the first time in a year, Lefarge felt pure happiness. Then he hesitated, reached into his uniform jacket for a cigarette. *Have to give this up again*, he thought. *At least until whatever habitat we build gets big enough.*

"Any news?" he asked softly. They both knew he could only mean his sister.

"Fred—" Stoddard returned to his chair, fiddled with the controls. "All we've been able to learn is that she's alive, they haven't penetrated her cover, and she's been bought up by a pilot officer who was there." He leaned forward, sorrowful and inexorable. "No, Fred, no. We will *not* expend assets— people!—trying to pull her out. And we won't try to trade for her, because we have to keep what bargaining power we have for situations where it's really needed."

There was more emotion in the old man's voice than Lefarge had heard in many years. "Fred, I love you both as if you were my own, you know that. Marya's tough and smart. It's not inconceivable she could get out. Or die trying. Until then, the only help, the only protection she has is that cover story. You will *not* endanger it, understood?"

"Yes. Yes, sir." Lefarge straightened, set his beret on his head. "I'm to report in a week? Well, if you'll excuse me, sir, I intend to go take advantage of the time. First, by getting *very* drunk. Safely, alone."

Stoddard sighed and dropped his face into his hands as the door closed. *I cannot weep*, he thought. *For if I do, will never stop.*

CLAESTUM PLANTATION
DISTRICT OF TUSCANY
PROVINCE OF ITALY
MAY, 1976

"Yolande?"

She stopped, caught between impatience and sick relief at the excuse for delay. It was John, looking grimmer than she had seen him in a long time, since Mandy got back from the last operation, in fact. Jolene was behind him, trying to make herself invisible. Yolande stopped, sighed, rubbed a hand over her forehead.

"Yes, John?"

He faced her, looked aside for a moment, then directly into her eyes.

"There's somethin' I'd like to discuss with yo', sister," he said. A nod in the direction of the plain door ahead; they were in a little-used section of the manor, only sketchily finished at all, suited for the use she had put it to. "That serf of yours, in particular."

The day was warm, but Yolande felt her skin roughen under her field jacket. "That's . . . not somethin' I care to discuss, brother," she said carefully, eyes on his face. The dappled sun-shadow patterns from the tall window at her back fell across the hard tanned planes of it, bleak and angry.

"*I* care to discuss it," he said. "Not just fo' myself. Fo' our parents, yo' sisters, for Mandy."

She opened her mouth to reply, then hesitated. The look on his face was enough to bring her out of self-absorption, with a prickle of feeling that it took a moment for her to recognize. *Danger.* This was the wrong context, the wrong person; this was her brother, Johnnie . . . and a very dangerous man, an extremely angry one. A cold-water feeling, a draft of rationality through the hot, tight obsession these rooms had come to represent.

"All right," she said, impatiently. "Say yo' say."

"Not here. In there."

Yolande blinked, conscious of her lips peeling back. Unconscious of her hand dropping to the butt of her sidearm, until she saw him copy her motion with flat wariness.

"If that's the way yo' want to discuss it, 'Landa."

"I—gods, Johnnie!" She shook her hand loose. "All *right*, then." Her back went rigid at the thought of another seeing this with her. She pushed open the door.

The American serf had been sitting at a table, picking listlessly at the wood. She looked up at the sound of the door opening, and scuttled to the far corner of the room; her hands caught up the tablecloth in passing, held it tented out in front of her as she scrabbled to push herself back into the stone.

"Noooooo," she said. They could see her mouth through the thin fabric, open in an O as round as her eyes. "Nooooooo. Ahhhhhhhh. Nooooooo." The serf's face looked fallen in, as if something had been subtracted from it, and her arms were wasted.

Yolande swallowed and turned her back; it was different, seeing it with John there. Suddenly she felt herself seized, the back of her neck taken in a grip as irresistible as a machine, turning her about.

"Look at that!" John said. "That is what I wanted to . . . This can't go on, 'Landa, it cannot. I will not allow it. None of us will."

The serf was making a thin whine, clutching the tablecloth to her with arms and legs, rocking. Yolande reached back, used a breakhold on the thumb to free herself, spun to face her brother, panting.

"Yo' disputin' my right to do as I will with my own?" she grated.

"*Not on my land!*" he roared, the sound shockingly loud. "*Not in my family's home!*" John reached over and pulled her pistol free, grabbed her hand, pressed it into her palm.

"Kill her, if that's what yo' want. Or get rid of her. Or if yo' want to keep actin' like a hyena, *get yo' gone.*"

Yolande looked at the weapon, up at her brother, her eyes hunting for a chink in his rage. "Are—" She fumbled the weapon back into its holster. "Are yo' tellin' me I'm not welcome in my family's home?" she said, in a small high voice.

"My sister Yolande is always welcome here," he said flatly. "My sister wouldn't do that"—he jerked his head at the moaning serf—"to a mad dog. It's your property . . . Don't yo' understand, 'Landa, yo' doin' this to *yo'self*. Every time yo' think of Myfwany, yo' takes it out on that poor bitch. Does that ease yo' pain? Does it? Is *that*"—he pointed again— "what yo' want your memories attached to? Yo've got to start livin' again. Not just goin' through the motions."

Yolande turned, braced her hands against the wall. Something inside her seemed to crumble, and she felt an overwhelming panic. *Gods, he's right. I'm poisoning all I have left.* That couldn't be right. *It's her fault . . . Or is it my fault?*

"All right," she said dully. "All right." His hand touched her shoulder gently, and she turned into his embrace. "All right." Her neck muscles were quivering-rigid, but her eyes stayed dry.

"Yo' want me to handle gettin' rid of her?" he asked.

She straightened, wiped her hands down her trouser legs, looked over at the serf. Appraisingly, this time. "No," she said calmly. "Yo' right. I won't use the controller on her any more. I'll try and have her patched up . . . but I'm not lettin' her go. Lettin' go isn't my strong point, brother. But thank yo'. Thank yo' all." A nervous gesture smoothed back her hair. "Iff'n she recovers, I'll . . . Oh, I don't know. Find somethin' else fo' her to do. That enough."

He nodded. "Welcome back."

She laughed, quietly bitter. "Not yet. Just startin', maybe." A glance at the sunlight. "I've got the afternoon, befo' I have to take the car in." She was on short-leave. "See yo' at dinner."

I am Marya.

"Oh, y'poor hurt thing."

Gentle hands were lifting her, holding a glass to her lips. She recognized the hands, the scent; they were surcease from pain. Black hands, sweet voice.

I am Marya Lefarge.

"C'mon, honey, we gets y' to the doctor. Give y' somethin' to sleep. Mistis isn't goin' do that no mo', she was just crazy, honest, no more."

I am Captain Marya Lefarge.

She was walking into a place that smelled half medicinal, half of country air, warmth. Children were playing outside, she could hear them. She was lifted into a soft bed; a pill was between her lips. Drowsy.

"No more painmaker, no mo'."

I am Captain Marya Lefarge, and nothing can hurt me. Because beside *that* there was no pain. She had felt the worst thing in the world, and she was still alive. *Nothing can hurt me.* I will remake myself. However long it takes, I will.

"Ah, Myfwany." The turf had healed over the grave, on the hill across from the manor. It was lonely here, not many graves in the Ingolfssons' burying ground yet . . . She looked up to the next space; that would be hers.

"I wanted to die, Myfwany, for . . . it seemed like a long time. Or to go away, go away from it all. And I had to . . .

keep goin', keep on doin' things. The things we talked about, the Astronautical Academy, qualifyin'. So . . . *dry*, it was like I *was* dead, dead on my feet and rottin', and nobody could notice. They say it heals . . . Oh, do I *want* it to?"

Yolande hugged her knees to her and laid her head on them; one hand smoothed the short damp grass. Somewhere she could feel a pair of warm green eyes open, somewhere in the back of her mind.

"Yes, love, I know. I takes things too much to heart." A rough laugh. "Yo' wouldn't have gone . . . hog-wild with that Yankee, the way I did. It should've been yo' that lived that night, love."

The Draka rose, dusting off her trousers. "I promise I'll do bettah now, Myfwany-sweet. Somehow I'll find a true revenge fo' yo'. And . . ." Her eyes rested on the far hills. *I think it would be better if I could weep, at least alone*, she thought. "I'll live, as yo'd have said. Make the memories live, somehow." Her eyes closed, and she felt scar-tissue inside herself. *Scars don't bleed, but they don't feel as well, either.* "Goodbye fo' now, my love. Till we meet again."

EUGENICS BOARD NATALITY CLINIC
FLORENCE
DISTRICT OF TUSCANY
PROVINCE OF ITALY
DOMINATION OF THE DRAKA
SEPTEMBER 1, 1976

"Now, shall we proceed, Citizen?" the doctor asked politely. He had glanced at the medal ribbons as she came into the office, and Yolande suspected he would look up her record again as soon as she left. A tall thin wiry man with cropped graying dark hair and brown eyes, with a Ground Command thumb-ring. *Technical Section*, she decided.

The office was a large room near the roofline of a converted Renaissance *palazzo* down near the Arno; the windows looked away from the river, out to the Cathedral with its red-and-white candystripe Giotto belltower and the green mountains beyond. It was cheerfully light, white-painted with a good tapestry on the inner wall, bright patterned tile floors, rugs, modern inlaid Drakastyle furniture. There was a smell of river and clean warm air from outside, faint traffic noises, the fainter sound of a group of brooders counting cadence as they went through their exercises.

"The brooder I sent in is satisfactory?" she said.

The doctor kept his eyes steady on hers as she turned back from the window, but could not prevent an inward flinch. You saw suffering in his line of work, but not like *that*.

"A little underweight, but otherwise fine," he replied, calling up the report. "The psych report indicates stabilized trauma, surprisin' recovery. Hmmm, primagravida . . . good pelvic structure, but are yo' sure a licensed Clinic brooder wouldn't do?" Yolande shook her head wordlessly. "The technicians report she's . . . hmmm, seems to have been under *very* severe stress. Good recovery, as I said, no biological agent; still, I'd swear she's been sufferin' from *somethin'*."

"She has," Yolande said, with a flat smile.

"What?"

"Me."

The doctor opened his mouth, shut it again with a shrug. It was the owner's business, after all. "Well," he said after another consultation with the screen. "We adjusted her hormone level, so she's ready fo' seeding anytime. Now, as to the clone." He paused delicately.

Yolande lit a cigarette, disregarding his frown. The new gene-engineered varieties of tobacco had virtually no carcinogens or lung-contaminants, and the soothing was worth the slight risk.

"I'd think it was simple enough," she said. The glassy feeling was back, a detachment deeper than any she had ever achieved in meditation. "My lover was killed in India. I want a clone-child, with *this* wench as brooder."

"Tetrarch Ingolfsson . . . yo' do understand, a clone is not a reproduction? All the same genes, yes, but—"

"Personality is an interaction of genetics an' environment, yes, I *am* familiar with the facts, doctor." She sank into a chair. It was odd, how the same physical sensation could carry such different *meanings*. The smooth competence of her own body; a year ago, it had been a delight. Now . . . just machinery, that you would be annoyed with if it did not function according to spec. "I realize that I'm not getting Myfwany back." Something surged beneath the glass, something huge and dark that would shatter her if she let it. *Breathe. Breathe. Calm.*

The medico steepled his fingers. "Then there's the matter of the Eugenics Code."

She stubbed out the cigarette and lit another. "I'm askin fo' a *clone*, Doctor. Not a superbeing."

"Yes, yes . . . are yo' aware of the advances we've made in biocontrol in the last decade?"

Yolande shrugged. "I've seen ghouloons," she said. "Bought a modified cat awhiles ago."

He smiled with professional warmth. "If yo'll examine that-there screen by yo' chair, Citizen." It lit. "Now, we've had the whole human genome fo' some time now, identified the keyin' and activation sequences." His face lit with a more genuine warmth, the passion of a man in love with his work. "Naturally, we're bein' cautious. The mistakes they made with that ghouloon project, befo' they got it right! We're certainly not talkin' about introducing transgenetic material or even many modified genes. Or makin' a standard product."

Double-helix figures came to three-dimensional life on the screen. "Yo' see, that's chimp DNA on the left, human on the right. Ninety-eight percent identical, or better! So a *few* changes can do a great deal, a great deal indeed." Seriously: "And those changes are bein' . . . *strongly encouraged*. Not least, think of how handicapped a child without them would be!"

"Tell me," Yolande said, leaning forward, feeling a stirring of unwilling interest beneath the irritation.

"Well. What we do is run analysis against the suggested norm, an' modify the original as needed. Saves the genetic diversity, hey? With yo' friend—"

His hands moved on the keyboard, and Myfwany's form appeared on the screen; it split, and genecoding columns ran down beside it. Yolande's hands clenched on the arms of the chair, unnoticed despite the force that pressed the fingernails white.

"See, on personality, we're still not *sure* about much of the finer tuning. We can set the gross limits—aggressive versus passive, fo' example, or the general level of libido. Beyond that, the interactions with the environment are too complex. With yo' friend, most of the parameters are well within the guidelines anyway. So the heritable elements of character will be identical to an unmodified clone.

"Next, we eliminate a number of faults. Fo' example," he paused to reference the computer, "yo' friend had allergies.

We get rid of that. Likewise, potential back trouble . . . would've been farsighted in old age . . . menstrual cramps . . . Any problems?"

"No." Even with feedback and meditation, those times had been terrible for Myfwany; Yolande had only been able to suffer in sympathy. The child—*Gwen*, she reminded herself—Gwen would never know that useless pain.

"Next, we come to a number of physical improvements. Mostly by selectin' within the normal range of variation. Fo' example, we know the gene-groups involved with general intelligence . . . Genius is mo' elusive, but we can raise the testable IQ to an average of 143 with the methods available. Fo' your clone, that would mean about fifteen percent up; also, we've been able to map fo' complete memory control, autistic *idiot savant* mathematical concentration, and so forth. On the athletic side, we build up the heart-lung system, tweak the hemoglobin ratios, alter some of the muscle groups and their attachments, thicken an' strengthen the bones, eliminate the weaknesses of ligaments—no mo' knee injuries—and so fo'th."

"The result?" Yolande said.

"Well, yo' know, a chimp is smaller than a man . . . and many times stronger. After the 'tweaking,' the average strength will increase by a factor of four, endurance by three, reflexes by two, twenty-five percent increase in sensory effectiveness. Greater resistance to disease, almost total, faster healin', no heart attacks . . . slightly lower body-fat ratio . . . perfect pitch, photographic memory, things like that."

"So." Yolande's chin sank on her chest. She had wanted . . . *He's right. Gwen has to have the best. As I'd have wanted for Myfwany.* "And?"

"Well, this is the most advanced part. We've been able to transfer a number of the autonomic functions to conscious control . . . Not all at once! Imagine a baby bein' able to control its heartbeat! No, we're keyin' them to the hormonal changes accompanyin' puberty, fo' the most part. Like any Citizen child learns, with meditation an' feedback, only it'll be *easy* fo' them, natural, able to go much further. Control of the reproductive cycle. Heartbeat, skin tension, circulation, pupil dilation, pain . . ."

He looked at the screen. "Yo' friend was in fine condition, but she had to fight fo' it, a lot of the time, didn't she? Your

. . . Gwen, she'll be able to set her metabolic rate at will. Eat anythin', and it'll be *easy* to stay in prime shape."

Yolande remembered Myfwany sighing and turning the dessert menu face-down. A wave that was dark and bitter surged up, closing her throat. *This is absurd,* she thought, squeezing her eyes shut for a moment before nodding to the man to continue.

"A lot of human communication's by pheromones: sex, dominance, anger, fear. We increase the *conscious* awareness of 'em, an' make the subjects able to deliberately govern their own output." He grinned. "Ought to make social life real interestin'. That's about it, 'cept fo' one thing." A weighty pause; Yolande endured it.

"We've been lookin' into agin', of course. No magic cures, I'm afraid. The whole *system* isn't designed to last. Normal unimproved variety, yo' and me, Tetrarch, we wear out at a hundred an' twenty absolute maximum. Modern medicine can keep us goin' longer, maybe right out to the limit by the time you're my age, but that's it. Then"—he shrugged—"yo' know that Yankee story, about the steamcar made so well everythin' wore out at once?"

Yolande felt herself snarl at the name of the enemy, hid it with a cough, nodded.

"Best we can do is stretch it. To about two hundred fifty years fo' the next generation."

Her eyes opened wide; that *was* something worth boasting about. "Show me," she said.

The column of data beside the figure of Myfwany disappeared; a baby's form replaced it. The infant grew, aged; limbs lengthening, face firming. Yolande stared, caught her breath as it paused at fourteen, eighteen, twenty. *Oh, my darlin'!* something wailed within her.

No. Not *quite* the same; the computer could not show the marks experience laid on a human's face. A few other minor changes, fewer freckles, slightly lighter hair. If you looked *very* closely, something different about the joints, in the way the muscles grouped beneath the skin.

"Gwen," she whispered to herself. For a moment the responsibility daunted her; this was a twenty-year duty she was undertaking, not a whim. A person, a Draka, someone she would have to play parent to as long as they lived. Give love, teach honor. Then:

"Yes. I understand, Doctor; that's entirely satisfactory."

She paused. "Just out of curiosity, what's planned fo' the serfs along these lines?"

He relaxed. "Oh, much less. That was debated at the highest levels of authority, an' they decided to do very little beyond selectin' within the normal human range. Same sort of clean-up on things like hereditary diseases. Average the height about 50 millimeters lower than ours. No IQ's below 90, which'll bring the average up to 110. No improvements or increase in lifespan, beyond that, so they'll be closer to the original norm than the Race. Some selection within the personality spectrum; towards gentle, emotional, nonagressive types. About what yo'd expect." He laughed. "An' a chromosone change, so that they're not interfertile with us any mo'; the boys can run rampant among the wenches as always without messin' up our plans."

"Yes," she said again, interest drifting elsewhere. "When can we do it?"

"Tomorrow would be fine, Tetrarch. The process of modifyin' the ova is mostly automatic. Viral an' enzymic, actually . . . Tomorrow at 1000 hours?"

Yolande looked down into her brandy snifter. It was her second, and she could barely remember tasting it. Barely remember tasting the meal, or even pushing the food around the plate; the *gelato* lay melting before her. It no longer seemed like treason that the body carried on; it *was* treason that the mind healed, kept trying to involve her in things. She took another sip, welcoming a numbness that was easier imposed from without than within. *I have to watch this*, some distant part of her mind told her. Myfwany's honor was part of her now; she bore it in trust. She must be faultless, at least in the eyes of the world and the Race, or that trust would be disgraced.

She looked up; it was full dark, here on the terrace beside the Arno. Little was left of the prewar town this close to the river, little except the timeless arcs of the bridges. Her people had turned the banks into parks and pleasances like this little outdoor restaurant; light globes on cast-iron stands were scattered among the tall dark shapes of the cypresses and the lush late-summer flowers. A few boats went by, and she could see folk strolling the colored-brick walks, hear low talking and music. Above, the stars were out, and the sickle moon. It was still warm enough to bring a slight prickle under the armpits of her uniform tunic.

Yolande strained her eyes. Was that a light, just across the line of the Lunar terminator? She decided not. Someday the city her folk were building there would be visible from Earth, but not yet. There were moving lights aplenty above, though; one to the west that might be a laser-lift from the Herakulopolis launcher at the Straits of Gibraltar.

It's there I should be, she thought. *Out where there's something to do. Where there's an enemy to kill.* You could forget a great deal, in war. Even loneliness.

"Excuse me, Tetrarch," a voice said. Yolande brought her eyes down and saw a man standing respectfully near the other side of the table. About her age, with an Aerospace Corps thumb-ring. Unremarkable, with close-cropped hair a dark-blond color, blue eyes, skin the startling white of someone not exposed to sunlight for some time. "Mind if I join you? Teller Markman, Centurion, Drive Officer on the *Conqueror*."

She blinked. That was the deep-space probe, the fourth Jovian expedition; it had just barely avoided the Americans on its return through the Belt. Yolande looked him up and down; he raised a brow at the coldness of it, then relaxed as she smiled lopsided.

"Why not?" she said. There were worse distractions.

"Sorry," Teller Markman said, easing out of her and away. Yolande gave him a final squeeze and unwrapped her legs from around his.

She sighed and rolled onto her back, stroking the knuckles of one hand down his cheek.

"Hmmmm, no, don't apologize, yo' were a complete gentleman," she said dreamily. *Freya, I'm tired. I think I could sleep now.* They were in her room at the hotel; it was dark, except for the light and breeze that leaked in around the curtains from the balcony. *Odd, how a man's sweat smells heavier than a woman's.* "I usually don't, not the first time with someone; always did enjoy givin' it as much as gettin'." A long yawn. "That's the closest I've come since India, anyways. Stopped tryin' altogether, fo' a whiles."

He offered an arm, and she curled closer.

"Want me to stay?" he asked.

"Yes, thanks. Nevah did like bein' alone after." *And you're actually quite sweet.* Far too many Draka males acquired bad habits, brought up on serf wenches, but Teller hadn't even wanted to enter, until she told him to. *Then again, there isn't much in the way of bedwench on a long cruise, is there?* He had had some fascinating stories to tell, things that didn't get into the official records.

Teller hesitated for a moment. "Mmmm . . . like to stay in contact?"

Would I? she thought. The immediate impulse was to lash out, to defend her solitude. *Pull yourself together,* she scolded internally. *Myfwany wouldn't want me to live a hermit. Wouldn't be good for the child, either, the effects on me.*

"Yes, Teller, I think so. Understand, though, I'll be honest with yo', a few things yo'd better know. First, do things work out well, it'd be my first time keeping company with a man fo' mo' than a single time. I'm about sixty-forty the other way, I think."

"I thought so, rathah," he said. Well, that would have been obvious from some of her responses; still, it *was* perceptive. "I'm not in a hurry, iff'n yo' not, Yolande."

She nodded against the resilient muscle of his shoulder and ran a hand over his chest; so strange . . .

"The othah, thing, let's keep it straight from the beginnin', this is just friendly-like. My lover who died in India, she was the one and only fo' me."

He nodded into her hair. "I understand." Yolande chuckled to herself; was that relief? *Well, I think we suit each other's needs for a while, friend Teller. And I think we will be friends.*

"Feel like talkin' about it?" he continued.

She sighed and closed her eyes. "Not much, but I should," she said. *Or so the alienist says. Besides, what is there to talk about, but what your mind turns on?* "Clonin', well, I think it's the right thing to do."

"Surprised yo' bein' so easy on this wench," Teller remarked.

"Oh—" Yolande stirred a little uneasily. "Well, she was at *fault,* but not to *blame,* y'know? It's a weakness of mine, I'm too easy on my serfs, I'll admit. Not with that one, though; I think I broke her mind with the controller. Trouble was, it made *me* feel like shit. Seeding her womb may quiet her down, and it'll be a way of her makin' amends without actually hurtin' her. Don't know if I'll let her nurse it, though. Depends on how she turns out."

"Don't think it's weakness, just a delicate sensibility," Teller said gallantly. " 'Sides, serfs aren't machinery, and I don't much like those who treat them like they were. They have to obey, an' be punished if they don't. Beyond that, no harm in kindness." He stretched. "Want to sleep?"

"Hmmm. Actually, not yet."

Yolande looked up as the serf walked into the room. Marya was dressed in a disposable paper shirt; the medical technician pulled it off and pushed her toward the couch. It was at the center of the room, surrounded like a dentist's chair with incomprehensible machinery, near a curved console with multiple display screens. The room was deep within the Clinic, far from the morning sun; the American captive's eyes blinked at the harsh overhead lights, reflected from gleaming white tile and synthetic. Her eyes darted from the doctor, busy at the console, to the other serf meditech in white who waited by the table.

She started uncontrollably as she saw Yolande rise from the corner.

"Nhhh!" she gasped, then clenched her teeth, staring at the palm-sized controller clipped to the Draka's belt. Her left hand hugged the left wrist to her stomach, as if she could bury the controller cuff on it into her flesh, away from the radio commands.

Yolande forced herself to watch the flinch, the eyes gone wide and white around the iris. *I should be enjoying this*, she thought, hating her weakness. Remembering the American's stubbornness. Instead it made her faintly nauseated, like a wounded dog. The faint medicinal-ozone smell of the Clinic was a sourness at the back of her mouth.

"Marya!" she said sharply. "Yo' won't be punished, as long as yo' obey. Do as these people tell yo'."

"Mmmmistis," the serf stammered. Docile but quivering-tense, she waited while the other technician laid a paper sheet on the table, then climbed onto it and lay back.

"Feet in the stirrups," the serf technician said. "Thatsa-right, little momma, this no hurt ata-all." She buckled the restraints at neck, arms, waist, knees, and thighs. "Now, we geta you ready for the visitor." She began to rig a visual barrier below the serf's neck.

"No," Yolande said, walking closer. The serf looked up with a respectful dip of the head. "No, I want her to see it all."

The meditech looked towards the doctor, mimicked his slight shrug. "*Sí*, Mistis." She touched controls instead, and the equipment moved. The couch bent into a shallow curve, raising Marya's shoulders and buttocks. The stirrups moved apart and back with a slight hydraulic whine, presenting the serf's genitals.

"Thisa no hurt," the meditech repeated. She pulled down a dangling line, attached it to Marya's throat.

The doctor looked up from his screens. "She's hyper-ventilatin' and on the edge of adrenaline-blackout," he said dryly, giving Yolande a resentful look. "One cc dociline." She could read his thought: *Damned amateurs messing up a medical procedure*.

Fuck you, she thought back.

Marya's straining relaxed a fraction, and sanity returned to her eyes. *Good*, Yolande thought. *It would be terrible if she went mad*.

"Wwwwhat—?" the serf shook her head angrily, as if trying to fling the stammer out of her mouth. "What are you doing to me?"

Yolande rested a hand on her stomach. "Seeding yo' womb," she said quietly, looking into the other's eyes. "Myfwany left me her ova. They don't have the egg-mergin' technique mastered yet, or I'd do that. So we're clonin' her; yo're to bear the egg."

The serf froze for a moment, then began to throw herself against the restraints, hard enough to make them rattle; it took Yolande a moment to place the sound she was making. A *growl*. The two meditechs frowned without looking up from their instruments, and the doctor swore aloud.

"Frey's *prick*, Tetrarch!" His hand touched the controls. "*Two* cc dociline, an' if yo' don't stop interferin', I won't be responsible fo' the procedure!"

Yolande nodded, but spoke once more to the serf. "Marya." She raised the controller box; the anger drained out of the serf, and she whimpered. "If the pregnancy an' nursin' go well, I won't use this on yo' again. *If they don't, I'll lock it on until yo' die!* Understand me, wench?"

A frantic nod. Then Marya's eyes darted down as the meditech touched her.

"Dona you worry, little momma," the meditech was saying from between the serf's legs. "This just take a *momento*." She had an aerosol can in her hand; with careful, swift movements she applied a thick pink foam to the genital area and lower stomach. "Now just wait a minute."

"Nnnnno!" Marya bit at the corner of her lip. Yolande looked up; the other meditech had rolled her sleeves back to the elbow and thrust both hands into a claver. There was a flash and hum, and when the technician withdrew them they were covered in a thin film that glistened like solidified water where the highlights caught it.

"Allll right, Antonia," she said.

"Hnnn!" from the serf on the table. Yolande followed her eyes; the meditech was wiping off the foam with cloths that had a sharp medicinal smell, moving down from belly to anus; the hair came with it. The Draka could see the muscles of Marya's belly and thighs jerk as the tech followed with a clear sharp-smelling spray. The pinkly naked flesh gleamed.

The serf with the molecular-film gloves replaced her co-worker. "Whata you think we win the bridge tournament?" she said casually, spreading the subject's vulva with her left hand. With her right she ran an experimental finger into Marya's vagina. "If that crazy Giuseppe no—Jesus-Mary-Joseph, she tight like stone!"

Yolande pushed down with the flat of her hand. "Marya, relax," she said in a clear, clipped tone. After a long moment she felt the serf loosen into obedience.

"Thank you Mistis, thata better," the meditech said. Her companion handed her an instrument like a speculum, giving it a quick spray of lubricating oil from another aerosol.

"Agg. Nhhhhnng." Marya's voice, as the meditech inserted it with a series of deft, steady pushes. She gave the threaded dilator at the base two turns and hooked fold-out supports over Marya's thighs to hold it in place.

"*Please! God, please!*"

The doctor whistled through his teeth. "Catheter now, Angelica," he said.

"Giuseppe, he crazy like fox," the other tech said, unreeling the end of a spool of what looked like black thread from a machine on casters. It rolled near. "Here. He say you play too cautious, you lose alla time."

The gloved meditech threaded the tip of the catheter through the instrument and into Marya. "Master Doctore?"

"Good, anothah ten millimeters. Careful now. Very slowly." Yolande stroked Marya's stomach and watched the wild, set eyes that stared down between her legs. "Good, that's it.

Hmmm. Acidity balance good, uterine wall looks good . . . getting a reading . . . Let's boost . . . All right, here we go."

Yolande looked down at the shuddering body on the couch, imagining a tiny form with red birth-fuzz lying in her arms; she smiled, and for a moment the weight of hatred lifted.

"Blastocyst's in the uterus. That's the egg in the womb to you laypeople," the doctor chuckled. "All right, Tetrarch, one seeded brooder. Virtually certain to take, anyway. Leave her here until tomorrow, she ought to be immobile. Intend to bring her back fo' the bearin'?"

"No," Yolande said, with a slight smile. "We've got a perfectly good midwife on our plantation. Look at me, Marya." The serf looked up, licked her lips. Wisps of hair were plastered to her brow, and Yolande pushed them back with one finger, and touched her navel with the other hand. "Yo're going to bear Gwen fo' me, Marya, an' suckle her. That's how yo' serves me and the Race, now. Understand?"

The serf jerked slightly. The meditech had withdrawn the speculum and catheter; the two technicians had laid a cloth over Marya's crotch and adjusted the stirrups so that her legs were together with knees up. One waited patiently with a blanket, while the other stripped the thinfilm gloves from her hands. The doctor rose.

"Yo' can pick her up tomorrow. Unless yo'd care to sit with her."

"No," Yolande said. The meditechs draped the blanket over the serf, tucking it around her neatly and freeing one hand next to a plastic cup of water. "No, I've got a date." This was better than inflicting pain, but she did not want to stay and watch. "And Marya here needs to be alone with her thoughts, hey?"

CHAPTER TWELVE

SUPERCONDUCTORS TO BE MANUFACTURED IN SPACE
[NPS] It was announced today from Alliance Space
Force headquarters in Monterrey that earlier,
unconfirmed reports of the manufacture of room-
temperature superconductors on the Freedom
One orbital platform were true. Intelligence
sources indicate that similar work is being done
by the Domination's space-fabrication researchers, and in any case the process has proven to
be so simple that any competent materials engineer could rediscover it given a sample.

The implications of this discovery are pro-
found, Space Force spokesman Josepha Sher-
man said. The midrange barium-copper-oxygen-
rare earth superconductors, which were discovered in the late 1950s and require liquid-nitrogen
cooling, have already found many applications.
The new compounds have unlimited current density capacities, and remain superconductive up
to the antiferromagnetic transition temperature,
in the area of 330 degrees Celsius. While they
require zero-gravity processing, the materials
required are common, and eventually the superconductors will be no more expensive than
aluminum cable. Applications in electric motors,
power transmission and storage, transportation
and computers are obvious and revolutionary.
Others too numerous to mention will be found; for
example, with the new materials shielding against
solar-flare radiation becomes much easier.

Space and Science Digest
"New Materials from Space"
March 20, 1966

SOUTH WING WAITING ROOM
CASTLE TARLETON, ARCHONA
ARCHONA PROVINCE
DOMINATION OF THE DRAKA
MAY 3, 1982

"Candidate Centurion Yolande Ingolfsson, please."

Yolande laid down the perscom board and nodded at the Auxiliary who stood waiting, hands folded and shaven head bowed. The South Wing was part of the original core of Castle Tarleton, two-story quadrangles of native sandstone and granite. These were buildings erected as garrison-fortress against tribesmen armed with spears; now the descendants of those tribesmen swept the floors, and decisions made here sent warriors and ships to fight beyond the orbit of the moon.

And determine the fate of junior officers, she thought nervously as she rose and settled the peaked cap on her head, following the serf out the yellowwood door and down the outside corridor. This hearing was something of a formality, for the members of the Assignments Board would have arrived at their decision days ago. *Not a formality for me! And I can still fuck it up*.

The corridor was the usual type in the Old Territories, solid wall on one side and arches on the other that looked in on the courtyards, on fountains and trellises and plants in giant stone pots. The inner wall bore trophies of arms and banners, faded cloth rippling in the thin highland air, noon sunlight bright on the old polished iron; shovel-headed Nguni spears and coats of Dervish chainmail, Mauser rifles and Spandau machine-guns. It was a perfect early-fall day, dry and warm with only a few high clouds. Yolande fought down a childish impulse to stop and check the alignment of her tunic or the polish on her boots; the garrison blacks were as immaculate as attentive servants could make them, and it was irrelevant anyway.

An antechamber of pale honey-colored stone, scattered with massive desk-consoles of polished granite; tall windows flooded it with sunlight, the smell of plants and cleaning-wax and old stone, a hint of the great city beyond. There was no sound save for the *tictic* of keyboards and two sets of bootheels. The final door was twice her height, dark red marula wood studded with copper rivets the size of her fist. Two Janissaries stood on either side, bulky and faceless in their impact

armor and face-shield helmets; they snapped to attention as
the doors swung open and the Auxiliary bowed her in.

"Candidate Centurion Yolande Ingolfsson, Aerospace Force,
detached!" the serf announced.

The doors slid shut behind her with a soft *shnnnnk*. The
great chamber beyond was dark save for the far wall, and her
eyes took a moment to adjust. The picture before her was a
hologram, a planetary shot taken close off Jupiter. The great
banded disk hung against the black, stripes of blue-white and
orange, the huge brick-red swirl of the Great Red Spot to the
lower right. Tiny globes against it were two moons, sulfur-
colored Io and silver-bright Europa. For a moment too slight
to halt her stride she was light-minutes from Earth, hanging
in zero-G before the viewport and lost in the vision of storm-
clouds greater than worlds.

The Board was seated at a horseshoe-shaped dais of black
stone with its open end toward her. She came to a sharp stop,
clicked heels and saluted, fist to breast.

"Service to the State!"

"Glory to the Race," came the reply.

She stood at an easy parade rest with her hands clasped
behind her back and boots apart; the Arch-Strategos was in
the center, the two lesser officers at either side visible with
trained peripheral vision. Smoothly, mind took control of
body, slowing her breathing and heartbeat, easing the con-
striction in her throat. There might be—probably were—
medical sensors trained on her. *They expect you to be nervous,*
she thought. *And to control it well.*

"Greetings, Centurion," the Arch-Strategos said. He was
an old man, an unmoving gaze whose pouches and wrinkles
she could just barely see by the reflected light of the hologram. The voice was dry and cold, somehow papery, suggesting a whisper despite the conversational tone and amplification.

"We are here to review your record and future service," he
continued. The hands moved over the screen in front of him;
with a shock, Yolande realized he was blind.

The rustling voice continued. Now she could detect an
Alexandrian accent, sharper-voweled than most, crisp and
hard. Folk of that city were prominent in highly technical
branches of the Forces.

"Excellent but uneven record at the Yalta Academy; academics slightly better than passable, flight record in the top
five percent; personnel evaluation as 'possibly lacking in nec-

essary ruthlessness.' Squadron service unremarkable until Indian Incident. Exceptional combat record in the later stages of that conflict. Southern Cross award, second class. Exceptional record since then, first-class honors from the Astronautical Academy course, faultless deep-space ratings since." A pause. "Evidently the events in India supplied a motivation lacking before."

Yolande felt sweat break out in a prickle along her upper lip, forced memories down beneath the surface. *Later, later.*

"Therefore, you are approved for promotion to the grade of Cohortarch in the service of the Directorate of War, least seniority."

A wave of relief made Yolande's skin itch, as if it had life of its own and wanted to crawl free and dance. This was the critical point in a career officer's progress, when you learned if you were tracked for command or not. A Cohortarch in the Citizen Force ground-troops commanded a unit of five hundred, or equivalent. Rather more in the Aerospace Command, where crews were rarely all-Citizen. This was the beginning of accomplishment, of her life's work of vengeance.

"Congratulations, Cohortarch," the general continued. "Now, do you have any requests as to your next assignment?"

Now what does the scary old bastard want? she thought frantically. Then: *best give them the truth.* "Deep-space warship assignment," she said crisply, from the iron mask of her face.

"Ah." A long wait. "Why?"

"Service to the State, sir. The best opportunity to inflict damage to the enemies of the Race."

"Commendable," the Arch-Strategos said; was it possible there was a tinge of humor in his voice? "Be warned, Cohortarch. You are on the verge of rank sufficient to hold independent command. The killing lust which is essential in a simple warrior of the Race, even in a junior officer, must now be controlled by a self-discipline more strict than any superior's orders." A long, considering wait. "What is the *purpose* of harming the enemies of the Race, Cohortarch?"

Oh, shit. He's wondering about my record from the alienist. "Suh, to break them to our Yoke."

"And?"

"Suh . . . when the last enemies are enserfed, there is no *limit* to the accomplishments of the Race! The transformation of human nature and the solar system—" She had let enthusi-

asm creep into her voice; a calculated move, but true still.
That had been her dream in the long ago, and Myfwany's.
She had simply underestimated the blood needed to accomplish it.

A chuckle. "Well enough. Simply remember this: that a
premature resort to the Final War will not produce the Final
Society. It will kill this planet.

"We do have a command for you, Cohortarch Ingolfsson.
Two cruisers of the Great Khan class, the *Batu* and the
Subotai. And several cargo and research craft, modified from
vessels of the same category."

Glory, glory! Yolande thought, keeping the same even,
steady rhythm of breath. Her old ship, the *Subotai*, where
she had been Squadron Exec; Teller must have gotten rotation to something bigger, a base command maybe. And *another* ship; the Fleet was expanding as rapidly as the orbital
construction nexus could manage, but this was something
else again.

"Suh!"

"Regard the far wallscreen, Cohortarch."

Her eyes flicked up to the holo; it was an older shot,
probably from the first manned expedition to Jupiter back in
'69. That had been a near-disaster, but others had followed,
and it was almost a routine voyage now. The screen changed
to a north-pole overview of the solar system out as far as
Saturn.

"Cohortarch, it's become a truism because it's true: who
rules space, rules Earth. Orbital sensors and weapons continually improve; even now they could destroy a single tank, or
ten thousand. Soon they will be able to strike an individual
soldier at will. We and the enemy race to outbuild each
other; but weapons imply factories, power sources, mines,
the whole structure of support necessary for that . . . There
are a hundred thousand of the Race and their servants beyond
Earth's atmosphere, and we hope to increase that by a factor
of ten in the next decade. Must if our goals are to be achieved.
There is a problem."

The picture changed again, shadings of different colors
blotching the orbits.

"Energy and Lunar materials are cheap, and now available
in large quantity to both us and the Alliance. The limiting
factors are those things which must either be brought from
the outer system, or out of Earth's gravity well. The latter is

prohibitively expensive, not simply in money but in foregone opportunities. Until now, both Powers have had ample supplies from the few cometary bodies we have been able to capture, and from the two Apollo asteroids. The Alliance are now starting to receive the first major shipments from the asteroid belt proper, which they largely control.

"We are not yet short of metals, although more would be welcome. Unfortunately, we *are* short of volatiles, water, carbon, nitrogen." A half-seen shrug. "Too many projects attempted at the same time; intoxication with the gigantic possibilities of space. Or simply hubris, our national weakness . . . especially the Aresopolis project on Luna. Useful, a monument to the Glory of the Race, but dependent on our undertakings in the Jovian and Saturnian moons. These are behind schedule. The distance is far; the difficulties, great."

Yolande remembered the radiation belts and their effect on superconductor shielding; ice-volcanoes; equipment designed for the Inner System failing in an environment given only the most cursory study because there was no time for the sort of in-depth investigation *really* needed. The sort that would find the killing surprises before they struck. Instead, full-scale exploitation as soon as the cargo-capacity was available, and learning by disaster. Loneliness in outposts where the sun was merely the brightest star, despair, madness, death by fire or cold or suicide.

"We will triumph there, our Will prevail, but time presses. Now, while the Yankees point their so-admirable farside reflector at other stars, we have been . . . alert. There is a body falling inward from beyond the belt." A line traced inward, crossed the path of Earth well behind the globe's passage, before heading out again. "It is only two kilometers in size; very dark, quite cold, off the plane of the elliptic. Unnoticed until now. Without intervention, it will bypass us by a considerable margin. Later in its approach, extreme measures would be necessary. But if we can capture it now . . ."

"Suh?" A two-kilometer rock was still *big*.

"A new method. A modification of the pulsedrive, using half-megatonne fusion bombs; we have no lack of *those*. The experts assure me that it can be brought into a stable, if eccentric, orbit around the Earth. Then they may settle their quarrel as to whether it is a burnt-out comet or an asteroid proper." A slight change in the wintry voice. "A small asteroid, by cosmic standards. Megatonnes of what we so desperately need!" The slow, calm tone again. "It is our estimation that if we establish possession, and maintain an escort, the Alliance will not intervene." More formally: "Cohortarch; do you accept this assignment?"

"Yes, *suh*!" It would mean many months away from Earth . . . away from Gwen. Forget that. It was something that needed doing, and they wouldn't have picked her if she weren't the best qualified. Even with expansion at the present rate, postings like *this* were not handed out to all and sundry.

Nor would she ever get anything better than dirtside anonymity if she turned this down.

The officers on the dais leaned their heads together for a moment, whispering. Their leader spoke:

"It is the order of this Board that Cohortarch Yolande Ingolfsson be appointed to the command of Task Force Telmark IV. You are to report to Draka Forces Base, Platform SkyLord Six two days from this date, for familiarization with the vessels and crew under your command; to depart thence for the Apollo asteroid Telmark IV approximately two weeks from this date, determine its composition and arrange, in coordination with Merarch Doctor-Professor Henry Snappdove of Technical Section, for its expeditious transfer to Earth orbit. And, of course, to cause such other harm and loss to the enemy as is compatible with the first objective."

"There is one more thing," the Arch-Strategos said before she could salute. This time his voice was almost human. "I note from your file that you haven't reproduced."

For a moment Yolande bristled, then relaxed. It *was* his business; a high commander's business was the welfare of the Race. And it was a compliment.

"I have a daughtah, suh, Gwendolyn Ingolfsson."

"She is adopted, and her genetic material is that of . . ." A pause to consult the screen: "Myfwany Venders, killed in action in India in 1975." Slight surprise. "A clone."

The wash of loss was fainter now, faint enough that she could feel what was underneath it: rage, and guilt.

"Suh. I had planned to seed a brooder with ova of my own befo' departin'." Well, she *had* thought about it.

"Excellent. I have read your poetry collections, Cohortarch." Was he smiling? "Both *A Grief Observed* and *Colder Than the Moon*. Your Archon's Prize was well deserved. The Glory of the Race is accomplishment, and beauty is as much so as power. Dismissed."

Yolande felt her ears turn red. "Service to the State!" she barked, to cover the confusion. *Would have sworn the old deathfucker had Helium-II for blood,* she thought, as she clicked heels and saluted with fist to heart. *Well, well.*

"Glory to the Race."

The family was waiting for her in the ringroad plaza by the south side of the Castle Tarleton grounds. Her brother John and Mandy, sitting at a table under an umbrella and talking. Looking exactly what they were, Landholders in from the provinces, down to the broad-brimmed hats and conservative Tolgren 5mm's . . . David, their latest infant, cooing and gurgling in the arms of stout Delores, his brooder-nurse; Jolene, Lele . . . and Marya, with Gwen. Gwen.

"Momma! Momma!" The small red-headed form bounced erect and ran toward her, toddler's tunic flying. "Momma!" She leaped up.

"Ooof." She was heavy, for a five-year-old; that was the denser bones. Incredibly strong. Yolande grabbed her under the armpits and swung her in a wide circle, laughing up into the face that smiled back at her.

"Zero-G!" the child cried. "Zero-G, momma!"

Yolande darted a look of apology at her brother, and tossed her daughter up with a swoop-catch. "There yo' go, spacer! And—*one* and *two* and *three* and *dockin' maneuver.*" She gave the child a smacking kiss and hugged her.

Gwen's arms tightened around her neck, and she pressed her head against her mother's. "Love yo', momma," she said.

"Love yo', too, my baby Gwennie," she said.

"I am *not* a baby! I'm *Gwen,*" she replied firmly.

"Indeed yo' are, light of my life." Yolande signed to Marya. "Here, now stay with yo' Tantie-ma for' a minute, an' hush."

John and Mandy were smiling indulgently at her, hands linked.

"I gathah the news is good," her brother chuckled. Mandy was using her beltphone to call for the car; the family had rented the latest for their stay in Archona, a superconductor-electric with maglev capacity on the few stretches of road relaid for that luxury.

"Yo' are lookin'," Yolande said, buffing her nails, "at the *newest* Cohortarch in the Directorate of War."

"Well, well, *well,* we Ingolfssons are movin' up in the world," he said, with a swift hard embrace. John had never been more than a Tetrarch, or wanted to be. He and Mandy did their Territorial Reserve duty, and that was enough distraction from Claestum and its folk. "Even as I dragged yo' appalling offspring through the zoo and amusement park. Wotan's stomach, the things they do with rides these days! While Mandy shopped the estate into bankruptcy; we'll need a Logistics Lifter to get the loot—"

He winced theatrically as the tall blond woman dug him in the ribs. "Gwen didn't enjoy those rides half as much as yo' did," she said. "Do I quarrel with yo' gettin' every toy Biocontrol dreams up fo' the credulous planter? Like those steakberries?" John winced more sincerely; the high-protein meat-mimicking fruit had proven a beacon for every vermin, pest, scavenger, and grub in Italy. Their son began to cry softly. "I could scarcely take Davie along with yo' and Gwen, now could I?"

They glanced over to the nurses. Delores was just lifting a full breast out of her blouse and brushing the engorged brown nipple across the infant's mouth; she rocked the child and crooned, smiling, as he suckled.

"That reminds me, yo'-know-who dropped a broad hint it'd be appreciated if I had anothah befo' shippin' out. Hmmm, Gwen? Yo' likes a little brothah or sistah to play with?"

The girl had been seated on Marya's lap, watching the adults and ignoring her cousin with five-year-old disdain. "Can't play with a baby," she said practically. "They just makes messes an' sleeps."

Yolande laughed, and glanced an inquiry at her brother and sister-in-law. Mandy nodded. "One more's no problem, 'Landa. Freya knows, what with ours and the two new ones ma an' pa are havin', we gettin' to be more of a tribe than a family."

Yolande's mother had borne four children naturally, but seemed to prefer the new method wholeheartedly.

"I'll have to pick a brooder," she said.

"No problem . . . 'Ship out'?" her schoolfriend said.

Yolande shrugged, spread her hands and looked from side to side in the universal Draka gesture for secrecy. Not that the Security Directorate needed to have spies hiding behind bushes these days.

"Be gone fo' quite some time. Months, leastways."

Gwen made a protesting sound, frowning and pouting, blinking back tears. Yolande moved over toward her on the stone bench, smoothing the copper hair back from her brow.

"Now, where's my big brave girl?" she said gently. "Momma has her work, an' I'll bring yo' back another piece of a star, sweetie." Gwen had been just old enough after the last voyage to understand that the light pointed out in the sky was where her mother had been, and the lump of rock from Ganymede was her most precious possession.

"I don' want a star. I want momma!" She tugged on Marya's hair. "Tantie-ma, tell momma she cain' go!"

"Hush, Missy Gwen. You know I can't tell your mother what to do." The serf wrapped her arms around the child and made soothing noises.

"Now, don't be a baby, Gwen," Yolande said. "Momma doesn't have to leave fo' a week yet"—which was forever to a child this age—"and when I go, yo' can come up to the station with me, how's that? Right up above the sky." No more risky than an ordinary scramjet flight, these days, and she could probably swing it.

"And yo'll have Uncle John and Auntie Mandy and Tantie-ma, too, and all the friends yo' makes at school next year. Oh," she continued, looking up at Marya. "I meant to tell yo'. I've posted bond, yo're moved up to Class III Literate." That meant non-technical and non-political literature, and limited computer access to menu-driven databanks; the classics, as well, most of them.

Marya looked down, flushing. "Thank you, Mistis," she whispered. For an instant Yolande thought she caught something strange and fierce in the wench's expression, then dismissed it. *Must have been boring, nothing much to read,* she thought. *Should have done this before.* Gwen subsided, looking up with nervous delight at the thought of flying to orbit.

"Well, what have we planned?" Yolande asked.

"Lunch," John said. "Then the Athenaeum, then dinner at Saparison's. Then there's a Gerraldson revival at the Amphitheater, the *Fireborn Resurrection,* and Uncle Eric used some pull to get us a box. We'll drop the children off first, of course."

"Nnooo, I think Gwen might enjoy it," Yolande said, considering. "The dancin', at least. Marya can keep her quiet, or take her out in the gardens if not." And it would be a treat for Marya as well; she had been behaving well of late. Gwen was certainly devoted to her, which was a good sign.

The electrocar had hissed up on the smooth black roadway

a dozen meters away. The main processional streets of Archona had been the first public places in the solar system to be fitted with superconductor grids, just last year. Their car floated by the curb, motionless and a quarter meter above the roadway as the gullwing doors folded up; it still looked a little unnatural to Yolande for something to hover so on Earth, without jets or fans. She reached out for Gwen's hand, and the child took it in one of hers and offered the other to Marya. Their eyes met for a moment over the child's head, before they turned to walk behind the others.

Strange, Yolande thought. *Life is* strange, *really.*

"I *did* it! Cohortarch, independent command, I *did* it!"

Jolene looked up smiling as Yolande collapsed backward onto the bed in her undertunic, the formal gown strewn in yards of fabric toward the door. The room was part of a guest suite in the von Shrakenberg townhouse, beautiful in an extremely old-fashioned way; inlaid Coromandel sandalwood screens in pearl and lapis, round water-cushioned bed on a marble dais with a canopy, a wall of balcony doors in frosted glass etched over with delicate traceries of fern and water-fowl. They were opened slightly, letting in a soft diffuse glow of city light cut into fragments by the wind-stirred leaves of ancient trees; it smelled of water, stone and frangipani blossoms, and the air was just warm enough to make nakedness comfortable.

"Congratulations, Mistis . . . again," the serf said.

Yolande shook her head wordlessly; it had been a perfect evening, after a stone bitch of a week shuttling from one debriefer to the next and wondering what the Board would say. Her mind still glowed from the impossible beauty of Gerraldson's music . . . *Why* had he killed himself, at the height of his talent? Why had Mozart, for that matter? And this mission, it was the *perfect* opportunity, for so many things. She rolled onto one elbow and watched Jolene. The serf was sitting on a stool before the armoire, brushing out her long loose-curled blond mane, dressed in a cream silk peignoir that set off the fine-grained ebony of her skin. And also showed off the spectacular lushness of her figure; the black serf had filled out a little without sagging at all. The Draka grinned.

"Yo' pick out a father fo' the new baby, Mistis?" Jolene asked. "That nice Masta Markman?"

Yolande chuckled. "No, not this time. We're giving it a raincheck fo' a while; different postin's." Teller had been a good choice for an affair; interesting and friendly without trying to get *too* close. "Myfwany's brother agreed to release sperm from the Eugenics banks when I asked. As fo' yo', wench, yo' just miss the variety." She and Teller had tumbled Jolene together a few times, and the wench had been enthusiastic.

"Mmmh." Jolene said, meeting her owner's eyes in the mirror as her hands brushed methodically. "It was nice." More seriously: "Nice to see yo' smilin' agin, Mistis."

Yolande shrugged, sighed. "Ah, well . . . Yo' can only grieve so long. Gwen deserved better, little enough she sees of me." Work could keep you busy, hold the pain at bay until it faded naturally; work and the things of daytime. Nights were worst, and the moments when the protective tissue seemed to fall away and everything came back raw and fresh. "Grief dies, like everythin' else." For a moment, her mind was beyond the walls, under the unwinking stars. *Except hate. Hatred is forever, like love.*

Jolene rose, arranged the armoire table, bent to pick up the gown and fold it, swaying and glancing occasionally at the Draka out of the corner of her eyes. Yolande watched with amusement, lying on her stomach with her feet up and her chin in her hands.

"Oh, fo'get the play-actin' and come here, wench," she said. "I know what yo' want." Jolene sank down on the padded edge of the bed and Yolande knelt up behind her, reaching around to open the buttons of the silk shift and take the serf's breasts in her hands; she traced her fingers over the smooth warmth of them and up to Jolene's neck, down again to tease at the pointed nipples. Her own desire was increasing, a soothing-tingling whole-body warmth.

"Mmmm, feels nice . . . Mistis? *Mmm*—" as Yolande ran her tongue into the other's ear. "Mistis, yo' picked the brooder yet?"

"Freya, yo' feel good. Up fo' a second." She drew the garment over the serf's head and tossed it aside. "Yo' first. The brooder? No, I'll look at the short list when we get back to Claestum." There were always plenty of volunteers to carry a Draka child; it meant a year of no work and first-rate rations at the least, often the chance of promotion to the Great House, personal-servant work or education beyond birth-status. Being a child-nurse as well as brooder was a virtual guarantee of becoming a pampered Old Retainer later. "Lie down."

The serf lay back and Yolande straddled her, running her hands from the black woman's knees up over thighs and hips, circling on the breasts and starting over. Jolene arched into it, squirming and making small relaxed sounds of pleasure. Yolande savored the contrasting sensations, the firm muscle overlaid with a soft resilient layer of fat. *Not flabby, but so different from a Draka*, she thought.

"Yo' do this with the brooder, Mistis?" Jolene asked through a breathy chuckle.

"Maybe," Yolande said, running her fingernails up the other's ribs. That brought a protesting tickle-shiver. "If she's pretty an' willin'. I'm goin' pick her for hips, health, an' milk, not fuckability."

She leaned herself forward slowly, until they were in contact, hips and stomach and breasts, then kissed her. *Mint and wine*, she thought languidly. There were times when this was *exactly* what you wanted: friendly, slow and easy. It might be the creche training, but with Jolene she always felt affection without the risk of the wench getting excessively attached, which was embarrassing and forced you to hurt them, eventually.

"Mhhh . . . I'd . . . I'd like to do it, Mistis," Jolene said. "Have yo' baby."

Startled, Yolande rose up on her hands and looked down into the other's face. "Why on earth?" she said. The movement had brought her mound of Venus into contact with the serf's, and she began a gentle rocking motion with her hips; the other slipped into rhythm.

"I . . . like babies, Mistis."

"Hmmm. Up a little harder. Yo' can have yo' own, anytimes; take a lover or a husband, I don't mind."

"Thanks kindly, Mistis, not yet. I hopes to travel with yo' sometimes, see them faraway places. But yo' away lots next little while. An' . . . well, yo' knows I gets friendly with Marya? No, not like this, just she don' have many to talk to. Other Literates at Claestum sort of standoffish, 'specially with her." Yolande winced slightly, remembering her early treatment of the wench. It would mark Marya with dangerous misfortune, in the eyes of most.

"Then, she don't have much to talk about *with*, with the

unClassed." The vast majority on a plantation, illiterate and forbidden even the most limited contact with information systems.

"Marya good with babies, but Gwen gettin' to be a holy terror; we kin"—she ran her hands down her owner's flanks, gripped her hips to increase the friction of the slow grind—"kin help each othah. 'Sides," she said, raising her mouth to the Draka's breasts, "I like the idea."

"Mmmm. All right, I'll take yo' in to the Clinic and have yo' seeded. Now shut up an' keep doin' that."

Bing. The bedside phone. Yolande raised her mouth from Jolene's. "Shit." *Bing. Bing. Bing.* "It isn't goin' away." Not that it was all *that* late; she had only been back from the Amphitheater two hours.

Her left hand went to the touchplate, keying voice-only. Her right stayed busy; not fair to stop now. "Yes?" she said coldly.

"Uncle Eric here." An older man's voice, warm and assured. "If I'm not interrupt—"

Jolene shuddered and stiffened, crying out sharply once and then again.

"Ah, even if I am, niece, I've got a gentleman here I think yo'd like to meet, an' some matters to discuss. Half an hour in the study? Strictly informal."

"Certainly, Uncle Eric," Yolande said, breaking the connection. "Senator, possibly Archon-to-Be, war hero, Party bigwig, darlin' of the Aerospace Command, he-who-must-be-obeyed by new-minted Cohortarchs, *shit*," she muttered, looking down. Jolene was smiling as she lay with her eyes closed, panting slightly. "Got to go fo' a while, sweet wench," the Draka said.

Jolene's eyes opened. "Half an hour, the bossman said," she husked, swallowing. "Five minute shower, five minutes fo' a loungin' robe and sandals. Ten-minute walk; that leaves ten minutes. No time to waste, Mistis-sweet, yo' just lie back there an' put yo' legs over my shoulders."

Yolande threw herself back and began to laugh. *I wonder,* she thought in the brief moment while thought was possible, *I wonder what he has to say?*

The study was book-lined, with the leather odor of an old well-kept library; there was a long table with buffel-hide chairs, and another set of loungers around the unlit hearth. A few pictures on the wall: old landscapes; one priceless Joden Foggard oil of Archona in 1830 with a smoke-belching steamcar in front of this townhouse; a nude by Tanya von Shrakenberg. A few modern spacescapes. The doors to the patio had been closed, and the room was dim; a housegirl was just setting a tray with coffee and liqueurs on the table amid the chairs. There were three men waiting for her. Uncle Eric; nearly sixty now, and looking . . . not younger, just like a very fit sixty; the hatchet-faced von Shrakenberg looks aged well. His eldest, Karl, thirty-six and a Merarch already, like a junior version of his father with a touch of his mother's rounder face and stocky build; also with more humor around his eyes.

They rose, and she saw the third man was still in evening dress rather than the hooded *djellaba* robes she and her hosts were wearing. A rather unfashionable outfit, brown velvet with silver embroidery on the seams and cuffs, and a very conservative lace cravat. An unfashionable man, only fifty millimeters taller than she, broad-built and bear-strong; you could see that he might turn pear-shaped in middle age among any people but Draka. A hooked nose, balding brow, and a brush of dark-brown beard.

"Greetin's," she said politely, gripping his wrist. "Service to the State."

"Glory to the Race," he replied; the return grip was like a precisely controlled machine. His accent was Alexandrian, like the Board chairman this morning, but with a human pitch and timbre. And a hint of something else, unplaceable.

"Doctor Harry Snappdove, my niece, Cohortarch Yolande Ingolfsson," Eric said, with a smile at her well-concealed surprise. "I am on the Strategic Planning Board, Yolande," he said.

They all sank into the chairs; the housegirl arranged the refreshments and left on soundless feet.

"I felt," her uncle continued, "that it was time yo' and I started . . . talkin' occasionally on matters of importance, beyond the purely social."

His voice was genial as they sipped at the chocolate-almond liqueur, and the other two turned politely toward her, but for a moment Yolande felt as tense as she had before the Appointments Board. Then the mellow contentment of her body forced relaxation on her mind, and she sent a thought of silent gratitude to Jolene.

"Hmmm. Ah, Uncle . . . am I to presume I'm bein' invited into the infamous von Shrakenberg Mafia?" The factional struggles within the Party had been getting fiercer these last few years, and it was well-known who led the controlling circle of the Conservative wing.

Eric laughed soundlessly. "Wotan, are they still callin' it that?" Seriously: "Yo're reaching the point where political commitments become necessary." Yolande nodded slightly; that was *almost* true. The Domination had never been able to afford real nepotism; you had to have plenty of raw talent to get promoted. Still, it had never *hurt* to have family and Party connections.

"The Party is goin' to split soon," he continued. Yolande felt a cold-water shock at the casual tone, the equally casual nods of the other two. The Draka League had always been there in the background of her life, like the atmosphere.

"How?" she asked.

"Oh, along the present factional lines. About thirty percent to my Conservatives, maybe twenty to twenty-five to Gayner and her Militants, the rest to the Center group; the Center will pick up what's left of the other parties, the Rationalists and so forth. Melinda"—she thought for a moment before realizing he must mean Melinda Shaversham, the present Archon—"hates the idea; she'll probably end up with the rump, the Center, and try to hold things together. The Center have the largest numbers, but they're short on organization an' leadership. We'll prob'ly have an unofficial Center-Conservative coalition, fo' a while at least. The long-term struggle will be fo' the Center's constituency."

"Well, if yo' lookin' fo' my vote, Uncle Eric—" she began dubiously. He shook his head.

"Somethin' far mo' fundamental, Yolande." He paused, looking down into his glass for a moment. "One thing the Militants *don't* lack, it's leadership: McLaren, Terreblanche, and Gayner. A thug, a loon, and a loony thug, but *smart*."

"Call themselves Naldorists, don't they?" she said.

Karl's snort matched his father's. "Naldorssen's been dead since 1952," he said decisively. "The Militants just wave her name, since we've all had her Will-To-Power philosophizing shoved down our throats in school."

"Well, son, she did put it mo' coherently than Nietzsche, even the formulations he made after he migrated to the Domination and calmed down," Eric said charitably. "And the Militants do have a point. All that *trans-human stage of evolution* thing was mystical drivel when Naldorssen made it up, back when. With modern biocontrol, it could happen." His mouth twisted slightly. "Under the *adjustment to circumstances* mealymouthin', what the Militants have in mind is reorganizin' the human race on a hive-insect specialization model."

"Gahh," Yolande said. *Maybe I should have been following public affairs more carefully.*

"Bad biology, too," the professor said. "The hive insects haven't changed an iota in seventy million years."

Karl laughed sourly. "Precisely Gayner's definition of success. Not surprisin'; the icebitch's never had an original idea of her own, anyways."

"But we live in a more challenging environment than insects do," Snappdove mused. "And . . . intelligence doesn't necessarily imply a self-conscious individual mind, y'know. Let the Militants get in control for three, four generations, and it'd be a positive disadvantage, even for the Race. We'd end up as empty of selfhood as ants."

"Loki on ice," Yolande said, alarmed. "I *have* been out of touch. Well, off Earth an' busy. Don't tell me the electorate is buyin' this?"

"Not directly, but then the Militant inner circle aren't spellin' it out in those terms," Eric said. "And it appeals to our national love of unchanging stasis, and the basic Draka emotion." Yolande looked a question. "Fear."

"Oh, come now, Uncle—"

"Why else would we have backed ourselves into this social cul-de-sac?" He rolled the liqueur glass between his hands. "Ever since the Landtaking, we've been in the position of a man runnin' downhill on a slope too steep to stop; got to keep going, or we fall on our face an' break our necks. Individual relationships aside, don't delude yo'self that the serfs as a group like us as a group. They don't. Why should they? We enslave them, drive them like cattle; because if we did any different, they'd overrun and butcher us."

Yolande looked from side to side, not a conventional gesture but genuine alarm.

"Don't worry," her uncle said dryly. "This place is swept daily by technicians personally loyal to me. It works, or I'd be dead."

"Well . . ." Yolande gathered her thoughts. "It's true, some aspects of the way serfs are treated is . . . unfo'tunate." She remembered deeds of her own. "I gathah yo'd like to increase the scope of those reforms yo've introduced, the serf tribunals an' such?"

Eric nodded. "Yes; but those are strictly limited. Administrative measures, really. They regularize the way serfs treat serfs . . . perhaps not so minor a mattah, since we use serfs fo' most of our supervisory work. It's certainly improved morale and efficiency, among the Literates . . . and they *still* provide the Headhunters with the most of they work. An ex-slave in America once said that a badly-treated slave longed fo' a good master, and a slave with a good master longed to be free . . . Not *entirely* true, thank Baldur the Good, or even mostly, but often enough to be worrisome. No, the *long-term* solution is to eliminate or reduce the fear. Do that, make the Citizen caste absolutely sure they're not in danger from the serfs, an' genuine reform becomes possible.

"Yo' see," he continued, leaning forward with hands on knees. The dim glowlight outlined the craggy bones of his face. "Yo' see, an outright slave society like ours is a high-tension solution to a social problem. Extreme social forms are inherently unstable; ours is as unviable as actual democracy, because it's as unnatural. It's too far up the entropy gradient. We have to *push*, continually, to keep it there. Remove the motive of fear and necessity, an' the inherent human tendency to take the path of least resistance will modify it. Eventually—perhaps in a thousand years—we'd have . . . oh, a caste society, certainly. An authoritarian one, perhaps. But somethin' mo' livable fo' everybody than this wolf-sheep relationship we have now. A better way out than Gayner's bee-hive, fo' certain. That's almost as bad as annihilation."

"Leavin' us Citizens as sheepdogs instead?" Karl asked rhetorically.

Eric grinned at his son. "Don't quote me back at mahself, boy. But yes, the human race will always need warriors and explorers, leaders even."

Yolande paused, picked up a brandied chocolate truffle and nibbled on it. "Uncle, with all due respect, Ah don't see *how* yo' could remove the necessity fo' strict control. It's been . . . well, the root of everythin'. Except by turnin' the serfs into machinery o' ghouloons."

Eric's grin became almost boyish. "We use *go-with*, on the Militants," he said. Yolande frowned in puzzlement; that was an unarmed-combat term, a deception-ploy which used an opponent's weight and strength against themselves.

"Yo've been in contact with the Eugenics people, fo' your daughter?" She nodded.

"The Militants thought they'd fought through a favorable compromise, a first step. We suckered them. Look—what are the biocontrollers removin' from the serf population? It'll take centuries more than the changes they're making in the Race, but what? Not intelligence; they're *increasin'* that, by eliminatin' the subnormal. Not creativity; Loki's tits, we don't *know* what causes that an' I suspects we never will, same as we'll never have a computer that does mo' than mimic consciousness. We're just removin' . . . that extra edge of aggressiveness that makes a warrior, from the subject races. We all know serfs that be no menace however free we let them run, right?"

"And Draka who aren't much mo' dangerous," Karl laughed.

Eric acknowledged it with a nod. "So, eventually . . . no fear. Not that the serfs would be without bargainin' power; they'll still outnumber us by eighty to one, and we'll still be dependent on them . . . but we could let the balance shift *without bein' terrified it'd shift all the way.* And *think* of what we could do if we didn't have to keep such tight clamps on their education an' such!"

Snappdove made a vigorous gesture of assent. "Better evolutionary strategy than Gayner's," he said. "More flexible. Couldn't count the number of species that've hit extinction by being overspecialized. Not that specialization's altogether bad; have to strike a balance."

She sipped at the drink again. Silence stretched into minutes. "Uncle Eric . . . Senator . . . yo've always been good to me, and honest with me. I'll be honest with yo'; it sounds good, and mo' or less what I've been thinkin', though I haven't articulated it. I've Gwen's future to think of, and my other children. But on foreign policy, as I understand it, the Militants stand fo' absolute, well, *militancy.* And that's my position, too, I . . . have reasons." She stopped, feeling her own fragility.

"Oh, so do we," Karl said.

"Absolutely. Political equations don't figure as long as the Alliance is in it," Snappdove rumbled, combing his beard with his fingers. "Adds too much tension and anxiety."

"Yes, I'm afraid so," Eric sighed. "I wish . . . well, we live as we must, and do what is necessary. Our prim'ry obligation is to our descendants, aftah all. As to the Yankees . . . we'll probably have to kill most of them." He set his glass down. "Gods, how sick I am of killin'!"

"I'm not," Yolande said grimly. To herself: *Is there anything I value more than that revenge?* Gwen, perhaps . . . A ghost opened green eyes at the back of her mind and whispered. *Don't borrow trouble, 'Landa-sweet. Or torment yourself with decisions you don't need to make.*

"Which brings us to the secondary mattah of Task Force Telmark IV," Eric said. "Incidently, Arch-Strategos Welber is one of us."

Us, Yolande thought. *So we make irrevocable decisions, without a spot you could stop and say—"Here. Here I did it."* She shivered slightly; the trip to Archona had been difficult enough when only an Appointment Board was at stake. Now she had joined a political cabal, and Draka politics was a game played by only one rule: rule or die.

"We—the inner circle of the Conservatives, that is—want to win the Protracted Struggle very, very badly. In the interim, we've got to be seen to *wage* it effectively; one hint of softness an' the Militants will be over us like flies on horseshit. This *is* an impo'tant mission. I think you can handle it. Wouldn't have recommended yo' fo' it, otherwise."

A wolf's expression. "Doesn't hurt that yo' a von Shrakenberg relation, from the Landholder class . . . and have been seen extensively in my company these past days. Politically profitable glory fo' all. If yo' win, that is. Fail, and it's a setback fo' me." *And a disaster for you, girl,* went unspoken between them.

"M-ha," Snappdove said. "Very important. If that object's what we think, our materials problems in the Earth-Moon area will be solved for the better part of a decade, *without* having to cut back on anything. By which time the outer-system projects will be on-line. Finally."

"We were over-hasty," Karl agreed. "Whole space effort has been. Those early scramjets, they were deathtraps." He shook his head. "Both sides'. The Yankees kept trying to model the airflows with inadequate computers, and *we,* we built a gigawatt of nuclear power stations, used the whole Dniester for cooling, to get that damned Mach-18 quarter-scale windtunnel. And we *still* had disasters."

Snappdove spread his hands. The gesture triggered something in Yolande's memory, and suddenly she could place the overtone to his accent. East European; his family must be one of the rare elite given Citizen status after the conquest. Scientists, mostly; that would explain a good deal.

"We needed the lift capacity, if we were to develop near-space in time," he said ruthlessly. "The only other way to orbit was rockets, and they are toys. Even those first scramjets could carry six tonnes to orbit; now they're up to fifty."

"The early pulsedrives were almost as bad," Yolande said. "We lost a lot of brave people, using them in the outer system."

Snappdove smiled at her, and to her astonishment began quoting poetry. Hers: *The Lament for the Fallen who Fall Forever*, part of the *Colder Than the Moon* collection. It had used a literary conceit, a fantasy, that the quick-frozen bodies retained a trickle of consciousness in their supercooled brains:

> "And those graveless dead drift restless
>   In the emptiness of space
> Who died so far from love and home
>   And the blue world's warm embrace . . .

"But now those problems are largely solved," he continued. "What remains is engineering. Wonderful engineering, though!" He warmed, eyes lighting. "Perhaps that is why we of Technical Section support the good senator . . . Did you know we have funding for the first Beanstalk project, now?"

"Ah?" Yolande said. That *was* news. "Where?"

"Titan!" He made the spreading-hands gesture again at her raised eyebrows. That was a cutting-edge project, lowering a cable from geosynchronous orbit and using it to run elevators to the surface. Daring, to put it on one of the moons of Saturn . . .

"Logical," the professor insisted. "The gravity there, that is nothing, only .14G, but the atmosphere is thicker than Earth's, and the problems of operating on the surface horrendous, lasers or mass-drivers out of the question. But a Beanstalk, that gives us even *cheaper* transit, and once we do—nitrogen, methane, ethane, hydrogen cyanide, all types of organic condensates! It will take nearly a decade, but even so, once completed we can pump any desired quantity of materials downhill to sunward. Better we had concentrated on Saturn's moons in any case; the distance is greater but the environment less troublesome than Jupiter." The giant planet had radiation belts that were ferociously difficult even with superconductor-magnetic shielding.

"Energy would be a problem, wouldn't it?" Yolande speculated. *This is part of the bait,* she thought without resentment, looking at her uncle sidelong. *They know my dreams.* That was politics, and the dream was shared.

"Well," Eric said easily, "there we've taken a tip from the Yankees. Here, look at this."

He slid a folder of glossy prints across the table to her. She flicked through them rapidly. They were schematic prints for some large construction; zero-G, or it would have collapsed. Circular, with two . . . large railguns? at either side.

"What is it?" she said.

"Somethin' the Yankees fondly believe is secret," Eric said, then glanced at his son. "Need to know," he added.

The younger man rose. "Goodnight, all," he said cheerfully. "I've got company waitin', anyhows. Less intellectual but mo' entertainin'."

Eric waited, then continued. "Example of how it's easier to do things in space," he said. "We *still* haven't got a workin' fusion reactor here on Earth. This is one—in a sense. Big empty sphere with heat exchangers an' superconductor coils in the shell. Throw two pellets of isotopic hydrogen in through the railguns, *splat.* Beam-heat at the same time. Hai, wingo, fusion."

"Ahmmm," Yolande said thoughtfully. "Sounds like what we're plannin' fo' the next-generation pulsedrive." A pause. "Crude, though, as a power source. Mo' like what we'd do. And why do they need nonsolar power sources in the Belt?"

"Yes," Snappdove said. "Patented brute-force-and-massive-ignorance method, very Draka . . . but it will work. Even useful for industry—the sun is fainter out there, microwave relay stations for the power . . . also typical of our methods. Here." He pulled out another of the prints, showing a long rectangle of some thin sheet floating against the stars. "And what our sources in the Belt say is being subcontracted for."

She read the list. "Superconductor coils . . . wire . . . *tungsten?*"

"Linear accelerators," Snappdove said. "Not for mass-driving, not for research. Antimatter production."

Yolande blinked. "Is it possible?" she said. "I thought . . . wasn't there an accident, a whiles back?"

"TechSec facility in the Urals." Eric nodded. "Equivalent

of a megatonne sunbomb. Discouraged us no end. Engineerin'
problems in laser coolin' and magnetic confinement, but antimatter is an old discovery on a laboratory scale, back as far as
the 1930s. Mo' sensible to do it in space, though. Question is,
why so secret?"

"Weapons?" she thought aloud.

"What point? We've *already* got weapons mo' powerful
than we dare use here on earth. Oh, yes, tactically useful in
deep space. Even better as a propulsion system, iff'n it can
be managed, the ultimate rocket, yes. Still, it's puzzlin'. This
has to be a long-term project, an' expensive as hell. The
maximum security approach makes it even *mo'* expensive an'
slow. Fifteen years even to start on large-scale production.
Probably mo'; it's doable but all sorts of problems. They'd put
it in the Belt, certainly." The Alliance was encouraging "home-
steading" there by every means possible. "We're goin' to
deuterium-tritium fusion pellets fo' pulsedrives soon, then
deuterium-boron 11. That's almost as efficient, all charged
particles. They can't be goin' to this much trouble just to
build a better pulsedrive fo' warships.'"

Snappdove snorted. "We have a pilot project, at the
Mercury-Shield Platform." That was a research settlement,
orbiting in the innermost planet's shadow. "Developing a
plan to mass-produce solar power farms for near-sun use.
Easily adaptable to powering antimatter production, perhaps
early next century. We do the usual, wait for the Yankees to
solve the tricky problems, steal their development, rejig it for
our needs. They get a little ahead but not much.'"

"So it *can't* be just what it seems," Eric said grimly. "Not
just a power source for Belt settlement, not just a try fo'
better drives. There's a *big* secret here. The sort that I have
nightmares about, knowin' some of *our* big secrets."

"Well . . . yes, Uncle Eric, but what's *my* part in it? I
thought the High Command was sendin' me to grab a rock?"

"Aha," Eric said, with a mirthless laugh. "A rock *comin'*
from fairly close to where a lot of Alliance personnel have
been *goin'*. And not comin' back, never. Now, we have
information on a launch . . .'"

CHAPTER THIRTEEN

PRIVATE ENTERPRISE IN SPACE

In a speech today to the North American Enterprise Institute, Commerce Secretary Ingrid Lindqvist called on the entrepreneurs of the Alliance to contribute to the humanization of space. Secretary Lindqvist noted that while pulsedrive ships will always be expensive, they are rapidly increasing in number and efficiency, while solar-sail and plasma drives (given the falling price of superconductor accumulators) put the system as far out as the asteroids in reach with a modest investment; given the tax credits and subsidies recently approved by the Alliance Grand Senate and the national governments, no more than the price of a merchant ship of moderate size. "Our entrepreneurs and companies are already present in strength in the orbital habitats and Lunar bases. Their diversity is our strength; we summon them to the contest for trans-Lunar space as well."

Under the new New Homestead Act (Alliance Grand Senate, Legislative Session 1976-77), private parties will now be able to claim any body within the interdicted Alliance zones provided they can develop it in a reasonable time. Survival equipment and surplus plasma-drive—equipped cargo shuttles suitable for conversion will be made available at Ceres Base. Facilities at the Alliance military outposts and scientific stations have now reached the point where full-time residence is possible, including centrifugal-gravity habitats for periodic exercise and child-bearing.

The larger asteroidal bodies will require intensive capital investment, but given cheap solar-powered vacuum refining methods, many smaller bodies will be accessible to partnerships or even individuals. Guaranteed markets exist, first with the Alliance government projects, then in Earth-Lunar space. Secondary activities, from manufacturing and food to services of all types, are expected to grow exponentially. Secretary Lindqvist added: "We have a crucial advantage here. We can trust our people with small spaceships, and appeal to the profit motive. What Draka Citizen will endure a prospector's life? And if they send out serfs, what is to prevent defection?"

> Capital Monthly
> Chicago Union Press
> July 11, 1977

LOW EARTH ORBIT
PLATFORM FRONTIER FIVE
ALLIANCE SPACE FORCE
MAY 6, 1982

Earth turned beyond the dome like a giant blue shield, streaked with the white of clouds, glowing softly with an intense pale light. The western coast of North America was on the edge of vision, turning toward night, and the sunlight glittered on the ocean through a scattering of cirrus. There were scattered spots of light across the surface, above the last azure haze of atmosphere, moving or drifting in orbit. Spidery cages of aluminum beam extended in every direction in a latticework that linked powersails, broadcast rectennae, machinery of less obvious purpose. Further out were docking arms of tubing connected to the main pressure-modules behind them; two held passenger scramjets, long melted-looking delta aircraft, featureless save for the big squarish ramjet intakes under the rear of their lifting-body shapes.

It was an old story to Frederick Lefarge. He twisted in the air to watch his wife's face instead. *How did I ever luck out like this?* he thought. The pale chill-blue light washed across the hazel-green of her eyes, the mahogany hair and olive-bronze skin. Tears glistened at the corners of her eyes.

"Listen," she said softly. Her voice had an accent that was a blend of her mother's South Carolina drawl and her father's Spanish-Mayan; soft and lilting at the same time. "You can hear it."

"What?" he said.

"The music of the spheres," she answered, then scrubbed the back of her hand across her eyes.

A bell pinged. *"All passengers, flight Hermes-17A, forty minutes to final call. Forty minutes to final call."*

"Damn, I wish you'd change your mind," he said fiercely.

"Honey," she replied, smiling. "How many times have we been over this? I wouldn't be anything but a burden for the next month; need-to-know, remember?"

She nodded to the scattering of people on the floor and sides of the domed lounge. Lefarge felt the familiar vertigo-inducing twist of perception, and now he was looking *down*, with the great curve of Earth above his head. A ground-ape's fear of falling passed through him unnoticed, and he studied the others. Several dozen. You could tell the Space Forcers and old stationjacks, and not just by their clothing; to them a floor was just another wall, and they used the ripstick pads on feet and knees and elbows to negotiate their way with innocent disregard for orientation. You never saw them drifting free without a handhold, either, like that hapless woman wearing a *skirt* of all things, thrashing in midair until a crewman anchored a line from the reel at his belt and leaped out to her.

Most of the rest were those who would be leaving on the *Pathfinder*. Forty of the eighty, come for a last look at the home that none would see again for years, many never again. The majority were young, more than half men, technical workers of every type. He saw tears, laughter, raucous good humour, nervous excitment among the handful of children. There was a scattering of older folk, married couples solemn with the thought of what this meant. His own two daughters were already aboard the *Pathfinder*, sleeping in their cocoon-cribs in Cindy's cabin. His stomach twisted at the thought.

"You'd be aboard a warship, if you waited," he said.

Cindy sighed. "Honey, it's important I get to know some of the project people without . . . well, without you around." There were a dozen recruits for the New America project aboard, the rest were leaving at Ceres. *But only one who has any inkling of the* real *project*, he thought. *In time, in time. Patience.*

His wife was continuing: "Free people don't like living under War Emergency Regulations, Fred. For things to work right, they've got to *want* them to work right, and for that they've got to see you as a human being, not some all-powerful bureaucrat. What better way than to get to know your wife and children, on a three-month voyage? There's only a few thousand people in the whole *belt*, darling, and a few hundred on the Project. We're going to be a *real* small town for a long while." Quietly. "Let me do my part for this too, Fred."

Cindy was cleared for the third-level version of the Project, but he suspected she had guessed more.

"It isn't *safe*," he said.

"Darling, it's *safer* than coming out on the cruiser. It's been years since there was a clash in the Belt, isn't it? And the only incidents have been between warships."

He ran a hand through his hair, sighed. "Okay, okay, you convinced me before. The only thing the Snakes have scheduled is an expedition out to Jupiter, anyway." Pulsedrive warships were still not common, and mostly very fully occupied.

"And we *will* get to Ceres about the same time," she continued with gentle ruthlessness. His ship would be leaving much later, but the *Ethan Allen* was a new-launched pulsedrive cruiser, vastly more powerful. This would be her shakedown trip, in fact.

"All *right*, Cindy! I just hope Captain Hayakawa understands how important a cargo he's hauling."

They linked hands, and she pulled herself closer, putting an arm around his waist and her head on his shoulder. The hair that drifted up around his nose was short-cropped (nothing else was practical in zero-G), but it shone in the Earth-light, smelling faintly of Colorado Mist shampoo and flowers. Her gaze went back out to the curve of the planet above.

"Well," she said, "he *is* carryin' part of something precious." At his glance, she added: "Hope, for our tired old mother here. Up here, where there's room to breathe." She dimpled. "Even if there isn't much air . . ."

"You're a romantic," he laughed. Somberly: "And the Snakes are here, too."

She nodded. "Like our shadows," she said, sadly. "Or like an ancient set of armor with nothing inside but a corpse that's rotting and pitiful and thinks it's alive, walking and clanking and killing and trying to eat . . ."

"For a nice person, you've got a way with images," he said, shivering slightly at the thought. It was appropriate, though. The Domination was something that *should* have died a century ago. *And it's my job to bury it,* he thought as they turned and braced their feet against the crosswire.

"Gently does it, honey," he said.

They pushed off, floating down the ten meters to the deck; he kept his arm around Cindy's waist as they twisted end-for-end and landed. The ripstick on their slippers touched down on the catch-surface of the floor, with a *tack* sound as the miniature plastic hooks and loops engaged. The crew supervisors from the *Pathfinder* were shepherding their passengers into one of the radial exitways. As they passed the dogged-open pressure door, he had another flash of twisted perspective, and now they were at the bottom of a long well five meters broad, lit by strips, with handholds in regular receding rows. It was lined with close-cropped green vines, part of the air system, and a contribution to the eternal rabbit protein of the spacer's diet. The joke was that you shouldn't leave gravity if you couldn't face rodent.

Or there was fish, of course. Frontier Five had a *big* watertank, like most industrial-transit stations with a population over a thousand; all you had to do was take a multitonne lump of Lunar silicon and point mirrors at it, inject some gas and continue to heat. *Voilá*, as Maman would say. An aquarium, a convenient heatsink regulator and fuel store. You could rent a facegill and go swimming there, if you didn't mind sharing the water with trout and carp . . . the *other* inevitabilities of life in space . . .

Why am I thinking about this? he asked himself as they passed a junction and caught a main-tube beltway. Cindy snuggled closer as they rode the strip of conveyor. Incoming traffic passed them on the left, and there was another set above. They could see the heads of the passengers whipping by three meters beyond. *Because it's a distraction, that's why,* he thought.

The departure lounge was thronged. Most of the exit docking-tubes led to the thrice-daily Luna shuttles, off to the moon-settlements of Freetown and Britannia, and New Edo. One of the larger tubes had a rosette of four MPs in Space Force blues hanging around it; they snapped his colonel's bars a salute, and the three men eyed Cindy with respectful appreciation.

Washington and *Simón Bolívar* were in, he remembered, downlined with skeletal crews for new thrustplates and repairs to their drive feed systems. The *Ethan Allen* was up at one of the L-5 battlestations, doing final calibrations on her drive and getting the auxiliary comps burned in; it was policy to keep as much of the deep-space fleet as possible away from Earth. Too many heavy lasers and beam-weapons between here and the moon, too many missiles and hardened launchers, too may sensors. A warship needed room to be effective . . .

Another exit, with the circular railing guard and a crewwoman in Trans-American silver. Briefly, his mouth quirked; the early skinsuits had been that color, for insulation. Someone had wanted to call the Space Force the Silver Service, back then, until a tabloid came up with the inevitable "Teapots in Space" headline. The display beside her was flashing: *Flight Hermes 17A—Trans-Am Ship Pathfinder—now boarding for Ceres.*

"This is it," he husked.

Cindy stood for a moment, then siezed him in a grip that nearly tore him loose from the deck. "I'll miss you, honey," she whispered, her forehead pressed into his chest. *"Vaya con dios, mi corazón."* Tears drifted loose and drifted like minor jewels; one landed on his lips, tasting of salt.

"I'll miss you and the tykes, too," he said, his own voice a little husky. Stepping back, he held her hands for a moment. "Go on then, have them all charmed silly by the time I get to Ceres!" he said.

"Will do, Colonel, sir," she said, smiling and wiping at her eyes with a tissue. She put a hand on the rail and stepped over, pulling herself down the access tube feet-first to keep him in view a moment longer.

"Shit," he whispered to himself, as she passed out of sight.

CLAESTUM PLANTATION
DISTRICT OF TUSCANY
PROVINCE OF ITALY
DOMINATION OF THE DRAKA
MAY 7, 1982

"Well, Myfwany," Yolande began.

The graveyard was empty now, save for the dead and her. Gwen had come, to solemnly lay her handful of wildflowers on the turf; she was down by the bottom of the hill now, playing with Wulda, their new ghouloon. He had been expensive, but her daughter was entranced; she could hear the happy high-pitched shrieks from up here, see the girl doll-tiny with distance and perched on the transgene animal's shoulders as they romped by the car. For the rest there was silence, and the warm sweet smells of early summer in Italy: cut clover, wild strawberries from the hedgerows. Bees hummed among the banks of trembling iris that lined the flagstone pathways.

"Gwen's growin' like a weed," Yolande continued quietly. She was kneeling by the headstone, a simple black basalt rectangle with name and dates inlaid in Lunar titanium; she thought Myfwany would have liked that. "And gods, she's smart. I love her mo' than I can tell, sweet. Goin' to be tough and fast like yo', but sunnier, I think."

She paused for a minute. You could see a long way from here, between the trunks of the big oaks and cypresses. Over the vale and the morning mist, past the terraced vineyards to the Great House shining in its gardens, into the bluegreen haze of the hills beyond.

"I'm havin' a baby, by yo' brother Billy," she said. "Took Jolene in fo' the seeding yesterday . . . don't know exactly why she volunteered, maybe she misses yo', too, darlin'." Suddenly Yolande pressed the heels of her hands to her eyes. "Oh, gods, I miss yo' so! I try, sweet, I try but I'm not strong like yo' . . . I wish yo' could tell me what to do." A shaky laugh, and she lowered her hands. "I know, darlin', I'm bein' soppy again like you used to say. Hated hearin' it then, and now I'd give mah soul to hear yo' rake me over the coals again. I've gotten a new command, though, love."

She rose to her feet. Her voice whispered. "And I swear, by yo' blood below my feet, Myfwany, I'll make them pay fo' yo'. Pay, and pay, and pay, and it'll still never be enough." Aloud: "Goodbye fo' now, my love. Till we meet again."

She turned to walk down the hill; there was the flight to catch. *Why don't I cry?* she thought. *Never, here. Why?*

LOW EARTH ORBIT
NEAR LAUNCH PLATFORM SKYLORD SIX
ABOARD DASCS *SUBOTAI*
MAY 23, 1982

". . . drive systems at one hundred percent," a voice was
saying in the background. The last of the checklist.

Yolande leaned back in the big crashcouch. Only the
elastic belts were buckled across her skinsuit; the massive
petal-like sections of the combat cocoon had folded back
into the sides. The bridge of *Subotai* was dark, lit mainly by
the screens spaced around the perimeter of the eight-meter
circle. A dozen stations, horseshoes standing out from the
walls with a crashcouch in the center, all occupied. Her own
in the center portside of the axial tube, surrounded by sections of console like wedge-shaped portions of a disk. Dozens
of separate screens—physical separation rather than virtual,
for redundancy's sake. Light blue and green from data readouts, pickups, graphs and schematics.

"*Subotai* on standby," said the First Officer, Warden
Fermore; she had voyaged with him before.

A screen before her flicked to the face of Philia Garren,
captain of the other warship. "*Batu* on standby," she said.

"*Marius* on standby."

"*Sappho* on standby."

"*Crassus* on standby."

"*Alcibiades*, on standby."

Cargo-carriers: the heart of this mission. A substantial proportion of the Domination's fast heavy-lift capacity, originally
built for work around the gas-giant moons. She tapped for an
exterior view. The Telmark IV flotilla were stationary a bare
kilometer from SkyLord Six and perhaps ten from each other,
touching distance in these terms. The armored globe of the
launch-station swung before her, with the 200-meter tubes of
the free-electron lasers around it like the arms of a spider.
The other ships . . . Yolande allowed herself a moment of
cold pride at the power beneath her fingertips.

"Status, report," she said. And there was a certain queasy
feeling, before any mission. Like having eaten a little too
much oily food—and it was worse this time. This time
everything was her responsibility . . .

"Time to boost, three minutes and counting," the First
Officer said.

She looked at the other ships. The *Batu* was a twin of her own. Two hundred and fifty meters from the bell of the thrust plate to the hemisphere dome of the forward shield; most of that machinery space open behind a latticework stretched between the four main keel-beams. The heat dumpers, running the length of the keels and the drive lasers; the long bundles that held the plutonium fuel-pellets; the jagged asymmetric shapes of rectennae, railgun pods, gatling turrets, launch-tubes. And the cylindrical armored bulk of the reaction-mass tank, with the smaller cylinder of the pressurized crew-zone half embedded in it. The transports were blockier, squat, similar propulsion systems but without the weapons, more reaction mass . . . A pulsedrive *could* run on just the fission reaction and the byproducts, but that was bad for the thrustplates and squanderous of fuel.

All of them clamped to strap-on boost packs, of course. It was not very nice to fire off a pulsedrive just outside the atmosphere; the EMP would destroy electronics over half a continent.

"Cleared for boost, SkyLord Six," she said.

"Guidance lasers locked. All locked. Excitment phase beginning."

An amplified voice, that would sound throughout the flotilla. "STAND BY FOR ACCELERATION. STAND BY FOR ACCELERATION. FIVE THOUSAND SECONDS, MAX AT ONE-POINT-SEVEN-EIGHT G. TEN SECONDS TO BURN. COUNTING."

She gripped the rests, let the fluid resilience of the couch enfold her. Far behind her back the supercooled oxygen in the strap-on booster would be subliming under the first teasing feathertouch of the station's lasers. A pulse to vaporize—

Whump. The *Subotai* massed 14,000 tonnes with full tanks; now that moved with a faint surge, growing as the magnetic equalizers between thrustplate and hull-frame absorbed the energy. And another pulse to turn vapor to plasma—

WHAM*whump*WHAM—too fast to sense, building to hundreds of times per second as the lasers flickered. The exterior view showed long leaf-shaped cones of white flame below the strap-ons, and the ships were beginning to move. Weight pressed down on her chest, building; the acceleration would increase as mass diminished. It was nothing compared to flying atmosphere fighters, but it went on much longer . . . 5,000 seconds of burn. Very economical, to save their own onboard reaction mass. It was liquid 02 and dirt-cheap here near Luna where the mines produced it as a by-product; more precious than rubies out where you needed it, at the other end of the trajectory. Even more economical to save on the tiny plutonium-beryllium-plastic pellets that powered a pulsedrive. Full load for a Great Khan cruiser was half a million pellets, which meant six *tonnes* of plutonium.

The world had been mass-producing breeder reactors for twenty years, to fuel ships like this.

Minutes stretched, and the pressure on her chest increased. She breathed against it, watching the time blinking on half a dozen screens and remembering. Other launches; her first . . . only six years ago? Assistant Pilot Officer, then. Not *quite* a record for promotion. There had been casualties, and a massive expansion program, and not everyone wanted space assignments . . . Uncle Eric had pulled strings to get Gwen allowed up for the launch, and she had actually been quiet when they showed her the ships through the viewport; there was one who was *definitely* going to go spacer herself.

The stars were unmoving in the exterior view, but the station was dwindling. Dwindling to a point of light, against the curved shield of Earth; that shrinking to a globe. Other spots of light around it, some things large enough to be seen: station powersails, then a real solar sail half-deployed near a construction station. Ten minutes, and the planet was much smaller. The terminator was sweeping over the eastern Mediterranean. Dusk soon at Claestum. Jolene was there, with Yolande's child below her heart; she remembered holding the serf's hand in the Clinic. Pinpoint lights from the darkness over Central Asia; possibly launches from the laserlift stations in the Tien Shan. City lights. Very faint straight lines on the northern and southern edges of the Sahara; one of the few things you could see from this distance were the reclamation projects.

The moon was swelling; they would use it for slingshot effect, about an hour after the burn stopped. Back in . . . '62, it had been, she remembered how exciting, the first moon landings. Going out with ma and pa on the terrace at home, the servants unfolding the 150mm telescope, ma showing her how to spot the tiny flame. The Yankees ahead—*may they rot*—but only by a few months. Strange-looking clunky little ships, hand-assembled around those first primitive orbital platforms. A dozen figures in black skinsuits and bubble-helmets climbing down the ladders in dreamlike slowness to plant the Drakon banner on the moon; she had stayed up past her bedtime, glued to the viewer, and no one had objected.

"How far we've come," she murmured. *Only a single generation. Of course, we had incentive.* Ten percent of GNP for decades could accomplish a great deal.

The First Officer responded to her words rather than the meaning. "Making eight kps relative, Cohortarch," Fermore said. "Twelve hundred seconds of burn to go; then a quick whip-round and it's a month to Mars." Minimum-burn, for pulsedrives. And you could pick up reaction mass, at the Draka station on Phobos.

She felt the weight of the sealed dataplaque over her breast. Sealed orders, and there were only six others in the flotilla who knew, of more than six hundred; she would tightbeam the course-change when they were a week out. A profligate trajectory, since it was necessary to deceive the enemy until the last minute, burning fuel and mass recklessly, but the prize was worth it.

BETWEEN THE ORBITS OF EARTH AND MARS
ABOARD DASCS *SUBOTAI*
JUNE 18, 1982

The wardroom of the *Subotai* was small and cluttered; it doubled as an exercise chamber, up here just below the bowcap of the cruiser. They would be a long time in zero-G, and the hormone treatments did only so much to slow calcium loss. Just now Yolande and Snappdove had it to themselves, their feet tucked into straps under a table. There was a lingering smell of sweat in the air, under the chill freshness the life-support system imposed.

"Your health," Yolande said, raising her bulb and sipping lemonade through the straw. Flat, but carbonated beverages in zero-G were an invitation to perpetual flatulence. *Such are the trials we face pushing back the frontiers of the Race,* she thought dryly.

Snappdove's beard had been clipped closer, for convenience in the helmet-ring of his skinsuit. "Our success!" he said, clinking his bulb against hers with a dull *tump* of plastic. "Not to mention our wealth."

"The news good as all that?" Yolande said.

"The core samples are all in now," the scientist said. "Definitely an ex-comet, somewhat larger and less dense than we thought . . . ah, there is so much we do not know! Always we discover theory-breaking facts faster than we can make plausible theories, out here." He shook his head ruefully. "Ex-comet, or at least something that came from the outer system, sometime. Complex orbital perturbations, collisions . . . Comet, asteroid—we impose definitions on nature, but nature does not always agree."

Yolande sighed inwardly. She had not had much time to get to know the head of the expedition's Technical Section crew—they had only been here five days and he had been madly busy, but it had been enough to know that he was unstoppable. *A true natural philosopher, out of time,* she thought. *The facts entrance him because he can think about them, not necessarily because they're of any use.*

"Yo' have a theory?" she said.

"Hmmm. Hmmm. Crude, but . . . several passes into the zone between Earth and Mars resulted in the loss of the outer layer of volatiles, various ices. The process was fairly gentle—I doubt if the Object ever came within 1.1 AU of the sun—and the solid material, the organics and silicates, were not thrown off. Instead it formed a protective crust; there must have been a truly unusual amount of such heavier materials. This was through many passes, you understand. Perhaps asteroidal material was incorporated. Now, though, we have a fairly complete crust, there may be some sublimation still, but nothing drastic." The slight foreign overtone to his accent became stronger as his animation grew. "We will have to be careful; ammonia or methane could still be present."

"The composition?" she asked, reigning in impatience.

"As favorable as could be hoped!" He spread his hands. "Carbonaceous outer layer, rock and organic compounds. Under that . . . ice! Over a *billion* tonnes of ice. Dirty ice at that, many complex hydrogenated compounds. And—an additional bonus—a rocky core with high concentrations of platinum-group metals. At a guess, the Object *did* encounter asteroidal material. At some time, the ice softened enough that . . . well, never mind." He chuckled, and parked the drink in the air to rub his palms. "My so-aristocratic colleague, has it occurred to you that we are now very, very rich?"

Yolande blinked. *Why no, it hadn't,* she thought. "Point-O-one percent of the value divided by . . . two hundred and thirty Citizens is that much?" A moment's pause. "Oh, I see what yo' means."

"Yes, indeed. This discovery will power our space-based development for half a decade."

The commander of the flotilla nodded, mildly pleased. Not that she had ever wanted for money; few Citizens did, and she less than most. Still, it would be pleasant; she was of Landholding family but not landed . . . A land-grant was free, but that meant raw territory you had to spend a generation licking into shape. Nothing like the opportunities her parents had had in Europe after the Eurasian War. With *enough* money you could get one of the rare plantations for sale, or pay for someone else to oversee development. A heritage for her children; and then, it would be useful to have an Archona townhouse . . .

"Can we move it?" she added practically.

"If it is possible, my crew can do it," Snappdove said with another chuckle. "They are well motivated, even the serfs."

Glory, she supposed, as well as wealth, for the Citizens. The serfs would get the satisfaction of exercising their specialties; these would be mostly Class V-a Literates already, many creche-trained for the military. And privileges, apartments, guarantees of education for their children. They would be eager for success, too.

"It is my ambition to get through a project without a single execution," Snappdove said, echoing her thoughts. "And yes, we can move it, I think. Monomolecular coating, reflective, to decrease the heat absorption. Single-crystal cable webbing. Then we set up that thrust plate—beautiful piece of work, astounding things they do with cermet composites these days—and it only has to last a month. Then *boom!* and *boom!*, we use our bombs. Earth orbit, very eccentric one, but the details after that are not our concern."

She nodded. "Sounds good," she said. "Very good."

He sighed happily. "Yes, every year the size of project we can accomplish increases. Geometrically. Did I tell you, we have nearly completed the long-range feasibility study for terraforming Mars?"

Her ears pricked. For a moment, she was back on the dark beach below Baiae School, lying around the campfire and watching the moving stars and dreaming of what they would do. Myfwany . . .

"No," she said hastily. *Gods, how it sneaks up on you,* she thought dismally. *Work, more work. That's what I need.*

"Oh, yes. We float big mirrors near Mars, melt the icecaps. Much water and C02 there. More mirrors, increase the solar heating. Then we blow up Callisto—"

"Wotan and the White Christ!" she blurted. "That was one of the major moons of Jupiter. "That's biggah than Luna!"

He nodded, and ran fingers through his beard. "But ice, only ice; much more than we need for Mars. And there is no limit to how big we may make our bombs. We drop pieces on Mars . . . comets also, if convenient. Already the atmosphere will be thicker and warmer. Water vapor increases the greenhouse effect; tailored bacteria and algae go to work cracking the oxides, the sun splits water vapor. An ozone layer. Nitrogen we get from various places, Titan . . . In a long lifetime, there is breathable air, thinner than Earth, higher percentage of oxygen. Then we build the Beanstalks, and work begins on the ecology; not my field. Many small seas and lakes, about half the surface."

His eyes stared out beyond the bulkhead. "And then we bring in serfs to till the fields . . . strange, is it not?"

"No," she said frankly. "Should it be?" For a moment she imagined condors nesting on the slopes of Martian canyons longer than continents, forests five hundred meters tall . . .

He snorted. "A matter of perspective. Me, I will buy an estate in perhaps south China, for my children. And a block in the Trans-Solar Combine, they have contracts in the project." Another shrug of the massive shoulders. "All this is moot. We must finish with the Alliance, first."

Yolande grinned. It was a much less pleasant expression than the intellectual interest of a moment before. "To business, then. Can yo' get me retanked on reaction mass? I ran it down somethin' fierce, matchin' velocities here."

"Oh, yes. Trivial. Do you wish water or liquid oxygen?"

"Hmmmm. No, we're rigged fo' 02, we'll go with that. How long?"

"Two days for your ship, and one to rig the stills. A week for the rest of the fleet."

"Do it, then. First priority. We need the intelligence data on that Yankee ship." *And an installment payment on the debt they owe me,* she thought. *A small, small payment on a very large account.*

ABOARD TRANS-AMERICAN SHIP *PATHFINDER*
EARTH-CERES
JUNE 12, 1982

The lounge of the *Pathfinder* had aquired a certain homey-
ness in the month and a half of transit, Cindy decided. It was
on the second-highest of the eight decks in the pressure
section, a semicircle on one side of the core tube, across from
the galley and stores. One corner was posted with drawings
and projects; she and several of the other mothers held
classes for the children there, around the terminal they had
appropriated. Young Alishia Merkowitz showed real talent in
biology; she really should talk to the girl's parents . . . There
was a big viewer, but the passengers generally only screened
movies or documentaries; the sort who moved to the Belt
didn't go in for passive entertainment.

There was a group mastering the delicate art of zero-G
darts, another arguing politics. The coffee machine was going,
scenting the air; it looked odd, but you did have to *push* the
water through here. A courting couple were perched by the
sole exterior viewport, but they were holding hands, obliv-
ious to the spectacle of the stars. Two young men were
building a model habitat from bits of plastic—scarcely a hobby,
they were engineers and had a terminal beside them for
references. She could catch snatches of their conversation:

". . . no, no, you don't have to use a frame and plating!
Just boil out the silicates, inject water, heat and spin and the
outer shell will . . ."

Dr. Takashi moved his piece. Cindy Guzman Lefarge started
and returned her attention to the *go* board.

"Oh, lordy, Doctor," she said. "You're never going to make
a *go* player of me."

"You show native talent," he said, considering the board. It
was electronic, and they were using light-pencils to move the
pieces; the traditional stones were a floating nuisance in
space.

"I'm surprised you don't play the captain," she said, frowning. A quarter of her pieces were gone . . . which still left her
with more than her opponent, who had started with a substantial handicap. But far too many were nearly surrounded.

"Ah." He smiled; Professor of Cybernetic Systems Analysis
Manfred Takashi was a slim man, fifty, with dark-brown skin
and short wiry hair. "Captain Hayakawa is impeccably polite,

but I doubt that he would welcome social contact. Not from me."

Cindy raised her brows. "Well, he is fairly reserved. I would have thought, though, you being Japanese—"

The professor laughed. "*Half* Japanese, my dear Mrs. Lefarge, *half* Japanese. Even worse, half *black*."

The woman winced, embarrassed. Overt racial prejudice was rare these days in the cities of North America, even more so in space. Of course, some of the family in the South Carolina low country were still unhappy about her mother's marriage to a Maya from Yucatan, even a much-decorated naval veteran of the Pacific campaigns back in the Eurasian War.

"Actually," the man continued, "it is an interesting change. In Hawaii it was the *Japanese* side of my heritage which created problems."

She nodded. The Imperial occupation in the early '40s had been brutal, and the angers had taken a long time to dissipate. Even now some of the older generation found it difficult to accept how important Japan had become in the councils of the Alliance.

"You must be eager to get to work, on"—she lowered her voice—"the Project." Best to change the subject.

"Indeed." He turned the light-pencil in his hands. "I—"

Tchannnng. The sound went through the hull, like an enormous steel bucket struck with a fingernail. Conversation died, and the passengers looked up.

"*Attention!*" the captain's voice. "We have suffered a meteorite impact. There is no danger; the hull was not breached. I repeat, there is no danger. All passengers will please return to their cabins until further notice."

"I must get back to Janet and Iris," Cindy said, rising briskly. She forced down a bubble of anxiety; a meteor strike was very rare—odd that the close-in radars had not detected it. "Continue the game after dinner, Professor?"

"I hope so," he said quietly, folding the board as he stood. "I sincerely hope so."

"Distance and bearing," Yolande said.

"100 k-klicks, closing at point-one kps relative," the sensor officer said.

Yolande could feel the strait tension in the ship, a taste like ozone in the air. A week's travel. Overcrowded, since she had dropped off most of the ship's Auxiliaries who handled routine maintenance and taken on another score of Citizen crew from *Batu*. The main problem with Draka was keeping them from ripping at each other. Constant drill in the arcane art of zero-G combat had helped. And now action. Not that the pathetic plasma-drive soup-can out there was any menace to a cruiser, but they had to *capture*, not destroy. Much more difficult.

"Bring up the schematic," she said. They would not detect the *Subotai* for a while yet; her stealthing was constructed to deceive military sensors.

Two screens to her left blanked and then showed 360 degree views of the Alliance vessel, *Pathfinder*. A ferrous-alloy barrel, basically, the aft section holding a reaction-mass tank and a simple engine. An arc broke the mass into plasma, and magnetic coils accelerated it out the nozzle, Power from solar-receptors or a big storage coil. Thrown out of earth-orbit much as the *Subotai* had been, then additional boost from a solar sail. That was still deployed, square kilometers of .05-micron aluminum foil, rigged on lines of sapphire filament; but soon they would furl it and begin velocity-matching for Ceres. A long slow burn; plasma drives were efficient but low-thrust.

Would have begun their burn, she corrected herself. It was odd, how vengeance always felt better beforehand than after . . . Sternly, she pushed down weakness. There was a duty to the Race here, and to her dead. If she was too fainthearted to long for it, then nobody else need know.

Yolande reached out a hand; that was all that could move, with the cradle extended and locked about her. The couch turned on its heavy circular base to put her hand over the controls. The schematic altered: command and communication circuits outlined in color-coded light. *Provided this is up-to-date*—

"When's their next check-in call?" she said.

"Five minutes."

There were no Alliance warships nearby or in favorable launch windows, but it was important not to give them more warning time than was needful. She wanted to have *Subotai* back with the flotilla long before anything could arrive; this was direct provocation, and it could escalate into anything up to a minor fleet action. Probably not. Still . . .

Her fingers played across the controls. "Here. See this

rectenna? Throw a rock at it first. Time it to arrive just after
they report everything normal."

"Making it so," the Weapons Officer said, keying. "Careless of them, all the comm routed though that dish." A low
chuckle from some of the nearer workstations.

"They like to mass-produce," Yolande said. A light blinked
on one of her monitor screens, echoing the Weapons Officer's.
On the outer hull a long thin pod would be swiveling.

"Monitoring call," the Sensor Officer said. "Standard garbage, messages to relatives." She paused. "Coded blip.
Recordin' fo' future reference." A minute passed. "End
message."

"Fire," Yolande said. A cold-flame feeling settled beneath
her breastbone. The first attack on Alliance civilians since the
Belt clashes.

The light blinked red. "Away," the Weapons Officer said.
In the pod, two charged rails slammed together. A fifty-gram
slug rode the pulse of electromagnetic force, accelerated to
ninety kilometers per second. "Hit." The target would have
vanished in a puff of vapor and fragments.

"No transmission from target, monitoring internal systems."

"With all due respect to ouah colleagues of the Directorate
of Security," Yolande said, "I'm not takin' any chances that
they got the plans exactly right. We'll cripple her first on a
quick fly-by, *then* get within kissin' range. Drive, prepare fo'
boost; pass at one kps relative, then decelerate an' match at
five klicks. Weapons, cut the sail loose, hole the control
compartment, wreck the drive." A plasma jet could be a
nasty weapon in determined hands. "Cut the connections to
the main power coil." There were megawatts stored in that,
and if it went non-superconducting all of it would be converted to heat, *rapidly*. "Then we'll see."

"Odd they don' have no suicide bomb," the assistant weapons officer said, as she and her superior worked their controls.

"Too gutless," the man replied. "Ready to execute."

"Drive ready to execute."

"Make it so," Yolande said.

The speakers roared: "PREPARE FOR ACCELERA-
TION. ALL HANDS SECURE FOR ACCELERATION. TEN-
SECOND BURN. FIVE SECONDS TO BURN. COUNTING."

Somewhere deep within the *Subotai* pumps whirred. Precisely aligned railguns charged as fuel pellets were stripped

from the magazines, ten gram bundles of plutonium-239 and their reflector-absorber coatings.

"BURN."

The pellets flicked out behind the cruiser. Her lasers struck and the coating sublimed explosively, squeezing. Fission flame bloomed, flickering at ten times per second. Nozzles slammed liquid oxygen into the carbon-carbon lined hemisphere of the thrust plate to meet the fire, and the gas exploded into plasma. The superconductor field-coils in the plate swept out magnetic fingers, cupping and guiding the blaze of charged particles into a sword of light and energy, stripping out power for the next pulse. The thrust plate surged forward against its magnetic buffers. And the multi-thousand-tonne mass of the warship *moved*.

"Burn normal. Flow normal at fifty-seven percent capacity. Point nine-eight G."

"Comin' up on target. Closin'. Preparin' fo' fire mission. *Execute*."

Needles of coherent light raked across the lines that held the sail to the *Pathfinder*. The single-crystal sapphire filaments sublimed and parted in tiny puffs of vapor, but no change showed in the giant bedsheet of the sail; it would be hours before the vast slow pressure of the photon wind made a noticeable difference. It was otherwise with the *Pathfinder* itself. A dozen railgun slugs sleeted through the control chamber, and the steel-alloy outer hull rang like a tin roof under hail. The missiles punched through and out the other side without slowing perceptibly, leaving plate-sized holes; the edges shone red as air rushed past, turning to a mist of crystals that glittered in the unwavering light of the sun. Light flickered briefly within as systems shorted and arced.

Other slugs impacted the nozzle of the plasma drive, turning the titanium alloy to twisted shards. A finger of neutral particles stabbed, cut across the lines that connected the arc to the main power torus. *Pathfinder* tumbled.

"STAND BY FOR ZERO GRAVITY." The subliminal thuttering roar of the drive ceased, leaving only the quiet drone of the ventilators. "STAND BY FOR MANEUVER." Attitude jets slammed with twisting force, and the cruiser switched end for end. "STAND BY FOR ACCELERATION. EIGHTEEN-SECOND BURN. THREE SECONDS TO BURN. *BURN*." Longer and harder this time; they were killing part of their initial speed and matching trajectories as well. The sound was duller, more mass going onto the thrust plate.

"Matched, closin'," the Drive Officer said. The attitude jets fired again, briefly. "Stable in matchin' orbit, five-point-two klicks."

Yolande keyed the exterior visual display, switching to a magnification that put her at an apparent ten meters from the Alliance vessel. "Well done," she said to the bridge; it looked precisely as she had specified. "Ah." Flames were stabbing out from parts of the can-shaped transport, and the tumbling slowed and stopped. "Nice of him." She hit the control, and the combat braces folded away from her with a sigh of hydraulics. "Number One, boardin' party to the forward lock. Sensors?"

"She's dead in space, apart from those attitude jets. Internal pressure normal except on the control deck, that's vacuum. Doan' think much damage to internal systems."

"Weapons, connectors away."

"Makin' it so. Off."

Two of her screens slaved to the Weapons station showed a rushing telemetered view of the enemy vessel, as the tiny rockets carried the connectors. Their heads held pickups and sundry other equipment; mostly, they were very powerful electromagnets. The cables themselves were no mere ropes: optical fibers, superconductor power-lines, ultrapure metal and boron and carbon, armored sheathing, the whole strong enough to support many times the cruiser's weight in a one-G field.

"Ah, human-level heat sources in the control chamber. Three, suited. Multiple elsewhere in the hull."

"Very well," Yolande said. "Maintain position, prepare to grapple when the target's secured." That was doctrine, and only sensible. The *Subotai* and her crew represented an unthinkable investment of the resources of the Race.

She rose, secured her boots to the floor. "Number Two, carry on. Boardin' party, I'll be with yo' shortly."

Janet had been squealing with excitment when Cindy returned to the cabin, Iris solemn and earnestly trying to remember what she had been told about emergency drills. It was still hard to believe, how different twins were; or how complete and yet alien a personality could be at five . . .

Then they both quieted, sensing her seriousness. She zipped

them quickly into their skinsuits; Fred had paid out-of-pocket for those luxuries, rather than rely on bubble-cocoons, and now she blessed the extravagance as she worked her way into her own. These were civilian models, little changed from the original porous-plastic leotards the first astronauts had worn. The fabric was cool and tight against her flesh, with a little chafing at groin and armpits where the pads completed the seal. She helped her daughters on with the backpacks, then checked her own; the helmets could be left off but close to hand, for now. God forbid they should have to use them, but if they did every minute could count.

"Come on, punkins," she said, guiding them to the pallet that occupied most of the sternside wall of their cubicle and strapping them in. "Mommy's going to tell you a story."

They settled in on either side of her; she had just begun to search her memory when the sound came. A monstrous ringing hail, like trip-hammers in a forging mill, toning through the metal beneath and around them, like being *inside* a bell. The *Pathfinder* was seized and wrenched, the unfamiliar sensation of weight pulling at them from a dozen different directions, inside a steel shell sent bounding downhill. The locking bolts on the door shot home with a metallic clangor, and even over the ringing of the hull she could hear the wailing of the alarm klaxon and the slamming of airtight doors throughout the ship. Her skin prickled.

"Mom! Mommeee!" Janet shrieked. Iris had gone chalk-pale, her eyes full circles, and her panting was rapid and breathy.

"Meteor swarm, O sweet mercy of God, let it be a meteor swarm!" she whispered under her breath. Their stateroom was the first-class model, with a porthole. The light that stabbed through it into her eyes was like mocking laughter; there was only one thing in the human universe that made that actinic blue-white light, that spearhead-shaped scar across the stars. A nuclear pulsedrive.

"Shhh, shhh, mommy's here, darlings." She used hands and voice and quieted them to whimpering by the time the reaction jets fired and the ship shuddered back to stability. *Just in time*, she found a moment to think. *I'm feeling sick and Iris looks green.* They were all on antinausea drugs, and it took some powerful tinkering with the inner ear to override those.

The *Pathfinder* drifted and steadied. Cindy looked out the

port again, blinking against the afterimage of fire that strobed across her sight, against the tears of pain. Then she jammed her knuckles into her mouth and bit down, welcoming pain to beat down the stab of desperation, the whining sound that threatened to break free of her throat. The shape that drifted model-tiny there was familiar, very familiar from the lectures she had attended before signing on with the Project—she was the Commandant's wife as well as a biologist. A Draka cruiser, the third-generation type. A Great Khan, and the only things in the solar system which could match it were a month's journey away.

Cindy Lefarge felt the world greying away from the corners of her eyes, a rippling on her skin as the hairs struggled to stand erect. Bile shot into the back of her throat, acrid and stinging as she remembered other things from those lectures. *No.* A voice spoke in the back of her mind, a voice like her grandmother's. *Y' got yore duty, gal, so do it!* She had the children to protect.

"Jannie, Iris, listen to me." The small faces turned towards her, pale blue eyes and freckles and the floating wisps of black hair. "You girls are going to have to be very brave for mommy. Just like real grown-up people, so daddy will be proud of you. This is really, really important, you understand?"

They looked up from where her arms cradled them against her shoulders. Iris nodded, swallowing and clenching trembling lips. Janet bobbed her head vigorously. "You bet, mom," she said. "I'm gonna be a soldier like dad, someday. So I gotta be brave, right?"

She pulled them closer. Twin lights sparkled from the Draka cruiser, seeming to drift toward her and then rush apart in a V. She closed her eyes, waiting for the final wash of nuclear flame, but all that came was two deep-toned *chunnng* sounds. The *Pathfinder* jerked again, rotating so that the Domination warship was out of her view. The overhead speaker came to life with a series of gurgles and squawks, then settled into the voice of Captain Hayakawa; calm as ever, but a little tinny, as if he was speaking from inside a skinsuit helmet.

"Attention, please. We have been attacked by a Draka deepspace warship. The engines have been disabled, our communications are down, and the sail has been cut loose. The main passenger compartment has not been holed, I repeat, *not* been holed. Please remain calm, and stay in your cabins. This is the safest place for all civilians at the moment.

Ceres and Earth will soon detect what has happened and *SKREEKKKKKAAWWK*—" The noise built to an ear-hurting squeal and then died.

Cindy Guzman Lefarge bent her head over those of her children and prayed.

"Assault party ready," the Centurion from *Batu* said.

Yolande nodded assent as she secured the straps on the last of her body armor. It was fairly light (weight didn't matter here but mass certainly did); segmented sandwiches of ablative antiradar, optically perfect flexmirror, sapphire thread, synthetics. Not quite as much protection as the massive cermet stuff heavy infantry wore on dirtside, but easier to handle. She settled the helmet on her shoulders, checked the seal to the neck-ring, and swiveled her eyes to read the various displays. She could slave them to the pickups in any warrior's pack, call up information—the usual data-overload.

The boarding commandos were grouped in Hangar B, the portside half of the chamber just below the nosecap of the cruiser. The Great Khans carried one eighty-tonne auxiliary, but it was stored in vacuum on the starboard, leaving B free as a workspace where systems could be brought up and overhauled in shirtsleeve conditions. Both hangars connected with the big axial workway that ran through the center of the vessel right down to the thrust equalizers, nine-tenths the length of the ship. Now this one was crowded with the score of Draka who would put this particular piece of Yankeedom under the Yoke.

Her lips drew back behind the visor, and she slid her hand into the sleeve of the reaction gun clipped to her thigh. A faint translucent red bead sprang into being on the inside of her faceplate as she wrapped her fingers around the pistol grip, framed by aiming lines. The bulk of the chunky weapon lay rightside on her arm, connected to her backpack by an armored conduit. It was dual-purpose: a jet for short-range maneuvering and a weapon that fired glass-tungsten bullets and balanced them with a shower of plastic confetti backwards.

"Right," she said, over the command push. "Listen, people." There were certain things that had to be repeated, even with Citizen troops. "This is a raid; we want intelligence data, not bodies or loot. Go in, immobilize whoever you find, get theys up to the big compartment just rearward of the control deck. Then we'll sweep up everythin' of interest, and get out.

Make it fast, make it clean, do *not* kill anyone less'n yo' have to, do *not* waste any time. Service to the State!"

"*Glory to the Race!*"

"Execute." There was a prickling feeling all over her skin as the pressure in the hangar dropped; nothing between her flesh and vacuum but the layer of elastic material that kept her blood from boiling—*except the woven superconductor radiation shield and the armor and the thermal layer and—oh, shut up, Yolande*, she told herself. An eagerness awoke, like having her hands on the controls of a fighter back in the old days.

The pads inside her suit inflated. Combat-feeling: a little like being horny, a little like nausea, a lot like wanting to piss. The surroundings took on the bleak sharpness of vacuum, but she knew the unnatural clarity would be there even if there was air. *Donar, I could have the suit monitor my bloodstream and tell me how hopped-up I am*, she thought.

The Centurion's voice. "By lochoi!"

Hers was first. "Follow me," she said, taking a long shallow dive through the hangar door. Out into the access tunnel, three meters across, a geometric tube of blue striplights and handholds two hundred meters sternward of her feet. She pointed her reaction gun toward the open docking ring over her head and pressed once. Heated gas pulsed backward; she stopped herself with a reverse jolt at the exit and swung around to face the enemy ship, adjusting perception until it was below her. The dark, slug-dented surface of the control deck swam before her eyes, jiggling with the distance and magnification. She fixed the red aiming-spot on the surface and reached across to key the reaction gun.

Locked strobed across her vision. "Slave your rg's to mine," she told the others, crouching. It would adjust the thrust nozzle to compensate for any movement short of turning ninety degrees out of line, now. Yolande took a deep breath. "Let's—*go*."

The hull of the Alliance ship thunked dully under their boots, sound vibrating up her bones for lack of air.

"Let's take a look," she said.

"Yo." A crewman slid a long limber rod through one of the impact holes.

She called up a miniature rectangle of vision keyed to the fiber-optic periscope, fisheye distorted but it would do. Dark, with the chilly silver look of light-enhancement. A drifting corpse, legs missing at the knee where flesh and skinsuit had fought a hypervelocity missile and lost badly. Grains of freeze-dried blood still drifted brown nearby. Wrecked equipment, a very elementary-looking control system, none of the fabled Alliance high technology. *Of course, they want to build these cheap and quick*, she thought. The Domination had no equivalent class of vessel; the closest were unmanned freighters. The Draka economy did not produce the same set of incentives as the Alliance's nearly laissez-faire system.

"Patch to their com," she said. A sound of voices in some Asian-sounding language; well, everybody who could have gotten a ship command would speak English. "Y'all in there," she said. "Surrender. Last chance."

Silence. She shrugged, looked up at the warrior who was preparing their entranceway, made a hand signal. That one finished drawing the applicator around the shallow dome of the spacecraft's nose. It had left a thick trail of something that looked very much like mint toothpaste.

"Secure." They backed off, tagged lines to protuberances on the surface. The *Pathfinder* was built smooth-hulled because that eased fabrication, but there were fittings a-plenty. "On the three."

"One. Two. Three."

A flash of soundless light, and the hull flexed slightly to push her up to the limit of the line. Then the cap of steel was floating away, dark against the mirror-bright surface of the sail; it would strike it, before the film could sweep away on the breeze from the Sun. The warrior nearest the giant circular hole freed a grenade from her belt and tossed it in, a flat straight line like nothing that could be done planetside. There was another pulse of light.

"Storm!" Yolande shouted, and the Draka slid forward, throwing themselves into the hole.

Thung. Yolande twirled in midleap to land feet first on the deck. A figure in a foil-covered skinsuit was thrashing, ripped by the shards from the grenade; his blood sprayed out, and she could see the scream behind his transparent bubble-helmet. Her eyes skipped, jittering. Another Alliance suit, rising from behind a spindly crashcouch, something gripped in both hands. The red dot pivoted toward him, but before she could fire the man's torso exploded in a corona of red and pinkish white. The bullets from a reaction gun were tungsten

monofilament in a glass sabot; they punched through hard
targets, but underwent explosive deformation in soft.

"Shit," she swore, seeing the rank-tabs on the man's shoulders. "That was the captain." Yolande batted a lump of
floating *something* away from her faceplate with a grimace;
zero-G combat was *messy*. Two others were zipping the
wounded man into an airbag and doing what crude first aid
they could.

"Labushange, Melder, stay here. Pull the compcore and
see if y' can patch through to log memory. Anderson, take the
door." That was a hatch in the middle of the floor. "Pressure-
lock it."

The warrior knelt and focused on the door, calling up a
schematic to show the vulnerable spots in his faceplate. Two
others peeled the covering off the base ring of a plastic tent
and slapped it adhesive-down on the deck around the hatch.
The lochos stepped inside, zipping it over their heads.

"Got it," Anderson grunted. "Ready?"

"Go," she snapped.

He locked his boots to the deck and pointed the gauntlet
gun. It flashed twice, and translucent confetti drifted back to
join the particles already rising out of the hole above their
head, mixed with a haze of blood. The deck sparked with
impact and glittered with a new plating of molten glass, and
there was the blue flicker of discharge. Yolande kicked the
lockbar of the door; it slammed down with blurring speed,
and air roared in to bulge the tent over their heads.

"*Bulala!*" she shrieked, and dove through the opening into
light.

"Shhhh," Cindy said again.

There had been sounds, clanging, shouts, screams, a sharp
ptank-tank rapping she could not identify, even pistol shots. *I
wish I'd taken the gun*, she thought desperately. She had had
the usual personal-defense training in school, though her
National Service had been in the research branch; even the
worn old high school submachine-gun would have been
something . . .

Probably just enough to get us all killed, she thought
bleakly. Even worse was the knowledge that that might be
the best thing.

The locking bar of the door moved a half-inch back and
forth. She started, then unstrapped the children and pushed

them back into the farthest corner of the cabin, bracing herself in front of them with her arms across the angle of the wall. There was silence for a second, then a bright needle of flame spat from beside the door. It swung open; she had a brief glimpse of the boot that kicked it, before a thin black stick poked in. A figure bounced through two seconds afterward and stopped itself with one expert footblow against the far wall. The fluted muzzle of a weapon fastened to the right arm pointed at her; she crowded her daughters farther behind her body.

Another head came through the doorway, then a body likewise strapped around with pieces of equipment. They were both in skinsuits and some sort of flexible armor that was a dull matte black, but a line of silver brightness showed along a scratch on one's chest. She swallowed through a mouth the consistency of dry rice-paper and tried to keep her face from twisting. Then they unlatched their helmets and pushed them back against their backpacks.

The first Draka she had ever seen in the flesh. For a moment she was surprised that they looked so much like the pictures. These two were both men, young, hair cropped close at the sides and slightly longer on top. One had a stud earring, the other a rayed sunburst painted about an eye—hard faces, scarcely affected by the usual zero-G puffiness, all slabs and angles, almost gaunt. The first one spoke, in a purring drawl hurtfully reminiscent of her mother's . . . No, more archaic-sounding, with a guttural undertone.

"All cleah." That into the thread-and-dot microphone that curved up from the neck-ring of his suit. "Yes, suh, these're the last. We'll get 'em secured an' up to the lounge."

"Yo'," he said. "Out of the skinsuit. The picknins, too."

The words flowed over her mind without meaning. *Can't be, can't be*, was sounding somewhere inside her. *Bad movie.*

"Shit," the man said in a tired voice; it sounded more like "shaay't." He reached across to do something to the weapon, and a red dot sprang out on the wall beside her head. It settled on her forehead for a moment, then shifted to the outer surface.

Bang!*ptank*. A hole the breadth of her thumb flashed into existence in the steel, and there was a shower of something flakey and glittering from behind his elbow. A brief whistling of air, before the self-sealing layer in the hull blocked it off. The red dot settled between her eyes again.

"To t' count 'a three, wench. One. Two—"

Trembling slightly, her hands went to the seals of her suit, then hesistated. *My god, I'm only wearing briefs under this.* The Draka made a gesture of savage impatience, and she stripped out of the clinging elastomer. "Help the picknin," he snapped.

"Come on, punkins," she said. The girls were staring enormous-eyed at the two Draka; Iris's lips were caught between her teeth as she fought rhythmically against her sobs. "We have to do what the man says."

"Mom!" Janet said, scandalized. "Those—those are *strangers*!"

The red dot settled on her daughter's face. Shoulderblades crawling, Cindy put herself between the gun and Janet, taking her by the shoulders and shaking her. "Come on, you silly girl," she forced herself to say, harshly. "Quickly."

The Draka in the doorway held up what looked like a medical injector. "Docilize?" he said to the other.

"Na, quicker if we let her handle the sprats," he said. "Don' have time to fuck around." He looked at her, up and down, and grinned. "Pity. Maybe latah." Reached out, quite casually, and grabbed her crotch.

Cindy closed her eyes and gritted teeth. Then something windmilled by her and struck the Draka with a *thump*. It was Janet.

"You bad man! Leggo my mom! Leggo!" The five-year-old was clinging to the man's harness with one hand and trying earnestly to punch him with the other, while her feet flailed at his stomach. "You let go, or I'll kill you!" Iris started to scream, shrill high-pitched sounds like an animal in a trap.

The Draka snarled, rearing his head back and raising the arm with the gun to club at Janet. Cindy felt a great calm descend as she readied herself; reach down and immobilize the left hand, strike up with the palm under his nose . . .

A hand snaked in with the injector and pressed it against Janet's side. It hissed, and the girl slumped; not unconscious, just drifting with her eyes half-closed. The Draka with the drug-gun laughed and reached around her to plant the muzzle against Iris's neck.

"Dociline," he said to her as the screaming stopped. "Trank. Haa'mless." To his companion: "Let's get on with it."

She huddled back with her children as they ransacked the cabin, giving the comfort of skin against skin that was all she had to offer. The two warriors went systematically through the tiny closet and the bulkhead containers. Cindy noticed what they took: books, letters, dataplaques, her new Persimmon 5 portable perscomp that Fred had got from the PX, all stuffed into a transparent holder. One of them came across her jewelry, but that went into a pouch at his belt.

"Right," the one with the face-painting said when they had finished. "Yo'. Hold out y'arms. Togethah." A loop went around her elbows, painfully tight; she could use her hands, but awkwardly. "Now, listen good. Yo' take the picknins, and we're goin' up to the top level. An' wench—any trouble an' we kill yo' spawn. Understand?" She gave a tight nod. "Go."

Cindy gathered her daughters with slow care; they had curled into fetal positions floating near her, and it would be easy to bruise them if she moved too quickly. She kicked her feet into the ripstick slippers on the floor and began to step out into the corridor. The man who had groped her earlier reached out one hand and stripped the briefs off her with a wrench as she went by.

"Later," he said

"Is that the last of them?" Yolande asked, as the woman steered the two children into the lounge.

"Yes, ma'am," the Centurion said. " 'Cept fo' the one who gave us trouble."

"Number Two," she said. "Target secured. Reel her in an' run a tube over to the airlock on this level."

"Makin' it so, Cohortarch. Twenty seconds to commencement."

"Silence!" she called to the crowd of prisoners through the exterior speaker on her helmet. "Everybody brace themselfs."

There were about eighty of them, milling about at the far end of the grubby lounge. Most had been wearing skinsuits, and so were nearly stripped; she looked at them with disgust. *This is the enemy? Flabby, soft-gutted rubbish,* she thought. A few had been docilized. Those thumped painfully against the wall when the ship lurched again, and so did a few of the fully-conscious ones. *Sheep.* There was an almost imperceptible feeling of sideways acceleration for a few minutes, and then the cables went slack; the *Subotai* would be backing off with her attitude jets, to reestablish zero relative motion.

"Line them up," she continued.

Her troopers moved in, prodding with their gauntlet guns. A moment of trouble from two young men, stocky-muscular;

they looked like they played—what was that absurd Yankee sport? Football? A flurry of dull thudding sounds and they were against the wall with the others, one clutching his groin, the other a flattened nose that leaked blood in drifting red globules. Three more figures floated up through the central hatch. A wounded Draka with a long cut through the belly-section of her armor, hands to a pad over the wound, helped by a comrade. Then a prisoner trussed hand and foot. Hand and elbows, rather; one forearm ended in a frayed stump covered in glistening sprayseal. Typical gauntlet-gun wound.

"What happened with *him*?" the Centurion asked.

"Had a fukkin' *sword*," the wounded Draka said, between clenched teeth. Soft impact-armor gave excellent protection against projectiles, but very little against something sharp and low-velocity. "Under his pallet covers. I blew his hand off on the backswing."

"Careless," the Centurion said. There were clanging noises and voices from the background, as the tube was secured and the airlock opened on the temporary seal between the two vessels. "McReady, get her back to sickbay. Bring up the rest of the bodies."

Yolande reached up to remove her helmet, wrinkling her nose at the proof that some of the prisoners had lost control of their bowels. She looked at the one-handed man. Black-Asian, she guessed, about fifty. Wiry and strong, stone-faced under her gaze. Shock, part of that calm, but that was one with a hard soul. It would not do to underestimate them all; few of the Alliance peoples were natural warriors, but they could learn, and the Americans in particular had a damnable trader's cunning that made them capable of all manner of surprises. *I wish they hadn't brought the picknins*. She pushed the children's sobbing below the surface of her mind. Now—

Cindy forced herself to take her eyes off the raw stump of Professor Takashi's hand. She tried to imagine what that would feel like, failed, raised her eyes to his face. He was smiling; that was almost as shocking as the wound.

The Draka commander was removing her helmet. A woman, she saw without surprise. The face was huge-eyed, triangular, delicately feminine, haloed in short platinum-colored hair. Then the eyes met hers, and she shivered slightly.

"This one?" the Draka said, to the man holding Takashi.

"Cybernetic Systems Analysis," the guard said.

"Lucky fo' us yo' didn't get killed," the woman said genially.

The dark man shook his head, smiling more broadly. "Not so—*ah!*" he shook once, slumped. The guard cursed, felt for his pulse.

"Dead," he spat. "Must've taken something."

The commander turned back toward the prisoners. "Listen," she said, and all fidgeting died away. The voice was deliberately pitched rather low, so that they would have to strain to hear it; it was soft, naturally light, Cindy thought.

"Yo' will, startin' at the right, go one by one to that table." She pointed to one where a group of Draka were going through the identity documents of the passengers. "Yo' will state yo' name and profession, and answer *all* other questions. Then go *back* to *that* end of the line. Understood, serfs?"

There was a rustling, and they glanced at each other. The Draka waited for a moment, then continued in a tone of weary distaste.

"Stubborn. Fools. All right . . . Who's a Yankee heah? I have a special and particular dislike of Yankees." The big eyes slid down the line. Gray, with a rim of blue. *Colder than any I've ever seen*, Cindy thought. She could almost have preferred a sadist's glazed sickness; it would be less intelligent.

The eyes settled on the Merkowitz family. A gloved finger pointed. "They two slugs look repulsive enough to be Yankees. Fetch me the pretty little bull beside them, an' make a steer of him."

A dozen of the Draka had been hanging ready by the opposite wall. Two crouched and sprang, blurring across the lounge, twisting end-for-end and landing one on either side of young David Merkowitz with balletic gracefullness; they grabbed his arms and leaped again, releasing him just before they touched down. The warriors let their legs cushion impact like springs, coiling; the teenager from Newark landed against the wall with a soggy impact. Stunned, he floated for an instant until they spreadeagled him on a table. Others moved in to hold and secure; one of the Draka reached over her shoulder and drew something as long as her forearm.

Cindy felt a glassy sense of unreality as she recognized the tool. It was a cutter bar, a thin film of vacuum-deposited diamond between two layers of crystal iron-chrome. Alliance models had the same backward-sloping saw teeth, although they did not come to the sort of wicked point this one did.

The Draka spun the tool in the air, a blurring circle, then reached in. The hilt slapped into her palm—bravado; that edge would go through fingers as if they were boiled carrots. She raised it in mocking salute to the prisoners and swaggered over to the boy; one of those holding him had stuffed a cloth into his mouth to muffle his screams, and was holding up his head so that he could not help but see.

The Draka with the cutter bar paused, turned, slashed the edge down on a metal table-frame. The steel tube parted with a ringing sound, and the woman smiled. She smiled more broadly as she pulled off the undersuit briefs, wet one finger and drew it up young Merkowitz's scrotum and penis. He convulsed and made a sound that was astonishingly loud; she gripped the testicles in her left and and raised the knife with taunting slowness.

"No." That from the man at the head of the line. He moved forward towards the table with the interrogators. Cindy looked at the Draka commander, who had been hanging relaxed, smoking a cigarette and looking up at the ceiling; the American saw a slight tension go out of the enemy commander's shoulders.

"Very well," the short blond woman said. "Hold it there, cut him if any of the rest make trouble." The Draka with the cutter bar lowered the weapon and waited, loose-alert as she faced the prisoners. Her other hand stayed on the teenager, stroking lightly. He began to weep.

"Name."

Yolande looked aside at the prisoner. A wench in her late twenties, with two picknins floating near; the children had been shot with dociline and were just coming to, still muzzy and vague. She was ruddy-olive, quite good looking in a slimmish sort of way, spirited from the calm tone she used, which was a relief. The sniveling from some of the others had been nauseating, even for feral serfs—especially when you considered that she had not *done* anything of note to them yet. Not that this whole business was very pleasant, at all; necessary, but distasteful. *Find it easier to kill them from a distance, eh?* she thought, mocking herself. *To desire the end is to desire the means.*

"Cynthia Guzman Lefarge," the wench was saying. She was the last of them. "My daughters Janet Mary and Iris Dawn. Master's degree in Applied Biosystems from the University of Anahuac in Mexico City. Going out to meet my husband on Ceres; that's his picture there."

Yolande looked at the timer display on the sleeve of her suit. Less than an hour from boarding, good time. A disappointment that the compcore had been slagged, but only to be expected. Still . . . She looked down at the picture in the booklet.

"Wait." Her hand slashed down. *Impossible*. She could feel herself start to shake as she looked at it. Impossible. With an effort greater than any she could recall, she took a deep breath. One. Another. The shaking receded to an almost imperceptible tremor in her fingers as she lifted the record book. Square face. Dark eyes. Dress uniform, not the mottled night-fatigues. Same face, the *same face*, the Indian night and its hot scents, the smell of Myfwany's blood. The broken body in her arms, jerking, mumbling the final words around a mouth filled with red. Gone. Gone forever, dead, not there, *gone*. The face in the night.

"Sttt—" She cleared her throat. "Stop." Her voice sounded strange in her ears. She leaned toward the wench, seeing with unnatural clarity every pore and feature and hair. There was a sensation behind her eyes, like a taut steel wire snapping.

"That's enough," she said. The tone of her voice had a high note in it, but it was steady. Somewhere, a part of her not involved in this was proud of it.

"Separate the prisoners," she said, without taking her eyes off the picture. "The aft section is cleared out? All the children, put them down there. Decurion, get a working party, transfer supplies from the foodstore; it's on this level. Enough, then weld the door shut, get the picknins down there and weld the hatch to *this* level shut. Wait, that wench and that wench"—she pointed at two of the mothers, ones who had listed no occupation—"with the children. *Move*. No, not these two picknins, leave them with the wench here."

There was a shift, movement, kicks and thuds and shuffling, wailing. A bit of confusion, before the prisoners realized that to Draka serfs were only children up to puberty. Yolande turned to consider them, the booklet gripped tight in one hand. "Docilize the adults," she said. Breathe. In. Out. "Shift them across." She keyed her microphone. "Number Two, how's the mass transfer goin'?"

"Should have the last of it in our tanks in 'bout ten minutes," he said. "Back up to sixty percent. Everythin' all

right?" That in a worried tone; he must be able to sense
something. Later.

"Good," she replied. "I'm sendin' ovah the prisoners,
docilized. Repressurize Hangar B, secure them to the floor.
Make arrangements fo' minimal maintenance until we get
back to the task fo'ce." There would be plenty of room there;
inflatable habitats had been brought along. "Set up fo' a
minimum-detection burn."

She turned to the Centurion. "Get those bodies," she said.
"Transfer them to the cold-storage locker on this level. Strip
everythin' else out, 'cept cookin' utensils, water an' salt,
understand?" He nodded, impassive; she had a reputation for
successful eccentricity.

Yolande reached back over her shoulder and drew the
cutter bar, handling it with slow care. She walked toward the
American woman, and held the booklet up beneath her face.

"I know yo' husband, wench," she said, almost whispering.
"It's an hereditary trust to hate all Americans," she continued. "But he . . . took somethin' . . . that I valued very
much. So much so that iff'n I had him in my hands, not a
lifetime's pain could pay fo' it." She halted, and waited immobile until the sounds of movement had died away behind her.
The last of the work party shoved the mass of cans and boxes
through the main hatch and into the cabin area beneath, then
welded the hatch with a sharp *tack* of arc-heaters. Then there
were only she and the Yankee and the two drugged children.
Forget them, they were *his*.

"So tell yo' husband, tell him my name. Yolande Ingolfsson,
tell him that. Tell him to remember the red-haired Draka he
killed in India; tell him he'll curse that day as I've cursed it,
and mo'. Because befo' I come fo' him, I'm goin' to take
everythin' he values and loves, and destroy it befo' his eyes;
his ideals, his cause, his nation, his family. And then I'm not
goin' to kill him, because . . . Do yo' know what the problem
is, with killin' people, slut? Do yo' know?"

Silence that rang and stretched, with her eyes locked to
the honey-brown of the prisoners. "*Answer me!*" Yolande
touched the cutter bar to the other's cheek. Skin and flesh
parted, a long shallow cut; blood rilled out, misting across her
eyes. *Carefully, carefully.* The other woman gasped, but did
not move. "Answer me."

"I don't know."

Yolande moved the cutter to the other cheek, sliced the

same controlled depth. "Because being dead doesn't hurt. It's in livin' that there's pain, wench." Another silence. "Do yo' understand? I'm leavin' yo' here. Lots of space. Plenty of water. Air system's good fo' two months, easy, an' they should be here fo' you in, oh, minimum three weeks, maximum seven. Yo' can even leave, iff'n walking buck-naked in vacuum dosen't bother yo'."

"But, but, how shall I feed my children?" the other asked.

Yolande forced herself not to look at the slight drifting forms, pushed the image of Gwen's face aside. Instead she smiled, and saw the American flinch as she had not at the touch of the knife.

"*Try the meat locker!*" she shouted, and leapt for the exit.

Twenty-nine days later, Colonel Frederick Lefarge was the first of the boarding party from the *Ethan Allen* through the airlock of the *Pathfinder*. His eyes met those of his wife.

They screamed.

CHAPTER FOURTEEN

DRAKA OFFICER CONVICTED *IN ABSENTIA* [NPS] The Alliance Global Court today announced that Yolande Ingolfsson, an officer in the Domination's Aerospace Force, had been convicted *in absentia* of war crimes and crimes against humanity during the notorious *Pathfinder* incident. Testifying at the trial were . . .

> *San Francisco Tribune*
> Editorial Section
> January 3, 1983

MERARCH YOLANDE INGOLFSSON RECEIVES SOUTHERN CROSS [DIS]

At a ceremony in the Archonal Palace today, Archon Melinda Shaversham awarded the Southern Cross, 1st Class, to Yolande Ingolfsson, daughter of Thomas and Johanna (née von Shrakenberg) Ingolfsson of Claestum Plantation, Tuscany. Merarch Ingolfsson was promoted to that rank at the same time, and decorations were awarded to several other officers and crewfolk of the now-famous Telmark IV expedition. Among the reasons cited for the award were Merarch Ingolfsson's organizational skill in securing the return of the Amor-group asteroid "Whiteridge" to Earth orbit, her timely repulsion of Alliance attempts to intrude on Domination-interdicted space (the so-called "*Pathfinder* Incident"), and tactical brilliance in the clashes with the Alliance cruisers *Washington* and *Simón Bolívar* in trans-Lunar space during the closing

stages of Telmark IV. The *Washington* was completely destroyed, and the *Bolivar* heavily damaged, while our casualties were very light.

When asked her opinion of the laughably presumptuous sentence recently passed on her by
a group of feral serfs styling themselves a "court,"
Merarch Ingolfsson responded with amusement.
"They've already tried to kill me, and come off
rather the worse for it," she said, on the steps
of the Palace. "They're welcome to try again."

Our heartiest congratulations to Merarch Ingolfsson and her kindred, and our gratitude for
showing that this frontier province has become
a breeding-ground of the true Drakon spirit.

> Leading Article
> *Nova Italia Magazine*
> Florence, District of Tuscany
> Domination of the Draka
> January 15, 1983

CERES BASE
SPACE FORCE MEDICAL CENTER
JULY 20, 1982

"How are the children?"

Frederick Lefarge reached up and touched the handhold
over the door. It was a pressure-door, and the wall around it
was rock; the hospital was in the oldest section of the base,
put in a decade ago when the Space Force had burrowed into
the heart of the rock to put five hundred kilometers between
their sick and an attack from space.

The specialist laid a hand on his shoulder. "We think . . .
no permanent damage," he said. "It's a miracle. Your wife
used the Dyleaze from the medical chest to keep them asleep
most of the time; it's one of the more recent ones, genuine
sleep, not unconsciousness. Just woke them up occasionally
for fluids, and they . . . did get some protein, after all. A year
of complete rest, with no stress, appropriate hormonal treatments, and there should be no physical ill effects except for a
little growth lag. And children are resilient, Colonel."

Lefarge swallowed again. "And my wife?" he husked.

The doctor looked aside. "Much worse. We've taken her
off the critical list, but—" He looked back at the officer. "We

can correct most of the cosmetic damage, replace the teeth with buds eventually. I'll be honest with you: she came as close to terminal coma as you can get and not actually die. There's kidney and liver failure, loss of function from other internal organs, *possible* neurological damage. The medics on the *Ethan Allen* did their best, and believe me, you were right to risk high acceleration."

"Was I?" Lefarge said wearily.

"Your wife would have died if it had taken longer to get here," the doctor said bluntly.

"I have extraordinary authority," Lefarge said. "I used it —and because of that, the *Allen* may not be back in the inner system in time, if she's needed." *The solitary non-disaster about all this is that Hayakawa managed to kill himself before they could question him in depth. So the Project isn't compromised.* "They had shifts going around the clock on *Washington* and her sister when we left . . . What's the prognosis?"

"We're bringing her back up to full metabolism for a day," the doctor replied, tone clinical once more. "Then down to fifty percent for six months. That way we may be able to restore function, or failing that get her well enough for transplants. I warn you though, Colonel, she's never going to be very strong again. Certainly, you won't be able to have any more children. And there *may* be irreversible loss of brain function, aphasia, or other complications. Not to mention psychological damage and trauma. Thank God that isn't my department."

"Let me see her," he said, waiting for the other's nod before ducking through.

Little of Cindy's body showed through the forest of tubes, wires and blinking screens. The room was silent save for minor noises of machinery, pumps and compressors. Most of the body functions had been taken over by the support mechanisms, to give the wounded organism a chance to recover. Her head was held in a padded brace, with only a nasal tube to hide what had happened. What he saw was nearer to a skull than a human face; the eyes were sunken, and wrinkled lips collapsed over an empty mouth. What hair was left was wispy and snow-white. He stood by her side and bent to kiss the brow with infinite tenderness.

Her eyes opened. Lefarge darted a glance at the doctor; the specialist checked the screens, exchanged a whispered word with the technician at the monitoring station and nodded, turning his back.

"Love . . . you." The words were faint and distorted, but the delirium was gone. "Girls?"

"I love you, too, honey," he said. "The doctor says they're going to be fine, you hear? Just fine."

The eyes closed again, the lids transparent and papery like an old, old woman's. "I . . . had . . . to," she said, a word with each fluttering breath. "Put . . . them . . . out . . . the . . . lock."

"Honey?" He wondered if her mind was wandering again.

"The . . . bodies . . . right . . . away," she said. "Didn' go . . . *away*." Her voice grew a little stronger, shriller. "They . . . floated outside . . . the ports . . . so *hungry*."

He swallowed. *The Draka didn't put them out the airlock after they'd killed them. Oh, sweet Mother of God.*

He looked down at the purpled bruises on his wife's arms, where she had tapped her own veins.

"Don't . . . tell them, ever." He nodded. "Told them . . . made soup." She sighed, and closed her eyes once more. He waited, was almost ready to leave.

"Message," she said at length. "You have to . . . hear." He bent his head to her lips.

"Sleep now," he said when she was finished. "Sleep now, honey. Get well."

The doctor sighed as he rose. "Well, no worse . . . six months *minimum*. Then we'll bring her up . . . Have to transfer to a spun habitat then, anyway; the costs of zero-G would start outweighing the benefits—"

He looked at the colonel's face and stopped, shocked.

BETWEEN THE ORBITS OF EARTH AND MARS
ABOARD DASCS *SUBOTAI*
JUNE 30, 1982

"Makin' remarkable progress, Merarch-Professor," Yolande said. They were teleconferencing, and the astroengineer was suited up; she could see segments of construction material behind him.

He waved a dismissive hand. "These are the heat dispersers," he said. Composite honeycomb sandwich, laced with superconductor on the interior, the same system that pulsedrive ships used; superconductors had the additional useful property of maintaining a uniform temperature throughout. Of course, this *was* a pulsedrive, it just used fusion bombs instead of 10-gram pellets. "We should start assembling the thrust plate soon."

Yolande linked through a view of Hangar B; the near-motionless forms of the prisoners were arranged in neat rows around the shrouded equipment. Skinsuited Auxiliaries were hosing the area down and hauling off the inert bodies; it had gotten quite noisome, with sixty drugged humans and a week's worth of high-G boost.

"We got yo' some additional labor," she said. "I know they don't look like much, but most of them have trainin' in zero-G construction an' so forth. We'll have to give a few to the headhunter to disassemble, of course."

"Good, perhaps it will keep him away from me," the scientist said, with an obscene gesture for any possible monitors.

"We'll put controller cuffs on them, maybe minimal-dosage dociline," Yolande continued. "You'll have to supervise them closely, but it ought to come out positive."

"Certainly. Hmmm, what to do with them when the project is completed?"

"Oh . . . take them back to Luna, I suppose. Maybe the political people can trade them off fo' somethin, or we can just sell them." Alliance-born serfs had a substantial curiosity value, for their rarity. "Hand them out as souvenirs, whatevah."

"Not to mention hostage value," her executive officer said. "Too much Yankee heavy iron in the Belt, fo' my taste."

Yolande chuckled. "Well, there are enough of *our* units further out," she said.

"Long ways off."

"Not so far as yo' might think," she said, and laid a finger along her nose. "Between yo', me an' the Strategic Planning Board, there are a few surprises fo' the damnyanks in this. Fo' one, we've got high-impulse orbital boost lasers in the Jovian system, which we're pretty sure they don't know 'bout. Multiple strap-ons, hey? Iff'n the damnyanks move, our cruisers can leave station around Himalia, boost on strap-ons with low mass." A pulsedrive ship could make much better acceleration with less reaction mass in her tanks—while the fuel lasted. "Do a quick-and-dirty burn to Mars orbit, arrivin' with dry tanks."

She called up a map of orbital positions. "An' notice, just

right fo' a quick stopover at Phobos to fill up? So unless the *damnyanks* is willin' to get here empty, leavin' them between us and the outer fleet, with nothin' to maneuver with—in which case we'd wipe them, then proceed to mop up the Belt piece by piece—they just naturally have to keep their iron floatin' out there by Ceres and Pallas."

"Ahhh," the exec mused. "Nice. That still leaves them with three Hero-class here in the inner system, though."

"Update?"

"*Ethan Allen* still boostin' fo' the *Pathfinder* like there was no tomorrow." He frowned. "Faster than we could, unless they're burnin' out their thrust plates."

"Well, the Heros have the legs on a Great Khan, but we've got mo' firepower. Anyways, that'll put her out of the picture fo' a whiles. The two in Earth orbit, we may have to see off. Note we're floatin' next to a fuel depot, though. Also, I've got a few ideas 'bout usin' some of our industrial equipment. Reminds me, staff conference fo' 1200 tomorrow, we'll go ovah it. Three weeks to encounter, minimum. Wants yo' there, too, Professor."

"Service to the State," he said formally.

"Glory to the Race," the two officers answered.

Yolande yawned. "Time to turn in, Number Two," she said, rising from the crashcouch.

"Just one thing, ma'am," he murmured as she passed his station; the offwatch was handling the bridge, minimum staff. "Yes?"

"Back there . . . when yo' saw those bodies come out the airlock, I was set up for a minimal-burn boost back to the flotilla. Yo' took us on a max speed trajectory, got us here dry. That was like hangin' up a big sign ovah the whole system pointin' to the *Pathfinder*. Why do it that way, ma'am?"

Yolande glanced at her fingernails. "Oh, better tactics. Impo'tant not to leave the Object unguarded." She thought again of the sleeping faces of the two children. *Yankee* children, she reminded herself again, but . . . "Or call it as close as I could get to changing my mind."

The commander's quarters of a Great Khan were luxurious, by Aerospace Command standards. Two cubicles, a tiny one for sleeping, a slightly larger one to serve as an office. A few pictures, the ones she took everywhere: her parents, siblings, three shots of Gwen, and her favorite of Myfwany. That showed them on the beach at Baiae, mugging and smooching for the camera . . . She sighed and finished stuffing her uniform into the cleaner slot; the black coveralls never got quite as ripe as the skinsuits, thank Baldur. Somebody keyed the door for admittance.

"Come in," she said.

The hatch swung out into the companionway. "As ordered, ma'am." It was a rating, with one of the prisoners.

"Oh. Oh, yes; just leave her here, thank yo'." The rating pushed the slight figure in through the hatch and dogged it.

"Alishia Merkowitz, aren't yo'?" Yolande asked.

"Yyyes, Mistis." A tiny whisper. About fifteen, Yolande estimated. Thinner, after a week spent comatose, but looking rather better for it; olive skin, curved nose, full lips. Still slightly damp from the hosing. "Please, don't hurt me!"

"Relax, I'm not *goin'* to hurt yo'." The captive huddled in the far corner of the office-space, twice arm's reach away, and stared at her huge-eyed, flicking an occasional glance about in an unconscious search for escape. "Or do anythin' else to yo', either." *Which puts me in a decided minority, wench.*

Yolande sighed. *Let's see . . . Oh, she'd probably be more comfortable wearing something.* "That's a locker behind yo'," she said. "Open it, hand me one of the overalls. Yo' can wear one of the spare shirts until I requisition some Auxiliary stuff fo' yo'."

The girl obeyed; she stepped into the clothing and Yolande pressed the seam closed. *Actually quite pretty, but far too frightened,* she thought, watching her struggle into the shirt and tie off the bottom. "Right. Now, that's sternward." She pointed to the padded floor of the cubicle. "Those black things are covers fo' the restraints. Iffn' yo' hear the acceleration warnin', get there fast, understand? Don't go near the terminal, or anythin' else with the circled-cross symbol on them, because they'll activate yo' controller cuff if you touch them." The prisoner cringed; they had already had the pain-device demonstrated along with the initial obey-all-orders-call-everyone-master lecture. "The nearest head is out that door with the red stripe uppermost, turn left, two hatches down. Now, stay out of my way."

Yolande hooked her feet under the terminal and activated, calling up the schematics for the Alliance Hero class; heavy cruisers in enemy terminology, although they massed slightly less than the Great Khans. Risky design philosophy, in her opinion. Not enough separate weapons systems, and too many interdependent elements in the beam-weapon guidance routines; fine when everything went perfectly, but dangerous and hard on damage control in action. She began to whistle silently through her teeth as she worked. The prisoner sank into the background of her consciousness; a Draka was used to being observed. A homelike sensation, since she had never been so much alone as on these deep-space voyages. It was several hours later when a bell chimed.

She yawned and stretched. "Time fo' bed," she said. The American girl flinched again. Yolande grinned. "I *said* I wasn't goin' to," she chuckled, as she leaned head and shoulders through the hatchway and rigged her sleeping net. Any flat surface would do in zero-G, but you needed something to keep you from drifting around when you moved in your sleep. "Yo' use the office floor. Draw the acceleration restraints out to max and lock them over yo', crisscross. Here. Like this."

She pulled herself through the hatch and swung around to fasten the net over herself; the bedroom cubicle was more or less useless during acceleration, but even a pulsedrive ship spent the vast majority of its time coasting. As she dimmed the lights, she could hear a hiccoughing sound from the other cubicle; crying, mostly in relief, she thought. *Oh, Freya,* she thought. *I hope she doesn't keep* that *up.*

"Mistis?"

"Yes?" Yolande sighed.

"What's . . . what's going to happen to us?"

"Depends. We'll put y'all to work until we head back insystem. Most probably trade y'all back, fo' somethin' or other." More sniffles in darkness. "To yo', nothin' bad, so long's yo' stays close to this cabin. Lot of bored, horny Draka out there, wench, so be careful."

"Can, um, can I ask a question?" Silence. "Why . . . why are you . . . doing this for me?"

Yolande smiled wryly into her private night. *That is complicated, and I'm not interested in explaining it. To you, or myself.* "Call it an offerin' to the gods of mercy," she said softly. "Loki knows, they get few enough. Go to sleep, girl."

"Status," Yolande said.

"Unchanged," the Sensor Officer said. "No relative motion."

"Good." *An odd situation to describe as static,* she thought ironically. *Bass-ackwards to the end of beyond.*

Not too untypical of a space-warship action, though. She looked at the screens again. An exterior view would have shown nothing but bright dots moving against the fixed stars, if that . . . The battle-schematic was much more accurate. A fixed dot, the asteroid; the regular five-minute pulses of its monstrous drive flaring back towards Earth. The flame was only partly shaped by the magnetic fields of the thrust plate; those forces were still too vast and wild for Earth's children, and it hid a good deal behind it from most sensors. An excellent place for her to conceal the vulnerable transports.

Yolande grinned like a shark in the darkness of the command center. *Subotai* and *Batu* were falling back toward the flotilla, with the two Alliance cruisers in pursuit; all on freefall trajectories, with their thrust plates presented to the enemy. That was the most heavily armored portion of a pulsedrive ship, *built* to withstand near-miss nuclear explosions. And the drive was the most dangerous weapon in itself; chasing a deepspace warship was a chancy proposition, since getting too close would mean self-incineration. Once you got within a certain distance, in a one-on-one there was virtually no choice but to flip end for end and coast until something changed the situation. You could disengage, of course, but that meant backing off and freeing your opponent from the menace of the nuclear sword.

Perfect, she thought. The Draka warships had drawn the Alliance craft on just enough; the enemy vessels were slightly faster than hers, and more nimble, but they were farther from base and so obliged to be sparing with their burns. A perfect matching-velocity flip, which meant they must pursue or quit, and pursue precisely in line with the Draka ships for fear of presenting a vulnerable flank. The asteroid was coming up rapidly; the fog of energetic particles around it negated her enemy's superior sensors, too; she did not *need* to detect much, here.

"Distance," she said.

"Two hundred twenty klicks. Transit of asteroid in seventy-one seconds, ten klicks clearance." Just enough to avoid the worst of the fusion-bomb explosions.

Nothing for it but to wait; all the orders were given, the personnel ready. Sweat soaked into the permeable fabric of her skinsuit, under the armpits and down the flanks, chill in the moving air the ventilators sent across her body. Sixty seconds. Life or death decided in one minute; victory and glory, or eternal shame. *Genius, or a goat. Which I wouldn't be there to see. Bones of the White Christ, this sort of thing sounds better in retrospect. Adventure is somebody else in deep shit far, far away.*

Fifty seconds. Snappdove had thought she was insane, for a while. *Maybe I was. Dammit, they are pressing home their pursuit.* The Alliance wanted to damage her; the only way to do it was to chase her cruisers off far enough that they could do a firing pass at the asteroid and its workforce as they turned and fled themselves. *A two-body problem with only one solution.*

Ten. Five. The pursuers maintaining position with beautiful precision; those were good ships and well-trained crews. Three. Two. Past.

"Now!" she shouted, superfluously.

"DECELERATION," the speakers sounded. It wrenched at her, throwing her to forward against the combat cocoon. Reaction mass was being vented from the forward ports, run through the heat dumpers to vaporize. Not nearly so powerful as the drive, but enough to check their headlong flight. The main drives of the Alliance craft lit in a brief blossom of flame, just enough to match.

And the asteroid was *turning*. A mass of billions of tons is very difficult indeed to move out of its accustomed orbit; it had taken dozens of fusion weapons to spend that much energy. It is much easier to pivot such a mass about its center of gravity; while the hydrogen-bomb flare had hidden them, the cargo vessels had nestled their bows into holes excavated in the rock and ice of the asteroid's crust. A cruiser could not have done it without self-destruction, but the haulers had been modified to act as pusher-tugs at need. Now four drives flared, and the lumpy dark potato-shape pivoted with elephantine delicacy. Toward *Subotai's* pursuer, blinded by its own drive for the crucial seconds. Fusion blossomed behind the rock's assigned stern, and the products of it washed out tens of kilometers; charged particles, gamma radiation striking metal and sleeting through as secondary radiation and heat. Through shielding, through the reaction-mass baffles around the command center; tripping relays, overloading circuits, ripping the nervous systems of the human crew as well.

"MANEUVER." *Subotai* flipped end-for-end. "DECEL-

ERATION." The main drive roared, a deeper thrumming
note as it poured reaction-mass onto the plate and spat out
fission pellets at twice the normal rate. The cruiser slowed
with a violence that stressed the frame to its limits, as if the
ship were sinking into some yielding but elastic substance.
Crippled, the Alliance vessel overshot. Weapons lashed out,
at ranges so short that response-time was minimal. From
both directions, for the wounded ship was not yet dead.

"Overheat, disperser three."

"Gatling six not reporting."

"Penetration! Pressure loss in reaction baffle nine."

"Wotan, get that missile, get it, *get it*." Rising tension,
until the close-in gatlings sprayed the homing rocket's path
with high-velocity metal. It exploded in a flower of nuclear
flame, and the radiation alarms shrilled.

Yolande felt the cruiser shake and tone around her, like a
vast mechanical beast crying out in pain. Sectors flicked from
green to amber to red on the screens; but the Alliance ship
was suffering worse, its defences shattered.

"Hit!" Railgun slugs sleeted into the *Washington*'s heat
dispersers. "Hit!" Parasite bombs dropped away from the
Subotai's stern, into the neutron flux of the drive; their own
small bomblets detonated, and the long metal bundles converted energy into X-ray laser spikes.

"She's losing air," the Sensor Officer reported. "Overheat in
her reaction mass tanks—pressure burst—losing longitudinal
stability—she's tumbling!"

Lasers raked across the enemy; armor sublimed into vapor,
and the computers held the beams on, chewing deeper. The
particle guns snapped; sparks flickered along the cartwheel-
ing form of the Alliance cruiser. Then the exterior screens
darkened.

"Something got through," the Weapons Officer said softly,
and consulted his screens. "Secondary effects . . . her fuel
pellets just went."

A cheer went through the *Subotai*, a moment's savage howl
of triumph.

"Stow that!" Yolande snapped. "Sensors, report."

"The *Bolivar*'s breaking and runnin' fo' it, ma'am." Only
sensible; with two ships to her one, the Draka could bracket
and overwhelm her.

"Damage Control?"

"Ship fully functional. Missin' one gatling turret. Three

dead, seven injured." Yolande winced inwardly. *Shit*. "Slow leaks in two sectors of the reaction mass tank. Seventy-one percent nominal, Drive full, remainder weapons systems full."

"Number Two, shape fo' pursuit." There was a momentary pause in the drive, and it resumed at normal high-burn rates. Stars crawled across the screens as the attitude jets adjusted their bearing. "If *Bolivar* gets back within the orbit of Luna, they'll do it with dry tanks an' scratches on that shiny new thrust plate." A pulsedrive ship could move on fuel pellets alone; the first generation had, using vaporized graphite from the lining of the plate as reaction mass. It was neither recommended, good for the frame, nor safe.

"Oh, and all hands," she said, switching to the command push. "Well done.

CHAPTER FIFTEEN

DATE: 12/11/82

FROM: Arch-Strategos Stephen Welber
        Assignments Board
        Supreme GHQ
        Castle Tarleton, Archona

TO: Cohortarch Yolande Ingolfsson
        Commandant, Task Force TelmarkIV
        Trans-Lunar Zone

RE: Further Orders:

You are instructed, upon the arrival of the relief force hereinafter specified, to return with DASCS *Subotai* to Geosynch Platform Padishah-One. You will there select a roster for skeletal watch-standing while the cruiser *Subotai* undergoes necessary repairs and consider yourself at liberty until 01/10/83, when you will report to this office for further assignment.

Please convey to all officers and crew of your command the warmest congratulations of the Supreme General Staff.

Postscript under personal code:

Dear Cohortarch: I, the Staff, and—I might add —your uncle, are extremely pleased with your performance. Not least the visible rage and frustration it has caused the Alliance; let certain parties accuse us of being soft on the enemy now! Still, it would be better if things were allowed to simmer

324

for a while. Your request for a permanent deep-
space command is accordingly denied, and in line
with what the High Command has in mind for
you, following debriefing you will be assigned
for the next year or two to the Astronautical War
College here in Archona. Then—perhaps—a Staff
appointment in the Mars-Jupiter sector.

Oh, you're getting a medal and a promotion;
do try to act surprised.

SPIN HABITAT SEVEN
CENTRAL BELT
BETWEEN THE ORBITS OF MARS AND JUPITER
JANUARY 4, 1983

Habitat Seven was the latest and largest of the Project's
constructs, half a kilometer across and two long; nickel-iron
was cheap, and easy to work with big-enough mirrors. Now
the former lump of metal-rich rock was a spinning tube,
closed at either end, with a glowing cylinder of woven glass
filament running down its center. There was atmosphere
inside, and part of the inner surface had already been transformed; gravity was .5 G, as much as was practical or necessary. Grass grew in squares of nutrient-rich dust, and hopeful
flowers. Individual houses were going up, foamed rock poured
into molds; there were dozens of different floor-plans.

"Goddamn circus," Frederick Lefarge said. "We're running
this like the bloody Los Alamos bomb project, back in the
'40's. Everything and the kitchen sink."

"Not really," the man beside him on the polished-slag
bench said. "In the long run, the actual construction will go
faster if we spend the time to get the infrastructure in place."
A sigh. "And even the . . . fourth Project will require a good
deal of preliminary groundwork. We are going to miss Dr.
Takashi very badly, as the years go by. I am more for the
crystals and wafers and wires, me; he was the instruction set
genius."

"Yes." He looked aside at Professor Pedro de Ribeiro: a
vigorous-looking forty-five, with the usual Imperial Brazilian
goatee in pepper-and-salt and an impeccable white linen suit;
the cane and gloves were, the American thought, a little
much. Very competent man, but . . . "I'd have thought that
was less so for the final Project than for the rest of the New

America enterprises. It's basically a set of compinstructions, isn't it?"

"Não." De Ribeiro's English was impeccable, but it slipped now and then. "I have been thinking much on this matter, since I was contacted . . . and have concluded that we must almost reinvent the art of information systems here, if we are to accomplish what we wish." He rested his hands on the silver head of his cane and leaned forward. "Abandon our assumption that because we have always done things one way, that is the inevitable path. Another legacy of the struggle with the Domination . . . Tell me, Senhor Lieutenant Colonel, what would you say to the idea of writing compinstruction procedures on a perscomp?"

Lefarge blinked, taken aback. "That's . . . Well, it would be like using a shovel as a machine-tool, wouldn't it?"

"Bim, but only because we have made it so." He tapped the ferrule of the cane on the ground. "Perhaps computers could only have started as they did, large machines used for cryptography, for the handling of statistics. Precious assets, jealously guarded. They have grown immensely faster, immensely more capable, even rather smaller—that first all-transistor model in 1942 was the size of a house! —but not different in nature."

"Well, how could they be?"

"For example . . . it is certainly technically possible to build central processing units small enough to power a perscomp. Yes, yes, quite difficult, but the micromachining processes we have developed for other purposes would do . . . if there were a strong development incentive. But our computers were always, hmm, how shall I say, *limited* in access. Perscomps were developed from the other end up, from the machinery intended to run machine tools, simulations, deal with the real world; only their instruction storage and the interfacers are digital, and the rest is analoge. We build them for a range of specific uses, and then develop the instruction-sets on larger machines; they are loaded into the smaller in cartridges. Complicated machines such as space warcraft have a maze of subsystems like that, linked to a central brain."

Wild speculation combined with restatement of the obvious, Lefarge thought. Then: *No, wait a minute. We've been too narrowly focused on immediate problems. The Project's going to need real ingenuity, not just engineering.* "But if we'd gone the other way . . . Jesus, Doctor, it'd be a security nightmare! Even as it is, we have to throw dozens of people in the slammer every year for illegal comping. There might be . . . oh, *thousands* of amateurs out there screwing around with vital instruction sets. The Draka could scoop it up off the market! Then think of the problems if you could copy embedded corepaths and instruction sets over the wires between perscomps, Lord. . ."

The Brazilian nodded. "Exactly! And who would find it more difficult to adjust to such a world, us or them? We must be radical, on our Project. That is an example."

He laughed as the younger man rocked under the question's impact. "Also, one of the reasons I have come here. Here we will be relatively free of the security restrictions—if only because we are already imprisoned, in a sense! For the first time, a completely free exchange of ideas and data."

Another tap at the metallic pebbles of the walkway. "The thing we wish to devise, it must be more than a set of hidden compinstructions. It must be a self-replicating, self-adjusting pattern of information, a . . . a *virus*, if you will. One able to overcome all the safeguards the Draka place on their machines; the redundant systems, the physical blocks, the many interfaces. We will have to reinvent many aspects of our art. Takashi agreed with me; it is better to start with a majority of younger men . . . and women, to be sure—ones free of the rather bureaucratized, specialized approach of other research institutes. And less dominated by us old men, who are so sure what is possible and what impossible! The *New America*, the starship, that is engineering. Wonderful engineering, many tests, unfamiliar challenges, but development work. In our Project, we must learn new ways to *think*. Ah, the senhora your wife."

She was walking now, with care and in this half-gravity. The forgetfulness was diminishing, and the crying fits; there would be no need for more transplants. The doctors were quite pleased . . . Something squeezed inside his gut, as he looked at her. She looked . . . a well-preserved forty, and moved with slow, painful care. Her face had filled out, a little, and she had gained back some of the weight, if not the muscle tone. The hair was cropped close, and only half gray; her teeth were the too-even white of implanted synthetic. Professor de Ribeiro rose and bowed over her hand.

"A salute to one so lovely and so brave," he said formally, bowing farewell to them both.

Cindy sank down with a sigh, and leaned her head against his shoulder. He put his arm around hers, feeling the slight tremor of exhaustion.

"Should you be up, honey?" he asked gently.

"I'll never get any better if I don't push it a little. I was with the girls," she said. "God, they're doing great, darling. Just . . . I get so *tired* all the time." He looked down, and saw that slow tears were leaking from under closed lids, made wordless sounds of comfort. "And I feel so old, and useless and *ugly*."

"You're the most beautiful thing in the solar system, Cindy," he said with utter sincerity. "I've never doubted it for a single instant."

She sighed again. "I like the professor. He's on whatever-it-is that's being hidden behind the *New America*, isn't he?"

Cindy laughed quietly, without stirring, as he tried to conceal his start of alarm. "Don't worry, sweetheart, I haven't been steaming open your letters . . . Honestly, I'm *sick*, not *stupid*. And I've had plenty of time to think, and anyway, we're all here for the duration. I do like the professor; he reminds me of Dr. Takashi—"

Suddenly she began to shake, and he turned to hold her in the circle of his arms. "Oh God, oh God, the end of his *hand* was gone and, and, *uhhh*—"

"Shhh, shhh," he said. "I'm here, honey, I'll always be here, I'll never let them hurt you again. Never again." The taste of helplessness was in his mouth, like burning ash.

At last she was still again. "Sorry. Sorry to be such a . . . baby," she said, gripping the breast of his uniform.

"God, honey, you're stronger than I could ever be."

She shook her head. "I get angry, and then I start feeling so *sorry* for everyone." A long pause. "Even her."

"Now, that's going a bit too far," he said, trying for humor. *Funny, hatred is actually a cold feeling. Like an old-fashioned injection at the dentist's.*

"No, darling. I tried to think how it would be, if somebody killed *you*, you know, what she said . . . "

"That filthy—" he bit off the words. "Sorry, honey."

"They can't help what their . . . way of life does to them. You know," she continued, "I think she really didn't want to hurt any of us, until she recognized your picture. It was as if she just . . . had a blind spot, couldn't *understand* why we weren't doing what she wanted, as if we were *making* her fight us. She . . . had them put all the other children in safely, with enough to . . . to eat."

He held her tighter. "Try not to think of it," he said. "And, honey, I'd do almost anything for you, except forgive the people who did this to you."

"I wouldn't want you to," she said unexpectedly, looking up at him bleakly. "I don't want you to become like that, eaten up with hate. But I don't want those people in the same universe as my children, either. Kill them all, Fred. Whatever you're doing here, *do* it."

The tension went out of her. "I really do feel sorry for them, though. What a life it must be, without a real home, without love—without even natural children. That's the first love of all, for the baby in your arms." Cindy yawned. "I feel sort of sleepy, Fred sweetheart," she whispered. "Take me home."

He bent and lifted her with infinite gentleness.

CLAESTUM PLANTATION
DISTRICT OF TUSCANY
PROVINCE OF ITALY
JANUARY 5, 1983

"Shit, I hope I'm in time," Yolande muttered to herself. She keyed the console and spoke:

"Central Mediterranean Control, Ingolfsson 55Z-4, here. Mach one-point-one at 9,985 meters, permission to commence descent."

"CMC here," an amused voice replied; one of the Citizen supervisors who had been following her dash from the orbital scramjet port in Alexandria. Being a national hero was proving more trying than she had expected, but it had its compensations. "Permission granted, we've cleared it."

"I'm not goin' need much room," she replied. Her hand hit the safety overrides *not designed for fighter pilots anyway* and kept the wings at maximum sweep-back; the Meercat turned on its side and dove.

"Right," she said. "Remember, this fuckin' *aircar* wasn't built fo' fighter jocks either." The ground swelled with frightening speed; she pulled the nose up in a half-Immelmann, vectored the belly-jets to loose speed, grunted as the craft seemed to hit a brick wall in the air. "Aaaaand again." The sonic boom must have rattled windows for kilometers around.

She shoved the wings forward and hit the spoilers; the speed wound down toward aerodynamic stall. "A little too much." That was the Monte Chiante ahead; she banked again, giving a touch to the throttle and hedgehopping. That was almost a forgotten sensation; amazing how much *faster* everything seemed with an atmosphere and planetary surface to reference from.

The Great House lay below her, like a model spread out on its hilltop. Nothing in the front court, and to *hell* with the pavement. Yolande rolled the craft in a final circuit of the hill, brought the vectored thrust fully vertical; the wings folded into their slots, and she could hear the landing gear extend as she let the aircar fall at maximum safe descent.

"God, I hope I'm in time," she said to herself. The canopy retracted and she vaulted out, hit the ground running, paused at the main stairs.

"Hiyo, ma, pa, I'm home. Am I in time?"

Her parents glanced at each other. "Everyone from here to Florence knows yo' home, after that approach, and yes. Only just. Run fo' it, girl!" her father said.

Yolande ran. Through corridors, hurdling furniture, once over a startled housegirl on her hands and knees scrubbing a floor. *Wotan and Thunor, I'm like lead, I should have worked out in the high-G spinner more*, she thought dazedly as she arrived at the birthroom door, breathing deeply. A voice stopped her.

"Clean up! Youa clean up before you come in!"

Middy Gianelli, no mistaking that bleak voice. Compelling herself not to fidget, Yolande hurriedly stripped off her uniform jacket and her boots, slipped on a sterile robe and slippers and stood under the UV cleanser until the buzzer sounded. Proper proceedure, after all. Almost certainly unnecessary, modern antibacterials being what they were, but there was no sense in taking chances with her baby. Suddenly nervous, she stepped through the door.

"Ma!" Gwen was on the other side of the table. "Ma, the baby's comin'!"

"Hiyo, dumplin'," Yolande said, distracted. "I know . . . How's it goin', Jolene?" she continued, stepping to the serf's side.

"Fine, M—*nnnnng*," she grunted. The black woman was resting on the birthing table; it was cranked up to support her upper body at a quarter from the horizontal, with a brace for her hips, raised pedestals for her feet; her hands were clenched on grips behind her head.

"You shoulda be asking me that, Mistis," the midwife said. She was an Italian serf, spare and severe; expensively trained, in her late fifties, much in demand on neighboring plantations. The Draka had never considered pregnancy an illness, and used doctors only when something seemed to be going wrong. "Dilation is complete, the water's justa broke; position normal, like the scanner said. Nexta time, use this wench again or picka one who's had her own *bambino*, it go easier."

"Glad . . . yo' . . . here," Jolene panted.

"No more talk; I been telling you what to do these six months now. Breath *in*, bear *down*. Yell if it helps."

The door opened again; Yolande's mother and father came in, and her brother John and Mandy; none of her brother's children were old enough to be here, of course; that would not be fitting until they were near-adult. The serf midwife scowled at the newcomers, snapped at her assistant-apprentice. Jolene filled her lungs and bore down with a long straining grunt, again. Again. Again. Her face and body shone with sweat, and her face contorted with her effort. Yolande laid a hand on her swollen belly, feeling the contractions through the palm. Time passed; Yolande looked up with a start and realized it had been nearly an hour. The other adults waited quietly; Gwen left her seat and stood, craning her neck to see around the two serf attendants.

"Oh, wow, ma," she said. "I can see the head."

"Quiet, Gwen," Yolande said gently. "Come on, Jolene, yo' can do it." The contractions were almost continuous now, and there was pain in the grunting cries.

She saw the crown of the head slide free of the distended birth canal, red and crumpled and slick with fluids. The stomach convulsed under her hand, and Jolene screamed three times, high and shrill. The baby slid free into the midwife's filmgloved hands. She cleaned the mouth and nose, then lifted it and slapped it sharply on the behind; it gave a wail as she laid it down on the platform, tied and severed the cord, began wiping the birthbloom, dipping the child in the basin of warm water her assistant held near. The crying continued as she dried and wrapped the child and handed it to Yolande.

"Ah," the Draka breathed, looking down at the tiny wrinkled form that quieted and peered around with mild, unfocused blue eyes. "My own sweet Nicholas; I'm goin' call yo' Nikki, hear?"

Gwen was tugging at her elbow. "Ma, can I see?" Yolande went down on one knee. "Why do they look so . . . rumpled up, ma? Did I look like that?"

"Just about, honeybunch. They have to squeeze through a pretty tight place, gettin' out. Here, see how perfect his hands are? Isn't it wonderful?"

The girl nodded, then looked aside where Jolene was shuddering and wincing as she worked to expel the afterbirth. "That looks like it really hurts, doin' all that. I'll never have to do that, will I, ma?"

Yolande spared a hard glance at Marya; what had the wench been saying to the child?

"No, of course not," she said to her daughter.

"No, Missy Gwen," Marya said, in her usual cool tone. "Your serf brooders will bear your eggs for you, just like this."

Gwen nodded, and Yolande rose and bent over Jolene. The serf was still panting, exhausted. She flinched slightly as the attendants cleaned her, slid a fresh sheet beneath her and wiped away the sweat before drawing up a coverlet and setting the controls to convert the birthing table into a bed; she would be moved later. Still, she smiled broadly as Yolande brought the small bundle near, reaching out her arms. "Can I?" she said.

"Of course," her owner replied, laying the infant gently on her abdomen. Yolande kissed her brow, then looked up to meet Gwen's eyes. "Remember, we owe Jolene a lot, daughter. We have to look after her always."

Gwen nodded solemnly, then gave her mother's hand a squeeze before she ran over to Marya; standing, her head was nearly level with the seated serf's.

How swiftly they grow, Yolande thought. Her daughter reached forward and hugged the American.

"Thank *yo'*, Tantie-ma Marya," she said earnestly. "I didn't realize how hard yo' worked, havin' me. Thank yo'."

Marya returned the embrace; the other Draka were smiling at the entirely proper show of sentiment. The serf stroked the red head resting on her bosom.

"You are welcome, Missy Gwen," she said. Then looked up, met Yolande's gaze, looked down at the child. "*You* are welcome."

Yolande felt a slight chill, then cast it aside. *Hearing things*, she decided, looking down at her son. A rush of warmth spread up from belly to throat, so overwhelming that her head swam with it. She was conscious of her family gathering around her, her father and mother's arms over her shoulders. John was popping a champagne bottle in the background, and someone pushed a glass into her hand. She sipped without tasting, watching the baby lying quietly with the dozing serf. Wondering, she stroked his cheek, and his head turned towards the touch, mouth working. "Why, he's an eager little one," Jolene said. "Mistis, help me?"

Yolande pulled down the sheet to bare the swollen breasts, and curled the infant into the curve of her arm so that he could take the nipple. He sucked eagerly, and Jolene closed her eyes with a sigh. "They been *so* sore an' tender. That feels good."

There was more quiet conversation as the infant nursed, and then the midwife cleared her throat. "Mastahs, Mistis', this not a good place for a party. An' this wench and the bambino, they needa their rest."

Thomas Ingolfsson rumbled a laugh. "True enough. Out, my children."

". . . so they sent out *Babur*, *Timur*, and *Mongke* fo' the final escort," Yolande was saying, some hours later. "The orbit's still eccentric enough that the damn thing swings outside Luna, so until we get it corrected, no sense in temptin' the Yankees to try anythin'."

"Think they might try anythin' closer?" her brother said sharply.

They were taking late lunch in the solarium. Yolande looked out through the clear crystal onto the winter gardens and the misty sere-and-green of a Tuscan winter. Rain had moved in, and falling curtains of silver hid the hills and the twisted black shapes of the vines. Inside there was a mild warmth, the tinkle of a rock-fountain, smells of coffee and seafood and fresh breads. Meditatively, she chewed another mouthful of shrimp.

"No," she answered, after a pause for thought. "There's too much at stake in their day-to-day lives that rests on what comes from near-Earth space. Too many vested interests would scream at the thought of disruption. Gwen, don't play with yo' food, if yo' goin' to sit at table with adults." John and

Mandy's eldest boy Eric was down at the junior's end of the family table, too, looking up from his plate occasionally with amusing hero-worship in his eyes; the other Draka children of the household were too young, and were off behind a screen of vines with their nurses.

"Yes, ma," Gwen replied. Slightly sulky, which was more like her; the birth had disturbed her a little. Only to be expected, but not to be cosseted. It was a natural enough process, after all.

Yolande sighed. "Well, it all came off reasonably well . . . except I hate havin' losses in my command. Score several points fo' us. That asteroid goin' to be real helpful, next five years or so. Still, I'm havin' doubts about whether we'll ever make a serious impact on the Alliance with this denarius-at-a-time policy. What the alternative is, I don't rightly know. Maybe they'll enlighten me at the War College."

"Mo' like to give yo' a severe case of paramathematical analytical holistic paralysis," her brother said lightly. "You'll be so aware of the consequences yo'll never do a damn thing again."

Johanna raised her wineglass. "A toast. To my grandson Nicholas Ingolfsson; may he serve the State and the Race as heroically as my daughter!"

There were laughter and cheers. Yolande smiled, but reached out and touched the glass. "The wish is appreciated, mother," she said seriously. "But no. I've got a different toast." She raised her own glass. "To Gwen and Nikki's future; by the time they're grown, may the Race rule from Sol to the Oort Clouds, unopposed!"

They clinked glasses.

Gwen's voice cut in. "But, ma . . . then who would I have to fight?" She sounded worried.

"Gwen, there's always space, an' that's enemy enough fo' all." A smile. "An' the telescopes say most stars like ours have planets, with air we can breathe. That means life, maybe with hands and minds. Yo' goin' to live a long, long time, honeybunch, hundreds of years. Yo' and Eric can go out to the stars an' conquer the aliens." *Who will hopefully have nothing better than spears,* she thought. *We've never gotten a message, not for all our looking, and the Yankees.*

Eric was gazing at her with a frown of serious thought. "The Yankees," he began, "they killed Aunt Myfwany." So she had always been called in this household, as courtesy to

Yolande. "They're really, really bad. I want to kill them all."
Gwen nodded vehemently.

Mandy and John turned to quell their son, but Yolande raised a hand. "Ah," she said, closing her eyes for a moment. "Eric, Gwen, thank yo' both." They were getting to the age of reason, and should be exposed to as much serious thought as they could handle. "But—remember this. When y'all are grown, yo' may have to kill to live. Remember, killin'—killin' people, even if they're not of the Race—it's not a good thing. We do it because we must, not because we hate, or because we like it. Eric, yo' don't hate yo' Tantie-ma Delores, do yo'?"

The boy shook his head.

"But she's Italian, and her people fought yo' grandma and grandpa. Gwen, Jolene's people fought us, long ago. Yo' Tantie-Ma is . . . was a Yankee. Don't want to kill *her*, eh?"

"Oh, no, ma. I love Marya."

"So yo' should, punkin. See, we're the Race, the Draka; it's our place to rule, an' fo' others to serve us and work fo' us. All this fightin' and killin', it's just because the wild ones don't know it yet. Once they've been brought under us and we've taught them that, we should protect them and treat them as gentle as we can, so they can be happy in their service." Yolande smiled indulgently as she saw the children's brows knitted in thought.

"And with that, maybe yo' should both go eat dessert at the children's table," Mandy said. Eric and Gwen slid from their chairs and came to give their parents the kiss of courtesy. Eating with the grownups was an honor but a strain as well, and less fun than joining their cousins and siblings.

"Gwen," Yolande whispered into her daughter's ear. "Did yo' like Archona? Quietly, now."

"Yes, ma, lots," the girl whispered back, her eyes glistening with excitment. "There was all *sorts* of things to do. Can we go again?"

"Well, punkin, don't tell anyone yet, but we're going to live there, yo' and yo' new brother and I, and I'll be home a lot more." *While I'm chained to a desk learning how at be a Staffer.* "And don't worry, yo' can still go to school in Baiae, and visit here lots." It was only a two-hour trip these days, anyway. "Now scoot!"

"Wisdom," her father said, when the children had gone. "Though there was damn-all fightin' here in Italy, at least." A laugh. "Bit of partisan trouble afterwards, though. Yo'd be too young to remember. Mo' like huntin' than combat, just a little mo' dangerous game."

Yolande shivered slightly inside herself; she had often wondered whether her generation had the iron of the ones who had fought the Eurasian War. India had been a sideshow, compared to that.

"That why yo' pushed to let those Alliance types yo' took go?" John asked. The servants gathered the plates and spread sweetmeats and pastries; her brother selected a walnut and cracked it between thumb and forefinger.

"Well, we traded them, fo' that lot of serf technicians." An embarrassing incident, when a robot personnel capsule had gone derelict on the way to the Phobos station; nobody but the Alliance had been in position to rescue them. "Left them with egg on they faces, too, when most of the serfs wanted back in."

Her mother snorted derisively. "Well, did they think we sent convicts fed on scraps into space?" she said. "Or that we'd select people without strong ties here to send to a risky frontier zone?"

"Quite possible they did think that," Yolande said, remembering. "I talked to some of the prisoners . . . they adapted pretty well; we only had to execute two or three . . . " *And none among the born-serf workforce; Harry was tickled pink about that.* "And they know less about us than we do about them." She frowned. "Of course, the type we got, near as yo' can translate they'd be Class IV or V serfs, here. Wotan knows, a serf learns as little about the Alliance as we can manage. I suppose their overlords do likewise."

"Never thought I'd see yo' talkin' down hatred and vengeance, sist—" John started, as his wife kicked him under the table.

Yolande's voice turned remote as her gaze. "I—I'll handle the vengeance, John," she said. "Hopefully, I'll handle the Yankees as well. Vengeance an' hate . . . that's my burden, and little joy of it I've had. None of it will give me back what I lost. *That's* what I want to spare our children."

There was a moment of awkward silence. "I hear yo' took one of the prisoners in fo', hmmm, *personal* cultural anthropology. Good? Wench or buck?" Mandy said, changing the subject with a joke.

The elder Ingolfsson's chuckle was strained. *Ah, the Race Purity Laws,* Yolande remembered. Fifty years ago, in *their* youth, it had been a hanging matter for a Citizen woman to lie with a serf male—an ancestral habit from which much else sprang. Contraception and equality of rights within the Citizen caste had made the law obsolete, and the new style of reproduction had rendered it outright silly, well before repeal in 1971. It had still been a matter for sniggering jokes when Yolande was a teenager; she found the younger generation appallingly casual about the whole matter. Mandy had always thought it vilely unfair, of course; but then she was just entranced with the male of the species.

"Wench," Yolande said, with a mock-severe frown of reproof at her schoolfriend and sister-in-law. "I'm an old-fashioned girl, myself. No, actually, I didn't touch her. Nice little thing, might not have minded keepin' her, but I sort of promised." She frowned, selected a confection of puff pastry and cream with fruit. "Coffee, Bianca. Did talk a fair bit; it got right borin' at times out there." She shook her head. "I'd *read* about them, of course. Seen viewers an' such. Still hadn't realized how downright *strange* they are. It'll be a relief when they're broken to the Yoke; the thought of it makes my brain hurt, frankly." She paused. "Might look little Alishia up, iffn' she survives the conquest."

"Oh," she continued. "I'm goin' to be needin' some staff, fo' the townhouse in Archona. Probably be based out of there for quite some time. Need a round score, good cook, assistants, set of housegirls, the usual. Driver, mechanic . . . hmmm. Junior nurses, to help Jolene; she'll be doin' clerical stuff again as soon as she's up. Glad to buy Claestum stock, if yo' can spare it." The plantation was actually overstrength; pa had been a little lax about enforcing birth control in the early years, and the chickens were coming home to roost. She saw the others exchange a glance and a smile.

"Well," said her father. "No problem, but it'd be unwise to stock a city home all from a plantation. Should buy some locals as well; maybe from a creche-trainer. Don't usually hold with the creche product, but yo' Jolene certainly worked out."

"Eric would help out," Johanna said. She sighed. "It *is* nice to see one's children doin' well," she added.

Yolande caught herself glancing out at the light, steady rain once more. It would be chill, out there. Misty and muddy, and the trees would be bare, and the smell would be of wet earth and rock and vegetation.

"I think," she said, "I'll get a slicker cape and a horse and go fo' a ride. Gods, if yo' knew how I'd missed fresh air, and the hills, and water I didn't turn on out of a tap. And I need the exercise, we used a 1.5-G spun minihab but it wasn't the same. Don't wait supper, I'll have somethin' sent up from the kitchens. See yo' in the mornin', I'll take the baby around then to show the ghouloons." The gene-engineered guardians trusted scent better than sight, and far more than words.

"Have a good time, darlin'," her mother said.

"And when yo' get back," her father said, to the others' laughter.

"Damn, I feel good," Yolande said quietly. The ride had been just what she needed, cold and physically demanding, a chance to feel at one once more with the earth that had born her, hour after hour until moonrise. And it had washed out the last of the tension from the ride down from orbit, cursing the interminable delays, the flight across the Mediterranean knowing that half the Citizens in the western provinces were following by viewer and smiling. The ride, and a long soak in the baths, and steam and massage from friendly expert attendants who had known her all her life. Now she felt alert and sharp-set, ready for her meal.

Shouldn't take long, she thought, opening the door of her suite by the tower. The kitchens always had someone on standby, and it wasn't as if the staff were overworked. *You know*, she told herself meditatively, *I'm even glad that Yankee bitch made it alive to Ceres*. That news had come through while the *Subotai* was making rendezvous with the relief flotilla.

Though more for the children's sake than hers. I really don't like hurting little ones, even when it's necessary. Uncle Eric's right, though; we hurt ourselves more than them if we . . . get out of proportion. Her eyes narrowed, lost in thought, as she walked through the lounging room and up the stairs, dropping her robe. Even then, she felt a minor surprise when something went *away* when you dropped it, instead of floating irritatingly at hand. *It's her man I want, anyway. I certainly don't regret the grief I've caused him. And he'll know they were under my hand, the rest of his days. Him, I'll kill. The rest of my revenge, it'll be enough to put the Alliance under the Yoke once and for all. Build a better world for mine and Myfwany's children.*

There was a fire crackling in the bedroom hearth, and a

meal laid out on a trolley table next to it. Her favorite, stuffed lobster with drawn butter, salad, and—

"Who the hell are *yo'*?" she asked the wench kneeling beside the table.

She rose, wearing a dazzling smile and a ribbon like a bandolier from shoulder to hip, with a large bow and a card attached to it. About twenty, raven hair falling to her waist, pale creamy skin; the straight delicate features and full-curved lips of a Michelangelo painting. The card was extended in one slender-fingered hand. *Nice fingers*, Yolande thought dazedly, as she unfolded it.

Enjoy, it read; signed by her kin.

"I am Mirella . . . Antonio the gardener's daughter, Mistis? And I am a gift, to serve you."

"Is that so?" Yolande said, falling back into the Tuscan of her earliest years and feeling laughter bubbling up beneath her breastbone. *Those impossible, presumptuous* — She shook her head helplessly. "Is that so, wench? And what do you think of the idea?"

"Oh, I wish very much to serve you"—a coy glance —"perfectly, in all ways, Mistis."

"Why?"

"Well . . . Everyone knows, you are kind, Mistis. And very beautiful. And . . . " the smile turned slightly urchin as the rest came in a rush. "And that you are going to the great city, Archona, and if I please you I will fly there away from here where nothing ever happens and see the lovely palaces and everything, and become a *head* housemaid before I am old and withered and not have to clean floors any more, and have a room of my own and pretty things and maybe even learn to read as they say all the servants do in the great city. Mistis."

Yolande sank into the chair, laughing until the tears flowed, then looked up at the wench's uncertain glance. "Well, Mirella, I like a serf who's honest. We ought to get to know each other better, before we settle your life." She patted the cushion beside her; there was plenty of room. It had been her favorite curl-up-in-front-of-the-fire-and-read-chair, when she was a child. "First, sit here and let's see if you like lobster."

CHAPTER SIXTEEN

The paradox of our times is that information has increased more rapidly than the capacity of the sciences to integrate it, and nowhere more so than in physics and cosmology. In the 1950s, we were still uncertain what lay under the clouds of Venus—swamps seemed a sound hypothesis—and the "canals" of Mars had only recently been debunked. Less than a decade later, spaceships and probes were studying every planet inside the orbit of Neptune. We exist in a world bear-lead by engineers, themselves driven by frantic necessity. Our theories are lame, limping things cobbled together to give some rough frame-work and mathematical basis to the huge con-structs we make, and the monstrous puzzles we encounter. And often we ignore vital areas of research simply because there is so much else to be done that is immediately promising. For example, only now are we developing a theory of stellar formation which has any predictive force, and this decades after the space tele-scopes proved the ubiquity of planets. We now know that planets with life—or at least oxygen-rich atmospheres and liquid water—are fairly common around stars of the general type of Sol; four have been confirmed so far within 50 light-years of Earth. Yet there has been no sus-tained investigation of Bigetti's Paradox; if life is common, *where are the intelligent aliens?*

A still more glaring example has recently arisen. Ever since the initial breakthroughs of the decade 1900–1910, we have been treating the quantum-mechanical paradoxes as useful mathematical fictions; some amuse themselves with thought-experiments such as Kubbelman's Rat and its half-life/half-death state in the sealed box. Now these questions are rising, as it were, out of the subatomic world and clamoring for attention—by biting us on the ankle, if nothing else. Our rule-of-thumb engineers stumbled across high-temperature superconductivity, and applied it widely, long before an adequate theory had been produced; we knew that the whole superconductor was in a single quantum state and left it at that. Only recently has it occurred to anyone to conduct the basic experiments necessary to show that quantum phase-shifts can create non-local events—action at a distance, without interval or an intervening exchange of particles.

Now we learn that a piece of superconducting material changes state *instantaneously*, regardless of distance. The whole basis of relativistic physics is shaken, and what is the response outside the scientific community? "Does this mean better telephones? Can we make a weapon of it?" What we need most urgently is a period of tranquillity, in which our species can assimilate and systematize the breakthroughs of this century.

> *History in a Technological Age*
> Ch.XX *Reflections and Conclusion*
> by Andrew Elliot Armstrang, Ph.D.
> Department of History
> San Diego University Press, 1995

CENTRAL OFFICE, ARCHONAL PALACE
ARCHONA
DOMINATION OF THE DRAKA
NOVEMBER 10, 1991

"That will be all," Eric von Shrakenberg said.

"Excellence," his aide replied, bowing and leaving.

Damned insolence of office, he thought with amusement. The Domination's chief executive was selected for a seven-year term, with no limits on reelection. Hence the Archonate staff tended to become used to an incumbent, set in their ways; he was still running into problems with that, except with the people he had brought in himself last year. The serf cadre were even worse . . .

"Five minutes," the desk said.

He sighed and seated himself, feeling a little out of place. This shape of carved yellowwood and Zambezi teak . . . how many Occupation Day addresses had he seen it in, from the other side? On film back during the Eurasian War, on screens of gradually increasing clarity since. *Wotlan, fifty years!* he thought, looking around the big room. Not overwhelming, although the view was spectacular, when the curtains were open; the dome of the House of Assembly was about half a kilometer away. History-drenched enough for anybody, he supposed, thinking of the decisions made here.

And now I sit here and hold the fate of the human race in my hands, he thought. *If anyone's listening at the other end of these communicators.* Having people obey when he spoke was the difference between being a leader and an old man in a room. *A fact not commonly known, and it's better so.*

"Incoming signal," the speaker said.

"Receive."

A spot of light appeared at head-height beyond the desk. A line framed it, expanding outward until it outlined a rectangle three meters by three; the central spot faded, and then the rectangle blinked out of existance. Replacing it was a holographic window into the interior of Washington House. Eric knew it was an arrangement of photons, as insubstantial as moonbeams, but still wondered at the sheer *solidity* of it. *Genuine progress, for a change*, he thought. You could get the true measure of an opponent this way, the total-sensory gestalt read from every minute clue of stance, expression, movement. The same applied in reverse.

"Madam President," he said, inclining his head.

"Excellence," she replied, with meticulous courtesy.

She may have been added to balance the ticket, but I don't think the Yankees lost when Liedermann slipped on the soap, Eric decided. President Carmen Hiero was the second Hispanic and the first woman to sit in the same chair as Jefferson and Douglas; before that she had been a Republican *jefe politico* in Sonora, still very unusual for a woman in the States carved out of Old Mexico. Fiftyish, graying, *criolla* blueblood by descent, mixed with Irish from a line of silver-mine magnates: that much he knew from the briefing papers. Old *haciendado* family, but not a shellback by Yankee standards; degrees in classics, history, and some odd American specialty known as political science, whatever that was. *A contradiction in terms, from the title*.

"I regret that I can't offer hospitality," he continued.

She shrugged. "Debatable whether it would be appropriate, under the circumstances. I hope you realize how much trouble with my OSS people I had to go through to allow Domination equipment here."

"And the political capital *I* must expend to let Yankee electronics in here," he added dryly. "Our Security people are still more paranoid than yours, not least because it is a field in which your nation excels us. Still, we can now be reasonably sure nobody is recording or tapping these conversations." He paused. "Why *did* yo' agree, Señora?"

The black eyes met his calmly. *Almost as much body-language control as a Draka*, he thought with interest. *Better than some of us do, actually. I wonder how deep it runs*.

"I suspect my reasoning was much like yours, von Shrakenberg. The convenience of dealing with essential issues without the circumlocutions essential where things are said in public, without the necessary lies of party politics. In addition, the chance of gaining personal insight into my enemy, set against the risk of him doing likewise. Well worth that risk. Always it is better to act from knowledge than ignorance." Eric nodded, spread his hands in silent acknowledgment as she continued. "Although, *por favor*, why did you not request such a link with the Alliance Chairman?"

Eric chuckled. "For much the same reason that you would not have agreed, had Representative Gayner's nominee been sittin' in this chair."

Her eyebrows rose slightly. "I would not compare Chairman Allsworthy to your Militants," she said.

"Not in terms of policy . . . a certain structural similarity in position on our relative political spectra. Perhaps a similarity in believin' too strongly in our respective national mythologies. Besides, the American President is still rather mo' than first among equals."

It was Hiero's turn to spread her hands silently. *Certain necessary fictions must be maintained even here*, he read the gesture.

"Turnin' to business," Eric continued, "was it really necessary to tow those-there gold-rich asteroids into Earth orbit? I admit it's industrially convenient havin' gold fall to the same value as tin, but the the financial problems!"

A thin smile; the Alliance currency was fiat money, while the Domination's Auric had always been gold-backed. "You could refuse to trade for gold, and maintain an arbitrary value," she said in a tone of sweet reason.

He snorted. "Thus sacrificin' the industrial advantages, and ending up with all the disadvantages of a metallic standard, all the problems of a paper-money system, and none of the compensatin' flexibility," he said. "Between me and thee, we're movin' to a basket of commodities, although with the general fall in prices—"

An hour later, Hiero leaned back. "Well," she said, "all this indicates several areas of potential agreement." They both nodded; technical discussions were easy, once the top-echelon political decisions had been made. "Perhaps we can move on to others, at later meetings. Certainly we have more of a meeting of minds than I could with your Militants."

Or I with Allsworthy, Eric inferred. Quite true; the chairman had what amounted to a physical phobia towards Draka, taking the nickname "Snake" quite literally.

"Please, don't misinterpret," he said softly. "On some issues of purely . . . pragmatic impo'tance, perhaps. On mo' fundamental issues of foreign policy, my Conservatives will follow an essentially Militant line."

"Why? If I may ask."

"Because . . . Madam President, the internal politics of the Domination can no way be interpreted in terms of what yo' familiar with; a word to the wise, to prevent misunderstandin'. The universe of discourse is too different. To call my faction paternalistic conservatives an' Gayner's biotechnocrats is a very crude approximation. Our real differences are on issues of domestic policy—very long-term domestic policy at that, arisin' after we dispose of yo'. Or yo' dispose of us, in which case it all becomes moot, eh? It's extremely impo'tant that we try to understand the parameters of each other's operations, otherwise things could get completely irrational."

"I see your point." A hesitation. "May I ask you a personal question, Excellence?" At his nod, she proceeded: "I've got the usual Intelligence summaries on you . . . and I've read your novels. Within limits, I received the impression of an intelligent and empathetic man. Which leads to certain questions."

Eric turned in his swivel chair and poured a measure of brandy into a balloon snifter, turned back, paused to swirl the liquid and sniff, sip.

"I assure yo', they've occurred to me as well," he said meditatively. "Why, in essence, don't I retire to my estate and let the world rave as it will?" He felt his lips twist into the semblance of a smile. "Well, in all honesty, Madam President, why don't yo'? It's in the nature of an ambitious politician to imagine all alternatives to himself are disaster. I flatter mahself I'm right."

"Duty," she said. "I'm . . . not indispensable, but there are worse people to occupy this chair. For my children, my nation, and for the cause of freedom, if that doesn't sound too pompous."

Eric laughed harshly. "Yo' Americans have been a lucky people, on the whole . . . what convenience, to have national interest an' high-soundin' ideals so congruent!" He made a gesture with the glass. "Forgive a slight bitterness. Leavin' aside the question of whether morals are objective reality or cultural artifacts, I'm left with some similar motivations. I have children, grandchildren. And my people. As my fathah once said to me, yo' nation is like yo' children; loved because they are *yours*, not necessarily because they deserve it. Moral judgment—that has to be made in the context of political and historical reality, not some imaginary situation where we start with a *tabula rasa*."

"Even in politics, surely moral choices are an individual's responsibility?"

"A true difference of national temperament, I think. Iff'n a Draka thinks of choice at all, it's as constrained within narrow bonds; human beings make history, but they don't make it just as they choose." He laughed again, this time with more genuine humor. "Interestin' question, whether perception is the result or cause of social reality . . ." He set the snifter down and leaned forward. "One thing is sure. Either of us would start the Final War *if we thought it was the right choice*. And neither of us wants to be *forced* into that decision prematurely. Which leaves us with certain common difficulties."

"*Bueno*, I am glad you realize this. This conflict—it has gone on so long, both sides, they have accumulated serious vested interests with a stake in waging it. Organizations, bureaucracies, careers are invested in it; power, vast profits. Always these push toward its intensification. We have a common interest then, in not allowing the instruments of policy to *set* our policy."

"True." He nodded decisively. "Very true. Although, hmmmm." He rubbed his chin meditatively, then decided to speak. It was no secret, after all. "Madam President, remember always that there is no true symmetry between our positions, here. There is an element in the Alliance which seeks to simply grow around and beyond us, reduce us to an irrelevance." She nodded. "This is precisely what much of our strategy has been designed to prevent. The border tensions, the convention we have allowed to grow up that there is no peace beyond Luna . . . It is yo' dynamism we fear. The tension inhibits it, forces yo' into military an' security measures where we can compete mo' easily."

Hiero's mouth clamped in a grim line. "Sí. So my analysts tell me. Let me warn you then, Excellence. This policy has its own dangers. Firstly, it makes the task you have, of restraining your military, more difficult. Secondly, both our societies are becoming dependent on resources and manufactures from space; this entails massive activities and investments beyond the Earth-Moon system. In turn, these create interests whose voices cannot be ignored. Also . . . when only explorers and pioneers were at risk, nothing vital was threatened by clashes in deep space. Now we are approaching the point where *vital matters of national security* are endangered in the heavens. We would not tolerate an invasion of Burma or England. Should we then regard Ceres as less?"

"Correct," Eric said, with soft precision. "As you point out, my task of control is mo' than yours; nor would I modify our tradition of decentralized decision makin', even if I could." He sighed. "A world bound in chains of adamant, that's our legacy. The stalemate becomes ever less stable. If nothin' else, inaction would give my opponents too much opportunity. The fact that I'm presented with an insoluble dilemma, and they know it, will not restrain them from takin' political advantage of it."

Hiero tapped a finger to her lip in polite skepticism. "I am to endure provocation from you, because if I do not, another even less restrained would take your place?" She continued with heavy irony: *"The whip is not so bad; fear instead, my brother, who will use scorpions?"*

"I see yo' point. So both of us looks for a means to *break* the stalemate; I don't suppose it's much consolation that I would use it with regret, while anothah in my shoes might do it with Naldorssenian glee and invocations of the Will to Power. But be careful, be very careful, Madam President. Neither of us wishes to destroy the planet. Don't rely too much on secrets—such as yo' New America project, out there in the asteroids. Conveniently on the opposite side of the Sun from Earth, most of the time, eh?"

She was shaken for a moment, he was sure of it: a thousand tiny signs said so. Then she rallied.

"Or your Stone Dogs, *sí?*"

It was his turn to feel a hand squeezing at the arteries in his chest. *Control yourself, you fool,* he said behind a smiling mask. *Ah . . . she didn't match my disclosure of* her *project's location.* Only a half-dozen knew the full to most of those charged with implementation. *And don't start flailing about to discover her source. The effort itself could tell them too much. Overwhelmingly probable they have discovered only that it is a secret, and important.*

He glanced polite inquiry. "Stone Dogs . . . an old nickname fo' our Janissary infantrymen. Perhaps a code name? I can't very well follow every project, of course." Their eyes met in perfect understanding of the game of bluff and double-bluff. "Well, we all have our little surprises," he said. "Tell me, do yo' ever suspect what yo' subordinates aren't tellin' yo'?"

She gave him a glance that was half ironic, half a reflection of shared fear. He remembered times when he had lain awake sweating with that particular horror, the worst of which was that there was no way to disprove it. A successful deception ploy was invisible by definition, and thinking of it too much that was the road to paranoia and madness.

"It has been, ah, interesting," the president said at last.

"At least that. Perhaps in another few months."

"Of a certainty. Excellence."

"Madam President."

The holo vanished, and Eric waited a long moment with the heels of his palms to his eyes before he touched a control on the desk. "Shirley," he said. "Send in the estimates, would yo'?"

His eyes sought the curtains. The sun had fallen . . . Perhaps next week there would be time for a visit home. *Stop reaching for the carrot, donkey,* he told himself brutally. *Bend your neck to the traces and pull.*

President Carmen Hiero shook her head thoughtfully as the aides bustled about, rearranging the room.

"*The poor man,*" she murmured, in her mother's language.

"Ma'am?" the Secret Service agent said.

"Nothing, Lindholm," she said, standing. It had been a long day, and there was a dull pain in her lower back. *And more dull pains to be endured at dinner,* she thought wryly. For a moment she looked again at the air the transmission had occupied. "Nothing that matters . . . in the end."

NOVA VIRCONIUM
COMMAND CENTRAL
HELLAS PLANITIA, MARS
DOMINATION OF THE DRAKA
NOVEMBER 17, 1991

Eerie, Yolande decided, watching her own image on the screen, on the bridge of the *Imperator,* the latest fourth-generation cruiser-carrier, flagship of the 2nd Trans-Lunar flotilla. *Watching an image of myself watching images,* she decided. Ghosts of ghosts . . . out there so far away, six months ago.

A dozen cruisers, plus the new stingfighter auxiliaries many of them carried. Dispersed so far that the reports took long seconds to arrive, almost as long as the blue-white visual signatures of nuclear explosions. Battle became a slow and stately dance, until the distances closed; then inertia made the commitment final, and the exchange of energies grew too swift for human reflexes to follow. *Lovely. Long enough for every doubt, then no time to do anything at the end.* She turned up the sound.

"Forward vessels reportin' . . . Wotan, look at the particle-beam intensities!" Data flowed across a screen.

"Well," she heard her own voice replying, "now we know the linear accelerators *are* dual-purpose. Pull them back if they aren't already." The big fixed installations had more punch than any ship, more than any ship's shielding could take. Not to mention neutral-particle beams, which were hard to shield against at all. "Report on the minor vessels, TacEval."

"Nothin' like as good as the stingfighters, but there are so *many* of them," the flotilla Tactical Evaluation Officer had said.

Well, the Alliance've certainly learned about arming their minor vessels, she reflected. There had been dozens of them around the secret project base; it was a major enterprise, with active traffic, at least outside the habitats where enemy personnel went in and nobody came out. None of the smaller vessels was up to military standards, and they were slow. But with the big installation lasers to provide emergency boost, and her own ships trapped in this narrow sliver of orbit, the warships did not have enough hands to swat them.

"*Batu*'s hit!" Flotilla Damage Control. Another stream of numbers, energy input and missiles from the enemy battle stations. "She can't—" Half a dozen screens went blank. The light-signature arrived seconds later, secondary explosions. "Gone, Merarch."

Yolande closed her eyes in remembered pain. Teller's ship. *Another friend. Another debit in your bill, Yankee.*

"Withdraw." She heard her own voice say it, and the bile-taste was back. There had been a vibration of protest on the command bridge of *Imperator.* "This was a reconnaissance in force, and we've learned what we came to find out." *That their New America project is important enough to warrant defenses as tough as Ceres—or Mars. That they're willing to spend lives like water to keep us off, even to keep us from pointblank observation.* "No point in expendin' further resources. The Great Khan's 're to cut trajectories fo' open space. *Imperator* and *Diocletian* will cover."

That had been the best decision; the deuterium-tritium pulsedrives gave the new ships longer continuous boost envelopes than the older cruisers could match. And were less vulnerable to combat damage, as well. Besides that, she hated to send warriors into a risk she did not share . . . It had been time to break off anyway, the Alliance fleet was burning their thrust-plates to get into action distance.

"End replay," she said, as the recording began to show the needlefires of the drives.

The office wall blanked for a second, then returned to a view of the outside. Command Central was actually burrowed far back into the basalt near the edge of the great lowland basin of the Hellas Planitia, but her favorite view was of the expanding base above.

Almost a city, now, she thought with pride. The late-evening sky was pink with the dust-haze and ice-crystals of the thin Martian atmosphere. Yolande could make out the disk of the setting sun, only two-thirds the size it would be from Earth. And the larger but dimmer circle of the first of the orbital mirrors. Just a proof-of-concept pilot project, concentrating the sunlight on a few hundred square kilometers around this equatorial base, but it had already made a difference in the nighttime temperatures.

"Record, fo' the Strategic Plannin' Board," she continued, standing with her back to the desk. "Note to previous reports. The other conclusion that we should draw from this is that the Yankees are spreadin' through the Belt like a cancer metastasizing through the bloodstream. Not only is this a long-range danger in itself, but it hampers every other operation of ours. Takin' direct counteraction may be impractical, but we should squeeze harder on their lifeline back to Earth-Luna, up their costs, an' cut into the profit margins of all those two-denarius outfits they're allowin' into space. Well worth any countermeasures, since we're not vulnerable to the same economic pressures."

A long pause, considering. "I know it's not my department, but the headhunters should be usin' the opportunities this presents to speed up their infiltration of the New America project, and the other nasty surprises they may be brewin' fo' us there. Hans, come in."

The door hissed open, and her secretary walked in. His shaved head made a token bow. He was a serf Auxiliary, of course; Dutch, if she remembered correctly. But there was less formality out here on the frontier, too much work to be done to waste time.

"Hans, take the recordin', dress it up suitable, plug in the numbahs. Just to remind them, add the latest graphics of increased enemy traffic flows, Belt-internal—I don't know how much the Statistical Section gets through to the Board—and have it on my desk Monday."

"Consider it done, Merarch." The Auxiliaries had the privilege of addressing their superiors by title.

She thought for a moment. "I won't be in tomorrow." Saturday; Yolande usually put in at least a half-day. "Oh, your son's gettin' married tomorrow, isn't he? To that systems tech?"

Hans bowed again, more deeply, smiling slightly. The serf was several years older than she, a longtime veteran of the Martian base. Old enough to have fathered the first generation to reach maturity; there were only a few so far, of course, but population was building up rapidly.

"Yes, Merarch," he said. "The authorization for the quarters came through. Thank you, Merarch."

She made a dismissive gesture. "Yo've given good service, Hans." This was her first major administrative post, and growing so rapidly that the Citizen executive staff were nearly as new to it as herself. Hans had been personal secretary to four Commandant-Governors, since the first minimal complex of bunkers back in '72: an invaluable element of continuity. "I may drop by the wedding fo' a minute or two. Get my car ready, would yo'?"

"At-at once, Merarch," he stammered, flushing with pleasure.

Well, it can't hurt, she thought, stepping into an alcove to change into a surface suit. There was a bedroom suite attached to the office, for the times when the Commandant-Governor had to stay near the levers. *I'll just stay for a few moments, any more would make them uncomfortable.*

The surface clothing was much less elaborate than a vacuum suit, a pressure-skin with temperature elements. Waste heat was less of a problem on the Martian surface than in space—the climate here on the equator ranged from chilly to Siberian, not counting the winds—but you did need warmth and protection from the UV. *Now, out of official mode,* Yolande told herself, and glanced at her wrist. 1800; the shuttle was due in an hour.

Gwen! she thought, striding through the open-plan outer office with the bouncy pace that covered ground most efficiently in one-third gravity. Most of the workstations were dark, the Auxiliaries at home except for the evening shift. The few there rose and bowed as she passed; then out into the corridors, past the entrances to the office suites of the Citizen staff; the Commandant's headquarters was the nerve-center of Nova Virconium, after all. *Gwen, baby,* she thought again. *Nikki.*

The shuttleport was several kilometers out from the center of Nova Virconium. New enough to include a few flourishes, including a terminal building finished in polished stone surfaces, combinations of colors Earth had never seen. Red in every shade from white-pink to blood-crimson, blue, black, swirling green. With a two-story-high central fountain, not really such an extravagance in a closed system . . . The VIP lounge was on the upper terrace, skylight ceilings and plants and light airy furniture of locally-grown bamboo; Yolande had an excellent view out over the runways. She suppressed an undignified urge to pace; there were too many official spectators. Sipping at the glass of white wine, she glanced down into the main lobby. Plenty of parents; the Transportation Directorate had advertised the first cruise of their spanking-new fusion-pulsedrive passenger craft as a Reunion Special.

"A milestone, in its way," she said to the aide in the lounger next to her. Kilometers away across the runways and dug-in hangars a finger of light probed into the sky with a ball of flame at its tip, a vertical-lift cargo pod rising on laser boost.

"Wotan, yes," he said. "Even if the Directorate of War did subsidize it." The liner *Sky Treader* was to double as a fast transport, in the event of emergency. "We'll be gettin' a flood of tourists, next."

"I— Here she comes!"

The Martian orbital shuttle was like nothing else in the solar system. Delta-shaped, but with huge slender wings that could only have flown under this light gravity and tenuous wisp of atmosphere. It swelled from the east, out of sky already gone purple and starlit, its riding lights bright against the dark ceramic of the heatshield. Just then the outline lights of the pathways blinked on, like a great glowing circuit-diagram across the plain, stretching out to the horizon. Daggers of brighter light appeared beneath and about the shuttle: steering jets and final breaking. The flat belly and underwing surface drifted down to maglev distance, fields meshing with those of the runway, and it slid frictionless at half a meter until the gentle magnetic tugging brought it to a halt.

Yolande rose, straightened her uniform. The others in the party bustled likewise as the windowless arrowhead slid its nose into the terminal docking collar. The band made a few preliminary tootles . . .

"Marya," Yolande said. The serf had been standing at the railing; she turned silently and faded into the background of the welcoming party. The doors below cycled open, and the passengers came through. A big clot of children, which dissolved like sugar under hot water as they scattered to the waiting families. A small group that hung uncertainly near the doors. Yolande recognized Jolene's blond mane first, then Gwen. Another girl next to her, and a smaller form next to Jolene . . . Nikki.

"Let's do it," she said.

The Martian Rangers decurion saluted with a grin, and called to his guard-party. They were ghouloons, of course; in surface suits and armor, but with faceguards swung back. Their muzzles dipped in unison as they wheeled, split into two lines of fifteen, and trotted down to take station in four-footed parade rest up the broad stairway that ran from the upper lounge to the lower. Yolande moved to the head of the stairs; the band struck up the *Warrior's Saraband*, and the decurion turned to the double line of inhuman fighters.

"Commandant-Governor's . . . *salute!*" he barked, as Yolande walked down the stairs. The ghouloon troopers threw back their heads and gave a short barking howl.

She was close enough to see her daughter's face now: flushed with a combination of delight and terminal embarrassment, as the crowd in the main terminal parted. There were cheers and claps; Yolande had come to the Commandant-Governor's post with a good reputation, and was popular enough . . .

"Ma. Ah, Service to the State."

"Glory to the Race." *Oh, Freya, she looks so much like her,* Yolande thought, with a brief twisting pain inside her chest. For a moment the years and light-minutes slipped away, and she was a rumpled teenager alone and lonely on her first evening at Baiae School. *Like that first time I saw her.* Gwen was fourteen now—a little taller than Myfwany had been, a little slimmer. Perhaps more relaxed about the eyes. *My own Gwendolyn,* Yolande thought.

"Hello, daughter," she said and opened her arms.

The hug was brief but bruising-strong, the New Race muscles squeezing her ribs. Yolande released the girl and held her at arm's length. "Yo' lookin' good, child of my heart." Nikki had been jittering at Jolene's side; now he tore free and threw his arms around Yolande's waist, smiling up gap-toothed. She ruffled the sandy hair and closed her own eyes for a moment; they were rare, these instants of true happiness. Best to seize them while you could.

Nikki was looking sideways at the Rangers. "Decurion Kang," Yolande said, "I think my son might like to review yo' guard-party."

"Yo' *bet*, ma!" the seven-year-old said enthusiastically.

Yolande nodded to her aide, saluted. "I think we can carry on from here, Tetrarch," she said, and turned back to her daughter.

"Ah, ma?" Gwen was pulling her companion forward. "This is my friend Winnifred Makers, I told yo' about?"

Wide blue eyes, a sharp-featured New Race face, dark-blond hair. Swallowing a little, but bearing up under the stress of meeting the planetary-governor mother of her schoolfriend. *Good*, thought Yolande, sizing her up. *All in order. I don't care what the younger generation says, it's unnatural to get involved with boys before you're eighteen. More than good.* They exchanged formal wristgrips.

"Don't be too intimidated, Miz Makers," Yolande said kindly. "It isn't a very big planet, and there aren't many people on it yet." The girl gave a charming smile.

They turned to walk up the stairs. The ghouloons were keeping eyes front, but their pointed ears had swivelled toward the officer and the boy with his earnest questions.

"Imp," his mother said fondly. "Ah, Gwen, here's yo' Tantie-ma." Yolande watched, was gratified to see her daughter give the serf an affectionate peck on the cheek.

"Glad to see yo' again, Tantie-ma," she said.

"I'm . . . glad to see you, too, Missy Gwen," Marya said. There was a smile on her face, slight but genuine.

Gwen slapped a hand to her forehead. "Oh, here, I brought yo' somethin'. Those books yo' wanted, from that store in Archona? Here's the plaque."

"This is the best time of day," Yolande said, nodding out the window of the car. "This and dawn." The sky was still the color of salmon to the west, with wings of paler color touching the jagged edges of the cratered highlands.

They were taking the long route around the city, along a ring-road of pink marscrete. Out to the left stretched the farms; those were enclosures two kilometers by one, with chest-high walls of native rock and inflated arch-coverings of thinfilm, double-walled envelopes filled with carbon dioxide for insulation. Most were lit from within, and they could see the shapes of plants, banana fronds, grape arbors, flowers, a dozen dozen shades of green, blue, yellow. A few held animals: the inevitable dog-sized rabbits, pigs, even a small herd of dwarf Ngama cattle.

"We feed the outer system from here," Yolande said. The children were supposed to be on a working holiday, from the volume of complaints in Gwen's letters about the assignments they had with them. As well to make a few gestures towards helping their on-site research. "As well as arm and equip it." A nod to the low mounded shapes of factory buildings on the other side of the road.

Winnifred frowned. "But yo' have to ship everythin' up out of a gravity well, ma'am?"

Yolande nodded. Off Earth, it made more sense to think in terms of gravity gradients and delta-V requirements than mere distance. "Not much of one, and this atmosphere is pretty thin. We've got a fusion generator now"—*the first planet-based one in the System, too*—"and of course the powersats, so launch energy is even cheaper than in the Earth-moon. There's Phobos and Deimos fo' materials in orbit, a couple of the Amor asteroids we've moved as well; the zero-G stuff we fabricate up there. Other things, it's mo' convenient to do under gravity, like food-production; easier to battle-harden them, too."

The best possible shielding was lots and lots of inert matter. "Also, Mars and Mars-orbit make a great base fo' operations among the gas-giant moons. Now *there's* a hostile environment fo' yo'! But a lot of stuff we need."

As if to underline her point, a streak of light cut the twilight out to the southwest, then slowed and dimmed. "That's a load comin' in, atmosphere brakin' and parachute. Possibly frozen nitrogen or hydrocarbons from Titan with an ablative shield. We've got a maglev railway out to the dropyard . . . All this is just a trial run fo' the terraformin' project, of course. But we expect the population here to double in the next five years." *My term of office.* "There's even Citizen schoolin' available here, now."

The two girls traded a look of alarm. "Don't worry," Yolande chuckled. "Wouldn't move Gwen, not from Senior School. Might bring Nikki out, though." He was riding in the rear car. "Lots of other projects here: the mass-driver up Olympus Mons, prospectin' . . . I've arranged fo' guided tours fo' yo' two, next two weeks. Should give yo' plenty of material for those papers Gwen was tellin' me yo' have to write."

*   *   *

The Commandant-Governor's Residence had started as a simple box, back when Nova Virconium had been a glorified research outpost, and had been added to substantially in the years since; much of that was domed courtyards, the primary luxury on Mars. Yolande had laid on the family dinner in her favorite, the one with the goldfish pond in the center, and the murals her city's first professional artist had done for her predecessor. They showed Martian landscapes, as they might look some centuries from now. A vastly larger Nova Virconium, streets lined with elongated trees, looking out over a Hellas Sea speckled white with the sails of pleasureboats. Children running on grass and flowers beneath birch trees. Skiers vaulting impossible distances on the slopes of Olympus Mons. The *lower* slopes, it was twenty-four kilometers high, and the peak would be out of most of the atmosphere, even when Mars had seas and breathable air.

Yolande smiled and leaned back in the chair, watching the houseserfs clear away the last of the dishes, sipping at her coffee. Nikki had gotten sleepy hours ago; not surprising, after an exciting day. Gwen and her Winnifred had been a delight. *Wotan and Thunor, was I ever that enthusiastic for . . . for life?* she thought wryly. *I remember it, I think. When does it slip away?* She shook her head, watching as one of the chrome-yellow carp in the pond leaped. It flipped half a dozen times end-for-end, then dropped back with what she could swear was a look of shock. *Embedded compinstructions.* She supposed there must be very little in a fish's repertoire of behaviors that was not instinct. *Poor little bastards will need a long time to adjust.*

It had really been quite nice of the girls to sit talking with her this long; it was nearly 2400. They had been sharing a stateroom with four others for the three weeks from Earth; very little privacy. With a fond sadness, Yolande glanced down the corridor they had taken. *Probably a lot of giggles and whispered confidences between the kisses, if I recall,* she thought wistfully. *Ah well.* What had the ancient Greek said, back when? "Comport yourself fittingly, and age will come not to you, but to another whom the God has prepared for it?"

"Bloody liars in bedsheets," she muttered, rising. Most of the household was quiet; there would be a duty staff on call over in the public section, and the guards, of course.

There was a light under the door of Marya's office; she had proven very competent, handling household accounts, now that Gwen was too old to need or want a nursemaid in attendance. *Probably screening those books Gwen got her*, Yolande decided. The serf was a fanatic reader, now that she was cleared for it. Also a churchgoer, which had surprised her owner considerably. Suitably modified, religion was all very well for the common ruck, but Yolande had not expected the American to be superstitious. *Ah, well, anything that helps*, she decided.

"Marya," she said, touching a finger to the door.

The serf looked around, raising her fingers from the keyboard. Symbols crawled across the screen; probably some game or other. Marya was not a bad chess player, and even better at *go*.

"Yo' go to that church, ovah on Chain and Barracoon, don't yo'?"

"Yes, Mistis." She bowed slightly. "I had been planning to attend the wedding there, your secretary Hans's son. With permission."

"Just what I was goin' to mention. The girls and I are goin' walkabout tomorrow. Gwen'll want yo' along, but that'll be in the afternoon. We'll pick yo' and Jolene up towards the end of the reception, when I drop in. Suit?"

"Thank you, Mistis." She inclined her hair until the black flow of it covered her eyes.

"Good to see her again," Yolande continued. "Got a warm heart, that girl. Glad I let yo' help raise her." The Draka nodded to the screen. "Certainly hasn't fo'gotten her Tantie-ma . . ." Curiosity moved. "Tell me, Marya. How do *yo'* feel about her?"

A minute's silence. Yolande saw the other's hands tighten on the edge of the desk. She suspected that lack of privacy was one of the things the American had found most difficult to adjust to. Citizens had little enough, in the Domination, and serfs less. "I love her, Mistis," the serf said, her voice softer than usual. "It's . . . She's the only child I'll ever have, after all."

True but not the whole truth, Yolande thought, regarding her quizzically. Marya had always refused to bear children of her own . . . *And I think that Gwen's the only thing in the Domination for which you have any affection at all. Understandable, of course.*

*   *   *

"One more minute, and then we leave," Yolande said to her daughter.

The family party had tactfully arrived just after the party moved from the chapel to the reception hall. Both were in the ground floor of a serf tenement. It was fairly well appointed; these people were elite serfs: Auxiliaries owned by the War Directorate, middle-level administrators, comp operators, cartographers, technicians, similar people from the Combines operating here. The Domination had learned long ago that a certain amount of privacy and comfort was essential for such, and these were family apartments with their own kitchens and even bathrooms. The lower floors held the communal facilities: game-rooms, viewers, the church, an elementary schoolroom. All attractively decorated in an amateurish fashion, but some of the handmade items were skillfully done.

From the brief glimpse, Yolande decided that the wedding entertainment was charming as well, in a homemade and rustic fashion, decorations and refreshments both. Very sedate, but then this type of serf tended to be quiet-living. The ruck of compound-dwellers were brutishly unrestrained, having nothing to lose; when the ferocious discipline of their existence was relaxed, little interested them but food, sex, alcohol, and *kif*. Allowing for elegance, education, and greater resources, there were similarities in the Citizen outlook on life, and their personal servants followed suit. These middle strata were strange to both, and she found them a little baffling. *No wonder the headhunters watch them closest of all*, she thought. There had been a green-coated Orpo, a member of the Order Police, in attendance until she glared him out.

Not much he could do when the Commandant-Governor showed up, she thought ironically. *Of course, there are probably informers and listening devices here*. Which was as it should be, of course. The priest would have been carefully selected and trained, as well; the Catholics had agreed to that, in order to be allowed to function in the Domination at all.

"Why do we have to leave right away, ma? It's sort of fun," Gwen said.

"This is their celebration, honeybunch," Yolande said quietly; they were standing by the door, at the head of the table. "I came here because Hans is a treasure. It gives him status, yo' see? More and they'd get uncomfortable. Remember, I don't own these, the State does."

She tasted her wine, which was surprisingly drinkable for the local product, and looked down the trestles. Hans was at a little distance; he glanced her way and smiled, bowing, and his plump wife flushed and beamed as Yolande raised her glass in reply. His son was gangling and blond, the new daughter-in-law petite and dark, Hindu by her looks; some sort of landing-field maintenance tech. The guests milled about tables set for a banquet, doubtless a potluck by the households of the guests; the presents were at the other end of the streamer-hung room. Yolande had contributed a diskplayer and a crate of wine, enough to please without embarrassing.

The speech had been the usual thing. Brief, praising Hans and his wife as skilled and valued servants of the Race, hoping the newlyweds would lead productive lives of service, and their children after them. Kissing the bride and groom had been no hardship, they were both quite pretty and radiantly happy . . . and now it was time. She looked around for Marya; the serf was over in a corner, talking to the priest. They both sank to their knees and linked hands, heads bent together; Yolande frowned at a vague memory. *Isn't that supposed to be some sort of private rite?* she thought. *Confession, or confusion or communion or something? Oh, well.* A glance at her watch, and Marya stood.

Hans came over. "Thank you again, Merarch," he said, and gave her the full bow, hands over eyes. There was a ripple as the room followed suit.

"No problem, Hans," she said, holding up a hand. "I know the difference between goin' through the motions and really tryin'." Which had helped her considerably, and this was an important career stop. "If there's ever any trouble, feel free to ask fo' help."

"Pretty weddin'," Jolene said, with a sigh.

Yolande yawned and stretched, wiggling her shoulders against the pleasant jasmine-scented smoothness of the sheets and looking up through the ceiling of her bedroom at the silver-bright circle of mirror in the sky. It kept the night moodily half-lit, but not enough to dim the stars away from its circle. *Like a moon,* she thought. One perfect and un-

stained, the first fresh idea of a moon dropped pure and
untouched from the mind of a god. *We did that*. That had
been the first; the second was down south, put up just last
year, warming the frozen water and carbon dioxide of the
south pole. It had already made a difference to the atmosphere, although you needed instruments to detect it. They
were the biggest constructs yet made by humans, although
gossamer-thin.

"Yo' saw mo' of it," she said. "Everythin' go nice?"

"Beautiful singing," Jolene said from the foot of the bed.
"They've got a really nice choir. Good fiddler, too, had fun
dancin' befo' yo' arrived."

"Sorry to drag yo' away fo' nothin'," Yolande replied. Nikki
had charmed Decurion Kang into taking him out with the
ghouloons on a carefully edited training patrol for the rest of
the day, and his mother into allowing it. Kang had confessed
that he was irresistibly reminded of a younger brother, back
on Earth . . .

"Oh, that was the fun part," Jolene said, and laughed. "I
don't know these here folks well enough to fit in at a feast.
Incidentally, think that nice Mastah Kang had an eye on me."

Yolande turned a critical eye on the serf. "Yo' lost weight
on the trip out," she said. "It suits."

Jolene touched her stomach. "Does, doesn't it. Only good
thing about not bein' able to eat." She had never been able to
handle zero-G.

"Shall I lend yo' to him, then?" *That* was not something a
junior officer would feel free to ask of a Merarch, frontier
informality or no.

"Mmmm. Maybe in a while, Mistis." She sighed again,
looking up through the bubble ceiling herself.

"Pretty."

"Jolene." She looked around. "Why did yo' never marry,
yo' self?"

"Oh . . . wanted to travel around, Mistis. See space, espe-
cial, even if it makes me sick." Not easy; plenty of serfs were
assigned to space, but that was with the military or the
Combines. Jolene had ample intelligence, but had been far
too expensive for such buyers. "That's difficult. Iff'n I got tied
down too hard, yo'd have moved me out of personal service.
I've got my Marybeth, anyhows." A year younger than Nikki;
Yolande suspected Teller was the father, but it wasn't particularly important. "Mastah Nikki's out like a light. Not surprisin',

after tearin' about like he does . . . That boy, he must have fusion power somewheres! Settled Marybeth in down by my quarters, too." A frown. "Yo' know, I was thinkin' . . . Folk there at the church, they say Marya goes regular. Didn't know her to be that religious, back to home, Mistis."

"People change," Yolande said, yawning again.

She was tired, but it was the pleasant fatigue of keeping up with two high-energy adolescents, not the nagging brain-tiredness of days spent fighting administrative problems. With a wry smile, she thought of enemy accounts she had read that depicted the Domination as a smooth well-oiled machine moving in perfect coordination. *If they only knew. Thank the Yankees for inventing the computer, otherwise the clerks would have locked us in* rigor mortis, *like a fossilized dinosaur.* She put work out of her mind; barring emergencies, that could wait until Monday. It was a relief to have only household matters to concern her.

"It's been, what, better than a year since yo' saw Marya. She's gotten a little moodier here, s'much as I've had time to notice. Good to have an outside interest." The Draka linked the fingers of both hands around a knee. "What I was thinkin' of, was those two pretties enjoyin' they weddin' night."

Jolene tossed back hair silvered by the mirrorlight; her brass-colored eyes were startling against the shadowed ebony of her skin. "Well, that we two can do somethin' about, eh, Mistis?"

SPIN HABITAT SEVEN
CENTRAL BELT
BETWEEN THE ORBITS OF MARS AND JUPITER
DECEMBER 28, 1991

"Aw, dad!"

Frederick Lefarge looked over at his wife. She was mixing them martinis, at the cabinet on the other side of the living room. Dinner was a pleasant memory and a lingering smell of guinea-chile and avocado salad—*God, what did I do to deserve a good cook, on top of looks and brains?*—and he wanted that drink, and his feet up, and more quiet than two teenaged daughters promised. On the other hand . . .

He glanced sternly at Janet and Iris. "Homework done?" he said. *Gods, they're getting to be young women,* he thought.

Haltertops, yet. And those fashionable hip-huggers . . . the damned things looked as if they had been *sprayed* on.

"Yeah," Janet said. Well, her marks had been excellent, particularly the math. It looked as if there *was* going to be at least one spacer in the family, if this kept up. Iris nodded. *Her* current fancy was composing. Well, at least she was still working at that, not like the other fads.

"It's a nice group," Cindy said. She finished shaking the cocktail pitcher, broke it open deftly and filled the chilled martini glasses. "From school, and a bunch over from Habitat Three. You know, the Martins and the Merkowitz kids?"

Lefarge pushed his chair back. "All right," he said, glancing at the viewer; it was set on landscape, with a time-readout down near the lower righthand corner. "But be back by 0100, latest, or I'll shut the airlock on you for a week, understand?"

"Thanks, dad!" Janet gave him a quick hug.

"We'll be back on time, daddy." Iris kissed his cheek. *"And they're playing one of my dance tunes,"* she whispered into his ear, giggling.

He sighed as he watched them fling themselves down the hall with an effortless feet-off-the-ground twist; they adjusted to the varying gravity of the habitat's shell-decks the way he and Marya had to the streets of New York.

"Next thing you know, I'll be beating off boyfriends with a club," he grumbled, accepting the drink. "Ah, nice and dry."

Cindy put hers on the table and went behind the chair. Her fingers probed at his neck. "Rock. Don't worry, they're sensible girls, and we've got a nice family town here." He closed his eyes and rolled his head slightly as she kneaded the taut musles. "At least we don't have to worry about juviegroups and trashing or having them go into orbit over Ironbelly Bootstomper bands," she continued.

Lefarge shuddered. "No, thank God. Sometimes I think the spirit that made America great hasn't died—just emigrated."

Cindy laughed and leaned over him; he felt a sudden sharp pain at the base of his cropped hair.

"Hey, cut that out!"

She held an almost-invisible something close to his eye on the tip of one finger: a gray hair.

"You don't have enough of these to be an old fogey yet, honey," she said, and kissed him upside-down. Her face sobered. "Something's really bothering you, isn't it?"

He reached up to run his hand through her hair, streaked with silver against the mahogany color, shining and resilient. "You're too old to be so indecently beautiful," he murmured. Then: "I have to take a trip back dirtside," he said.

"Oh. That chair big enough for two?"

She picked up her drink and settled in against him, curving into the arm he laid about her shoulders. The silk of her blouse and skirt rustled, and he smelled a pleasant clean odor of shampoo and perfume and Cindy. "Uncle Nate?"

"He's sharp as ever, but not getting any younger," Lefarge said grudgingly. "You know how it is, anyone in his position so long makes enemies." The executive positions two or three steps down from the top in an agency like the OSS were coveted prizes. Not high enough to be political appointments, but they set policy. "Those who want his job, if nothing else; the problem is they're all disasters waiting to happen."

He paused to take another sip of the martini. "I have to blather to a couple of select committees. On top of that, Nate's afraid the new people in charge over in Archona are foxy enough to let up the pressure. That von Shrakenberg's a cunning devil; he knows how quickly some of us will go to sleep if they're not prodded." A frown. "I don't like it, when the Snakes get quiet. They're planning something. Maybe not now, maybe in a decade; something big."

Cindy shivered against him, and he held her closer. "No more raids, at least," she said. "Oh God, honey, I was so frightened."

And went straight from your office to your emergency station and had the rest of them singsonging and playing bridge, he thought with a rush of warmth. *Jesus H. Christ, I'm a lucky man.* Grimly: *And we took out a major warship, too. They may be pulling back their fingers because we singed them.*

"There's something else, isn't there?" she went on.

"Witch." He sighed. "In the latest courier package from Uncle Nate." The Project was on the AI-3 distribution list; this was as secure an OSS station as anywhere in the Alliance, if only because so little went out. "They're in contact with Marya again."

"Bad?" Cindy said softly.

"No worse than before. That Ingolfsson creature's spawn . . ." He turned his head aside for a moment, then continued. "Anyway, Marya's been taken to their main Martian settlement. Working in household accounts, but even better, she's made some social contacts with the HQ office workers . . . just rumor, gossip, but priceless stuff. Contact's a priest; Christ, it's dangerous, though!" More softly: "And I miss her, sweet, I really do."

"Mmmmh. So do I. She was always like a big sister to me . . ."

The diskplayer came on, with a quiet Baroque piece that Cindy must have selected beforehand. The lights dimmed, turning the homey familiarity of the living room into romantic gloom, and a new scene played on the viewer. He recognized that beach, with the full moon over the Pacific and the swaying palms. Surf hissed gently . . .

"Why, Mrs. Lefarge," he said, looking down at her face. She grinned. "If I didn't know better, I'd say that a respectable matron was trying to seduce her husband again."

She wiggled into his lap. "Why, Mr. Lefarge," she whispered, twining her arms around his neck. "Why do you think I was so eager to get the girls out of the house?" She nibbled at his ear. "And if *you* are too young to be a fogey, *I'm* too young to be a matron. So there."

CHAPTER SEVENTEEN

The Protracted Conflict has a brutal simplicity; the Final War will start the moment either side feels it can attack without risking unacceptable losses. The Draka definition of "acceptable cost" is much higher than the Alliance's. These two facts have driven most human endeavor since 1945, aeronautics included. Average speeds of 200 mph in 1930 increased to about 400 mph by the beginning of the Eurasian War. By 1942 prop-engine fighters had reached their maximum of around 480 mph, but the first swept-wing turbojets were already in service, and by 1946 maximum speeds of 620 mph were common. German rocket-boosted experimental aircraft had reached nearly twice the speed of sound, providing invaluable aerodynamic information to both the Domination and the Alliance. They had also launched research into high-altitude rockets, and rocket-boosted ramjet unmanned vehicles.

After the Eurasian War ended in a blaze of nuclear fire, the contending powers were left with weapons of unprecedented lethality, and inadequate delivery systems. For strategic purposes, what was needed was a means of striking deep into the continental heartlands of the enemy with little or no chance of interception; and the primitive fission and fusion bombs of the 1945–1955 era were massive and clumsy to boot. Jet bombers were useful for tactical purposes, but were too limited in range and easy to intercept to be really satisfactory for delivering the new "sunbombs." Rockets had abundant speed, but inadequate payload. The solution both sides developed was the ramjet, which was light, theoretically simple, and had excellent performance in the Mach 2 to Mach 7 envelopes. Desperate need drove both sides to solve the incredibly complex materials and engineering problems; by the early 1950s, unmanned ramjet missiles following high-suborbital trajectories at speeds of up to 4,000 mph were in production on both sides.

These use-once missiles pressed the materials technology of the day to its limits; the Alliance had a lead in precision-formed refractory alloys, and used it to produce the first reusable, manned ramjet craft. The Draka "leapfrogged" with fiber-matrix composites and high-strength ceramics; the Alliance in turn used its superior computers to successfully model supersonic airflows and achieve scramjets (supersonic-combustion ramjets) in the late 1950s. Combined with liquid hydrogen fuel/ coolant and pure-rocket boost, this gave the Alliance the ultimate "high ground" of orbital capacity. As might be expected, espionage and frantic catch-up prevented either side from gaining the last, crucial edge needed for assured survival. Once out of Earth's gravity well, it was clear that the answer to the high-atmospheric missile was orbital weapons and sensors; these in turn suggested massive counter-measures. Space-based manufacturing and energy were obviously necessary, even after laser-launch and mass drivers became available in the 1960s; this made Luna an indispensable source of raw materials. Once orbital and lunar stations were in place, expeditions to deep space became relatively easy, and neither side could allow the other to monopolize either the material treasures or the knowledge to be found there. Nuclear-pulse engines opened translunar space, and beyond the orbit of the moon the Protracted Struggle could and did flicker into active clashes.

Perhaps as revolutionary were the *spinoffs* of this rivalry . . .

History in a Technological Age
by Andrew Elliot Armstrang, Ph.D.
Department of History
San Diego University Press, 1991

We're never going to win this race unless we trip
the fuckers somehow; all this effort isn't doing
anything more than bailing out a sieve. We've
got to stop playing to their strengths.

Representative Louise Gayner
Minutes of the Long-Range Strategic
Planning Board
Senator Eric von Shrakenberg, presiding
Archona, Archona Province
April 16, 1962

DRAKA FORCES BASE ARESOPOLIS
MARE SERENITATIS, LUNA
MARCH 25, 1998
2000HOURS

Yolande turned her head to scan the other side of the Wasp
class stingfighter. *This is what it's like to be a ghost*, she
thought. She ran her hand through the solid-seeming bulk of
a crashcouch, looked down to see her shins disappear into the
deck. A Wasp had room for exactly two crew, clamped into
their couches for most of the trip. *Or what it's like to be a
time traveler*. The events she was experiencing were nearly a
thousand hours in the past. She watched the movements of
the pilot's gloved fingers on the rests.

"Coming up on pod," the pilot said. "Twelve kay clicks and
closing. Status." The wall ahead mapped trajectories and ran
digital displays.

"Locked," her Weapons Officer said, his voice tight but
steady.

So young, Yolande thought. *Gwen will be that old in a few
years. So young.*

"Unauthorized craft, identify yourself." That from a resona-
tor film somewhere in the cabin. Flat, grating Yankee accent
with the mechanical overlay of a simple AI-interactive system. "You are on an intercept trajectory to within prohibited
distance. Identify yourself or alter course."

"Visual," the pilot said.

"Acquisition," the Weapons Officer replied, and called it up on the screen.

A rough cylinder of slag-surfaced metal, surface pocked with bubbles and lumps from the vacuum-condensation refining process. A pod at one end with sensors and the guidance system, and rings of low-velocity hydrazine steering jets, a minimal course-correction system to send a hundred thousand tonnes of whatever from the asteroid belt to the Alliance smelters and factories, here on the Moon and points inward. These days, a good deal of it might end up on Earth, headed for splashdown sites in the Sea of Cortés or the Cook Strait or the Inland Sea.

"Composition," the pilot was saying.

There was a second's pause and the Wasp's computer replied: "Iron, fifty percent, nickel twenty-one percent, chromium group, sixteen percent, tungsten ten percent, fissionables three percent, volatiles and trace elements."

Valuable, Yolande thought. The Yankees were stronger in the asteroid belt; their initial lead in deepspace pulsedrives had given them an opening they had never relinquished. Much cheaper to drop heavy elements down into the solar gravity well than boost them out of Earth's pull and atmosphere, even now that freight costs were coming down so low. The Alliance would trade metals for the water and chemicals the Draka took from the Jovian and Saturnian moons, of course, but it was cheaper to hijack where you could. Better strategy, too, since it hampered their operations and forced them to divert resources to guarding their slingshot modules and scavenging the asteroids for scarce volatiles . . . She had had a hand in formulating that policy.

At least it's been better strategy until now. A rectangle appeared in the "air" in front of her, an exterior simulation of the two spacecraft. The Wasp drifted, a blunt pyramid tapering from the shockplate at the rear to the crew compartment at the apex. Slim tubes rose from each corner of the plate, linked to the pyramid with a tracing of spars; asymmetric spikes flared out to guide the parasite-bombs riding in station around the gunboat. The simulation limned the outlines, since like any warcraft this was armored in an absorptive synthetic that mimicked the background spectra.

"Closing," the pilot said. The outside view showed a needle-bright flicker behind the gunboat, deuterium-tritium pellets squeezed into explosion by the lasers. Yolande started, almost surprised not to feel the acceleration that pushed the crew back into their cradles. "One-ninah kay clicks, matchin'."

"Unidentified craft, this is your last warning," the robot voice droned.

"Eddie, shut that fuckah up, will yo'?" the pilot said, exasperated. The man grunted, touched a control surface.

The control chamber vanished, leaving a blackness lit only by the face of the investigating officer in the central portion. "That's it, Strategos," he said, shrugging. "End datalink. The fighter went pure-ballistic from then until we grappled what was left." Yolande gestured, and the black turned gray, then faded into her office. She motioned again.

"All right," she said, as the rectangle expanded to occupy a square meter above the surface of her desk. "Give me the record of the recov'ry action."

"Well, the Yanks scrambled once they'uns realized what was happenin'," the Intelligence Section merarch said. The three-dimensional image lifted a cigarette to its lips. "Two Jefferson-class patrollers, with six and four gunboats respectively, in position to do somethin'. Thirty personnel, all told."

Yolande nodded: Yankee gunboats were single-crew, and the Jeffersons had ten apiece. The Alliance military relied more on cybernetics than the Draka did. "That was all they had within range."

Space was *large*, and even with constant-boost pulsedrive units it took a *long* time to get from anywhere to anywhere, compared with on-planet applications. There were times when she thought it was more like the situation back in her great-grandfather's time, when it could still take weeks to cross an ocean, months to traverse a continent. Then trouble blew up, and the soldier on the spot was left with their ass hanging in the breeze and no way to call for mama.

"Luckily, we'n's had three Iron Limper corvettes on, ah, patrol." *Corsair duty*, her mind added sardonically, using the crew slang. "This's what happened."

The view shifted to points and data-columns, a schematic of the corvettes and their twelve—*no, eleven*—gunboat outriders, and the machinery's best guess on the Yankees. The usual thing for space combat, a long gingerly waiting before a brief flurry of action. A pulsedrive was sort of hard to hide anywhere in the solar system unless you had something the size of a planet to shelter it, but that told you very little except the past position and a fan of possible vectors. Space-

ships were another matter; between stealthing and datamimic
decoys, long-range detection had always run a little behind
the countermeasures.

"Well, both parties knew they'd have to intersect somewhere along the trajectory of the cargo pod and the stingray."
A section of the curve that looped in from beyond the orbit of
Mars turned red, the area where either set of warships could
match velocities. "The Yankees went into constant-boost,
figurin' to overrun us on the pass, then go back fo' it. We
went silent, coastin'; had the advantage, comin' out-system
from sunward."

"Ah." She could guess what came next. You could think of
a pulsedrive as a series of micro-fusion bombs and field-
shielding and reaction mass heated to plasma—or as a sword
of radiation and high-energy particles tens of kilometers long.

That was the Staff way of seeing it. Her imagination flashed
other images on the inner screen of her consciousness. The
matte-black shapes of the Limpers falling outward. A shallow
disk perched on a witch's maze of tubing like some mad oil
refinery, all atop the great convex soup-plate of the pusher.
The dozen crewfolk locked into their cocoons of armor and
sensors, decision-making units in a dance of photonics. Units
that sweated with fears driven down below consciousness; the
ripping impact of crystal tesseract-mines scattering their high-
vee shrapnel through hulls and bodies, blood boiling into
vacuum. The pulse of a near-miss and secondary gamma
sleeting invisibly through the body, wrecking the infinitely
complex balances of the cells. Tumbling in a wrecked ship,
puking and delirious and dying slowly of thirst . . .

Fears carried down from the ground-ape; hindbrain reflexes that twitched muscles in desperate need to flee or
fight, pumped juices into the blood, roiling minds that must
stay as calm as the machines that were master and slave both.
Yolande swallowed past dryness, and used the inward disci-
plines taught by those who had trained her for war. The
slamming impact of deceleration; railguns, lightguns, mine-
showers, missile and counter-missile, the parasite-bombs driving their one-megaton X-ray beams like the icepicks of gods.
The drives punching irresistibly through fields and shield-
ings; perhaps a single second for the stricken to know their
fate as plasma boiled through the corridors.

Silence. Long slow zero-g fading past, waiting for the
sensors to tell you if you were already dead . . .

She shook her head. "*Hugin* totalled." Sheer bad luck, a parasite-bomb impact just as her drive was cycling out a new pellet. Twelve dead. "*Lothbrok* mostly made it." If the biotechs could repair tissues so riddled. "*Ragnar*, no losses."

"A successful engagement," the Intelligence Officer said. "But . . ."

"*But* we still don't know what the *shit* happened with that-there original intercept."

"Strategos . . ." The merarch hesitated, then continued. "Strategos, admitted all we've got is what downloaded to optical storage befo' they bought it . . . but *somethin'* catastrophic *did* happen. Iff'n I didn't know better, I'd say pointblank parasite bomb hit, with a chain-fire in the feed tubes fo' the drive. But there weren't no parasite bombs travelin' with that cargo pod."

"Incorrect, Merarch. There were five."

For a moment the man looked blank, then his eyes widened slightly in shock. There gaze met in silent agreement: *With the fighter, its own weapons.* "This is speculation, an' not to go on record. Understood?"

He nodded. They were silent for a moment; his voice was slow and musing when he continued: " 'Bout the prisoners . . . We kept them in filterable-virus isolation an' did a complete scan, as per usual."

Security had gotten even more paranoid of late, now that Alliance nanosabotage capacities were approaching the size level of Draka gene-engineering skills. Not to mention the ever-present nightmare of dataplague contamination; the Alliance's superiority in compinstruction was indisputable. The Domination took what precautions it could—offline back-up systems for all essential functions, manual overrides, physical separation—but there were limits to what could be done in an environment as dependent on computer technology as space.

"Well, somethin' sort of odd came up. *Very* damn odd. The biotechs *found* somethin' on six of the seven livin' prisoners, some sort of latent . . . weeell, virus or *somethin'* back in the central nervous an' limbic systems. Very tricky, very, they only found it on 'count the discrepancy in the neural DNA analysis was the same on each. Wouldn't have found it say, two years ago; it would have come out as the usual noisegarbage." The cellular codes of any mammal have far more information capacity than they need.

"So we blipped the info to Biocontrol Central." Yolande waited while the man moistened his lips. "Order came back, freeze in place. Then about two hours latah, a priority-one command to wait fo' a courier. One came direct, with orders to turn them ovah to the headhunters. That an' wipe the data an' fo'get we'd ever seen it."

"Castle Tarleton?"

"No; from the Palace. From the Archon's office, an' under his personal code." They exchanged another glance; he had placed his life in her hands with those words. A calculated risk; that Eric von Shrakenberg was her uncle was widely known. That she met regularly with him on more than family matters was not.

"Well." For the first time in the interview, Yolande smiled, a slow cold turning of the lips. "Well, we can't argue with *that*." Normally there would have been a bureaucratic bunfight; Aresopolis was War Directorate territory, after all. "Not that I don't love to trip our esteemed colleagues up as much as anyone, but in *this* case . . ."

She grinned at the thought of the slow disassembling the Security Directorate would use on the prisoners, and the other officer turned his eyes aside slightly. Yolande Ingolfsson's feelings concerning the enemy in general and Americans in particular were well-known, but still a little disconcerting to meet in practice.

The grin faded, to be replaced with something resembling a human expression. "And, Thomas . . ." the first name was a signal, and he leaned forward, an unconcious expression of attention ". . . I have an odd feelin' about this. That data had better *really* disappear. Or I think *we* might."

"What data?" he said.

She nodded. "Ovah. Service to the State."

"Glory to the Race," he replied formally, and the rectangle went blank.

"Fade," she said, and the lights dimmed. "Review, casualties."

Her mouth thinned; this was a disagreeable chore. Theoretically, the unit commander . . . No, she had ordered the action. The general policy was set higher up, but she made the operational decisions. It was her responsibility. A figure in the form-fitting vacuum skinsuit blinked into existence before her, turning toward the pickup and laughing, bubble-helmet in one hand. A cat hanging in mid-air beside it, obviously unused to low-G and falling in spraddle-legged panic. The figure was young, with fair hair cropped close. Data unreeled below: Julian Torbogen, born . . . Very young, only a year older than her oldest. A face with the chiseled, sculpted look the Eugenics Board was moving the Race toward, but an individual for all that. The dossier listed it all: pets, hobbies, grade-evaluations, favorite foods, friends, love-affairs, hopes (. . . *habitat design is so complete an art!* . . .), hates.

Yolande called up the medical image and placed it beside the laughing youth. Explosive decompression is not a pleasant way to die, especially combined with a wash of radiant heat that melts equipment into flesh across half the body. Two-thirds of the face was still there, enough for the final expression to survive.

A long moment, and then she closed her eyes and began to dictate. "Dear Citizens. As your son's commanding officer, I . . ."

It took an hour to complete the messages; they were brief, but it was crucial to give each one the individual attention it was due. These were Citizens, the hope of the Race. *Cells must die for the whole to live. But we must mourn them, because we are cells who* know *what we are. That is our immortality.*

She shook off the mood and rose, calling the lights back to normal. *Coming home,* she thought wryly. Half her existence these days seemed to be spent in illusion and shadows, riding the silica threads and photon pulses, until she could hardly tell waking from sleeping.

"Call Tina," she said to the machines that always listened. "Brandied coffee, please." Absurd to use a form of courtesy with a computer, but it was another connection to real life.

This outer room of her sanctum—was this home? *As much as anyplace, the last five years.* A long box-rectangle, her desk at one end. Lunar-basalt tiles, covered by fur rugs from animals created by biotech. Leather-spined books, and shelves of real wood, expensive on Luna, but Loki knew there were *some* compensations for this job. The outer wall was set to a soft neutral gray for concentration's sake; it was a single blank sheet five meters by ten, a thinfilm sandwich holding several hundred thousand thermovalves per square centimeter. It could be set to display anything at all, well enough to fool even an expert's eye until you touched, but she was suddenly weary of vicarious experience. And of the fresh clean recycled air.

"Transparent and open," she said. It blinked clear and slid up with a minor *shhhh* as she walked out onto the balcony.

That was near the top of the ring wall, a lacy construction of twisted vitryl, filaments of monocrystal titanium-chromium-vanadium alloy and glass braided together. Those were words; the reality was smooth curves of jade-green ice, thin as gossamer, stronger than steel. The sky above was of the same material, a shallow ribbed dome across the hundred-kilometer bowl of the crater. A thousand meters over her head one of its great anchor cables sprang out, soaring up and away until it dwindled into a thread and disappeared into the distance; the sky was set to a long twilight now, and she could just make out the bluewhite disk of Earth. She walked to the waist-high balustrade, looked out and down.

The crater was in natural terrace-steps to either side and sheer cliff below, nothing but air and haze three kilometers to the tumbled jungle-shaggy hills at the base. To her right a river sprang out of the rock, fell with unearthly slowness in a long bright-blue arc until it misted away into rain; a lake gathered underneath, and the river flowed like silver off through the mottled greens of the landscape below. Clouds drifted in layers, silver and dappled with earthlight; they cast shadows over fields, meadows, forest, roads. There was no horizon, only a vast arch that melted green into blue. Lights were appearing here and there; far and far, she could just make out the high spike of the mountain at the crater's center, bright-lit, with the thin illuminated streak of the elevator-tower rising to the landing platform on the airless side of the dome.

"Mistis."

A presence at her elbow; she took the cup without glancing around, murmured abstracted thanks, propped one haunch on the balustrade, sipped. Kenia Mountain Best, diluted with a quarter of hot cream and a tenth of Thieuniskraal. Warmth and richness flowed over her tongue, with a hint of bite at the back of her mouth and down her throat. It was very quiet, the thunder of the falling water far enough away to be a muted background. The soft wind that flickered ends of her gray-blond hair about her face was louder; she ignored their tickling caress. All about the balcony, rock that had lain lifeless since the forming of the Earth was covered in rustling vines that bore sheets of pale-pink blossoms; they smelled of mint and lavender.

As they had been designed to do. So had the multicolored birds that flitted through the flowers been designed for the intricate flutelike song they trilled; farther out a yellow-feathered hawk banked on four-meter wings and called, a long mournful wailing. Yolande sipped again, feeling a sensation that was half contentment, half the repletion that followed the end of a poem. This *was* a composition, and she one of its manifold creators; part of what she had dreamed, as a child looking up at the new lights in the sky over Claestum. The Glory of the Race was more than power; that was just the beginning. It was accomplishment; it was to *do*.

She closed her eyes, squeezing them against a flash of old remembered pain. *Myfwany, darlin', if only you could be here to see it with me,* she thought. Then somewhere far back in her mind a ghost met her gaze with sardonic green: *Freya, what a sentimentalist yo' are, Yolande-sweet, to let me haunt yo' so. One thing I never aspired to be was the drop of gall in yo' cup; yo' alive, so live, girl.*

"Such good advice, and as always easier to give than to follow," she murmured to herself.

"Mistis?"

"Nothin', Tina," Yolande said to the serf who squatted at her feet and peered through the finger-thick rods of the balustrade.

The wench rose. Tina had a glass of milk in one hand, and a white mustache of it on her upper lip that she licked away with unselfconscious relish; then drank more, taking the slow care needful in one-sixth gravity. Eighteen and softly pretty in a doe-eyed Italian way, big-hipped, the four-month belly just starting to show. Yolande smiled and laid a hand on it; the serf smiled shyly back and put her hand over the Draka's in turn. For a moment Yolande wondered what it must feel like, to bear a living child beneath the heart. She was too old herself, of course, even if there had ever been time, and bearing your own eggs was eccentric to the point of suspiciousness now, anyway. Strange to think that she herself was of the last generation of the Race born of their mother's wombs.

She rubbed her serf's stomach affectionately. "Time to get yo' home to Claestum, Tina," she said.

The later stages of pregnancy did not do well below .3 G; in theory, regular centrifuge was enough to compensate, but she did not intend to take any chances at all. Strictly speaking, there was no need to get involved in the process to this extent; a lot of people just sent the fertilized ova in to the Clinic and picked up the baby nine months later. Yolande had always found that too impersonal; she insisted on being present at the implantation and the birthing, and used only family servants as brooders, volunteers from the plantation. It seemed more . . . more *fitting*, somehow. Birth was no less a miracle because the Race had mastered its secrets, after all. And this was the most important of all, truly hers and Myfwany's, now that the ova-merging technique was perfected.

"Yes, time to get home, Mistis," Tina said with a sigh, leaning into the caress and looking out over the crater. "I will miss this. It so pretty."

And such a vanity, Yolande thought. Oh, not *so* difficult, not when you could use fusion bombs and bomb-pumped lasers for excavation; not when energy poured down in vacuum, to be stored as pressurized water or liquid metal in superconducting rings . . . Anything local and not too complex was cheap, given autofabricators, and the whole construct was basically titanium and glass. Oxygen and silica and light metals were abundant on the moon; launch-lasers and magnetic catapults at Gibraltar and Kilimanjaro and in the Tien Shan were part of the War effort, and might as well be kept to capacity with cargo loads; an abundance of water and volatiles was coming in from the outer system. Also, a closed ecosystem was a tricky thing; the bigger you made it the easier it was to manage.

Also a chance to put the Drakon's eye up here on the Moon, looking down, she thought. *And wouldn't the Yankees love to stick a thumb in it.*

Which was why the bulk of Aresopolis was burrowed kilometers deep into the lunar crust, factories and dormitories, refineries and chemosynthesis plants, the fardown caverns with their stores of liquid hydrogen, oxygen, methane, ammonia, metals, a Fafnir's horde gathered from as far out as Saturn. The orbital battlestations clustering about Earth were largely armed and built from here; so were the outposts at the L-5 points, the far-flung bases, Mercury, the Venus study-project, Mars, a scattering of outposts in the Alliance-dominated asteroids. Half the two million souls the Domination had sent into space lived here, in this strange city of warriors and warriors' servants; a third of them free Citizens, the highest ratio of any city in the Domination.

All of them beneath her command—and able, in their leisure, to come out here to walk naked under living green, swim in water that bore silverspeckled trout, to fly with muscle-powered wings as no humans before them had ever done. She flicked the last droplets from the cup out into the void, watching the long dreamy slowness of the fall.

"They say the neoredwoods we've planted down there will grow a thousand meters tall in another fifty years," Yolande said, softly. "I'll bring the children here, and we'll rent wings and fly off the highest branches like eagles." She should still be hale, then, with modern biotech.

"Will you bring me to watch?" Tina asked, and snuggled another question.

"Yes," Yolande said. "That's a promise. And no, get yo' off to a nice, quiet bed, wench; mind yo' health."

The serf left with the long glide-bounce of an experienced Aresopolite. Yolande lingered for a moment, yawning and rolling the still-warm porcelain of the cup between her palms. The sky had gone true-dark, and the hard bright stars were out; the clouds below reflected blue-silver earthlight back into her eyes. Moving stars, many of them, and she could see another rising swiftly to join them from beyond the crater rim, a laser-boost capsule from one of the emplacements that studded the mountains around the city. That was one of their functions; another might be to rip targets as far away as Earth, one day.

Suddenly she was on her feet, shaken with a wild anger. The flung cup arched out into emptiness with maddening slowness; there was nothing on the planets or between that could express the wash of loathing she felt. *They* were there, too, the Yankees, the destroyers of all happiness, the oaf-lump impediment that stood always in the Race's path. This single city, an ornament above a fortress, when the Moon might be laced with them like living jewels. Scorched meat made of lordly golden boys who should be here playing tag with eagles, or going out to make green paradise of frozen Mars and burning Venus. Always intriguing, threatening with their sly greasy-souled merchant cunning, menacing the future of her blood. Gwen, Nikki, Holden, Johanna still un-

born, whose years ought to stretch out before them like
diamonds in the sun . . .

"I *will* be back with them, in yo' despite," she said in tones
quiet and even and measured. "Everythin' yo' are, we'll
bring to nothin'; we'll grind yo' bones to make our bread, and
yo' children will serve mine until the end of days."

With an effort she turned back into the office. *A consum-
mation devoutly to be wished,* she thought. *To which end,
I'm going to get Uncle Eric to tell me precisely what's been
goin' on here.*

"Message:" she said to the sensors. "Strategos Alman Witter,
Vice-Commandant; Allie, I'm droppin' down to HQ fo' the
week. Yo' step in as per, stay on top of the patrol incident an'
keep me posted soonest. Message: Transport, Aresopolis to
Archona"—She looked at her desk: 2140—"departin' 1100 to
1200 tomorrow. Message: private, code follows—"

"*One-hudred-forty*-nine, *one-hundred*-fifty," Marya Lefarge
gasped as she finished the series of situps, and sank back on
the exercise table, panting.

No more. That finished her daily three-hour program, but
there was a druglike pleasure to exhaustion as hard to fight as
sloth. The 1-G exercise chamber was crowded and close, a
slight smell of sweat among the machinery that glistened in
the overhead sunlamps. The floor had a slight but perceptible
curve; it was a wedge section of a giant wheel spinning deep
beneath Aresopolis. Dual-purpose like most things offplanet,
a flywheel storing energy for burst use, but time here was
still limited and rationed. Most of the occupants were pregnant brooders, wearily putting in their minimum on exercise
bicycles, with a scattering of others whose owner's credits
allowed or tasks required high-gravity maintenance. Mostly
they leafed through picture-books, listened to music on ear-
plugs or chattered among themselves, leaving her in a bubble
of silence.

Cows, she thought bitterly, looking at them as she swung
her legs off the table. Then: *That's unfair. Not their fault.*
Some of them looked back at her out of the corners of their
eyes, then away again. She felt the slight ever-present tug of
the controller cuff on her right wrist, more than enough
reason to shun her; who knew what she had done, to need an
instant pain-paralyzer? Guilt was contagious, especially here,
where every word and gesture was observed by the never-

sleeping senses of the computers and the endless probing vigilance of the AI programs.

There was a man working with springweights near her who did not look away. Handsome, younger than she, a Eurasian with smooth olive skin and bright blue eyes; he smiled, lifted his brows. Lithe-bodied and strong, he could be anything from a dancer to a Janissary . . .

Why not, she thought, hesitating a second, then shook her head as she smiled and left, towel thrown over one shoulder. She felt his eyes on her neck, memorizing her number. Probably he could reference it through Records, probably he would sheer off when he learned who owned her.

And it would be too easy, too easy to make yourself comfortable with little compromises until there was nothing left. Better not to start, just as it was better not to talk too much. When every word could kill, talk meant fear. Fear until you censored the words, then the dangerous thoughts to make that easier, then stopped *having* the thoughts. Better to talk to yourself, in the safety of your head.

Marya walked inward from the hub, up steps that gradually flattened into floor as the centrifugal force weakened and lunar gravity took over. She ignored the faint ferris-wheel feeling of disorientation from her inner ears and halted before the gate; it slid open, and she stepped into the narrow chamber and pressed her back against the antispinward wall. There was a brief pressure as the inner ring of the wheel slowed and stopped; the inner door opened, and she walked through into the hub.

Showers and sauna were crowded, too, but at least they were not open-plan. She stripped off the exercise shorts and threw the disposable fabric into a hamper, nodding to a few persons she knew as she waited in line for a cubicle, studying herself in the mirrored walls. *Not bad,* she decided. Especially for fifty; not much sagging, although of course the light gravity helped, and the daily exercise she had kept up as a silent gesture of self-respect . . . and the fact that Strategos Yolande Ingolfsson bought her personal servants top-flight Citizen Level medical care, which meant the best in the solar system. Viral DNA repair, cellular waste removal, synthormone implants, calcium boost, the works. There were strands of silver in her long black hair, crow's-feet beside her eyes, but for the rest she could have passed for mid-thirties.

A woman in her mid-thirties who had borne a child and

breast-fed it. Her fingers traced lightly over the cracked-eggshell pattern on the taut muscle of her stomach.

"Not now," she murmured to herself, her eyelids drooping down as she turned attention within, finding the pattern of calm. Her gaze was cool as she raised it back to the mirror. *Yes, not bad. That could be important,* she thought with cold realism. *Things are moving to a crisis; you've got to know.* Clandestine-ops mode. *Think of yourself as a sleeper.* She grinned sardonically at the joke as she stepped into the vacated cubicle.

"Sector three, level two," the transporter capsule said.

The lid hissed up, and Yolande stepped out into the station, past the unmoving guards. Probably unnecessary; the machinery would simply not obey unauthorized personnel. On the other hand, there were ways to fool machinery, and it was not in the Draka nature to trust too completely to cybernetics. The Orpos were the regular pair, and saluted briskly; she blinked back to awareness of her surroundings and returned it. Downside there might have been actual physical checks.

Lucky we're not quite *settled enough to start importing surplus bureaucrats,* she thought wearily. Sector Three was command residence country, Civil, War Directorate, Security and Combines both; status was being close to the main transport station. Yolande sighed slightly as she palmed the lock of her outer door; the inner slid open as the corridor portal cycled shut, another emergency airlock system. It might have been more efficient to pack everything close together in one spot, but this *was* supposed to be a fortress. Carving rock was no problem either, not when the original function of Aresopolis had been to throw material into Earth-orbit to armor battlestations. So the city-beneath was a series of redundantly-linked modules, any of which could function independently for a long, long time.

"Hiyo, Mistis," Jolene said, waiting with a hot lemonade. The entranceway was a circular room ten meters in diameter, with a domed roof over a central pool and fountain. The walls were holopanels between half-columns, right now set to show a steppe landscape: rolling green hills fading into a huge sky, wind rippling the grass, distant antelope.

" 'Lo, Jo," Yolande said, accepting the glass.

Machiavelli IV came bounding into the room and raced

around the wall to reach her, running with innocent uncon-
cern across what looked to be empty space and soaring to
land on the foamlava floor by her feet. Two housegirls followed more sedately with her lounging robe and slippers;
Yolande sipped moodily at the hot sweet-tart liquid while
they removed her uniform and redressed her, moving only to
transfer the glass from hand to hand.

"We're leavin' tomorrow," she said abruptly. Then, to the
apartment: "Walls, blank." The holo panels dimmed to a
neutral pearl-gray color. Yolande spared them a moment's
irritation; she would have preferred mosaic, but the necessary skills were still scarce on Luna, and anyway this *was* the
Commandant's quarters. Furnished rooms, in a sense.

"Tomorrow, Mistis?" Jolene asked, puzzled. It was a month
before leave was scheduled.

"I said so, didn't I?" Yolande snapped, then sighed and
drew a hand across her face. "Sorry, Jo. Somethin' came up.
Down to Archona, stayin' with Uncle Eric, then a quick trip
up to Claestum to drop off Tina with John an' Mandy, then
back here. Call it fo' days; just pack an overnight bag an'
Tina's things."

She looked down at the housegirls, kneeling with hands
folded in their laps and eyes downcast; both rather new, and
still a little shy, especially at hearing the Archon referred to
as "Uncle." "Run along, there's good wenches . . . I'll take
Lele, none of the other staff." No point in carting a dozen
servants along for a visit, and Jolene hated space travel.
"Light supper, an' . . ."

The inner door sighed open and shut. Yolande looked over
her shoulder; it was Marya. ". . . An' set up the chess game
fo' after, Marya."

King's pawn to knight four, Yolande decided. She moved
the carved-ebony Janissary and leaned back in the lounger,
sipping at the white wine; it was Vernaccia. *Checkmate in,
hmmmm, seven moves*. She was not doing as well as usual
tonight, and it was getting a little late. *Damn, I'm not sleepy,
either*, she thought.

The lounging room was arch-roofed, a relic of excavating
techniques in the early days, back in the mid-1960s; the
Commandant's quarters had been enlarged but not moved as
the city grew. There were a few pictures, some hangings, but
she had had most of the walls left in the natural white-

streaked black rock interspersed with hand-painted *azulejos* tile; the furniture was modern and local, spindly shapes of lacquered bamboo and puff-pillows. The room seemed cavernous and dim now, yet somehow cramped despite space enough to guest a hundred. Perhaps it was subliminal knowledge of all those kilometers of rock above. Yolande stirred restlessly.

What was it Michelangelo said about Vernaccia? she thought, sipping again. *It "kisses, licks, bites, thrusts, and stings." There's my subconscious telling me what I want.* That was a little awkward; she had told Tina no . . . She was not in the mood for Jolene's friendly complaisance, and the rest of the staff were unsuitable or too new, too much in awe, to be very interesting. *Maybe a man?* That was nice occasionally; unfortunately, no Citizen she knew well enough was available, probably. Well, she could have a nightspot send a buck around—perfectly legal nowadays; the Race Purity laws had been updated back in the '70s.

No, maybe I'm old-fashioned, but no. Ah well, there's always the headset. That brought sleep without chemical hangovers.

"Mistis." Yolande blinked out of her reverie and saw the serf's next move.

"Thought so. Yo' shouldn't be so . . . schematic about yo' pieces. See." She took the other's last bishop and indicated the alternatives. "Neither of us's up to scratch tonight."

"Ah, Mistis." There was an unusual note in the serf's voice. Yolande looked up, saw that she was studying a piece held in one hand. A pawn in ivory, in the shape of a German soldier of the Eurasian War. "Ah, can I ask you a question?" The fall of her hair hid most of her face, and the tops of her ears were pink.

The Draka blinked puzzlement. "Certainly."

"Were, ah, were you planning on going to bed alone tonight, Mistis?"

Yolande's eyebrows rose, and she spoke with a chuckle in her voice. "Is that an invitation, Marya?" *I hope so. Have for years; wonder what changed her mind?*

A nod. "Well, well, that *is* a surprise." She cleared her mind and looked. *Rather nice. Not young, but then, neither am I anymore.* It was getting to be a little embarrassing, bedding teenagers. Granted they were only serfs, still . . . *And I've wanted you for a while.*

She rose and extended a hand. "Shall we?"

"*Ah!*"

Yolande went rigid as the orgasm flowed over her like waves of warmth, felt the world swim blue before her eyes. She was straddled kneeling across the other's shoulders, arched back on her heels with her shoulders resting on the serf's upraised knees. Now she leaned forward and sank lower, linking her hands behind her neck and smiling down at the face between her thighs. "One mo' time, pretty pony," she said softly, moving her hips in languid rhythm to the sweet wet friction of tongue and lips. The serf's eyes were closed below a frown of concentration; her head moved with the arching of Yolande's pelvis, and she gripped the Draka's hips with a clench that whitened her fingernails.

"Ah. Mmmm*mmm*." Yolande moved more quickly, shuddered, locked immobile with a long hiss between clenched teeth. This time the color went beyond blue to indigo, shot through with veins of red. She nearly collapsed forward—would have in normal gravity.

"Wonderful," she sighed as she eased herself down beside the other and reached up for the wineglass. Blood pounded in her ears like retreating drums, and the dreamy relaxation was like flying in dreams. Marya's eyes fluttered open, dark and unreadable. Yolande poured the last of the wine on her lips and kissed her, savoring the pleasant mixture of tastes. The room was dark except for a wall set to show a landscape of lunar mountains jagged across the three-quarters Earth; that cast a pale silver glow over the circular bed. The air was lightly warm, and she could smell the roses in planters around the walls, musk, a slight tang of sweat and warm flesh.

Marya turned on her side and laid her head on her owner's shoulder; Yolande stroked her back. *At least the third-arm problem is less up here,* she thought drowsily. *Gods, I haven't felt this relaxed in months.*

"I'm glad you liked it, Mistis," the serf said, yawning into the curve where neck met deltoid.

"Freya, yes. I's so tense without knowin' it, I went off like a sunbomb. That damn stingfighter's got me tied in knots . . . *can't* figure out how the damyanks did it." She was muttering, half thinking aloud; absently, she set the glass down on the fused stone of the headboard and began stroking down Marya's flank. "And on *top* of that, those fuckin' prisoners.

Why is *Biocontrol* gettin' into the decison-makin' loop? They're just a research institute, even if they're so almighty impo'tant these days . . ."

She paused, hand lingering on the firmness of the other's hip. "Lift yo' knee . . . Did *yo'* like it, Marya?" Her fingers trailed down the inside of the serf's leg and lightly cupped her groin.

"Couldn't you tell, Mistis?" the other said. She smiled and rolled onto her back, raising and spreading her legs.

"Hmmm, I could tell when yo' came; that isn't the same thing." Yolande slipped her free hand under the serf's neck while she kneaded softly with the other, rising on one elbow and bending her head to Marya's breasts. The nipples were dark and taut, the large aureoles around them crinkled, ridged smoothness under her tongue.

"I . . ." Marya caught her breath as Yolande bit gently. "I volunteered. This time."

There was quiet for a few minutes, broken only by the increasing sound of the serf's panting. Yolande leaned closer, studying the other's face. The dark eyes were wide, iris swallowed in the pupil. *Ah, nearly,* she thought, laughing and increasing the featherlight pressure of her fingers. Marya's arms went back, gripping the headboard, as her knees pulled up and wide; the cords in her neck stood out as she gave a series of gasps and then a sharp cry.

"I think maybe yo' *do* like it," Yolande said. "Pity yo' don't like me; it increases the pleasure." She wiped her hand on the sheet.

Marya sighed. "You've been . . . You haven't been as . . . strict with me these last few years, Mistis."

Embarrassed, Yolande lay back. "Oh . . . Well, I wasn't thinkin' straight, fo' a while after Myfwany was killed. Yo' sort of stood fo' the Yankees, in my mind. But that isn't fair, of course; yo' aren't a Yankee anymore, yo' my serf. Not fittin' to abuse yo'. Besides,"—she patted the other's stomach for a second, then took her hand—"yo' bore Gwen. Not willingly, of course, but yo' still carried an' nursed Myfwany's clonechild; I couldn't keep up the hatin' after I saw her at yo' breast, could I?"

She was silent for a moment, letting drowsy thoughts sift through her mind. "Still . . . playin' chess, yo' get to know a person somewhats." She yawned. "Yo' strange to me. As different as two bein's of the same species can be. Draka I understand, an' serfs. Yankees I meet in structured situations, like battle; logic of objective conditions forces a certain amount of similarity to they behavior. Most of my serfs like me well enough; I'm a good owner. Yo' . . ." She shrugged. "Yo' wasn't raised to think that way." *I think I'm still the enemy, in your heart,* she thought. *What do they taste of, the kisses of an enemy?*

"Mistis; take me with you, on this visit?"

"Why fo'?"

"I . . ." Marya turned her head away from the one on the pillow beside her. "You're right, everyone here is still strange to me, even after all these years; but you less than the born-serfs."

" 'Kay," Yolande muttered. She turned on her side and threw an arm and leg across Marya's body. "Sleep now." Her eyelids fluttered closed.

Marya's right arm was free; she raised it in the dim light of the reflected earth, letting it shine on the imperishable metal of the controller. Then she brought it to her lips, opening them to the cool neutral taste, slightly bitter. She lay so, motionless except for an occasional slow blink, as the hours crept by and the sweat cooled on her skin.

CHAPTER EIGHTEEN

The opening of space was a military measure, but its only *military* effect to date has been to maintain the stalemate at a higher level. The truly revolutionary impact has been, as so often, the *unintended* and *unforeseen* consequences. The most obvious has been the flow of new materials, products which could not be produced at all on Earth or only at prohibitive cost. Monocrystal materials, ultra-pure silica wafers and optical fibers, bearings and alloys close to the theoretical maxima, room-temperature superconductors, all are flowing in abundance from the plants built to sustain the orbital defenses. More surprising than this has been the sheer *scale* of developments. In space, our industrial machine is suddenly relieved of crippling, blinding burdens, burdens of which we had never before been aware. We have only recently learned to control nuclear fusion on a planetary surface, but in space fusion power—the Sun—is freely available on an unlimited scale. With unlimited power, vacuum, zero gravity, and no environmental problems, manipulation of materials becomes vastly simpler. Solar sails and plasma drives make space transport cheap, while pulsedrive with its constant high acceleration makes rapid interplanetary travel possible. The flow of fissionables from the asteroids in turn reduces the cost of transport; much cruder methods, involving fusion warhead-type bombs, can be used to move massive objects such as comets and asteroids of moderate size.

Scramjets were the first step; Earth-to-orbit

launch with ground-based power sources such as lasers and magnetic catapults came next. Once significant manufacturing and mining capacity had been established in space, growth became exponential. The use of space-generated power beamed to the surface for launch energy closed the circuit; and cybernetic mass production of solar cells is reducing energy costs to the point where only the very cheapest hydroelectric power can compete. From a few hundred in the early 1960s, the number of humans resident in space grew to perhaps ten thousand in 1970; hundreds of thousands a decade later; by the beginning of the 1990s, probably nearly a million. This is the most significant development in human history since the American Revolution and its counter-creation of the Domination. It has altered the terms of the Protracted Struggle; the two-tiered economy of the Domination has had to contort itself into knots to adapt to space; and while illiterate slaves on the Moon tend hydroponic crops in the tunnel-colonies, there are limits to the process. It has or will soon free humankind from the threat of complete annihilation which haunted the generation after the discovery of atomic energy.

Perhaps most important in the long run, it has freed industrial civilization from the constraints of the terrestrial environment. Metals and fossil fuels are nonrenewable, and the ability of Earth to absorb contaminants and by-products was already being strained by our present stable global population of 2,800,000,000. The problem of raising the serf population of the Domination to Alliance standards hardly bears thinking about—if the terms of reference are limited to Earth. They no longer are, and there is no longer an argument from necessity for poverty.

History in a Technological Age
by Andrew Elliot Armstrang, Ph.D.
Department of History
San Diego University Press, 1995

NEW YORK CITY
HOSPITAL OF THE SACRED HEART
FEDERAL CAPITAL DISTRICT
UNITED STATES OF AMERICA
APRIL 7, 1998

Nathaniel Stoddard grinned like a death's-head at the shock in Lefarge's eyes.

"Happens to us all, boy," he said slowly. "Ayuh. And never at a convenient time."

Lefarge swallowed and looked away from the wasted figure, the liver-spotted hands that never stopped trembling on the coverlet. *I've always hated the way hospitals smelled*, he thought. Medicinal, antiseptic, with an underlying tang of misery. The private room was crowded with the medical-monitoring machines, smooth cabinets hooked to the ancient figure on the bed through a dozen tubes and wires; their screens blinked, and he knew that they were pumping data to the central intensive-care computer. Doling out microdoses of chemicals, hormones, enzymes . . .

"I'd have told them to stop trying two years ago, if I hadn't been needed," Stoddard said. The faded blue eyes looked at him with an infinite weariness, pouched in their loose folds of skin. "But if I'm indispensable, the nation's doomed anyway, son."

Lefarge looked up sharply; that was the first time the old man had ever used the word to him. He reached out and clasped the brittle-boned hand with careful gentleness.

"My only regret is that you couldn't take over my post," Stoddard said. "But what you're doing is more important. Janice and the boy all right?"

Lefarge smiled, an expression that felt as if it would crack his cheeks. "Janice is fine. Nate Junior is a strapping rockjack of thirty now, Uncle Nate. Courting, too, and this time it looks serious. We'll have the Belt full of Stoddards yet."

The general sighed, and closed his eyes for a moment. "The Project? What do your tame scientists say about the trans-Luna incident?"

Well, at least the information's still getting through, Lefarge thought. *I might have known Uncle Nate would arrange to keep a tap into channels.*

"They . . . " He ran a hand through his hair, and caught a glimpse of himself in the polished surface of a cabinet. *God-*

dam. I show more of Maman every year. His cropped hair was as much gray as black, now; no receding hairline, though. "Well, the consensus is that it . . . mutated. They had to make it so that it could modify itself, anyway. The trigger is multiply redundant, but it's just data, and if something knocks out a crucial piece . . ." he shrugged and raised his hands. "No estimate on spread, either. Slow. Maybe ten percent penetration by now, if we're lucky. Two years to critical mass. Absolutely no way of telling if there'll be more, ah, mutations. Or if they'll figure it out." He shrugged again. "The Team says de Ribeiro was right; we took a . . . less than optimum path in computer development, way back when. Too much crash research, too much security. Though they practically end up beating each other over the head about what we *should* have done! Anyway, even the Project can't redevelop an entire technology. They've pushed the present pretty well to its limits, and what we're using is the product."

Stoddard's eyes opened again. "Fred . . ." He fought for breath, forced calm on himself and began again. "Fred, don't let them throw it away. We can't . . . The Militants will win the next Archonal election in the Domination. Coalition . . . we're pretty sure. War . . . soon after. Inevitable . . . fanatics. Think of the damage if they attack . . . first. Remember . . . *Nelson's eyepatch.*"

Fred felt the hair crawl on the back of his neck. Admiral Nelson had been signaled to halt an attack; he put the telescope to his blind eye, announced that he had seen no signal, and continued.

A red light began to beep on one of the monitors. Seconds later a nurse burst into the room.

"Brigadier Lefarge!" she said severely, moving quickly to the bedside. "You were allowed to see the patient on condition he not be stressed in any way!"

He leaned over Stoddard, caught the faded blue eyes, nodded. "Don't worry, Uncle Nate," he said softly. "I'll take care of it."

"Brigadier—" the nurse began. Then her tone changed to one he recognized immediately: a good professional faced with an emergency. "Dr. Suharto to room A17! Dr. Suharto to room A17!" Her hands were flying over the controls, and the old man's body jerked. More green-and white-coated figures were rushing into the room; Lefarge stepped back to the angle of the door, saluted quietly, wheeled out.

* * *

The office in Donovan House was much the same, missing
only the few keepsakes Nathaniel Stoddard had allowed himself; even the Parrish landscapes were still on the wall. Something indefinable was different, perhaps the smell of pipe
tobacco, perhaps . . . *I'm imagining things*, Frederick Lefarge
thought, as he saluted the new incumbent.

Anton Donati was holding down Stoddard's desk now.
Lefarge had worked with him often over the years; less so
since the New America project got well underway and he was
seldom on Earth. About his own age, thin and dark and
precise, with a mustache that looked as if it had been drawn
on. Competent record in the field, even better once he was
back at headquarters. But a by-the-book man, a through-
channels operator. The other man in the room was a stranger,
a civilian in a blue-trimmed gray suit and natty silver-buckled
shoes; the curl-brimmed hat on the stand by the door had a
snakeskin band and one peacock feather. A whiff of expensive
cologne; just the overall ensemble that a moderately prosperous man-about-town was wearing this season.

"Anton," Lefarge nodded. He continued the gesture to the
civilian, raised an eyebrow. His superior caught the unspoken question: *Who's the suit?*

"Brigadier, this is Operative Edward Forsymmes, Alliance
Central Intelligence."

Fucking joy. He is a suit. Still, this was no time to let the
rivalry with the newer central-government agency interfere
with business. San Francisco was capital of the Alliance, and
the Alliance was sovereign. The OSS had been founded as an
agency of the old American government; it was only natural
that the Grand Senate wanted an intelligence source of its
own. *And the suits still couldn't find their own arses with
both hands on a dark night.*

Lefarge extended his; the ACI agent rose and shook with a
polished smile. There was strength in the grip; the man had a
smooth, even tan, and no spare weight that the American
could see; thinning blond hair combed over the bald spot,
gray eyes.

"Jolly good to meet you," he said pleasantly. *British?* Lefarge
asked himself. *No. Australasian; South Island, at a guess.
Possibly Tasmanian.* A quarter of the British Isles had moved
to the Australasian Federation over the past century, and the

accents had not diverged all that much, especially in the Outer Islands. "Shall we proceed?"

The ACI man sat and clicked open his attaché case, pulling out a folder. It had an indigo border, Most Secret. An OSS code-group for title; the New America designation. Lefarge shot an unbelieving glance at his commanding officer.

Donati shrugged, with a very Italian gesture. "The Chairman's Office thought the Agency should be involved," he said in a neutral tone.

Christ, Lefarge thought with well-hidden disgust. Not enough that San Francisco was getting involved, but the Agency *and* the Chairman's office. The Chairman was an armchair bomb-them-aller, and the Agency were a band of would-be Machiavellis, and the two never agreed on *anything*—except to distrust the OSS.

"Well," he said. "What's the latest on the hijacking incident?"

Donati waved a hand to the civilian.

"Really, quite unfortunate," the ACI man said. "Your boffins did say that this would be a *controllable* weapon, did they not?"

Lefarge flicked a cigarette out of his uniform jacket and glanced a question at Donati. "Sir?"

"Go ahead, Brigadier."

"It's *largely* controllable," Lefarge explained patiently, thumbing his lighter. "Christ, though, look at what it has to penetrate! We're trying to paralyze the whole Snake defensive *system*, not just one installation, you know. That means we have to get into the compinstruction sets when they're embedded in the cores of central-brain units; then it has to jump the binary-analogue barrier repeatedly to spread to the other manufacturing centers where they burn-in cores. Talking *sets* here, not just data. *Plus* the continual checks they run against just this sort of thing; they're not stupid." He drew on the tobacco, snorted smoke from his nostrils. "One replication went a little off, and responded to a specific-applications attack command instead of the general-emergency one. If we could get more *original* copies into fabrication plants . . . What've we got on reaction?"

The Australasian tapped his finger on the file. "The SD are running around chopping off heads," he said thoughtfully. "But rather less than we expected. It seems they had the beginnings of a tussle over those prisoners of ours they took in the hijacking, the usual War-Security thing they amuse themselves with . . . and then their top politicals stepped in. Closed everything down; shut off all investigation; had the core from the stingfighter they lost, *and* the prisoners, *and* the bodies, all shipped to Virunga Biocontrol. We did catch an unfamiliar codegroup; all we could crack was the outer title. *Stone Dogs*, whatever that means." He smiled at the two OSS officers. "You chappies wouldn't be holding out on us, would you?"

Lefarge and Donati exchanged a glance.

"We've never gotten a handle on it," Donati admitted. "The name's cropped up"—he paused to consult the terminal in the desk—"five times, first time in 1973. Again in '75, '78, '82. Then you, which is the first time in nearly a decade. It's about the most closely-held thing they've got, and all we can say firmly is that it's tied to Virunga . . . which *might* mean something biological. Or might not."

"Those damned Luddites!" the ACI man exclaimed. Donati and Lefarge nodded in a moment of perfect agreement; the anti-biotech movement had crippled Alliance research for a generation. It was understandable, considering the uses to which the Draka had put the capabilities, but a weakness nonetheless.

"Still," he went on musingly. "*Why* is *that* involved . . . when we know that it was our little surprise that caused the incident with the stingfighter?"

"Let's put it this way," Lefarge said grimly. "The Stone Dogs, whatever they are, are as closely held as . . . the Project. What's the Project? Our ace in the hole. Now, what's wrong with this picture?"

The agent winced slightly. "I say, bad show. Well, not our affair, what? There's no compromise of the Project; they'll go over that stingfighter's core, but their standard search models won't find a thing." He thumbed through the file. "We *are* getting some interesting data, from the deep-cover agent with the Commandant of Aresopolis." He laughed. "A deep-cover agent between the covers, eh? From the pillow-talk, she must be fantastic—"

Lefarge was dimly aware of Donati wrestling him to a standstill, of the ACI man scrambling backward snarling, with a hand inside his jacket.

"*That's my sister you're talking about, you son of a bitch!*" he shouted. Coming back to himself, shuddering, smelling the sudden reek of his own sweat.

Inch by inch, they relaxed. "Look, Fred," Donati said. "He didn't know, all he saw was a code description, he's got no *need* to know, he *wouldn't* know if you hadn't blown up!"

"Right," Lefarge said, shaking off the arm and straightening his jacket. *Breathe. In. Out.* He pulled a handkerchief out of his pocket and split the package, wiping his face down with the scented cloth and sinking back into his chair.

"I apologize, Brigadier," the ACI agent said.

"Accepted. You had any experience inside, Operative Forsymmes?" The other man shook his head. "Then don't make comments about those who have to operate in the snake farm. For your information, my sister was missing-in-action in India in '75. She contacted the OSS again, on her own initiative. *Twenty-four years in there!*"

"I apologize again, Brigadier," the man said patiently. "The fact remains, the *New America* Project is not compromised, as far as we know. Time to saturation remains on-schedule, and then we will be in an unassailable bargaining position."

Lefarge smiled with a carnivore's expression. "Certainly we will. After we've pounded their strategic installations into glowing rubble and destroyed everything they have off Earth—" He paused at something sensed between the other two. "There's been a change of plan?" he said, in an even tone.

Donati looked down at his linked fingers. The agent spoke in the same smooth tone.

"No, of course not. Your Project will finally give us the top hand, and we'll use it, never fear. Not in an all-out surprise attack, of course. That was '70s strategy. We'll demonstrate it; with the balls cut off their space defense capacity, they'll have no choice but effectively to surrender. With guarantees for the personal safety of their top people, of course."

"Ah." Lefarge glanced over at the other OSS officer. "General Donati, is it just this suit, or are they all fucking insane out there on the West Coast?" He glanced back at Forsymmes. "Are you? Completely fucking insane, that is?"

The agent's tone grew slightly frosty. "Brigadier Lefarge, I'm going to charitably assume that your personal . . . background and losses have made you somewhat unbalanced on this subject. Are you aware, my dear sir, of what even *one* hypersonic surface-skimmer could do to a major city? Even given the most optimistic possible projections, the Project could only disable eighty percent of their space-based systems, less on Earth. That's primarily the defensive systems, at that. The Project's little photonic bug can't *fit* into anything smaller than a shipcomp core, and the enemy use more distributed systems than we do, which can be decoupled from their core computers. They would still have some capacity to operate their ships by manual linkage, and their installations. Furthermore, even if we wait *three* years, some of the older backup cores would be uninfected. They are not, as you pointed out, fools. We will show them they can't win an exchange, and offer terms."

Lefarge shook his head in sheer wonderment. "You . . . *Somebody* thinks the *Snakes* are going to be deterred by *casualties?* You look old enough to remember the fall of India, even if you haven't read any history. Perhaps you recall them shooting the top fifteen thousand officials of the Indian Republic's government in batches, on the steps of the goddamn Archonal Palace, and broadcasting it worldwide? How many millions more were slaughtered or chemically brain-scrubbed?"

"There's no need to spout propaganda at me, Lefarge!" Forsymmes snapped.

"Oh. Then maybe you've tuned in to their public execution channel? Impalements in living color; I'm told the breaking-on-the-wheel is—"

The agent sighed with elaborate patience. "Brigadier, I'm fully aware of the enemy's contempt for *other people's* lives. We are talking about putting their *own* lives at risk."

"And maybe you think it's a myth their troops commit suicide rather than surrender? What about Fenris?"

"The so-called doomsday bomb? Nobody's ever been able to prove that it's active; self-evidently a bluff."

Donati intervened. "In any case, we're talking in a vacuum, here," he said mildly. "None of us are exactly at policy-making level, are we?"

"No, that's true," Lefarge said calmly. The discussion became technical.

"Lefarge, do you really want to be taken off the Project?" Donati asked, turning on his subordinate as the door closed behind Forsymmes.

"No, sir, I do not," Lefarge answered.

The black eyes probed him. "If you don't, I'd better not see another performance like that," the general warned. "Stoddard's protégé could get away with things, because Stoddard had been here longer than God and knew where all the skeletons were buried. They were terrified of him, from the chairman and the president on down . . . at least the chairman was; I don't know if Hiero's scared of anything. Herself, probably, like all the rest of us. But—and this is the important *but*—her attitude to the constitutional relations between the presidency and the Alliance is correct to a fault. Hell, Fred, the president knows Allsworthy's a horse's ass as well as you or I do. But he's the bossman."

"We're neither of us a General Stoddard," Lefarge agreed. "Does that mean we have to swallow this horseshit?"

Donati shrugged and lit a thin black cheroot in an ivory holder. "As far as it goes. You know the ACI, they like to use scalpels where a sledgehammer's needed."

"Christ, Anton, that so-called strategy of theirs could lose us a dozen cities—if we're *lucky*. Fenris is as real as this table." He rapped his knuckles on the wood.

"You know that. *I* know that. The people in San Fran, they don't believe it because it's . . . 'fucking insane,' to their way of thinking."

"Not to a Snake . . . Yeah, Anton: '*I* know—' " He shook his head. "Of course, we could be in a use-it-or-lose-it situation before that. If the cover goes, or they spring *their* surprise on us, whatever it is. What do you think our Great Leaders will do then?"

"If the Project's cover's blown? Back off, if it's before saturation point. Dither a little and then use it, after that. If the Snakes attack first, everything gets used."

"I wish Stoddard were here. You going to the funeral?"

"Yes." Donati drew on the cheroot, his hollowed cheeks giving a skull cast to the thin face. "I never thought he'd die, you know?" There was compassion in his voice as he continued. Everyone had known Lefarge and the old man were close: "I'm glad you made it back before the end; it was so sudden . . . What did you talk about?"

"Nothing. Personal things." *And Nelson's eyepatch*, Lefarge thought with chill satisfaction, as the other man nodded agreement. A soldier's duty was obedience, but there were other duties. *I'm glad Uncle Nate reminded me of that*, he thought. It would have been a lonely burden to bear alone.

"And, Fred, remember you've gotten out of touch with the institutional balance while you had your head up there in the clouds all these years. Stoddard kept the wolves off your back while you pushed the Project through." He rose and crossed to the sideboard. "Scotch?" Lefarge accepted the glass. "Here's to him." They clinked glasses. "You're going to have to walk a little smaller, for safety's sake. The view's great, but there *are* disadvantages to having your head in the clouds, you know."

It's still better than having it rammed up your ass, Lefarge reflected, as he raised the glass in bland acknowledgment.

"We'll all do our jobs," he said. *Whether the suits want me to or not.*

DRAKA FORCES BASE ARESOPOLIS
MARE SERENITATIS, LUNA
1100 HOURS
MARCH 26, 1998

There were dozens of launch-sites around Aresopolis, and swift linear-induction subtunnels to all of them. Yolande chose to exercise a Commandant's privilege and use the central dome exit when possible, and to travel aboveground. They left from another of those privileges, a small private villa on the lip of one of the natural terraces that rimmed the crater. It was daywatch, and the sky was set to a bright blue-green that dimmed everything but a ghost-outline of the three-quarter Earth, and the unwinking fire of the sun. The house gleamed white and blue and its roofs russet-red; the walled hectare of garden smelled of damp earth and plants from the nightwatch rain.

The staff were lined up before the round doorway; they bowed with hands before eyes as she drew on her gloves, this being a formal occasion.

"Good-bye," she said. "Yo've served well, and while I'm gone, y'all can stay here in the villa servant's quarters an' grounds." They brightened; it was a rare treat, they were usually only here when the Mistress was in residence.

"Maintenance work only, an' Jolene's authorized to draw supplies fo' an entertainment, yo'selves and a guest each." Cheers at that.

She nodded at Jolene. "Keep 'em in order, hey?"

"Yo' command, Mistis," Jolene said, bending to kiss the Draka's hand.

Yolande put the palm under her chin and raised her to meet her lips. "Be seein' yo'."

Marya sank back on the cushioned seat beside Tina and watched the Draka board the airsled. Yolande ignored the steps, vaulting over the side in a complete feet-uppermost turn that looked slow-motion in the .16 G, landing neatly in the bucket seat; she turned and smiled broadly at Marya, with a wink.

The serf smiled back. *It's like method acting*, she told herself in some cold inner pocket of her mind. You had to construct a part of you that actually *was* what you portrayed; only here, you had to write the role as you went along. Impossible to do consciously—there was no way to concentrate long or hard enough; eventually you would slip up fatally. More a matter of creating and living in a persona. She suspected most born-serfs did the same from infancy, less consciously; it was impossible to tell how many retained anything beneath the role, how many *became* it.

Careful, she dosen't expect you to fawn, Marya reminded herself. Yolande turned to the controls and stretched, cracking her fingers together over her head before dropping them to the sidestick. *Just keep her happy and relaxed, and she'll keep talking. Why not? You're only a serf.*

Knowing people was useful in ordinary life, the margin of survival for a spy, life itself to a serf. Yourself most of all. *She isn't cruel by their standards*, Marya told herself. *Nor stupid. As for last night* . . . The shame was less than she had expected; decades spent in the Domination could not help but rub off on your attitudes. *It wasn't rape. You asked her.* And while it was not something she would have otherwise chosen to do . . . *Face it, it was physically pleasant.* Yolande had been gentle, and took pleasure in giving pleasure as much as in receiving it—from what she knew, not something a serf could count on. The irritating part had been remembering always to let the other take the lead. *Oh well, call it waltzing.*

No, not unpleasant, she thought, letting her tired body relax into the cushions. Apart from the lack of sleep, she felt fine; the body had its own logic. Expecting it, she could handle the irrational rush of friendliness. That was a common pattern as well; hopefully, her owner would see no reason to suppress it. Yolande liked to be liked, even by her chattel, when possible.

She's not evil, Marya thought with analytical dispassion. Neither was an apple full of cyanide.

It was simply too dangerous to be allowed to exist.

Yolande took the airsled straight up from the courtyard. It was basically a shallow dish of aluminum alloy built around a superconductor storage ring, with seats and windshields and small noiseless fans. Lift and drive were from pivoting vents on the rim, a dozen of them making the little craft superbly responsive. She glanced up into the rearview mirror.

Not the only thing that's superbly responsive, she thought happily. *Freya, but I needed my clock cleaned. That was different, not as bland as most serfs. More push-back.*

A sensor went *ping* at three hundred meters: echosounder, of course. Air pressure here was uniform right up until you ran into the sky. The aircraft slid forward at sixty kph, beneath a light scattering of fleecy pancake-shaped clouds.

There were times when you had to step back from a problem, turn your mind to something else, before you could see it plainly. She had climbed the command-chain faster than anyone before her; native ability, connections, luck, and sustained drive. That because she had seen that the deadlock on Earth would squeeze resources into space, where they could at least accomplish *something*. For more than a decade, ever since Telmark IV, the knowledge that there could be nothing better here than a stalemate at a higher level of violence had eaten at her. Her mind prompted a list.

Item: Uncle Eric and the others aren't stupid. They must realize that as well as I.

Item: Only something on the order of technological surprise could break the stalemate. And if it went on long enough, it would be the Alliance that came up with the winning card. She grinned at the thought, not an expression of pleasure, but the outward sign of a hunter's excitement. So the Final War had to come before then—but it would be a disaster, as things stood. *Seemed* to stand.

Item: The Supreme Command knew that, too.

Item: Commandant of Aresopolis was high enough up the command structure to be on the verge of the circles that made policy, political decisions. High enough that she would get hints of purpose, not just code-verified orders.

So. Perhaps the incident with the Yankee prisoners was something significant. Perhaps not; there were a thousand clandestine programs going on, everything from espionage to cultural disinformation. But perhaps this was different, and they had promoted her to the level where they had either to bring her into the picture or shoot her. Nor could her appointment be an accident.

I'm competent, she told herself judiciously. *More than competent; but even so, there are dozens of others with qualifications as good.*

Uncle Eric and his Conservatives knew where she stood; foursquare with them on domestic policy. She was a planter and an Ingolfsson and a von Shrakenberg connection, after all, and besides that she agreed with them. On the other hand, in foreign policy nobody could doubt she followed the Militant line; nobody at all.

Yolande began to hum softly under her breath. This promised to be interesting, very interesting indeed, when she got some data to work with. Her mind felt as good as her body, loose and light and flexible, ready to the hand of her will like a well-made and practiced tool. Quite true what the alienists said: celibacy was extremely bad for you, as bad as going without proper diet or exercise or meditation, and as likely to upset your mental equilibrium.

I must do something nice for Marya, she thought as the crater slid by below.

This view always heartened her. Most of the Domination off-Earth was like being inside a building all the time at best, or more commonly imprisonment on a submarine. Efficient, necessary, even comely in the way that well-designed machinery could be, but not beautiful; difficult to love. Space and the planets *were* lovely, but they were unhuman, beyond and apart from humankind and its needs, too big and too remote. Here were reminders of what she was fighting for.

There was a river beneath them, meandering in from the rim, weaving between broad shallow lakes that had been subcraters once. Reeds fringed the banks, brown green, except for a few horseshoe shapes of beach. The water was intensely clear, speckled with lotus and waterlily, and she could see a fish jump in a long, slow arc that soared like an athlete's leap. Trees grew along the shores, quick-growing gene-engineered cottonwood, eucalyptus, and Monterrey pine, with a dense undergrowth of passionflower and wild rose.

Beyond was a rolling plain of bright-green neokikuyu grass, the plant of choice for first establishment, rolling in long thigh-high waves beneath the warm dry air. Beneath that, earthworms, bacteria, fungi, helping grind dead soil into life with millennial patience.

Yolande grinned and sideslipped down to ten meters over the grasslands. A herd of springbok fled, scattering like drops of mercury on dry ice, their leaps taking them nearly as high as the belly of the car. Two grass-green cats a meter long raised implausible ear-tufts and yowled at her with their forepaws resting on a rabbit the size of a dog. She banked around them, skimmed over a boulder-piled hillock planted in flattopped thorn trees that exploded with birds.

"*Mistis.*" She looked back as her hands straightened the aircraft and put it on an upward path. Tina was looking green and swallowing hard.

"Sorry, Tina," she said. Morning sickness had struck the brooder hard, and she was still easily upset.

They flew more sedately across tree-studded plain, then a section still mostly bare whiteish-brown soil—*regolith*, she reminded herself. Vehicles and laborers moved over it in clouds of dust, spraying and seeding. Then over another waterway, a stretch of forested hills beyond that curved out of sight on either hand. The area within was more closely settled, networked with maglev roads and scattered with buildings: lodges, inns, experimental plots, landscaped gardens. Ahead lay the central mountain.

Long ago an asteroid had struck here, carving the crater in a multi-gigatonne fireball; a central spike half as high as the walls had been left, when the rock cooled again. For three billion years it had lain so, with only the micrometeorite hail to smooth the sides; then the Draka engineers had come. The dome they built required an anchor-point and cross-bracing; the mountain was bored hollow, and a tube of fiber-reinforced metal sunk home in it. That rose from the huge machinery spaces below through the ten-meter thickness of the dome itself, and the long monofilament cables that ran in from the circumference melded into a huge ring kilometers overhead. Yolande looked up, tracing their pathway. Thread-thin in the distance, like streamers of fine hair floating in a breeze; swelling, until they bulked like the chariot-spokes of a god.

The slopes below had been carved as well, into stairs and curving roadways, platforms and bases for the buildings, or left rugged for the plantings and waterfalls that splashed it with swathes of crimson and green and slow-moving silverblue. The buildings were traceries of stone and vitryl and metal, like an attenuated dream of Olympus, slender fluted columns and bright domes. Yolande brought the airsled in towards the main landing field, a construct that jutted out in a hectare of flange from a cliffside. She sighed at the sight of the reception waiting; *some* ceremony was inevitable. *I am Commandant, after all*, she thought reluctantly, and let the sled sink until it touched the gold-leaf tiles.

She touched down. Waiting Auxiliaries pushed up two sets of stairs, one for her and another for the servants. She stepped onto the red carpet of the first, and a band struck up "Follow Me," the anthem of the Directorate of War. A cohort in dress blacks snapped to attention: human troops, Citizen Force. Her own Guard merarchy. Bayoneted rifles flashed, drums rolled, feet crashed to the tiles in unison. *Not easy to do without kicking yourself into the air, here*, she thought ironically as she saluted in turn, right fist snapped to left breast.

"Service to the State!" she called.

"Glory to the Race!"

The Section heads were waiting, with their aides and assistants. Aresopolis was still organized like a War Directorate hostile-territory base, although that was growing a little obsolete. Commandant, herself. Vice Commandant and Operations Chief, Alman Witter. Weapons, Power, Lifesystems, Construction, Civil Administration. The Security commander, in headhunter green—a surprisingly reasonable sort, she had found, with a weakness for terrible puns. The Aerospace Command chief. The civil administrators. In four years she had come to know them all quite well; twelve-hour office days were something they all had in common. Except during emergencies, when it was rather more.

There's irony for you, she thought. Yolande Ingolfsson was niece to the Archon, an Arch-Strategos, and scion of two of the oldest Landholder families in the Domination. Wealthy in her own right even by Landholder standards, owner of several dozen human beings directly, and of thousands if you counted interests in Combine shares and other enterprises. And she actually had less leisure than a State-chattel serf clerk toiling away in one of the anonymous offices below her feet, and not much more in the way of personal freedom. *Well, a little more. I have all sorts of choices. Who I go to bed with, and what clothes I wear.* She looked down at her uniform. *Sometimes.*

"For this we conquered the world," she muttered under her breath, then looked up. The Earth was in its invariant place on the horizon, and she could make out the shield-shape of North America. *Not all the world; it will be better once we have.* Her teeth barred for a moment, and then she forced relaxation. *Ah, well, it would get boring with nothing more to do than swim, hunt, and make love.*

"Strategos Witter," she said formally to her second in command. "Citizens," to the others, "I expect to be back in about a week."

There was the usual exchange of civilities, but only Witter stayed with her as the metal rectangle rose a handspan and floated off into the three-story arch in the cliff; there was a mesh of superconductor laid below the tiles.

"Thomas was notably uncommunicative about the patrol incident," he said.

The skid was moving through a long corridor cleared for her use into a great circular hall, overlooked by ramps and walkways. The hall stretched out of sight in either direction, encircling the launch stations; crowds thronged it, away from the Orpo-cordoned path to her gate. Arches were traced on the walls, covered in brilliant mosaics; the sights of the solar system, mostly. Jupiter banded in orange and white, or the rings of Saturn against the impossible sky-stalk rising out of the hazy atmosphere of Titan. A few landscapes from Earth. And endlessly repeated above, the Drakon with its wings spread over all. She heard murmurs, foot-slither: a troop of new-landed ghouloons following their officer, peering about and hooting softly in amazement. One forgot himself and bounced two meters in the air, slapping at his chest and shoulders for emphasis as he spoke.

"Ooooo," he burbled. "Big big. *Big.*"

"Merarch Irwine had his orders," she said.

"Meaning, shut up?" the other Draka replied.

"Not quite. But all is not as it appears, Alman. I'm goin' down to find out. I may find out something; I may not. In any case—"

"There are Things We Were Not Meant To Know," he replied. The skid stopped before a final door. "Exactly," she said, stepping off the platform as it sank to the floor. "See yo' next Thursday."

"Service to the State."

"Glory to the Race." She turned to the doorguards. "Scan."

One of them touched a control; something blinked at her eyes, like a light flashing too quickly to be noticed.

"Arch-Strategos?" the tetrarch said. "Ah, ma'am. Yo' serf, the tall one." Yolande turned; he was indicating Marya. "She's cuffed, but yo' don't have the controller-activator on yo'."

"Thank yo', Tetrarch, but I think I'm safe from my housegirls," she said dryly, tapping her fingers on her belt. He flushed and stepped back with a salute.

"Yes, ma'am," he said. "Straight through, Arch-Strategos."

"Tell yo' the truth, I'd forgotten the bloody thing," Yolande said, as they seated themselves.

"I . . . never have, Mistis," Marya said, touching the cuff with the fingers of the other hand.

The capsule was the standard passenger form, a steel-alloy tube five decks high. There was an axial passageway with a lift platform, a control bubble at the bow and a thrust nozzle and reaction-mass tank at the other. There were the usual facilities, and a small galley. Nothing elaborate—cargo versions didn't even have a live pilot—but quick and comfortable. The usual load was several hundred passengers, although this flight would be hers alone; a seven-hour flight, under 1 G.

She sighed and looked around the lounge, empty, save for herself and Marya; Tina had gone to lie down in water-cushioned comfort. This was a wedge-shaped section of the topmost passenger deck, set with chairs and loungers and tables. A long section of the wall was crystal-sandwich screen. Yolande touched a control, and the wall disappeared. Smooth metal showed a half-meter away. Clanking sounds, and it began to move; magnetic fields were gripping the capsule. They slid sideways with ponderous delicacy, then into a vertical shaft. A slight feeling of acceleration, like an elevator. That lasted five minutes, past more blank metal; they were rising through one of the many passages that honeycombed the central lift-shaft.

"Ah." They were out, on the hectare-broad pentagonal metal cap; flat and empty now, no other launches just now. The dome stretched around them, and dimly through it she could see the landscape below. From above and close-by the structure of the dome was more apparent, the layers of gold foil and conductor sheathing.

"Stand by for boost, please."

She swung the lounger to near-horizontal. Not that the acceleration would be anything to note. Below her lasers would be building to excitation phase, mirrors aligning. A rumble, as the pumps began pushing liquid oxygen into the nozzle. *Whump.* Thrust, pushing her back into the cushions, building to Earth-normal. She sighed again, glanced over at Marya.

"Marya," she said. The other woman looked up. "What am I to do with yo'?"

"What you will, Mistis."

Yolande laughed with soft bitterness. "What I *will*? Now, there's a joke." She brooded, watching the Lunar landscape grow and shrink behind the windowscreen, the ancient pale rock and dust, the roads and installations her people had built. "Duty . . . I was raised to do what is right; duty to the State, to the Race, to my family and my friends and to my servants. For the State and the Race, I've helped preside over a useless non-war that shows no signs of endin' except in an even mo' useless *real* war that will destroy civilization, if not humanity. My best friend I failed . . . not least, by failure to let go of grief. My family?"

She sighed and stretched. "Well, my children have turned out well. And I've been a good owner to my serfs, with one exception. Yo', of course. It was wrong to torture yo', hurt yo' beyond what was necessary to compel obedience. Actin' like a weasel, to assuage my own hurt."

"Are . . . " Marya hesitated. "Are you *apologizing* to me, Mistis?" There was an overtone of shock in her voice.

Yolande opened one eye and grinned. "It's rare but not unknown," she said. More seriously: "Marya, I know you've never accepted the Yoke, not in yo' heart. But yo' behavior's been impeccable for more than twenty years, which means my obligation is to treat yo' as a good serf. I . . . seriously violated that, back when." Her smile turned rueful. "I'd consider letting yo' go, were it practical. Or just giving yo' a cottage on the Island and letting yo' live out y' years." She owned one of the Seychelles islands outright, but seldom visited it.

"Mistis? May I speak frankly?" Yolande nodded, and the serf continued. "You don't feel in the least, ah, disturbed about enslaving me, but using this"—she raised the controller cuff—"makes you feel, mmm, guilty?"

Yolande linked her hands behind her neck. "Slightly *ashamed*, not guilty; such a bourgeois emotion, guilt." She frowned. "Not about—yes, enslavin' is the correct term, I suppose—no. Yo' not of the Race; I am. My destiny to rule, yours to obey and serve. Obedience and submission: protection and guidance. Perfectly proper."

The Draka studied the serf's face, which had taken on the careful blankness of suppressed expression. "One reason besides Gwen I've kept yo' around, not off somewheres clerkin' or something. Yo' so *different*. It's refreshin', keeps me on my toes mentally, like doin' unarmed practice against different opponents. Here." She snapped open a case on the table beside her, brought out two pair of reader goggles. "I'm promotin' yo' to Literate V-a."

That gave unlimited access to the datastores. Except for information under War or Security lock, of course, and Citizen personal files; it was the classification for top-level civilian-sector serfs. Very rare for someone not born in the Domination. Yolande tossed the other pair to Marya and put on her own; they had laser and micromirror sets in the earpieces, so that you saw the presentation on an adjustable "screen" before your eyes.

She sighed again. *One more time at the data, and maybe I can make sense of them.*

CHAPTER NINETEEN

Planet AC-IV: Code-Name *Samothrace*

Samothrace is terrestroid to a high degree. Diameter is .97 Standard, and density indicates a metallic core with a shell of silicates, as with Earth. Atmospheric analysis shows an oxygen-nitrogen atmosphere, with somewhat higher concentrations of the noble gases and slightly less water vapor; there is a small icecap in the north polar region, although none in the south. Continental outlines are compatible with a plate-tectonic model; land area is 40% of total, rather higher than Earth, but there is no large mass comparable to Africa/Eurasia at present. Surface area is markedly concentrated in the North Temperate Zone. There are twin satellites, each of roughly .5 the size of Luna; these have been provisionally named "Thoreau" and "Emerson."

Current planetographic theory indicates that the observed data can only be accounted for by a developed biosphere based on sea- and land-growing photosynthetic plants, presumably with analogs to the animal phyla as well. There is, however, no indication of intelligent life: no industrial-era changes in the atmospheric composition, no observable engineering works or large-city lights, and certainly no space travel or even modulated emissions in the electromagnetic communications wavelengths. However, the Committee wishes to point out that even space-based VLT[1] and electromagnetic scanners have their limitations, and an investigation of Earth from similar distances would have revealed no indications of intelligent life as recently as 1800.

Furthermore, while the oxygen-rich atmosphere indicates roughly similar patterns of biological development, very wide differences in detail are to be anticipated.

Leaving aside the outer planets and what orbital perturbation indicates is a substantial population of asteroids, there are four other large rocky masses. The three inner ones appear to be roughly comparable to Mercury: subterrestrial in size, and airless. Beyond Samothrace, at 1.7 AU, is another planet of approximately .57 Standard diameters, showing signs of a predominantly carbon dioxide-inert gas atmosphere at a surface pressure equivalent to the 5,000-meter level on Earth; there are also indications of liquid water and water vapor. Mars is the obvious parallel in the solar system, but this planet—preliminary name "Jefferson"—is nearly twice the size and rather closer to the primary; conditions more closely resemble the current theory's picture of Mars several billion years ago. Terraforming operations would be much simpler than the ones projected for Mars, however.

The asteroidal bodies . . .

From: The Alpha Centauri System
Fifth Study Committe Summary
Recruit Orientation and Introduction
New America Project, Level III
Most Secret
July 17, 1997

CENTRAL OFFICE, ARCHONAL PALACE
ARCHONA
DOMINATION OF THE DRAKA
MARCH 27, 1998
1700 HOURS

"*Sweet—Mother—Freya*," Yolande said, looking wide-eyed at her uncle. Rank and station, the slight residual awe this office evoked, all vanished. "Shitfire!"

Footnote #1 Very Large Telescopes, including the 10-kilometer Farside instruments.

"Both appropriate," he said, rising stiffly and walking to the sideboard. "So is a drink . . . Arch-Strategos."

For a moment even the news she had just heard could not block a stab of concern. *He looks so much older.* Nearly eighty, but with modern medicine that was only late middle age. Still straight, but he moved with care, and the lines were graven deeper into the starved-eagle face, below the thick white hair. It was a killing job, this; his pallor was highlighted by the dark indigo of his jacket and the black lace of his cravat. Then the immensity of what she had heard swept back, and she felt her stomach swoop again. *My teeth want to chatter.*

She accepted the glass and knocked half of it back; eau-de-vie. The warmth spread in her belly, and she closed her eyes to let the information sink in.

"Uncle, this is the best news I've had since . . . Loki, I don't know."

"Is it?" He sank down behind the desk. "Is it really?"

Yolande looked up, met the cold gray eyes, and refused to be daunted. "Uncle Eric—Excellence—I've spent the past decade dead-certain convinced that we were headin' fo' the Final War without a *prayer* of comin' out on top. Yo' just gave me hope fo' myself, not so important. For my children and the Race, rather more so!"

He nodded and rested his face in his hands for a moment before raising his drink.

"Now yo' know, daughter of my sister, what only a dozen other people outside Virunga Biocontrol know—and we've kept the ones who worked on the project locked up tighter than a headhunter's heart." For an instant his voice went flat-soft. "Yo' realize, even the *suspicion* that yo' *might* reveal this would mean a pill?"

Yolande one hand in a gesture of acceptance. A bullet in the back of the head was an occupational risk, at the highest levels of command and power. "And when is acceptable-saturation?" she continued.

"Well . . . " Uncle Eric seemed oddly reluctant. "This year, accordin' to projections. No way to be absolutely sure, so they put a large margin of error in. Didn't want a whole-sale infection; that would increase the chance of detection too much. We coded a stop; it replicates a certain number of times and then goes noninfectious. Then we used unknowin' vectors for the various targets: their command an' control echelons, Space Force and so forth. There may be some spillover to the bulk of their military, even civilians, but not much. Yo' little brush beyond Luna gave us a random sample that fitted right in with our best-case hypothesis."

"Trigger?" she said.

"Coded microwave; resonates, activates it. Irregular period beyond that, but once it starts, stress accelerates the process."

"No way of shieldin'?"

"Not unless yo' know. Heavy tranquilizers an' psychotropics can mitigate the effects, until the thing cycles itself out; takes about four, five days iff'n the subject is restrained that way. But even so, yo' not worth much in that condition. Questionin' the test subject indicates it's like . . . a combination of *Berserkergang* and paranoid schizophrenia, with some mighty nasty hallucinations thrown in. Works best on the highly intelligent."

Yolande sipped again at the fiery liquid, imagining the consequences. In the crowded workstations of a battle platform, in the tight-knit choreography of a warship's control center. A hard grin fought its way toward her face, was pressed back.

"Effectiveness?" she asked.

"Depends . . . they're more automated than we are, but they still haven't cut humans out of their action loops, not at the initiation stage. Given surprise, an' an all-out attack along with it, the projections indicate we could take out their Earth-orbit capacity to about ninety percent, and still come through with enough of our own to block what little of their offensive strength survived. We've built redundant, fo' exactly that purpose."

"Ah," Yolande exclaimed. "The Militants, they must know, too! *That's* why they're confident enough to talk openly about startin' the Final War."

"Their top triumvirate. Gayner was in on it from the beginnin'. The rest, no, of course not. They're just the bloodthirsty nihilistic loons they come across as."

"Shitfire," Yolande whispered again. The alcohol seemed to slide down her throat without effect. "Gayner nearly lost it right there on the viewer when yo' got the reelection vote, back in '97," she said.

Eric smiled thinly. "One of my mo' pleasant memories. She was wild to be in this chair when we reached go-level." A harsh laughter. "What immortality, fo' the Archon who led the Race to victory in the Final War? Someone in that position could do anythin', get any program put through. Trouble would be to keep the Citizenry from electin' him—or her—to godhood."

"When do we attack?" Yolande said.

"Yo', too," the Archon said with resigned bitterness. "I've been hearin' that question with increasin' frequency fo' six months now. Accompanied by thinly veiled threats, from Gayner and her cutthroats."

She looked at him bewildered for a moment, then felt her eyes narrow. "Why *not*, fo' Wotan's sake?" she said. "Every moment we hesitate longer than we have to is deadly-dangerous. Use it or we risk losin' it."

Eric gave a jerk of his chin. "Oh, yes. They behind in biotech, but makin' slow progress . . . and computer analysis is basic to that, too. The rate of increase in computer technology is slowin'—the experts say it's pushin' the theoretical limits with known architectures—but it hasn't *stopped*. Sooner or later, they'll get a clue; if nothin' else, from the strategic deployment choices we've been makin'. On the other hand . . ." He looked up at her and tapped his fingers on the desk. "This incident of yourn, it wasn't the bioanalysis of the prisoners that got yo' interested initially, was it?"

"No. *Somethin'* destroyed that stingfighter. Some sort of interference with they infosystems."

"*Our* nightmare. And they've been *matchin'* our deployments. Increasin' the proportion of orbit-to-ground weapons. Exactly the sort of thing yo'd put in, if yo' expected to be in a position to hammer Earth from space with impunity."

"Wait," Yolande said with alarm. "They *could* just be matchin' us tit fo' tat. Their buildup didn't start until well after our current six-year plan."

"But it points to *somethin'* they are doin' to *us*. And . . ." he hesitated. "I saw the results of nuclear weapons, in Europe, back at the end of the last war. Stoppin' *almost* everythin' isn't the same as stoppin' *everythin'*." He looked out through the wall, at the lights of the city winking on below, and continued very softly. "Not to mention how many of them we'd have to kill. Not to mention . . . " He looked up.

"Arch-Strategos, the final decision in these matters is mine; the responsibility comes with the office. We will move when I authorize."

Yolande rose and set the peaked cap on her head. "Understood, Excellence," she said, saluting. Then: "I'm takin' a week's leave, Uncle Eric. That all right?"

"Oh, yes. We won't begin the war without you, niece," he said. "Besides, it'll keep the enemy from wonderin' what yo' doin' back on Earth."

Yolande grinned at the sarcasm; it was just like Uncle Eric. *A little too squeamish*, she thought. *But basically a good man.*

"Service to the State," she said.

"Glory to the Race," he replied.

She left, and he turned down the lights, watching the multicolored glow of Archona below. Minutes stretched, and he sat motionless. "Glory indeed," he said. His mouth twisted. "Glory."

SPIN HABITAT SEVEN
NEW AMERICA PROJECT
CENTRAL BELT, ALLIANCE INTERDICTED ZONE
BETWEEN THE ORBITS OF MARS AND JUPITER
MARCH 31, 1998

"First-rate dinner," Manuel Obregon said.

Cindy Lefarge nodded thanks and finished loading the dishes into the washer. She touched a control and the cylindrical hopper sank into the counter-top. A quiet hum sounded through the serving window. The Lefarge living-dining area was open-plan in the manner that had become fashionable in the '70s, when the price of live-in help rose beyond the budgets of the upper middle class. *It always was, here in the Belt*, she thought with slight cynicism. *Amazing how fast domestic gadgets got invented when it was really necessary.* The thought was a welcome distraction from what would be said tonight. She picked up the tray with the coffee and carried it around to set on the table.

There were six others dining at Brigadier Lefarge's house that night, four men and two women. Department heads, or in two cases shockingly *not*, a few steps further down the chain of command. They shifted uneasily, buying a few more minutes passing sugar and cream around until everyone was settled; these were people of authority, but not military, not conspirators. Scientists for the most part, or scientific administrators at least, engineers, used to hard-material problems and juggling workers and resources. This smelled political, and not office politics either.

"All right," Fred said abruptly. Cindy could feel a harshness behind the tone, the same force that had been hagriding him since his return from Earth. There were new lines graven in the heavy-boned face, down from nose to mouth. "First, let me say you're all here because I trust you. Your intentions, and your ability to keep your mouths shut. We've all worked together for . . . at least a decade now. You've all shown that you are willing to cut yourselves off from the outside world to work on the Project in its various phases." He paused, looked down at his hands for a moment. "I think most of you who haven't been told have guessed; the *New America* is not the only purpose of this installation."

Ali Harahap nodded. "Indeed so," he said in his singsong Sumatran accent, lighting a cigarette that smelled sharply of cloves. "But what is not said, cannot be betrayed." There were more nods around the table.

"Good man." Fred nodded, satisfied. "That was the right attitude. It isn't anymore. Before I go on, I want to make clear that what I'm about to say is unauthorized. If this ever gets out, I could be shot." A slight intake of breath among the others. "And all of you could be ruined, your careers ended. Does anyone want to leave?"

Colin McKenzie laughed shakily and wiped at the sweat on his high forehead; he was Quebec-Scots, a heavy-construction man. "Wouldn't do any good, would it, unless we finked? And you're the OSS rep here, Fred."

The security chief waited. When a minute had gone by, he turned to de Ribeiro. "Fill them in, professor."

"We all know we have been building a starship," he began, stroking his goatee, "with surprising success—Although the only way to test it is to undertake the voyage. Scarcely a low-risk method! Many of you have suspected that the reason for this is as a last-ditch guarantee against defeat, to preserve something if the Alliance falls."

Patricia Hayato nodded. "We've all gotten used to secret projects," she said. "Since the War, every five years another group of scientists drops out of sight. The Los Alamos Project pattern. Mistaken, in my opinion. It sacrifices long-term to short-term; more suitable for wartime than the Protracted Struggle."

De Ribeiro inclined his head graciously. "What is the best disguise? A disguise that is no disguise at all. Here we hid the *New America* within a series of concentric shells of secret projects, each one genuine. Within the *New America*, the ultimate secret. A weapon."

Hayato threw up her hands. "Oh, no, not some super-bomb!" Everyone else winced slightly; the rain of fission weapons that had brought down the Japanese Empire to-wards the end of the Eurasian War was still a sensitive subject. "Just what we need, more firepower. What have you discovered, a way to make the Sun go nova?"

Lefarge rapped sharply on the table. "Ladies, gentlemen, we've all been cooped up with each other so long our argu-ments have gotten repetitive. Let the professor speak, please."

The Brazilian examined his fingertips. "We've developed a weapon that is no weapon—which should appeal to you, my dear colleague." Hayato flushed; she took neozen more seri-ously than the founders of that remarkably playful philosophy might have wished. "You were quite right; bigger and better means of destruction have reached a point of self-defeating futility. But consider what *controls* those weapons."

"Dataplague," Henry Wasser said. He was head of the antimatter drive systems, and worked most closely with the Infosystems Division de Ribeiro directed. "I always did think you had too much facility for what we needed."

De Ribeiro beamed; he had always had something of the teacher about him, and enjoyed a sharp student. "Exactly." A sip of coffee. "To be more precise, contamination of the embedded compinstruction sets of mainbrain computers, the cores." The white-haired Brazilian sighed. "Their complexity has reached a point barely comprehensible even to us, and the Domination's people are somewhat behind." He brooded for a moment. "The paranoia both sides labor under has been a terrible handicap. Both in designing our little infovirus, and in spreading it. The absolute barrier between data-storage and compinstruction . . ." Another silence. "Still, perhaps our errors in design have spared us certain temptations, certain risks. Often I feel that computers might have been as much a snare, a means of subverting our basic humanity, as the Draka biocontrol. As it is, we have reached a limit and will probably go no further—" Lefarge rapped on the table again, and he started.

"Sí. In any case, it was unleashed perhaps a year ago. It

spreads slowly, from one manufacturing center to another, as improved instruction-sets are handed out. In the event of war—" he grinned—"The Draka will find their machines . . . rebellious."

"And when enough are infected, the Alliance would move. That was the original plan." Lefarge looked around the table. "We're cut off here. Not from the latest fashions or slang; we get those coming in. But from the movement of thought, opinion, the climate of feeling. They've relaxed, down there, this past decade. They've started to think there might be some alternative to kill-or-be-killed. Fewer and fewer clashes, no big incidents. The Draka have been cutting back on their ground forces; these so-called 'reforms' . . . "

His fist thumped the boards. "They know enough to see that *tanks* aren't going to win them any more wars. And a better-treated slave is still a slave . . . Hell, I don't have to tell *you* all this. The crux of it is, they've changed the plans, there in San Fran. They're thinking in terms of an ultimatum; demonstrating our capacity, then demanding that the Draka back down, accept disarmament as a prelude to"—his mouth twisted—"*gradual reform*."

Their eyes turned to Hayato. The lifesystems specialist fiddled with her cup. "No," she said. "It wouldn't work." Meeting their regard: "Yes, I know I've made myself unpopular by saying Japan would have surrendered without cities being destroyed by nuclear weapons. I still think so. The Domination is a different case entirely. The old militarist caste in Japan, they could surrender, sacrifice themselves for the benefit of the nation. The Draka, the Citizens, their caste *is* their nation. If that's destroyed, everything worthwhile in the universe is gone, and they'd bring the world down with them out of sheer spite."

Lefarge turned his hands palm-up. "Anyone think different?"

McKenzie hesitated, then spoke. "Fred . . . Look, I'm just a glorified high-iron man. What the hell do I know? That's what we've got spooks like you for, and a government we elected, come to that. Policy's their department."

Lefarge opened his mouth to speak. Hayato cut in: "That's bullshit, Colin, and you know it. We've got the power; that means we have the responsibility to make a decision, one way or another. And it *is* a decision, either way."

He slumped. "I've got kin back on Earth," he said.

"We all do," Lefarge said. "Every indication of the way

they've configured their off-Earth forces, every intuition I've built up about Draka behavior, tells me that the Snakes have some sort of ace in the hole comparable to us. It's a race, and we know for a fact that they won't hesitate a moment once they're ready; *they* aren't going to suffer from divided counsels. That's why we've got to act. Right, let's have a show of hands."

One by one, they went up. McKenzie's last of all, but definitely.

"I hope everybody realizes we're committed? Good, here's what we do. First, we make *multiple* insertions of the infovirus; we're set up for it. Next—"

Cindy Lefarge held her husband's hand. The grip was strong enough to be painful, but she squeezed back patiently, waiting in the silence of the emptied room.

"Am I doing the right thing?" he asked at last, in a haunted voice.

"It's what Uncle Nate wanted, honey," she whispered back.

"Yes, but . . . he was an old, *old* man by that time."

"And he'd taught you to think for yourself!" she replied sharply. He looked up, startled, as she continued.

"You wouldn't be doing this if you didn't think it was right," Cindy went on. "For what it's worth, I agree . . . but you know what Uncle Nate always said: 'you take the choice, you bear the responsibility.' " More gently: "I can't be sure that what you're doing is right, Fred. But I'm behind you, and I always will be."

"I know," he said, and raised her hand to his cheek. His shoulders were still slumped, as if under an invisible weight. "I'm left with another question. Is what I'm doing *enough*?"

INGOLFSSON ISLAND PRESERVE
SEYCHELLES DISTRICT
ZANJ COAST PROVINCE
DOMINATION OF THE DRAKA
APRIL 2, 1998

Marya Lefarge shaded her eyes and looked out over the waves. It was a clear day, and the afternoon sun was white light on the hammered indigo metal of the ocean; there was enough wind to ruffle it, throwing foam crests on the waves and up the talc-fine powder sand of the beach. The endless background hiss of the light surf was the loudest sound; above her the wicker sunshade thuttered, and the fronds of the coconut palms rustled over that.

Out in the water the three Draka were playing, and she could see their bodies flashing through the surface layers. Then they were in the shallows, and Gwen and her young man swept Yolande up between them. They came trotting up the beach with an effortless stride; New Race muscles could do on Earth what ordinary humans did in low-gravity.

She studied them as they washed off the salt under a worked-bronze waterspout and walked over to the blanket and deckchairs. You could see the differences better nude and wet; slight variances in the way the joints moved, the pattern of muscles sliding under tight brown skin. It was natural; they could secrete melanin until they were at home under this equatorial sun or pale to cream white at will; tablets had done that for Yolande and herself. No body hair, save for the scalp and the pubic bush. They walked unconcerned over sand that had made the elder Draka slip on thong-sandals. Yolande moved with the studied grace of a lifelong athlete in hard training; the younger pair had the fluid suppleness of leopards.

Oh, Gwen, she thought. *It was easier when you were a child.* A saddening thing, not to be able to wish luck and happiness to one you loved.

"Remind me not to play tag with yo' New Race types," Yolande was saying, her hands resting on their shoulders. "I wonder that yo' puts up with us fossils."

"Oh, we've got time," the man chuckled. He was a handspan past six feet, with a head of loose white-gold ringlets.

That they do, Marya thought with a slight shiver in the warm tropical day. They were in their early twenties, and it would be two centuries before they showed much sign of age. *How can even Draka bear to cut themselves off from their descendants so?*

Gwen gave her companion a good-natured thump on the ribs. "A little mo' respect for my momma, there," she said. "See yo' up at the house, Alois."

"Gwen. Miz Ingolfsson," he nodded to the two.

Yolande threw herself down on the blanket and stretched. "Nice boy," she said. "Drink, please, Marya."

Marya smiled to herself as she opened the basket and took

the pitcher from the cooler. Yolande regarded her daughter's newfound enthusiasm for the opposite sex with tolerant indulgence, as appropriate for her age. To the elder Ingolfsson, Marya suspected, men were nice enough in their way, often pleasing, but with some exceptions basically rather stupid and prisoner to their emotions. Not an uncommon attitude among female Citizens . . . She glanced up and met Gwen's eyes; for a moment they shared amusement.

"Ma," Gwen said, taking one of the chairs. "Do me a favor?"

"Anythin', child of my heart," Yolande said, accepting the chilled papaya juice. "Thank yo', Marya. Have what yo' like."

"It's that damned controller cuff," Gwen was saying. Marya froze for a moment, with a feeling of insects crawling on her skin, then made her hands busy themselves in the basket. "Tantie-ma's never said much about it, but it makes my backbone crawl. Take it off her, would yo'?"

"Ah." Yolande rose on one elbow and considered the serf. "As a matter of fact . . . Hand me that case from the bottom of the basket, would yo', Marya?"

There was a thin leather binder about the size of a small book; the serf's hands shook slightly as she handed it to her owner, kneeling beside her. She had not noticed it, slipped in among the bowls and packages and softcover volumes of poetry brought along for a day by the ocean. Yolande opened it and took out a slim jack on the end of a coil cord.

"Hold out yo' hand, wench," Yolande said.

It was shaking worse as the Draka took it and slid the jack into an opening on the front edge of the thin metal circlet. The bright sun darkened and the world blurred before Marya's eyes. She saw Yolande's fingers touching controls within the opened binder. There was a tingling in her wrist, and a subdued *click*. Marya heard herself whimper slightly as the metal unclasped; the skin beneath it was very white. Angry, she caught her lower lip in her teeth as Yolande turned her palm up and dropped the cuff into it. The metal was still warm from her skin.

"Do what yo' want with it," the Draka said.

Marya looked at it. Feeling the tears cutting tracks down her cheeks, and making herself remember the *pain*. It had been twenty-four years, and not a day had passed when she had not suppressed that memory; now she let the holds crack. The two Draka were looking politely aside as she rose unsteadily to her feet and walked out into the light, down to the edge of the water. The sand was scorching through the thin sandals, the waves cool as she walked into their knee-high curling. There was an intense smell of ocean, of iodine from the seaweed along the high-water mark. A gull went by overhead, shadow against dazzle, *grawk-grawk-grawk*. Her arm went back, seeming to drift. Forward with an elastic snap, and the cuff was soaring until it was a dot. Hesitating at the top of its arc, then dropping down at gathering speed. A last *plek* as it broke the smooth curve of a wave in a tiny eruption of white.

Gone. She dropped to her knees and bent forward, heedless of the ends of her hair trailing in the foam. *Gone.*

Yolande looked back to her daughter with a smile. "That seemed to go well, honeychile," she said.

Gwen nodded and lay back on the deckchair to spare the serf intrusive eyes. "Thank yo', ma," she said.

Yolande shrugged. *How strong and beautiful, and how sweet with it*, she thought. It was an ache in the chest, pride and love beyond bearing. *Me and Myfwany—you have the best of us both*, she thought. *Of both your mothers.* Marya was still down by the water's edge. *Or all three.*

Gwen took a fig from the basket and nibbled. "Almost a shame to be leavin'," she said happily. "It's been a good three days, just yo' and the sibs, ma."

"Liar," Yolande said amiably. "Y'all are indulgin' me, and I know it. Yo' thoughts are divided about equal between the new ship an' dancin' the mattress gavotte with Alois; he's likewise, and polite to me because he's got long-term designs on yo'. Holden is bored in the manner of six-year-olds, and Nikki"—she shrugged again; her oldest son was fifteen—"likes it here because there are a whole new set of housegirls to lay. Plus good spearfishing."

Gwen laughed, turning her eyes skyward. "*Lionheart's* a real beauty, though, ma," she said musingly. "Gods, when we took her out fo' the shakedown! Deuterium-boron drives've got it all *ovah* the older types, the exhaust's *all* charged particles." Her voice took on a dreamy tone. "Fifty thousand tonnes payload, she's fitted out like a liner! Even a spin-deck at one G. Only—"

"Gwen."

"—two months to Pluto! Granted we'll be there a year settin' up the base, but—"

"Gwen, honeychile, *I was on the design committee.*"

Her daughter laughed and waved acknowledgment. "Sorry, ma."

"You've been noble not talkin' shop, Gwen. I recognize true love when I hears it."

"And, well, I *am* sorry to be leavin' yo'. And not . . . Know what I mean?"

"Oh, yes, child of my heart, I know *exactly.*" A long laugh, and she reached up to squeeze a shoulder. "Fo' reasons too numerous to state, I'm feeling first-rate just now. But yo' are always a . . . string of lights around my heart, child. Ah, here comes Marya."

Gwen rose. The serf stopped at arm's length and threw back her head; she had never stooped, but Yolande thought she saw a different curve to the neck. "Thank you, Missy Gwen," she said.

The young Draka embraced her. "Always welcome, Tantie-ma," she said. "Well—"

Her mother made scooting motions. "Alois and yo' have notions on how to spend the afternoon. Honestly, with an eighteen-month cruise ahead of yo'—"

"Ma!"

"But youth will be served. Or serviced—"

"*Ma!*" Mock-indignation.

"Run along, yo' Tantie-ma and I will find *some* way to pass the time." Yolande winked, and thought she caught a hint of real embarrassment on her daughter's face. *One thing that hardly changes*, she thought. *It never seems quite natural when the older generation doesn't lose interest.*

"Strange, Mistis," Marya said, watching the child she had borne walk away into the palms and oleander and hibiscus.

"How so?" Yolande turned her attention back to the serf. Her half-hour by the waves seemed to have composed her, at least. The coffee-brown synthtan suited her, as well.

"When . . . when she was little, she was so helpless as I held her. Now I can feel how gentle she's being hugging me, and she could crush me like an eggshell. Strange to remember her so tiny."

"True enough. Lie down here."

Marya sat beside the Draka, wrapping her arms around her shins and laying her head on her knees.

"You want me?" she said, smiling faintly.

"Yo' and a snack and a nap befo' dinner," Yolande said. "Settle for the snack and nap if yo' tuckered out."

"Not yet," Marya said, with the same slight curve of her lips. "You have been very . . . energetic, since Archona."

"Good news does that to me, and no, I can't tell you what."

CLAESTUM PLANTATION
DISTRICT OF TUSCANY
PROVINCE OF ITALY
DOMINATION OF THE DRAKA
APRIL 4, 1998

"Hello, Myfwany," Yolande said, sitting by the grave with her elbows on her knees. Wind cuffed at the spray of roses.

There was another nearby, now, her father's. There were a few clouds today, white and fluffy. The air was just warm enough to be comfortable sitting still, with an undertone of freshness that was like a cool drink after the tropical heat.

"Tina's coming along well," she continued. "Gods, it'll be interestin' to see what a merger of my genes and yourn comes out to! With all the little improvements they puttin' in these days."

The wind ruffled the outer leaves of the flowers. They were still a little damp from the sprayer in the arbor where she had picked them. Yolande leaned forward to smell the intense wild scent.

"And Gwen . . . ah, love, yo'd be proud of her. Assistant Com officer on this new ship, the *Lionheart*. Exploration voyage, really; establishin' a study-base for the outer system and the Oort clouds. Cold out there . . . Hope it works out for her. Hope she settles with Alois, he's a good sort."

She smiled and touched the flowers and the short dense grass. "And there's somethin' else. Wotan and the White Christ, it's so secret I hardly dare tell *yo'*, sweet! Gods witness, I'd begun to despair of the whole Domination, we seemed to be goin' nowhere, until Uncle Eric let me in on the secret. Been in the plannin' since"—she swallowed—"since befo' India. A chance to put an end to the struggle, once and fo' all."

Yolande stopped for a moment. *This is the most painful pleasure of my life*, she thought. "I'm . . . worried, though.

About Uncle Eric. He's . . . not frightened—it's just so *easy* to be indecisive at these levels, love! Always easier not to decide. He hates the idea of usin' it, takin' the risk. Even of the killin' involved." Slowly: "I admit it, love, I don't like the idea either. The fighters . . . they take they chances, same as I. Always hated hurtin' the helpless, and as fo' throwin' sunfire across the land . . ." she made a grimace of disgust, looking out across the hills of her birth-country. Birds went overhead, a flock almost enough to hide the sky for an instant.

She hammered a fist on her knee. "But what can we *do*, love? I could live with the thought of everythin' bein' destroyed, when there was no choice. Now there *is*. And the longer we wait, the worse. Ah, Myfwany, it's so hard to know what's *right*."

Shaking her head, she rose and dusted her uniform. "I wish yo' were here, honeysweet," she said. "I promise . . . I'll do my best fo' the children. Goodbye fo' now, my love. Till we meet again."

"What the hell is *that*?" Marya exclaimed. "Mistis," she added hastily.

"That," Yolande replied, "is the most expensive toy evah built."

She had managed to shake most of the crowd of officials at Florence Airhaven; even the officer from TechSec, who was reasonably interesting when he got onto the yacht's construction. *Enough of crowding back on Luna*, she thought, and besides, she had checked out fairly thoroughly on the simulators. They were almost alone on the floater; even this backwater had modernized maglev runways, now. The craft before them was *not* something it had seen before, or most other airhavens in the Domination, either. Ninety meters long, a slender tapering wedge; the bottom of the hull curved up at the rear into the slanted control fins. There were control-cabin windows at the bow, scramjet intakes below the rear edge. And what looked like a huge four-meter bell pointing backward at the stern.

"It's from the test program fo' the fifth generation pulse-drives, the Rex class." A sliver of afternoon light fell within the thrustplate, and glittered off the lining. "Synthetic single-crystal thrustplate, stressed-matrix/mag equalizers, deuterium-boron-11 reaction. They had two of the first units left ovah. Decided to try matin' them to a heavy scramjet assault-transport; first Earth-surface to deepspace craft ever built, is the result." A Yankee might have junked the test units, but Draka engineers had a rooted abhorrence of throwing anything that still worked away.

"The power-to-weight's good enough yo' could take off on the pulsedrive," Yolande continued, as they came to the lift and stepped on board. It hummed quietly and swept them past the black undersurface heatshield; the top of the craft was dark as well, but the texture was subtly different. "Though that wouldn't be neighborly. Actually it's a waddlin' monster in atmosphere, and mostly fuel tank inside; liquid hydrogen, of course. Got good legs, though; that reaction is *energetic*. Yo' could make it to Mars or even the Belt, iff'n yo' didn't mind arrivin' dry."

They stepped through the open door. It swung shut behind them, and she took a deep breath. Filtered air, the subliminal hum of life-support systems; pale glowpanel light, and the neutral surfaces of synthetic and alloy. *Space*, Yolande thought. Even though they were still on the surface, it had an environment all its own. She ducked her head through the connecting door into the control cabin. There were comfortable quarters aft; it was essentially a very expensive yacht.

Not that they're likely to become a hot item anytime soon, she thought wryly. Even discounting the cost of the drive as part of the research overhead, the *Mamba* would price in at about the combined family worth of the Ingolfssons and the von Shrakenbergs. For now, the Archon and the Commandant of Aresopolis were assigned one each.

She returned the pilot's salute. The control deck was horseshoe shaped, with pilot and copilot forward, Weapons and Sensors to either side on the rear. Only the two pilots were here now, of course.

"Pilot Breytenbach," she said to the number two. "Yo' can go aft; I'll sit in on this." Yolande grew conscious of her servant hovering behind. "Well, come in, wench." Marya flinched slightly, fingering the bare strip on her wrist; the controller cuff would have shocked her away from activated military comp systems like this. Yolande saw her take a deep breath and step forward. *Good wench*, she thought.

"That crashcouch," she said, indicating the Sensor station. She swung herself into the copilot's seat and pulled the restraints down. "All yourn, Pilot," she said. He nodded briefly, running his eyes in a last check over the screens.

"Highly cybered," Yolande said, indicating the control panels. " 'Less yo' has to fight her"—*in which case yo' bumfucked, because those lasers are a joke*—"menu-commands to take yo' anywheres within range."

She settled back happily. "I'll take ovah out of atmosphere," she said. They would be back to the world of the Commandant's office soon enough. *TechSec designs a toy, I might as well use it,* she reflected. The big vehicle lifted off the runway with the peculiar greasy feel of maglev and turned toward the long reach.

CHAPTER TWENTY

All human beings are conscious of the process of choice, of choosing between alternative courses of action. Yet we are also and inevitably conscious of the *limits* of choice; if we see a three-tonne weight falling towards us, we have the "choice" of jumping or being crushed. Free will may appear absolute in the abstract, but in the real, concrete world in which we live it often seems a mere illusion, a mental construct. My own opinion is that both propositions are true, and that reality reflects this in a number of ways. First, the constraining situation within which an individual finds himself is itself the result of countless *previous* decisions. It is their sum total, forming an interacting field which we can never escape. So instead of an unconstrained fan reaching out in all directions, our choices are more in the nature of a set of tracks within canyon walls. For the most part, the walls are narrow; we can veer a little to one side or the other, but the main direction is fixed. Moreover, even to use this small degree of latitude takes *effort*, to move the "wheels" of our path from one set of tracks to another.

Sometimes the canyon walls open out for a time; *then* the fan of possibilities spreads, into a delta of radiating alternatives. Time presses. One or another alternative must be chosen. Once the choice is made, the course of a life—or a nation, or a world—is set on a new path. And the choice an individual makes becomes in turn immutable destiny for others, foreclosing *their* alternatives.

Such changes of path may be the result of continuous effort, or an ever-vigilant readiness to seize the moment. Most terrifying of all, they may be the result of nothing more than raw accident . . .

Meditations on a Life
by Eric von Shrakenberg
Central Press, Archona
2003

DRAKA FORCES BASE ARESOPOLIS
MARE SERENITATIS, LUNA
NOVEMBER 1, 1998
0930 HOURS

"Sector Seven, Level Twelve," the transporter capsule said. The lid hissed open, and Marya stepped out.

"Ident," the guard said. The room was a narrow box with only one exit, brightly lit and completely bare, smelling of cold rock. The guard was in Security Directorate green, battle-armored and carrying a gauntlet gun; his head turned toward her like a mirrored globe, her own distorted face reflecting off the helmet shield.

She stepped up to the exit and laid her hand against the screen set in the wall beside it. "Marya E77AI422, property of Arch-Strategos Ingolfsson, Commandant, on personal errand."

Her mouth was tissue-paper, and the pulsebeat in her ears roared louder than trumpets. This was action, covert action. It was impossible to disguise, impossible to cover, no matter her skill on the infonet. Recognition sets were embedded in the central brains, and flagging from a station with this priority was direct-routed down to read-only memory. It would stand out, stand *out*, the minute anyone did a search on her activities today. Even the most dimwitted Orpo would notice someone being in two places at once.

Only for you, my brother, she thought, controlling the impulse to shudder. The message had been like none she ever received. Far longer. Not just instructions on a new drop, a new contact-code; orders to *do*. The thing she carried at her belt. *Something is very wrong here. Fred's never been in the loop before, neither of us would dare.*

The screen flicked light at her eyes. A laser read the pattern of her retina; the information sped away as modulated light. Another scanned her palmprint, the abstract of her voice. Information flowed into a central computer's ready-storage peripheral; embedded instruction sets were tripped. Data from deep storage was copied, run through a translator into analog form, compared. Another code-phrase tripped a set in the response machine.

"Confirmed. Marya E77AI422, property of Arch-Strategos Ingolfsson, Commandant. Literate Class V-a. Delay, query." The idiot-savant routines would be calling her owner's private quarters. Marya breathed in, calmly. That was where the interception loop she had established would work; or not. The machine spoke again: "Query, confirmed. E77AI422, proceed."

The guard nodded. "Confirmed. Present, wench," he said. Marya turned and bent back her head to bare the serf-tattoo beneath her right ear. There was a box clipped to the serf policeman's waist; he pulled free a light-pencil on a coil cord and ran the tip down her tattoo. The box chirped, encoding her ident on a dataplaque within; another footprint.

With a slight hiss, the door opened. Marya noted the thickness of it, featureless sandwich-armour alloy. The corridor beyond was plain, but there would be instruments and weapons in the walls. Another door, and she was out into a vestibule of the factory; more guards, crewing control-desks. They waved her through. She walked on, past color-coded doors and more corridors. Through a transparent tube, over a long room where workers bent to their micromanipulators and screens. They were assembling circular electrowafers in tubes, building the precoded stacks that contained the instruction sets for major computers and their closed-access internal memories. Others fitted the pillars of wafers into the rectangular platforms of the logic decks; she could imagine the submicroscopic tools soldering their gold-wire and optical-thread connections.

All familiar enough; the basic technology had not changed in a generation, despite vast improvements in detail. *And I've heard Draka complain the Alliance isn't introducing as many refinements for them to steal lately,* she recalled. Exterior data storage, translator/interfacer unit, memory, instruction sets, logic deck. And beyond this complex, the most crucial area of all, where the design teams' compinstruction data was turned into physical patterns for embedding in the cores . . .

"Hello," she said to the receptionist in the office area. Polite but not servile; she was a command-level officer's personal servant. Not as formally high-status as this expensively trained technical secretary, but they were both Class V-a's, and her owner outranked the Faraday Combine exec who ran this facility. "Is Master MacGregor in? The plant manager?"

The receptionist looked up from his keyboard, looked Marya up and down. "Your message?" he said. "Master MacGregor can't be interrupted, he's in conference."

He's checking my clothes, Marya thought. Silk shirt, pleated trousers, jeweled clasps on the sandals and belt. Obviously a houseserf, equally obvious from someone not to be offended.

"It's an invitation," she said. "From the Commandant." Marya held out a folded parchment sealed in gold with the Drakon signet, then pulled it back when the man reached for it. "Personal service." That *was* one of her duties, keeping track of the obligatory social functions Yolande hated, and seeing that the invitations were in harmony with the relative status of each participant. A personal hand-delivery to a Commandatura reception was just slightly more than MacGregor rated; just enough that no underling of sense would endanger it.

"Oh, excuse me." The serf's heavy Arab features knotted. "Ahhh . . . " There was a waiting area behind the desk, but that was for Citizens. "Here, I'll take you to his office. You can wait there, and give the invitation."

"Will he be long?" Marya said, with a frown of concern. "Mistress the Arch-Strategos Ingolfsson expects me back." *Sometime this evening, probably, but the rank ought to make you sweat*. Marya's owner took her lunches at her office, and it was vanishingly unlikely that her absence would be noted. Even less likely that anything would be made of it, Marya was authorized to leave the household and entitled to do so at discretion, so long as her work was done. *But every minute is another chance to be missed.*

"It's right this way," he continued. She followed; there was carpet here, muffling even the light sound feet made under Lunar gravity. He touched the wall, and a section slid upwards; *that's right, lay on the courtesy*. He *could* have made her wait in the hall, but it was never wise to antagonize one who had the ear of your superior's superior. She stepped through. A typical office chamber, big enough for pacing, with a holowall landscape, desk, workstation. That was activated, notes and papers left carelessly around the terminal. The release of tension was like nausea or orgasm. She turned that into a one-two-kneel motion, sinking down on her heels and closing her eyes, hands and invitation folded in her lap. The Perfect Servant, concentrated on the task in hand. *Go away,* she thought with deadly concentration at the receptionist. *Don't try to make polite conversation, don't offer me refreshment, go away.*

He did; she waited until the door closed, and sixty heartbeats beyond. When she rose, it was with a smooth economy of motion that wasted no second of time, time that she was buying with her life. There was no turning back; it could be months before she might have to use the pills carefully hoarded in her room, even years, but the clock was running from this moment.

Exec MacGregor had been careless, leaving his terminal up. A violation of procedure, even here in the heart of a guarded facility. Even behind a door only those with authorization could access. She took the dataplaques from the pouch at her waist and touched the keyboard.

-Work in progress-, she typed.

[Core memories. Actuation sequences.] A long string of codes; she picked out the ones she knew, the ones on the plaque she should have wiped but could not bear to, the one with her brother's image.

[Cr-ex 5-5 Btstation orbital: launch sequence. IFF.] *There.* Her fingers moved. *-Halt. Memcheck, active-.* Then the only time embedded sets were held in access memory. While they were being *transferred* to the cores. Feverishly, she checked the work-in-progress table on the status of the sets; they were finished, ready to be templated for the master-pattern in the assembly hall.

-Modification,- she typed.

[Delay.] Seconds of white terror. [Accepted. Load sequence.]

Marya stared at her hand until the slight tremor disappeared. She pushed the first of the palm-sized synthetic rectangles into the receptor.

-Create parallel file temp:1-

[File standing.]

-Load receptor D: seq-

An almost inaudible whine, as the reader/translator loaded the contents of the plaque into the virtual space she had created. Another. Another. There were five of the plaques. Three minutes in all; now for the difficult part. She gave silent thanks that the Domination used a standard working compinstruction language. There were three in the Alliance, not to mention illegals.

-Run temp:1 *comparison* workfile: *Cr-ex 5-5 keyphrase com; master-*

The screen flickered, as the computer matched the sets. [Congruence sector core: code exe.] The master recognition commands, friend-foe.

-Mergeset: modify workfile: *Cr-ex 5-5 keyphrase com: master-*

[Merging.] Long seconds, while the machine knitted the new symbols with the old, matching smoothly where the coded ends fitted the set. [Complete. Workfile 2temp:1.]

Shit, she thought. It was making duplicate drafts, not substituting.

-Compare workfile / workfile 2temp:1-

[Congruence 99.73 abs.]

-Wipe workfile-

[Query?]

-Wipe workfile-

[Query?]

"Oh, shit, shit, shit!" she said. *Think. Think, damn you, wench. What are you, Draka cattle or a human being?* The station and the table around it were littered with paper notes; this MacGregor was a worrier. Hated to do anything irrevocable. *Calmly. There are only a few ways you can alter the procedures.* Designer compinstruction sets were embedded as well, after all. A single note at the bottom of a stack, old and faded, in pencil.

Marya gave a shark-grin and returned her hands to the keyboard.

-Wipe workfile-

[Query?]

-coverass-

[Execute *-wipe* workfile-]

-Load workfile *seq all mainmem-*

[Unfind: query? namefile.]

"I got it, I got it!" Quickly now, but carefully.

-dename workfile 2temp:1 / *rename* workfile-

[Execute -*dename* workfile 2temp:1 / *rename* workfile-all.
Wipe wordfile 2temp:1?]
  -*command aff*-
[Execute -*wipe* workfile 2temp:1-]
Now to check; only an anal-retentive of the first order
would log under a code like this, but . . .
  -*time/work log* coverass *perscode/master*-
[Query? coverass unrec Logtime/work MG-A1?]
Marya looked at the time display in the lower right corner
of the screen; 09:41, exactly eleven minutes since she entered
the fabrication complex.
  -*time/work log thisdate MG-A1*-
[Inlog 08:00 01/07/98 lastsrk 09:29 dto MG-A1]
"Exactly why only designers get these free-access memories," she muttered to herself. "Too easy to cheat a little."
Her handkerchief dusted across the keyboard, no use making
it easy for the greencoats if things blew soon. A quick pass
across her face left it damp; nothing she could do about the
trickles from her armpits down her flanks.
I have just condemned myself to death, she thought, as she
settled back on the floor—*can't pollute the Race's holy chair
with my serf ass*—and folded her hands. "And I haven't felt
this alive in decades."

"No, I don't want anything." Yolande snapped, then forced
herself to calm. *The housegirl isn't to blame*, she thought. It
would be alarming enough that she was back here at the
Commandant's quarters at 1200, only four hours after she
left. The serf was looking at her wide-eyed. *Be gentle. They're
frightened when the routine is upset.* "Run along, Belinda.
I'll call later if I want lunch."
The memory of the message from Archona was a sour taste
at the back of her mouth as she stalked past the fountain into
the lounging room. *No party planned. Invitation superfluous.*
"He isn't going to do a fuckin' *thing*," she told herself, lost
in rage and wonder. Months past saturation point on the
Stone Dogs, and no action whatsoever. *Be honest with yourself*, she thought, flinging herself down on a couch and staring at the ceiling. Throwing yourself down was curiously
unsatisfying on the Moon; like punching pillows, there was
no thump.
*It's two months into Gwen's voyage. She's out of the inner
system, out of any possible combat.* And Gwen was the only

one of her children old enough for military service. Short of a catastrophe that wrecked the planet, the others would be safe. The Draka prided themselves on being a foresighted people; since before her birth they had been building deep shelters, every plantation and school, city and town in the Domination was *ready*. And the facilities had been improved constantly. They would work, provided there was a living world to return to.

"All right," she asked herself, coldly realistic. "What can yo' do, Yolande?"

Very little. It was bitter knowledge. She knew of the Stone Dogs, now; perhaps two dozen others did. *Could I get in touch* . . . No. The only others she knew of for certain were Gayner and the two Militant leaders; they would not trust a niece of the Conservative bossman. *And it would be like shooting Uncle Eric in the back.* Morally unthinkable, and . . . you did *not* betray Eric von Shrakenberg and enjoy the consequences. Perhaps it would be worthwhile, if there was no alternative. Not *until* there was no alternative. She had a year until the *Lionheart* returned from the edge of the System. For that matter, Gwen would not thank her for being sheltered from danger. *So she's as stupid as anyone else that age. No more essential to the State than a hundred thousand other junior officers.* A fine balance, duty to the Race and to family, but clear in this case.

"I'll have to fuckin' *wait*," she hissed to herself, and then clamped down on her own mind. *The Will is Master*, she repeated. Breathe . . . Presently she won to a degree of calm.

"Belinda," she said to the air; the housecomp would relay it. "Lay out a fresh uniform in my changin' room."

"Marya!" she said, pushing open the door. It had no lock, of course. "Yo'—"

The room was empty, and there was no sound from the others. Yolande stopped, blinking slightly in surprise. *Could have sworn the comp said all servants present*, she thought in puzzlement, looking around. It was a fairly standard upper-servant's suite, bedroom, sitter opening off the corridor through a nook, and a bathroom at the rear. The lights had come on as she entered, but the air had the slightly dead feel of space not used for several hours. *I wonder where she is?* It was annoying; grabbing a quick nooner was not something she did all that often, and there was nobody else in the household right now she would feel that relaxed with; Jolene was down dirtside, visiting her daughter and Nikki back at Claestum.

Oh, well. It was no great matter; she turned to go, and then hesitated. *I've never actually been in here*, she thought.

No reason to visit the servants' quarters, really, except a sudden impulse to surprise . . . Nothing in the bedroom but a bed with a quilt coverlet; there was a signed holo of Gwen by the bed, and a book left open beside it. The sitter was a box-room about four meters by three, lit by a glowceiling, walls of foamrock and tile floor covered by throw rugs. A couch along one wall, a couple of spindly low-G chairs, cushions. The viewer screen, and a bookshelf with a dozen titles, mostly classics; a row of dataplaques beside it, with the garish covers of serf entertainment. The new perscomp on a table, with a chair still pushed back as if in haste; the screen was dark, but the indicator was on, something running.

"Careless," Yolande chuckled, and walked over to it. There was a wrap-robe on the back of the chair. The Draka picked it up and brought the cloth to her face; there was a faint scent of Marya on it. *Damn, I wish she was here*, Yolande thought, sitting and picking up the dataplaque lying on the table.

" 'Serving Pleasure #15,' " she read, and laughed again. An erotic-instruction sequence. *No wonder she's getting so imaginative*, she thought, flattered. *Wonder what's on it.* Impulsively, she snapped it into the port and hit the DIVIDE command on the keyboard. The perscomp was a fairly capable one, the type midlevel serf bureacrats were issued. Embedded accounting, typescribing, datalink and display functions. A million-transistor logic deck, two hundred thousand bits of core storage besides, and a plaquereceptor.

The screen blanked to light-gray, then lit. Yolande watched in growing bewilderment. *Sodomy? Basic Passive Sodomy?* she thought, watching as the instructor showed the young buck how to brace his elbows on his knees before stepping behind. *What in Freya's name is Marya doing with—*

The screen blanked again, the grunting figures replaced by a man's face. In an Alliance uniform, with Brigadier's shoulderboards. American eagle, OSS flashes. Unremarkable face, square, rather dark, big-nosed; in his fifties, plenty of gray in the flat-topped black hair, eyes black too, so that the pupil didn't show. Deep grooves, ridged forehead, the face of a man hagridden for many years. Yolande heard her own breath freeze in a strangled gasp, felt a sheet of ice lock her diaphragm.

Him.

"Marya, my sister, you must realize from this how desperate the situation is."

Him. India. The cool Punjab night, and the missiles arching up from the trees. *Pssssft*-thud, and Myfwany's graceful stride turning to a tumbling fall.

"This plaque must be wiped as soon as you've read it. Likewise the others. *Those most of all.* Here are your instructions."

Him. The face, under the upraised visor. That single glimpse.

". . . je t'aime, ma soeur," the voice concluded. A moment of blank screen, and the instruction sequence cut back in. She touched the controls. Her own face reflected dimly in the darkened screen. Eyes gone enormous, lips peeled back until the gums showed. A trickle of hoarse sound escaped her throat.

"His *sister. His* sister. I've had his *sister* in my own household fo' *twenty-five years!*" A bubble of laughter escaped her, and she ground her teeth closed on it, feeling something thin and hot stabbing between her eyes.

I'm dead. The thought was almost welcome. *I'm a walking corpse.* Nothing and nobody could save her from Security after *this.* The message had mentioned previous drops; even if nothing vital—*there couldn't be, I hardly talked to her for years until*—"Until she volunteered to play pony, gods damn me for a *fool,* why else would she suddenly decide she wants to lie down with me," she said. And now a sabotage operation.

I could kill her, Yolande thought. Just one quick bullet, and call disposal. Or indent for some drugs, get the information, *then* kill her. Perfectly legal—*no, the headhunters would smell something immediately.* The Directorate of Security was an unofficial arm of the Militants, or vice versa. They watched the von Shrakenberg connections like vultures around a dying camel. For an Ingolfsson to kill a houseserf was a break in the pattern, a red flag that something unusual was going on. They would ferret it out if it took them a decade.

No, it was her duty to report this. Put down everything she knew and suspected, write up a report, then one quick bullet of apology to the temple. *The family will be involved,* tolled through her with dreadful knowledge. A knot like the claws of something insectile hooked under her ribs. *Gwen will be disgraced.*

Duty—

"Oh," she breathed. There was a way to use this. *A spy you know about is an asset, not a liability*, she reminded herself. A slow, calm smile touched her lips. *It's even personally fitting*, she reflected. *He's known I had his sister as my serf. Used her for a brooder, probably knows she's been serving pleasure. Torture, to a Yankee.* Her hands touched the keys; she would have to find out what the perscomp was running. *Carefully, Yolande, carefully. She can't suspect, not for a moment.*

This evening.

"You *bit* me, Mistis," Marya said.

Yolande bent and kissed the U-shaped bruise on the inside of the serf's thigh. The bedroom was dark, and she had set the wall for a winter landscape in Tuscany.

"I was excited," she said, lying back. *True, by Loki lord of lies. I didn't expect that. It was odd, she felt no hatred. I suppose I burned all that out long ago, for her.*

"It usually dosen't take you like that, Mistis."

"It's the news," Yolande said. "Here, rub my back." She rolled on her stomach, felt the serf's breath warm on the damp skin of her neck as her fingers kneaded at the muscles along her spine.

"What news, Mistis?"

Yolande made herself hesitate. "Well, it can't hurt now. No point in bein' overcorrect. Remember the good news I got back when, in Archona?"

"I thought it must be important," Marya said calmly, with a hint of a wink. "Certainly set you at me, Mistis."

Are her fingers trembling? Yolande thought. *Good. Sweat, a little. Don't stop to think.*

The Draka laughed. "It's our secret weapon," she said. "There really *is* one. I always knew they must have somethin' planned . . . A biological, to disable the Yankee crews in near-orbit. Really nice piece of work; codename *Stone Dogs*. It's a stone killer, too! Delicate trigger, modulated microwave emission. We go to War-Condition Alpha tomorrow."

The serf's hands *were* shaking now. Yolande put a raised eyebrow into her voice. "What's the matter, Marya? Don't worry, yo' aren't in any danger. Should be a cakewalk, and anyways, this is the best-defended place on Luna." She pulled the other close and kissed her. "Think I'll get a landgrant in California, after," she continued. "Anyways, stay close to the quarters, the tubeways'll be closed down." The lights dimmed toward sleepset.

"On second thoughts, I've got a few things fo' yo' to do. There may be some surface damage, worst-case. That crate of Constantia '87 Uncle Eric sent, fo' that cruise on the *Mamba*." She felt the serf jerk slightly at the mention of the yacht. "Be a shame to lose it, even if that damned toy's not here when Gwen gets back fo' the victory party. Go on out tomorrow, and supervise strippin' all the personal effects out, bring them back to quarters. No droppin' hints, now!"

"What?" Yolande looked up from her desk at the holo image of Transportation Central, the traffic control nexus for Aresopolis.

"The *Mamba*, Commandant. We would have appreciated notification of a lift!"

Yolande felt a cold pride at the expression of mild surprise on her face. *Of course, it's a good thing they don't have a medical sensor going on me*, she thought stonily. The face in the screen was New Race; they *could* control their heart-beats. She wondered how it felt . . .

"So would I," she replied dryly. "Since I am *here*, and have authorized no such mission. Where is the pilot?"

"I . . . " The hawk-featured young face took on an imperceptible air of desperation. She knew the feeling; the sinking sensation of bearing very bad news to someone far up the chain of command. "Yo' pilot is in his quarters, Arch-Strategos. That was why we assumed, ah—"

"Don't assume, Tetrarch, *do*. I presume yo've hailed?"

"Of cou—Yes, ma'am. No response."

There wouldn't be, Yolande thought. She had very carefully had all the com systems decommissioned for preventitive maintenance. An investigation would find that significant, but far too late.

"Well, we'll have to assume an unauthorized lift," she said, frowning with the expression of a high-ranking officer forced to intervene in trivial matters. "Issue a warnin' to the *Mamba* and whoever's aboard, to surrender or be fired upon. Alert the orbital platforms."

"Ma'am, it's, ah, the trajectory indicates a boost for translunar space. Mars is, well—"

"I'm familiar with orbital mechanics, Tetrarch," she said. *Stop tormenting the poor boy.* Her fingers touched the desktop. "On that burn, the Belt would be the logical destination. Hmmm. The *Mamba's* fairly valuable, but there's nothin' on board we'd be all that embarrassed fo' the Yankees to get . . . Worth a chance on not scrubbin' it. Dependin' on who's aboard. Get Merarch Tomlins on the screen, we'll see if we can set up an intercept."

"Yo' *what*? Yo' pillowtalked a bedwench *that*, and then let her *escape*?"

The Archon's image was alone before her. For a moment Yolande felt a sensation she had not known for many years: raw, physical fear.

He looked down at the copy of her report, and the fury on his face went cold and blank. "This had to be deliberate on yo' part. Usurpation of command prerogative, as well as treasonous incompetence."

"She was an agent, Excellence," Yolande continued expressionlessly. "If yo'll examine the appendix to that report, yo'll see we found clear evidence of dataplague sabotage. No way of knowin' how long this has been goin' on, either." A skull grin split her face, below eyes that were edged in red. "We went aftah the Yankee personnel. They planted a, a virus in our comps. Typical, isn't it?" Her hand twitched slightly as she reached for the glass of water. "The fact remains, Excellence, that we no longer have an intercept or strike option on the *Mamba*. Inside of three days, the Alliance craft *will* intercept, and shortly thereafter they'll know about the Stone Dogs."

She waited the seconds it took for light to reach Earth and return, on this most secure of links.

Eric von Shrakenberg rose behind his desk, and she felt his will beating on her like waves on a granite headland. "I will have yo' *shot*. I will have yo' fuckin' *shot!*"

"That is yo' prerogative, Excellence," Yolande said. *And I don't care nearly as much as I thought I would*, she realized. Yes, the body reacted: sweat rolling down from her armpits, muscles tensing in millennial fight-flight reflex. But somewhere deep in her soul, she would accept it. "If yo' wishes to relieve the Commandant of this installation just befo' the . . . outbreak of hostilities."

She saw that ram home. "Use it, or lose it," she continued.

Silence, for long minutes. At last he looked up again, older than she remembered. "Why?"

"I—" A pause, while she considered how it could be said. "I disagreed with yo' hesitation, but I would have accepted that. On a professional level. But yo' gave me a weapon, Uncle Eric. And I decided to use it. Fo' . . . personal reasons. Love and hate." Another pause. "And afterward—if there is an afterward—" she laid her sidearm on the desk, in range of the receptor—"I'll save yo' the trouble, iff'n it's still important."

The ancient, weary eyes stared into hers. "The fate of worlds, fo' *personal* reasons?" he said, wonderingly.

"Are there any other kind?" she answered.

At last: "Go to Force Condition Seven, and await further orders, Arch-Strategos." With a touch of ironic malice: "Service to the State."

"Glory to the Race, Excellence."

CHAPTER TWENTY-ONE

DATE: 01/07/98

FROM: Supreme GHQ, Castle Tarleton
         Archona, Archona Province
         by order of His Excellence the Archon Eric von
         Shrakenberg
         Commander of the Destiny of the Race

TO: All commanders Classification 7-Z and above

RE: Force Condition Seven

         Be advised that as of this instant, the Domination
         is moving to Force Condition Seven, as per War
         Plan Zebra-Kohln. Sealed orders are to be opened
         and all prepared measures taken. An Archonal De-
         cree of War Emergency Status is in effect as of this
         communication, and all civil and Security organs
         are to consider themselves under the authority of
         the Supreme General Staff and the Directorate of
         War. Where necessary, exemplary measures may
         be taken to secure public order and the speedy
         implementation of evacuation. The highest readi-
         ness must be maintained, but on pain of immedi-
         ate execution no hostile measures toward the enemy
         are to be taken until the receipt of orders moving
         to Force Condition Eight or until the enemy initi-
         ates action.

         This is no drill.

DRAKA FORCES BASE ARESOPOLIS
MARE SERENITATIS, LUNA
NOVEMBER 2, 1998
0600 HOURS

"Whew." Yolande collapsed into the chair. For a few minutes she forced herself to sit quietly, breathing, letting the wash of cool air from the vents help her body flush out the hormonal poisons. Then she reached for the communicator.

"Staff conference, immediate," she said. "Forcecon 7."

". . . And all nonessential traffic between sectors has been closed down," the civilian administrator was saying.

Yolande looked around the table. "Mark?" she said.

The Aerospace Command Strategos shrugged. "We've moved all the available units into sheltered orbits," he said. If there was one thing that a generation of skirmishing in space had shown, it was that ships were helpless in confined quarters with high-powered energy weapons.

"Move them out further," Yolande said. "Outer-shell orbits fo' the Cislunar Command zone. Sannie, start pumpin' down the bulk water in the dome habitat, fill the reservoirs."

"That'll play hell with the Ecology people's projects," she warned.

"Don't matter none." The other officers around the table glanced sidelong at each other; Yolande saw carefully controlled fear. This was the nightmare that had haunted them all from their births. "And yes, that means I knows somethin' y'all don't. Somethin' bad—and somethin' good, too."

"Now, and this is crucial"—she paused for effect—"startin' *immediately*, and *while* yo' moving to full mobilization, bring yo' redundant compunits on-net. Then do a *physical separation* of the main battle-units, and run simulations of actual operations—everythin' but the final connections to the weapons units." She held up a hand to still the protests. "Y'all will find malfunctions, I guarantee it. Report the make an' number of the malfunctionin' cores, *immediate*, to Merarch Willard here, who's now Infosystems Officer fo' Aresopolis. We'll patch across to maintain capacity. Believe me, it's necessary."

CLAESTUM PLANTATION
DISTRICT OF TUSCANY
PROVINCE OF ITALY
NOVEMBER 2, 1998

"*Vene, vene*, keep movin'!" The serf foreman reached out to stop a fieldhand family; one of the children was cradling a kitten. "No livestock in the shelter, drop it." The girl began to cry in bewildered terror.

The bossboys were as ignorant as the rest of the serfs, but they had caught the master's nervousness. John Ingolfsson whistled sharply to catch the man's attention and jerked his head; the foreman's rubber hose fell, and the line began moving again as he waved the serf girl through with her pet.

Makes no nevermind, the master of Claestum thought, watching the long column disappearing into the hillside. He swallowed to moisten a dry throat, pushed back his floppy-brimmed leather hat, and wiped at the sweat on his forehead. It was a clear fall day, and still a little hot here in the valley below the Great House. The shelter was burrowed under that hill, quite deep; begun in the '50s, and refined and extended in every year since. This entrance was disguised as a warehouse, but behind the broad door and the facade was a long concrete ramp into the rock. The elevators were freight-type, and the thousand-odd serfs would be in their emergency quarters in another hour or so. Armorplate doors, and thousands of feet of granite—

It should be enough, if we have an hour, he thought. There was hatred in the glance he shot upward. Nothing but the coded messages over the official net, but you could tell . . . *I always grudged the money and effort.* Full shelter for all the serfs, sustainable if crowded; fuel cells, air filters, water recyclers, and food enough for three years on strait rations. He had had just time enough to put most of the farming equipment under wraps; the sealed warehouses held seed grain. There was even room for basic breeding stock, on the upper level.

The last of the fieldhands passed through, and the overseer looked up from the comp screen by the door. "That's the last of them," she called. Rumbling sounded within, as thick metal sighed home into slots.

Silence fell, eerie and complete. Nothing but the hot dry wind through the trees, and the tinkle of water from one of the village fountains. He stood in the stirrups and looked around; the land lay sere and dry with autumn, rolling away in slopes of yellow stubble, silver-green olives, dusty-green pasture and the lush foliage of the vineyards. Commonplace, infinitely dear. Yesterday his only worry had been the falling price of wheat and the vintage.

"Run one mo' check," he said. "Wouldn't want to leave one

of they brats out by mistake." The overseer was taut-nervous herself, but her fingers were steady on the keyboard.

"All of 'em."

"Right." He ran a soothing hand down the neck of his horse as it side-danced with the tension. "Sooo, boy, easy. Now, let's go jump in a hole and pull it in aftah us."

WASHINGTON HOUSE
NEW YORK CITY
FEDERAL CAPITAL DISTRICT
UNITED STATES OF AMERICA
NOVEMBER 3, 1998
0700 HOURS

"Could it be a drill of some sort?" one of the figures in the screen said.

The Conference Room was nearly empty; the president, and a few of her chief aides. The Alliance Chairman was in the center of the holoscreen, with the military chiefs and some of the most crucial administrators. In theory the other Alliance heads of government were co-equal, but this was a time for practicalities, and the American head of state was still much more than *primus inter pares*.

Carmen Hiero forced herself not to sigh in exasperation. "*Amigo*, they've started closing down factories and evacuating the population to the deep shelters," she said. "Look at the reports; there are abandoned dogs walking through the streets of Alexandria! You think they're doing this—it must be costing them astronomically—for a *drill*?"

Allsworthy tapped his fingers together and looked to one side, toward his pickup of the ACI chief. Hiero frowned slightly; she thought the chairman tended to rely on his Intelligence people rather too much. *Enough*, she thought. *Listen*.

"Anything congruent? Any reason for it to start *now*?" the chairman said.

The ACI man licked his lips slightly. "Nothing we can spot on short notice, Mr. Chairman," he said; his face was calm, but the tendons stood out in the hands that twisted an ivory cigarette-holder. His Australasian accent had turned slightly nasal.

You too, my friend, Hiero thought.

"But . . . " he continued. "Well, something jolly odd *did* happen yesterday, up on Luna. The *Mamba*—that's the personal yacht of their Commandant of Aresopolis—did an unauthorized takeoff and is running for the Belt. Continuous boost trajectory for Ceres; should be there in about ten days."

"That quickly?" Johannsen, the Space Force CINC.

"Well, it's got one of their new fifth-generation pulse-drives," the ACI commander said. "And whoever's piloting it isn't leaving any reserve for deceleration, we think. They've got two Imperator class cruisers trying to catch it, and they've been beaming a series of demands that the *Mamba* stop, and warnings to everyone else to stay clear. We've no earthly idea what it's about, really. The yacht is either unwilling or unable to communicate."

Hiero leaned forward and touched the query button on her desk. "Can they catch it? Can we?"

"No; and yes, if we have something start matching velocities *now*. Considerably sooner than it might reach Ceres, if we use one of the *New America*'s auxiliaries." A collective wince; that would mean blowing the Project's last line of cover. "Under the circumstances, I'd say it's justified."

"I say we do it," Hiero said.

"Sir?" The ACI man looked to the chairman, who nodded abstractedly.

"Ah, sir?" That was Donati, the OSS chief of staff; he was looking off-screen, and his fingers were busy. "We do have—yes, we do have something significant, just now. They're . . . ah, yes. Trying very hard to keep it quiet, but our ELINT is picking it up. They're pulling up their backup comps on . . . hell, one sector after another. Running some sort of check program on the central comps. Then—they've just put out an all-points to their military, to downline the AV-122 series. That's their most recent battle-management comp."

Hiero's own fingers moved; yes, everyone here was cleared for the fourth layer of the *New America* project.

"Is that one of the ones we managed to infect?" she said. Chairman Allsworthy's question came on the heels of theirs.

There was a long moment of silence. "*Mierda*," she whispered. "A leak."

Allsworthy grunted, as if someone had hit him in the belly. "We . . . " He looked down at his hands. Hiero felt herself touched with sympathy, and a moment's gratitude that the final decision was not hers. The life of the planet lay in those palms. "Recommendations?" he continued.

"Attack immediately; we're already at Defcon 4," Hiero said.

"Attack." Donati, more decisive than usual.

"With all due respect, Mr. Chairman, that would be premature." The ACI commander's balding head shone. "If . . . A leak in the Project security would not be enough to put them up to this level of alert. They'd know it would focus our attention; they'd try and isolate the infected comps clandestinely, so that we wouldn't *know* it's been done. There's another factor here, one we haven't grasped . . . Maybe the *Mamba* has the answer. Whatever it is, *God*, sir, even if we *win* with the present inadequate level of infection in their infosystems, we're talking *hundreds* of millions of dead. *Everybody*, if they use Fenris. We have to play for time."

Hiero sat silent, listening to the debate. This was not a committee, could not be, and she had said what she believed . . . At last the chairman raised a hand for silence.

"We'll present an ultimatum," he said. "How long until the *Mamba* is intercepted?"

"Twenty-four to thirty hours, sir."

"I authorize immediate interception. Take whatever measures are necessary. Secretary Ferriera, draft an immediate note to the Domination; their mobilization is an intolerable provocation and threat, and we will consider ourselves in a state of war unless they begin withdrawal by exactly" —his eyes went to a clock—"1000 hours tomorrow. General Mashutomo, all Alliance forces to Defcon 5, and proceed on the assumption that hostilities begin as of the expiration of the ultimatum." He looked around. "Any questions?"

Hiero waited until she was sure there would be none, before she spoke. "No. I disagree with this course of action, but we must have discipline or we are truly lost." A weary smile. "And I very much hope I am wrong and you are right, *Señor* Chairman."

"Roderigo," she said, as the last of the president's council were leaving. "Wait a moment." When they were alone. "Miguel and the grandchildren are still on Ceres. Send a message, tightbeam, priority. *Stay*. He will understand."

EAST TENESSEE
UNITED STATES OF AMERICA
NOVEMBER 3, 1998
1500 HOURS

"Captain, what the hell *is* this place?"

The trooper was nervous. They all were, after the sudden Defcon Four and the scramble of orders that had sent them haring off into the hills, away from any news of what was going on.

The Ranger officer looked up from his maps; they had walked the last half-mile, up into the hills. The air was cool here in the high Appalachians even in summer, chill with winter now the steep mountain ridges were thick with oak and maple and fir, the scars of the mines long healed. He had been born not far away, and he remembered the deep woodland smell of it, a little damp and musty, deeply alive. There were few enough left who could call the mountains home. Unforgiving hard country to scratch a living out of, once the pioneers had taken the first richness; the timber companies and the coal-miners had passed through, and then the people had followed, down to the warm cities and the sun.

"It's a disused coal mine, son," the captain said. *They're supposed to be independent-minded,* he reminded himself. *And they're feeling lost, yanked out of their regular units.* Most of the Rangers were helping with the last crates, up from the disused road and through the carefully run-down entrance. The shielding started a little way beyond that, and then the storerooms and armories. "You married, son? Close relatives?"

"Nnnno, sir," the soldier answered. He was in his late teens, with a fluffy yellow attempt at a mustache standing out amid the eye-blurring distortions of a chameleon suit that covered his armor. "Not really."

"Nobody here does," the officer continued. "And in that cave there's everything we'd need for a long, long time."

The soldier swallowed. "Yessir. I get the picture." The officer noted with pleasure that he did not ask if there were other refuges like this. *I suspect so,* the captain thought. *But neither of us needs to know.* One of the noncoms below called with a quietly menacing displeasure, and the young Ranger saluted and turned to go. That gave him a glimpse of the last contingent, looking unaccustomed to their fatigues and carrying various items of black-boxed electronics.

"*Girls?*" he squeaked, then remembered himself and saluted again.

"Technicians," the captain said softly to himself, looking up. "Edited out of the comps, like all the rest of us. Unlikely to be missed. Not on paper either, anywhere."

The last chameleon-suited troopers were following up the trail, replacing bent branches and disturbed leaves, spraying pheromone-neutralizers. He folded the map and tucked it into a shoulder-pouch. It was going to create the biggest administrative hassle of all time, getting this set up again when they had been stood down.

"I hope," he murmured. "I sincerely hope."

NORFOLK, VIRGINIA
UNITED STATES OF AMERICA
MALVINAS SSN-44
NOVEMBER 3, 1998
1700 HOURS

"Take her down to a hundred meters," the captain of the submarine said. "All ahead full."

Commodore Wanda Jackson glanced around the command center. It was up forward, near the bows of the metal teardrop. Only half a dozen in the bridge crew, a score more in the rest of the vessel. The drive was magnetic, superconductor coils along the length of the hull; most of that was filled with the nuclear power plant, essential life support, and thirty torps. Hypervelocity sea-skimmers with multiple warheads, on a ship that could do better than fifty knots, or dive as deep as the water went, in most places. The finest class of submarine the Alliance had ever built, and the last, nearly obsolete.

"Well, they seem to have found *some* use for us," she said. "Number Two." The Executive Officer came to stand by her chair. "We'll open the sealed orders now." Their squadron were spraying out from Norfolk like a fan of titanium-matrix minnows, each with their own packet of deadly instructions.

"Yes, ma'am."

Her thumbnail hesitated for a moment on the wax of the seal. *I'm glad we never had kids*, she thought; her husband was in Naval Air, out of Portsmouth. The paper sprang free with a slight *tock* sound.

The commodore's eyebrows rose. "Make course for the Angolan Abyssal Plain," she said. "Down to the bottom, and wait."

ABOARD DASCS *MAMBA*
TRANSLUNAR SPACE
NOVEMBER 4, 1998
0300 HOURS

"God," Marya muttered. The new trace on the screen was matching velocities *fast*.

She was in the pilot's couch of the yacht, where she had been since the takeoff. Never leaving it, except for a few dashes to the head. The floor around her was littered with the wrappers of ration-bars; it was important to keep up the blood sugar. Sleep you could avoid, by popping stim, even when you were accelerating at a continuous 1.3 G. Over forty hours now since the last sleep, and *things* were beginning to scuttle around the edges of her peripheral vision. The icy clarity of her senses was growing disconcerting, a taunting, on-edge *twisting* that left you wondering if the information coming in to the brain was accurate. Could she really smell so sour already? *Am I thinking straight?* The dimmed lights still seemed hurting-bright.

Her eyes flicked back to the board. The Draka cruisers were still there behind her, three of them. Not gaining much; this ship was *fast*. Grotesquely overpowered, and the hydrogen-boron-11 reaction was fantastically efficient. The first drive that really didn't need reaction mass; all it produced was charged particles for the coils to squeeze aft . . . Those cruisers were fourth-generation, deuterium-tritium fusion. This much continuous boost was probably doing their thrust plates no good at all, they must be using just enough water-mass to protect the diamond films. Still, eventually they *would* get close enough to get parallax and bring their beam weapons to bear.

An alarm chimed; one of the warships' lasers was impinging on the *Mamba's* thrust-plate. Marya's fingers touched the board, and the magnetic fields twisted slightly against the fusion flame. The *Mamba* skittered sideways . . . The Draka craft were still light-seconds away, enough to make dodging easy. Missiles and slugs were out of the question without matching or intersecting vectors; not enough sustained boost.

"Oh, shit, no *way* I can fight this thing," she muttered, looking over to the vacant couches. One untrained person could just barely pilot it, on an idiot-proof minimum time, maximum thrust boost, if they knew the theory and how to stroke computers. A quarter of the screens were dead anyway, the comm systems, *all* of them down, and no time to check why without getting sliced into dogmeat by the pursuit. In the meantime she was half-delirious and wholly terrified.

She laughed. "And I feel *great*. Fucking wonderful!" Because she was doing, accomplishing; perhaps only her own death in a quick flare of plasma, but that would be something. It was helplessness that was the worst thing about being a slave. Not abuse, not privation, not the ritualized humiliation; it was not being able to *do* anything except what they wanted. This was the most alive she had felt in twenty years.

The new trace was still closing. Marya blinked and recalibrated; her eyes felt dry, but the lids slid up and down as if lubricated with mercury. Whatever it was was boosting at 2 G to match velocities, and had been for the better part of a day. Better than the *Mamba* herself could do. Again she looked in acid frustration at the dead comm screens; there was probably enough information flying back and forth, threats and warnings and demands, to tell her everything she needed to know. *I might as well put a message in a bloody bottle and throw it out the airlock*, she thought. *3K klicks and closing at 1k per second relative.* Soon they would be in visual distance, as something more than a point of light . . .

"Visual," she muttered to herself, unconscious of speaking aloud. "Maybe, if they're looking —"

Impatiently, she called up the maximum magnification and waited. Presently it appeared, no class of vessel she was familiar with. For a chill moment she thought it might be another like the craft she was flying; the tapered-wedge shape was plainly meant to transit atmosphere. Then she saw the Alliance colors, the Space Force blazon. Even the name: *Sacajawea.* It was bigger than the *Mamba* as well, corvette sized, a couple of thousand tonnes payload. Her hand touched a section of the consol.

Airflight mode

CURRENTLY IN VACUUM, the computer replied with electronic idiot-savant indifference to circumstances.

Airflight mode, landing lights, exterior.

OPERATIONAL: ON/OFF (Y/N)?
She touched on. Off. On . . .

"Sir."

Frederick Lefarge looked up from the plotting console. The *Sacajawea* was one of a dozen shuttlecraft the *New America* would carry, mirrormatter powered, equally suited to atmosphere or deepspace work. That was easy enough with a power supply as energetic as antihydrogen. If the *New America* ever sailed, it would be a one-way trip with not much hope of return, and a long time before a functioning economy could be established at the target star. Her auxiliaries had been designed to last a century, and do everything from lifting kilotonne-mass loads out of a terrestrial-sized gravity well to interplanetary freighting. This one could cross the solar system and back in forty days, without refueling.

And it could fight an Imperator-class cruiser, quite handily; hence the large bridge crew. Lefarge looked hungrily at the spread of trajectories on the board before him. Those Snakes were going to get a *very* unpleasant surprise, if push came to shove.

"Sir?" That was the *Sacajawea's* captain, Ibrahim Kurasaka.

"Sir?" Lefarge said in turn. He outranked the other man, but there was only one commander on a bridge. For that matter, his manning a board here was irregular, but there were times when the book didn't matter all that much.

"Ah . . . Brigadier Lefarge, I'm getting a damned odd pattern of visuals from that Snake pleasure-barge."

"I'll be glad to take a look," Lefarge said. An image blinked into the center of his screens, and he narrowed his eyes. Not a random pattern . . . Suddenly, he chuckled harshly.

"You didn't go through the National Scouts, did you, Captain?"

"No, Brigadier, I didn't," Kurasaka said. He was Javanese-Nipponese, and the Indonesian Federation had not been advanced enough for a universal youth-movement back then.

"That's an antique system; Morse, it used to be called. Probably in the datastore; let me . . . yes." He raised one hand with enormous effort against the drag of acceleration and began keying. After a moment: *"Oh, my God."*

"Marya, Marya! *Ma soeur, ma petite soeur*—"

For a moment she was lost, content simply to hold him.

Then she pushed herself to arm's length. There was shock in his eyes, enough that she was startled. *Do I look that bad?* Forty hours of stim, but still—

"Fffff—" Appalled, she stopped. The stammer she had overcome so long ago was back. *Not now, not now!* A medical corpsman was floating down the connecting tube behind her brother, crowding along the wall to let the squads of Intelligence types past as they headed for the quick ransacking of the *Mamba* that was all the available time would allow. She had an injector in her hand, and the single-mindedness that went with the winged staff that blazoned her elbow. Antistim and trank.

"NNnnnnno!" Marya stutterred, pointing. Her brother half-turned, cut off the medic's protest with an angry gesture.

"You need rest," he said. The words were banal, not the tone, and there were . . . yes, tears at the corners of his eyes.

Tears are for later, she thought, and felt a flat calm return. A deep breath in.

"Liii-sten," she said slowly. "Therrre is a bbbbiological . . ."

CENTRAL OFFICE, ARCHONAL PALACE
ARCHONA
DOMINATION OF THE DRAKA
NOVEMBER 4, 1998
0500 HOURS

"So." Eric von Shrakenberg looked around the circle of the table. "Is that the consensus?"

Louise Gayner snorted and snapped a thumbnail against the crackle-finish of her perscomp. The others glanced sidelong at each other; the Supreme General Staff representatives, the Directors of War and Security, the Council members. No teleconferencing, not for this. A dozen human beings, and they were all those who must be consulted in this matter.

Silence. Nods. At last the head of the Staff spoke:

"Excellence, we've *already* lost twenty percent of our capacity to this damned comp-plague, and there'll be mo'. *Must* be mo'. The Stone Dogs are our only hope. If we lose that there's nothin'. There's no *time*, Excellence; every moment we wait is a nail in our coffin."

The Archon looked down at his fingers. *They're waiting for my decision, my choice.* The thought was hilarious, enough so that he did not know whether laughter or nausea would be more fitting. *All my life I've wanted to set us free*, he thought. *Free from a way of life based on death. Now my only chance of it is to inflict more death than the combined totals of every despot and warlord in the whole mad-dog slaughterhouse we call human history. My choice.* Could it be Yolande's fault? Could it be *anyone's* fault that it had come to this, the whole of human history narrowing down to this point? Ten thousand generations, living, rearing their children, working, dreaming, going down to dust, and now . . . He would say the words, and they would lie like a sword across all time, no matter the outcome. If there were humans at all, a generation hence, they would call this the decisive moment. The ultimate power, and in his hands.

A leader is someone who manages to keep ahead of the pack, he knew bitterly, feeling the cold carnivore eyes on him. There was exactly one practical choice he could make, within the iron framework of the Domination's logic, and the Draka were nothing if not a practical people. Or he could refuse it, and the only difference would be that he would be safely dead in twenty minutes. For a second's brief temptation he wished he could; it would spare him the consequences, at least.

No. At seventh and last, I am a von Shrakenberg, and I have my duty. Besides that, if nothing else it would give Gayner too much pleasure.

"Activate the Stone Dogs," he said; his voice had the blank dispassion of a recording. "Force Condition Eight. Service to the State."

"Glory to the Race," came the reply. There was another brief pause, as if the men and women gathered around the table were caught in the huge inertia of history, the avalanche they were about to unloose. Then they rose and left, one by one.

Gayner was the last. Eric watched her with hooded eyes as she snapped the perscomp shut; time had scored his old enemy more heavily than he, for all his extra years. Only traces of red in the gray-white hair, and there were spots on her hands.

"Happy?" he said, at last. There was a curious intimacy to a perfect hatred, like a long marriage.

"Not particularly," she replied, straightening her cravat. Their eyes met. "The Yankees . . . that's not personal. They're cattle." Then she smiled. "Yo', on the other hand. Ahhh, come the day, *that* will make me happy."

"Nice to know Ah can afford anothah human being such satisfaction," he said. There was no particular hurry now; neither of them was much involved in implementation. The snow was moving down the slope. Still glacial slow, but there was no stopping it. "Headin' fo' y' bunker?"

"No." She looked up at the wall. "I've got a transsonic waitin'. I'll sit this one out in Luanda. Home." Gayner looked at him again. "But don't worry. *I'll be back.*"

DOMINATION SPACE COMMAND PLATFORM MOURNBLADE
LOW EARTH ORBIT
NOVEMBER 4, 1998
0900 HOURS

The commander of the battle platform looked up sharply. "That's the code," he said. His second nodded, confirming. They were in the centrum of the platform, and the Chiliarch allowed himself a moment's pride; this was the newest and best of Space Command's orbital fists.

"Initiate Zebra," he said.

There was a heavy tension on the command bridge, but no confusion, no panic. This was what they had trained long years for; if any of the operators at their consoles were thinking of homes and families below, it made no difference to the cool professionalism of their teamwork.

"Preparin' fo' launch," the Weapons Officer said.

The commander touched his screen.

[Detonation sequence activated]

"What the *fuck*—that's not the launch protocol." There was controlled alarm in his voice. "Weapons, pull that sequence!"

Frantic activity. "Suh, it's not respondin'! The central comp's not acceptin' input."

[Ten seconds]

A warning sent through Security crept into the Chiliarch's mind. "Dump the core, over to dispersed operation." A sound of protest from the Infosystems Officer; that would reduce their combat capacity by nine-tenths. "Do it, do it *now*."

"Initiatin' . . . suh, it won't respond. Null board."

"Get in there and slag the core, physically, now."

[Seven seconds]

Fingers were prying at access panels. Hands tore bunches of wire free, and sparks flickered blue.

[Five seconds]

Sections of screen were going dark. He could see globes of fire rising and flattening against the upper atmosphere, down below on Earth. Vortexes of black cloud were gathering.

[Three seconds]

Even now there was no panic. Desperate effort . . . *Impossible*, he decided. The Chiliarch closed his eyes, called up a certain day. He was small again, and his father was lifting him . . .

[Two seconds]

. . . up so high toward the tree . . .

[One second]

. . . with Mother smiling, and . . .

[Detonation]

WASHINGTON HOUSE DEEP SHELTER
FEDERAL CAPTIAL DISTRICT
NEW YORK CITY
UNITED STATES OF AMERICA
NOVEMBER 4, 1998

"This had better be worth it, *compadre*," Carmen Hiero said, fastening her robe. It was the early hours of the morning, and she reached grumpily for the coffee. Then she saw her aide's face, and gulped without tasting. "Something more about those broadcasts?"

"No, still just harmless modulated signals," the aide said. "But there's something else . . . Madam President, the chairman's gone to the Denver War Room." Thousands of feet under a mountain; she felt something clutch at her windpipe. That was where the real decisions would be made, as was right and proper; the Alliance was sovereign, not the member states. "Please, the briefing's being prepared." It was a short walk to the War Room; even after all these years, she still found the salutes a little incongruous for an elderly Sonoran lady in a housecoat.

"What's the status?" she asked, sinking into the command chair. There was a tired smell of cigarettes and stale coffee, under the artificial freshness.

"They've gone to Force Condition Eight," the general said. "Full mobilization. Evacuations in progress; nearly complete, in fact. Nothing overt, not yet; we're matching, of course. No panic . . . " Unspoken, the knowledge that the civil defense measures were inadequate passed between them. *Yes, yes, general. I did my best. Pray that we will not see how far short of enough that is.*

"And they're continuing that crazy broadcasting. The experts say the only thing it's going to affect is the homing sense of pigeons. Evidently that's in the same range, planetary magnetism or some such. And . . . yes, Denver says the Project people in the *Sacajawea* did match velocities with the *Mamba*."

Hiero nodded. She had always felt that name was a little ill-omened; Sacajawea had led Lewis and Clark on their expedition to the northwest. Heroic, if you looked at it from a Euro-American perspective, but even if the family did not talk about it, there were *indios* in the Hiero background. And from their point of view, of course— She forced her mind back to the present. Best not to think too much of the past, here and now. That way lay thinking that somehow she could have prevented this.

"They're—" He frowned. "That's odd, they're making a Priority A broadcast, *from the shuttle.*"

She snorted. "Get me Orbital Three. Split screen, and call up the *Sacajawea* broadcast."

Reason fought with sick dread. It made no *sense*; the balance had not changed. Von Shrakenberg was still in power over there, and still a rational man, for a Draka. They had been counting on that, on him keeping the Militants out until the Alliance was ready . . .

How could they have found out about the Project? she thought; *that* was enough to send a stab of pain from the incipient ulcer through her stomach. "Milk," she said. *No. It must be more. They would know we are not ready.*

"Madam President, we're having a little trouble with the link to Orbital One," the comtech said, puzzled. "The signal's odd. Here's the Project broadcast."

It was Brigadier Lefarge. She sat bolt-upright at the sight of his expression. "To all Alliance bases and personnel. To all Alliance bases and personnel. The Domination has engaged in a"—his voice paused, as if searching for words—"an act of bio-psychological—"

She felt a sudden quietness spread from the tech's desk, rippling out. "Put them on central screen, and *get Orbital One*," she said. *Oh, my children.* "Now. *Vamos.*"

The communications desk of the orbital battlestation came on, but there was no one behind it. Silence, then a flicker. Then the image on the screen jumped, to the command deck. A man turned to look at them, and Carmen Hiero crossed herself reflexively. There were screams, and one of the techs started vomiting on her console. The man on the screen wore the uniform of an Alliance general; there were deep nail-gouges down the side of his face, and an eye hung loose on a stalk along his cheek.

"*Urrrrrrr,*" he said, advancing on the screen pickup. They could see the body behind him, broken and floating in the zero-G chamber. Little else; too much blood was coming from the throat. More floated around the general's mouth. "*Aaaaaaaaaa*" The mouth swelled enormous, and a slick grating sound came through the speakers; the sound of teeth on crystal sandwich. The general was trying to gnaw his way to the command room on Earth. Wet mouth on the screen, and the teeth were splintering now. Chewing, with shreds of tongue hanging between the jagged ends. "Ah. ah. gggggg."

Below her in the War Room the tech was screaming again, but now he was standing, tearing out handfuls of his hair. The president lifted her hands against the sight, and the fingers turned on her. They smiled, showing their fangs. Burrowed toward her face and began to feed, smiling.

Pain. That was the first thought. Then, absurdly: *So this is what madness is.*

She stood, floated upward, landed on feet that rooted themselves deeper than the world. That was terrible, because she must run, she must hide, the *Anglo* girls at Mt. Holyoke had sprinkled brown sugar over her sheets again and—

—She was walking down the corridor towards the elevators, and the wall kissed her shoulder wetly. A tech was kneeling in a corner, hands locked around her feet, shivering with a tremor that sent waves of blue into the air in time with her whimper. Hiero pulled her own hands away from her face, feeling the tendrils stretch and pulse. A man stumbled toward the tech and squatted before her. He had a fire-ax in one hand, and mass of bloody tissue in the other; the spurting wound between his legs showed what it was. He held it out to her, and Hiero wanted to weep with the numinous beauty of the motion that smelled of pomegranates.

Instead she walked into the elevator and keyed for the surface. It shot upward and inward, compressing her into a fetal curl. Bones snapped and flesh tore as it masticated her, rolling her into a ball that it spat out into the corridor. Tissue and fragments flowed together and she crawled along a carpet that moaned in pain and writhed away from her. Something grabbed her and jerked her upright. Insect-stick limbs, oval body, buzzing wings, centered in a face she knew. *What is this monster doing with Roderigo's face?* she thought, and felt rage seep wetly out her stomach. Words spattered around her, heavy with evil oils. She lunged forward and it ran, ran before her out onto a balcony beneath a sky that shivered and thundered.

Light blossomed, and there was a moment of total clarity as her melted eyeballs ran down her cheeks. Then—

SEABED, ANGOLAN ABYSSAL PLAIN
MALVINAS SSN-44
NOVEMBER 4, 1998
1005 HOURS

"Damned fragmentary, Captain," the Exec said. The lines scrolling up the screen were the long-wave relay from Hawaii. "What the hell does that mean?"

"The first part's an all-points from some Space Force johnny," Jackson replied, rubbing one hand across the other. She felt a little off, as if things were blurring at the edges. *Christ, I can't be coming down with the flu* now *of all times.* "The stuff after that is completely garbled. Rerun the first, the comp ought to have decoded it by now." That was NavCommand for you, nothing better to do than cryptography.

Wanda Jackson read the report over, once and then again, then turned her head to look at the Exec. Her hand reached for the controls, and she keyed the general circuit.

"*Now hear this,*" she said. "All hands. This is the captain speaking. All hands will proceed to the nearest medicomp and take the maximum waking trank dose, *immediately.* Remain calm. Once you have taken the medication, report to sickbay by watches."

The Exec handed her an injector; she pressed it against her neck and felt a cool bite. A wall of glass came down between her and the world, imposing an absolute calm. *That was close.* The sick feeling at the edge of her vision was still there, but now she could feel it as something apart from her. The captain touched another control, this time to sickbay.

"Dr. Fuentes?" she asked.

"Sí, Capitán," he answered. Dull, heavy tone. Good.

"Have your psychotropic basket of tricks ready. You understand?"

"Sí."

Still with the flat lack of caring; trained reflex would take over, when motivation was gone. That would be enough, until they took the counteractants. Paranoia and schizophrenia were reasonably well understood, and you could suppress the symptoms quite readily, for a while.

It would reduce their efficiency, of course. But they could do the job. *Good thing I don't care much what must be happening,* she thought idly, and rose to head down the corridor.

OFF THE COAST OF NORTH ANGOLA
2,500 METERS ALTITUDE
NOVEMBER 4, 1998
1035 HOURS

"Oh, shit, oh, shit," the pilot of Louise Gayner's aircar was saying as he fought the controls.

"Pull yourself together, man," she snapped, and looked down at her wrist. 1035, November 3rd; not a day she was going to forget very soon.

Perhaps that was a little unfair, she thought, as he quieted. The aircraft was down low, no more than two thousand meters, and doing better than Mach 2; not bad, considering the turbulence since the blast front hit. That had probably been Lobito, considering their position on the coast; a medium-sized port city. *Pity. Thought they'd stick to counterforce.* The weather outside was turning strange, with cloud patterns she had never seen before. Nothing on the standard channels, nothing but the roaring static bred by the monstrous electromagnetic pulses that were rolling around the earth. High-altitude detonations. Her aircar was EMP hardened, of course . . .

Nothing but cloud above, choppy blue-gray ocean below, visually. The radar was crawling with images, higher up: hypersonic craft, decoys, suborb missiles, bits and pieces of this and that. She swallowed, and realized with a start that her throat was dry; her flask was steady as she raised it to her lips. Wine and orange juice; to hell with the doctors. Two more traces, lower down, *fast.* From off to the west, only a few kilometers ahead of them. Something lanced down out of the sky, a pale finger that touched one of the traces. The explosion was a bright *blink* against the sea; the other trace was gone away, over the horizon.

"I don't think . . ." Gayner began. Another dagger from the sky, this time brighter and more ragged. *Ablation track,* she thought, and sipped at the flask again. *Missile, trying for the submarine.* As if to punctuate the identification, the sea erupted in a dome of shocked white, kilometers across. A low-yield fission weapon, tactical type. "I don't think there's much point in continuing on to Luanda," she continued.

The canopy went dark, and showed only the blossoming sunrise in the east. For a moment there were two suns; Gayner braced herself, and felt the automatic shockbars clamp down around her body. "Not much point in trying to reach home," she whispered. "We'll divert east and land in the Kasai." *If we make it.*

A fist struck.

DRAKA FORCES BASE ARESOPOLIS
MARE SERENITATIS, LUNA
NOVEMBER 4, 1998
1200 HOURS

Yolande Ingolfsson felt the rock tremor beneath her. "What was that?" she asked sharply. For an instant she felt bitter envy of the operators crouched over their screens. They had no *time* to think.

"Sector Ten," one replied. "Levels one through eight not reportin'. Penetrator." That was serf housing, she remembered. The breakthroughs seemed almost random; the last hit had been a fabrication plant. This would mean heavy casualties, ten thousand or better. Crushed, burned, explosive decompression. *Probably fairly quick, at least.* It was a good thing that grief was not cumulative; impossible to really feel more than you did for an individual. If you could pile one up on top of another, human existence would be impossible.

"Incoming." Yolande looked up from her warship-style crashcouch to the main screen. Another spray was coming into sight over the mountains, fanning out in blinking tracks. Some vanished even as she watched, but that quadrant's main battlecomps were down, the weapons reaching for the warheads were under individual control.

"Those three are going to—" The faint vibration again, then a louder, duller sound. "That's the dome gone."

A hand closed on her throat. *Don't be ridiculous, it's only an artifact,* she told herself.

"Outside comm?" she asked.

"Very irregular, from Earth," the officer replied. Yolande looked over to the main view of the mother planet, routed in from a pickup well out. Cloud reached unbroken around the northern hemisphere, and large patches of the south. Even as she watched a light blinked blue-white against the night quadrant. Decision firmed.

"Order to Ground Command," she said. That was the Army CINC here in Aresopolis—*what's left of it,* her mind japed at her. The Damage Control board's schematic of the city showed nearly half red; the residential sectors were mostly still blue, but much more of this and there wouldn't be enough afterwards to maintain the people. And there would probably be very little help from Earth. "Activate Contingency Horde-Two."

"Ma'am?" The Tac officer looked up from his board. *"Now?"*

Yolande keyed the releases of her combat cradle and stood, pushing herself up with a brief shove of one hand. "The troops will be safer dispersed on the surface," she said dispassionately.

Her chin jerked toward an overview of this area of Luna. "Most of this garbage is comin' from New Edo. It must be civilians or reservists, takin' over from incapacitated military personnel; we didn't get complete exposure fo' this Stone Dogs thing. That's why it's so irregular an' uncoordinated, we can *almost* handle it even crippled up as we are. That bein' so, they can't noways be in a position to stop us if we go in, dig out their perimeter on the surface, an' then blast down to get at the inhabited levels."

She thought of forests frozen-dead in the dome, and then of ghouloons hunting the enemy through their own tunnels. There was a certain comfort in it, dry and chill though it was.

"Oh, and please to info'm Strategos Witter that I'll be with the assault brigade." The Tac officer made to protest, shrugged, fell silent. "Don't worry, Merarch, he'll object, too, but all the policy-level decisions've been taken. This is our last throw. I'm certain-sure not needed here."

CENTRAL OFFICE, ARCHONAL PALACE
ARCHONA
DOMINATION OF THE DRAKA
NOVEMBER 4, 1998
1700 HOURS

"Excellence, they're getting some of the birds away," the liaison officer said pleadingly. "Please, it's important that yo' get to the shelter."

Eric von Shrakenberg shook his head. "We didn't expect to disable all the submarine launchers," he said quietly. "But if they get Archona, then it's pointless anyway. I'll live or die with my city . . . Call it an old man's fancy. Status report."

The Palace infosystem was excellent. Not that he was in the command loop, of course. Today he was a spectator.

Have I ever been anything else? he thought wearily. The lines traced over the globe. Somewhere outside there was a mammoth *crack*, like thunder. Manmade thunder, a laser burning a trail of ionization through the atmosphere, and a particle beam following it.

"We got the sub!" someone shouted. Lines were spearing out from somewhere off the Cape of Good Hope. "Four skimmers away." Hypervelocity, low level. "Sweet mercy of the White Christ, that's Mournblade's sector."

"The close-in will stop it . . . One down. Two. Three. Come on, baby, come on —"

The voices cut off, as if sliced. An awed voice spoke. "That's Cape Town gone."

The mother city, Eric thought. *Cradle of the nation. Taste victory, old fool. Savor it.*

"Status," he said, without opening eyelids that felt heavier than worlds.

"Excellence, we've lost . . . Wotan, we've lost nearly half the discrete platforms out to L-5. Alliance, ninety percent down an' falling fast. Freya bless, Excellence, if it hadn't been fo' the Stone Dogs"—a quaver, hastily surpessed—"there wouldn't be anythin' *left*, Excellence."

Another stone-shaking roar of manmade thunder through the walls. Eyes darted to the screens, relaxed; the last salvo had been at low-orbit targets, ones that were unlikely to respond. Eric forced his eyes open, onto the screens. Forced his mind to paint the full picture of what the bloodless schematics meant, through the hour that followed. *Your doing. Your responsibility.*

A man was cursing softly. "Oh, shit, oh, shit, that's Shanghai. Penetrator. Two. Another."

"Northern hemisphere stations report high-incidence cloud cover—"

"I don't believe it," somebody said. Eric looked up; that had been soft awe, not the hard control that had settled on most. "London's gone."

Eric slammed a hand down on the arm of his chair. "Who ordered that? Get me their name!"

"Excellence—" the operator looked back over his shoulder; the New Race control of hormone levels must have slipped, inattention, because there was a sheen of moisture across his forehead. "Excellence, they did it themselves."

Eric sighed and sat back, reluctantly letting go the balm of anger. "It'll happen, if yo' inflict insanity on those in charge of nuclear weapons," he said quietly.

"Multiple detonation, Japan." A toneless voice, lost in procedure. "High-yield groundbursts. Sublevel." A pause. "Jacketed bombs. Prelim'nry sensor data indicate radioactivity—"

The Archon listened through the figures. "Schematic on distribution, given projected wind patterns," he said. "Give me an intensity cline, geography an' timewise." The deepgraven lines beside his beak nose sank a little deeper as the maps twisted themselves. "Note to Plannin' Board: we'll probably have to evacuate the survivin' shelters from the Korean peninsula up through the Amur Valley, minimum. Draw up estimates." The Japanese had been true to their tradition, and had taken a good deal more with them to the land of the *kami* than their home islands. *They never liked the Koreans, anyhow,* he thought.

Minutes stretched into hours, as the quiet voices and screens reported. The thunder spoke less often now, outside; more of it was being directed offensively, into space, to make up for battlestations left derelict. More and more often his eyes went to the screens that showed the cumulative effects, graphs rising steadily towards the red lines that represented estimates of what the mother planet's biosphere could stand. *Conservative estimates . . . we think,* he reflected.

At last he spoke. "Strategos, a directive to the Supreme General Staff. No mo' fusion weapons within the atmosphere. Kinetic energy bombardment only, on Priority Three targets and above." Active military installations. "Throw rocks at them."

"Excellence—" A glance of protest from the Staff's representative.

Suddenly Eric felt life return, salt-bitter but strong. "Gods damn yo', that's *our planet* yo' fuckin' over, woman!" A dot expanded over the Hawaiian islands. "There goes 25% of Earth's launch capacity! Do it, get them on the blower, do it!" *What's a few more million lives in this charnel house?* he asked himself mockingly. *Go on, finish the job.*

"If only it were that easy," he muttered to himself. "If only." Aloud: "I'm goin' to catch some sleep." Chemicals would ensure that, and these days they could bring true rest. *Whether you deserve it or not.* "Wake me immediately if we get any substantial info'mation on the Trans Lunar situation."

Even this day had to end, sometime.

BEYOND THE ORBIT OF MARS
ABOARD DASCS *DIOCLETIAN*
NOVEMBER 5, 1998

The bridge was still chaotic, but it was a more orderly confusion now. Merarch Gudrun von Shrakenberg took another suck at the waterbulb and glanced over at the console that had housed the main compcore; there was an ozone and scorched-plastic stink from it even hours after they had crashed it with two clips from a gauntlet gun. A bit drastic, but it had worked . . . Now the circular command chamber was festooned with jury-rigged fiber-optic cables, and a daisy chain of linked perscomps floated in the center.

"Ready?" The Infosystems Officer looked up from his task. *Goddam New Race bastard* still *doesn't look tired,* she thought, then caught herself. It was amazing how habits of mind stayed with you, long after the circumstances had made them irrelevant. *Now everything is irrelevant, with two exceptions,* she mused.

"Ready," he affirmed, and looked down, flexing his hands.

"Sensor Officer?"

That one spoke without taking her eyes from screens that had to be manually controlled. "They're still matching at what they think is a safe distance." There was a vindictive satisfaction in the tone, and Gudrun nodded in agreement. Safe distance from the standard suicide bomb, but not from everything on the cruiser rigged to go at once.

She felt very tired, herself. "The rest of the squadron?"

"Still acceleratin', Cohortarch; looks like they'll be able to break contact."

The Stone Dogs had scourged the enemy fleet even more drastically than the comp-plague had crippled the Draka; it was the Alliance's civilian jackals who were closing in on the helpless *Diocletian* now. Miners and haulers and prospectors, fitted with a few haphazard weapons and crewed by irregulars . . . gathering like buzzards around a prey they would not dare to approach if it were hale.

"Cleon," she said conversationally, "yo' were at Chateau Retour last leave, weren't yo'? Met my mothah?"

"Yes, Cohortarch," he said, making a final adjustment. "Always admired her paintings." And he was probably sincere, considering what they were about to do.

That had been a good leave. *It would be good to see home again*, she thought. The vintage would be in; the fruity red of Bourgeuil, the Loire Valley Pinot Noir that smelled ever so faintly of violets.

"Actually, I was thinkin' of somethin' she told me about the Eurasian War. She was in tanks then, the Archonal Guard."

"Oh?"

"Yes, they had a sayin' . . . Is that damn fool still comin' in to board?"

The Sensor Officer nodded. "Makes sense, actually. We've been givin' a pretty good imitation of a dead ship. Be quite a prize if they could get it."

The Infosystems Officer made an affirmative sound, then asked: "About that sayin', Cohortarch?"

"Oh. 'If yo' tank is out of fuel, yo' becomes a pillbox.' " Her hand closed on an improvised switch, and her eyes went to the screen. Nothing fancy, someone had chalked a line on the surface. When the blip crossed it . . . " 'If yo' out of ammunition, become a bunker. Out of hope, then become a hero.' Service to the State!"

Her finger clenched.

"Glory to the R—"

CENTRAL OFFICE, ARCHONAL PALACE
ARCHONA
DOMINATION OF THE DRAKA
NOVEMBER 14, 1998

"So," Eric said, looking at the head of Technical Section.

The table was more crowded for this conference than it had been for the final one on the Stone Dogs. "Strategos Snappdove, what yo' sayin' is basically that we in the position of a man in a desert with a bucket of water. There's enough to get us to safety, but we got a dozen holes in the bucket and only one patch." Somebody actually managed to laugh, until Eric stared at her for a moment with red-circled eyes.

The Militant Party's man frowned. "None of the problems seem insoluble, on the figures," he said suspiciously.

Eric kept his face impassive; somewhere within him, teeth were barred. *You'll be dancing to our tune for some time, headhunter,* he thought coldly. The wall-screens were set to a number of channels; one showed the streets outside. Rain was falling out of season, mixed with frozen slush . . . *We humans may have earned this,* went through him. *The plants and the beasts did not.* His hand gestured to the scientist.

"Ah." Snappdove tugged at his graying beard. He looked as if he had not slept for a week, and then in his uniform, but that was common enough here today.

"Hmm," he continued. "Strategos, you are missing the, ah, the *synergies* between these problems." His hands moved on the table before him, calling up data. They scrolled across one wall, next to a view of Draka infantry advancing cautiously through a shattered town. The troops were in full environment suits, ghosting forward across rubble that glistened with rain. It was raining in most places, right now.

"We lost some fifteen percent of our Citizen population," he went on.

Unbelievable, Eric thought. *Worse than our worst predictions.*

"And twenty-two percent of the serfs. Three hundred million in all. But these losses are concentrated in the most highly skilled, educated components, yo' see? Then again, half our Earth-based manufacturin' capacity is still operable. But crucial components are badly hit. And to rebuild, we need items that can only come from zero-G fabricators: exemplia, superconductors and high-quality bearings. Not to mention the electronics, of course."

"Ghost in the machine," the Faraday exec half-mumbled. They all glanced over at her. "We *still* haven't gotten certain-sure tracers on that comp-plague," she went on, and returned her gaze to her hands. "May have to close down all the fabricators commissioned in the last decade—what's left of them—an' start from scratch."

Snappdove nodded. "So we need the orbital fabricators. But we lost mo' than *eighty percent* of *those*. And of our launch capacity. We must rapidly increase our launch capacity, but—" he spread his hands "— much of the material needed for all forms of Earth-to-orbit launch is space-made. And so it goes."

"Not to mention mo' elemental problems. Miz Lauwrence?"

The Conservancy Directorate chief raised her head from her hands. "We stopped short of killing the planet," she said dully. *There's someone who looks worse than I do*, Eric thought with mild astonishment. "Just. Lucky the worst effects were in the northern hemisphere, where it was winter anyways. Even so—" she waved a hand to the screen that showed freezing rain dripping on the jacarandas and orange groves"—damn-all crops this year from *anywheres*. Not much in the north fo' one, maybeso two years. Oceanic productivity will be way down, we got ice formin' in the *Adriatic*, fo' Freya's sake. Even half normal will take a decade; it'll be a *century* befo' general levels are back to normal." A death's-head smile. "That's assumin' some beautiful synergism doesn't kick us right ovah the edge."

Eric looked over to the Agriculture Directorate's representative. "We can make it," he said. "*If* the transport system can get back to somewhere like thirty percent of normal in a year or two. And *if* there's no more excess demands, and we impose the strictest rationin'. We'll have just enough in the stockpiles to tide us ovah without we have to eat the serfs." A few hollow chuckles. "We're already freezin' down the livestock that died. Best we get control of the enemy territory's grain-surplus areas as quick as may be."

The Archon nodded to the Dominarch, the head of the Supreme General Staff. He was coolly professional as he took over control of the infosystem.

"Well, we made a mistake tryin' fo' immediate landings in North America," he said. Casualty figures and losses in equipment flashed on the wall; his tone became slightly defensive at the slight but perceptible wince. On the screen beside the schematic a firefight was stabbing bright tongues of orange-red through the gray drizzle.

"Too much of our orbital capacity is out; reconnaissance and interdiction we don't have. Not all that many organized fo'mations to oppose us, but we're hurt badly, too; also, we've had to keep back a lot of troops to maintain order an' help with relief efforts." He paused. "An' they had a damn good fallback force waitin'," he said grimly. "Couple of cases, it was like stickin' our dicks into a meatgrinder. It goin' be a *long* time befo' we get that area pacified. 'Specially iff'n we have to give priority to economic uses of our launch capacity. We're occupying a few strategic areas, stompin' on any major concentrations, an' otherwise pullin' back. Fo' one thing, we still haven't gotten the last of those subs."

Snappdove joined in the general nod; Trincomalee had taken a hypersonic at short range only yesterday. "In any case, the survivors in North America would be almost as much trouble in labor camps," he said. "Making better progress in some other areas we are, but . . . these are territories dependent on a mechanized agriculture. We cannot support it, and the industries that did we have smashed. Also, ground combat devours resources we need elsewhere, not so much of matériel as of trained personnel."

"Aerospace?" Eric said.

A nod from another of the Arch-Strategoi. "Well," she said, "in Cis-Lunar space, we won—iff'n yo' consider bein' *almost* wiped out as opposed to *completely* wiped out in those terms. Only Alliance installations survivin' are in Britannia an' New Edo, with our people from Aresopolis sittin' on them. Aresopolis came off surprisin' well, which is a good thing because fuckall help *we* goin' give them these next few years."

"Outer system."

A shrug. "Excellence, Mars is pretty safe, not least because what's left of the Fleet is mostly in orbit around it. A lot of them with their compcores blown. Not much direct damage to the Martian installations; the comp-plague hit them bad, wors'n here, but they on a planet, which makes the life support easier. Trouble is, the Fleet units down are our best, the most modern." Another shrug. "As fo' the gas-giant moons, we be lucky just to keep them *supplied*, and that's assumin' no hostile action."

"And in the Belt?"

"We lost. They whupped our ass, Excellence. We hurt them bad, totaled Ceres, but they've got pretty well complete control in there now. No offensive capability to speak of, but plenty of defense, all those tin cans with popguns an' station-based weapons. And that starship. We don't know much of *its* capacity, but we do know its auxiliaries are Loki on wheels; roughly equivalent to what's left of our Fleet. Less the *Lionheart*, but they're out of the picture and runnin' their systems on the research computers."

"Dominarch," Eric said formally, "is it yo' opinion that, as matters stand, we can break the remainin' enemy resistance?"

The head of the Domination's military looked to either side at his peers, then nodded. "Depends on yo' definitions, Excellence. In Cis-Lunar space, not much of a problem, for what it's worth. On Earth, we can prevent any organized military challenge, yes. Dependin' on the resources made available" —he inclined his head towards Snappdove—"we can pacify the last of the Alliance territories in twenty to fifty years. Pacify to the point of bein' open fo' settlement; I expect some partisan activity fo' a long, long time."

He bit his lower lip and tapped at the table with a stylus. "Problem is Trans-Lunar space. There's maybe half a million ferals still left in the Belt, an' they have that starship and the facility that built it. We have our own antimatter production, just comin' on stream near Mercury, but the transport an' guardin' problems . . . And they are standin' above us on the gravity well." A long pause. "All factors considered, yes. We'll have to devote everythin' we can spare to it beyond survival, but yes. Certain advantages to bein' nearer the sun, and we do grossly outnumber them, in production as well. Long, long war of attrition, though. Possibility of technological surprise, although I doubt it; rate of innovation was slowin' down even befo' the War, and they won't have nearly as much to spare fo' research now."

Eric tapped his fingers together, looking around the table. The Draka were not a squeamish people, nor easily frightened—but the magnitude of this was enough to daunt anyone. *Myself included*, he thought, and surprised them with a harsh laugh.

"Come now, brothers and sisters of the Race," he said. "These are the problems of *victory*. Think how our enemies must be feelin'!" He turned to the Dominarch again.

"Consider as an alternative that we get a year's grace," he said. "In addition, that that starship actually *leaves*."

"Oh. Much better. Same prediction here on Earth; then . . . oh, say forty years to mop up the Belt. Still difficult an' expensive, but it would give us some margin."

Eric tapped the table lightly. "Here is my proposal. We

offer terms to the remainin' enemies in Trans-Lunar space. The, ah, *New America* to be allowed to leave; we can guarantee that with exchange of hostages an' so forth. They turn ovah the complete schematics on the comp-plague. In addition, we offer Metic Citizenship to any who surrender on Luna an' beyond." That meant civil rights but not the franchise, with full Citizenship for their children. "Between the ones who leave, and the ones who take our offer, we cut the problem down to size."

Shock, almost an audible gasp. The Militants' spokesman burst out: "Inconceivable!"

Thank you, Eric thought. *Gayner would have been more subtle.* "There's ample precedent, aftah the Eurasian War, fo' example." Everyone there would be conscious that Snappdove was the child of such.

"No precedent fo' that *scale*. And many of them would be racially totally unsuitable."

Eric smiled thinly. "Is there any precedent fo' the size of this *war*? Fo' the extent of our *losses*? Fo' the *situation*? We need those skills, fo' sheer survival's sake. War to the knife now might bring down the Domination." He paused at that, for the political implications to seep home. *That's right, think on the fact that I'm the Archon who's winning the Final War. Who'll be seen as the prudent one, and who the reckless, if you push this issue.* "As to the cosmetic problem, the Eugenics Board can see that their children have suitable exteriors." *And they will know which party to throw their support behind, a factor not to be dismissed.*

"But—letting them establish a colony, on the nearest star; an insane risk!"

"Nearest? With a forty-year transit time?" Eric said mordantly. Heads nodded; most of those here had a reasonably good idea of the sheer immensity 4.5 light-years represented. The whole solar system was a flyspeck by comparison. "Strategos Snappdove?" The Militant flushed, knowing this was collusion and unable to use the fact.

"Ah. Well, we estimate that they could take no more than a hundred thousand, assuming they use our Low-Met process. No matter how well equipped, this is a very small figure to maintain a technological civilization, the specialists required . . . The Belt itself is not self-sufficient, not really; it is almost impossible to fully duplicate a terrestroid ecology without a terrestroid planet . . . Using worst-case analysis, that is best-case fo' them, a century after arrival befo' they are established firmly enough to think of anything beyond bare survival. Therefo' we can expect no hostile action for a century an' a half, at an absolute minimum. Mo' probably a century beyond that.

"Besides which," he went on, "our studies indicate conclusively that attackin' a defended planetary system is virtually impossible. Interstellar war at sublight speeds is an absurdity; so is interstellar government. In two centuries, we'll be fully recovered, mo' powerful than a strugglin' colony could possibly be, and I'll stake my life and soul *we* wouldn't have the slightest chance of successfully attackin' *them*. If they did attack us, we could swat them like mosquitoes. Far mo' rational to put a fraction of that effort into colonizin' stars further out; which, incidentally, we'd be doin' as well."

Eric waited until the expressions showed the argument had been assimilated, weighted the balance of doubt and acceptance.

"And finally," he said, "a meta-political point. We Draka have always lived fo'—not necessarily war—but to excel, to dominate, to prove ourselves. As far as we can tell, there's no other sophont race within reach. Leastways, none with a technological civilization. The universe isn't enough of a challenge, it isn't conscious; without some rival, even if it's a rival we can't fight directly, what is the Race to measure itself against?"

He cleared his throat. That was a good concluding note; he had shown them just how grim the situation really was, and a way to simplify it considerably. And besides the practical reasons, a philosophical one squarely in line with tradition.

"We'll need to study this in far mo' detail, of course" he went on. "And a number of factors depend on the enemy's reaction. But I take it we have a preliminary consensus to present to the Senate and Assembly?"

CENTRAL OFFICE, ARCHONAL PALACE
ARCHONA
DOMINATION OF THE DRAKA
JANUARY 14, 1999

The face of the man in the screen was haggard-blank. Eric suspected that that was more than the psychotropic drugs thwarting the viral saboteurs at the base of the American's brain; it would be enough, to see a world perish while you stood helpless. *There is something worse than these ashes of victory*, he thought, moved. *Defeat*.

"You are a son-of-a bitch even for a Snake, you know that?" the American said.

"Those are the best terms yo' can expect," Eric said, making his voice gentle. The minutes of relay time were an advantage; his brain felt gritty with lack of sleep. "Oh, yo' mean my little offer of Citizenship?" He raised an eyebrow. "Well, yo' can scarcely blame yo' compatriots—ex-compatriots—on Luna for mostly fallin' in with it. Considerin' the alternatives."

"It's not altogether over," the voice from the screen grated. "We . . . hold the Belt. We're standing over your head, Snake."

"The war is ovah. Was over befo' it began, or the human race would be dead. It couldn't be fought, only finessed. We both knew that; yo' lost, General Lefarge." *For reasons you'll never know.* "Even assumin' yo' support in the Belt stays rock-firm, all you can do is hurt us befo' we drag yo' down. Which we will in the end; to kill the Race yo'd have to kill Earth. Meanin' two billion innocents; any one of whom, of course, can exercise the option of dying on they own initiative any time they wants. In terms of yo' own ethic, sacrificin' them for victory is one thing. Deprivin' them all of they personal choice just to make the Draka suffer mo' is a little questionable, isn't it?"

"Not as questionable as trusting a Draka's word on allowing the *New America* to leave peacefully."

I've won, Eric thought. It brought a workman's satisfaction, if no joy. "We don't expect that. What I'm asking is fo' yo' and I to work out a way which doesn't *require* that yo' trust us." He spread his hands. "To be absolutely frank, we don't really have the capacity to stop y'all, only to make the best departure orbit unworkable and slow yo' down. Which yo' can send observers to verify. In any case, my offer *has* split yo' community. To the brink of civil war, if yo' refuse this option."

Slow minutes of waiting. He felt the chill; it was colder than it should be, here in Archona, much colder. *Not too much. Near the edge, but we pulled back in time. Our Mother is wounded, but she'll recover, if I can buy her time.* Eric used the opportunity to study the other's face while the message arrived. *That is a dangerous man*, he decided. *Am I doing the right thing?*

"We accept, pending the details," Lefarge spat. "And your sympathy isn't worth shit, Snake." He recovered an icy possession. "Tell me, though. Why not just offer admission to the Snake farm to our traitors?"

Eric spread his hands in concession. "Two . . . no, three reasons, Brigadier Lefarge. First, many mo' will *take* the offer, if they can salve they consciences by knowin' y'all have a place to go." He smiled.

"Sun Tzu said that one should never totally block an enemy's retreat; retreatin' refugees are less troublesome than a last stand, at the moment. Second, and this I used with my colleagues, what are the Draka without an enemy, however distant? We won't be able to follow y'all anytime soon—that's anothah thing we can arrange to verify—but we'll *know* that yo' there. Third, fo' my private consumption . . . Well, let's say that the Domination . . . forecloses certain options, as a path of human development. Better that not all the eggs be in one basket, fo' Earth's children."

A curt nod, and the screen blanked. Eric sat in thought, watching the chill non-summer rains beat against the window. Then he keyed the office com again.

"Put Arch-Strategos Ingolfsson on," he continued. There was work yet, before he could sleep. "Secured Channel Seventeen, and leave me, please."

Yolande looked up from her desk, her hand shaking as she took another stim and swallowed it dry. *Got to watch these*, she thought.

"Excellence." *Wotan, he looks worse than I do. Of course, he's eighty.*

"Arch-Strategos. This is on Channel Seventeen, yo' can speak freely. In brief, yo' are relieved and ordered to return to Archona." The starved eagle face leaned closer to the pickup. "Seven hundred million dead," he continued quietly. "Includin' millions of our own people. How does it feel, bein' the greatest mass murderer in human history?"

Yolande squeezed thumb and forefinger to the bridge of her nose. "If this is victory, perhaps defeat is preferable," she said. "I'm ready fo' yo' firin' squad, Excellence."

"I've seen defeat just recently, and yo're wrong," Eric said, and laughed; she shivered slightly. It was the laugh a hanged man might make. "And I'm not lettin' yo' off so easy as that."

She looked up, and he was grinning at her.

"A third of the human species dies, and *Louise Gayner* survived; accordingly, I can't spare the 'Hero of the Tunnels.' And y'are kin, aftah all . . . I *ought* to send yo' to Australasia to pacify it."

A pause. "No, I'm givin' Gayner that joy; it's butcher's work, she'll enjoy it. And hopefully do it badly enough to give me an axe-swing at her neck . . . No, yo', dear niece, are comin' home to put the remnants of our space capacities together. We need them, if we're to get this planet back on its feet."

Another corpse smile. "Just to help, I'm goin' to be sendin' yo' lots of qualified personnel. We're goin' to be handing out Citizenship fairly liberal; some millions, as many as I can swing. Awkward to have them around here—off to yo'. Now yo' can *really* learn how to handle Yankees." Flatly: "And that firin' squad is in abeyance, not dismissed."

She looked up sharply. "Think about it, niece. *I just 'won' the Final War.* I've got a decade at least in which to use that, politically, and I intend to *use* it. And yo' . . . yo' troubles are just gettin' under way."

Yolande nodded. It was difficult to care, when you were this tired. "Was that smart, lettin' the *New America* go?" she said. *And are the Lefarges escaping me, or have I taken the most complete vengeance any human being has ever achieved?*

"I think so," he said, nodding heavily. "Keeps us on our toes, makes sure the Race goes to the stars as well. And . . . maybe this *victory*"—his mouth twisted at the word—"means Earth is goin' down a dead end, much as we try to see otherwise. The *New America* means an insurance policy fo' our species, at least. See yo' soon, partner in crime."

CHAPTER TWENTY-TWO

Could things have turned out otherwise? My father went to his grave blaming himself for the Fall. Some others who should have known better still do so. Yet how far can any individual be blamed or praised for a historical event so large and complex? Here on Samothrace we have developed an exaggerated idea of what one person can do, perhaps. An entire solar system with less than a quarter-million inhabitants will do that; we are on our own, on a frontier whose homeland has been eaten by time and history. And our heritage is one of belief in individual responsibility, the sacredness of choice, in the human being as the embodiment of humanity. Rightly so; even to the extent of renouncing the temptations of the trans-human, whether electronic or biological. We make our own destiny here.

So we see our history-become-myth in terms of heroes and villains. My father was a very great man; the *New America*'s completion is his monument, for without his driving will it might well never have been ready to carry our saving remnant. This *world* is his monument, as much as any single man's, for his leadership in the first terrible years of the Settlement. Yet in those final months around Sol the lovely and the lost, how many separate acts—of cowardice, heroism, treachery, honor, love, hate, stupidity, inspiration—went into the making of the Fall? The past we do not know; the future we cannot. I knew the living man, and know he never did less than his utmost. Perhaps that should be added to our new Republic's proud motto: *Ad Astra et Libertas*.

A Hertiage of Liberty
by Iris Lefarge Stoddard
Adams University Press
New Jerusalem, Planetary Republic of
Samothrace
Alpha Centauri
2107 AD (109 Dispersal)

EPILOGUE I

CLAESTUM PLANTATION
DISTRICT OF TUSCANY
PROVINCE OF ITALY
DOMINATION OF THE DRAKA
JUNE 1, 2000

Yolande Ingolfsson paused and looked back from the entrance of the graveyard. The hills looked raw, without the ancient olives; the new plantings were tiny shoots of green, and she could see the workers still piling the black stumps and branches together for burning. There were gaps in the fruit orchards as well, despite all the anticold bacteria, and the sheep were few and sickly. The winds out of the west had been cold, these past winters; cold and full of death. But the land would recover, if not fully in her lifetime; the grass stood green, and the thin rumpled grainfields were beginning to show yellow with promise. She shivered slightly, pulling the collar of her coat closer about her; it would be a long time before Italy was as warm as it had been.

The grave was a little ragged, neglected when so much else needed every pair of hands. She knelt and laid the roses on the shaggy grass. *That's all right*, she thought, smoothing it with her hands. There were small white flowers blooming in it; they smelled of peppermint. *It's life, is all*.

"Myfwany," she said, and found herself empty of words for a long time. The sun moved, and her shadow crept across the living flowers and the ones she had brought.

"Myfwany, sweet," she whispered at last. "I don't know what to say. They're calling me a hero, now. Even Uncle

Eric, in public." She shook her head again. "The world is so full of mourning, it should make my own griefs seem small. And yet . . . I'm lucky, I suppose. Gwen's safe; our children are safe. There's no war hangin' over they heads now. But —" she beat her fists together. "Oh, love, did I do right, or did I fuck it all up?"

Warm wet slid down her cheeks, into the corners of her mouth. She raised her hand to her face, reached out to lay the teardrop on the roses. It slid onto the crimson petal, lay glittering.

"Oh, honeysweet," she said, her voice shaking with the sobs. "All the tears I never cried, would they have made a difference? My love, rest yo' well. Rest ever well. Till we meet again, forever."

EPILOGUE II

CONTROL DECK
ALLIANCE SHIP NEW AMERICA
PAST THE ORBIT OF PLUTO
OCTOBER 1, 2000

"That's it," Captain Anderson said with a sigh. "If we needed any more confirmation." He eased the earphones from his wiry black hair; a stocky pug-faced Minnesotan of Danish descent, and a physicist of note as well as a Space Forcer. "Over to you, JB," he continued formally.

The Second Officer nodded and touched a control. Anderson turned to the gaunt man who stood behind him, watching the receding light of Sol in the main tank-screen in the center of the control deck. It was set to show what an unaided eye would see from this distance: no more than an unusually bright star.

"So they're keeping their word, for once," Lefarge said softly. "Not that we left them any choice, the way we had it set up." It was surprising enough that von Shrakenberg had trusted *him* to broadcast the final specs on the comp-plague . . . He pushed the complexities out of his mind. It was difficult; that was something he was going to have to learn all over again, to live for the future. Cindy would help, and they would both offer what they could to Marya.

"They couldn't touch us at this range, anyway," Anderson said meditatively.

"That's true," Lefarge agreed. His voice had an empty tone, to match his eyes. "They'll probably follow, one day. If not to Alpha Centauri, to other places."

"We'll be ready," Anderson said, coming up beside him. There was no other sound besides the ventilators, and the subliminal tremor of the drive. That would continue for months yet . . . "Or we . . . our descendants could go back, first."

"No. No, not if they have any sense. There'll be nothing here worth coming back for; we're taking all the valuables with us. All that's left."

The ship's commander cleared his throat. His authority was theoretically absolute, until they reached the *New America*'s destination, and he knew Lefarge would obey as readily as any crewman. But there was something in that lined face that made him reluctant to order; it would be an intrusion, somehow.

"Brigadier—" he began.

Lefarge looked up and smiled; it even seemed to touch his eyes, somehow. "Fred," he said. "While we're off duty, Captain."

"Fred. Look, man, there's no real need for you to stand watches; yes, you're qualified, and it'll be only five years total." The bulk of the colonists would be in low-met all the way; there were five active-duty crews, who would work in rotation. "But it's at the other end we're *really* going to need you. Hell, why waste your lifespan? You're going to have a life's work there, and barring catastrophe the crew's doing routine. For that matter, I'm going to have time to finish that novel at last."

"I think I am going to have a life job, when we get there," Lefarge said, nodding. "And to do it properly, I'm going to have to be looking forward." He met the captain's eyes again, and his were like raw wounds. The other man had seen more than enough of grief, these last few months, but it was still shocking. "So I need time for . . . thinking. And to get the saddest words in the English language out of my system." He laughed bleakly at Anderson's silent question. "If only. If only."

EPILOGUE III

OBSERVATION DECK
DASCS *LIONHEART*
NEAR PLUTO
OCTOBER 5, 2000

The bright dot of the *New America*'s drive was another star among many, in the screen that fronted the darkened chamber. Gwendolyn Ingolfsson hung before it, lost and rapt, unconscious even of the man whose arm was linked with hers.

"Oh, gods," she whispered; starlight broke on tears. "How I envy them!"

APPENDIX

Note to readers: First mention of placenames not common to our timeline and that of the Domination are given with their equivalent in brackets, thus: Virconium [Durban, South Africa]

Excerpts from:
The Economy of the Domination: Historical and Regional Perspectives by Sandra de Varga, Ph.D, Department of Economic Geography, San Diego University Press, 1991.

Industrial Power Systems and Transportation

The development of the steam engine followed rather different paths in the three most important centers of innovation during the Early Industrial era—Great Britain, the USA, and the Crown Colony of Drakia.

Steam Engines to 1850

The Watt engine had assumed its mature form by the early 1780s; a double-acting reciprocating engine with D-slide valving, a centrifugal governor, a separate condensor and steam pressures of no more than 5 psi, capable of delivering reciprocating or rotary action via sun-and-planet gearing. This engine was very suitable for the British market, which was small, coal-rich and had an excellent transport infrastructure by the standards of the time. Watt engines were extensively exported to Drakia in the late 1780s, and put to a number of uses in mining and agricultural processing, particularly sugar milling, and also in civil engineering—principally harbor dredging.

However, the Watt engine had serious disadvantages in the Southern African environment. The coal was abundant and cheap but the mines were far inland and out of the reach of water transport; water itself was often scarce and highly mineralized. Unlike the Americas, there were virtually no navigable rivers. The centers of economic activity—plantations, ranches, harbors, gold, coal, and diamond mines—were very widely scattered, islands in a sea of thinly-populated grazing country. By 1796 there were over 250 Watt engines at work in the Drakian colony, a number second only to that of Britain herself, and these problems were becoming acute. Boulton & Watt, the manufacturers, were far too distant to understand the needs of the Drakian market, and uninterested in the sort of research program necessary to solve the manufacturing problems involved; after all, they were selling every engine they could turn out and more.

It was at this point that Richard Trevithick arrived in Virconium to take up a post as inspector of steam engines for the African Mining and Metals Combine. The young Cornish engineer had little formal education, like many of the entrepreneur-inventors of the time; unlike them, he also had virtually no business sense to speak of. What he *did* have was an almost instinctive grasp of the thermodynamics and mechanics of steam engines, and a matchlessly fertile imagination. In Africa, he found a patron with limitless capital and driving needs.

Trevithick's first accomplishment was a simple modification of the Watt engines used for pumping water and crushing ore in the Combine's gold mines in eastern Archona province; he substituted a riveted-iron double flue boiler for the earlier copper model, inserted the cylinder in the boiler itself, and tripled the operating pressures. The drastic increases in fuel efficiency led directly to his promotion to Inspector-General of Engines for the Combine.

Shipping shortages produced by the Napoleonic Wars, coupled with high prices and demand, had already prompted a coalition of investors to start a coal-fired iron smelting plant on the site of the future city of Diskarapur [Newcastle, South Arca], where suitable coking coal and iron ore occurred in close proximity. The colonial Assembly had financed its expansion to include a Court-process puddling plant and crucible-steel facility for munitions production; there was a large Wilkinson-type cannon boring mill, imported from England, as well. The Mining Combine was sufficiently impressed with Trevithick's talents to propose a merger, and the setting-up of a Ferrous Metals Combine which would produce mining equipment—steam engines in particular.

Trevithick was in charge of the new operation, and recruited extensively in the British Isles for mechanics and engineers. Improved products followed rapidly, particularly since Drakia was too remote for Boulton & Watt patent-protection lawsuits. Pressures of up to 25 psi were quickly achieved, and smaller and more precisely-bored cylinders produced. Trevithick's next crucial innovation was the external feedwater condensor, which permitted recycling of boiler water (1799) and the uniflow valve system, which raised fuel efficiency another order of magnitude by separating the steam entry and exhaust areas of the cylinder. By 1800, Trevithick high-pressure single-cylinder engines were being produced in some numbers and were replacing or supplementing the Watt engines then in use.

However, Trevithick was not content with fulfilling his original mandate. The new engines were now compact and rugged enough to be a credible power plant for locomotive purposes. In 1800–1801 Trevithick and his team of assistants (which included a number of instrument makers familiar with precision metalworking) produced working scale models of road-engines and rail locomotives, as well as an experimental paddle wheel steamboat. The backers of the embryonic Ferrous Metals Combine were sufficiently impressed to provide funding for prototype development. While slow and cumbersome by later standards, the resulting locomotives and "road autosteamers" were an obvious and vast improvement on animal traction. Capital from gold production and the export trades flowed into further investment, and the first production models were in use by 1803. Steam-powered gunboats on the Nile proved the military utility of the new engines, and were crucial to the rapid pacification of the province of Egypt after the uprising of 1803. Steam dredges of Trevithick's design helped to build the Suez Canal in 1803–1810, and coastal steamers and harbor tugs. Steam gunboats pushed Draka control up the eastern coast of Africa and into Madagascar. As early as 1810, "drags" (steam haulers pulling wagons) were being used to transport troops.

The next important innovation was in the fuel and boiler systems. Power-driven drills had been an early application of Trevithick's work, searching for underground water in the extensive arid regions of southern Africa. When Egypt was overrun, drilling teams began operating in its Western Desert—and discovered petroleum in the deserts west of Alexandria, natural gas in the Nile Delta. There were no convenient coal mines in Egypt, and local engineers quickly modified their machinery to use at first crude oil, and then distilled products, as a fuel source. Once the greater convenience and heat-density of petroleum became apparent, most road-engines and an increasing number of nautical ones were converted to liquid fuels. At the same time, "water-tube" boilers (in which the furnace fire circulates around water-filled tubing to produce steam) were introduced, lowering the weight and bulk of boilers.

Power Distribution Systems

Meanwhile, Trevithick had not forgotten the special needs of his original Mining Combine patrons. The gold mines were quickly running deeper, and this was the hardest of hard-rock work. While unskilled labor was plentiful and cheap, costs still rose with depth. Trevithick and the team of apprentices and subordinates that grew around him experimented with direct-acting steam drills and borers, as well as with improved pumping and hoisting systems. However, piping hot steam without loss of heat (and therefore pressure) proved to be extremely difficult and dangerous, especially in underground situations.

Trevithick (and Edgar Stevens, his principal assistant) turned to compressed-air systems instead. The basic mechanical principles were already familiar, and local experiments with native rubber provided a solution to the problems of gaskets and flexible connectors. Large reciprocating double-action compressors were set up, enabling each mine (or later, factory) to have an efficient central power plant. Regenerative systems (using the heat generated during the compression of the air to warm the feedwater of the steam engines) provided greater thermal efficiency. Compressed air was stored in central reservoirs, then distributed by iron piping to dispersed locations with only minor frictional losses; drills, pumps, winches, and crushers could be placed as needed and flexibly operated.

Once developed, this had obvious applications outside mining. Mobile compressors were developed to power rock drills and other equipment in road building and construction work; powered rock-saws drastically reduced the cost of masonry, despite the lack of trained masons and quarrymen. Central-factory systems, particularly after the development of the rotary-vane air motor in the 1820s, superceded the clumsy, friction-ridden and dangerous belting and shafting the British pioneers of the Industrial Age had used. Whole new categories of machine tool proved possible with the flexible and precise control which air motors could offer with a simple manipulation of valves, and powered equipment could now be used in locations—e.g., the home—where direct steam drive was out of the question. Air transmission systems had few moving parts and were easily centrally controlled, leading to low maintenance costs. Compressed-air auxiliaries greatly simplified the operation of autosteamers.

Technology and the Sociology of Industry

By the 1830s, most Draka mining-industrial plants were using centralized pneumatic transmission systems, operating at standardized pressures. Given the vastly superior efficiency of such systems, the question arises of why the other industrial countries, particularly Britain, did not follow suit to anything like the same degree. (For example, several of the larger Draka cities installed mains systems delivering metered compressed air via understreet tubes in the 1840s and 1850s; the first European city to do so was Paris, in the 1880s—and that system was installed by Draka engineers.) A digression into industrial organization is necessary to establish the causal links.

The overwhelming majority of European and American industrial firms—even in heavy industry—were organized on a family business basic until well into the twentieth century; corporations were closely held. Before about 1870, railroads aside, this was the *only* form of business organization in those countries. These firms, mostly small, were obstinately self-financing, which sharply limited their capital reserves; and they were almost pathologically averse to debt and the supervision by banks it entailed. This form of organization responded quickly and intelligently to shifts in consumer demand; it was matchlessly efficient at supplying a diverse and "atomized" market.

In the proto-Domination, by contrast, industry developed to serve *production* rather than consumption; mines, heavy transportation, the armed forces, the Landholders' League and its agricultural processing plants, were the primary customers. The primary demand was for metal goods, principally tools, rather than the textiles and other end-products which were the staple of British industry in the period. When consumer goods manufacture did become important, it was mostly as a part of the Landholders' League's drive to capture value-added by following its members' crops "downstream" through processing to final sale. Even here, orders were "lumpy" by contemporary standards; for example, the Combines bought standard products in immense quantity for their basic serf labor forces. After the League went into cooperative wholesaling/retailing for its members (at first by mail order), plantation demand was largely aggregated as well— the League bought uniform goods in bulk, e.g., agricultural machinery or cheap shoes for fieldhands, later canned goods and power systems. Thus markets were simple, and on the whole quite reliable, making it possible to utilize economies of scale with little risk. The production units were large, from the beginning, and operated by salaried mangers. The government, and the especially the League, dominated the banking system, which served to funnel the surplus capital of agriculture into concentrated locations.

Thus Draka enterprises could afford to be of *technically* optimum size (indeed, sometimes larger); sales were reliable enough, and capital abundant enough, that long-term planning and research became a feature of their operation two generations before the Germans followed in their footsteps. The concentration of all money incomes in the top 4%–8% of the population kept the savings rate extremely high, usually in the neighborhood of 30%–50% of GNP, which meant an economy that was both awash with capital and furnished with abundant opportunities for productive investment. Land, unskilled and semi-skilled labor, and raw materials were all superabundant and cheap; the perennial shortage of managerial personnel led to an early emphasis on higher education—influenced by the German tradition of many of the early immigrants.

At the same time, this was not a pure command economy. Prices were set by the market, which was completely open to world trade; the high export propensity exerted continual pressure on even the largest organizations. The consumer and service sectors that served the Citizen population were characterized by much smaller individually owned enterprises. The ideology of the corporate State came later; in the early period, roughly to 1840, it was a matter of "sleepwalking" through to a solution to a set of isolated problems. Only when the essentials were in place did the fact that a system existed become obvious.

The result was what the great classical-liberal economists of the 19th century regarded as an utterly perverse economy: one in which human beings and their food and clothing were intermediate production goods, and machine-tools and cannon end products. To function it required a militarized society regimented by terror. But for the sort of brute-force, quantitative, capital-goods intensive industrialization the Domination needed to power its relentless expansion, it was ideal.

Power System Development, 1840–1910
Steam Turbines:

The low operating efficiency of reciprocating steam engines was obvious, both intuitively and from the growing knowledge of thermodynamic and mechanical analysis in the early 19th century. Even with pneumatic transmission, the reciprocating action of pistons lost efficiency every time it had to be transformed into rotary action, and there were annoying limits to the size, speed, and power-output of steam pistons. Attempts at direct rotary engines (steam turbines) were made in a number of countries, but the manufacturing difficulties were many. A multi-stage turbine was obviously essential if the expansive power of steam was to be utilized, but this required precision machining of unprecedented quality. Furthermore, for maximum efficiency operating speeds and temperatures whole orders of magnitude greater than the piston engine were needed. Wrought and cast iron, and direct-contact oil lubrication, had sufficed for Watt and even Trevithick; they were not enough for the turbine.

However, the Draka did have one advantage in the race to perfect a working steam turbine. Their extensive use of pneumatic systems had led to an early interest in axial-flow air motors, which is to say, air turbines. While it was much easier to manufacture a workable air turbine (operating temperatures were low, and for most uses a relatively low degree of efficiency was tolerable), the basic operating principles and problems were quite similar. The development of roller-, ball-, and air-bearings from the 1840s was largely done in the course of work on air turbines, and so was the development of larger precision-machined steel alloy rotor blades—especially for the large boring machines used in heavy-artillery manufacture. By the 1860s, materials technology had advanced to a stage where steam turbines were a distinct possibility.

While industrial demand might have provided incentive enough, it was a military-transport need that provided the final impetus. Powered dirigible balloons had been experimented with in Alexandria and Diskarapur from the 1850s. During the Franco-Prussian war, the besieged French garrison of Paris improvised semi-rigid dirigibles powered by a Draka-made industrial compressor (reciprocating type) and propellors driven by air turbines. These were capable of speeds of up to 60 kph for several hours, and were used to ferry passengers and messages, and even to bomb the Prussian artillery; during the Paris Commune, they were also used to bombard Communard positions before attacks by government troops.

This success resulted in desultory research in a number of European countries (particularly the new German Empire), and a crash project in the Domination. Using a single-stage expansive steam turbine, extensive construction with the newly-available aluminum alloys, and pneumatic transmission, dirigible airships proved to be an expensive but practical weapons system during the Anglo-Russian war of 1879–1882. Shortly thereafter heavier models of steam turbine were used to generate electricity, to power turbocompressors for large-scale pneumatic systems, and to power ships through mechanical and pneumatic gearing.

Internal Combustion Engines:

The possibility of using combustion gases directly in the cylinders of a prime mover, rather than indirectly by heating a working fluid such as steam, had been theorized as far back as the 17th century. The attractions—simplicity, since there was no boiler system, and greater inherent thermal efficiency—were obvious. Again, manufacturing limitations prevented widespread use until well into the 19th century. In this field, French and German researchers established an early lead; the very efficiency of the central engine–pneumatic transmission system in the Domination inhibited research on alternatives. Andre Charbonneau (1820–1887) and Rudolf Diesel (1858–1920) established the workability of internal-combustion prime movers (using a flame-ignition and compression-ignition system respectively); by the 1880s, such "gas engines" were in quite common use in Europe, mostly as single-cylinder factory engines, especially in steel plants where they could be run on blast-furnace gas. The German General Staff's Transport Section, in conjunction with Diesel, made the first serious application to transportation, with a compression-ignition system for their experimental dirigibles of the mid-to late-1880s. Meanwhile the French were perfecting the lighter spark-ignition engine, leading to the first practical heavier-than-air flight by Edouard Sancerre in 1898.

Once alerted to the possibilities, the Domination's armed forces and Institutes quickly eliminated the Europeans' early lead in piston-action internal combustion engines. By the 1890s, Diesel-type engines (largely of aluminum-alloy construction and running on a mixture of kerosene and hydrogen gas from the lift cells) had become the standard engine for dirigible airships worldwide. The spark-ignition engine was largely limited to airplanes; there were experimental applications to automobiles, but the industrial inertia of 60 years kept the steam engine dominant on the road, especially considering its greater range of fuels, ease of manufacture and maintenance, and greater reliability. However, the greater power-to-weight ratio of the internal combustion engine did maintain a certain degree of interest for ground applications, particularly in armored fighting vehicles.

The next step was obvious, by analogy from the progress of steam engines: a gas turbine. The Domination's researchers first attempted (by about 1900) a "pure" turbine, with a rotary compressor delivering air to a combustion chamber, whence the gases exited through an expansive power-turbine. This proved to be a monumental engineering task, and the speeds and especially temperatures involved were beyond the manufacturing technology of the day—particularly when the corrosive nature of the combustion gases was considered. Developing an axial compressor that did not consume more power than it generated also proved frustratingly difficult. A further analogy suggested itself, however: the steam piston-compressor, air-turbine combination which had always been the mainstay of the Domination's industrial machine. Using a conventional compression-ignition cylinder as the gas-generating unit, a high-pressure gas of moderate temperature could be obtained, and then delivered through a power turbine. This gave many of the torque advantages of a turbine engine, an excellent power-to-weight ratio plus the fuel efficiency of Diesel's engine. This "turbocompound" engine was demonstrated on a trial basis in 1914, and was first applied to war dirigibles in 1917, and to armored fighting vehicles in 1917–1918. While easier to make than a pure turbine, the turbocompound was still a formidable proposition; American and European manufacturers continued to develop the reciprocating IC engines, until pure turbines became available in the late 1930s.

Electricity:

By the 1840s, the basic technology of Draka 19th-century industrialization—reciprocating steam engines, with direct or more commonly pneumatic transmissions to various machines and machine-tools—had been established. The next two generations saw a continuous refinement, increased efficiency, and vast expansion of scale; installed horsepower in the Domination probably surpassed that of Great Britain in the 1850s, and by 1910 it was equal to that of the United States, or equivalent to Germany, France, and Russia combined.

In the meantime, experimentation had shown itself to be a paying proposition, and the overlords of Drakia were nothing if not practical men; accordingly, they subsidized research lavishly. Furthermore, developments in mechanics and especially in industrial chemistry were obviously moving beyond the inspired-tinker stage. Drawing on the partly Germanic educational tradition of their ancestors, both the regular universities and the Technological Institutes (which had originally been craft training centers and lending libraries) increasingly emphasized direct, systematic research in well-equipped laboratories. The largely illiterate and unskilled nature of the industrial workforce paradoxically reinforced the drive for efficiency; by mass-production, assembly-line methods and by "building in" skills into specialized machine tools, it was possible to substitute rote-trained machine tenders for the all-around skilled craftsmen of European countries.

The next major development in power systems was electricity. The initial interest was for communications purposes, and secondarily for electrochemical and electrometallurgical work. Copperwire telegraphs were introduced in the 1820s, and spread quickly, in the Domination as elsewhere. Long-distance transmission and underwater cables, however, required more theoretical work. The University of Archona [Pretoria, South Africa] succeeded in acquiring the services of Michael Faraday (born 1791, Newlington, Surrey, died 1872, Archona, Archona Province) in 1824. As Director of Electrical Research, he made a number of discoveries, including the basics of electromagnetic induction, and the first electric dynamo and electric motor (1830–33); students under his supervision perfected the lead-acid storage battery. During the 1830s and 1840s, fresh discoveries included electrolytic refining of a number of metals (principally copper and magnesium), electric arc-lights, improved direct-current motors, and electromagnets. In 1838 a new industrial firm, the Faraday Electromagnetic Combine, was established to manufacture and market the new discoveries; Faraday himself was granted 10% of the capital gratis, the remainder being supplied by the government, the Ferrous Metals and Trevithick Autosteamer Combines, and the Landholders' League and individuals.

The combination of dynamo/motor and storage battery made many applications common, although pneumatic-transmission systems remained predominant in most industrial use for several generations. The dynamo was usually powered by axial-flow air turbines, which gave the steady high-speed rotation needed. Carbon-arc lamps quickly took over the high-intensity outdoor and factory lighting roles, and by the 1860s incandescent bulbs had been developed. At roughly the same time small electric generators became common on autosteamers and trains, mainly for lighting purposes. Initially, electric power was generated on the spot in plants, factories and mines via the existing pneumatic transmission methods; there was little incentive to develop central-plant distribution systems until home-lighting became common, or until electric motors began to supplement or replace pneumatic transmission—the latter awaiting the perfection of alternating current motors in the 1870s.

The first large-scale electric power development project was the Quattara Depression Scheme. Located about 120 kilometers west of Alexandria, much of this area of salt marsh was hundreds of meters below sea level. Studies from the 1850s on had reviewed the possibilities of digging a canal through to the Mediterranean and tapping the resulting hydraulic energy, but the distances involved made pneumatic transmission impractical. In 1878 a hydroelectric format was selected, and construction began in the same year; by the mid-1880s, a yearly production of 250 megawatts was reached, climbing to 500 MW by 1890. Initial applications were mostly electrometallurgical, particularly aluminum refining by the newly discovered cryolitic process; large-scale plants were set up on site, and underground DC power cables were laid to Alexandria itself. The discovery of natural gas and oil beneath the half-flooded Quattara, and the growth of chemical plants associated with the evaporation of brine, led to further expansion; in the end, to the explosive growth of the Alexandria connurbation westward, a solid block of factories, refineries, artificial harbors and residential developments along the shore from the Delta to El Alamein.

With the discovery of the alternating current motor and generator (1870s, largely in the US and Germany), the mercury-arc rectifier for easy conversion of AC to DC power (Alexandria Technological Institute, 1880), and the Tesla transformer (Archona University, 1891), large-scale use of electrical power as a general power source became possible. The concurrent development of steam turbines provided another suitable prime mover.

Developments in the Domination followed a rather different path than those in Europe and the US. As usual in Draka practice, a central agency was established for power generation; the Electricity Supply Combine, in 1890, with financial backing from most potential industrial consumers. Distribution systems within urban areas were mostly AC from about 1895 on. Africa proved to be supera-bundantly supplied with hydroelectric potential—the Inga falls on the lower Congo alone had 10% of the potential of the entire planet—although it was often rather inconveniently placed.

The period from 1880–1910 saw continuous investment in hydroelectric and hydroelectric/irrigation projects, and continuous improvements in transmission efficiencies and range of uses (e.g., electric trains, 1890, fluorescent lighting, 1903, arc furnaces for alloy steel production, 1893). Comprehensive basin projects for the Orange River (1884), the Nile (1889), the Chad/Benue (1893), and the Congo (1900) were launched, with radical innovations in high-dam and large-scale water-turbine technologies. These were long-term projects; the Zambezi-Cunene scheme, which supplied water for the central Archona Province industrial zone, irrigated 9,000,000 hectares, provided deep-lift barge traffic as far inland as Kariba and generated over 2,000 MW, was started (piecemeal) in the 1880s and not completed until the 1930s. Nevertheless, by 1914 the Domination produced over half the world's electricity, 80% from hydropower, and had a commanding lead in electrochemical and metallurgical technology—producing approximately 90% of the world's aluminum and aluminum alloy production, for example. Supplementary sources of electrical energy included coal- and natural-gas-fired steam turbines; North Africa in particular proved very rich in natural gas, which came on stream in increasing amounts after the discovery of the Libyan and Saharan petroleum fields in 1880–1900. Along the Great Rift, experimental development of geothermal power began in the last decade before the Great War, and theoretical studies of deep-ocean convection taps and oceanic currents as power sources were launched.

One notable feature of the Domination's power-grid was the use of compressed-air storage systems to even out demand. This grew naturally out of the central compressed-air delivery systems which had preceded electric power, and which had left a complex of underground ferroconcrete tanks around most of the Domination's cities. Since demand for electric power was irregular on both a daily and seasonal basis, costly excess capacity had to be kept idle during "off" periods to meet peak demand. The Draka used the power generated in the off hours to pump air into the storage tanks in highly compressed form. When demand rose, the hot dense air was released through pneumatic turbines to generate power; there were frictional losses in the system, but it still allowed savings of up to 25% in comparison to the cost of keeping additional fossil fuel plants on standby, and it was more flexible as well.

Immediately after the Great War of 1919, these storage systems also proved an ideal way of making solar-powered electricity generation practical. Solar water-heating systems had been in operation in the Domination and the US since the 1860s, and the constant sunlight of the arid tropics was an obvious energy source. It was also frustratingly irregular. In the period 1910–1916, researchers at the Kolwezara Institute developed a new sun-powered generator: black-painted insulated pipes, running above parabolic steel mirrors that were moved by electric motors to keep the pipe at the focal point. With a suitable working fluid, this was an economical method of power generation, and one that was extremely suitable for automatic operation and required no nearby water source. Adding compressed-air storage made it possible to even out the power flow, and mass-production brought the cost of the equipment down to levels competitive with any but the lowest-cost fossil fuel and hydropower plants; the flexibility of location was an added advantage. Large areas of low-value desert land in the tropics and subtropics were available, and long stretches of remote railroad and many isolated mining settlements were so equipped. By the 1920s, remote plantations without suitable hydropower sources were buying prefabricated units through the Landholders' League.

The period after 1919 saw an enormous expansion of the Domination's power grid as the New Territories were settled. Hydro developments were very extensive, often as part of multipurpose flood-irrigation-power projects. The petroleum resources of the Persian Gulf, Iran, Central Asia, and Ferghana were also brought on-stream, but very little of the oil was used for central power generation; instead, the natural gas was burned *in situ* and used as the basis of a very extensive electrometallurgical and electrochemical complex along the Gulf.

The most startling development was the Bosporus Project. Theoretical studies had been done before the Great War, and had shown that the Gallipoli–Golden Horn strait between the Mediterranean and the Black Sea contained two consistent and very powerful currents, one at depth flowing into the Black Sea and one on the surface flowing out. From 1920–1937, a series of enormous underwater structures, a steel and ferroconcrete grid, was inserted into many miles of the strait, often in conjunction with elaborate surface structures amounting to a minor city suspended over the water. Large low-speed turbines fixed to the underwater frames were driven by the currents, and the power transferred to generators by hydraulic pressure. Initial capacity (1927) was approximately 1,000 MW, and the final total was in the 6,000–7,000 MW range.

Railways and Road Transport

Railways:

Railways—in the sense of roads with rails and wagons running on flanged wheels, had been in use in mines for centuries before 1800. In the 18th century a number of British coal mines built small railways to link their pits with water-transport; traction was by gravity or horse-power. The mines of the Crown Colony of Drakia quickly adopted internal rail systems, and shortly thereafter built small surface lines—to transport ore to central crushing and smelting plants, or to bring coal short distances to the fixed engines.

Application of steam power was an obvious development, but practically impossible until a better prime mover than the Watt engine was available. Trevithick conducted a number of experiments using the existing mine railways, and once the correct road-bed was developed (crushed rock, timber crossties and iron I-section rails spiked to the ties) began developing locomotives to replace the existing animal-traction systems. Once the concept was proven on a local scale, he lobbied for the first main-line systems; the Archona-Virconium was begun in 1805. Like all subsequent main-line railways in the Domination, this was built to a 1.75-meter gauge and was government owned and operated. The locomotives were much simpler than the road-engines being developed at the same time, and the inflexibility of a fixed route was offset by the lesser rolling friction on iron rails. Railways were used for traffic between towns, and for heavy-goods haulage: coal, stone, grain, metals and so forth. Local distribution from the railheads was by animal traction, or increasingly by autosteamer and steam drag. The primary initial limitation was the shortage of iron rail, but after the conclusion of the Napoleonic Wars excess capacity in England and the increasing domestic production removed this bottleneck.

Railway mileage, Domination:		Railway mileage, U.S.A.:	
1810	50	1810	nil
1820	500	1820	100
1830	2,500	1830	1,000
1840	10,000	1840	3,500
1850	25,000	1850	12,000
1860	48,000	1860	40,000
1870	60,000	1870	55,000
1880	90,000	1880	100,000
1890	140,000	1890	195,000
1900	200,000	1900	230,000
1910	270,000	1910	310,000

The Transportation Directorate was organized in 1822, and became the major shareholder in the Drakian Railroads and Harbors Combine, sole operator of rail transport outside a few narrow-gauge specialty lines. Since DR&H quickly became the world's largest single railroad enterprise under one management, it was a short step to becoming the world's greatest manufacturer of locomotives, rolling stock, and other equipment; however, this was so closely tailored to local conditions that it had surprisingly little effect on worldwide practice.

The first Trevithick locomotive engines had vertical cylinders driving gear-trains which in turn powered the wheels. By the mid–1820s, horizontal cylinders linked directly to cranks on the outside of the driving wheels had become standard. The Diskarapur Works began turning out standardized "classes" of locomotive at about this time, with interchangeable parts. Power and size gradually increased, with fast-express passenger trains reaching averages of about 40 mph by the 1840s. Condenser cars (where the exhaust steam was recondensed into water to feed the boilers) became an early feature, as did petroleum fueling in the northern provinces. Other notable innovations were pneumatic-powered stokers and air brakes, introduced in the 1830s. The nature of traffic on the DR&H (mostly long-distance heavy minerals, coal, and agricultural products) resulted in innovations in handling and marshaling techniques, such as "unit" trains and multiple locomotive use. Railway stations were usually located on the outskirts of urban areas, with passengers and goods distributed by autosteamer or later by mass-transit systems.

Fast pneumatic-drive express trains were introduced in the 1850s, with the Cape Town-Archona "Gold Train." This was powered by a locomotive mounting an industrial-type three-cylinder uniflow reciprocating compressor, with a regenerative heat-pump to transfer the waste compression heat to the feedwater. Transmission was via axial-flow air motors on all wheels, including those of the ten passenger cars; speeds of up to 110 kph were achieved, especially on the long straight stretches of the interior plateau. The ultimate development came in the great trans-continental expresses of the 1890s, the Apollonaris-Suakim (Atlantic-Red Sea) and Cape-Alexandria (Indian Ocean to Mediterranean) runs. These huge passenger specials were radically streamlined, constructed largely of new alloy-steels and light metals, and powered by giant steam turbines driving turbo-blowers; the wheels ran on frictionless air bearings. Average speeds of 170 kph, with bursts of up to 200 kph, were achieved.

The period 1890–1910 saw a further burst of innovation. The increasing use of electrical power in industry naturally provoked interest in the Transportation Directorate. Experiments with electric locomotives had been going on in a low key since the 1860s, but it was not until large-scale power generation and long-distance transmission got underway in the late 1880s that main-line use became practical. The first line to be electrified (on a 3,500-volt AC system) was, understandably, the Alexandria-Quattara line, in 1884. Some sections of the southern network were converted to electric traction in 1886–90; in particular the perennially overloaded Archona-Virconium and Archona-Shahnapur. Electric traction showed numerous advantages: central power stations were more efficient than locomotive prime movers, electric locomotives could operate well above their rated horsepower in "burst" mode, and with regenerative braking they fed power back into the net on downslope runs. As additional bonuses electric locomotives required no water supply, were indifferent to altitude and temperature; they proved to be simpler to maintain than the various steam engines and, once the techniques were mastered, easier to build. In 1900 the 25,000-volt overhead system was standardized and a 10-year plan to electrify most of the heavy-traffic main lines was launched, and by 1914 30% of the Domination's mileage and 50% of the ton-miles were electrified. The all-electric Cape Town to Alexandria express of 1912 maintained an average speed of over 190 kph.

Direct-drive steam engines remained popular everywhere, due to their huge numbers and industrial inertia if nothing else. The European networks (particularly in Switzerland and other countries rich in hydropower) had installed significant mileage of electrified line by 1914, and were experimenting with direct and hydraulic-transmission diesel systems. The Americas had some electrification, but were pioneers in internal-combustion/electric (particularly diesel-electric) traction. The high-speed diesels developed for airships in the 1880s and 1890s proved to be ideal for this purpose, and by 1910 were supplanting steam engines on fast express runs.

There were also important advances in fixed way and rolling stock in the period before the Great War. Central traffic direction was introduced (Domination, c. 1900; US, a few years later) and made much higher traffic densities safely possible. The Domination began converting to ferroconcrete ties and welded rails in the 1890s, re-laying about 40% of their track by 1914 and making considerable savings in maintenance costs. Improved suspensions were instrumental in raising average speeds, and specialized cars of all types grew in number and complexity. Sealed freight-containers of standard size were another innovation, originally (1895) German, but rapidly taken up in other European countries and the US; they also spread to shipping and the new intercontinental airfreight services in the same period.

After the Great War, the Domination's primary problem was extending its rail net to the 3,000,000 + square miles of additional territory gained in 1914–1919. A Draka-financed line had been built between Bandar Abbas and Tehran in 1905–1910, and was within 100 miles of the Russian network in Turkestan at the outbreak of the war. The Domination also inherited some 10,000 miles of Turkish and 3,000 miles of Russian line, although these were of different gauges and substandard quality. Between 1917–1940 approximately 100,000 miles of line was built to the 1.75-meter, all-welded standard in the new territories.

Electric traction was also extended, but was risky in imperfectly pacified areas, as the power lines were easy to sabotage. Because of this, and for use in areas where traffic density did not justify the capital cost of electrification, in 1920-22 a new series of locomotives using turbocompound-electric power were brought into service. These gradually replaced the remaining steam fleet; construction of new steam locomotives was phased out in the 1940s, and the last engines removed from service in the 1960s. With advances in power transmission and construction, the vastly increased network of the post–Eurasian War period was mostly electrified; by the 1960s, speeds of up to 240 kph were common for intercity express trains. Total mileage exceeded 1,000,000 by the time construction was complete in 1990.

Urban mass-transit systems developed concurrently during the 1850s. After experimenting with steam-powered street tramcars, the municipal governments of Archona, Shahnapur, and Alexandria decided to switch to elevated pneumatic-powered rail systems. These were supported on ferroconcrete pillars, and ran with rubber-tired wheels on single concrete "rails"; essentially a monorail. Propulsion was supplied by a tube in the fixed way, kept at overpressure by central pumping stations and with a longitudinal slit sealed by rubberized fabric. The cars were attached to pistons in the tubes, fastened to the bodies by L-shaped bars which lifted and replaced the fabric cover as they moved. Systems of this type were built in the larger cities, usually to link suburbs with central business districts, as "ring roads" around the urban perimeter, and to shuttle crowds to and from railway stations, harbors, and later airship havens and airports. The rights-of-way were usually park zones (since the system was pollution-free and relatively quiet) with escalators at widely-spaced intervals. The original pneumatic system was replaced with electric motors in the 1880s, and these in turn by linear induction in the late 1930s.

Road Transport:

Trevithick's initial experiments had included both road and rail engines. Rail quickly proved to be more efficient for long-distance bulk transport, but initial capital costs were high, and the fixed rail lines required a "catchment area" large enough to provide a constant stream of traffic. Since much of the Domination was thinly-populated, with most freight (e.g., agricultural goods) available only seasonally, rail lines were impractical for local transport. Road engines were the obvious answer, since they could flexibly collect goods from scattered locations and "bulk" them at convenient locations for rail transport. Roads were cheaper to construct than railways, particularly on the extensive flat plateau surfaces of the interior, and road-engines proved to be much better at handling steep grades than rail. Since roads (especially after the appointment of John L. McAdam as Chief Inspector) could be built by chain-gangs of unskilled labor, the advantages were obvious.

The original vehicles were simply coaches with cranked axles driven by steam cylinders; the heavier models (drags) pulled one or more wagons, while the lighter and faster models transported passengers and high-value goods. The spread of condensors freed autosteamers from their dangerous dependence on local water, and liquid fuels gave added range. Continuous improvements were made in the 1805–1825 period in steering, suspension, gauges and auxiliary systems; e.g., oil-lamp headlights with mirror backing. By the late 1820s, autosteamers had become common enough (a total of over 2,000) that rudimentary traffic codes became necessary, and there was some export of luxury models and intercity steamcoaches to Europe and America. Bad roads (America and central-eastern Europe) and vested interests (Britain and Europe) slowed the adoption of steam road-transport outside the Domination. In Africa neither of these factors were important, and the expansion of the mining/slaving frontier into areas where sleeping-sickness (ngana) made animal transport impossible was a further spur.

The next major innovation was in transmission systems. Direct drive to the rear axles was simple but unreliable, as the necessary long connecting rods and cranked axles often broke, given the erratic forging techniques and rough suspensions of the day. The development of pneumatic power systems for mining and industry suggested an automotive application. In 1829 Edgar Stevens redesigned a popular light autosteamer. Instead of power cylinders driving the wheels, a three-cylinder expansive uniflow compressor was installed and linked to air motors in the wheel hubs. All four wheels were independently sprung and steerable, and all could be powered. A reservoir evened the supply of compressed air, and there were automatic venting and shunting systems to prevent overpressure. The boiler feedwater, as had become standard practice, was preheated by being used as the cooling-water for the compression cylinders.

Fuel consumption proved to be roughly comparable to the direct-drive models, and the power-to-weight ratios were drastically improved. Pneumatic transmission also proved to be much more reliable, more flexible, and to offer better tractive power on steep slopes and rough ground, and maximum speed was increased. The resulting machine was, however, somewhat more expensive and required more sophisticated manufacturing techniques.

Concurrent advances in materials and machine tools (the universal borer, the turret lathe, planing machines, and diamond-tipped cutting tools) resulted in a mutually reinforcing process. As autosteamers and drags dropped in price and increased in reliability, the market increased. This permitted increased economies of scale in production (leading to full-fledged conveyor-belt mass production with interchangeable parts by the 1850s), which in turn reduced costs—including fuel and maintenance as infrastructure and skills built up— and increased reliability. The willingness of the Legislative Assembly to vote funds for road-building and maintenance was a tribute to the precious importance of powered road transport in the Domination's growth.

Another factor pressing for mass-production was the bulk nature of demand. Private passenger autosteamers were fairly common, but well into the 1870s remained a luxury for the very wealthy, even among the Draka aristocracy. Steam drags for transport purposes, and steamcoaches for urban mass-transit, were the most common types, and these were ordered in bulk by municipal governments and by the embryonic Combines. The Landholders' League was also a steady customer; for example, the sugar plantations of the Natalian coastal zone rarely processed their own cane. Instead, League-owned heavy drags collected the cut and bundled cane from the fields and transported the produce of dozens of plantations to central-powered crushing mills, a crucial factor in the successful battle for the world sugar market; by the 1850s, 90% of Europe's cane sugar, molasses, and rum were Draka grown. When the more prosperous planters began buying steamtrucks and drags for their own use in the 1830s and '40s, they almost invariably ordered standard models through the League's cooperative purchase program, if only because they could do so on credit—an early example of hire-purchase.

Steam road transport spread slowly outside the Domination-to-be, but it did spread. Besides the opposition of other forms of transportation, and the poor quality of roads, there was the problem of climate (the early autosteamers were very suscep-tible to freezing weather, being designed for Africa) and infrastructure. Until fuel, spare parts, and trained mainte-nance technicians were available, there was little incentive to buy autosteamers; until people bought autosteamers, there was little incentive to invest in infrastructure. The Combines had been able to introduce the technology gradually, and in any case they had capital reserves (and government backing) unmatched elsewhere in a world of Victorian laissez-faire. Accordingly, the first non-African use of autosteamers was as toys for the rich in Great Britain; this almost led to a com-plete ban in the 1820s, and did result in punitive speed limits. France then established an early lead, since it was comparatively large and had good roads by the standards of the day; Paris was connected with Lyon, Orleans, Strasbourg and the Channel ports by autosteamer coach services by the 1830s, although these had difficulty competing with the rail-ways in later decades. Most European states gradually copied Draka autosteamer and road-building technology, and steam power gradually supplemented horse traction in local transport.

By the 1850s, autosteamer taxis were common in most large Euro-American cities (London had over 1,000); a major-ity of these were imported from the Domination, but Britain, the United States, Brazil, France, Belgium, and Prussia had the beginnings of indigenous industries—see, for example, the crucial role played by steamcoach schedules in Dickens's masterpiece *The Drood Detective*. The technology was now not very demanding, and any country with an up-to-date ferrous metals and steam engine industry could manufacture passable vehicles. In the United States, with its weak federal government and poor roads, autosteamers tended to be limited to urban use, and to prairie-plains areas (such as the Midwest and the Far West) where flat hard ground was available. Everywhere, autosteamers were a driving force in industrial development; machine tools, precision engineering, lubricants, and bearings, all benefited from the demand and served as learning-centers for industrial skills. The prominent roles of smaller industrial coun-tries such as Belgium (from the 1840s) and Sweden (1860s) were made possible by the initially rather small scale of autosteamer output. The fuel requirements of the new form of transport also encouraged first process-coal industries (especially in Germany, where chemical byproducts were important) and then the French, Romanian and Russian petroleum producers.

The Prussian military, always among the most flexible of European institutions, saw the potential of steam transport as early as the 1840s; the use of improvised armored warcars in the suppression of the revolutionaries in 1848, and the use of railways and steamtrucks in shuttling troops between centers of insurrection, were exemplary. At the same time, Britain and Prussia (both areas characterized by large estates and labor shortages) experimented successfully with mechanized traction in agriculture. By the 1870s, some British landowners and east-Elbian Junkers had consolidated single farms of up to 5,000 acres worked by autosteamer traction power and powered harvesters; these attracted much attention from Karl Marx and his followers, but remained exceptional. In the United States, the demands of the Civil War (1860–1866) transformed the small-scale autosteamer industries of Pittsburgh and Cincinnati, leading to the formation of the predecessors of the great Stanley Motors, Angleheim, United Autosteamers and Carnegie companies. The Confederacy remained dependent on imports from the Domination and Europe, a crucial handicap after the Union succeeded in closing most of its ports in 1863–64. Pittsburgh-made warcars, artillery tractors and steamtrucks, plus limitless numbers of Mexican conscripts and European mercenaries, ended the Confederate experiment.

By the 1880s, with alloy-steel and light-metal construction, electric light/ignition/heaters and cheap light-oil distillate from the newly opened fields of Texas, Ploesti, Baku, and Libya, autosteamers had become a mature technology. Pneumatic tires gradually replaced solid models, bodies contained less wood and more metal, safety glass was introduced . . . but these were detail matters. Costs remained high—$1,500 for a six-seater Trevithick in 1885, equivalent to four times the average per capita wage even in the US—but steam transport was gradually replacing the horse and ox throughout the developed world. The postwar surge in road construction in the US laid the foundations of American supremacy in passenger-steamer production, and by the 1890s America was also the only country to introduce steam-powered farm machinery on a large scale; however, this was limited to the large grain-farms of the Midwest and Great Plains areas. The Domination had already decided, for a mixture of social and economic reasons, effectively to ban direct use of powered traction in agriculture, and lacked a mass market for light passenger steamers; Europe remained uneasily poised between the two models. The next great breakthrough was in production technology rather than design—the reduction of prices in the US to the point where, by the 1890s, tens and then hundreds of thousands of the middle classes could afford the light four-wheel models pouring out of the Midwestern factories.

Air Transport:

Hot-air and hydrogen balloons were a product of the 1790s, with the experiments of the Montgolfier brothers in France. While there were some military applications (e.g., for artillery observation in siege operations) the lack of directional control limited their usefulness. Later development of hydrogen-inflated balloons lead to valuable experience in how to balance ballast and gas-valving, and in gasbag materials.

By the 1860s, the steam engine (especially the automotive types) was making some sort of powered balloon possible if not practical. Individual inventors tinkered with a number of models, usually with Domination-built autosteamer motors, but these remained one-off curiosities. Several Combines in the Domination experimented also, but while providing valuable experience these studies also indicated that a long and expensive process of trial-and-error would be necessary before anything useful resulted.

The first major impetus came during the Franco-Prussian War of 1870. Paris, which by this time had an autosteamer and compressor industry of some size, was surrounded by Prussian troops and under siege for several months. Powered semi-rigid dirigibles (craft with a fixed keel but a gasbag whose shape was maintained by internal pressure) were built to restore communication with the armies in the field and the National Government in Bordeaux; these were powered by automotive engines driving wooden propellors through air-turbine motors, and provided a power-to-weight ratio just sufficient for controlled flight in calm to moderate winds. The dirigibles were also used for counter-battery fire and artillery observation, and on a small scale for bombing Prussian positions. The Prussians retaliated with light cannon, firing upward and mounted on autosteamers; there were several dramatic chases cross-country. After the French government admitted defeat, the Paris Commune uprising saw the "Versailles" use the two surviving powered craft to bomb the communards.

The dramatic role of the dirigibles attracted military attention in many quarters. The new German Reich copied the French models, with improvements, regarding them as principally useful for scouting and artillery observation. Britain tended to regard them as "unsporting," and also a menace to sea power, and tried to have their use banned by international convention. Small pressure blimps became a curiosity in many parts of the world, but the high accident rate—particularly on landing—prevented any widespread civilian use. The early models were small, few being over 50–80 meters, and had very limited range and cargo-carrying capacity.

The Domination's researchers were galvanized by the news from France. They quickly realized that the problems of range, speed, and ability to stand adverse weather could only be solved by a vehicle much larger than the blimps or semirigids; a hull whose shape was dependent on internal pressures had sharp limits of size and weight-bearing capacity, and was also very vulnerable to bending stresses in the thunderstorms of the continental interiors. The solution they developed was an internal frame, covered with a cloth outer coating and with the gasbags within. The elongated teardrop shape of the new craft "airships" was based on that of whales and birds, a bit of inspired empiricism that later aerodynamic analysis proved right. The basic frame was made from two spirals of light, strong laminated tropical woods running in opposite directions from the nose of the dirigible to the tail; the spirals were glued together every time they crossed, with a reinforcing circle of wood on the joint; four to six internal circular braces and a keel strengthened the whole. The lower section of the interior was sealed off to form engine rooms, crew quarters, and cargo holds, while the interior of the hull was divided into cells for the gasbags, which were contained by a network of steel wire.

Power was provided by a steam turbine, a radical high-pressure design mostly manufactured from the new, and as yet very costly, aluminum alloys. This was coupled to a compressor, which supplied high-pressure air for six external pneumatic turbine pods driving large wooden propellors. The fuel was hydrogen from the gasbags, mixed with petroleum distillate, balanced so as to have a neutral effect on buoyancy. The compressor also powered pumps for compressing the gas into cylinders, and an electrical generator, which could, at need, crack extra hydrogen from the water in the ballast tanks along the keel. Steering was via large cruciform control fins at the rear of the vessel, and longitudinal control could also be achieved by pumping ballast water between different tanks. The gondola was entirely enclosed in the hull, and the bridge was a glassed-in section of the dirigible's lower nose section. The nose itself had extra bracing and a large metal eyebolt for fastening the craft to a mooring tower; permanant stowage and repair was done in huge hangars, and the deflated craft was hung from the rooftree of the hangar while undergoing construction or maintenance work.

The first craft were quite small, 200–400 feet in length, and served mainly for experiment and training; several were lost, in storms or to fire. Hydrogen proved inherently risky, but not impossibly so provided careful precautions were taken to prevent the buildup of an explosive air-hydrogen mixture inside the envelope of the dirigible. Maintaining a slight overpressure within the gondola, and keeping the outer fabric envelope permeable (so that any escaped hydrogen would quickly rise and diffuse into the atmosphere) sufficed to bring safety to acceptable levels. By the time of the Anglo-Russian War of 1879–1882, the Alexandria Institute's craft had reached the point where voyages of some hundreds of miles, carrying payloads of several tonnes, were routine.

The Northern War (as the Draka called the conflict) broke out in the spring of 1879; its basic cause was Russian pressure on Turkey, and the Czar's desire to push his frontiers farther south in Central Asia at the expense of Afghanistan, which was the last of the Muslim khanates between his dominions and British India. The Draka were involved first as members of the British Empire, and secondly because their possessions in the Mediterranean (Cyprus, Crete, Rhodes, the Ionian Islands, and ultimately Egypt) would be menaced if the Russian Empire took Constantinople and the Straits.

The war went badly for the British in the first year, with Russian armies laying Constantinople under siege and advancing as far as Kabul in Afghanistan; the Russians were embarrassingly ahead of the hidebound British armed forces in their application of autosteamer transport to logistics. The Draka entered the war only when they were given ironclad assurance of overall command, whereupon 750,000 Janissary and Citizen troops were poured into the conflict. The war on land is outside the scope of this paper, but it was the conflict in the air that captured the imagination of the world.

The first massed attack was launched from Draka bases on Crete; ten 600-foot Lammermeyer-class dirigibles bombarded the Russian siege lines around Constantinople, in conjunction with the landings at Thessalonika. The Russians had balloons, and a few French-style semirigids, but nothing like these purpose-built aerial warships. Subsequent raids on both military and civilian targets disorganized the Russian rear echelon and played a substantial part in the eventual Draka victory. They also brought the dirigible well and truly into the public eye, and in the postwar period every major power rushed into dirigible research, often with catastrophic results.

The next major steps in dirigible design were the substitution of aluminum alloys for wood in the frame and of internal-combustion engines for steam turbines as the motive power. Both occurred in the mid-1880s, as the Alexandria Institute's research program pressed relentlessly for improved efficiency. The first transatlantic flight (1882) was made in a Northern War–style craft, crossing between Apollonaris and Recife, Brazil, where the South Atlantic is narrowest. This was a spectacular success, but not of much practical importance, as the fuel and ballast requirements left little cargo capacity.

Aluminum had been available for specialty use since the 1840s, refined by an offshoot of the cyanide-process gold-refining methods developed for the refractory ores of the Whiteridge. The early 1880s saw the electrolytic process perfected, and the Domination proved very rich both in bauxite and hydropower. Prices fell continuously, and a wide variety of aluminum alloys were developed. The first metal-frame dirigibles had duralumin skeletons and cloth coverings, with internal gasbags. By 1900, a new type with gas-tight aluminum-alloy shells, reinforced within by spiral bracing, had become predominant. With multiple turbo-compound engines, airships were capable of speeds in excess of 120 kph, and unrefueled flights of several thousand kilometers.

Excerpts from:
> "A History of Weapons and Warfare"
> by Colonel Carlos Fuete, U.S. Army (Ret,)
> Defense Institute Press, Mexico City

Small Arms Development: The Draka Experience

[Note on terminology: until roughly the 1820s, the inhabitants of the Crown Colony of Drakia were commonly referred to as "Drakians"; after that, as "Draka." This article follows that usage.]

The initial migrants to the Crown Colony of Drakia in 1781–1785 included a number of Loyalist and Hessian regiments; most of these were stood down when their members took up the land grants issued by the Crown, but they remained active in the Militia reserve forces.

The original armament of the newcomers was a mixture of breech-loading Ferguson rifles (25%), muzzle-loading rifles of both the "Kentucky" and "German/Jaeger" varieties (10%), and ordinary Brown Bess smoothbores (65%). All of these weapons were flintlocks, but their performance differed widely, as follows:

Brown Bess

Caliber: .75 inch
Weight: c. 11 lb.
Range: 75 yards effective, 150 maximum
Rate of Fire: 2–4 rounds per minute
Operation: Muzzle-loading

Kentucky Rifle

Caliber: .50 inch
Weight: 9 lb.
Range: 150–200 yards effective, 400 maximum
Rate of Fire: 1–2 rounds per minute
Operation: Muzzle-loading

Ferguson Rifle (with round ball)

Caliber: .45
Weight: 10 lb.
Range: 200–250 yards effective, 400 maximum
Rate of Fire: 6–8 rounds per minute
Operation: Lever-operated screw plug

The Ferguson rifle, invented by General Patrick Ferguson (b. 1744, Pitfours, Aberdeenshire, d. 1807, Cape Town, Crown Colony of Drakia), was obviously far and away the more efficient weapon. The breech was blocked by a vertical plug, coarsely threaded like a giant bolt. The lower end was attached to the front of the movable trigger guard of the weapon, which had a wooden handle affixed to the rear behind the hand-grip. A complete 360-degree turn lowered the plug and exposed the chamber of the rifle; a ball and paper cartridge of black powder were then loaded, the flintlock primed, and the action reversed to seal the breech. The weapon was then ready to fire.

The Ferguson rifle—"the gun that broke the tribes"—had all the advantages of Brown Bess and the Kentucky rifle, with features uniquely its own. Unlike the Kentucky rifle, it could carry a bayonet, a factor of some importance in the 18th century, and unlike Brown Bess the "sticker" did not interfere with loading. Not only was its rate of fire substantially better than the smoothbore, but it could be loaded comfortably while in the saddle or lying down behind cover. The threaded plug gave excellent gas sealage, and the lighter bullet meant that more ammunition could be carried. Unlike muzzle-loaders, it could not be multiply loaded by mistake in the confusion and noise of battle. Best of all, it could be manufactured with the rather primitive gunsmithing technology of the period; the plug had to be turned on a lathe, but this was the only unorthodox part.

In Europe and America, military conservatism kept the Ferguson rifle confined to specialist units; the British army was satisfied with its volley-and-bayonet tactics, the French enemies never showed any sign of initiating an arms race, and the Americans preferred smoothbores and the vastly inferior Hall breechloader for reasons of national pride and lack of competition.

The Drakians could not afford such luxuries. Faced by native opponents capable of fielding armies of tens of thousands of fanatically brave spearmen, they needed a weapon that could hit hard, fast, and far. Armories were established, using skilled gunsmiths from among the Loyalist population and later European immigrants, and enough breech-loaders were produced to reequip the entire militia. Drawing on the experience of the Dutch colonists before them, the new masters of the Cape rapidly formed units of mounted riflemen, supplemented by light fast-moving horse artillery. With Fergusons, a few dozen colonists were a match for regiments of black spearmen. Fighting from mobile wagon-forts, a few hundred could shoot down thousands without loss to themselves. By the mid 1780s, the Drakian soldier of the early conquest had taken on the characteristics that were to last for most of the next fifty years: mounted on a small hardy pony and leading a string of remounts, equipped with a Ferguson, two double-barreled pistols, knife, and saber. Regiments of black slave-soldiers filled garrison and infantry roles.

The Ferguson was a weapon of revolutionary importance, but it was not perfect; for example, the hot gases eventually eroded the seal between the threads of the plug and the drilled breech, requiring a new plug and remachining. It required careful maintenance to prevent a buildup of fouling in the chamber and barrel, and the plug had to be wiped and oiled after every use to prevent corrosion, which could ruin the gas seal. Prolonged heavy firing could heat the chamber and cause disastrous "cook off" detonation of the loose powder during loading. Like all flintlocks, it had a tendency to misfire, which required a lengthy and frustrating drill to clear the touchhole, and it was vulnerable to damp. Furthermore, the round ball used was very inefficient aerodynamically, limiting range and accuracy.

The first important improvement was the McGregor bullet. Captain Angus McGregor, a North Carolina loyalist of Scottish background, had been using an heirloom "stonebow" (crossbow adapted to throw small stones or lead bullets) to hunt duck on his estate near Virconium. It occurred to him that the same force threw a pointed quarrel much further and more accurately than a round stone; in 1792 he patented a "cylindro-conic" bullet, a short blunt-headed round with a hollow pointed head. McGregor had anticipated the effect of reduced air resistance, but not the even more important reduction of cross-sectional diameter in relation to total weight.

Range was increased to 500 yards against individual man-sized targets, and 1000 against massed formations; as an added bonus the hollowpoint round had much greater wounding power than the round ball. The colonial forces were rapidly converted, since the only modification necessary was a new type of bullet-mold. Performance was altered as follows:

Ferguson Rifle (with McGregor cylindrical bullet)

Caliber: .45
Weight: 10 lb.
Range: 500–600 yards effective, 1000 maximum
Rate of Fire: 6–8 rounds per minute

This was the rifle that the Drakian expeditionary force took north to Egypt in early 1800. Egypt, formally part of the Ottoman Empire, had been occupied by a French army of approximately 15,000 in 1798; the force was originally under the command of Napoleon Bonaparte, but he had returned to France in early 1800. At the Battle of the Nile Delta in March of 1800, 6,000 Drakians (mostly Janissary slave-soldiers) faced 9,000 French troops under the command of Jacques Menou in a flat, sandy area immediately east of the irrigated zone. The Drakian infantry were deployed in a single-line formation, flanked by mounted rifles, while the French attacked in company and battalion columns—relying on shock action, and preceded by skirmishers. The Drakians opened volley-fire at 400 yards, firing by tetrarchies [platoons]. None of the French formations came closer than 150 yards to the Drakian line, and only a few of the skirmishers were even able to open fire. The French columns broke and reformed for the charge several times, eventually suffering casualties of up to 75%; the crews of the French field-artillery were practically annihilated before they discovered that the Ferguson rifles out-ranged their fieldpieces.

The battle had begun around dawn; by 1000 hours, the French were in full flight, pursued by the Drakian mounted infantry. Less than 200 of the French expeditionary force ever returned to Europe. Drakian casualties numbered less than 150, of whom only 30 were free citizens. Oddly, this shattering demonstration of the superiority of the breech-loading rifle over the muzzle-loading smoothbore had little impact on the course of the war in Europe. The Egyptian theater was remote, and little attention was paid to it; the details were simply not known. Furthermore, the contending powers in the Napoleonic Wars were stretched to the limits of their manufacturing and logistical capabilities, sup-porting armies larger than any Europe had known before. The British equipped some of their specialist light infantry regiments (the Royal Greenjackets, for example) with Drakian-made Fergu-sons; the French, towards the end, issued the superior brass-cartridge Pauly-type rifles to their equivalents. In the postwar cutbacks, innovation became even slower.

The final refinement of the Ferguson rifle was the adoption of percussion ignition in 1804; a copper cap containing fulminate of mercury was used. The inventor—a sporting Anglican clergyman by the name of Forsythe—had been bothered by the delay between pulling the trigger and ignition in flintlock weapons, which made wing-shooting birds difficult. Percussion caps proved useful in military applications because they were immune to damp (unlike the priming powder of flintlocks) and because they were much less likely to misfire—one in several hundred rounds rather than the one in twenty typical for flintlocks.

The war faction in the Drakian Legislative Assembly had suc-ceeded in hanging on to Egypt, despite strong British efforts to return the territory to Turkey; the result was war between the British and Ottoman empires in 1807. Since all available British forces were engaged in Spain, the Drakians had free rein in the Mediterranean theater, and seized Cyprus, Crete, Rhodes, the Ionian Isles, and Tunis. The Peace of Vienna in 1814 confirmed these transfers, and the Ottoman Empire renounced its territo-rial claims in North Africa in favor of Britain, in return for 1,000,000 British pounds in gold (paid by the Drakians) and a large loan.

The T-1 (Teillard-Pauly) rifle:

The next step in Draka small arms resulted from the conver-gence of two factors: the campaigns in North Africa, and the immigration of substantial numbers of French after the fall of Napoleon. The lowlands of Tunisia had been overrun and occupied without much difficulty, and by 1820 they had been divided into plantations and the native inhabitants enserfed. However, to the west stretched thousands of kilometers of the Maghreb: plain, mountain, and desert, inhabited by several million hardy, warlike Arabs and Berbers. The North Africans were technically backward but not to the same degree as the sub-Saharan tribes; they had a literate class, firearms, horses, some cities, and a tradition of large-scale organization in states and tribal confederacies. To conquer and pacify this enormous area required two generations of hard campaigning—the Berber mountaineers of Kabylia and the Rif Atlas were not subdued until the 1850s—and the outnumbered Draka forces needed every advantage they could get. The Ferguson rifle was vastly superior to the native weaponry, but something better was eagerly sought.

From 1812–1816 a French inventor, Samuel Jean Pauly, had worked on the problems of breech-loading rifles. His solution was a cartridge case with a brass base that would expand to seal the breech, then contract when the gas pressure in the barrel fell after the bullet left the muzzle. This was an almost perfect solution—the one used for virtually every small arm from the 1850s on—but rather ahead of its time. In particular, seamless drawn-brass tubing was expensive and its quality unreliable. Pauly also invented a centerfire primer, a percussion cap set into the center of the rear end of his cartridge.

Pauly lived and died in France, apart from a brief visit to England to register a patent. However, his work inspired two disciples; Dreyse, who developed the Prussian "needle gun," the first breech-loader to achieve general issue by a European power, and Francois Teillard (born Lyon, 1772, died Bon Esperance plantation, Nova Cartago province, 1842).

There had been some French immigration to Drakia in the 1790s; refugees from the slave uprising in Santo Domingo (many of whom settled on the sugar coast of Natalia and northwestern Madagascar, then just being opened to settlement), and aristocrats dispossessed by the Revolution. Few of these ever returned to France, but news of how they had prospered in the new land did. After the restoration of the Bourbons, there was another wave of French settlers, this time largely to Egypt and the newly-opened North African territories, consisting mainly of Napoleonic veterans and their families, discontented with a drab peacetime existence or ruined by the fall of Napoleon's Empire. Along with them came others drawn by the same stream, among them Teillard.

Teillard first settled in Diskarapur, in 1816; at that time it was a rapidly-expanding center of iron and steel production, and also of machinery and armaments. Employed as an "overlooker" in a factory manufacturing Ferguson muskets, he took advantage of the Ferrous Metal Combine's policy of making facilities available for after-hours experiments by its technical staff. (Diskarapur's free population at this time was only 3,000, and matters were more informal than they later became.)

Judging from his surviving notes and drawings, Teillard attacked the problem of improving on the Ferguson rifle from two angles. The first was to eliminate the separation between primer and charge (loading the round and placing the cap on the vent), and the second was to find a method of breech sealing which was as good or better than Ferguson's screw-plug.

The solution had the simplicity of genius. Teillard designed a single-piece cartridge, consisting of three elements. First was a rather long, pointed bullet. This was set firmly into a tube of stiffened gauze soaked in nitrate; the tube was then filled with a dough of moistened gunpowder, and a percussion cap set in a cardboard disk was placed over the open rear of the tube. Carefully dried, the round then contained primer, propellant, and projectile in one piece, was strong enough to be handled, and was reasonably water-resistant, due to the shellac then applied to the exterior.

The loading and sealing mechanism was equally simple. A turn-bolt system was used, shaped exactly like a door-bolt. To load, the bolt was turned up (unseating a locking lug at the head of the bolt, immediately behind the chamber) and withdrawn; the same motion compressed the spring within the bolt and readied the firing pin. A round was thumbed into the chamber, and the bolt driven forward and turned down to lock firmly behind the cartridge. When the trigger was pulled, the firing pin shot forward and struck the percussion cap.

This left the problem of sealing the breech against the escape of gas; experiment proved that a metal-to-metal seal eroded quickly. Teillard then thought of Pauly's solution. Individual brass cases were impractical, but Teillard developed an alternative. A brass tube was made, open at both ends; midway between them was a metal disk, completely blocking the tube except for a hole in the center exactly the size of the head of the firing pin. One end of the tube was threaded, and screwed onto the head of the rifle's bolt. The other (very slightly smaller in diameter than the inner end of the rifle's chamber) was open. When the bolt was pushed forward, the open end of the tube cradled the base of the cartridge. Upon firing, the hot gases pressed against the inside of the tube, expanding it to firmly grip the walls of the chamber with a gastight seal. When the bullet left the muzzle and the pressure dropped, the elastic brass contracted, the bolt was turned and withdrawn, and the whole cycle began again.

Together with careful redesign of the bullet, the results were as follows:

Teillard-Pauly Rifle (T-1):

Caliber:	.45
Weight:	9 lb.
Range:	800–1000 yards effective, 1500 maximum
Rate of Fire:	8–10 rounds per minute
Operation:	Turn-bolt with obturator ring

Field trials in 1820 produced strong demands from the commanders in North Africa for more of the new rifles. The design was not perfect; the cartridges required moderately careful handling, very rapid fire could produce "cook-off," and the machining required for mass production of the weapon stretched the limits of available technology. After a time the brass cup became brittle and inelastic; the tube then had to be unscrewed (with a special wrench kept in a compartment beneath the buttplate of the rifle) and replaced. The advantages were so overwhelming, however, that by the mid-1820s the Draka armed forces were completely reequipped with the new weapon.

Teillard himself was granted a commendation, 50,000 aurics prize-money, and a 4,000-acre plantation in the Cap Bon area of Tunisia. After a further productive decade (during which he developed the world's first practical revolver and was instrumental in organizing the Diskarapur Technological Institute), he retired to his estate to breed horses and experiment with viticulture.[1] After the adoption of the Teillard-Pauly rifle, only minor improvements were made for the next thirty years. The next breakthrough was the development in the 1840s of techniques for cheap mass-production of seamless brass tubing; this was the result of improvements in automotive steam engines, but had a military application. West and Central Africa were being conquered, and the hot wet climate was having unfortunate effects

Footnote 1. His son, William Teillard, was the author of *Ravens in A Morning Sky*, the first notable Draka novel, as well as other works, and his granddaughter Cynthia Teillard played an instrumental part in the campaign for women's suffrage.

on the permeable cartridge of the T-1; also, repeated attempts to design a workable repeating rifle had broken down on the fragility of the T-1's ammunition. A drawn-brass cartridge was perfected in 1847, and the opportunity was taken to further reduce the caliber of the weapon. The feed mechanism was a steel box beneath the bolt, holding eight rounds and with a Z-shaped spring attached to a riser plate beneath the ammunition. Moving forward, the bolt "stripped" a round out of the lips of the magazine and chambered it. After firing, the bolt was turned, grasping the cartridge with a wedge-shaped extractor on the bolt face and withdrawn. As the bolt withdrew, so did the empty cartridge case, striking a milled "shoulder" and being flung out of the rifle. With the bolt left back, the magazine was exposed and could be reloaded, initially with individual rounds and later with clips of four rounds in a beveled zinc strip holder.

Performance was as follows:

T-2 Rifle

Caliber:	.40
Weight:	9.5 lb.
Range:	1000 yards effective, 1800 maximum
Rate of Fire:	10–12 rounds per minute
Feed System:	Fixed box, 8 rounds
Operation:	Turn-bolt

With the T-2, the black-powder rifle had reached its ultimate refinement. The disposable cartridge helped to reduce the heating problems endemic to earlier models, and also removed fouling from the chamber of the rifle; it was also virtually unaffected by water. The only remaining serious problems were those inherent in the black-powder propellant: fouling of the barrel, requiring frequent cleaning (difficult in the heat of battle), and the large output of smoke, which disclosed the firer's position and could blanket an entire battlefield.

The T-2 proved its worth in the final conquest of the interior of Africa, and in the two major overseas expeditions of the 1850s, the Crimean War and the Indian Mutiny. In the first, Draka infantry equipped with T-2's repeatedly savaged far larger Russian forces armed with a mixture of muzzle-loading and single-shot breech-loading rifles. In India, the prompt intervention of 20,000 Draka troops saved the British position. (These conflicts also taught the Draka valuable tactical lessons, particularly concerning the necessity for dispersed formations and the obsolescence of cavalry shock action.)

Machine-Guns: The Gatling Gun

Richard Gatling (born 1818, Maney's Neck, North Carolina; died 1905, Archona, Archona Province) was a Southern-born inventor. His first career was in the field of agricultural machinery (his seed-drills were ingenious and widely used). His second began in the late 1840s, when he developed the first version of the ten-barreled crank-operated machine-gun that later made his name famous. Gatling failed to interest the American government in his invention, and went to London in the spring of 1850 to test the European waters. He found little interest, but happened to meet (in a City chop-house) a junior member of the staff of the unofficial Draka embassy, Marius de Witt, who had worked in the Naysmith Machine Tool Combine's design section in Diskarapur.

De Witt interested his superiors in Gatling's designs, and he was encouraged to move to Diskarapur. There, in cooperation with engineers from the Naysmith and Ferrous Metals Combines, he quickly perfected his designs. The new metallic cartridge proved ideal for this use, and a reliable weapon with a rate of fire in excess of 600 rounds per minute was quickly produced. General issue to the Draka armed forces began in 1855, and Gatling guns were used with devastating effect in the Indian Mutiny.

The T-2 in the American Civil War

The next major test of the T-2 came, oddly enough, in the American Civil War. While relations with the US had always been rather chilly, many Draka had family ties with the Southern states; in addition there were ideological links, strengthened in the 1830–1860 period as both the South and the proto-Domination became conscious of their isolation in an increasingly bourgeois world. Accordingly, when the war broke out, Draka sympathy was overwhelmingly pro-Confederate. Direct intervention was impossible; the Domination was still formally part of the British Empire, and had only recently acquired "Dominion" status, with full control of the Executive branch of government. Furthermore, the Draka had no navy to speak of; however, they *did* have shipyards capable of turning out very modern steel-hulled steamships. Draka yards built commerce-raiders for the Confederate government, and Draka and miscellaneous European volunteers and mercenaries manned them. Draka blockade runners funneled huge amounts of aid into the Confederate ports.

The American armed forces had started the war with the Hall-Springfield rifle, a percussion-cap, single-shot breechloader with a lever action sealed by a Teillard-style brass obturator. Cheap, simple, rugged and easy to maintain, this was an excellent weapon of its type, and both sides used it as the predominant infantry arm. The Confederacy also received substantial numbers of T-2's, enough to arm all its cavalry and many of its elite infantry formations (e.g., the Stonewall Brigade). These—together with the thousands of Gatling guns and hundreds of Meercat armored steam warcars, cast-steel artillery pieces from the forges of Diskarapur, tinned food from the Cape, and cloth from the mills of Alexandria—were instrumental in prolonging the Confederacy's doomed struggle against the superior numbers and industrial resources of the North. Not until 1866 did Richmond fall, and the North lost more than 700,000 dead in the process.

Smokeless Powder and the T-3/T-4

Mining had always been an important part of the Draka economy, and when the Swede Alfred Huskqvist (b. 1820, Uppsala, d. 1890, Kenia province)[2] perfected his method of stabilizing nitroglycerin by absorption, it was quickly adapted as the main explosive in the Domination's mines. Dynamite (as the new compound was called) exploded far too readily to be used as a propellant, but proved to be very suitable as a bursting-charge in shells. After settling in the Domination, Huskqvist developed a mixture of nitroglycerin and nitrocellulose that could be extruded into various shapes, and which gave a much more controlled "burn" than black powder. The new compound was patented in 1872, and known variously as "cordite" (from the string-shaped pieces initially used), 'white powder' (from its color) and, usually, "smokeless" powder. The War Directorate immediately noted the superiority of the new propellant (less fouling to build up in the chamber and barrel, no smoke to give away the rifleman's position, higher velocity, and flatter trajectory). The first attempt at use was the T-3, in which double-base smokeless powder was substituted for the original 250-grain load of compressed black powder.

Footnote 2. Huskqvist settled on a coffee plantation in Kenia province, and the Huskqvist family have remained as Landholders on the estate ever since. Huskqvist's daughter, Karen Huskqvist, was the author of the noted *Into Africa*.

Performance was as follows:

T-3 Rifle

Caliber:	.40
Weight:	9.8 lb.
Range:	1500 yards effective, 2200 maximum
Rate of Fire:	10-12 rounds per minute
Feed System:	Fixed box, 8 rounds
Operation:	Turn-bolt

However, there were serious problems, and the T-3 was withdrawn from service within four years. Recoil was excessive, and the velocity so high that the bullet tended to melt in the barrel, lining it with smears of lead. The rifling also tended to "strip" the exterior of the bullet.

Design studies were undertaken, and the opportunity used to redesign the service rifle from the ground up. A smaller-caliber weapon was used, since it was obvious that the higher velocity reduced the need for a large bullet to achieve severe wounds. The shape of the bullet was redesigned (a "boat-tail" to reduce drag), the round itself was made of lead swagged into a jacket of harder alloy (except for the nose, left bare to expand inside the target), and the feed mechanism was altered to a detachable clip with 10 rounds, which made reloading easier under battle conditions.

T-4 Rifle

Calibre:	7.5 mm x 60 mm
Weight:	9 lb.
Range:	2000 yards effective, 2500 maximum
Rate of Fire:	10-12 rounds per minute
Feed System:	Detachable box, 10 rounds
Operation:	Turn-bolt

The T-4 was the weapon used by the Draka armed forces during the Anglo-Russian War of 1879–1882, and proved to be a war-winner; simple, light, rugged, and very hard-hitting. Widely copied in Europe (e.g., the German Mausers of 1888 and 1898), it remained standard issue until 1906.

Automatic and Self-Loading Weapons

While the Gatling gave excellent service, it was inevitably large, bulky, and heavy, and usually mounted on a modified field-gun carriage or steel tripod. In vehicle mounts with an exterior power source its very high rate of fire and reliability made it nearly ideal, but for infantry service it had severe limitations.

After the adoption of smokeless powder, the Draka Gatlings were modified to fire the new round, but it was obvious that new possibilities were opened by the new propellant—especially by its reduced waste residue and the more efficient "long push" that its slower burn gave as compared to black powder.

The first application was in a heavier weapon, a 25 mm automatic cannon designed for armored-vehicle use and as an antiairship defense. Developed by Charles Manson of the Army Technical Section in 1882–86, it used a form of blowback operation, combined with advanced primer ignition. The breechblock was flanked by two metal arms, themselves attached to a strong coil spring in a sheath around the lower barrel of the weapon. When released, the block was pulled forward by the spring, stripping a shell out of the metal-link feed belt and firing it slightly before reaching the full-forward position. The recoil force thus had to stop the forward intertia of the breech, then move it backward against the mass of the breechblock, the two flanking arms, and the force of the coil spring.

While efficient, the mechanism was not directly transferable to small arms. It did inspire a good deal of experimentation, and in 1890 Dr. Alexandra Tolgren, of the Shahnapur Technological Institute, made the first serious application of the gas-delayed blowback principle which was to be the foundation of Draka small-arms design for two generations.

The Tolgren automatic pistol used a rimless modification of the standard 10 x 15 mm smokeless-powder pistol round adopted in 1881. The feed device was a 12-round staggered box clip in the grip. Operation was as follows: the bolt, which was machined to wrap around the barrel on three sides, ran forward, chambered a round and fired when the trigger was pulled. Above the barrel was a short cylinder, the rear end of which was sealed. A gas port was drilled through to the barrel, and a piston-head and rod were inserted in the tube forward of the port. The operating rod ran forward through a further, slotted portion of the tube which contained a coil-spring, and at the forward end was fastened to two steel pins that ran in grooves back along the outside of the gas tube and attached to the bolt.

At rest, the spring held the breech sealed. When fired, the

recoil of the weapon began to blow the bolt backward, against the force of the coil spring and the inertia of the bolt and operating rods. These alone would not have sufficed to keep the breech sealed, but as the bullet fired, high-pressure gas filled the tube above the barrel and prevented the piston-head from recoiling. Once the bullet had left the muzzle, the pressure in the cylinder dropped and the piston traveled backwards, forcing the remaining gas into the barrel. The bolt recoiled, then moved forward again as the coil spring expanded, stripping another round from the clip and repeating the cycle.

Tolgren Automatic Pistol, model 1890:

Caliber:	10 mm x 15 mm
Weight:	2.6 lb.
Range:	50 yards effective, 100 maximum
Rate of Fire:	60 rounds per minute, theoretical
Feed System:	Detachable box in grip, 12 rounds
Operation:	Gas-delayed blowback, semi-automatic.

The gas-delayed blowback system proved to give a reliable operation, particularly after it became possible to chrome-plate internal parts subject to gas-wash.

In 1891, a design team from the Technical Section decided that the Tolgren action could be scaled-up to produce a "machine pistol"—a portable, automatic short-range weapon suitable for police and close-quarter military use.

Machine Pistol Mk. I, model 1891:

Caliber:	10 mm x 15 mm
Weight:	7.5 lb. (with collapsible steel stock)
Range:	150 yards effective, 200 maximum
Rate of Fire:	600 rounds per minute, theoretical
Feed System:	Detachable box in grip, 35 rounds (75-round snail drum for special roles)
Operation:	Gas-delayed blowback, selective fire.

This proved a great success—although somewhat over-elaborate, as European experience in the Great War showed that a simple blowback weapon with a heavier bolt would do quite satisfactorily. It should be noted that the Draka armed forces initially found little role for the machine-pistol/ submachine-gun, since current tactical doctrine envisaged infantry combat at greater ranges. The Draka War Directorate issued it fairly extensively to personnel for whom a full-sized rifle was inconvenient: armored vehicle crews, gunners, and the women's auxiliary branch. The Security Directorate found it much more useful, and equipped about one third of their Order Police with it. No European power showed any interest until after the outbreak of the Great War in 1914.

In 1900 it was decided to develop a full-power semiautomatic rifle. The Tolgren action was adopted; there was initially some doubt that a system without positive mechanical locking of the bolt could operate using a powerful full-bore rifle cartridge, but experiments proved the contrary. A notable feature was the semi-closed bolt; at rest, the bolt was set slightly back from the closed position. When the trigger was pulled, the firing pin struck the primer and the bolt was simultaneously freed to complete its run forward; this absorbed a considerable share of the recoil and made it possible to build a very light action. The resulting weapon, adopted for general service in 1906 and standard issue until 1936, was the T-5.

T-5 Rifle

Caliber:	7.5 mm x 60 mm
Weight:	9.7 lb.
Range:	2000 yards effective, 2500 maximum
Rate of Fire:	25 rounds per minute, theoretical
Feed System:	Detachable box, 15 rounds
Operation:	Gas-delayed blowback, semi-automatic.

The T-5 was produced in enormous quantity, over 11,000,000 being turned out during its period of general issue; no substantial modifications were made, apart from minor alterations to simplify manufacture. The action worked very smoothly, and the advanced primer ignition and semi-elastic "gas cushion" effect of the delayed blowback gave minimal recoil. The result was a rifle that was very pleasant to fire, nearly as accurate as its bolt-action predecessor, and had twice the firepower. In fact, the T-5 proved to be another classic weapon, its only drawback being the extensive machining necessary for manufacture. In the field, it gave the Draka infantry a density of firepower none of their opponents could match, particularly in combination with its companion-piece, the SAW-1.

The Technical Section team that designed the T-5 also saw an oportunity to develop the first really portable machine-gun. Simply modifying the trigger-mechanism of the T-5 gave an automatic weapon, but magazine capacity was too small, the barrel tended to catastrophic overheating (and attendant cook-off), and the weapon was violently unstable in full automatic mode.

Modifications followed. A heavy barrel was fitted, with a carrying handle and quick-change facility, the forestock of the rifle being replaced with a slotted metal guard and grip. A bipod was attached to the gas-regulator, a straight-line butt and pistol grip was fitted, and the operating mechanism was made more robust. In addition, a pawl-and-ratchet belt-drive device was installed, with provision for quick conversion to magazine feed. The "Squad Automatic Weapon, Mark I" could then take the standard disintegrating link belt feed (usually in 75-round belts packed in a box that clipped beneath the weapon), or 15 or 30-round box magazines inserted from the top. Specifications were as follows:

Squad Automatic Weapon, Mark I model 1907:

Caliber:	7.5 mm x 60 mm
Weight:	19 lb.
Range:	2000 yards effective, 2500 maximum
Rate of Fire:	600 rounds per minute, theoretical
Feed System:	Disintegrating-link metal belt/15- or 30-round box
Operation:	Gas-delayed blowback, automatic.

With these two weapons the Domination fought the Great War of 1914–1918 and carried the Drakon banner from Constantinople to Xian.

The infantry squad of the Great War was equipped with a mixture of SAW-1's, T-5's, and machine-pistols; subsidiary weapons included rifle grenades, hand grenades (stick and "egg" types), flamethrowers, heavier water-cooled machine guns, and light mortars. After the winding-down of the Pacification Wars in 1925–26, the Technical Section decided to run a detailed tactical analysis of the actual operation of these weapons in the field; the Draka armed forces generally were anxious to avoid "victory disease" and self-criticism was being encouraged.

The T-5 had been very popular with the actual users, and was widely imitated in the postwar period; the American Springfield-7 (1927), the British Lee-Shallon (1921, almost a direct copy), the French MAS, the Russian Tokarev . . . In fact, by 1939 the only major power not to convert to the full-power semiautomatic format was Germany, where investigators were advocating a subcaliber compromise weapon.

Much to their own surprise, the Small Arms Study Project run by Sven Holbars of the Alexandria Technological Institute determined that the T-5 was far from perfect. The average range of infantry combat had decreased, even in open desert country, and all major combatants had adopted the Draka/ German system of dispersed infiltration infantry tactics. The full-power cartridge was superfluous at ranges within 800 meters, and 90% of all infantry engagements were at that or less. Beyond that range, crew-served weapons were more effective. Furthermore, the venerable 7.5 x 60 mm made a true selective-fire rifle impossible; a weapon light enough to be useful was uncontrollable in full-automatic mode, and the barrel overheated disastrously.

The Project therefore decided to "reinvent the wheel" and design a new weapon from the ground up. Since the rifle was merely a delivery system for the true weapon—the bullet—ammunition was the first priority. The design parameters emphasized the smallest and lightest possible round which would have good wounding characteristics within the 800-meter envelope and would still punch through the average steel helmet at that range. A small-caliber, high-velocity round was found to give the best effective combination of characteristics (a caseless round would have been even better, but this proved extremely difficult). The caliber settled on was 5 mm (about .2 inch), with a bottle-necked 45 mm cartridge case of aluminum alloy.

The gas-delayed blowback action of the T-5 and SAW-1 was used for the new rifle. The design was actually based more on the SAW-1 than on the rifle, as automatic fire and an integral bipod were part of the specifications. The feed device was a matter of controversy; with the 600 rpm cyclic rate envisaged, a box clip was of doubtful use—it tended to become unmanageably bulky and unreliable with capacities over 34–40 rounds. A 75-round disintegrating-link belt, prepacked in a conical drum, was settled on, using aluminum for the belt and the feed lips of the drum, and the new glass-fiber resin for the box itself; the rear face was made semitransparent, so that the soldier could see at a glance how many rounds were left. Performance was as follows:

Holbars T-6 Assault Rifle, Model 1936

Caliber: 5 mm x 45 mm
Weight: 9.7 lb.
Range: 800 yards effective, 1000 maximum
Rate of Fire: 600 rounds per minute, theoretical
Feed System: Disintegrating-link metal belt, 75 round drum
Operation: Gas-delayed blowback, automatic; optional
                  3-round burst.

Careful engineering and extensive use of high-strength alloys
reduced the loaded weight to less than 10 lbs.; combined with
the low recoil force and soft action, this made the Holbars fully
controllable even when fired from the hip on full automatic. A
bipod was attached below the gas port, and when not in use
folded into a slot on the bottom of the laminated wooden foregrip.
The stock was a metal frame, with a robust folding hinge; when
collapsed, it lay along the left side of the weapon. There were
post-and-aperture sights, but the main system was an optical x4
sight; this was optimized for quick use, and encased in a rubber-
padded "shroud." Most troops carried their optical sights perma-
nently clipped to the weapon, although they could be removed
with the standard maintenance tools. Folded, the weapon was
only 30 inches long, an important point given the increased use
of armored personnel carriers. The Holbars was usually carried
across the chest on an assault sling.

A companion SAW-2 was developed concurrently; this was
very similar, but used a 150-round drum and had a heavier
quick-change barrel attached to a carrying handle. This two-
weapon combination was used throughout the Eurasian war, and
remained standard issue for the Domination's forces until the
early 1970s.

With the Holbars, the metallic cartridge selective-fire rifle had
reached the endpoint of its development; detail improvements in
materials and performance were possible, but a fundamental
improvement required a complete redesign. The basic breakthrough was a successful caseless cartridge—in essence, a high-
tech version of the old T-1. Research began as early as the 1920s,
and continued for forty years in a desultory fashion. Apart from
gas sealage (no longer a problem with modern machining) the
primary difficulty had to do with ignition and heat-disposal. The
metallic cartridge served not only to seal the breech of the
weapon but to carry off much of the heat of the combustion. The
final answer to the problem was to abandon the dual-base propel-

lants that had been in use since the introduction of smokeless powder, and go over to an actual explosive—previous propellants had really been very fast burners rather than explosives proper. To keep chamber pressures within acceptable limits, the explosive was diluted with a combustible synthetic, which also acted as a matrix to provide mechanical strength for the round. The projectile, the bullet proper, was almost completely enclosed in a rectangular block of propellant, greatly easing the design of magazines and eliminating waste space. Ignition was electrical, and the chemical mix was designed to be very resistant to heat and shock-wave detonation.

At the same time, the traditional stock-action-magazine-barrel design was abandoned, and the pistol grip was placed *forward* of the action. The buttplate was immediately behind the action (next to the user's face when the weapon was shouldered), which posed few problems since there was now no need to eject spent cartridges.

The resulting T-7 entered field trials in the mid-1960s.

Holbars T-7 Assault Rifle, Model 1971

Caliber:	4.5 mm x 40 mm, prefragmented, other options
Weight:	10 lb.
Range:	800 yards effective, 1000 maximum
Rate of Fire:	2000/600 rounds per minute, theoretical
Feed System:	100-round spiral cassette
Operation:	Recoil; optional 3-round burst.
Notes:	Most T-7's incorporated a single-shot 35 mm grenade launcher below the main barrel; this was loaded from a slot near the buttplate, and there was a selector switch above the trigger group to change from regular to launcher.

Author's Note:

COMPUTERS AND TECHNOLOGY

The development of computer technology and electronics in general followed a rather different course in the timeline of the Domination. The precocious development of pneumatic power systems and machine-tools made Thomas Babbage's mechanical computer a marginal success in the 1830s, rather than a marginal failure. Mechanical-analog computing was a fact of life by the 1840s, controlled by punch-card memory systems analogous to Jacquard looms. They were expensive and cumbersome, but they gave a distinct impetus to many types of research and to engineering.

Next, the vacuum tube came along rather earlier, by about a generation; the same is true for the transistor. Analog data-manipulation technologies (e.g., for numerically-controlled machine tools) were therefore more advanced when digital computing techniques were achieved. All-digital systems are therefore much more limited.

In consequence, the research methods followed by both Alliance and Domination were quite different from our history's. The climate of the Protracted Struggle bred an obsession with security that sharply limited the flow of information and ideas even in the democratic nations of the Alliance. It also resulted in a "crash project" attitude towards research in general; the result was very quick progress in fields where the possibilities were known, but less serendipity, less of the shotgun approach. As an analogy, if there had been a Manhattan Project attack on polio in our 1950s, the result would probably have been a magnificently advanced iron lung. The fact of stable, rather than expanding, population also altered the market structure and reduced demand for innovation in the Domination's timeline.

Consequently, computers in the timeline of the Domination developed on a "big brain" basis. Software—what they called compinstruction sets, or instruction sets—was "burned in" to central core units, embedding the program. The central cores were generally sealed, with their own internal memories; an interfacer unit translated data from the external memory storage for the central unit to manipulate. The thought of "open" programming was rarely brought up, even as a theoretical possibility—it gave counterintelligence agencies the willies.

Personal computers—perscomps—evolved up from sensoreffector systems like those used on machine tools, rather than down from big-brain computers. They too had embedded programs, and they were mixed digital/analog rather than digital systems. Large, complex jobs like running a spaceship were handled by a central brain, which acted as a coordinating node for a number of perscomp-type subsystems, each handling something like a weapons mount or fuel-flow monitor. Note, however, that the sophisticated use of digital/ analog systems was an advantage in some fields like voice recognition.

This computer system had built-in limitations. Many of the embedded programs were very capable, and the manufacturing facilities in space permitted the use of quite exotic materials— silicon/sapphire sandwich wafers, and gallium arsenide—but there was less innovation and less pressing need for miniaturization. The existence of heavy-lift missile and orbital launch facilities alone removed a powerful incentive, and nothing like the hacker subculture of our timeline ever emerged. Research was limited to a number of large companies and government institutes, and the number of participants was very small, a few thousand at most. The spillover effect of widespread perscomp *use* was restricted, because only the largest central-brain units could be used for "software" design or programming of any sort; new programs were bought as physical components and inserted into the core. Computer applications were many and crucial to most aspects of war and business, but they were vastly less flexible than in our continuum; by the 1990s, capacities were approaching a plateau, a dead-end.

In some respects, this was true of science and technology generally. The precocious development of heavy-lift space capacity biased technological development towards bigger and better applications of known principles; so did the constant rivalry between the powerblocs. The overall result was a technology more powerful than ours, but also rather cruder—as if the technological visionaries of the 1930s had been given unlimited funding, and as a result the course of development had been littered with a series of "roads not taken" because attention was focused on the immediately achievable. By the 1960s, there was a built-in bias (on both sides) towards projects which were obviously *possible*, given massive applications of personnel and funding. The basic mentality was that of engineers rather than scientists, and dam-building, metal-bashing rule-of-thumb engineers at that.

In the end, the world of the Domination achieved what might be called "yesterday's tomorrow."